THE LEGEND OF THE GRIZZLY SPIRIT

THE LEGEND OF THE GRIZZLY SPIRIT

CHARLES L. HOLCOMB JR

ARPress
45 Dan Road Suite 5
Canton MA 02021
Hotline: 1(888) 821-0229
Fax: 1(508) 545-7580

Ordering Information:

Quantity sales. Special discounts are available on quantity purchases by corporations, associations, and others. For details, contact the publisher at the address above.

Printed in the United States of America.

ISBN-13:   Softcover   979-8-89356-532-4
                eBook   979-8-89356-533-1

Library of Congress Control Number: 2022905900

Table of Contents

Introduction

A few years after the Civil War in the fall of 1877 there were still great changes going on as the settlers expanded west. With the big cities being crowded more people were looking for open spaces and business opportunities while others just sought adventure. Matt Saxton had felt the pressure from all three. But, he'd been determined to make his own way, which had caused conflict between him and his family. He'd already shown himself to be a natural in many ways and had adapted to some special training with ease. Even though he was fairly large, he was agile and very quick. He also possessed instinctively light feet and a highly prevalent sixth sense.

Matt Saxton's adventure starts in the city of New York from there he travels west to encounter storms, Indians, and beasts. Through his adventures he encounters seven special women that affect his life greatly. In the process, he finds a hidden valley then builds a home for himself and establishes a legendary name for himself. Along the way, he enforces what he believes is just and right. This leads to many exciting conflicts with Indians and bandits. Also, unknowingly, Matt has an arch enemy that tries to destroy him and his close associates.

He makes many friends from the people he encounters, as he builds a small empire in his hidden valley. He develops cattle ranching along with other business opportunities that end up making him very wealthy which makes it possible for him to hold his gold supply in reserve for emergencies. With the help of the best engineers and workers he is able to develop his hidden valley and buildings. Matt Saxton brought all of the modern conveniences that had been developed in the east to his hidden valley. He hoped to make it the showplace of the west. For the most part he's able to establish most of his dreams with help from the rest of his family before he reaches his final resting place.

<h1 style="text-align:center">CHAPTER ONE</h1>

<h2 style="text-align:center">THE HUNTING TRIP</h2>

It had been a mild day for the late fall season in the Catskills. The sun had shown through the clouds, off and on, all day; but it looked as if it could rain at anytime. With the cool gust of wind coming out of the north, it could even start snowing in a few hours. Matt Saxton had really enjoyed the day of hunting. He'd always done what he could to get out of the big city. He was a young man of seventeen and was already turning the heads of the women folk, young and old. He was already over six feet tall with a strong physique, long legs with arms to match along with his wide shoulders and a flat stomach. But it's his features that have the women talking. He has dirty blonde hair with eyes that were of the most amazingly hazel imaginable, which could change colors mysteriously at times.

Today had been special since it was the first time that Connie Maxton, Matt's buddy since they both could walk had gotten a deer. Connie was gorgeous with long blonde hair and bright blue eyes. She was five foot six inches tall and still growing. She had pretty long legs with a thin waist, but she wasn't too skinny. Her figure was well developed for a girl of sixteen.

They'd spent a lot of time together, a lot more than their parents knew about. They'd both learned how to get away without their parents knowing where they really were. At first it was just little escapades around the place for which they always got their hides tanned. Later because of the fights with the other kids in the city, they were just scolded and patched up by their parents.

1

Matt and Connie always liked to go places and see things even if it was on the dangerous side of the city. New York City was getting worse. Of course, Matt didn't always have to go out into the city to get in a fight. He could always go home and get into one with his brothers Mark and Michael the older of Randolph and Ann Saxton's sons.

Mark and Michael were very similar in looks. They were both around six feet tall medium built and brown eyed. The biggest difference between them was their dispositions. Matt was violent compared to his brothers who were quite temperate compared to him but had enjoyed picking on Matt. Matt had been easy to pick on as he was quick to take offense when something was directed his way.

In the last fight with his brothers, he'd held his own, even though they'd ganged up on him again. He knew they'd never have any chance against him now since he'd met Lee Chan. Lee Chan was five foot three, in excellent shape even at the age of fifty-two. He was of medium build. He was still quick and very agile.

Matt and Connie had come across Lee Chan who had helped them out of a bad scrap they were in when they had been greatly out numbered. They had been on a visit to the wharfs to see a new ship that had come in. They had heard some talk of how grand it was. They had decided to take a short cut as they had wanted to be in time to make it home for supper. They had gotten into a rough neighborhood and some thugs had thought to rob them of anything they had. Matt had been taking a real beaten. Connie had tried her best to help and had got smacked around real good a few times. It looked like they would be lucky to get away with their lives.

That's when Lee Chan came to their rescue. It had taken him only a few well, delivered blows, and in less than a minute had dispatched the thugs. After helping them up and making sure they had no serious injuries. In broken English, he persuaded them to follow him home to clean, and bandage them up. After meeting the family and being invited back several times they had become friends.

The Chan's had even told then of the events that had brought them to America. Lee Chan had been one of the elite guards for the Emperor's daughter. They had spent most of their time at the palace. He had been one of the youngest of the imperial guards that had been assigned to her. He had learned quick and had been considered to be one of the hand-full of guards to be at the top, as far as their ability in Martial Arts.

There had been attempt to overthrow the Emperor. As word came to them Lee Chan with a few guards had barely escaped with the Emperor's daughter and a close cousin Mia Su Yin. With fighting there way out and on the run a lot of the time. With the rest of the time hiding out it was over a week before the hostilities had come to a stop. They had then returned the women back to the palace reuniting them with the rest of their family.

Lee Chan had been the only guard of the six that had survived the last fight. He had received a couple of deep cuts that had to be sewn up. He had run a fever for a couple of days. With the help of some medicine it had been brought down along with the help of Mia Su Yin who had been an expert nurse for the most part. With the close proximity Lee Chan had become infatuated with her. Mia Su Yin had fallen for Lee Chan also.

But once back at the palace it had been forbidden for them to be together because he was not of royal blood. They had been so infatuated with each other they had forgotten about their cultural differences and had been surprised when they had been informed that the palace priorities were back in affect.

Over a few months they finally decided to risk all for their loves sake. With the help of a couple of trusted friends they had put into action a plan of escape. One was a palace guard and the other was a diplomat of the Royal Family. They had helped them make arrangements for their departure. Instead of using the normal shipping routes they had disguised themselves as peasants and worked their way from one province to another. They did what work they could find and at time it was only for a place to get their meals and have a place to lay down. It had taken them a little over sixteen months to travel and save up enough to purchase their fares to America from a little known seaport.

To help stretch out their budget Lee Chan had made a deal with the ships Captain to help out aboard the ship. They had not really cared where they were going as long as it was to America. They soon found out that they destination was to be a place called New York. The Captain of the British Freighter was trust worthy and had not demanded more than they had agreed to. They had not been shanghaied as was the custom of many captains. The Captain had tried to persuade Lee Chan to stay aboard as he was liked by the crew and had done more than his share.

The Emperor had given up of finding them by the time they had left China. Still being careful of what they said soon after they had arrived in New York they had found a Monk to marry them in the custom of their religion. They had found jobs and rented a room. After a couple of months they found a place to rent. In a couple of years they had made a down payment for the place that was there home now.

They had made a few close friends and had three children. Lee Chan had trained them in the art of Martial Arts. They had been instructed not to use it unless it was a last resort and not to talk about it. They still did not what any word to get back to the Emperor. So, it had been a family secret until Matt and Connie had been rescued by Lee Chan.

It had taken a lot of persuasion to talk Lee Chan into teaching them something he called Martial Arts. Lee Chan had taught him what he could about Martial Arts he'd told Matt that he was very fast and agile. Matt added some variations of his own and Lee Chan had told Matt that he was better than him. Connie determined not to be outdone, had persisted and became exceptional also.

Today though, Matt had been real proud of Connie, for she'd stood on watch for a couple of hours as the temperature had dropped. Somehow though, she'd managed to keep from moving a muscle, until she'd raised her rifle, to make the shot.

From the advantage of a higher bank she'd seen the deer come from behind a hill as it traveled into the wind. He was sneaking through the brush a good two hundred yards away. She heard what sounded like horns click on a couple of little limbs as the deer went through some real heavy brush. When he had reached a little clearing she'd caught a glimpse of his rack and slowly raised her rifle. She felt the adrenalin start to flow. As he eased on through some more thick brush she saw a lane that opened up that was twelve yards wide. In a few seconds the buck reached the lane she lined the sights up right behind his front shoulder, taking a deep breath and releasing half of it concentrating on getting him lined up in her sights she slowly squeezed the trigger. The rifle bucked against her shoulder and she watched him drop. She relaxed for fifteen minutes or so to make sure he was dead before she slowly approached him.

Matt hearing the shot had gotten the horses and returned to where he thought Connie had been when she made the shot. She heard him coming and shouted out to guide him to her. When Matt got there and he spotted her kill said, "Very good shot! You got him right through the heart. Where were you standing when you made the shot?"

She pointed and told him all about it. She was excited and he had the buck nearly gutted out before she got done telling all about it. He couldn't get over how she had made the shot from at least two hundred yards away. It was a good clean kill and a nice ten- point that would dress out at around one hundred eighty pounds.

Working together, they put the deer on the packhorse, and then headed to the Sockett's hunting cabin to meet Vern and Jimmy. Vern was a retired gunfighter, a little rough around the edges. He walked with a slight limp from an old wound, but he managed to carry himself well. You could tell he had spent a lot of time outdoors because of his weather beaten look. He had dark black hair with sharp, narrow brown eyes, and small lips. Vern was of medium build with long legs and arms for his height and he had quick hands for his age. Jimmy resembled his father with his dark hair, and was a good three inches taller. With eyes of hazel like his mother he usually had a charming dimpled smile.

As Matt and Connie approached the cabin Vern and Jimmy stepped out since they'd heard the horses. Spotting the deer Jimmy said, "See you got a nice one we heard the shot."

Matt seeing that both of them were looking at him shook his head then said, "Connie got him. She made a real good shot on him. Connie go in and get warmed up I know you've got to be freezing. Jimmy would you mind helping with the horses and the deer?"

Jimmy answered, "No problem, be my pleasure."

He then tipped his hat to Connie as he stepped forward to take the reins of her horse as she stiffly dismounted. As Connie walked up to Vern and the cabin Vern put his arms around her giving her a sweet little peck on her cheek saying, "Good job I'm proud of you. Come on let's get you warm."

Then putting his arm around her they walked into the cabin. Matt and Jimmy took only twenty minutes to care for the horses and hang the deer. They had always worked well together and enjoyed each other's company. As they walked back to the cabin from the horse shed, they could tell that the temperature had dropped a few more degrees.

When they got inside the cabin they saw that Connie was sitting at the table and sipping on a cup of coffee. Vern was working at the wood stove stirring up something in a pot that smelled good. Matt was sure that it was venison stew and Vern made it as good as any Matt had ever eaten. As of yet Vern had not shared his recipe of what species he put in the stew to add some extra flavor to it. They always enjoyed it when Vern put the stew together.

Vern looked over his shoulder and said, "I thought it was the least I could do, seeing that Connie made the kill. I didn't think it was right for her to do the cooking, too. Connie, tell us how you got him."

Matt walked around the table and benches to get a cup out of the cupboard then to the stove to filling it. Taking a sip Matt knew that Vern had brewed the coffee; he always made it real strong. It took some to get used too, it did grow on you though. Matt had gotten so he really liked it now.

As Connie told them about her hunt Matt on his way with his cup of coffee grabbed Connie's rifle along with some cleaning materials. When she'd finished telling them Vern said, "Girl it sounds like you did real good I'm so proud of you."

"Oh," (shyly) "thank you but that's enough."

With a blush she looked at each of them seeing the pride shining in their eyes. She felt another rush of adrenaline go through her. When she glanced into Matt's eyes, they were shining with an intense flash of light that always affected her greatly.

Then Matt said, "You know this would be a good story to tell your parents."

Connie glared at him out of the corner of her eye, and said, "You wouldn't. They wouldn't dare let me out of the house again if you did."

Matt smiled then, as they all chuckled, except for Connie. She then realized that Matt was just teasing her, so she forced a smile but didn't laugh.

Jimmy, getting into the mood of things said, "Well Matt, if you're going to tell her parents about the hunt you might as well tell them how she straddles her horse and wears men's jeans."

Connie said, "Hush Jimmy or I'll give you a thump! Matt doesn't need any ideas!"

"Don't let the boys hurrah you." Vern turned slightly from the stove, "That's why I decided to do the cooking. Cause I've had theirs and it wasn't any good."

"Now Pa it wasn't that bad. It was just a little burnt but it was still edible."

"Well son your teeth must be a whole lot tougher than mine cause it was like chewing on a piece of shoe leather to me."

Connie giggled and Matt started to laugh a little himself then said," Sorry Jimmy but your Pa is right."

"Matt if I remember right the time you fixed the beans it was like eating a glob of hot paste."

Everyone laughed except for Matt he just smiled good-naturedly. Vern turned from the stove and carrying the pot of beef stew he had been warming, he said "Get your bowls, the stew is ready."

Everyone got their bowls and returned to the table. As they ladled the stew into their bowls Vern offered, "Its Matt who needs to worry though."

Matt looked at Vern, and asked, "Why's that?"

Vern then said, "I'll tell Connie's parent's that you spent the night with her in the cabin. You'd be the one with a lot of explaining to do."

Before Matt had time to realize what he was doing he reacted with, "Oh, no! Don't do that, you'll ruin everything," Surprisingly Connie had joined in at the same time with the same exact words.

Then Matt said, "You and Jimmy were here also."

Vern said, "Jimmy and I might forget that little detail."

Both Connie and Matt gave them a look then said together, "You wouldn't!"

In a flash Connie and Matt looked at each other and smiled as they realized Vern had just gotten the best of them. They finished their meal and cleaned up. Then they laid out their bedrolls to settle down for the night.

After a good restful night and a good morning meal they saddled their horses and put the venison on the pack horses along with their bedrolls they'd started out for the Sockett's home. Vern and his family would use the venison. Matt and Connie's family didn't care for it. Besides it would be hard to explain how they'd gotten it since they weren't even supposed to be out of the city. The night had been cold and windy and had left behind two to three inches of snow. However, the sun was out and it was warming up nicely. It looked like they would have a pleasant ride back to the Sockett's home.

They got to the Sockett's about noon. Betsey and Diane came out to meet them looking proudly at all of them and the deer. Betsey was always aglow when she looked at Vern. Matt always noticed that Vern rode taller in the saddle when he saw Betsey. Everyone could tell that they just adored each other.

Diane asked, "Who got him? He's a nice one."

Vern said, "Connie."

Jimmy with a nod said, "A real good shot too."

He handed his horse's reins to Diane and went to the packhorse starting to untie, the deer. As Matt stepped down Mrs. Sockett took the reins of his horse so he could help Jimmy take the deer to their smokehouse. After everything was taken care of everyone sat around the table drinking lemonade except for Matt and Vern who were drinking coffee.

Connie and Matt knew they were in for a good supper; Mrs. Sockett always prepared a real good meal. She had fixed ham and potatoes with a freshly baked apple pie. Connie and Matt always enjoyed their visits, and Mrs. Sockett always welcomed them like they were her own. While Mrs. Sockett and the women folk were putting the finishing touches on the meal Jimmy and Matt were listening to Vern and not to the women folk. They had persuaded Vern to tell them what it had been like out West.

Diane questioned Connie, "It didn't bother you to shoot the deer?"

Connie answered, "No, it was exciting...but sad at the same time."

Diane said, "Well, the gun is too loud for me."

Mrs. Sockett replied, "Diane, don't bother Connie."

Connie stated, "Oh its all right if the meat wasn't to be used I wouldn't have shot it but neither would the men."

Mrs. Sockett agreed, "No they wouldn't."

Diane said, "I don't think I'd like to do all the walking setting or waiting. It is just to cold."

"That is the best part. Seeing the country listening to all of the many sounds and wondering what you hear. Then he's standing right there in front of you."

"I still think I would get bored. "Diane commented.

Connie added, "I don't think many people do like it but to me it's exciting."

Just loud enough for Connie to hear Mrs. Sockett asked, "Connie does Matt know you love him?"

Connie turned red as she'd stammered, "Ho--How did you know? No, I don't think he does."

Diane just stared.

"I see how you look at him. Don't give up on Matt. I think he feels the same, but I don't know for sure."

"Oh, I hope so," declared Connie, "but he just keeps saying we are the best of friends."

Betsey added, "I've never heard him talk about another girl. Now, Diane you keep this girl talk to yourself."

Diane said, "Yes, Ma." Diane wouldn't thing of disobeying her mother.

To get things back in focus Mrs. Sockett said, "Well, let's get this food on the table, I am sure the men folk are hungry."

They sat done to a real good meal, then sipping their drinks they had conversed late into the night. For Vern, was a real good storyteller upon the rare occasions when they were able to get him in the mood, to express what it was like out west. He had told them of one time he had come across the tracks of a large mountain goat. He was sure it was a ram and had tracked it for nearly a week before he had been able to get close enough to have a decent shot. Vern told them it was the biggest one he had ever seen with the most magnificent set of horns he had ever seen. Vern had described in detail the mountain passes and lofty cliffs they had traversed. Spending a night above the tree line with the full moon illuminating much of the mountain side. The bright stars had enhanced the effect of the thin air. Vern explained that he felt that he could almost reach up and touch them. Vern had told them he had let the ram go and had never regretted it or even all of the effort that he had spent tracking him down.

The next morning after Matt and Connie enjoyed a good breakfast and said their goodbyes. They got in the Sockett's buggy so Jimmy could take them to the train station. When they'd arrived they said a quick goodbye, grabbed their bags and made a run for the train as it was getting ready to leave.

They found a seat away from most of the others so they could talk about their trip and how much they always enjoyed their visits out to the countryside with the Sockett's. They talked about their luck of running into Vern at the riding stable where he worked part time when the construction jobs slowed down. They had met him one Saturday when they were able to talk their parent's into letting them out of the city one of the few times they hadn't had to sneak away.

They reflected back when Matt had noticed a man working with a young two year old stallion that the stable owner had been having a problem with. What had attracted Matt was that the man was being real gentle calm and patient as he worked with him. Even at times it was like the man let the stallion have his way to a certain extent. They had watched for a long time and when the man had taken a break to get a drink he had spoken to Matt and told Matt to hold a tight reign on the horse he had and for Connie to be alert as sometimes the horse she was about to ride liked to pretend to spook so as to throw its rider so it could come back to the stable.

When they had returned from the pleasant ride they'd had the man had come out to claim the horses to put them up. Being attracted to him Matt had told him that he would help. Matt had been told that it was not necessary. Matt had told him he did not mind as he liked being around horses anyway. Connie had followed and after some conversation had exchanged names and made a quick growing friendship.

Matt and Connie had taken to Vern right from the start; it appeared that Vern felt the same for he had invited them out to his place. After getting to known more about all of the Sockett's, especially Vern, Matt had been able to persuade him to teach him all about the guns and their uses. It had not been easy. Vern had said he did not see how Matt would have any use for them. That had been another time

Connie had gone along as she was always determined that whatever Matt did she would do also. Matt had thought that the guns would be too much for her that the noise or the recoil of the gun would be more than she wanted to handle. He had been wrong she had done just fine.

CHAPTER TWO

A NEW DIRECTION

They ended their conversation as they arrived at the station in the city, taking their bags Matt flagged down a carriage to take them to their homes. Since their homes were next to each other they both got out at Connie's. Matt carried their bags as he walked Connie to her door. Mr. McBain the butler opened the door to welcome them as he said, "Miss Connie, Master Matt, welcome home. Did you two have a good time?"

Mr. Brad McBain was five foot seven medium built. He had brown hair and brown eyes with a nose that was short over a pointed chin with a light complexion. Connie respectfully answered, "Yes, Mr. McBain. I have always enjoyed the country. Are Mother and Father home yet?"

"No. But they should he home soon. Master Matt, I saw your family go by just a few minutes ago."

Thank you, Mr. McBain. Connie, I'll see you soon. I might as well go face the music."

"Goodbye, Matt."

Matt handed Connie's bag to Mr. McBain then left.

Matt got home at his door to be welcomed by Mr. James Fallon the Saxton's butler. "Did you have a good time out in the country Master Matt?"

Matt answered, "Yes, the fresh air is a lot better than what the city has to offer."

"I think you enjoy a lot more than the fresh air. Your family is home."

"Yes, Thanks. Mr. McBain told me he'd seen them go by."

Breaking with propriety Matt took his own bag to his room and cleaned up. Then he'd hurried to the dining room where he received stern looks from his family. He sat down then cheerfully said, "Hi." Everyone nodded, kind of. Matt helped himself to the ham and potatoes.

After awhile Randolph Saxton Matt's father firmly reprimanded him with, "It's time you stop running off every chance you get and spend some time with your family."

Randolph was five-foot-ten two hundred forty pounds with grayish hair and a gray beard. A little heavy built with medium features a blunt nose brown eyes and constant frown.

Matt signed, then replied, "Father all we do is argue and disagree."

Randolph sternly said, "Well its time you grew up and start taking on some responsibilities."

"That's not what I want to do yet."

Randolph getting perturbed asked, "Why not?"

"Father I'm sure I never want to go into business with you."

Randolph getting more upset said, "Well you can't be a bum the rest of your life."

Ann Saxton Matt's mother cut in, "Okay that's enough. Let's finish eating in peace. Matt it would be nice if you did go to church with us once in a while."

Ann had strawberry blonde hair with sharp intelligent blue eyes. She had the cutest perky nose and in fact at her age she was still quite good looking. When she smiled you couldn't help but smile back at her.

Matt looked at his mother and felt uncomfortable when he saw her stern look then he answered, "Yes ma'am."

Matt then heard his sister-in-law Margaret (Mark's wife) snicker. But he didn't give her the satisfaction of one glance. They had never gotten along well. He still couldn't see how she and Mark got along. They were completely different and on top of that Matt thought she was snobbish. Margaret Saxton was five foot six with spitfire red hair. She had a pale freckled complexion, green eyes and a buxom body; she also had a very high opinion of herself.

Things were more pleasant during the rest of the meal as each of them reframed from any serious subjects. After everyone was done eating Matt went along with his father and brothers to the den. His father got his pipe and filled it up. As he lit it Betty Green a house servant brought in a tray of drinks. Matt liked cider after his meals. The others liked whiskey with water and ice. The ice was hard to come by and to keep. Randolph had a small room that had been insulated with sawdust in between the double walls just inside the cellar near the outside entrance. The ice was delivered once a week. The ladies usually didn't join them because of the smoke.

Randolph asked Mark, "Is Chris going to be over?" Chris Maxton was Randolph's business partner along with Mark and Michael.

Mark answered. "He should be here anytime."

Matt's interest had peaked for it was unusual for them to discuss business at home on Sundays. Just then they heard footsteps in the hall to be followed by Mr. Maxton coming into the den.

Chris Maxton was five foot six with sandy brown hair and a medium build. His arms and legs where just a little long for a man of his size. He had a trimmed mustache with a real thin face and blue eyes. His nose was a little longer than normal.

After he nodded his greeting to everyone he then inquired, "Where do we stand? Are we going to expand or are we going to play it safe?"

Randolph looked at Mark and Michael who nodded at him, he then replied, "We have decided to expand. Are you sure you want to be the one to make the move?"

Mr. Maxton countered, "My wife and I think the change would be nice. We know it will be a hard trip and a lot of work. Now is the time to try it. It sure would be nice to get a start out there and if we start having some of our ships land on the Oregon Coast it would be cheaper than having all the goods transported overland. If we start importing out there we can get a big jump on everyone else."

"Okay, we have a lot to plan. Are you sure you want to go overland instead of by sea?"

"Yes if we can get there by next fall we should be able to have a storehouse built for the following season ready to receive the goods from the first ship."

"Are you sure you'll be safe I heard its quiet a wild trip."

Chris Maxton added, "Valerie said the only way she'll go is by land. She gets motion sickness very easily. From a couple of trips we have made on the ferry out to visit some friends on Long Island she has gotten awfully sick."

Matt listened intently for the next few minutes. As it started to get dark and the meeting started to break up Matt said, "Mr. Maxton when you leave in the spring I will be going with you."

Randolph, Mark, John, and Chris were startled. They had forgotten he was even in the room because it was the first time he had spoken since the meeting started.

Matt continued, "Before you finalize all the details you should talk to Mr. Sockett. He came here from the west and he'll know what you will need to prepare for the trip along with everything you will need to take along. Also, he will know of what dangers too watch out for."

The four looked at each other and then Mr. Maxton said, "Randolph he's right, we can never know too much and the more prepared we are the better it would be all around. It may even make it safer."

"Okay I guess you're right. We are really concerned about your safety. Matt when do you think we could meet with Mr. Sockett?"

"I can see him at work and invite him and his family here for this weekend."

Randolph looked at Chris and his other two sons to see them nod in agreement.

Chris said, "Well I guess we have decided; now we need to get everything into motion. We will keep things quiet at work a while longer to keep the people from getting nervous."

Randolph said, "We talked about that and we think it would be better to wait until we have everything planned. When its right we will be able to give everyone concerned an accurate plan so there will not be any confusion."

After Chris left Mark and Michael went in search of their wives. Randolph looked at Matt and then said, "What makes you think I'll let you go?"

Matt looked hard at his father then said, "I don't intend to be rude but I am going with your permission or not."

Randolph's face got red then he amplified, "Why all of a sudden are you interested in the business."

"I'm not; I just want to see the country."

With his temper rising Randolph blurts out, "Well! I thought you might be getting interested. But I should have known better. I guess you will be a bum the rest of your life."

"Think what you want." he spurted as he walked out on his father, "But this is doing no good."

Randolph yelled, "I'm talking to you young man!" following Matt he met Ann in the hall and she asked, "What's the matter?"

"Matt he never listens."

"You know he's always been different."

"Yes, but he needs to decide on something to do except playing all of the time. At some point every boy must become a man. His time has already passed."

Ann speculative responded, "We have been through this many times, just give him some more time."

Randolph firmly said, "The time is now, he's past being old enough."

"We just need to be patient. I'm sure he'll decide what he wants to do when he is ready."

"I just don't want him to end up never amounting to anything. I can't see that he has one interest besides running around all over the place."

Ann stated, "At least he's not getting into fights now."

"That's a wonder."

Niftily Ann said, "Well let's get a piece of pie to eat I've been waiting for you."

"Oh I'm sorry. I'm glad you waited for me but you shouldn't have."

Randolph took a deep breath trying to get calmed down some. With a forced smile he hugged Ann tightly. He even shook a little as he made a large effort to control himself. Grabbing Randolph's arm Ann snuggled her five-foot-five shapely body close to him leading toward the dining room saying, "I wanted to wait for you so as to let the others finish theirs so we can have some time to ourselves."

Meanwhile Mark and Michael found their wives after leaving the den. Getting their deserts they went to the balcony to watch the sun set.

Mark said, "Boy Matt sure surprised all of us."

Margaret asked, "What now?"

Michael said, "Matt just listened saying nothing during the meeting, then he told Father he's going out West."

Mark said, "I thought Father was going to have a fit."

Michael said, "Yeah if Chris hadn't been here you would've heard him yelling no matter where you were."

Margaret said, "I don't know how your father puts up with him. He always does just as he wants no matter how much trouble he gets into."

"Matt has always been head strong; I think Father wore out several belts on him." Michael said with some humor.

Mark said, "In all fairness we prodded him into a lot of it though."

Michael expressing wonder then said, "Mark he never told on us, not one time."

Mark replied, "In a way, I do respect him an awful lot."

Margaret revealed, "Well I just don't like him. All he thinks about is himself."

Sue finally said, "Well I'm the newest member to the family. Matt has always been decent to me. I can't say that we have been real friendly but he has always been pleasant to me."

Sue Saxton was five foot two inches with pretty black hair and a darkish complexion with plain features. Her nose was a little to long for her face. It was, highlighted by her deep brown eyes. She had long legs with a short body and short arms. She was always primping for she didn't think she was attractive at all.

Margaret said, "Oh you always have a hard time seeing any bad in anyone."

Sue said, "Well possibly. But I don't think I'd want Matt really mad at me."

The three stared at her then Michael asked her, "What do you mean by that?"

Sue surprised said, "Well you never hear him come or go it's like he just appears."

Michael and Mark looked at each other then Michael replied, "She's right now that I think about it. I guess it has always been like that as long as I can remember."

Mark said, "That's Matt sure enough...never looked at him as being spooky though. I just got used to him coming and going as he pleased."

Sue said, "Matt is just different. Michael has tried to sneak up on me before but I could always tell most of the time."

"Matt is just scary to me," Margaret said, "I never know what he's thinking."

They settled down to discuss some of the local events. Some of the party's that was the gossip of the town. They had brought up what was being performed at the Opera house while they watched the setting sun. The men had snuggled up to their wives. On the way to his room Matt saw light as it shined under Meaghan's bedroom door, so he stopped and knocked on her door. Meaghan asked, "Who is it?"

"Me Matt" Just a minute." Meaghan said then while he'd waited Matt heard sounds like some things were being hurriedly moved around. After a couple of minutes Meaghan opened her door, then took a couple of steps back. Matt stepped in and looked around. With a questioning look at Matt Meaghan asked, "Well?"

Meaghan was five foot six inches with long golden hair that had a natural curl at the ends. She was of medium to thin build with all her curves in the right places. She had bright blue eyes that highlighted her sweet smile making her incredibly sensuous figure seem to glow.

It had been a long time since the two had just talked to each other...a lot longer since he had been in her room. Matt said matter-of-factly, "Father and I just had another argument."

"That's not new."

"I don't know...this one was different."

Meaghan answered, "Maybe it's just because there is so much going on."

"You knew?"

Meaghan said, "Yes I've heard some talk for quite a while...they just got serious though."

Matt sat in Meaghan's chair as she sat on her bed. Matt looked at her and then replied, "I didn't know."

"Well you're hardly ever here except to eat."

His thoughtful reply was, "Well I'm restless I guess."

"I get restless sometimes too I get up in the middle of the night." Meaghan retorted. "However, I don't disappear. I don't turn into a mist."

Matt looked intently at her then asked, "What do you mean?"

"I've seen you sneaking in and out sometimes very late."

Matt asked, "How come you've never told?"

"It just seemed that you had enough problems with Father."

Matt said, "Yep."

"I think Mother knows."

Matt quickly stood and as he paced he quickly added, "She's never said anything to me."

"Matt, I think she realizes you have a lot of stored up energy.

Matt asked, "You've talked?"

"A little Mother and I have come to realize that you just like to be independent."

"Oh, I don't think it's that so much. I just don't want to be tied down in the city."

Meaghan asked, "You don't like the idea of working inside?"

"That's for sure." Matt sat down again with a sigh and then said, "I told Father I was going out West."

"Good Mother thought it would be good for you."

Matt asked, "Oh when?"

Meaghan answered, "When she first heard of the plans. She told me that she thought you'd like it and also that it might relax Father. Maybe if you were out of each other's lives for a while you two would get calmed down some."

"Well I am glad you talked."

Getting up he spotted some books and folders that had been stuffed in Meaghan's desk drawer that she hadn't quite gotten closed. Curiously he asked, "What's all this?"

Meaghan's face showed some embarrassment as she responded, "What?"

Matt pointed, "All of the books and folders."

"Oh! nothing really."

As Matt started to open the drawer to look Meaghan got off the bed and tried pushing the drawer shut as she yelled, "No, Matt.! It's just some books."

"No, they're study books. Look like engineering. Where did you get them from?"

Meaghan whispered, "S--h...be quiet." Meaghan then quietly answered, "Mother is the only one who knows she's been helping me."

"Oh! in what way?"

In an exasperating tone Meaghan muttered, "Well, I've been studying at college in the evenings with a Professor friend of Mothers."

Matt asked, "Do you like all that paperwork?"

Meaghan answered, "Yes but not all of it is inside. Professor White has been able to sneak me on some jobs so I could get some actual hands-on work."

Matt asked, "How was he able to pull that trick off?"

"He had me dress up like a man."

"Boy if Father finds out he'll really blow his stack."

"That's why no one has been told."

Matt said, "Watch Margaret."

"I do as Mother does also."

Matt asked inquisitively, "When did you decide to do all of this?"

"Two years ago, I wanted to do something and not end up being just a wife and mother."

Matt said, "Good for you."

"Wonderful you don't think I'm out of bounds." For Meaghan had believed, that she would not be able to find any man that would approve. Not even her own brother. Most seemed to thing she'd stepped over some invisible line even her other brothers as she had questioned them once about what they thought of a woman being in such a position.

"You should do what you want to do."

"But I'm a girl."

Matt said, "I don't care about that; just do the best you can then no one can say anything."

Meaghan gave Matt a big hug and kiss then said lovingly, "You don't know how good you just made me feel, I haven't had a whole lot of support."

Matt uncomfortably said, "I won't tell," then walked out.

She laughed. She thought to herself as big and virile as her little brother was he was just a big teddy bear.

Matt timed his visit with Mr. Sockett at lunch, time. Mr. Sockett was a foreman and the job he was working on was going to be a shoe factory. The smell of sweat from man and beast filled the air. The horses were used to hoist up the lumber and other building material with the use of pulley assembly's to get the material to the height they wanted and to make the horses work a little easier. Matt thought it would probably bring his father some more business.

Shaking hands as always, Mr. Sockett said, "Glad to see you but this is not your usual place to be. I thought maybe you were scared of real work."

Matt smiled realizing that Vern was teasing he explained the future plans of what his father and partners where about to venture into.

"Well if your father wants us to stay that would be good but he doesn't have to put us all up. I'll still help but I have to be back home before it gets real late. There's no trains running out of the city that late in the evening."

"No that's not necessary. We have lots of room."

"Okay we'll be there. If you sure it's all right. See you Friday night then?"

Matt answered, "Yes no problem."

"That'll be good my family can meet me at the train station and we'll come to your place together."

Matt shuck Vern's hand and started to leave when Vern said, "Matt if you're going out there I'd really like you to get in some serious practice. I'd like to teach you some sign language and some more about tracking."

Matt had stopped then puzzled he asked, "Why? I thought you said I am already pretty good."

"You are but I've been around you long enough to know you pretty well. You never back up from anyone. Going out there I want you to be the best you can possibly be."

"Oh okay. If you really think that way then be tough on me."

Vern grinned and added, "You can count on it."

Matt then went to Connie's place and was welcomed by Mr. McBain, "Hello Master Matt. Connie is out back in the garden."

"Thanks."

Matt going through the house found Mrs. Maxton, Connie, and their servant Mrs. McBain digging up carrots. Matt and Connie had made their greeting with their eyes. Mrs. Maxton was five foot-three with darkish blue eye and blond hair. Mrs. McBain was five foot three slightly on the thin side. She had dusty brown hair with blue eyes with a pleasant face. Her ears were a little big which she covered with her curly hair. She was the Maxton's maid.

Matt after greeting them had helped them finish. Using the potato fork Matt loosened the soil for them. It had really helped to speed things up for them. Since he was bigger and stronger than they were. It was a little warm with a cool breeze and the exercise felt good to him. The smell of the fresh dirt was good after his visit to the construction sight. Matt saw that most of the garden was harvested except for three rows of potatoes that were still green with growth as they had not had an early frost yet. After they were done and resting on the back patio facing the cool air from the clear blue sky Connie said, "I thought you'd be here earlier."

Matt told her why he wasn't there then asked how long she had known about the plans being made to go out West.

Connie told him, "Last night."

"I'm going." He confessed.

"I know father told us."

"Vern believes by working me really hard with shooting and tracking he can get me to be better. Then he said something about some kind of sign language."

"Oh, did he say why?" Connie asked.

"He just wants to be absolutely sure that I'm well trained in everything."

Connie said, "I also intend on learning everything." Then she asked, "What is sign language?"

"Yep, I expected that. I don't really know but he told me it had something to do with a common language that the Indians used with the motion of their hands. Do you think you can get out so we can go visit the Chan's?"

"Stay here I'll go ask my Mother."

A few minutes later Connie returned and said, "We're clear let's go."

"She didn't make a fuss?"

Connie answered, "It's been a lot better after last night since they've decided to go ahead with expanding their business and start importing out west they have been preoccupied making plans. I think that is why."

"That's good."

At Lee Chan's after they had flagged a passing carriage they had noticed quite a few people were taking advantage of the pleasant day. The home the Chan's had was not far from the ship yard. When they had purchased it had been a single structure of three rooms. It had been small but solidly built and the best feature to them was that it had a vacant lot that had become part of the property. They had one of the bigger lots in the area as far as land. It was nearly three quarters of an acre. When they had paid it off they had started to add on to the main building to make room for their growing family. The addition had been built to look like the type you would see from their homeland. As far as that went they did followed the customs of their home land at their home. Matt and Connie had adapted to the Chan's customs. With the customs still being kind of new to them. It added to their joy when they visited. Mrs. Mia Chan had let them in with a big smile. She hugged Connie then bowed to Matt. Mia said, "Welcome things are ready. Please help yourself"

Mia was still learning English. She was five-feet and very attractive for her age and short stature. She was of medium build with a mild temperament and motherly affections. She gestured to them as much as she spoke inviting them into her home

Matt and Connie thanked her then went to their separate rooms to change. After they had changed into clothes that gave them freedom of movement they started stretching to loosen up. After working out through some routines with each other for about an hour, Lee Chan arrived home and watched for a while with a look of pride. After a little he responded, "Very good."

Matt and Connie grinned. They took a break and wiped the sweat off their brows. Matt and Connie had both bowed out of respect for Lee Chan and his children. Lee Chan didn't really demand them to do so. But they respected Lee Chan's children enough to do as he had taught them to do so. Matt then told him of the latest news. Lee Chan said, "That is good, very good. Too have adventure when you're young. I'll change and be right back."

Matt and Connie decided to rest awhile as Lee Chan went to change. It wasn't long before he returned with his daughter Su Chan and his two sons Lee Chan Jr. and Sawn Chan. Su Chan who spoke the best English of the family said, "Father wants to teach you some new moves. Then he wants Matt to try it out against the rest of us. Then he wants Connie to do the same."

Su was five foot three inches and looked much like her mother. She was one hundred fifteen pound's in excellent condition and very quick. Lee Chan Jr. was of like shape, looking almost like a carbon copy of his father, he was one hundred thirty five pound's, and three inches taller than his father's five-foot-four. Sawn was the tallest of them at five-foot-nine, and the slimmest of them. He was in just as good of condition as the others. The only one of the Chan's that could beat him was his father even at his advanced age he still didn't have any problem keeping up with them. Matt and Connie looked at Lee Chan who nodded, then said, "Okay, don't worry. This will be very good."

After three hours of intense training, with different fight routines that had them moving more to make them less predicable. He had instructed them to shorten their punches while at the same time putting more power behind their blows. Lastly, he worked on speeding them up while making sure they still kept their good balance. Finally, Lee Chan called out, "Enough."

Matt and Connie both tiredly looked at each other Lee Chan had kept all of them at it real hard.

Matt asked Lee Chan, "How come all the new techniques and why did you work us so hard?"

Lee Chan replied, "For the two of you to be at your very best. You want to be good. Yes?"

Matt and Connie bowed with respect. Then they cleaned up and after a super meal of meat and fried vegetables mixed together with some seasoned herbs that Matt and Connie had really enjoyed. After some good conversation they'd departed for their homes.

CHAPTER THREE

THE PARTY

The winter months had gone by quickly and all the plans had been worked out.   Everything was on schedule. Vern had talked to everyone that was going out west into letting him instruct them in shooting. Mrs. Maxton had done quite well. He had them all use forty-four caliber rifle's and pistol's so they would not have to worry about putting the wrong ammunition in any of the gun's.

Vern had helped them with a detailed list of what they would need for provisions on the trail. What kind of wagon that would be best for them. Vern then tried to explain to them what they could expect on their overland trip.

The business partners had decided to take some extra wagons filled with some of the things they were sure they would not be able to find at Portland. Chris and his people would have to make the trip and have the warehouse built by the end of spring the next year as a ship load of supplies would be arriving then. They had brought all of the local people that worked for them up to date. Everyone had spent a lot of late nights attempting to make sure everything would be ready.

As for Matt and Connie they were the only ones who concentrated on the pistols. Vern had worked with them one at a time. Matt had worked out a way of practicing on his own so that he was able to draw and shoot by instinct or reflexive action. It worked so good he had showed Connie what he was doing. The pistols were big and heavy in contrast to her small frame but before long with some hard work she was able to handle them quite well and had gotten quite accurate with them.

Vern had pushed Matt a little because he felt that Matt was holding back. Matt hadn't wanted to embarrass Vern. But Vern had picked up on that. Vern had been fast and Matt thought he still was but Matt had gotten to where he was much faster than Vern. He also had gotten to where he hardly ever missed.

Vern had made sure they had the best new rifles and pistols that money could buy. He made sure they had some good Bowie knifes also. Everything was then packed away in crates with the other tools and goods that Mr. Maxton, Mr. Saxton, Mark and Michael thought they would need. All of the supplies were shipped by train close to Saint Louis to be stored there waiting for them.

Vern had really put all of Matt's abilities to the test in tracking. He had also tested his ability to spot ambushes by having all the Sockett's under his guidance try to stage a few surprise ambushes.

Matt and Connie had spent their spare time at Lee Chan's place getting into excellent shape doing pushups, setups, and jump rope along with a lot of stretching. Lee Chans' children worked with them when they had gotten home from their jobs. With the weeks of training they had gotten in real good shape. The best they had ever been in their young lives. They had quite a lot of freedom and figured it was because their families were too busy making plans to worry about them.

They had said their good-byes with the Chan's family two evenings ago. It had been a real special occasion with a lot of talk and the best oriental food. Mia had steamed some potatoes and made some fried rice. She had marinated some beef in some of her special herbs. She had made a pudding that neither Matt or Connie knew for sure what all the ingredients were but had smelled so good they could not refuse trying it. The pudding had even tasted better than it smelled. Matt and Connie had become close friends with Su, Sawn and Lee Chan Jr. who had spent all their extra time helping to get them in tip top shape. Most everyone's eyes where glistening when they had said their goodbyes.

They spent the next evening at the Sockett's with another good meal of venison that Betsey had canned along with beets. Betsey had fixed some sweet potatoes and even baked one of her special apple pies. They had a good evening of friendly helpful conversation. Vern had told them that they were as prepared for their trip as anyone could be and hoped they didn't have any trouble. It had been a blessed evening with many different emotions for all of them.

Matt, Connie, and Vern decided to take a walk outside so their food could settle and have a private talk. Matt had thanked Vern for taking time to work with him and Connie. But Matt still couldn't get over the look he'd gotten from Vern who said, "I'll speak real plain, you two are just as much a part of this family as my wife and children. I know I pushed you two real hard to make sure if there was, any trouble you would be able to handle it. You've even done better than I ever expected."

Matt and Connie then took turns giving him great big hugs and Connie kissed him on the cheek making Vern' face as red as a beet. Vern had started back in as he then said, "Enough let's go in and get you settled for the night so you'll have plenty of rest before you have to get up and catch the train in the morning."

It had been a great night but with all of the food, talk, and emotions, Matt and Connie were sleepy. Saying their goodnights they went to their assigned beds. The next morning their eyes were puffy as Matt and Connie had found little sleep as they were excited about the coming trip. Matt was gratified that Vern must had made the coffee that morning as it was extra strong. With a quick breakfast and some more tearful hasty goodbyes between Betsey, Diane, and Connie, Jimmy rushed them to the train station.

By the time they had arrived in the city Matt and Connie had quietly talked about how lucky they were know two wonderful families like the Socketts and the Chans that met the world to them. They were sure that they would miss them a lot. But Matt and Connie were excited about the trip that awaited them along with the new adventures. Matt carried their bags as he flagged down a carriage. On the carriage ride home they had discussed the big party that was to be held that night. It was taking place at the Saxton's. For Randolph had insisted on giving the Maxton family and all of the people that where going along a big send-off.

As Matt was going to the kitchen to find something to drink he met his mother in the hallway, "Oh Matt, I had your suit cleaned and it's laid out on your bed."

"I don't really want to wear a suit; I just planned on dressing up real nice." He stated.

"Oh, please your father would really like it."

"Father is the one that's insisting then."

"Yes, but it would really please me too," his Mother shared. "Oh, I think you would be real handsome in it and it will be a long time before I get to see you again. It would be so nice to see you looking your best."

Coming upon their conversation Meaghan asked, "See who looking their best mother?"

"I was trying to convince Matt to wear his suit tonight."

"Oh yes, Matt please I'm begging you, oh I know you would be the most handsome one here tonight please." Meaghan's plea was quite heartfelt.

"Matt, you know your father will make a fuss. I would like for everything to be perfect tonight; so if you won't do it for us do it for Connie. I 'm sure she is going to wear a pretty gown. Valerie's mother told me she bought her one."

"All right mother I'll wear it just to please you and Meaghan. I'm not going to like it though."

Meaghan hugged Matt and gave him a little kiss saying, "Oh good this is going to be such a wonderful evening. Oh, I can hardly wait you'll put all the other guys to shame."

"Thank you, son."

Matt's face was still a little red from Meaghan's little assault but managed, "I was headed to get something to drink you need any help with anything?" "No everything has been taken care of."

Matt was real uncomfortable in the suit they had talked him into wearing. He was glad his mother and sister had finally gotten him to go along with it though. He figured it was worth it because he had never seen Connie looking so good. She was wearing a gown of deep blue that matched her eyes. Matt was used to seeing her in pants or just a plain flannel skirt and shirt. He had to take a couple of looks to make sure his eyes weren't playing tricks on him. Every time he looked at her; and especially when they danced his stomach started churning. He would suddenly feel feverish which left him weak-kneed. He spent some time trying to figure out why he was being affected that way, but finally gave up.

What really got to him was when he saw how Connie's eyes just seemed to flash sparks at him; so much that he felt like jumping out of his skin. He had to admit his father had gone all out and everyone was having a grand time; even Margaret had seemed to mellow. Matt guessed she was in her element. Matt had danced with his mother and sister who looked their best. But as far as he was concerned there was no one that looked even half as good, as Connie did.

Matt wanting to cool off and get some fresh air away from some off the smoke that, had accumulated in the parlor. So he'd gone out to relax on the balcony. He gazed at the moon and the stars as he sipped from a glass of lemonade. He then heard some steps and turned as his brothers joined him. Michael said, "Great party."

"It sure is."

Michael looked at Matt then said, "You take care of yourself, be careful if you can. From the reports we have heard it can be dangerous out west. Also it is a long trip."

"I will." was his short reply.

Michael said, "We know you better than that don't we Mark? I mean it don't just jump into things. What I really mean is for you to be cautious, you have always gotten into enough problems here. Out there you could really get hurt."

"I had some help sometimes."

Michael smiled as he looked behind them then replied in a lower tone, "Yes, but you had a choice and you never backed down once. You even seemed eager. That's why we are so concerned."

"I'll try to be careful. I'll try not to rush into anything."

Mark added, "Guess we should get back to out wives," then he took Matt's hand as he earnestly pleaded, "Do be careful."

Michael gave him a quick hug and said, "Take care. Do be careful."

Matt thought that was the first time he had seen his brothers ever show concern for him. Matt stayed and looked up at the moon and stars thinking about his family. Except for his mother and sister he had thought the rest were kind of cold. Not that his mother and sister really expressed a lot of love but he could at least tell that they really cared.

With his father and brothers it seemed like their only concern was just for the business.

Reflecting on the Chan and Sockett families' he didn't have to guess for there love for each other was plain to see in their families. They had hardly ever said a bitter word to each other. It even seemed like they tried to guess what they could do to make things better for each other. Each family had treated Connie and him the same way. They did tease each other in a playful way but it was never hurtful.

Hearing steps again Matt turned around to see Connie. She asked, "Getting some fresh air?"

"Yes it was getting pretty warm down there."

Connie then said, "Me too. I needed to get cooled off. It was just too full, hot and smoky down in the parlor."

"I saw all the guys waiting to dance with you." proffered Matt

Connie flushed as she asked, "You don't mind do you?"

Matt a little startled said, "No."

Connie smiled just a little with her eyes really twinkling. Thinking to herself that was not what Matt wanted to say and hoped even more that she was right. Matt seeing her eyes sparkling had to take a deep breath. Thinking man she was so beautiful. "Let's dance; okay?" He'd gathered enough strength to say.

"Love to."

Matt had all he could do to keep from jumping as he heard the word love. It sent the blood surging through his veins. As Connie put her arm in his Matt led into the upper floor then down the stairs to the parlor.

As they danced they got a lot of glances for they looked grand together. With a glance toward his mother and sister Matt saw that they were being watched with approving smiles directed at them. Matt was concerned when he saw Meaghan whisper in his mothers ear saying, "They are so lovely together. I hope they realize pretty soon that they are a match for each other." Ann had nodded her response.

Connie did feel good in his arms. He was proud of her beauty and grace as well as being proud that she had chosen him for most of the dancing which had really gratified his heart which confused him as he tried to understand why. The party went on past midnight. Matt and Connie ended up dancing quite a few times. Matt had to admit that he had a lot better time than he had believed he ever would before the party started.

The next day after the short night most felt a little better as they had been tired enough from the party and dancing they had actually slept some. It had turned a little colder overnight and most had heaver coats on and some even had scarf's around their necks. It was actually cold enough to barely see their breaths. Upon arriving at the train station they had a big surprise. The Sockett's and the Chan's had taken time to come in to see them off along with a lot of friends and employees of the families. They received hugs and well wishes all around. Most of the women ended up being teary eyed. The men had lumps in there throats.

Matt had even felt the effects in his throat as he had gotten big hugs from Mrs. Sockett, Mrs. Chan. His mother and even his sister had hugged and kissed him. His father had even surprised him with a big hug asking Matt to be careful and to stay out of trouble.

They were traveling light as most of the tools and supplies had been sent ahead to be waiting for them at St. Louis in the Missouri Territory.

The conductor had yelled all aboard which broke up the travelers from their well wishers. Matt had escorted Connie aboard followed by Mr. Hart, the Mcbain's and then the Maxton's. Connie found a seat next to a window and Matt had lowered it so she could wave her good-byes through it. Chris had lowered a window for Valerie as the train started to depart. There were a lot of shouts and Matt was sure nobody could hear the person that was shouting at them. Some of the women continued to wave until they had gotten out of sight.

CHAPTER FOUR

SAINT LOUIS

They saw a lot of new country as they headed west. The early spring had brought with it a lot of deep green colors. There were a few blossoms as the trees were just starting to bud. As much as they enjoyed the passing scenery the flip side was that they had to rush off the train and back on to get sandwiches and something to drink at some of the stops. The seats were uncomfortable as well after a day. They had heard some talk that maybe one or two of the companies were going to make some special passenger trains with sleeper cars and even a dining car.

By the time they got to the mid-west the train had made several stops for passengers to get off and others to get on. The train's crew had to load on some more coal as well as take on water which did not seem to last long at all. It took them the better part of three days to make the trip and the conductor had told them it had been a good run. No matter they were well ready to get of the train. They all were looking forward to getting cleaned up and have to place to lay down. They hoped it would be a long time before they had to breath coal ash. Their cloth's where blackened with it also.

After arriving in the St. Louis area Mr. Maxton with Matt had taken a paddle wheel boat across the Mississippi River to go in search of a hotel that would be safe. They also wanted something that would be decent enough for the women. It took a couple of hours even with the suggestions of some of the locals. They finely settled on the Monroe Inn then made sure everyone was signed in. The Inn was not as fancy as a couple they had checked out but it was very clean and the proprietor had been very pleasant. It had a dining room and did serve liquor but did not have a bar. It was three stories high with a board walk across the front of it. A balcony from the third floor went all the way across supported by large pillars. It appeared to have been painted white within the last year or so and had a light green trim.

Signaling for a carriage they returned to the paddle boat. Mr. Mcbain and Mr. Hart had secured their luggage from the train. Mrs. Maxton was quite pale by the time they had crossed the river. Returning back to the inn they had decided to make sure Mr. Hart, and Mr. McBain would stay with the women for their safety as they noticed a lot of rough looking characters around.

Mr. Hart was five-foot-eight of slim build yet muscular for his size. He had black hair with a full beard and brown eyes. Back at the Maxton home he had been the driver for the household.

Mr. and Mrs. Maxton would share a room with Connie. Matt and Bruce would share a room while Mr. and Mrs. McBain would have a room to themselves.

They noticed that things were booming. They could see a lot of rough, unkempt looking people rushing all around. They decided to make sure that Chris or Mr. McBain would always be close to the women. Mr. Maxton told Matt not to be running off by himself either. Matt agreed so as not to cause any problems. Matt's father had told Mr. Maxton he was in charge of Matt who had agreed to the arrangements.

Matt decided to go with Mr. Maxton to look up Captain Jeff Taylor the wagon master who was to be in charge of the wagon train they were to travel with. Chris had asked for directions to the area where the wagons were being assembled. They caught a buggy ride and along the way they passed several taverns then the driver had to stop for a fight in front of them. The two fighting were using knives even though they were still wearing guns. After several cuts appeared on both of them finally one got the best of the other with a thrust through the heart.

Mr. Maxton asked the driver as he started out again, "Do they have a lot of fights?"

The driver replied, "Yep nearly every day."

Mr. Maxton had a worried look when he looked at Matt then said, "Maybe we should have left the women back home." "Do you really think Mrs. Maxton would have let you?"

"No probably not we talked about it and she got pretty stubborn. She said she wouldn't be left. She did mention that Connie could stay. Connie decided she would not be left behind though." He paused, "They knew it could be dangerous but they were both looking forward to starting over in a new place."

"We'll just have to be real careful."

Chris looked at Matt, "You started to say something else."

"Well it isn't my place to say anything."

"Matt I know you and your father have never seen eye to eye, but he's not here. This is a different environment than any off us have been in before."

"Yes sir. It is wilder here than anything we ever had back home."

Chris agreed, "Yes we've already seen that. Matt Valerie and I have watched you and Connie pretty closely."

Matt gave Mr. Maxton an intense look.

Chris held up his as Matt started to speak then said, "Don't worry I've never told your father, his biggest interest is the business. That's why Valerie and I wanted to branch out on our own a little."

"Guess I just thought you all wanted to expand."

Chris replied, "Yeah; but now I'll be making all the decisions.""Yes sir."

"But Matt. I want your input especially on this trip."

Matt looking at Mr. Maxton puzzled, "How do you mean?"

"I know that you and Connie spent a lot of time with the Sockett's." Chris held up his hand because Matt couldn't keep the surprise out of his eyes. Chris then said, "Oh Connie never said anything. Valerie and I on the way to a party stopped where Connie was supposed to be and wasn't. So the next time she left I followed."

Matt still surprised said, "You never said anything."

"No after I finally found a ride and got direction's I had a talk with Mrs. Sockett. She told me you two along with her husband and son had already left on a hunting trip. She assured me you were no trouble, and how much she enjoyed your company."

"She never said anything to me."

"I asked her not to. I just wanted to make sure Connie was okay. She's always been almost as wild as you Matt."

Finally, Matt had to grin, "Mr. Maxton, I think sometimes she was leading me."

Chris looked at Matt then said, "She's like her mother leading but making sure you think you are the one in charge."

"I hope I haven't been fooled that much." uttered an embarrassed Matt.

Getting back on the subject Chris said, "What I wanted to tell you is I'd appreciate your input. I was impressed with Mr. Sockett for he was real patient; he really knew how to teach us about guns as well as what life would be like on the trail. I know he worked extra hard with you and Connie."

"Yep, we always enjoyed our trips out to his place."

Chris said, "Matt what I mean is I think he taught you and Connie a lot about what to look for out here. I'll admit I'm the greenhorn. So, anything you see that might make things better for us let me know."

Matt was surprised, but with a respectful look he said, "I'll try to remember all that he told me."

"I'm not worried; Mr. Sockett told me you were a very good student."

Matt somewhat embarrassed admitted, "Well he was tough, he made me do better than I thought I could."

Coming to a clearing that opened up before them they noticed it had been nearly filled up with wagons that had canvas tops. Smoke drifted through the area from several cook fires. Horses, oxen and some other livestock were all around the area too. Chris pronounced, "It looks like we're here. Don't be afraid to say something."

"The biggest thing Mr. Sockett told me is never let anyone make you back down, because after that you'll be easy-pickings."

With concern showing in his eyes Chris responded, "Thanks you may have already helped."

Their driver came to a stop just inside the camp which was busy with children running around playing. The rest of the people were looking over and checking equipment for the trip west. All kinds of stock were grazing at some grassy spots around the area close to the camp.

Chris and Matt got out of the buggy. Chris finally got the attention of a man and asked where he could find Captain Jeff Taylor. The man pointing into the middle of the camp saying, "He's on the big white stallion."

"Thank you,"

They started working their way through the camp. It took them about fifteen minutes to work their way through and around wagons along with all the livestock. Chris eventually spotted the stallion and yelled at Captain Taylor as he waved to get his attention. After a couple of times he got his attention. Captain Taylor worked his way over to them then asked, "Can I help you?"

Captain Taylor was six foot and appeared not to have an ounce of fat on him. He was slim built and looked rawhide tough. He had long legs for his body size with long arms to match. He had an honest chiseled-looking face with a long nose. He had black hair, brown eyes that could be expressionless. He was an ex-cavalry Captain who looked like he knew how to handle the well worn pistol that was strapped around his hips. "Yes I'm Chris Maxton this is Matt Saxton."

Captain Taylor replied, "Oh, howdy," with a brief look at Matt he then said, "I thought only one of you was going. I was expecting Mr. Saxton to be a lot older."

"Oh, this is Randolph Saxton's youngest son, he wanted to come along."

Captain Taylor then said, "Let's get out of all this dust and noise." He led them off through the crowd to a big shade tree. Chris and Matt had an easy walk after Captain Taylor's horse opened up a path for them. Getting to the tree Matt saw Captain Taylor ease effortlessly out of the saddle, then drop his horse's reins. Matt could tell the horse had been taught to ground tie.

Matt had walked a step or two behind Chris they were welcomed by Captain Taylor with a friendly handshake to Chris he said, "Glad to meet you." Captain Taylor then said, "You too son." Matt could feel a lot of reserve strength in Captain Taylor's hand but as Matt watched Captain Taylor's eyes they seemed to brighten just for a second.

Chris said, "I see you're real busy so we don't want to take up a lot of your time. I would like to start getting all of our things together."

Captain Taylor said, "Fine you can call me Jeff forget about all the other. I'm not a captain anymore you'll find out that titles don't mean much. It'll be your actions that count."

"All right just call me Chris."

"Well I've got your wagons stored down at Griffin's Stable. Your goods are at the station warehouses on the east side of the river. I decided it was the most secure place to have everything stored."

Chris queried, "You didn't have any trouble getting our draft cashed then?"

"No, the bankers know me. Of course, being a cashier's check made it easy."

"Good. How long before you expect to be leaving?"

"My scouts should be back in a week. If the grass looks good and we can get everything together we should be on our way. The sooner we can get started the better."

"I need to buy some horses to pull our wagons."

Jeff said, "Not to insult you but are you going to know how to pick out some good ones?"

"Well" suddenly Chris's expression showed how green he was, "Thought I'd just tell them what I needed and they'd supply them."

Jeff gave Chris a hard look then said, "Well it's your money but I'm responsible for all the lives on the train." He paused then said, "I'll meet you at your hotel to have some breakfast. Then I'll go along to help make sure you get some good animals."

Chris a little red faced muttered, "I'd appreciate it. I admit I don't know much about all of the things out here. I know there's a lot I need to learn and I'd be thankful for any help I can get."

"I didn't mean to offend you but the biggest thing is being able to admit it. Just watch and listen you'll catch on."

Chris said, "Thanks we'll be open for any advice."

"Well not everyone. I'll make sure to introduce you to a few of the better people to get you off on the right foot." Captain Taylor replied.

Then Chris asked, "Do you have some people in mind for drivers like we had telegraphed each other about?"

Jeff answered, "Yep I was able to get five good hands. Thought I had another but I guess he decided to do something else."

Chris said, "I think they will probably be enough. My driver from back home decided to come along."

"Is he good?"

"He never had any problems at home."

Jeff said, "You'll have two teams for each wagon. You think he can handle them?"

"Oh well. I don't know."

"See you in the morning. I'll check out your driver then to make sure he can handle them. See you at six sharp okay?"

"Six! I don't usually get up till around eight." Matt had just been able to hold back a little chuckle.

Jeff said, "You'll need to get used to it. On the trail we'll be getting up at four or five and be on the trail by daylight."

"Okay. There's a lot I need to learn I guess. Hope I can." Chris gave Matt a stern look this time to keep him from laughing. He knew he would find getting up at four in the morning was going to take some getting used too.

"Don't worry we'll get you squared away. I better get back to the others. I'll see you in the morning."

Chris and Matt shook hands with Jeff as they said there good-byes. As Jeff watched them walk off he took a good hard look at Matt and thought he might be all right. Even though Matt hadn't said anything except hello and good-bye he thought that Matt didn't miss a thing. Mostly he couldn't get over the way Matt carried himself. He acted like he could explode in any direction in a moments notice not because of nervousness though. Also, Jeff couldn't get over Matt's grip. Not that Matt had hurt his hand. Jeff realized Matt had just evened his grip and he was sure that there'd been a lot left reserved.

Once back in the buggy Chris told the driver to take them back to the Monroe Inn. Chris said, "I see there were a lot of people wearing guns on their hips."

"Yeah, I saw that too. I think there will be a time for all of us to have our guns handy, but I don't think we need to worry about that now."

"I have to admit they make me nervous. Do you think I said anything wrong?"

"No Mr. Sockett told me being honest and willing to learn is what the people like most out here. Second not to be afraid of hard work."

"I guess they'll be a lot of things we will have to adapt too. I can already see that a lot of things are different out here."

"We'll be fine. I like Mr. Taylor. I think he'll be very helpful. But when he wants something done I think he is going to mean exactly what he says."

"Yeah, I do think he could get awfully serious."

They had all eaten a steak with some potatoes at the Inn. Matt had ordered a custard pie to finish off his meal. Even though it was early they had gone to stretch out on their beds. Matt had slept a little after the sun had gone down. But not used to the noise of people partying all night he had not slept long. However, he was refreshed from laying on a bed and not hearing the clatter and being bounced from side to side. The others had a comfortable night for the most part.

Chris met Matt and Bruce in the dining room and had just ordered breakfast when Mr. Taylor walked in to join them the next morning. Mr. Taylor had a pleased look on his face when he spotted them. He walked over to their table and shook their hands as he said, "Nice morning; isn't it?"

Chris, Matt and Mr. Hart smiled sheepishly as Chris replied, "Seems like it, but we haven't been out yet. This is Bruce Hart."

Jeff responded, "Glad to meet you Bruce. I'm happy to see you're up you'll get used to it after a while."

Bruce replied, "Good to see you."

They all nodded sleepy-eyed, as they sipped their coffee. Chris offered, "We just ordered." Taken a seat Captain Taylor gave his order of ham and eggs with an extra helping of potatoes. When the waitress had returned with a cup of coffee. Matt had ordered a large meal also and did not feel so much out of place. They were the only ones in the restaurant at the time. Captain Taylor was all business when he ate and the others were still waking up and it didn't take long for them to eat. With nobody saying much they finished their meal shortly. As they finished Chris said, "I'll pay up then we can be on our way."

Matt and Bruce stood along with Jeff and followed him outside. The sun rose as Jeff eased into the saddle and Chris came out to join them. Jeff then turned his horse guiding it up the street as they followed along behind on foot.

At the early hour not many people were up and about yet so they reached Griffins Stable in about twenty minutes. As Jeff eased off his horse Mr. Griffin came out and they shook hands. Jeff turned to them as he said, "I would like you to meet Chris Maxton, Bruce Hart and the youngest there is Matt Saxton. They're here to pick up the wagons and some animals to pull them with."

Mr. Griffin replied, "Mm-mm sure everything's out back Captain. I just got a new supply of good animals in. Are you looking for horses or mules?"

Chris looked Mr. Griffin in the eyes than said, "That's why I brought Mr. Taylor to help oversee and make sure I get some good animals."

"Oh sure," said Mr. Griffin. Matt had noticed that some of the glint had left Mr. Griffin's eyes. "Well, my best animals are in that corral over there," Mr. Griffin had motioned over his left shoulder.

Mr. Taylor picked out four mules for each wagon, explaining to Chris why he liked each one and why he had rejected some of the others. Mr. Taylor said, "Well; your drivers will be here pretty soon. I'll let you haggle over the price with Mr. Griffin. Just don't give in too easily."

"Mr. Taylor," Chris said, "I'd like to get some riding stock also. The ladies decided that they would be more comfortable riding along on horseback instead of bouncing around on the wagons. We also thought seeing as though we have enough drivers we may as well ride horses also."

"Oh, I'm sorry." said Mr. Taylor, "That does make sense. Most of the women and children walk they can't afford that luxury. Are they experienced riders?"

"Yes, my daughter is very good," said Chris. "My wife and Mrs. McBain are good enough."

Jeff asked, "Well how many horses do you need then?"

"Seven," said, Chris.

Matt asked, "Mr. Griffin is that horse in the coral by himself, for sale?"

Mr. Griffin looked in the direction Matt was pointing then responded, "Yep but he's a wild one. I don't know what happened to him. I paid too much for him but he is a looker. No one has been able to handle him though."

Mr. Taylor, Chris and Bruce stood close and started to pick out the ones that looked good by checking their teeth, legs and hoofs. They rejected a couple that had tight tendons. Captain Taylor explained to Chris what he was looking for and why he rejected them.

Chris went over the horses and had to admit Mr. Taylor really knew what he was doing and responded, "Mr. Taylor I sure thank you. I don't think I had any horse sense at all but you've been real patient and explained things to me plain enough so I could understand what I needed to know."

"Well you've made it easy for me by listening real well. I don't mind at all helping when someone really wants to learn and also it's for the welfare of the whole wagon train. We will be on the trail a long time so we all need the best animals we can get. Where's your young man Matt?"

They were all surprised as they searched all around then saw Mr. Griffin stiffen. They followed his gaze as he stared at the corral where the big roan horse was. He opened his mouth to yell when Mr. Taylor put a hand on his arm and said, "Quiet." He eased his way toward the corral with his right hand on the butt of his pistol.

For as they watched Matt was standing in front of the big roan which had come up to within ten feet of him. The roan was snorting and stomping his feet but had not made his final charge at Matt yet. They could hear Matt talking to the horse in a real calm voice. They all stared for as they watched, Matt calmly turned his back on the horse. The horse snorted and pawed the ground then took a few steps toward Matt but still didn't charge him.

Mr. Taylor looked at Chris as he asked, "What the hell is he doing!"

Chris with his eyes glued on the scene didn't respond at first then still not moving his eyes he said, "Don't ask me but he's scaring me to death. That horse looks like he wants to trample all over him."

Mr. Griffin said, "Well I'll be dang. I sure never seen anything like that. If anybody else was in there that horse would have already stomped him to death."

Chris' head spun around to look Mr. Griffin in his eyes as he asked, "You're not kidding are you?"

Mr. Griffin answered, "Nope it's got me stumped."

Mr. Taylor added, "He's right. Everyone out here has heard about that horse and comes by to see him. I think that's why Mr. Griffin keeps feeding him so he can attract business."

They all gasped as the horse lunged the last few feet toward Matt. Matt didn't move a muscle. The roan relaxed a little and started to sniff Matt's back and neck. They could hear Matt as he spoke in a quiet calm voice so as not to scare him. The roan relaxed a little more. Then Matt slowly started walking toward the rails closest to the men holding a hand up slowly to keep them where they were. As Matt got to the rails he leaned his arms on the top rail and then said, "Mr. Griffin I'd like to purchase the horse, if I can have your permission to use your corral."

Mr. Griffin nodded. For Matt had spoken just loud enough for them to hear. He didn't' want to scare the horse.

Matt looked at Chris and said, "If you really need me I'll go with you and the wagons to help load, but I'd like to stay here and work with the roan as much as I can."

Chris just above a whisper said, "I don't know Matt your father would skin us both alive if he could see what you are doing right now."

In a low voice Matt said, "Sorry to put you in a spot, but I intend to have the roan one way or another."

As Chris was deep in thought the others didn't say anything either. They were tense with the strain of waiting for something to happen. They all expected the horse to leap on Matt and destroy him any instant.

Chris at last said, "Alright; but you be damn careful. I can see you got a lot of work to do, to get him ready. You think you'll have enough time?"

"It won't be easy, but I think I'll have time. Not to be rude, but I think it would be better if the roan and I where left alone now."

They all nodded moving back away from the coral slowly. Mr. Griffin quietly said, "You really going to leave him alone with that man-killer?"

"I don't know what else I can do. Matt is not my son, but I think I understand him better. When Matt is determined I don't know of any way to stop him."

Captain Taylor quietly said, "I think you did do right. As dangerous, as it is in that corral. I do think young Matt meant what he said."

"Oh, I have no doubt about that," Chris responded.

Captain Taylor led them off and then speaking to Mr. Griffin, "That makes up all of the animals that Mr. Maxton is going to need. Oh, I see the drivers are here. I'll have them hook up the wagons. Chris by the time you settle on a price they should be hooked up. Oh, I almost forgot, don't let this buzzard take you for too much."

"Now Jeff," speaking directly to the captain, "You know I always try to be fair."

Captain Taylor mounted his horse as he said, "Well I'm just trying to make sure Chris doesn't get scalped before he even sees his first Indian."

Catching on Chris laughed so hard he almost choked, but recovered with, "Thanks Captain Taylor. I need all of the help I can get."

Mr. Griffin finally smiled then said, "Jeff get back to your wagons before you have me going bankrupt."

Captain Taylor mounted his big white stallion and rode over to the cowboys to converse with then a couple of minutes. He then put his horse into a trot headed for the camp grounds.

Chris and Mr. Griffin took twenty minutes to agree on a price. Chris stepped out of the little office for a while to make sure Matt was all right. While he waited for the bill of sale he watched the roan ease up and muzzled Matt. Matt acted like the horse wasn't even there. The roan using his nose nudged Matt and he slowly turned and talked to him for Chris could see Matt's lips moving. Matt started stroking the stallion on the head and neck. Chris saw the stallion tense then relax again when he realized Matt wasn't hurting him.

Mr. Griffin came out and handed Chris the bill of sale. Then he looked at the corral and shook his head saying, "If I wasn't seeing it, I wouldn't believe it."

Chris asked, "What's that?"

Mr. Griffin responded, "I've seen that horse cripple a lot of the men around here and he hasn't even chased that youngster out of the corral."

"You think Matt will be able to tame him?" Chris worriedly inquired.

Mr. Griffin nodded and replied, "Before today I would have bet no one could have tamed him, but that youngster has already done more with him than anyone else I've ever seen. I do think they'll be all right."

One of the cowboys walked up then said, "Mr. Maxton we're ready," then startled as he stared at the corral he barely got out, "Who's in that killers corral?"

Mr. Griffin answered, "That's something I thought I'd never see; that's Mr. Maxton's friend."

"Oh! I'm sorry. I can't help worrying about Matt. My partner would skin me alive if he knew I'd let Matt in there with that wild animal."

Mr. Griffin responded, "If I remember right he did it on his own. After I said he was too wild for anyone to do anything with."

Chris said, "That's Matt, always trying to prove everyone wrong."

The cowboy was still starring. Then he responded, "I'm looking and I still don't believe what I'm seeing."

Chris said, "I'm sorry, but I don't know your name. You can call me Chris."

The cowboy answered, "You can call me Tex."

Tex was five-foot-nine with a lean raw-hide tough build; long dark hair that had just been cut to shoulder length as well as a dark sun burnt complexion. He kept clean shaven when he could. Sharp blue eyes behind a narrow nose, thin face which most of the time had a stern expression on it. He spoke with a Texas drawl and was slow of movement, but very efficient which made it appear he moved faster than he actually did. He wore a well used six shooter, in a worn holster that was tied down low on his right hip. The other cowboys walked up staring into the corral. One of them said, "That horse must be sick he just isn't acting natural."

Tex said, "Something I thought I'd never see. Mr. Maxton this is Slade. That skin and bones over there is Slim. The darkie over there is Bones. The last fellow there is Ben."

Slade was five-foot-two with dirty blonde hair, stocky built with a slight limp caused by a right leg that had been broken and not set right. It was still crooked, but didn't seem to slow him down. He had brown eyes with a big nose that had been broken and was pointed to the left side of his face. He was another Texan with a well worn pistol tied low on his right hip.

Slim was five-foot-seven slim built with a tough wiry strength. He had long legs his arms where short for his body size. He had black hair with blue eyes he was left handed and wore his pistol on his left hip.

Bones was five-foot-four of medium build, strong for his size. He was of the black race and wore his gun on his right hip. He was a little shy around people he didn't know, especially white women.

Ben was five-foot-five with a medium heavy build thick black hair he had blue eyes with a long jagged scar on his left check. He was a bear of a man the strongest of the cowboys. Quiet, but liked being around people. He wore his two pistols low and tied down.

Chris shook hands with everyone then said, "I'm sorry, but I've been worried about Matt being in there."

They all glanced at the corral, Slim said, "Yep if he was my youngster, I'd be worried too."

Tex said, "Well Chris. Not to rush you, but we can watch them or go load these wagons and get them ready for the trail."

Chris a little red faced said, "Yes, yes. Of course. I guess we need to be going." After a slight pause he continued, "Don't any of you be afraid to let me know if I'm doing something wrong or even if anything needs to be done. This is all new to me."

Chris could see all of them relax a little as Tex said, "That's good. Chris the boys decided I'd be in charge of our little group if it was okay with you."

Chris rather pleased said, "I think that'll help me a lot. I think Mr. Taylor has done right by me in everything. Oh, where's my manners I'd like you to meet Bruce Hart. They seem to be getting along alright but I can't help but worry about Matt."

Tex responded, "Yeah I don't blame you. That horse has gotten the best of a few riders. As far as the Captain you can't do any better than Captain Taylor. I have known him along time. Bruce and the rest of us have already introduced our selves. Don't worry yourself about it we can see why you would have your mind elsewhere. Well, I think we better get moving, we have burnt enough daylight already."

It took them just a few minutes to harness and hook up the wagons and get them in motion. Bruce wasn't having any problems it looked like things where falling into place. Chris was still worried about Matt, but didn't know of anything he could have done differently.

Matt spent the whole day working with the stallion. He didn't even leave to get anything to eat or drink. Basically, Matt just stayed near so they could get used to being in each others company. Eventually Matt had gotten so he could walk around in the coral and the roan stayed calm. Matt felt like they would end up being real good friends now. They had already learned a lot about each other; now they just had to learn how to work together.

Toward the end of the day Matt saw the wagons return and head out to the camp grounds. About an hour before dark Matt left the corral. The roan had watched then walked toward the fence and gave a low neigh.

As Matt was going by the stable Mr. Griffin said, "Looks like you made a lot of headway."

Matt replied, "Yeah; I'm trying to make him think it's his idea to be friends."

"That's clever where'd you learn that?"

"Just observing people, they do more if they find someone who is willing to help instead of being forced to. With animals, I just try to make them think it's their idea."

Mr. Griffin said, "Well you messed that horse up by not being afraid."

"Oh. I was scared to death I didn't think he'd stop when he came at me the first time. But I knew if I was to ever win him over that I couldn't let him realize it in any way. That's why I decided to turn my back. I was afraid if he saw my eyes, they would give me away."

Mr. Griffin slapped his leg as he laughed. Then he said, "Well I wouldn't have had the nerve to turn my back and from where I was standing I didn't see no fear."

"Well; I'd better go they're probably waiting on me to come for supper."

Mr. Griffin said, "You got a lot to do before the weeks out; night."

Matt got to the inn and went up to his room to clean up. He had just finished when there was a knock on his door. He opened it to Chris who said, "Howdy, glad to see you're in one piece!"

"I'm fine. I was on my way! Sorry if I delayed all of you."

Chris replied, "You're not late. We just got ready our selves, but I wanted to let you know that we've decided to go to the Victorian Hotel to eat. Captain Taylor suggested that we move out to the campground so we'd have time get used to doing the things that we'll have to do instead of having to learn everything on the trail. So, we are going to move out in the morning."

"Are you going to have one of the wagons coming in or are we going to have to rent one to take the things out?"

Chris answered, "Tex told me he would be out here a couple of hours after daylight, so as to give us time to pack up our things. Then we'll go on out. Captain Taylor is probably waiting. I invited him to join us. I'll get the rest and be right along."

"Sure, see you downstairs."

Matt looked around the hotel lobby for Captain Taylor as he went down the stairs. Once he spotted him he walked up to him and shook hands. They already had a fast growing respect for each other. Captain Taylor smiled at Matt then said, "I see the horse didn't get the best of you; yet."

"No, I think we're getting used to each other. I think we can get a lot done now."

Captain Taylor said, "If you can tame that horse you'll have one of the best in the whole country."

Matt said, "I don't think his spirit has ever been broken and he does have a lot of energy. I think if we can get to be friends and learn more about each other we will be able to get a lot done."

"Well I've never seen your approach before, but from what I've seen so far with a lot of patience on your part. I think you have a real good chance of taming him."

They heard steps on the stairs and turn to see Connie, Mrs. Maxton, Mrs. McBain, and the rest coming down the stairs.

Matt said, "I'd like you to meet Connie Maxton." Captain Taylor stepped forward then lightly shook her hand.

Then Matt continued, "This is Mrs. Maxton, Mr. McBain, and Mrs. McBain, everybody this is Captain Taylor."

After Captain Taylor had shaken hands with all of them he responded, "You just call me Jeff or Captain. I'll answer to either. We're not much on long names or titles out here. Besides I'm not a Captain anymore, that's just a honorary title now."

Connie always real friendly said, "Jeff it's nice to meet you," They all talked for a while. They were joined shortly by Chris and Bruce. When they had walked up Chris said, "I'm starving let's go get something to eat."

Captain Taylor started toward the dining room. When he did Chris countered with, "Jeff I'm sorry, the ladies have been talking to some of the other guests and they wanted to go up the street to Ted's Steak house at the Victorian Hotel."

Captain Taylor stopped and then replied, "Oh...ladies...that might be real nice. I heard that their food was real good I've never been there myself though. I was told that it was real expensive."

Why hadn't he realized it before, Chris began beating himself up. In a firm manner yet completely gracious Chris let the captain know his meal was taken care of since he was part of his crew. While Captain Taylor wanted to argue the matter as a matter of pride Chris found a unique way to ease all of his uneasiness and they left the hotel and started up the street. The men put the women in the middle of their little group as they escorted them along. They had picked the best way along the wooden walkway and used it whenever they could. They did have to step down in a few places in order to cross a street or when one of the stores or saloons didn't see any need to build a better walkway. There were still a lot of people out and about. As they passed one of the saloons there was a couple of mean looking characters in front of it who started eyeing the ladies and being loud. One said, "Wow! Look at them, they are some real fine looking fillies."

Connie nudged Matt in the ribs with her elbow for she had felt him tense up. Matt merely strengthened his grip and continued to escort her as they walked up the street. Captain Taylor had put his hand on his gun butt then looked the two in the eyes and told them in a hard voice to back off. They gave him a hard look back but didn't say anything else.

They arrived at the restaurant with no further problems. They where led to a table toward the back, that was big enough for everyone. They all ordered then had one of the best meals they had eaten in quite a while. They really stuffed themselves knowing it would be along time before they could get such a good meal again.

Finished with there supper as they sat back to sipping their coffee and drinks of lemonade or some juice which some of the ladies preferred. They started to question Captain Taylor about the trail to Oregon and he told them. He didn't lie to them. He told them that they would get little sleep they'd be up early and stay up late. That they'd be out in rain, droughts, wind and mostly have to endure the same boring routine day after day.

Finally, Mrs. Saxton asked, "How bad are the Indians?"

After a slight pause Captain Taylor answered, "Well there's good ones and bad ones then there are some that are really bad. Not going to say there won't be any trouble, but we do have a few advantages. First the wagon train is bigger than most. I was also able to get two of the very best scouts."

Mrs. McBain said, "Well we decided to go along with the Maxton's because it was getting awfully crowded back home in New York City. Now we see a lot of people here."

Captain Taylor responded, "Its springtime here now and there are a lot of drifters. Also, the trappers have come in to sell their hides. A lot of the people you have seen are traders here to get trade goods, to take back out to trade with the Indians and anybody else they run across. Then there's just a lot of people here to get supplies and head out to places all over the west, looking for somewhere to settle. That's why there's so many people here right now."

Chris interrupted, "Well I guess we better get the ladies back. Might be the last good night of rest we all get for a while."

Captain Taylor nodded then said, "Yes I'm sorry. I'm not used to having such a good meal and such pretty company." He nodded slightly to each of the women with respect and appreciation. The ladies smiled back at him with a shining glow on their faces in response.

Chris excused himself to pay for all their meals, something on which he had insisted. They finished their drinks, got up and worked their way to the front of the restaurant which was now crowded. Chris caught up with them as they reached the front door. It was now an hour after dark. The street wasn't very well lit, for there were few lamps and most of the light was coming from store fronts that where still open.

On their return trip back to the hotel as they approached the same saloon, where they encountered trouble earlier. They saw that the same two men where still there, but now four others had joined them. Captain Taylor put his hand on his pistol then to Chris he said, "I wish we had another gun or two. They look like they're looking for trouble."

Matt handed Connie over to Mr. Hart to escort as he said, "Don't let go of her and keep all the ladies together. If anything happens don't stop. You Mr. McBain and Chris get the ladies back to the hotel as quick as you can."

Matt then quickly stepped up beside Captain Taylor then whispered, "I'm watching your left side."

Captain Taylor responded, "Thank you; but I wish you had a gun."

Matt answered, "Crowd them and don't give them time to think. When we get even with them, we'll let the ladies through then follow them. If it looks like there is going to be trouble jump them, don't let them have a chance to get set."

The Captain said, "Okay that's about as good as anything I'd come up with."

As they approached one of the men that had talked to them before started in again, "Why are you people so high and mighty? The way you act someone would think we had some kind of plague or something." The others laughed and cheered.

Matt and Jeff were about twenty feet away. The six men looking like they had been drinking for many hours. They seemed to realized the intentions of Matt and Jeff and formed a line across the walkway.

"Just keep crowding them." Matt uttered just loud enough for Jeff to hear with his lips hardly moving.

Another one of the ruffians said, "We just want to have a real good look at your fillies." They all tensed up as Matt and Jeff just keep walking right at them. One of the men then said, "Maybe they'd like to have some fun with some real men." They all guffawed loudly which started to draw a crowd. When Matt and Jeff got six feet away from them one of the men started to make a move for his gun. Matt saw the movement. He leaped forward and gave him a hard chop on his forearm as he tried to jerk his gun clear. Matt's hand had just been a flash. They heard the bone snap as the brute immediately started screaming. Matt let his momentum carry him as he spun on his right foot and kicked out with his left foot catching the man to his right on the left side of his knee. There was a loud pop as the knee was blown apart. He started howling very loudly. Letting his momentum carry him on Matt used the edge of his left hand. Matt hit the next man on his right as hard as he could on the back of his neck. There was a snap as he fell on the sidewalk. Not a sound had come out of his mouth. With Matt's next move as his left foot had hit the ground he pivoted on it then using his right foot with a back kick his leg fully extended was able to catch the man that was the farthest to his left on the mans Adam's apple with the back of his heel as the man made a grab for the gun on his hip. He dropped his gun and put both hands to his throat in an attempt to get some air. Matt getting his balance back under him saw that Captain Taylor had the other two men under control.

When Matt had jumped forward Captain Taylor had drawn his gun and hit the man in front of him on the head. As he fell Captain Taylor had pointed his gun at the last man left standing. In a mean voice full of threat told him not to move a muscle. The man froze completely sober now; he looked at the two that were still howling. The other two had stopped struggling. His friend closest to him was unconscious. He was in a state of shock now with his eyes full of fear.

Quickly Matt blurted, "Get the ladies to the hotel. Captain Taylor and I will be right behind you."

Chris looked at Matt with astonishment clearly showing in his eyes. He just nodded and then he turned, and hurried them on headed for the hotel. After the rest of the group had passed through Matt and

Captain Taylor followed. They turned to cover the last man from the fight and anyone else that might want to cause trouble. Matt glanced at the hotel to make sure their group was all right. Captain Taylor was still holding his gun on the only man that was left standing.

Captain Taylor watched as a crowd started to gather with their mouths drooped and their eyes full of wonder, "Tell the Marshal that we'll be at the hotel."

They got to the hotel without any further trouble. As Matt and Jeff got to the hotel lobby Mrs. Maxton hugged Matt than stepped back asking, "Are you all right?"

"Yes Ma'am."

Chris his eyes still filled with wonder asked, "How did you learn to move like that?"

Matt answered, "From some friends back in the city. I was tired of getting beat up all of the time."

Captain Taylor, said, "I've never seen anything like it. I thought we were going to have a lot harder time getting out of that trouble than we did."

Mrs. McBain confessed, "I couldn't believe that they'd be so rude."

Captain Taylor said, "Ma'am there's a lot of bad people out here and not just the men. For the most part they treat women with respect out here even the outlaws."

"Well, I am glad none of us got hurt. Guess we should be getting to bed. I'm tired." Chris sighed.

Captain Taylor said, "Yep you ladies should go on to bed. Chris we need to wait for the Marshal to get here." Captain Taylor saw the worried look appear in the ladies eyes; so he said, "No! no don't worry. I'm sure there won't be a problem."

The women reluctantly said goodnight then went up to their rooms with Mr. McBain and Mr. Hart escorting them.

The Marshal showed up about fifteen minutes later. Spotted Jeff he said, "Captain Taylor," came out almost by habit as he walked up then shook his hand, "You left quite a mess out there."

Captain Taylor said, "I'm sorry, but they crowded us I was afraid there'd be gunplay. But they never got a shot off."

The Marshal said, "That's what the other people said." The Marshal looked at Matt as he continued, "You must be the young fellow that jumped them when they started for their guns."

"There was only one started for his gun first but I didn't want to let him get the advantage on us."

The Marshal said, "You did right. But you don't need a gun by what I saw."

Captain Taylor nodded, then said, "I told them that I wish we had another gun or two, but I had never seen how fast he could move nor how much damage he could do in such a short time. What I still can't get over is how easy he did it."

The Marshal responded, "That's what I was told. They will be burying two of them. One looked like his knee was going to split his pants. Another one has a broken arm. Of course, the one you hit Captain is going to have one hell of a headache. The last one was real humbled. He told everyone that he was glad he didn't get a chance to make a move."

"We didn't want them to get the upper hand." replied Captain Taylor.

"Well take care and goodnight," the Marshal said while shaking hands with them.

Captain Taylor in turn said, "Goodnight,"

After Captain Taylor left Chris and Matt gratefully went upstairs to bed.

CHAPTER FIVE

LEARNING TO SET UP CAMP

The rest of the week had gone by without any trouble not that everyone didn't have their trials. Mr. Maxton and the rest of the city people had all pulled together by doing their share. (City people) is what, they were called by the rest of the other settlers on the wagon train.

Mr. Maxton had insisted that his drivers teach him how to harness and hook up the wagons and also how to drive them.

Not to be outdone the women had started doing the camp chores and cooking. They learned to build a fire pit and set up the iron tripod to hang the kettles on. The Gates family had the camp site next to them, so they had helped teach them what was needed to be done and how to cook over an open fire. They had earned the respect of most of the people, for they all worked hard and wouldn't quit even when they had gotten blisters on their hands and muscle cramps in their arms, backs, and legs. However, they just where not used to doing all the things that were required to have a good campsite. Connie had fared the best and as far as her mother and Mrs. McBain could tell even liked being out in the wild. At first Mr. Maxton had tried to keep her from helping him and the drivers harness the horses and hooking them up to the wagons, but she had persisted until she got her way.

Today had been a day of rest. There was a preacher and his family with the wagon train so they had a service and some singing accompanied by a couple of fiddle players.

The scouts made it back and told the Captain that they thought the grass was doing good and they could start anytime he wanted. They also said that as far as they had gone the rivers and streams had a plenty of water.

Connie really was enjoying herself she thought, maybe more than the rest of her group, except for Matt of course. She knew that things weren't going to be easy. Connie had spent enough time at the Sockett's to know how things where. She also knew the Sockett's could have had a lot better life style than they did and that different circumstances can change everything for a family. She thought how the family wouldn't be as happy or close as they were if they lived in the city. She already missed them a lot and thinking about them made it worse.

Connie missed Matt more than she wanted to admit. She knew that was one of the reasons she had stayed so busy. For Matt had decided to stay at the stable with his horse. "Damn," she mumbled as she thought about him. "He's probably sleeping with that horse."

"What?" asked Judy Gates.

Judy Gates was a quite girl of twelve and the Gates youngest daughter. She was slimly built maybe a little short for her age she was starting to show signs of sprouting out. She had light red hair and brown eyes with a cute face.

Surprised Connie said, "Huh?" Then with cherry cheeks blooming she blurted, "Oh, I'm sorry. I was just thinking out loud I guess."

Judy pointed and said, "There are some flowers over there that we haven't seen before."

Connie responded, "Oh they are pretty and all different colors. They look like painted flowers don't they?"

"Oh yes. I'm glad you asked me to come along for a walk."

"Well we need to head back. I know we're not far, but we better not take any chances. I was just tired of sitting."

"I'm glad to just walk. Even though today is Sunday, "Judy said. "My mom would have found something for me to do."

As they walked back Connie wondered if Matt knew that they were starting out tomorrow.

On their return back toward the camp Matt was just riding in. He thought it had been a real productive week working with the stallion he had named Flame. Matt had borrowed a horse blanket from Mr.

Griffin and remained in the corral and only leaving to use the outhouse or to get some food. After the first couple days they had become well accustomed with each other. He was really looking forward to getting a bath and scraping the whiskers off his face. They were starting to itch. Matt had made friends with Flame and worked with him like he had never been handled by anyone else. After that the stallion responded well and they both seemed to reach on understanding. Matt thought he learned as much from Flame; as he had taught him.

When Matt was able to put the saddle on Flame without him getting upset he found he was able to ride him without bucking or making a fuss. Matt was teaching Flame to neck and knee rein as well as ground tie. Flame was quick to learn and the two of them challenged each other with some games they both liked to play together. Matt was sure every one had to have some play time even animals.

Matt had taken Flame out on the open range the last couple of days and found out that Flame had a smooth, effortless stride. Flame was very fast and Matt thought he had still had some speed left if needed.

Matt couldn't have been happier. Flame still didn't like other people and got tense around them. As long as Matt was in the saddle Flame was okay and behaved as long as he was close by. Matt was sure that no one else would be able to handle or steal him, right now anyway. He also taught Flame to respond to his whistle and in a couple of days the stallion recognized his name.

Mr. Sockett said that Matt had a magical touch with animals and especially horses. He commented that Matt was firm, friendly and patient with them which the animals seemed to recognize. Matt eased Flame toward camp leaning forward enough so he could pat his neck and spoke to him in a calm voice. This was now the most people Flame had been around. Flame stayed calm, but his ears kept flipping back and forth. The stunning pair had drawn the eyes of several of the people, for Matt had been brushing Flame down every night and his coat was looking magnificent.

Matt guided Flame around the camp until he could see the wagons belonging to his group. Subconsciously he felt his glance pull around to make eye contact with Connie as she and Judy were coming back to camp. For as long as he could remember he new when Connie was around without hearing or even seeing her. He wasn't sure how or why he just knew it.

Connie and Judy walked toward Matt and Flame. Matt stopped Flame and waited; wanting to see how close they could get before Flame tensed up. Connie and Judy got to within fifty feet before Flame started to tense up. Matt quietly said, "Stay still just a minute."

Matt eased out on the saddle and spoke to Flame while rubbing his neck. After a little while Matt said, "Real calm and with your best friendly voice see if you can ease up to us."

Judy started to come also Matt said, "Sorry miss, just Connie please."

Connie got to within five feet before Flame started fidgeting. Matt held up his hand and Connie stopped. Matt was able to calm Flame down again and then Matt eased Flame ahead. Matt was proud of Connie for she just waited patiently not moving. She quietly spoke, "Nice horse pretty horse."

When Matt stopped Flame started to sniff Connie's hair along with the rest of her.

Matt was still rubbing Flames neck. Connie slowly raised her hand to rub Flames nose and forehead. Flame relaxed and Matt said to Connie, "He likes you. I named him Flame."

Connie spoke quietly, "That fits him. He is real pretty. Can he run?"

Matt nodded, "Yeah he can really move."

Just then Flame jerked his head up. Matt and Connie looked up and saw Captain Taylor with two others riding their way. They had stopped when they saw Flame's head come up.

Matt said to Connie. "Probably be better if you eased off a little. We're still in our training stages."

Connie eased back to stand next to Judy again. Matt turned Flame so they were facing Captain Taylor and the two riders. Matt could see Captain Taylor saying something to the other two and then he walked his horse forward alone. Flame stood in place until Captain Taylor got within fifteen feet then he tensed up and snorted.

Captain Taylor stopped his horse and quietly said, "You've really done it. He's still a bit skittish, but if you can control him for a week or so he'll get used to things."

Matt nodded, "He's a quick learner. I think he knows now that not everyone is mean and brutal."

Captain Taylor nodded, "Is he as fast as he looks?"

"Faster I think."

Captain Taylor's eyes flicked, then he nodded without saying anything. He raised his hand and motioned for the other two riders to come forward. They walked their horses up even with Captain Taylor and stopped. Flame was fidgeting a little, but not bad.

Captain Taylor quietly said, "I'd like you to meet our scouts. This one on my left is Dan Wade and on my right here is Hawkeye."

They both nodded and said, "Hi."

Matt nodded then said, "Hi."

Dan wade was five foot six with a stocky build and had green eyes. He had short legs but a long body with long arms. He wore a mustache complemented by an old scar on his left cheek suspiciously like it was made from a knife. He had a jagged scar on his right cheek running up into his hairline. When he smiled you could see a gap in his teeth where they had been knocked out. He wore his pistol tied down low on his right hip. He also wore a big bowie knife behind his left hip.

Hawkeye was of the Delaware Nation and taller than most of his people. He was five- foot- eleven with a dimpled square chin long nose and sharp black eyes. Medium in build, but well muscled with raven-black hair.

Dan said, "Captain Taylor tried to tell me you were taming that man-killer. He'd never lied to me before, but until now I thought he was pulling a woolly on me. Now I'm seeing, but still not believing it."

Matt responded, "He's real friendly once you get acquainted with him."

Captain Taylor said, "Chris was worried that you'd be killed by that horse; I told him I thought you'd be able to tame him. Hell; he let you in the corral with him. That was a good sign."

Matt nodded and replied, "Yeah, that was the hard part. I still get goose bumps thinking about that."

Captain Taylor laughed quietly and nodded, "Yep that sure was something to see."

"Well, I'd like to get him settled down for the night."

They all nodded and gently reined their horses away. Matt decided to walk to the wagons, which weren't far away. Connie and Judy let Matt and Flame go past and then followed at a safe distance. They said their goodbyes with each going to their own camp.

Matt picked a spot just outside the wagons to unsaddle Flame, then picketed him out to graze. Matt could see some people inside the circle of wagons still watching them as he finished rubbing Flame down. Then he walked toward the campfire.

He went to the wagon where his gear was stored and got a change of clothes. Guessing at Matt's intentions Chris pointed to a bend in the river where he could go to bath and told him it had a nice deep hole with a sandy bottom. Matt with his change of trail clothes and boots that he had been using when he went hunting back east. The Sockett's had seen to that, for city clothes didn't last long in the woods. Matt shaved and got all cleaned up, then he returned back to the wagons just as the women where finishing the evening meal.

He put away his dirty clothes and walked to the campfire to find a plate and some utensils helping himself. He then took his plate of food to a log not far from the fire. After they had eaten Matt checked on Flame. Matt took him to get some water and then took him out to some fresh grass. When he returned to camp he saw that Captain Taylor was sitting on a log sipping coffee by the fire. Matt came into the light and Connie who had watched Matt leave was waiting with a cup of coffee all ready for him. Connie walked to meet Matt handing it to him.

Captain Taylor followed her with his eyes as he was talking to Chris. The Captain said, "We'll rotate the wagons each day so no one is always in the rear eating dust." he jerked when out of the corner of his eye he spotted Matt walking into the camp, spilling a little hot coffee on his leg he jumped up sluicing some more on his hand. Holding the cup he said, "Damn, ouch! Sorry ladies." His face turned red as he stared hard at Matt, with a look at his feet he said, "You shouldn't sneak up on a person like that; you'll get hurt."

Chris said, "Captain Taylor, he wasn't. I guess Connie was taking him a cup of coffee, so I knew he was there. Maybe we're all used to him, for its normal to us that know him. As long as I can remember we have never heard Matt come or go. Guess I did think it would change out here, with so much under foot, but I see that it hasn't."

Captain Taylor responded, "Well, he needs to let out some kind of noise or something to let a body know he's around. If he's not careful somebody will be shooting him by accident. If we were already on the trail I would have been going for my gun."

Matt took the coffee from Connie and walked to the log and sat down. Captain Taylor just stood watching still not hearing Matt make a noise and could see that it did look like his normal walk.

Matt said, "Sorry, Captain Taylor. My folks always said they had to get used to me when I was real young. I forget sometimes when I'm around new friends to let myself be heard."

Chris responded, "Captain, guess I should have said something. I didn't know he'd startle you so, but even when he was a toddler he was light on his feet. We all just got used to it."

Captain Taylor said, "Well, I guess I need to apologize," looking at Matt. "It's my job to know and see everything that's going on and wasn't expecting anybody coming or going that I couldn't hear. Hawkeye isn't even as quiet as you are"

Matt sipped his coffee then replied, "I'll try not to scare you again."

"You didn't. Well, you did startle me." Changing the subject, "Do you think you can control your horse?"

"Yes. He's getting pretty calm now; I think he likes it out here already. Better than that corral he was in."

Captain Taylor responded, "Well, you might be all right if he doesn't run off on you."

"I think he'll be all right. We've gotten to be pretty good friends. I didn't break him; we just learned to work with each other."

Captain Taylor rose as he said, "Well, I better get back to my camp. I need to get up early; I want to have the wagons ready to be moving by daylight. Goodnight folks."

Connie sat down next to Matt and said, "Flame is beautiful."

Matt looked at her noticing that everybody else was going to their wagons or bedrolls leaving Connie and him alone.

"I was hoping you'd like him. I know you just met today, but I think he already likes you."

"Oh, I hope so. I can tell he really likes you. From what I've heard you've done wonders with him. Father was worried to death he'd hurt you."

"I think Flame was looking for a friend. He is awful smart, so once we got to be friends it was pretty easy to train him."

Connie said, "Well, we've made friends with that nice family over there," She had pointed over her shoulder at a campfire just a (little ways) from them.

Matt nodded, "I hope we can be friends with a lot of people."

Connie nodded in agreement, but she knew that Matt didn't make friends very easily. Thinking that the Sockett's and Chan's were the only ones Matt really had for friends outside of his family and he didn't really get along that well with his family.

"Dad likes you."

"Why, what did he say?"

"Oh, he hasn't said so in words, but he's always bringing your name up one way or another. I can tell he respects you, especially after what happened in town."

"Well, time we got some sleep."

As Matt got up, Connie did also, she knew they were done talking. She took his cup then said, "Goodnight."

"Goodnight."

Connie knew she needed sleep for they would be days upon days without a lot of rest. But she was restless, all she could think about was Matt and how much she cared for him. She had over the years learned that to know him, you needed to listen very well, for he didn't say much. She knew that he didn't want to talk about the fight in town and liked him even better for it. She knew that most people would like to brag about it. Then she thought about Captain Taylor and how he hadn't repeated anything about the incident either. She decided maybe that was what separated the dangerous people from those that just thought they were. As she drifted off to sleep she was glad that in the letter she had written to the Sockett's she hadn't told them anything about the fight.

It seemed like her eyes had just closed when Connie heard the call to rise. When she got to the fire, her mother and Mrs. McBain were already cooking and she noticed Matt bringing in some firewood. Mrs. Maxton said, "Matt, we've got lots of wood."

"Yes Ma'am, but we should keep an extra amount of dry wood; there'll be times it'll be hard to find. I'm going to drape a canvas under the wagon then make sure it stays full."

The food and coffee was almost done and the men were harnessing the horses and hooking them to the wagons. Connie decided to help Matt drape the piece of canvas he'd found under the wagon and fill it with wood. It was all stacked under the wagon and the teams hooked up with the horses saddled for the women as the morning meal was ready.

Chris waved Matt over as the drivers of the Maxton wagons approached the fire. He said, "Matt, you got so busy back at the corral you didn't get to meet our drivers. The tall lanky one is Tex and then Slade, next to him is Ben, then Bones, and Slim. Fellows, this is Matt."

They all shook hands. Then Tex muttered, "I saw you come in last night. A lot of people saw you with that horse, he sure is pretty to look at."

Matt nodded, "He can really run, but I don't know how much bottom he has yet. He's smart, too."

Slim said, "I can't believe he let you ride him."

"Well, I just kind of made friends with him, after that it was pretty easy."

Chris said, "I admit, I was worried to death. Everyone told me that horse was a man killer. Your folks would skin us both alive if they ever found out about it."

Matt responded, "He's still a little nervous with all the people around, but he is relaxing some. I think in a few days he'll be fine; I have trained him so he will knee and neck rein. He picks up on things quickly."

The men finished their meal and coffee then went to their respective wagons. Mr. Hart went to the wagon where they stored the extra gear for repairs--wheels even an extra axle, harnesses and most any other part. The Maxton's and the McBain's went and mounted their horses. It was the first day on the trail to a new life for many of them. There would be many sleepless nights a head of them due to the tension and excitement of the unexpected. After a few days the excitement would be replaced by boredom, from the slow pace. A few of them where just looking forward to the adventure and the scenery. Matt was one of them and he couldn't think of a better way than on the back of the grandest horse he had ever seen.

CHAPTER SIX

STARTING ON THE TRAIL

It had taken a little over three weeks to get to St. Joseph, Missouri. While they were there, they replenished their supply of goods. The weather had been decent, although there had been a couple of thunderstorms, which held them up a day or two.

Flame had really taken to the open country and Matt had him well trained now; he would even ground tie. Flame wasn't so gun shy anymore; Matt was able to get flame to lower his head with a touch of his knee, so Matt could shoot straight ahead and nor worry about shooting him in the head.

Matt had made friends with the Gates family. He was helping them whenever he got a chance. He retrieved water and wood for their cooking fire often, even though Helen Gates told him it was her job.

Robert Gates was a good prosperous farmer five-foot-four of a husky medium build, reddish blonde hair. His brown eyes and short blunt nose accented his face. He had a strong back big hands with a calm temperament and thought before speaking.

His wife Violet was five-foot-two of medium build with just a few excess pounds. Her very feminine hair was a rusty red color and her dark blue eyes nearly turned to violet when she was angry. She was blessed with a pretty face, her legs and arms in perfect proportion to the rest of her body and nibble hands a little smaller than appropriate for her frame.

His oldest boy Billy was five-foot-two on a frame of muscular medium-build. From his early growth it appeared he would be much taller than his father. He was handsome with bright red hair, and big hands. A little big for his age at fourteen with a demeanor calm and thoughtful, much like his father.

Plain-faced Joe his youngest was a little on the cubby side for a ten-year-old. He was a good worker for his age, liked farming and made good use of his long legs and arms.

Helen Gates was sixteen years, old five-foot-three and just a few pounds light for her well-proportioned body of medium build. She was very shapely with nicely formed hips, narrow waist, and well-formed shapely breasts. Her petty face much like her mothers. She had long bright red hair with some blonde mixed in.

Matt discovered he liked being around Helen as much as possible. They came to be on a first name basis and he talked to her as much as he did Connie. He had noticed that even though their eye color was different; both had the same brilliant sparkle in their eyes when they got excited about something.

It did seem lately Connie's eyes had something more intense in them. The normal sparkle he was used to see plus a little something he hadn't seen before. He noticed it when she looked at Helen and him together; he caught a couple of looks that held an intense brilliant flash of which he was trying to understand the meaning of. Matt thought that Connie was being sort of moody lately.

Connie had enjoyed their trip so far. She knew it was hard on everyone. Long trips were hard on the animals also, especially after a hard rain or at river crossings. The rain was still very cold, but she couldn't get over the clear skies and how big and bright the stars where. At first, she had been a little frightened of the animals sounds at night, but had finally gotten used to them. She asked Mr. Wade and Hawkeye to explain to her what they were and was able to pick them out nearly as quick as they could.

Captain Taylor and the scouts had gotten so they took their meals with the Gates family or the Maxton's. When they got ready to lie down for the night they'd just throw their bedrolls around whichever campfire they came too.

The Gates, Captain Taylor, and the Maxton drivers had all gotten used to Matt's silent comings and goings, now. Matt did try to make more noise, but still was as silent as ever, as far as they could tell. Connie smiled to herself. At last they weren't spilling coffee all over themselves.

Matt, even though he spent most of his time on horseback hadn't taken to wearing spurs like most of the men did.

What time she spent with Matt she could tell that he really was enjoying the trip. He spent most his time training Flame and now she thought that Flame would follow Matt around like a good pet dog. She and a few others had watched in fright as Matt and Flame played tag or something when they thought they were alone. Connie knew now that Flame would never hurt Matt. She had even gotten to ride Flame and boy she couldn't get over the power, she felt underneath her when she was on his back.

Flame had gotten sociable with a lot of the people and animals, but Matt and her were the only ones that had ridden him. Not even Helen had gotten to ride him, Connie thought with pride. Oh; she thought; sometimes she got so mad at Matt and especially Helen. She really did like Helen; she even let Helen ride her horse, when Helen's parents allowed it. She knew Helen liked her a lot too, she still helped Connie and her mother in chores around camp whenever Helen had a little extra time. She knew she couldn't help feeling like Helen was taking Matt from her. But being honest with herself; she couldn't blame Helen, because Helen had asked her if Matt was her guy. Connie had told her that Matt had never laid claim to her. She explained they'd been good friends forever; and knew that was true; but couldn't get over the ache in her heart. It had taken awhile, but Connie finally realized how much she really loved Matt and how proud she was of him. When he was with Helen, her feelings were not so complimentary.

Matt had at one time or another helped almost everyone on the wagon train. Her father had hired drivers for the wagons, but had not given Matt a job. So Matt had just taken it upon himself to help wherever he could. Driving a wagon or fixing a broken wheel or axle, or just taken over when someone was sick or needed something. Most everyone liked Matt and said he was handy with his hands and as strong as anyone they had seen.

There were three wagons of trouble-makers though; always trying to make sure they had the best spot or crowding to water their animals first. As of yet, nothing bad had happened. One wagon with a family of six and the other two had two men each that were on the mean side. The one with the family had two cows; they pulled along behind their wagon. The wife and four children were always yelling at one another or fussing about something. They were tolerated and most everybody just stayed away from them. The thing was; every once in a while things came up missing; but nothing could be proven that linked them to the items. The way the men looked at Connie and some of the other women, made her stomach turn. It was like they were looking at them as if they were completely naked.

Nobody ever heard what the troublemakers last names were, but Connie for one now realized that names out here didn't mean much anyway. It was what a person did that mattered. For that reason and to get Matt off her mind; she insisted on driving one of the wagons every once in a while, over her fathers protest. She tried to stay busy doing anything she could. Connie realized that her mother knew; or suspected she was upset with Matt, so she was avoiding her unless they were so busy they didn't have to talk much. Her mother couldn't help her not to suffer and she sure didn't want her mother feeling sorry for her.

Helen hadn't wanted to move west when her family had decided to. She'd been happy where she was. She had decided she would teach school or get a job at one of the businesses offices as a secretary in the small town of Hebron Ohio they had come from. She hadn't ever really been boy crazy, as her mother would say. Oh, she liked a good dance, but she had made up her mind that if she ever got interested in a guy. He was going to have to be something real special. Helen smiled to herself and admitted that she was really attracted to Matt. He was so handsome it almost took her breath away every time she looked at him. All of his facial features were just perfect she thought. Those nice thick lashes of light brown, almost blonde; his nose not too long or short. She thought, it was just right and his eyes were the most perfect hazel she had ever seen. They could change colors mysteriously at times. Every once in a while, he'd smile or show some other emotion that she didn't understand and his eyes would really sparkle with flashes of light going through them. Matt had nice full lips, but not too big and his ears were a perfect shape also. Helen thought she couldn't improve a thing to make him look better in any way. She Knew he was over six feet tall; but didn't know how many inches. He had long legs and arms to match, wide shoulders with a flat waist. Helen thought that Matt was heavier than he looked because she didn't think he had an ounce of fat on him. As big as he was, it seemed like he moved with the ease and lightness of somebody half his size.

Helen thought of Connie and was a little sad, she had really taken to her. They had gotten along very well and were close friends now. Connie was so pretty she thought; much prettier than herself. Connie had long blonde hair and was five-foot-six and could probably grow a little still. She realized that Connie had long legs. As she thought of Connie she wondered if her own hips were as big, she knew Connie's were not so big, but she thought that they fit her pretty well with her thin waist; not really skinny. It was obvious she had a real nice chest and no one had to wonder what was there. She knew that Connie probably looked better than she dressed, but Connie couldn't hide her build completely. She thought Connie resembled her mother more, but had gotten her height from her father. Connie's father was six feet with medium brown hair. His face encompassed a chin which was a little square with a long nose, his eyes the same blue as Connie. Mr. Maxton had broad shoulders and carried a little excess weight, but she could see that he was already thinning up, and had built up some muscle too. Helen felt sorry for Mrs. Maxton and Mrs. McBain, for it was easy to see they where not used to the hard work. There was an awful lot for them to learn about living outside and doing the chores that needed to be done. Helen was proud of them for they insisted on looking after and doing their own work.

She had always been proud of her family, for they where well respected by their neighbors and her parents had volunteered to help out the Maxton's right from the start. Now they were all friends and always made sure their fires where close together. It had been suggested that they make just one fire, but Mr. and Mrs. Maxton said it wouldn't be right for them to be fixing food for all their people.

Helen did admit the five cowboys, especially Matt ate a lot. Some of the other people really didn't like the Maxton family or the cowboys; especially at first. Everyone knew the Maxton's where fresh out of the city. They where looked on as just another bunch of high rich class city people. The cowboys didn't help either because they always wore their pistols on their hips like they knew how to use them, which made a few of the people nervous. There hadn't been any trouble, but people just stayed away for the most part. She thought that a lot of them where jealous. Mr. Maxton hadn't spared any on his expenses; for he had bought the best, wagons, tools, rope, mules and horses. Everything was in top notch condition.

Helen had to admit that all of the guns and the cowboys themselves had made her nervous at first, but now she thought she'd trust any of them. They all had been respectful and if anything even acted shy or afraid of the women. Her brothers Billy and Joe along with her sister Judy were getting along with them real good.

Tex was almost as tall as Matt, not as heavy built. But she figured he would be dangerous in any kind of fight. Tex seemed to like the kids and didn't seem to mind having them around. Helen thought Slade was short at five-foot four, stocky built. But he would not be one to mess with she thought. Joe really liked him. Slim was what his names sake said he was. He liked to talk and had done so right from the start. He told great stories and laughed a lot. Helen didn't think he'd run from a fight either. Bones, the dark one was a little shorter than Tex, but had big broad shoulders, long legs and a narrow waist. It was obvious he was strong and very healthy. He was shy around the women and had been real quite at first with everyone, except the other cowboys. He was cautious around the children also, until he felt like he was accepted.

Ben, the last of the cowboys who worked driving the Maxton's wagons; was quiet and stayed to himself. He was very pleasant and not a bit rude. Helen thought he might have been highly educated somewhere; for once or twice he had slipped up and spoke some very good English, instead of the Western or Texas drawl. Ben wore two guns and always made sure they were cleaned every night. Helen was really happy, that they were all getting along so well. Helen's thoughts then went back to Connie and, she felt a little sad again. She didn't know what to do. Helen knew, or was pretty sure that Connie was in love with Matt. When they first met he was all she talked about when they were alone. Then Matt finally made his appearance with Flame and she couldn't blame Connie. Now it seemed like Matt spent a lot of time with her and even though Connie tried to hide it. She could see the hurt and anger in Connie's eyes. Connie had tried not to let her see it, but Helen had caught it out of the corner of her eye a couple of times. Helen knew they were still friends, but it was a real tense friendship and neither one of them talked about Matt any longer. Helen got up from the rock she'd been sitting on and went back to camp, which was just a short walk away.

There had been a Bible reading that her father had led. Then they had taken the rest of the day off just to rest. They were to move out again in the morning. The Maxton's and Matt sat in on the Bible reading. So had the McBain's and Mr. Hart and even Captain Taylor. The cowboys, Mr. Wade and Hawkeye had stayed back, but were quiet and respectful. After eating everyone just seemed to go to their own spots and either took a nap or simply watched the wind blow through the grass and trees. It had been a pleasant afternoon.

Helen saw Connie get up and walk away from camp. As she watched she knew instantly where she was going. She didn't even have to turn her head. She knew Matt and Flame were coming back. They had taken the day off like the rest. She assumed even though they had not known each other long, that they where more able to relax by taking a gentle easy ride. Helen was sure that with all the energy Matt and Flame had, they would have been a bundle of nerves if they had stayed in camp. Helen thought that Connie and her could always feel Matt's presence long before seeing him. She thought that was why as quiet as he was, they where not surprised like the others when he walked up on them.

Connie didn't realize she had been going to meet Matt until she saw him and Flame come over the little rise about a quarter of mile away. She stood and waited for them to come up to her. Matt smiled at Connie and said, "We really had a good run and Flame still has a lot of bottom left in him."

"It doesn't look like he is breathing hard at all."

Matt dismounted and started walking beside Connie with Flame following close behind them. "Connie, I like it out here. There is so much to see. Flame and I get along fantastic together."

"Yeah, it's been nice, the fresh air most mornings and the new growth, it's been pretty. You know the…flowers and the new blossoms on the trees."

"Well, things are going to a change now. We're going to be heading out on to the plains and then after that we go across the mountains."

Connie sighed, "Yes, it's been just like Mr. Sockett told us so far and I remember him saying that sometimes it got pretty dry."

"Well, Hawkeye said that he thought this would be a better year than most."

"He doesn't say much, but he don't miss anything that's going on. I've seen him watching you; I think he and Mr. Wade are good scouts."

Matt said, "Yep, Captain Taylor has done a super job and I've noticed that few complaints of any kind have been directed his way. So, I'm sure he'd pick the best he could find; your father's drivers have already proved to all of us how good Captain Taylor's judgment is."

"Yes, Dads very pleased with them. He doesn't think things could be going any better, we are ahead of schedule, and the first wagon train to cross this year."

As they approached the camp site Matt picked out a spot of nice plush green grass to picket Flame on. Matt as he unsaddled Flame and gave him a good rub down said, "Everything's been so good; we haven't had many delays or breakdowns; so luck has been on our side so far."

They walked up to the cook fire which for one time the Gates and Maxton's had decided to combine to make one big meal. Matt and Connie were the last to arrive.

Captain Taylor said, "Matt, I'm going to have to restrict you from riding off from now on. It's not going to be safe for a single rider anymore."

"Yes sir. I understand, but I am careful and I watch very close."

Captain Taylor said, "Well, it could get pretty dangerous for some one not armed."

Connie cut in on them and said, "Matt will be all right, especially if he's armed," she smiled with pride showing all over her face.

"Okay, I know he can handle himself. I've seen that first hand."

Chris and the rest of the Maxton's group nodded in confirmation. The Gates and all the cowboys stared at Matt and Captain Taylor.

Matt then responded slightly embarrassed, but with a firm voice said, "That is in the past, I would like to forget about that."

Matt's statement had put a real curious look on their faces.

Mrs. Maxton seeing Matt's precarious position announced, "Well, the food is ready; lets eat."

Matt so he wouldn't be questioned stayed back as everyone helped themselves. After they had eaten Captain Taylor sitting near Matt reassured him with, "It isn't your abilities I'm questioning. It's just that things are a whole lot different out here. You have to notice and see everything that's about you or you'll lose your hair."

Connie not realizing her pride in Matt was controlling her cut in again saying, "Mr. Sockett said that Matt was as good as anybody he'd ever seen. He worked very hard to make sure Matt was ready and also made sure I could do nearly as well."

Captain Taylor in exasperation said, "I hear you people mention his name a lot. Just who is he?"

Mrs. Maxton insistently said, "He's the one that taught all of us to shoot--a rifle anyway."

Captain Taylor said, "No! No! I mean, what is his first name?"

Mr. Maxton with a slight grin replied, "Thought that's what you meant. The little we were told about him before we left from the East was that he had a bad fight at Great Falls Idaho and got shot up pretty bad. Then how a young school teacher; new from back East; helped save his life. After he recovered because of his reputation; she insisted they go to the East coast if they where going to get married. That was the only way she would and he loved her enough also, so he agreed."

"Yeah, yeah," said Captain Taylor his cheeks puffing a little. "That's fine, but you still didn't mention his first name."

Chris with a little short laugh said, "Sorry, it's the first time I've had a chance to get in a good story that would hold your interest. We've heard so many from the rest of you, so I thought it might be my turn. We call him Mr. Sockett which upsets him and he keeps telling us to just call him Vern."

Captain Taylor about to speak couldn't form a word; with opened mouth he just stared at Chris.

Dan Wade excitedly said, "I heard he died after that fight. It was said he got shot up bad Captain; that's what I heard!" Tex said, "Never heard of him. What's the big story?"

Dan said, "Oh if we're talking about the same man, you've heard of him all right."

Slim said, "Tex is probably right, we mostly spent are lives in Texas and Mexico Territory, that is a long way for word to get to us about something that happened in Idaho."

Dan with slight nod said, "You tell them Captain."

Captain Taylor looked at Chris and then asked, "Do you know if he was the town Marshal?"

Chris nodded, "Yeah, he did say he was the Marshal for two years before the gun fight. He didn't like to say much about it though."

Tex a little loudly asked, "All right, you two seem to know. You going to let us in on the rest of the story."

Captain Taylor nodded as he looked at Dan who nodded for him to do the talking, "Yelp, I just wanted to get some fun out of it too."

Dan grinned as he said, "Yeah, and he was."

Tex and Slim gave them pleading looks and acted like they were about ready to jump up and down. The Gates and the rest of the cowboys looked anxious as they nodded pleadingly.

Captain Taylor said, "Okay, most people weren't interested in details as far as his given name, but he was known as the Idaho Gun Wizard."

Nobody said anything for a couple of minutes while the Captain and Dan just sat waiting for their response with smug looks on their faces.

Finally, Tex with amazement in his voice said, "Man, I heard he was really something. They say you couldn't even see him draw and he could still shoot the eye out of a needle."

Slim said, "Yep, heard he was hell on wheels once he got started. Oh, sorry ladies, didn't mean to curse."

Mrs. Maxton smiled, "That's okay, Slim. Chris and I suspected there was a lot they hadn't told us."

Ben who never spoke much with a serious tone in his voice said, "I heard about that fight. Heard he took seven of them with him that day. I did hear he died though."

Dan said, "I heard eight and it was said he hit some others pretty bad, but they were able to get away."

Captain Taylor said, "The few that seen it said, Mr. Sockett was taking lead, but just kept shooting until his guns were empty."

Tex said, "I heard he was a one gun man."

Captain Taylor said, "Yeah, as a rule he wasn't known to wear two guns, but I did hear that on occasion he wore two and could hit what he aimed at with either hand."

Slim said, "Heard he was awfully good and nobody to mess with."

Mr. Gates added, "Yeah, we even heard about it four or five years ago from a traveling salesman that stopped by one day. We thought it was exaggerated though."

Captain Taylor said, "No, he was something. Sure does my heart good to know he's still alive." Looking at Chris he asked, "He doing well?"

Chris answered, "Yeah, he has a lovely wife and a very nice girl and boy."

Hawkeye who had really been attentive said, "Heard he was a real good tracker."

Dan said, "There is that. It was said he could trail an ant across solid rock."

Tex asked, "Captain, do you know what started that ruckus?"

Captain Taylor answered, "Well, what I heard was there was a gang of claim jumpers, that were holding up the ore wagons. Mr. Sockett was really crimping their style, so they all got together and rode into town. They thought if they had enough guns, it would be a piece of cake."

Captain Taylor paused to catch his breath then continued, "Well, Mr. Sockett suspected something was up. Story is he was crossing the street. Instinctively he knew or spotted them coming out of the stable area. It was said as they charged he didn't give them a chance. He just started knocking them out of their saddles. Of course if I was going up against fourteen or fifteen riders, I don't think I'd let them get set either."

Slim said, "You'd have thought they would have made sure of him."

The Captain answered, "From what I heard he was emptying saddles real quick and with all the noise from the gunfire and all the lead that was flying around everywhere the one's that didn't get hit; left like the Devil himself was after them."

Bones said, "Lucky he was wearing both of his guns."

The Captain said, "Most think he had heard something was up. He had been wearing two guns for a week leading up to that day."

Slim asked, "Captain, do you really think that Mr. Sockett did all the things that have been told about him."

Captain Taylor responded, "Pretty much. Had an old friend of mine that was from up that way. He never told me a lie that I know of and I always took any information he had given me as gospel."

Bones said, "Heard about him, all good as far as I'm concerned."

Wade said, "Never heard anything bad about him, except that he didn't know how to back down from anything or anybody; if that is bad."

The Captain said, "Not out here it's not. Just make sure it's for right."

"Captain, Captain! There's a fight!" yelled someone from the wagon train as he came running up.

Captain Taylor got up as, he walked off he tipped his hat to the ladies excusing himself. Then he asked, "Where?" He was told straight across the far side. Matt jumped up and hurried after him. Dan seeing Matt get up rushed to catch up with Matt. He took the gun loop off the hammer of his pistol as he caught up with Matt saying, "I think maybe your are right."

When they got within hearing distance they could see the Captain pulling people apart, and telling some of the other fellows that had been standing there watching to do the same. Matt was impressed, he hadn't realized the Captain was still as strong as he was. For he was just grabbing people and throwing them aside.

Things where beginning to settle down. So Dan and Matt stayed back on the edge of the ruckus. Finally with everyone calmed down the Captain gave angry looks at the men involved in the fight and said, "I know all of you know what the by-laws are on this wagon train." controlling his temper as he pointed, he added, "You and you find all the whiskey and destroy it. From now on I see a bottle that's not being used for medical purposes you'll be left at the next town we come to. I don't care which side you fought on, but that war is over. I had friends on both sides."

Dan listening and watching intently hadn't noticed when Matt left his side.

Captain Taylor trying to make eye contact with everyone said, "I hope there aren't any more problems, because any other infraction of any kind I'll throw you out of the wagon train."

Just then there was a yell! "That's my whiskey you're having them destroy. That cost me a lot of money. I'll kill you." He shouted as he reached for his gun and had just cleared leather when they saw a flash of movement. Suddenly his gun went flying through the air and they heard a snap. He let out a loud yell as he grabbed his arm. Suddenly two younger men in there mid twenties leapt at Matt. One of them yelled! "That's my dad you son of a bitch."

Matt spun catching the closest one with a foot in the chest so hard he went flying back almost where he had just come from. As his brother rushed in Matt's right hand caught him in the center of his chest. Matt had been so quick, and accurate it was hard to tell which one hit the ground first. It took each them about a minute to get air back into their lungs. Then both moaned saying, "U-h I think he broke my chest. Oh, I hurt!"

Captain Taylor, very angry now; was pointing at all three of them as they sat on the ground in a lot of pain. He grumbled. "When we leave in the morning you don't put your wagon in line. This is as far as you go."

A friend of the three said, "Man you can't just leave them here all alone."

Captain Taylor said, "They'll just have to cross back over the Missouri river to St. Joseph, I don't really care."

One of the boy's still moaning pointed at Matt asked. "What about him?"

Dan Wade, who was holding his hand on the butt of his pistol said. "He was stopping a murder and defending himself. I hope you're not dumb enough to think we should do anything about him!"

Someone in the back of the crowd said, "They are our friends, we can't just abandon them."

One of the three men who had been sent to destroy the whiskey returned and said, "Captain we destroyed all of the whiskey that we could find--as much as was visible easy-like-anyway."

The Captain roared, "Okay thanks! Well everybody you all should get back to your wagons. It will be daylight before you know it, if any of you want to go with them it's up to you. But this is as far as they go."

There was not a one that objected. For by the tone of his voice he left no doubt. He meant to be precisely obeyed in every detail. Matt had quietly eased off back to his campfire. Captain Taylor waited a little for the crowd to disperse. After a little everyone had calmed down as they broke off into small groups talking about the incident. Most went back to their own wagons and campfires. Captain Taylor satisfied that things had settled down walked up to Dan. After a quick glance around asked, "Where's Matt?"

Dan turned and looked around. Surprised he said, "Damn he was just here. I swear he's unnerving. It seems like he just vanishes."

"Well, I'm glad he was here."

Dan said, "Sorry Captain, I thought I was seeing everything, but I sure missed that fellow when he went for his gun."

"I know Dan. Matt took care of him, that's all that matters."

"Captain, I have never seen anybody move so fast."

"He is awful sudden. Dan, I didn't see it this time, but I've seen him in action once already and know for a fact how quick he is."

"Captain, I've never seen anybody fight like that. Not sure I really saw everything that happened, but I did hear that one fellow's arm snap than saw the gun go through the air. Then the other two jumped up, but they would have been better to have stayed put. They just ended up going right back where they came from; real quick-like. "

"Yeah, that's a fact. I don't think I'd ever what to face Matt in a fight."

Dan exclaimed, "That's for damn sure. Matt's not far from having me spooked."

"Dan, you don't have anything to worry about from Matt."

"Captain, I know that, I just can't think of another word for him right now, he's just spooky. You don't hear him come or go and he's so damn fast.

They had come up to their bed rolls. So they said their good nights and laid down.

The third night out from St. Joseph they came to the Delaware River in Kansas territory. They camped a little early as Captain Taylor wanted everybody to make sure all their canteens and water kegs were full. Also, he passed the word to carry all the extra wood they could find to build their fires with. No one complained for they were seeing very few trees and where also coming up on less water all the time. There was a lot of grass and it was still green. It resembled waves on a sea when the wind was blowing, which was most the time. It would die down toward the evenings most of the time. It hadn't gotten awful hot, but was getting so they didn't need blankets to sleep.

Connie spotted Captain Taylor coming when he came back to camp after checking all the wagons. She got up and poured a cup of coffee and handed it to him. He wasted no time in saying "Thank you." After taking a sip, he gave Chris and Matt a look and said, "I'd like to talk with both of you; in private."

Captain Taylor with coffee cup in hand walked away from the supper fire a little. Matt and Chris followed him as Connie with a possessive frown on her face sat back down. Captain Taylor glanced around then stopped. Then he said, "I don't think anybody's within hearing."

After giving Chris a hard look he stated, "Chris, it's Matt I really wanted to talk to. But I remember you saying that Matt's father had put you in charge. I'll get right to the point. I've got a couple of more wagons I want to check on before it gets dark."

Matt just stood listening intently.

Chris said, "Thank you Captain. I'm curious, but I do appreciate your thoughtfulness."

"Well Chris, you may not after you hear me out."

"Well go ahead, get it done."

Matt didn't show it, but he was curious. The Captain then looked hard at Matt as he said, "Matt I had a chance to talk to a couple of Trappers that came in off the plains at St. Joseph. They were headed for St. Louis to sell their fur's. They told me they came across a lot of Indian sign, especially for this time of year. They felt like it might be a bad year for Indians. I'd appreciate it if you kept this to yourselves. I don't want everybody getting nervous before there's anything to really be concerned about. Matt what I'd like and I'm kind of in a tuff spot. I've ask a few who could do the job, but was told they felt like they needed to stay with their families. You see I had another scout in mind that I wanted, but he didn't make it. I hoped I could run into somebody that could fill in for him. So, Matt I'm asking you if you'd try to fill in. I'll pay you of course. I had that figured in when I agreed to take this wagon train west."

Captain Taylor held his hand up as Matt started to answer. "The rest of it is I want you to ride with Dan and Hawkeye to make sure you can read sign and not run into an ambush. I want you to be armed from now on also."

Captain Taylor looked back at Chris and then said, "That's it. If you say no I'll treat it like we never talked."

Chris didn't respond right away, he then asked, "Do you really think Matt can take care of himself out there." He then looked quickly at Matt kind of apologetically he added, "Matt, I've already seen you in action and know you can take care of yourself, but I'm not sure you can handle things that you may not know anything about. I think there's a lot you need to know yet."

"Your daughter told us that Mr. Sockett said he was as good as anyone he knew."

Chris worriedly frowned, then said, "He might have said that just to flatter her."

The Captain said, "You believe that Mr. Sockett did say that then."

Chris answered, "Oh yes, I heard him also."

The Captain said, "Well Vern meant it then or he wouldn't have told you so."

"Okay, Matt's father wouldn't approve, but he's not here. Besides, he really never took the time to know his own son. If I told him no, more than likely we probably couldn't keep Matt in camp."

Captain Taylor looked back to Matt and then asked, "Well what do you think?"

"I'd like to try it Captain."

Captain Taylor nodded with a glint in his eye, that was the first time Matt had dropped his last name. He then said, "Good. Ride out with Dan in the morning. Well armed and if you can; find some clothes that blend in with the land. That would be a big help. Color is more important than anything."

Matt said, "I'm sure I can find every thing I will need."

"Okay, thanks Matt, just be careful. Dan's real good, so he will check you out. Hopefully, there will be something you can pick up on."

Matt flatly said, "I'm sure I will."

The Captain replied, "Well thank you. I got some things I need to check on, I'll see you after dark."

Chris and Matt went back to their cook fire. When they got there Chris in firm voice said, "Listen up, I know you're curious. Matt is going to be helping the scout's, so he'll be getting up early and back late. I just didn't want anyone to be in a panic when you don't see him tomorrow."

Tex said, "Do you think he'll be all right." Then holding his hand up to stop everyone so he could finish he quickly said, "No insult Matt, I'm just kind of fond of you, I don't want to see you get hurt…or worse."

Matt said, "That's okay, Tex. I won't be by myself for a few days yet. They'll make sure I'm good enough before turning me loose. Besides I'll be extra careful."

Connie said, "Oh yeah, and when did you start that?"

Matt looked at Connie as he frowned, then asked, "What do you mean by that?"

"Matt, I've followed you around a lot of places in the city we weren't supposed to be. I have never seen you run from a fight."

Connie a little red-faced spun her head around to see her mother and father looking at her with a knowing smile on their faces. She knew she had just told on herself, thankfully they didn't seem to be upset. As she wondered about that she relaxed. Matt just got up and walked to the wagon that had his personal things in it. Connie in exasperation got up saying to everyone and maybe to no one, "He just got up and walked away. I wasn't done talking to him."

Helen walked up just then, a little concerned she asked, "Is everything okay? We saw Captain Taylor, Mr. Maxton and Matt talking in private. It looked like something serious was going on."

Connie still excited cut the others off as she said, "All I was trying to do was talk some sense into Matt."

Helen puzzled said, "What sense does he need? I'm sure you mean well, I don't understand; he needs to have sense about what? Oh I'm sorry, but you got me upset and confused."

Connie said, "Helen, I told you Matt don't scare."

Helen said, "I know what you told me, I don't see how he's any worse of than the rest of the men that are here with the wagons. We will make sure of that. I mean we can watch out for trouble too head him off."

Connie calming a little, then cut her off again as she said, "No, no! He's going to start riding out front to start scouting for the wagon train."

Helen said, "Oh no! I don't know what I can do, but I got to stop him." She started to go after Matt. Connie quickly stepped in front of her saying, "No; don't do that."

"But we have to do something. He could get hurt."

"No," Connie getting calmer continued, "He could get hurt here also."

Mr. Maxton as he stood back up said, "You two need to relax. I'm sure Dan Wade will make sure Matt understands what he needs to do."

Both girls looked back to see everyone around the campfire watching them with their mouths wide open. Their faces turned red as they realized everyone at the fire had heard them. Connie the first to respond by taking Helen's arm lead her away from the fire a little ways so they could talk in private.

Slim said, "Looks like maybe Matt would be safer out yonder. It's bad enough when one woman is getting her cap ready to put it on a man, let alone two. But when they start getting their head's together and ganging up that don't seem fair to me."

Most of them chuckled.

Tex said, "Well I guess they'll be a lot of excitement around here now. Maybe more than Matt can handle."

Everyone did laugh then.

Mrs. Maxton said, "I have been sure that Connie is in love with Matt, now I Think Helen is also. Oh! the poor dears."

Bones said, "Yes ma'am! It's as plain as the nose on your face. The only thing is, does Matt know it yet."

Mrs. McBain said, "Oh dear, Connie has been like a daughter to me. I really like Helen too."

Mr. Maxton said, "Well there's nothing we can do, but hope they don't start fighting."

Slim said, "Guess Connie might have lost some of her confidence in Matt now that he's going to be out there by himself."

"I think it is just that she realizes that she won't be around to caution him," Mrs. Maxton offered.

After fifteen minutes Connie came back to the campfire while Helen went back to hers. The cowboys said their goodnights and headed for their bedrolls. Mr. Maxton looked intently at Connie and asked if everything was all right. Connie simply answered, "Yes" and headed to her wagon. On her way she saw Matt with his bedroll headed to where Flame was staked out.

The next morning when Matt looked up at the moon for the hundredth time he could tell it was still early, around three o'clock, but he wasn't sleeping anyway. He was too excited for sleep, he couldn't wait to be able to scout for the wagon train and just hoped he didn't do anything wrong. He was thinking of Vern and how hard Vern had worked to make sure he knew how to read trail signs and not put anybody in jeopardy because he missed something. He wasn't concerned so much about embarrassing himself as he was about letting Mr. Sockett down. Especially with Vern's reputation out here in the west. Back at the Sockett's home in the East no one had ever told them much of his earlier life out here in the western part of the country. Now that his name had come up after so many year's, most of the talk had been one story after another about the Idaho Gun Wizard, around their evening campfires.

Connie's wifely attitude had Matt confused. She had never stood up and talked back to him like she had last night. Not that Connie wasn't right in some ways. He knew that he did jump into action to quickly sometimes, but he had learned early on that surprise and being the first one to move made it a lot easier to come out on top. Especially when you were out numbered. He thought that Connie had more confidence in him. He knew she may be worried that he might get hurt or something, but he wasn't worried about getting hurt. He just wanted to make sure he didn't do anything wrong that might get someone else hurt. Besides if there really was trouble, he was confident that if he pushed Flame real hard. That he could outrun anything on the plains. He glanced at the moon and noticed that it was about three thirty, then he heard Connie get out of her wagon. She got a cup and filled it with coffee. As Matt rolled up his bedroll and stood, she came up handing it to him. Matt took it then looked at her directly. With wonder in his voice asked, "What are you doing?"

"Giving you a cup of coffee silly. When you want more let me know."

Matt was about to say something when his eyes where drawn toward the Gates campfire to see Helen start toward their camp caring a hot plate of food; that was stacked high. When she handed it to him with wonderment in his eyes that he was unable to hide he asked, "What's this."

Helen cheerfully said, "It is beans and bacon. I was even able to find a couple of biscuits left over from last night also."

As Matt started to say something Helen cut him off sternly saying, "S-h s—h, go sit and eat up. You'll have to be leaving soon."

Connie nodded at Matt and then took his cup to fill it up again.

As Matt ate his food he glanced at the girls several times. They just sat watching to take care of anything he wanted. Once when Matt paused to say something Connie asked, "Is there something else you want?"

He just shook his head and finished his plate of food. As soon as he was done Connie handed him his freshly filled cup of coffee. He had seen Helen looking him over closely. As he sipped his coffee she said; "I'm glad I got to see you before you left. With the moccasins, leather pants and shirt I would never have recognized you."

Before Matt could say anything Connie asked, "You're still going to wear your hat?"

Matt said, "Yes to keep the sun out of my eyes."

Matt looked toward the Gates campfire to see Dan and Hawkeye as they started out leading their horses. Matt gave a low whistle Flame responded and came up to stand behind him. Matt had already saddled him and put his rifle in its scabbard as soon, as he had gotten up earlier.

Connie said, "Just a minute," and hurried off. She quickly returned with something wrapped in paper as she handed it to Matt she said, "Hears some lunch for you."

Dan glanced at Matt and saw he had his guns on and they where hung low and tied down. He looked a little closer then he had intended as he saw that the butts of Matt's pistol's where exactly even with his hands so it would take just a slight movement to pull them and get of a shot. He thought to himself that Matt could be in action faster than anybody he had ever seen. Dan glanced at the ladies touched the brim of his hat, tipping it to both of them as he said, "Good morning Ladies. Matt; are you ready to ride?"

Matt with a quick look at Connie and Helen nodded saying, "Bye, see you."

As they smiled cheerfully at Matt, both girls quietly told him goodbye and to have a good day. The three men mounted up and rode out from the light off the campfire. As Matt looked back he saw the girls wave. He waved back to them.

CHAPTER SEVEN

THE LADIES DECLERRATION

They had traveled for six hours. They were looking for a place to camp that would have a little water. The grass was still green, but looked like they would have a dry camp for the most part. Dan decided that the wagons should be able to make twelve to fifteen miles, since they wouldn't have any rivers to cross or a steep hills; just the rolling plains. They sought out a little dip or small basin to camp in so as not to be sky-lined, if possible. They had eased along watching for any sign that would show if anyone else was out and about. They weren't really expecting any trouble yet, but Dan and the Captain weren't taking any chances. It wasn't just Indian's they had to watch out for; there were gangs of white people who would prey on small wagon trains; more so if there were only a couple of wagons out on their own.

So far, they hadn't seen anything to show that anyone else was out on the plains. They had just found a campsite like Dan was looking for, so they decided to have lunch. They found a little ledge to sit on just below the horizon looking over their back trail. They planned afterwards that Dan and Matt would circle back to the wagon's one way while Hawkeye went the other way. At the end of the day they would come up on the wagons from behind, making a big circle around the wagons. When they had finished lunch Dan said, "Matt, you looked like you had a lot on your mind to day."

Matt replied, "Oh! I'm sorry! I hope I didn't miss much."

Dan looked at Hawkeye who seamed to read Dan's mind. He shook his head no. Dan looked back at Matt and said, "No we haven't seen anything that you missed, I had Hawkeye watch you also. As a bird flew up off the ground we saw you glance to see if something had scared it into flight. We saw you look at the tracks of the deer and Antelope when we crossed over any of them."

Matt nodded, "Oh I hoped I wouldn't come up short. I thought maybe you might have been testing me, so I watched real close."

As Dan saw Matt frown he asked, "What?"

"You didn't say anything about the wild horse tracks."

Dan looked at Matt sharp to see if Matt was trying to play a joke on him. He decided Matt was serious. Dan asked. "Where?"

"They were about five miles back when we were going around the marsh that had a little water from the run-off of the ravine. I saw the tracks of an unshod horse where he had gotten some water."

"What makes you think he was wild?"

"His tracks weren't deep. It didn't look like he was being lead or guided. I was pretty sure it was just a young stallion that had been driven out of a wild horse herd."

Dan looked at Hawkeye who hadn't taken his eyes off of Matt when Matt had started talking. Dan looked back at Matt then said, "Wish you had pointed them out to me."

Matt said, "I'm sorry I was just about to when I decided you had to have seen them. I figured that you would probably just make fun of me for not knowing it was just another wild animal."

Dan said, "No, No! Well, not really, but I guess. Well damn, Hawkeye damn it, help me out."

Hawkeye grinned a little as He said, "I was told to be quiet. I was told let's see if the pilgrim talked all day and asked a lot of dumb questions."

Dan turned his head to give Hawkeye a hard look, as his face turned red he said, "That's not what I meant damn you."

He turned back to Matt and watched closely. "Okay I've got to admit that I was testing you and maybe I hoped you would act like a green horn. I have to also admit it's hard for me to get used to you." (Dan held up his hand as Matt started to respond) then continued. "With you being from back east moving like a shadow; plus you fight different from anyone I have ever seen. Then this morning I see you in buckskins with your gun belt on, that big bowie knife and two guns hanging low and tied down. I guess it is just hard for me to put them all together. I know now some way or somehow that you're far from being a greenhorn. I guess I'm apologizing to you. I should have discussed things with you more, but I guess I kind of hoped to trip you up. It looks like you tripped me up though."

"That's okay. I expected to be tested. Mr. Sockett would test me also. He never talked much, especially when riding. But he would make sure I had seen everything when we got back to camp."

Hawkeye said, "Well he did a real good job with you. I'd like to meet him one day."

"I think he would like you Hawkeye. He has an instinct for knowing people and he told me that I did to. We seemed to reach the same conclusion about people we came across."

Dan asked, "How long have you known him?"

Matt took a few seconds before he responded, said, "It's been just about three years now."

Dan nodded his head, "Well we need to be heading back."

Just as they mounted their horses Dan remembered and asked, "Why where you in such deep thought most of the day Matt? I noticed that you were frowning a lot."

Matt took his time as he thought everything through. He realized Dan had been very plain and honest with him, just like Mr. Sockett had always been. Now he knew he had made another real friend. Trying to pick his words carefully Matt said, "Well I have been trying to put things together all day, about the way things happened back at the camp."

Dan and Hawkeye looked at Matt with puzzlement in their eyes. Matt looked at them like they should have known what he was talking about, but then realized they didn't have a clue. Matt confessed, "Well first off, Connie gets madder than I've ever seen her. Then, Helen seems to get upset and they both just walked off. This morning it was like I had given them both the biggest, and the best gift they have ever had. But I didn't do anything for either one of them at all."

Dan and Hawkeye looked at each other with disbelief as tears filled their eyes. Then they both burst out laughing. Dan almost fell off his horse, which started bucking. He was just barely able to stay seated. Hawkeye barely controlling his horse laughed even harder. Matt had stopped Flame. His face had turned red. He was now a little bit dismayed with his two new friends as he said, "I don't see anything funny at all!"

The response he got was even worse. They both pulled rein and stopped their horses falling on their horse's necks laughing like hyenas. Matt was starting to get a little mad kneed Flame lightly and rode on looking straight ahead. Shortly Matt heard them ride up. As they caught up with him Dan said, "I'm sorry Matt, you just caught us off guard, I don't think there's much we can do to help you. About the best thing I can tell you to do is just take Flame and head out in a bee line till you reach the Pacific. It will save you a lot of problems." With a chuckle he questioned, "Right Hawkeye?"

Hawkeye said, "Maybe you could find a big boat to get across the water, then maybe you will be safe." Then he chuckled.

Matt realizing he is being ribbed now returned, "Thanks; but I thought I would get some expert advise."

They both started laughing hard again.

Dan said, "But Matt that was."

Hawkeye just nodded his head.

Matt decided he was getting nowhere, so he clamped his mouth shut.

Dan and Hawkeye finely got themselves under control.

Dan gave Hawkeye a nod who then reined his horse off to the south to make his half of the circle. Dan and Matt took the northern route. When they get half way around their part of the circle they saw the dust from the wagon train. When Dan spotted the dust he pulled up. When Matt stopped beside him he said, "Matt, I'll let you go on. I'll go into the wagons so I can lead the Captain to the camp sight we found. Be careful and ride light."

Matt just nodded that he understood as he kneed Flame into motion. Dan saw the Captain riding toward the front of the wagons on his side as he approached. He saw the Captain spot him, then head his way. So, he reined his horse to a stop and waited so they could talk without being around all the noise and dust. The Captain pulled up, and then slapped some of dust off his clothes. When he was done he sat back in his saddle and asked, "Did Matt do Okay."

"Matt was fine. He did real well and I don't think there will be any problems with him."

Captain Taylor asked, "How far is it to our next camp ground?"

"About five miles."

Captain Taylor said, "Good. We should be there about an hour before dark. That will be good. Do we need to change our direction any?"

"No, if we keep straight we should be within a half mile of where we what to be for the night. When we get close we'll make the slight change then. But it's going to be a dry camp tonight."

"I expected that. Seeing your back so soon I guess Matt checked out alright."

Dan's face tightened just a little with a tint of red. He had hoped the Captain had accepted his brief report of Matt. So Dan started to give a more detailed report, "He doesn't miss anything. I think if he did, that horse of his wouldn't. Those two are as alert as any I've seen. The only thing that I can think of that would make him inefficient is Matt's lack of experience, and there's only one way to get that."

"Good! I guess I'm of the same opinion too. You check him out to see if he could hit anything with his shooting irons?"

Dan hesitated then said, "No I didn't Captain. Hawkeye and I watched him close to see if he was any good at tracking and see if he missed anything. Well… he saw some sign that we missed. I admit we put him to the test. But he ended getting the best of us. I could tell an expert has trained him, so I guess he can shoot also. I just couldn't get myself up to being embarrassed twice in one day."

"I guess I can't blame you and I'll bet your right anyway. I think all of them can shoot and hit what they aim at."

Dan said, "Well I don't know about the rest, but even without seeing it, I'd bet all I got that Matt can."

"If Vern Sockett taught them to shoot I have no doubt of their marksmanship and they have all been honest to a fault; even to the point of embarrassment to what they don't know. They haven't been afraid to ask for guidance when they didn't know something. Did you notice none of them hesitated to nod when they where asked if they could shoot. Mrs. Maxton even acted like she was proud of her marksmanship. I would almost bet she can drive in nails with her rifle."

"Well I'm not going to bet against you."

Captain Taylor said, "You can go on out in front and guide us to where you want us. I have a couple of wagon wheels I want to check. I might have to make sure there are some repairs done tonight so there won't be any problems tomorrow."

"Oh Captain, I almost forgot. Pass the word to the guards to expect Matt to come in after dark. Make sure to tell them he is wearing buckskins and not to get trigger happy."

"Ok Dan I'll pass the word, when you go back out in front let the lead wagon know the direction you want him to go."

After their private talk both Connie and Helen admitted to each other they each loved Matt with all their hearts. So they decided that the best thing to do was to work together. Then just let things happen, whatever the outcome would be they decided to just accept it.

In a short while after coming to their agreement they become the best of friends again. They made up their minds that they would take care of Matt's every need when he was in camp. They kept everyone that was close to the two families guessing. Especially Mr. Maxton's cowboys. For everybody had been sure there would be a falling out between the two girls; they had all seen how both of them had taken to Matt. Most were sure the two girls would be jealous of each other and end up having a big fight. So when people noticed the girls being real chummy with each other everyone was confused. They just weren't acting normal.

The girls had taking a nap in the wagon that Connie and her mother had been sleeping in. Even though it had been warm, dusty and ruff that day they decided they could make up for some of their lost sleep. They knew that for Matt to do his job he would be coming in late and leaving early a couple of hours before any of the others, except for Dan and Hawkeye. But they were determined he would always have hot coffee and food, not just leftovers either!

After they had done their camp chores that evening, they had gone to work making room in the wagon that Matt used to store his things along with the other supplies. They used it as an overflow for the things they didn't need on their horses or close at hand. Like the cowboys' saddles and other stuff. By moving some things around some they were able to make enough room to lay down some blankets to make a bed.

When Mr. Maxton saw the girls come out of the wagon he asked, "Connie, what are you doing in there?"

Connie, with a stern voice looked him in the eye as she said, "That is where Helen and I are going to sleep. So, we won't be waking anyone up when we make sure Matt gets a hot meal and coffee, when he gets in late and leaves early."

Mr. Maxton was about ready to reply and then saw the intensity in her eyes. He just closed his mouth, turned and walked off.

The Captain had been right about the two wheels. Mr. Gates, Mr. Maxton, and Dan helped repair the two wagons. They had to take the wheels off and re-grease the axles and put the wheels back on. When they were finished they cleaned up, and went to the Maxton cook fire. Mrs. Maxton and Mrs. McBain had food ready for them. The rest where just sitting around sipping coffee and talking. It had been the warmest day they had seen yet. It had cooled off just enough though that the heat from the campfire made it pleasant to be by. After he ate Mr. Gates arose and thanked the women for the food and coffee. As he headed for his wagon he spotted Helen sitting by Connie. He said, "Helen it's time we got some sleep. It will be time to get up soon."

Helen responded, "Father, I'm going to sleep with Connie in Mr. Maxton's wagon."

He stopped and then turned to look at Mr. Maxton.

Chris was caught by surprise and answered, "Well I knew they had fixed up the wagon, but I thought they had already talked to you about it."

"This is the first I have heard anything about it."

Then to Helen he said, "You need to come on daughter. You got chores to do and we shouldn't be imposing on the Maxton's."

Helen knew when her father used daughter instead of her name that he wasn't pleased with her. This was the first time she had done anything without talking to either one of her parent's. She had been expecting a little argument, but not in front of everyone. She had made up her mind with Connie and she wasn't going to give in. She learned from Connie that back home she had a lot of freedom. So, Connie had gotten used to having her way from time to time. Connie wasn't bad just more independent.

Helen replied, "Father, we have made up our minds. I won't neglect my chores. We'll be safe in the wagon. Nobody is going to bother us."

Robert's face turned red and he gulped like a fish out of water; he was completely caught off guard with Helen's disobedience. For Helen had always obeyed, she never talked back to him. He finally got his thoughts back together then said, "Uh Helen uh, uh, let's go to our camp and talk about it."

Helen said, "No, I've decided. My mind is made up."

Robert started to get mad as he demanded, "Look you are just sixteen, I will decide what you are to do."

Helen started to get flustered and upset as she replied, "Father, I'm not doing anything bad. It's just that Connie and I like each other's company. So we decided we would like to be together as much as we can."

"Disobeying me is not bad?"

"Well…yes…I…guess you're right about that. But my mind is made up."

"Girl, if there weren't so many here, I'd take a belt to you."

Mrs. Maxton slightly raised her voice as she said, "Mr. Gates it's okay. I'm sure they'll be all right. I don't think Helen will slack off any in doing her chores. We are all good friends. Why don't you two calm down before you say something that you'll regret?"

Mr. Gates looked at her, but held his tongue. After a couple of deep breaths he spit out through clenched teeth, "All right!" He then realized that everyone had been listening. With his face almost beet red he responded, "Ma-am I'm sorry. I didn't mean it. I have never had a problem with her before."

Helen wisely stayed quiet. It had gotten very quiet.

Robert just stood where he was for a minute looking at his feet. Then he looked up as he said, "Yes Ma-am. Thank you! I better be going now."

Helen sat back down by Connie. Everyone around the fire had gotten very quiet. A couple of the Cowboy's got up to refill their cups. The rest just sat and sipped their coffee. Dan finally broke the silence as he said, "Guess I'll stay up to welcome Matt back. I don't want one of the guards shooting him by accident. With his leather paints and shirt on he looks like an Indian except for his hat, but being so dark out here they still might not recognize him."

Before she had time to think Connie said, "They better not or I'll shoot them."

Dan said, "Don't worry Ma-am I'll make sure nothing happens to him."

The Captain asked, "How long do you think it will be before he is due in."

"Another hour at the most, he could be along anytime."

"Do you think we can let him go out to scout on his own tomorrow?"

Dan replied, "Yes, he'll be okay. I'll go out ahead of the wagons, but no more than four or five miles. So, I won't be far from you."

Captain Taylor nodded, "Yeah, just like we discussed before."

Dan said, "Yeah, Hawkeye and Matt can start out ahead then angle off a little. That will leave the middle for me."

The Captain replied, "That would be good. With them leaving a couple hour's before we do they should be able to spot any trouble soon enough to be back, to warn us before anyone could surprise us."

Dan said, "Before I go to the front, I'll take a good look at our back trail."

Mr. Maxton commented, "They will have to cover a lot of ground in a day then."

Dan replied, "Yeah! But with Matt helping out it will be safer and will not be so hard on Hawkeye and me."

Connie asked, "What if they see something, then what?"

Captain Taylor replied, "Connie Ma-am, Uh, Miss Maxton, they will slip back and alert us so we can circle up the wagons and be ready."

Connie said, "You be sure to tell Matt to do that."

The Captain looked at Dan.

Dan responded, "I'm sure he knows. I don't think you're Mr. Sockett would have neglected to teach him that."

Connie in a stern voice said, "Just be sure to tell him."

Dan answered, "Yes Ma-am!"

Captain Taylor said, "Well, it's late. It's time I got some shut eye."

Matt and Flame had made a full circle to come up behind the wagon train. As it became dark he'd come across the wagon train's tracks and thought he might see Hawkeye. But the darkness had closed in around him first. He was sure the wagons where only about five or six miles ahead. He knew he could be there in only a few minutes, but was not going to take a chance on getting Flame hurt in a gopher hole or something. So Matt just let Flame pick his way. After a half hour or a little more he could see the campfires. He remembered the lay of the ground in and around the basin, so he made a wide circle. He knew where the Maxton's wagons should be located as the wagons took turns being up front so that from time to time did not have to eat dust all day. The Maxtons would be to the west side of the circled wagons. The next day or two would see them at the end of the wagon train. When Matt got to where he thought he would find the Maxton wagons he eased Flame toward the circle of the wagons. He had figured just about right, and after a bit recognized the wagons. He hailed the camp and to his surprise he heard Dan reply and tell him to come on in. He eased on in, then after guiding Flame between a couple of wagons he dismounted. As he dismounted he recognized Bones who was on guard duty.

Bone's looked Matt over real good, but didn't say a thing.

Dan asked, "Did you see anything?"

Matt answered, "No it's still clear. Did Hawkeye make it in yet?"

Dan answered, "Yes, just a few minutes ago. He's probably already eaten and hit his bedroll though. You know if you run into something you need to get back without a fight if you can; to warn us."

Matt stopped walking then looked at Dan as he barked, "Yes I know that!"

Dan replied, "Just wanted to make sure."

Just then Connie came up to them, to Matt she said, "I'll take Flame to unsaddle and rube him down, then I'll picket him out."

Matt said, "That's okay, I'll take care of him."

"No, Flame will let me take him," As she spoke, she reached, and took the reins out of Matt's hand. As she walked off with Flame following over her shoulder she said, "Helen has got your food ready."

Matt with Dan still by his side saw Bone's go back out to his spot; just outside the circle of wagon to stand his post. Matt just starred at Connie for a couple of seconds. He just whished that Dan and the others weren't there to see everything that was going on. Everything was bad enough with the girls. He sure didn't need everyone hearing every word that was being said. Matt walked to the campfire and sure enough Helen handed him a cup of coffee as she said, "Set on that stone over there. I've got your food all ready. I just got to put it on a plate for you." Matt took the coffee, then sat down. He starred at her as he sipped the coffee. It was good it reminded him of Mr. Sockett; then thinking of Connie he knew that the coffee was no mistake. Connie knew how much he had gotten to like Mr. Sockett's coffee.

When Helen returned with a plate of food she said, "Eat that, I've made some biscuits and I got some honey to put on them for dessert."

Dan had followed Matt to the campfire. After Matt started eating he said, "In the morning you and Hawkeye ride out a mile or two, then break off at a slight angle to go out straight for fifteen to twenty miles. Then when you come back make your circle. I will ride out straight in front of the wagons. That way we can cover a lot more ground. We should be able to come across anything that would be of any danger to the wagon's long before anyone would be in a position to do us any harm."

Matt as he ate just nodded. Dan seeing his nod continued, "When the wagon's start out I'll cover our back trail before I circle around to get out in front. After that the Captain will check it out each time he is on a trip back to the end of the wagon train."

Matt just nodded again. Just as he finished his last bite of food Helen put two biscuit's covered with honey on his plate. She got his coffee cup, refilled it and returned it to Matt. As Dan stood up with a slight grin on his face he said, "Ride light I'm turning in."

"Okay, goodnight!"

"Goodnight!"

Just then Connie came to the campfire bringing his rifle and sat on an empty crate. She had found some rags in Matt's wagon earlier that day. So with her cleaning materials she went quietly to work--unloaded the rifle and started cleaning it. Matt finally had, had enough. In a quiet, but stern voice he said, "Okay that's enough, I appreciate all you two are doing, but you should be in your beds and getting your rest."

Helen tried to be as quiet, but just as sternly said, "We are going to make sure you have a good meal and get as much rest as possible. So sit, relax and sip your coffee. Give me one of your pistols. I'll make sure it's clean."

Matt handed her his left hand gun. Then he was upset with himself for he had done it on command like she was in charge. Besides, he thought he should be the one cleaning his own weapons. Helen sat beside Connie, then unloaded the pistol and started cleaning it. Connie had made quick, but efficient work cleaning his rifle. She got up handed it to him then asked for his other pistol. Matt took the rife and reluctantly gave her his other pistol. As he sipped his coffee he watched out of the corner of his eye. He had to admit that they both where safe and did a good job. He knew he had nothing to worry about as far as Connie was concerned. She had been taught to be safe and always did a good job. But he reluctantly saw that Helen was doing just as good. In just a few minutes Helen handed him his pistol back clean and loaded. After he took the pistol she reached for his coffee cup. Helen quickly went to refill it. Giving it back to Matt she sat down by Connie. After a short time Connie finished his other pistol, got up and then handed it back to Matt. She then returned back to Helen and sat down beside her again. They just sat contented-like as they watched Matt sipping his coffee. When Matt was about done Helen asked, "Do you want some more to eat or drink?"

Matt answered, "No that's plenty. You two don't need to do all of this. I can take care of myself."

Connie, with some of the pleasantness leaving her face, got up. As she took his cup she said, "I have your bed roll all rolled out for you next to the bushes not far from where I picketed Flame. As far as us taking care of you, you can darn well get used to it. That's the way it's going to be."

Exasperate he stood and headed for his bedroll as he muttering to himself. He then tensed a little as he was sure he heard Bone's make a slight chuckle from where he was on guard duty.

Connie and Helen got the eating utensils and quickly cleaned them up. Then they headed for the bed they had put together in the Maxton wagon. Connie and Helen fell asleep shortly, they were very sleepy. But they were not going to let Matt know.

Matt was tired and restless; it had been a long day. It had also been the first time he had been in the saddle all day. He found muscles he had never used before or realized he even had. Even though he was in much better shape than most, he had a lot of sore places to let him know that he was still human. He new he would get use to it in a few days, so he wasn't worried about it. It was just something more he would have to adapt to. What really had him a uncomfortable was the change in Connie. Helen too for that matter had made a complete change. For all the time he had been around the Gates she had always been obedient, almost to the point of being too submissive. Always saying yes ma-am, or yes sir to all the duties her parents had given her. Shoot the girl's were treating him like he was an invalid or something. As these thoughts continued to run through his mind he concluded that maybe it was not that bad. But it was more like he was a king or something. He tried to think of some way to change their minds. People might get the wrong idea. He thought they acted like they were his mother or even worse, like nagging wives. He almost sat straight up when the thought hit him. Then he tired to relax thinking to himself that was the last thing he wanted right now. He wanted to be free and there was so much he still wanted to see. He had seen so many married people and most of them had been changed by their marriage. Especially the descent men who had had to settle down to take care of their wives. He thought that was what a man should do once he made the commitment. He admitted to himself that he did like both girls. At one time or another each of them had made the blood rush through his veins a little too quickly; but he thought that it was just because they where so attractive.

Matt woke with a start, not knowing when he had finally fallen asleep. Glancing at the moon he realized he had almost overslept. As he shook out his boots; to make sure there were no bugs or anything in them. He checked the moon again and saw that it was just three-thirty. He relaxed a little, he had time to saddle Flame and get a cup of coffee. He put his gun belt on with the twin forty-fours in their holsters moved his rifle to roll up his bedroll when he heard someone coming up quietly. As he slowly turned he said, " Connie what are you doing."

"S-h! not so loud. Most everyone is still asleep. Go eat, Helen has got your breakfast ready. I'll make up your bedroll and saddle Flame for you."

Matt whispered between his clenched teeth. For he was afraid he would wake up the whole wagon train if he tried to talk. He said, "This is not right, I can do it, you two should be helping your own folk's. You need to be getting your rest not baby-sitting me."

Connie didn't say anything she just pointed her hand at the cook fire. Matt stood over her as he looked at her stern pose. He tried to read her eyes, but he couldn't. There wasn't quite enough light.

"You need to hurry. Hawkeye will be ready to leave soon."

Matt turned and walked off with frustration showing on his face. Connie smiled a little as she got Matt's bedroll together.

CHAPTER EIGHT

MATT'S FIRST GUN ACTION

They had followed the Little Blue, then along the Platte River to Fort Kearney. A rainstorm had made everything muddy, which had slowed them down some. They had to circle the wagon's to fight off some Indians. The natives had given up pretty quickly though, thanks mostly to the Maxton's and their cowboys. The deadeye firing that came from their part of the circled wagons had been devastating to the Indians. That was where most of them had fallen. Captain Taylor told them to hold their fire and to watch closely while the Indians picked up their dead and left. The word quickly spread through the whole camp about how well the Maxton crew could shoot, it was not long before the news made it around their camp and from then on they were known as sharp-shooters. From what the ones close to him had seen they were sure Matt did not miss often if at all. The fight had lasted for the better part of the morning. The Indians had made three attempts at breaking through the circled wagons. After each attempt they pulled back well out of rifle range. The scouts had given Captain Taylor enough time to pick out a place to circle the wagons that had a lot of open land so the Indians had nothing to hide behind to sneak up on them.

Connie had taught Helen how to shoot and handle a rifle very well. After a few shots she was hitting her mark. The men tried to keep the women down and out of sight. But Mrs. Maxton and Mrs. McBain had stood there ground and didn't pay much attention when they where told to stay under cover. The cowboys where proud as peacocks and kept saying it was the best shooting outfit they'd ever been around.

Matt and Hawkeye had made it back well in advance to warn them of the coming attacks on the wagon train. They then filled in where they thought the strongest attacks where being attempted and where they felt like they were needed the most. Matt was especially noted for not missing. The word had gotten around that every time one of his guns spoke; rifle, or pistol, one of the Indians fell.

When the scouts were in camp they stayed around each other. Matt's only problem was when he was in camp the girls always kept him in sight and waited on him constantly. He'd finally given up on getting them to let him take care of himself. At first he had heard a lot of chuckles and they teased him constantly about not being able to control his women. He tried to tell them they weren't his women, but they just laughed at him.

They stayed next to the river so they would have water for their camps. They had crossed over the South Platte River at Ogallala. It had been twenty-two days since they had left St. Joseph Missouri.

The Captain was pleased with the trip so far. They had stayed in camp a day or two along the way to rest up the animals and people as well. It gave them a chance to get their clothes washed and to have a good bath. Matt had been able to take a bath just before he returned to camp most of the time.

The people had gotten used to Matt and his clothes. It still amazed them that he could come and go without anybody hearing him. He had taken to wearing his knee high moccasins, which made him quitter than ever.

Connie and Helen's friendship had grown and they were together all the time now. They were talked about and there was some laughter around them from time to time. They really created a lot of attention; for almost everyone knew they BOTH had eyes for Matt only. That had made a lot of the single men on the wagon train unhappy and they had a dislike for him without cause; for many thought they were the prettiest women on the wagon train. The girls had made sure they got all of the chores they were responsible for done for Helen's parents; they even did their share around the Maxton's camp. Everyone was using the fire only for cooking, since it had gotten pretty warm. It was getting a little hard to sleep at night too. Because of the heat the Captain held them to no more than ten or twelve miles even though the days were longer; so they wouldn't wear the animals out.

Dan and Hawkeye where amazed at how good a scout Matt had turned out to be. Connie had heard them talking about it and with pride in her voice she said, "Mr. Sockett told me Matt was a natural and had gotten much better than anybody he had ever seen."

The two men nodded. Then Hawkeye said, "I still can't get used to him moving around without making a sound."

Connie nodded as she said, "I guess all of us that have been around him for such a long time must have gotten used to him; we just don't give it a second thought. As far as I can remember he has always been that way."

Dan replied, "Well it is still kind of spooky. Just never had anybody come up on me that I couldn't sense, or at least hear, even if they where trying to sneak up on me. He does it in his natural walk; that's what's so scary."

Matt and Hawkeye had been riding with extra caution the last few days. There still was a lot of grass, but it had gotten very dry. Captain Taylor made sure everyone was extra careful with their fires. It had gotten hard to tell fresh tracks from old tracks. So they had to be very careful not to miss anything. Flame was a big help. Matt learned he had a real keen nose and when it seemed like Matt wanted to follow a certain trail; he took to it almost like a bloodhound. Matt and Flame were so well acquainted with each other now; it was like they could read each other's thoughts. Matt and Hawkeye had varied their directions each day, so as not to fall into any predictable patterns. They were trying to make it very hard for anyone to set up an ambush. They were now about half way between Fort Laramie and their crossing back at Ogallala. For the last hour or so Matt had been riding with extreme caution. He hadn't spotted anything, but was sure he could sense a presence that he hadn't been able to locate yet. The last few minutes Flame had gotten tense, but Matt felt maybe that he was responsible for that. He pulled rein to bring Flame to a stop. Matt took his hat off and held it in front of his eyes to pinpoint the suns location, then decided it was close to high noon. He wiped sweat from his brow and put his hat back on. Making a quick decision, Matt reined Flame off to his right into a little draw that he'd been riding next to. He found a good spot to hide

Flame among some sagebrush and then guided him into the middle of a tall bunch of it. Before dismounting, he tied the reins loosely around the saddle horn. As he eased out of his saddle he grabbed his riffle. He didn't have to work the lever of his forty-four-lever action rifle for he already knew there was a round under the hammer. When he was away from camp he always made sure of that, and he always had all six rounds in each pistol. He didn't play with his weapons. The only time they were out of his holster was when he actually used them or they were being cleaned. He told Flame to stay and knew he would, unless Flame was approached by another presence, man or beast; also if Matt whistled he would come to him in a flash. They had practiced on such things and the two trusted each other completely now. Matt worked his way back-trailing the way they had just come, sticking to cover when he could. He had covered about a mile already and was able to stay in the slight draw as he moved noiselessly along and was glad he had taken to wearing his moccasins. He had covered ground quickly and finely, he spotted what he was looking for. It was a tree that had been blown over and was laying down over a wash out. He backed in under it and squatted down. He thought he was in a good spot and it would be hard for anyone to see him. Anyone trailing him would have to go around the turn which would be past him in two or three steps. That would be the only time he was in danger of being visible. He had been waiting just over an hour when he sensed, more than actually hearing someone coming. Now knowing for sure, he tried to decide how to get away without letting anyone know they had been spotted. His mind racing, he decided anything he did would give him away. So he stayed completely still as he hoped there was just one.

Just then a large Indian in nothing but moccasins and loincloth holding a knife in his right hand with a bow and quiver hanging on his back appeared, moving along quietly watching out across where Flame and Matt had passed through earlier. Making up his mind Matt made three quick steps keeping low. The Indian sensed or heard Matt and started to turn with the reflexive action of a cat spinning with the knife coming right at him. Matt had the advantage of moving first and with his speed the Indian didn't have a chance. With a hard down-sweep of the side of his hand Matt hit the Indians forearm. He heard the bone snap as a slight groan came from the Indian. Matt let the momentum of his body carry him past. But he rolled his hips as he went bye spinning with all the speed and force he could, caught the Indian in the chest with his heel. He heard more bones snap and the breath rush out of the Indian. Matt stayed on the ground where he had landed and quickly looked around to spot any others. The Indian hadn't moved. When Matt took a close look he saw that the Indian's chest wasn't even rising. After fifteen minutes had gone by, he got up and retrieved his rifle. He quietly retraced his steps back to Flame. He was thinking hard while he alertly watched the area all around him. When he got back to Flame he climbed aboard. While leaving the reins tied to the saddle horn, he used his knee's to guide Flame away at a good clip to the south, hoping to cut across in front of the path Hawkeye would be taking on his return trip. He not only watched for ambushes, but surveyed the land as he tried to figure out where Hawkeye would be making his return trip.

After going ten to twelve miles he slowed Flame down. He started looking for the tracks from Hawkeye's horse as he was sure, he was close to where Hawkeye should have gone on his trip out. He had traveled another mile when he kneed Flame to a stop. He took the rifle with him as he dismounted, then he quickly walked forward to the top of the hill they had been climbing up. Dropping to his hands and knees he crawled forward as he took his hand and moved some of the tall grass aside. He was relieved to see tracks of Hawkeye's horse. He took a sharp look around again; close first then far out. Something had made Hawkeye nervous. Matt new he would never skyline himself unless there was a very good reason. Something had really bothered him. Matt was sure he was only an hour or two behind Hawkeye. With that information he knew that Hawkeye would be getting ready to make his outer trip back to circle behind the wagons.

With another quick decision he retraced his steps to deftly mount Flame. He kept the rifle in hand and kneed Flame into a fast trot straight south. He hoped to cut across Hawkeye's trail again, or even be ahead of him. He knew he was riding a little to fast for safety's sake, but tried to get a good glance at every bush, rise, or little depression he got remotely close too.

After a couple more miles he started to knee Flame to a quick stop, then realized he didn't have to--Flame had already started to do so. Matt still held his rifle as he quickly dismounted. He saw the track's of a dozen unshod horses. With a quick glance he could tell most of them were being led. He jumped back in the saddle and kneed Flame slightly more to the west in the direction Hawkeye should be coming from. He still stayed to the highest ground; even though it did skyline him. He hoped Hawkeye would spot him. He kept far away from anything that would give anyone cover. When he broke over the next rise he spotted Hawkeye riding slowly and very cautiously. He could tell from where he was that Hawkeye suspected something. Flame's ears perked up and then turned his head to the right of them. Matt glanced that way and saw the ponies with two Indians holding them. With his quick glance he counted fifteen ponies. Matt looked back to his front again, not at Hawkeye; but in the grass all around them. He noticed that some of the grass wasn't waving like the rest; like it should when the wind was blowing through it. Matt didn't wait to spot any other signs. He urged Flame into a good speed--a controlled speed that would give them a chance to maneuver. They where really flying. Matt took in the whole area by keeping his eyes straight and concentrated on not being focused on any one spot. He tried to let his peripheral vision work for him. He noticed that Hawkeye had spotted him. Hawkeye slid off his horse taking his rifle with him.

Matt eased his rifle back into its boot slipping the hammer loops off his pistols, then drew them. Matt spotting movement to his left; trusting his instinct he flipped his left pistol toward it and squeezed off a shot. Almost instantly he caught movement to his right. He flipped his right hand gun and squeezed the trigger. He saw Hawkeye take aim, then heard Hawkeye's rifle bark. In just a short time Matt and Flame slid to a stop beside Hawkeye's horse. All business Hawkeye whispered, "Three down, how many more?"

As he glanced around Matt said, "Thirteen that I'm sure of. We need to get to the wagons."

Hawkeye just nodded as he quickly mounted. Matt turned Flame and retraced their tracks as Hawkeye followed. When they cleared the rise from which Matt had first spotted Hawkeye from. Hawkeye urged his horse up next to Flame, then hollered, "You go on ahead! Don't wait for me. You need to warn them!"

Matt looked hard at Hawkeye and then nodded. He reloaded his pistols, settled them in their holsters and put the hammer loops over them. After his was sure they were headed back in the direction the wagons should be coming from he had untied Flame's reins from the saddle horn. Then Matt let Flame have his head. Flame kicked up a dust storm behind them. Matt then knew he was going faster than he'd ever been before. He had thought nothing could move that fast; not even Flame. In just five minutes as he glanced back, he saw that Hawkeye was a mile behind them already.

After riding for an hour Matt was able to confirm what he had thought was dust from the wagon train was factual. Fifteen minutes later he spotted Dan. When Dan looked in Matt's direction, Matt took his hat off and made a circular motion. Dan immediately spun his horse around and headed for the wagons. Matt eased Flame into a slow trot to let him cool off some. He was really impressed with Flame. It was hot and the stallion was covered with sweat. Matt was too for that matter. But Flame wasn't breathing that hard at all and this had been the hardest Matt had worked him. The last mile he had slowed him down to a walk. Flame had gotten cooled off enough now so he wasn't sweating badly at all. After a half hour Matt would make sure he had a real good taste of water. Not too much though. Not till he was cooled off more.

Captain Taylor and Dan had the wagons circled in short order. Matt spotted the Maxton wagons and headed in that direction. A few yards from them he slide off Flame to walk the rest of the way. He spotted Captain Taylor just as he got up to the wagons. He noticed that everyone had their weapons in hand. Captain Taylor stepped outside the wagons with Dan a couple of steps behind him. Matt and Flame came to a stop as he thought the Captain would want to converse with him for a minute, away from the rest of the people.

Matt nodded as he said, "Captain, Dan. I'd like to put my saddle on another horse and check the perimeter before we take the wagons out of the circle again."

Captain Taylor said, "I take it we have company."

Dan watched Matt very closely.

Matt said, "Yeah we got company, I don't know how bad it is yet."

Captain Taylor nodded as he turned to Dan, and said, "When Matt goes back out you go with him."

As Captain Taylor turned back to the Wagons Dan and Matt followed. Matt led Flame through a gap between two wagons. When he got through he spotted Mr. Maxton saying, "I would like to borrow one of your horses."

"Sure Matt," Chris turned, then said, "Tex get my horse please. It's our next best one."

Tex nodded and hurried off. By the time Matt had his saddle off Flame. Tex had returned with the fresh horse. Bones on watch where they had come in through the circle of wagons as he kept his gaze out over the land in the direction Matt had come from. He said, "Look's like Hawkeye is coming in."

Matt had the saddle on the fresh horse when Connie came up and said, "Matt, I'll rub Flame down and finish cooling him off."

Matt said, "Don't give him any water for a half hour."

Connie answered, "I know! I remember what Mr. Sockett taught us."

Matt just clamped his mouth shut and then turned to go back to The Captain and Dan. A few of the men had come up to see what was going on. Matt had made it only a couple of steps when Helen stepped up beside him saying, "Matt, here is some fresh water. You look like you could use it."

 Matt grateful, but aggravated with a tense voice said, "Thank you,"

Slim close by had noticed Matt's reaction. To Slade who had just walked up he snickered a little as he said, "Looks like to me that Matt's getting about ready to pop."

Matt gave Slim a hard look; it had only lasted a split second. His eyes had flashed full of sparks. Then a little embarrassed he just walked off.

In a quite serious voice Slade said, "Slim, I think you better not prod him anymore."

Just as quietly Slim said, "Yeah, I saw that look. I didn't think he would hear me."

As Matt led his horse up Captain Taylor said, "You two wait and relax. Let's see what Hawkeye has come across."

In a few minutes Hawkeye rode up and dismounted off his tired horse.

Captain Taylor asked, "Guess you came across some sign also?"

Hawkeye with a startled glance at Matt nodded to Captain Taylor; then said, "Yeah! Crows!"

Captain Taylor asked, "How many?"

Hawkeye at a loss, took some time before he answered. After a thoughtful minute, he said, "Three for sure. I don't know how many more."

Captain Taylor asked, "Matt, how many did you see?"

Matt answered, "Seventeen for sure. I know there were more around though."

Captain Taylor asked, "What do you two think? A hunting party or some scouts from a war party?"

Matt said, "Ambush, I think they're from a big war party."

Hawkeye nodded as the Captain with a frown said, "We haven't seen a thing. How far ahead are they?"

Matt said, "Captain, I don't know the answer to that. That's why I'd like to go right back out. I thought we better have the wagons circled while that's being done. I want to make sure everything is clear before we start moving out again. So I hurried back here to warn you. I was afraid they'd already hit you. But I think they wanted to take Hawkeye and me out first in the hope of surprising you back here."

Hawkeye nodded, as he said, "I think Matt is right. I would like to borrow another horse to go along with him."

Chris Maxton along with some others had come up to listen. He said, "Hawkeye, pick out any horse you would like."

Hawkeye as he led his horse of said, "Thank you."

Captain Taylor said, "If there's that many guess I ought to go with you."

Tex who had been close bye and listening said, "Captain with Mr. Maxton's permission. I think it would be better if you stayed. My men and I will ride along. Besides it would be good to get off them wagon seats for a while."

Dan cut in before Captain Taylor could respond, and said, "Captain; I think that's a good idea."

Mr. Maxton nodded in agreement as he said, "I do think that would be the right thing to do. If anything happens back here we can hold our part of the circle. But, I'm sure; they would be back before we got attacked back here. Sounds like the more that go right now, the safer it would be."

Captain Taylor said, "Okay get your mounts."

The cowboys gave a hoot and holler and ran to saddle their horses, and get their gear together. In just a few minutes everyone was ready. Dan gave everyone a good glance as they had come up to make sure everything was in order. Satisfied when he noticed that they all had brought their rifles, he led them off. After a short distance he motioned for Hawkeye and Matt to come up beside him. As they did Dan said, "Matt, you take the lead. I think you have the best idea on where to pick up their sign."

When he spoke, he glanced at Hawkeye surprised, but pleased to see him nod in agreement. Hawkeye then said, "Yes he found more sign then I did."

Matt nodded and then urged his mount out in front. Hawkeye and he had returned to the wagons coming in from the southwest. Matt considered all that had already taken place, after a minute of thought he led them more to the northwest. As he led them he kept to low ground so they wouldn't be sky lined; he was depending on his instincts as much as anything. After they traveled for about an hour, he pulled his horse to a stop. No one had spoken since they had started out. Dan reined his horse up beside Matt then said, "We could of missed their sign; we been riding pretty hard."

Matt still by instinct as much as definitely knowing anything, looked at Dan as he said, "No! I just think Hawkeye and I should ease ahead on foot a little."

Putting action to his words Matt quickly dismounted and took his rifle with him. Hawkeye heard what Matt had told Dan threw the reigns of his horse at Tex grabbing his rifle to catch up with Matt. Dan with a big frown then told the other's to step down and give all the horses a breather, but to keep a sharp eye out. There was a pretty good breeze that made the grass look like waves on an Ocean.

Tex as he stood next to Dan, said, "I don't know how long they will be gone. But it would make me fell better if we had someone crawl up to the top of that hill to keep a lookout, till they returned."

Dan nodded, "Yeah Tex. That would be a good idea. I should have done that right off."

Before anyone else spoke Bones said, "I got it!"

He handed the reins to Slim, took his rifle, then worked his way almost to the top before he dropped to crawl the last few yard's. When he made it he gave a hand signal that all was clear. Since they had left the wagons they had all whispered so as not to be detected. Sound especially when carried by the wind could be heard for a long way. It was at least two hours before Matt and Hawkeye returned. They both had worked up a good sweat. Dan happened to be looking right at them when they came back around the slope. He could barely hear them and then he realized he only heard one. As he looked at Hawkeye He said, "Damn Hawkeye, your are getting almost as quiet as Matt when you want to be."

Hawkeye smiled with his white teeth showing, then whispered, "Matt is a good teacher."

Dan asked, "Well what do we have? Anything?"

Matt nodded for Hawkeye to speak. Taken a few seconds to get his thoughts together Hawkeye said, "I understand a little Crow, which they were speaking. They have a big war party of maybe eighty warriors. I think maybe half of them had new rifles. Not all of their Scout's have returned, so they were nervous. Some think there medicine has gone bad."

Dan asked, "Why is that! They haven't even attacked the wagon's yet."

Hawkeye answered, "Two or three of the scout's are really scared. They have influenced some of the other's and are not so eager to make an attack on the wagons."

Dan said, "I still can't figure that out. What would have them so spooked?"

Hawkeye a little uncomfortable said, "I didn't understand every word, but they told of a man on a horse of fire, like they were a spirit. How the man could make someone dead without leaving a mark. I don't know. Then how his guns spoke without him even looking at them; and did not miss."

Everybody except Bone's and Matt had gotten closer to hear Hawkeye.

Dan said, "That don't make sense."

Hawkeye said, "The first part I don't know about. The second part I can understand."

Tex asked, "How's that?"

Hawkeye said, "When Matt saved me from the ambush. They where hiding in the tall grass. As he came riding up on them he looked straight ahead. When one on his left moved, Matt shot him. Then one on his right moved, he shot him. He didn't move his head. So his eyes caught all the movement. That's what has scared some of them. That's why they think of him like a spirit. They also said that when Matt and Flame left where they had set up their ambush for him it was like spirits led them straight to where I was."

Everyone had gotten real quiet as they took turns looking from Hawkeye, then back at Matt. Matt not liking the attention started to feel uncomfortable. Dan thought through the information he had been told by Hawkeye as the others tried to understand what they had just heard. After a short time, coming to a decision he said, "Well I guess we should get back to The Captain and let him knew what is up."

After a hard look at Hawkeye Matt said, "If they are already really spooked why not circle around to come in behind them. Down the draw we saw them camped in. We would be up wind and I think we could be on them before they knew what hit them. If we were lucky, we could scatter all their horses."

Dan answered, "I don't know, it's risky. The Captain would have my hair if something went wrong. Tex what do you think? I can't ask you to take the risk. Right now if Hawkeye has heard right. They may back off, and leave the wagons alone."

Tex looked at his friends. He could see the eagerness in their eyes. He knew that he could use a little excitement. Riding the wagon seats was getting to all of them. They still had a long way to go. If Mr. Maxton hadn't agreed to pay them so much, they'd surely not have waited. Plus with their good relationship with The Captain they'd been persuaded it wouldn't be much of a gamble or they would already be back on some ranch-punching cows. They were making more on this trip than they could have in two years of nursing cows. The Captain had persuaded them because he had told them that Mr. Maxton needed loyalty and trust more than anything else.

Tex finely said, "Well, I know the boys want to; but the only thing holding me back is that it is my job to make sure the Maxton's get all their wagons through."

With a cautious calculating look at Hawkeye Tex asked, "Hawkeye, what do you think? You saw what we would be up against."

Hawkeye said, "I think Matt's right. But it must be a surprise or we would be in a bad spot."

"I would like to hit them real bad too," muttered Dan, "But to much is at stake if something was to go wrong."

Matt just listened after he had made his statement. Once their minds were made up; he retrieved the reins of the horse he had borrowed, put his rifle in its boot and then mounted up with the rest.

Bone's heard them mount up slide back down the slope to his horse and climbed aboard. Dan started out back the way they had come looked back at his riders to make sure everything was in order. He noticed that Matt hadn't moved yet. Just loud enough for Matt to hear Dan said, "Matt we need to be going?"

Matt retorted, "Thought I would hang back a little just to make sure no one comes up behind us."

Hawkeye said, "Think maybe it would be a good idea if Matt and I did drift behind you a little just in case."

Dan with a slight pause decided it was all right. It fit in with their job of being scouts, so he nodded as he offered, "Don't drop too far behind. I'll tell The Captain to keep wagons circled until you get in."

Matt waited until they had ridden out of sight. Then he put his horse in motion in the direction Hawkeye and he had just scouted. Hawkeye rode up beside Matt and then just loud enough to be heard above the horses said, "It will be a lot of fun. But I hope it don't get me fired; because I do like my job."

With sudden reservation Matt said, "You should have gone with the rest. I don't want my decision to hit them get you in trouble. I just can't ride off knowing they will probably just wait and attack us a little later. Then maybe someone on the wagons would end up getting hurt.

When if I raise a little cane with them right now, maybe it will make them decide not to bother us at all."

"Oh! I don't want to miss the fracas for anything in the world. I have already seen you in action once. Besides you saved my life."

Tex rode next to Dan as they worked their way back toward the wagons. They kept to low ground and as much cover as possible. Tex suddenly pulling rein brought his horse to a stop. Reacting to Tex's action Dan pulled rein to stop also and then asked, "What!"

Tex just sat in his saddle in deep thought as his facial expression turned into a frown. Before he answered the others had rode up. They had been scattered out some, just in case they rode into an ambush.

"Matt's going to hit the Crow's,"

Dan said, "No! Hawkeye knows better. Besides we decided not to."

Tex said, "Yep, we did; but not Matt."

Slim and Bones almost together turned there horses and put them into a gallop to head back to where they had last seen Matt. Dan shouted at their backs as the rest turned, "You will be to late. It will be over before you can get there; if that's what they're doing; damn!"

He realized they had all left him behind and he was just shouting at himself. He spun his horse and rode after them.

Hawkeye and Matt had just returned to their horses after taking out the guards that had been on lookout with the horse herd. Matt held his hand out and Hawkeye froze. Then they both heard the hoof beats of horses at a gallop and they were headed right at them.

Matt said, "We got to go now! It may be a hunting party that has discovered our tracks. I think the attack we planned is still the best way out. "

Hawkeye just nodded. They quickly mounted and headed straight at the horse herd. On a dead run they started shooting there rifles a couple times each. Matt yelled, and Hawkeye gave a war cry. The horses were off in a panicked run in a heartbeat. They headed straight for the Indian camp. Several of the Indians only had just enough time to get out of the horses path; some were trampled. Only a third of them got away with any weapons and with no injury of any kind. The Crows fired some shots trying to turn the horses.

Matt and Hawkeye rode tight behind the herd so the dust would cover them. But it made it hard for them to see out too. Matt guided his horse left a little so he could see better. He saw a few Indians looking hard into the dust. Finally, some of them spotted him, he saw them draw back the strings of their bows while others tried to get a bead on him with their rifles. As it cleared some he was able to pick out a few of the Crow as they scrambled away. Making sure of his balance he started shooting every time the horse was in the air before his feet hit the ground again. He thought he could hear Hawkeye's rifle bark a few times on the other side. He shot fast and was pleased that at a gallop on a horse he hadn't rode before he was still hitting more than he missed. However, he had gotten pretty close to them. He heard a few bullets and arrow's go by, but so far none had hit him or the horse. When Matt's rifle ran dry he put it up and drew his pistols. He had seen a couple horses go down to be trampled. He had shot up all the rounds in his right-hand pistol and then emptied his left-hand gun. When he passed the Indian camp he slowed his horse down, then spun him around to look back. Matt returned the pistols to their holsters. Then he quickly got his rifle back out of its boot and reloaded it. As he did so Matt looked back through the camp. He saw that it was Dan with the cowboys that he and Hawkeye had heard. As they rode through the camp Matt started covering them. Even though it was a long shot he was able to make some more hits or at least close enough to drive them to cover. The cowboys were all shooting as they rode through the camp. The dust had settled down pretty well now and they had pretty easy pickings as the Crows scurried to cover. It had cleared up enough for Matt to see most of the camp now. He felt a lot better; when he was able to spot Hawkeye and breathed a big sigh of relief. It looked like the camp was a disaster. Bodies were scattered everywhere, some moved while others were as still as the ground they laid on. Most of them looked like they lay pretty much where they had fallen. It appeared that only six or eight had made it completely intact. Matt then quickly reloaded all his weapons and put them up. When Dan and the rest rode up Hawkeye was able to catch up to them. Matt reined his horse in beside them as they reloaded their weapons.

Matt looked back to make sure there wasn't any danger from the Indians. They were trying to catch some of the horses, but none seemed to have any interest in coming after them. Matt saw that Dan had a real stern look on his face so he didn't say anything. As he glanced at Tex he thought his eyes and face showed the excitement of the action. Matt thought he was able to read some disbelief there also. Matt ran the events through his mind. He still thought he had done the right thing. He was a little surprised that the rest were here, but he hoped above all that he hadn't gotten Hawkeye in trouble. He knew that Hawkeye had come with him because Hawkeye felt that he owed Matt his life. Matt didn't feel that way though, he had just done what he thought was right. He did figure that he was in for a good chewing out though, especially from Captain Taylor. He was glad that nobody had gotten hurt as far as he could tell.

The sun was far to the west when they made it back to the wagons. Nobody had made a comment as they seemed to have picked up on Dan's mood. Matt eased to the rear; he figured with the anger that showed on Dan's face it was the best thing to do. As they made their way in between the wagons, Matt saw Dan spot the Captain, then dismount to lead his horse toward the cook fire. Dan had stopped a little distance away to let The Captain come up to him away from the rest of the people. As Captain Taylor approached Dan, Matt had dismounted to lead his horse up to stand beside Dan. Matt thought he caught a hint of surprise from Dan's eyes as the rest of the riders went on by to take care of their horses and check all their equipment. However, Tex did walk up to Matt saying, "I'll take care of your horse for you."

Matt started not to agree and then he saw something in Tex's eyes. So he relented, and replied, "Thank you."

Tex had gotten a hard look from Dan. But Dan had just clinched his jaw tight.

Captain Taylor caught the little exchange. As no one acted like they wanted to open up the conversation the Captain offered, "It looks like you boys burnt some gun powder."

In a tight voice Dan said, "Yep."

From the talks Matt had with Mr. Sockett he remembered being told. That people out west didn't tell on somebody, especially if they were friendly with them.

Therefore, Matt blurted, "Captain it's my fault. First, I probably did wrong when I went to make sure Hawkeye didn't get caught in an ambush before I came back to warn the wagons. The next thing is, after we found the Indian camp it appeared that they decided not to bother us. But I decided to go ahead and jump their camp anyway."

Dan gave Matt a surprised look. With his voice full of stunned anger he said, "You knew you were to return to the wagons first."

Quickly the Captain cut in, "Okay Dan! Matt not to excuse you, but I would like to hear your thinking."

Chris Maxton had walked up in time to hear the last comment. He said, "I heard the last part. I won't interfere, but Mr. Saxton's put Matt in my charge."

Captain Taylor nodded saying, "Sure, sure, Chris no problem. You do have a right to hear."

In answer to Captain Taylor Matt said, "Captain, I felt I was being followed. So, I found a spot to leave Flame. I backtracked on foot to make sure. After I found out I was being followed by an Indian on foot I took care of him. Then I figured they had planned to ambush me. Returning to Flame as quickly as I could I was sure that they were going to do the same to Hawkeye. I figured they tried to make sure they got rid of both of us so as to make sure they could hit the wagons before you had a chance to circle up. As for attacking the camp according to Hawkeye they were in mass confusion. I just wanted to hit them before they got settled. So I decided to attack them."

Captain Taylor looked at Dan, then asked, "What did Hawkeye say?"

Dan said, "That they were talking about their medicine. Some were sure it had gone bad. Some even talked of a spirit that they thought had killed their scouts."

Confusion showing all over his face, the Captain asked, "What spirit?"

Dan pointing at Matt said, "Him!"

Chris asked, "Sorry I don't understand. How would they think that Matt's a spirit?"

Dan had calmed down quite a bit, he said, "From what Hawkeye heard, Matt must have killed one of them without leaving a mark on him as to how he had been killed. He got the other two without looking as far as they could tell. To them it was like his guns had a mind of their own."

It was quiet for a while as they tried to understand what they had just heard. Captain Taylor looked at Matt, then back to Dan. Then with a glance at Chris. After a moment the Captain asked, "Dan. Do you think they will cause us any more trouble?"

Dan answered, "No, not that bunch. We left them in such a shambles it will take them a week just to find their horses and get all their things back together again."

Captain Taylor nodded then said, "Okay, Dan get something to eat. Matt I would like a few words with you in private."

"Yes sir!" Matt followed Captain Taylor a few steps from the fire until they were out of every ones hearing. Chris returned back to the campfire with Dan, found his cup and poured some coffee in it to freshen it up. Before he could find a spot to sit down to sip his coffee Connie with Helen close behind her came up. Very interested Connie asked, "What's going on? It looked like you were having a serious conversation. Wouldn't it be better if we all knew what's going on?"

Tex had gotten back from making sure the horses were being taking care of. Bones told him they would. Finding his cup he started toward the coffee pot as he gave a quick glance at Helen, Connie, and Chris, but he didn't say anything. He decided it was better to just get his food. Connie had noticed his actions, though. She became flustered as she saw quick glances from some of the others. They even rushed by to get their food, as if it had been a week since they'd had anything to eat. Getting perturbed she put her hands on her hips saying, "Father something happened or something's wrong. We have a right to know."

Helen was acting just as anxious as she listened intently. Mrs. Maxton came up and noticed that Connie was confronting her father. It was something that Connie had never done before. With concerned in her voice Mrs. Maxton inquired, "Is everything all right?"

While the conversation was going on at the fire, Captain Taylor told Matt that he could understand Matt's actions. But told him that from now on, for better or worse Matt's only responsibility was to the wagon train. Also, if they rode out in a group again, Dan's decisions right or wrong had to be abided by.

Matt answered, "Yes sir! Sorry sir!"

Captain Taylor responded, "Just Captain! Or Jeff. You don't have to sir me. I'm not an officer anymore. Besides I'm not used to it. Now let's get something to eat. Also, we can forget about our little talk. Just be sure we understand each other."

Then after a slight pause, before they headed for the fire, Captain Taylor said, "As much ground as you covered today you must have pushed Flame pretty hard."

Matt relaxed he felt relief. But he also had some guilt for his actions. For he knew if he had failed in helping Hawkeye or if things had gone bad at the Indians camp. It would have put the wagons in a great deal of jeopardy. A lot of things could have gone wrong. Matt had even more respect for Captain Taylor. The Captain had listened. The Captain hadn't condemned him. Matt also realized he better not make another mistake.

His father would have yelled and screamed, then would have tried to belittle him which in turn just made Matt mad. That's one of the reasons why they never got alone very well. Matt's thoughts raced through his mind comparing the facts and differences. After a short pause he thoughts reflected on Flame. With his voice full of pride he said, "I really did. I think he still had a lot left if I had needed it."

The Captain said, "I thought so. Let's go. You need to eat then you should be able to get a good nights rest. I could use another cup of coffee myself. All this talk has made my throat dry."

As they walked back to the fire Captain Taylor noticed the Maxton's were in the process of being confronted by Connie and Helen. He had noticed like everyone else that had been anywhere around Matt and the girls that they had set their caps for Matt. From Matt's actions the Captain thought that maybe the only peace Matt had was when he was out riding. He concluded that Matt was putting up a good fight though. He had not appeared to have giving in yet. Captain Taylor was sure Matt and the girls didn't know bets had been made on which one would win or how long it would be before Matt would finally give in. So as Captain Taylor and Matt approached he decided to stir the pot a little saying, "Evening ladies nothing to get excited about. Everything is fine and dandy. There were a few Indians around, but it looks like they will be moving on."

Chris gave such a sigh, that most everyone could hear it. Connie looked at Captain Taylor. Her lips moved, but nothing came out. She was confused; she had been ready to demand that her father tell her everything. Captain Taylor had just taken all the wind out of her sails and scrambled all her thoughts. Helen also had a surprised look.

Not to miss the only chance he'd had in days. To get some control back over the girls Matt said, "Thank you Captain. You couldn't have explained it better."

Connie knew they wouldn't learn anything right then. She tried to control herself, but she still ended up stomping her foot. She started to say something twice, but was still unable to form any words. She gave up and walked away with anger all over her face. She went to stand just outside the circle of people. Helen stood, confused and at a loss for words. As she looked around she became embarrassed; she then turned to the fire and started dishing up Matt's food. Both of the girls heard the cowboys as they tried to hold their chuckles back. As the girls heard them it made them feel worse. After a while, almost simultaneously they both sucked in a big breath of air. Getting their composer back they went about their routine of taking care of Matt. So Matt's reprieve hadn't lasted long. Helen had his food and coffee ready for him before he had a chance to get it himself.

Connie had gone and retrieved Matt's rifle. Then sitting on her crate started cleaning it. In a short time Helen was cleaning one of Matt's pistols also. Both girls after drawing the cleaning cloths through the barrels noticed how dirty they were. They both had glanced up and looked at Matt and the Cowboys. But they didn't make a single remark. Captain Taylor after making his comment had been in deep thought as everyone ate. He suddenly said, "Chris I've been thinking. If you could see fit to turn them loose, I would like to use a couple of your drivers if I could."

"Sure, what do you have in mind?"

Captain Taylor said, "Well, after today seeing there is so much Indian activity, I would like to keep Hawkeye and Matt out in front. I'd like Dan and another covering our rear. Then I with another could be on each side of the wagons."

"Okay, that makes sense. I can drive one of the wagons. Then Connie can drive another one. There shouldn't be a problem."

Captain Taylor said, "Well thanks. I'll pick up their pay."

Chris said, "Tex you know your men. You can decide which ones should go out with them if you don't mind." Then he turned to his daughter as he asked, "Is that okay with you Connie?" Are you up to driving one of the wagons?"

"Yes father!" Still hurting over her earlier treatment she retorted, "Now aren't you glad I insisted on learning to handle the teams."

Chris smiled knowingly with pride as he said, "I sure am daughter."

Connie in spite of herself felt her chest fill up with pride; while she was still upset with her father and the others.

Tex after conferring with the other Cowboys came back to Mr. Maxton and the Captain saying, "Bones and Slade will be your best ones Captain. Bones is the best at reading sign though."

Captain Taylor replied, "Good, Bones can ride behind with Dan. Try to keep each other in sight. I would like you to stay four or five miles behind the wagons. Slade you can stay up front of the wagons two to three miles. Hawkeye, Matt, you only need to leave an hour before the wagons move, then go out only five or six miles from now on; no further. I'm going to check the guards then get some shuteye. Goodnight!"

They all said, "Goodnight!"

The next morning they got a big surprise. When Matt with his bedroll got to the cook fire the girls were already up. He thought they wouldn't be up so early since Connie was going to be driving one of the wagons. She was wearing pants, which was something women just didn't do. He took a good look around. Then when he looked back at Connie asked, "Are you sure? You will really get your father upset and a lot of the people may think that it's unladylike."

Connie smugly asked, "What about you?"

"You know it's never bothered me."

Connie retorted, "What's your problem then!"

"I was just thinking about what the other people might think."

Connie said, "Well if they think any different of me, then that will be their problem. If anybody say's anything I'll just ignore them."

With his thoughts on some of the men, before he took much time to think Matt said, "If they do; they'll have me to face."

Both Helen and Connie had glanced at Matt as he'd spoken. They saw the steely glint in his eyes and knew instantly he was dead serious. Helen felt a chill run down her spine just then. She now realized how dangerous Matt could be. She said, "Matt we talked it over last night. I'm in agreement with Connie. If she's going to be driving a wagon she needs to be able to move about without worrying about getting her skirts or dress caught on anything. If the women say anything because she's wearing pants we'll try to explain. Besides even if they don't like it, I'd rather she wasn't handicapped in any way. I want her safe."

"I agree. But it's not the women I was thinking about. It's the men."

They both exclaimed. "Oh,"

Then a little red in the face Connie said, "Mr. Sockett, and Jimmy never acted like anything was wrong."

"They were decent." Then as he looked at Helen Matt said, "I agree with you. Doing what she's going to be doing. I think it's only right that she wears britches."   With a hard look at both of them, Matt said, "You let me know if anybody bothers her. I mean that!"

They both saw that steely glint again; along with the warning they had heard in his voice. They knew he was very serious and that he was talking to them with complete honesty. They realized they would be in trouble with Matt if he found anything was said or done from someone else. That made a warm feeling flow through their bodies to realize how protected they felt by Matt. Matt confused himself by his statement; he knew he meant what he had told them. But he just didn't understand why he felt that way.

At that moment Captain Taylor, Dan, Bones, Hawkeye, and Slade, approached the fire. They all stopped suddenly. Well at least Captain Taylor did, he was the first in line, with Dan right behind him. The Captain stopped so quickly Dan run his left eye into The Captains right shoulder as Dan's hat went flying. Dan tried to step back quickly to keep his balance. In doing so Dan's head caught Bones right on the end of his noise. Bones yelped trying to rub his noise. Bones had quickly stepped back to get away from Dan's head only to get tangled up with Hawkeye's feet. Hawkeye in the process of trying to regain his balance banged his head hard into Slade's elbow. Slade had tried to spin away from the colliding bodies. Slade's left elbow had flown out to catch Hawkeye's head right on his funny bone as Hawkeye fell to the ground. As Hawkeye got back up, they all yelped in pain as they rubbed their sore spots. All of them were cursing except for Captain Taylor who just stood with his mouth wide open as he stared at Connie. No one understood what Hawkeye had said. But they had an idea it wasn't pleasant. When they looked past the Captain to see what had caused their mishap they froze. It suddenly got quite. They all stood with their mouths dropped as they stared at Connie. Not a one of them remembered they had been hurting just a second ago.

Connie could tell from their expression's what they saw. At first she was embarrassed. Then with all that had happened; as they had fallen all over each other she laughed out loud as tears filled her eyes. In short order Helen laughed out also. Matt smiling was just barely able to keep from laughing out. He didn't want to be the one to wake up the whole camp. The girls had calmed down to a giggle now. The men rubbing their sore spot's as they realized their mouths where still wide open. They knew how goggle-eyed some of them had been. They had cussed in front of the girls also. They were all completely embarrassed. They all tried to apologize at the same time. Helen was the first to recover as she said, "Gentlemen the coffee is hot and the food is ready."

That made them all feel worse, for they all knew they had acted nothing like gentlemen. They all went quickly to get their cups and eating utensils. They quietly sat down to eat. None of them looked at anything except for their food or the ground. The Captain had been caught of guard like the rest and had found a particular interest in his food also.

Connie turned and walked away from the fire. First, she did it to go over her emotions. The look she'd gotten from the men had been of nothing but admiration. Second, if anything it had embarrassed them more than it had her. So out of kindness and to get herself under control she thought it would be a good time to get Flame ready for Matt. After a few minutes she returned back to the camp fire. As she got close to Matt, she told him that Flame was ready. Matt nodded as his eyes were drawn toward one of the Maxton wagons. Getting up just loud enough for Hawkeye to hear he said, "Hawkeye, it's time to go."

Hawkeye looked at Matt as he swallowed the last of his coffee. He stood and hurried up behind Matt. When he caught up he asked, "What's the hurry? It's early yet?"

Matt just pointed at the wagon as he walked on. Hawkeye looked where Matt had pointed. As Matt was still ahead of him Hawkeye had nodded to himself in agreement saying, "I do think maybe you're right."

Hawkeye most of the time was quick at figuring things out. For as they stepped into the darkness Chris Maxton walked up to the cook fire. As he rubbed the sleepiness out of his eyes he said, "The coffee sure smells good this morning." Helen had spotted him just before he had spoke got up, found his coffee cup and filled it. As Chris approached, she handed it to him.

"Thanks, I thought maybe you girls wouldn't be up so early this morning." As Chris took a good sip of coffee he spotted Connie. With the coffee cup still at his lips he sucked in too big of a swallow. He choked and then coughed spitting coffee down his chest. His whole body shook as he gasped for air. In the process he spilled the hot coffee all over his hand. As he dropped the cup he pointing at Connie asking, "What the hell are you doing? You get some clothes on." As soon as the words left his mouth, he realized all the men had seen and heard. His face turned red. Connie glanced around to find Matt. She wanted his support; just his presence always calmed her. She was completely astonished not to see him within sight. It was one of the few times she hadn't seen him leave. She noticed that Hawkeye had gone too. The others followed her glance and their face's showed their wonderment. They had been unaware of Matt and Hawkeye's departure also. Not realizing what they were doing they had followed the action that was being played out before them. Their heads turned from side to side. Connie had hoped that Matt would be there to support her. But he had snuck away--coward she thought. Finally, she said, "Father please, you'll wake everyone up. Let me try to explain."

Captain Taylor glanced off. Connie followed his eyes to see her mother appear. As she waited for her mother to walk up she received a look from her mother. Then her mother looked at her father. Mrs. Maxton had seen at once what the stir was all about. Helen spotting Mrs. Maxton got a cup of coffee for her. Having taken it Mrs. Maxton sat down as she nodded her thanks to Helen. Mr. Maxton still upset gave Mrs. Maxton a hard look as he asked, "Aren't you going to say something to your daughter."

Mrs. Maxton calmly said, "So she's my daughter now."

Chris said, "You know what I mean, I have told her she needs to get some clothes on."

Valerie said, "Well, I think when I walked up she told you she'd explain."

Captain Taylor and the other men were uncomfortable. They knew this was a family matter. But none of them moved; because they didn't want to interrupt in any way. So not knowing what they should do. They just ended up acting as though they weren't even there.

Connie got her nerve up some. Then she said, "With me driving the wagon I need to be able to move around without worrying about getting my dress caught. In case I have to get up or down in a hurry. Also when I'm around all the harness, hooking and unhooking the horses."

Valerie nodded then said, "That makes sense to me dear."

Chris not believing his ears said, "You mean; you think she's decent."

Valerie said, "Yes, I've always thought so. We know she hasn't always done right. But yes I think she's decent."

Chris said, "You know what I mean. The way she's dressed."

Valerie said, "I don't know about that, but if she's going to be driving a wagon it does makes sense to me."

Chris said, "Well I think there will be talk. It probably will be the cause of some trouble."

Captain Taylor coughed, and then as he cleared his throat said, "There will not be any trouble. I'll see to that."

Helen said, "Matt already told us nobody better bother her. He told us real plain too."

Captain Taylor said, "No, No! Any trouble you let me know. Sure, as hell don't let it go! Oh, sorry, excuse me ladies. But you let me know. If Matt ever got started, there won't be a wagon train left." Then Captain Taylor looked straight at Tex as he said, "Tex, if there's any sign of trouble you let me know. If you don't have time to get me handle it however you see fit."

Captain Taylor then looked at each of them to make sure they all understood him. He then said, "Thank you ladies. I need to make sure everyone's up and getting ready to go."

CHAPTER NINE

KIDNAPPED AND RESCUED

It was now the first part of July. The trip had become very strenuous for everyone. Some of the animals had been replaced when they were available at a fort or some other little settlement, when they came near one. At one river crossing they lost a wagon that was swept downstream into some deep water by the swift running currant. A mother and father that did not know how to swim had perished with it. The three children that were left orphaned were adopted by a nice couple that had not been able to have any of their own. There was a boy of four, a girl of six and another boy of ten. After a few days they had gotten pretty close and where quickly becoming a family.

Wagons had broken down and needed to be fixed. There had been a few more scraps with Indians and they had lost another ten people to arrows and gunshot wounds. One child that had just turned two, a boy of ten and three women had been taken from their husbands and children respectfully. The other five had been men, which left their families to morn for them. They were doing their best to go on without them. No one had turned back though. All of them explained there was nothing to go back too. It was hard on everyone, especially hard for the ones that had lost the man from their families. Between the children that had taken on the extra burden and with the help of some of the other men folk, when it was really needed; everyone was making out.

There were a few wounded who were still on the mend. Tex had gotten a bullet through the fleshy part of his left shoulder. He had told them at least it wasn't my shooting arm. They hadn't been able to keep him away from his duties though. Slade had taken an arrow through his thigh, but after having it pushed on through he rode out the next morning with Captain Taylor over the protest of all the Maxtons and the Gates'; of course. After a couple of days he was heard to have said that it was worth it. For when in camp, if any of the women thought he wanted a cup of coffee or something they got it for him. Mrs. Maxton gotten creased by an arrow at the top of her shoulder. The men had gotten upset with her for she hadn't told anyone. She had kept shooting until the fight was over.

They were about seventy miles out of Fort Steele in Wyoming territory and getting close to Table Rock. The grass had dried up, which was making it hard on the animals. The streams had gotten pretty low also. Luckily, a slow moving thunderstorm had built up during the night, which freshened up both man and beast. They had spent two days in camp, except for the scouts. It rained awfully hard and they ended up paying for it the next couple of days, as the mud took a toll on everyone and everything. Fresh meat had been taken, when Captain Taylor knew it was safe to send out a small hunting party. Mostly they were able to hunt deer and every once in awhile they were able to take a stray buffalo.

The days had gotten shorter. To make up some of time they'd lost along the way. Captain Taylor had the wagons moving from daylight to dawn. They did stop to rest the animals every couple of hours. They didn't want to wear them out completely. Captain Taylor told them if nothing else they couldn't afford to lose another week or two. Not if they wanted to make it over the big mountains. They told him these were big Mountains. He corrected them replying, "The ones we have crossed were just the babies."

Matt and Hawkeye, depending on which valley they were in or mountain they crossed, rode along together sometimes. They separated whenever they could depend on the terrain. They had gotten so they almost knew each other's thoughts. Dan and Bones seemed to be getting along very good too.

It was well after dark before Matt and Hawkeye had returned to the wagons. After Matt and Hawkeye had eaten and were sipping their coffee Captain Taylor sat down on a rock with his coffee; across from them. Helen took Matt's cup to refill it. Connie was making sure Matt's second pistol was clean. No matter what he had tried they still waited on him hand and foot; so to speak.

Captain Taylor asked, "Ok, What do we have?"

Hawkeye responded with, "I think Matt can explain better."

They had been separated for most of the day. But they had traveled back together.

Matt relayed, "There's a lot of Indian sign. They don't seem to be hiding it; but they are making sure they keep out of sight."

The Captain nodded, "Yep! Dan and Bones gave me the same report. Every time they sneak back they have seen fresh tracks. But they haven't been unable to spot anyone yet."

Matt said, "Captain; I think they got more than one tribe or an awful big tribe. It feels to me like they are trying to set us up for something."

The Captain gave Hawkeye a good look. Hawkeye just nodded. The Captain then asked, "Do you think he's right? Do you know which ones?"

Hawkeye answered, "No, not yet. There's lot's of pony tracks. But they are being extra careful not to leave any other sign."

Matt said, "I could try to follow their tracks back to their camp; then we would know."

The Captain said, "No, I can't wait for you to go off. The main camp could be more than a day off. Also, I just don't dare to have the wagons moving without having my eyes out in front."

Matt said, "Captain I am just asking and pardon me if I'm getting to nosy. But you seem like you are awfully worried."

The Captain said, "I am! I think they plan on ambushing us in a couple days. We have a narrow pass we have to go through. Once we get into the pass; there will be no place to circle the wagons. The livestock would have to be fresh to make it through in a day. We do have a bigger wagon train than usual. Most of the time it has helped. But under the conditions we are in now, it could be a big problem."

Matt said, "If we had a place with graze and water to let the animals rest. Maybe with a few hand-picked men we could scout the pass before we go through."

Captain Taylor thoughtful asked, "Hawkeye, do you know of anything at all; off the main trail a little ways."

Hawkeye said, "I think in another day we will be in a position where we would be able to head north. From there it would be about another half day of travel. The place almost always has good grass and there is a real good spring that runs into a good-sized pond. There's a big bluff to put the wagons up against. It would be a good place to make a stand."

Captain Taylor said, "Maybe that's where they are camped."

Hawkeye said, "I think not. Most of the trails run east and west. Most of the white men stay on the trail. Not many Indians know about the spring, unless they travel through here a lot. The land lays in such a way that it kind of funnels most travelers from going into that area."

Matt said, "They might attack us before we get there. If they did they would have us short on water and grass."

"The more I think on it that's why they are leaving so much sign for all of us," Hawkeye had cut in. Taking a breath he continued, "They may be trying to scare us into making a run for the pass."

Matt asked, "Is it too late to turn back and find another way?"

Hawkeye answered, "We would lose too many days. Snow would have the passes full by then."

Captain Taylor said, "You boys get some rest. Let me think on it tonight. I'll have the other scouts along with a few of the other men up early; then we'll talk some more. Goodnight." Captain Taylor and Hawkeye headed for their bedrolls. Matt finished his coffee, then headed for his. In passing he told Connie and Helen goodnight. Their response was just a big smile. After he'd lain down he couldn't help but think of their problems. He knew they were in a bad spot, even with all of the wagons and people. If the Indians' plan was to wait and attack when they tried to go through the pass. All they would have to do was hide on the cliffs among the rocks.

His thoughts drifted to the girls--he was proud of both of them. Helen was driving as much as Connie was now and both of them could handle the team almost as well as any of the men could. They seemed to pick up on things very quick. Helen had borrowed some jeans from Connie which had stirred things up a lot with her parents. Matt knew with all they were doing it had to be wearing them both out. But no one had ever heard a single word of complaint from either of them. He finally heard about Tex pulling a gun on one of the men when they had made a comment about one of the girls. Nobody told him which one or what was said. It was long after the incident that he found out; so he let it pass. He did however make a lot of people nervous; for from time to time they would see him starring at them like he was trying to read there minds. So, they pretty much stayed away from the two camps. Of course, it helped that Matt was gone out from them most of the time. Besides; they now knew with Tex around that he'd not put up with any nonsense as far as the girls where concerned. Many of the people close by had stated that Tex's gun had appeared faster then any of them had ever seen before. They were glad he hadn't gone ahead and pulled the trigger. He hadn't had to; for the ones that had been involved had a complete understanding in an instant.

The story of the raid on the Indian camp and some of the other things Matt had already done had made it through the whole camp. Matt as easy going as he was most of the time; was getting a reputation that he was not one to be messed with. The more they heard about Matt, the less Tex had to watch the girls. Hardly anyone looked at them anymore, let alone talk to them. When they had the wagons circled defending themselves Matt had gotten the reputation of not wasting a single shot. The trip was really starting to wear on most of them now. It had been hard and no one had gotten a lot of rest, especially Hawkeye and Matt. Matt liked the wild open land a lot better than the city. Matt thought Connie felt the same. Helen being brought up on a farm was used to some things. But unlike the farm, there was no routine. The rivers and mountains passes they had crossed made sure of that as each one had a different challenge to overcome to make it across.

Matt decided that just coming across Flame had been worth all of the money in the world as far as he was concerned. Nearly everyone else commented that they thought Flame was the best horse they had ever seen. He had a thought or two about how people looked at him. He did hope that they thought he was decent. He did what to do the right things. Matt then let himself doze off to sleep.

The next morning as Matt approached the cook fire he spotted Captain Taylor just sitting with a cup of coffee in his hands. Captain Taylor had glanced at Matt as he smiled, "I'm finally learning to pick up on you. I still didn't hear you, but I knew you were coming. Of course; it probably was Connie that gave me that sign. I have noticed that she always seams to know when you are near."

Connie blushed as she handed Matt a cup of coffee. She said, "It's just because I've been around him more than the rest of you. The food will be ready shortly."

Before long the rest of the Scouts along with a few of the other men came up to the fire. Spotting them the Captain stood up. Most of them had brought their own coffee.

Captain Taylor looked everyone over; satisfied that everyone was accounted for he began, "Most of you already know that we have a big problem. I have decided we need to try and take care of it before we go through the next pass. If we don't we will be in danger of loosing a lot of people; if not all of us. I have decided to move out like we've been doing. But at the end of the day we'll circle the wagons a little early to make like we are going to settle in for the night. Then after it gets real dark we'll move out again. I know it's going to be extra work; but we must make it look like we're staying for the night. Matt and Hawkeye will go out the same as they have been. But instead of coming back to camp they will try to give the Indians watching us the slip. Then they are going to try to find the Indian Scouts and take then out to clear the way for us." The Captain paused as he made eye contact with each one of them. He then asked, "Any questions?"

Everyone shook their heads as they responded, "No, Captain."

Captain Taylor then said, "All right; we need to make it work. There are a lot of lives at stake."

Connie with Helen close by had heard that Matt and Hawkeye wouldn't be in that night. They quickly put some food together along with another canteen for each of them. As the others left the fire Captain Taylor gave Matt and Hawkeye a stern look as he said, "You two need to make sure you act like nothing different is going on. Then tonight you need to clear out our path without firing a single shot; if you can. I'll try to have the wagons in place and circled a couple of hours before sunset. That's going to give you two maybe three hours at the most to sneak back to find anyone that is scouting us. Start at the north side first; if Dan and Bones can sneak out they'll try their fate on the south side. With some luck we'll be where we want to become daylight. When we get there we can set up our defensive positions. You two be careful because we're all depending on you. I guess I've held you up long enough; good luck!"

They'd finished eating by the time Captain Taylor was done; so they were ready. As Matt got up Connie handed him the food and canteens. With his hands full he had no way to stop her as she stepped up close and gave him a hug. Then before he knew what was up she kissed him full on the lips. Then she said, "You better be careful or I'll skin you alive. I mean it."

Matt saw her eyes as they flashed like lightning. He felt somewhat embarrassed as his heart started pounding. Before he had gotten his thoughts together he stammered, "Yes' ma'am."

Connie had stepped back with her heart racing as she saw Matt's eyes. They in return shot lightning-like flashes at her. Helen before he had a chance to move with her eyes flashed like Connie's; quickly stepped up, hugged and kissed him on the lips also saying, "That goes for me too."

Her heart was beating so fast she thought she'd pass out. She had seen the intense look that Matt had given her. After the assault by the girls Matt was froze in place like a statue. At first; it was like the girls had taken all of the air from his lungs. It felt as if they had taken his life with them. Just as that feeling hit him it was replaced with all the compassion they had given him. His chest filled up with enough energy he felt like he could almost soar away. In a husky daze he said, "Yes' ma'am."

Hawkeye said, "Time to go now." Then turned and strode off.

Matt said, "Oh, yeah," and quickly turned to follow.

Captain Taylor's eyes had really brightened, for he liked all three of the youngsters and thought the world of them. He also knew the wagon train needed them to be successful. Matt and Hawkeye where going on as dangerous of a mission as any he had ever sent anyone on. He then said, "I guess that's the plainest talk I've heard in a long time."

Hawkeye just laughed as Matt's ears got so red it felt like they were on fire. Connie and Helen were blushing with their faces red and their countenance all aglow for everyone to see. Dan gave Bones a good look as he said, "The way Matt was when he left here I don't think there are enough Indians. They don't know it yet; but they are in real bad trouble."

Connie looked at Dan as she said, "S-h… he'll hear you. He already thinks he can handle anything."

"Man or beast I'll agree; I can't think of anything or anybody I'd bet on against Matt," Bones proclaimed, "But he's no match for you two women." He stated.

Captain Taylor laughed, "You two will be getting your hides skinned off your back sides if you don't stop picking on the Ladies."

Dan said, "Yep, guess you're right. Bones let's go."

Dan and Bones both tipped their hats as they left. As the rest of the camp started, to come alive Captain Taylor tipped his hat explaining, "Ladies; don't worry too much. Matt's got more bark on him than most any three of the best men I know."   They both thanked him. Helen saying, "That is some comfort." Connie had quickly spoken, "I agree; I hope he is cautious."

Watching the sun Matt had circled back to a spot that he and Hawkeye had agreed to meet. He felt sure he had been watched most of the day. He'd looked for a place to get away from them. He finally found one that gave him a chance to sneak away undetected. It had worked out fantastic. It was a gully that had run for a couple of miles with fairly easy going. He had been able to go through some water to hide Flame's tracks for a while. He had hoped they'd think he'd stumbled on to it by accident. He waited about twenty minutes. He had just about made up his mind he'd have to go when he finely spotted Hawkeye. Matt knew he would have had to try to carry out his mission even if Hawkeye hadn't showed up. When Hawkeye had worked his way up to Matt keeping to as much cover as he could he just said, "Good idea." Then leapt off his horse to do as Matt had.

He took his leather shirt off to cut four circles along with four strips for strings. In a short minute he had put them on his horses hoofs to help cover up any sign the Indians would be looking for.

Matt knew they'd be cold before morning, but the sun felt good to him as it was still pretty warm; for now. It wouldn't be for long. The sun was already getting low in the sky. Way back over the mountain he thought he'd seen a dark cloud, but wasn't, sure. As they took another glance at the sun they started out. Matt lead on Flame who must have picked up on Matt's cautious manner; for he snuck along like a cat.

With his hoofs covered Flame was hardly making a sound. Also, there was hardly any sign left showing that they had passed through.

Hawkeye followed Matt a little off to one side or the other as he tried to stay just in sight. Hawkeye shook his head to himself in amazement as he had never seen a horse and rider that knew each other as well as the two he followed. They seemed to be gliding along like ghosts. Hawkeye shook his head again, then decided they were a perfect match for each other.

There were pony tracks from the Indians ponies all around. Most had been left, in the last few days. They were sure that the main body wasn't far away. They had begun to pinpoint a direction. They would let the Captain know that they had a pretty good idea where to look. Then maybe with enough men to make a good force they would be able to surprise them.

They had been going straight north for three or four miles. Matt stopped to make sure Hawkeye was okay and could see him start east. It had gotten pretty dark now and Matt new they where running a little behind, but he still didn't dare to rush. They had to be careful so as not to give themselves away. After another three miles he stopped. Five minutes later Hawkeye eased up. Matt whispered, "You head toward the wagons from here, then work your way east. I'll angle off toward the north ahead off the wagons. We're late."

Hawkeye nodded as he angled in toward where the wagons should be. It was going to be a deadly game now. If some Scouts were watching the wagons as they suspected; they had to be dealt with.

After a mile Matt dismounted; he needed to be afoot. He tied the reins to the saddle horn whispering a couple of commands to Flame. Silently he set out again. Matt had trained Flame to follow behind him at a distance of a couple hundred yards.

One thing he was grateful for was that the breeze was drifting in from the southwest. The sounds and smells would be in his face. As Matt caught a glimpse of the campfires he froze. He was sure he hadn't made a sound. He was being extra careful and using all his senses. After a little, even though he hadn't heard a sound concentrating like Lee Chan had taught him. He angled a little more to his right.

After a good three hundred feet not making a sound. He spotted a shape that wasn't natural. Soundlessly he stepped behind some brush. In a few seconds he spotted someone watching the fires. Easing his knife out he made sure not to make any noise as he glanced around. Then he checked to be sure the Indian was still in place. He made an extra effort not to stare so as not to arouse the Indians senses. Matt was sure he could crawl up behind the Indian undetected. He didn't think he had the time though. So on the balls of his feet feeling the ground before he put his weight on each foot he crept up behind the Indian.

He had closed to within five feet when he saw the Indian tense and glance right. Matt went down low and left. At the last split second the Indian felt his presence and tried to spin around to meet the attack. The Indian moved very fast; but just a bit too late. Matt flashed by with knife held high in his right hand. The Indians throat had nearly been slashed completely through. The Indian had made some noise when he hit the ground; but the Indian had stayed motionless.

Matt then heard an Indian pony stir. Matt quickly found him then made sure he was tied well; he didn't want the pony running off. He eased off to the east a short distance then stopped to listen. After a minute he was sure all was quiet. With a little luck the Indians would have left only one or two to watch them at night. Even then there still might be one around just in case someone from the wagon train got careless doing something outside the circle of the wagons.

Matt had worked around pretty much to the south of the wagons now. He had come across three more and taken care of them in a similar fashion. Matt had then spotted a pony all by itself. Careful not to make a sound he eased over a little rise. As he settled into some brush he spotted the fires inside the circled wagons. He had waited only about five minutes when another Indian approached. With a quick glance back at the camp he saw why. Captain Taylor had started to break up camp. The wagons were being put into motion.

As the Indian hurried by Matt stood and caught the Indian under his chin with his arm. Then he threw his feet out behind him with his arm held tight under the Indians chin. With their combined weight hitting the ground he heard the Indians neck snap. Suddenly Matt spun drawing his right hand pistol. Then he heard Dan's urgent whisper, "It's me Matt; don't shoot!"

With Dan's first word Matt had been able to hold his fire.

Dan then whispered, "Damn; I didn't know you were anywhere around. I spotted his pony and was working into position to get him when all of a sudden you got him."

Matt whispered, "You should be clear now if Hawkeye made it around his side."

Dan still whispered, "I didn't see the gun in your hand when you got him."

Matt holstered his pistol and then whispered, "It wasn't!"

Dan just stared at Matt as he nodded.

Matt heard Hawkeye's owl hoot which you would have thought was flying through the air by the sound of it. Matt answered it but knew it was nowhere near as good as Hawkeye's. Hawkeye with Bones soon appeared. Matt could see that Hawkeye was bleeding from a cut across the left side of his ribs.

Matt asked, "Is it bad?"

Hawkeye answered, "No, I'm okay."

Dan said, "Let's get you to the wagons and let somebody look at that."

Hawkeye said, "No, No! I need to find my horse and get out in front of the wagons."

Matt said, "I think he'll be all right Dan. The wagons are already on the move. We need to be also. You should be careful in case we missed one. They'll be coming from behind you."

Matt then gave a soft whistle and shortly Flame came up. He hardly made any noise at all. Matt mounted and then asked Hawkeye where his horse was.

"Almost back where we were together last,"

Hawkeye at a brisk run headed to the north so as to angle in front of the wagons Matt then knee-reigned Flame slightly to the left as he followed. Dan and Bones rushed off to find their mounts and catch up with the wagons.

After they had gotten past the wagons Matt went to the east a little while Hawkeye headed west to get his horse. They stayed within sight of the wagons and a little out front on each side. They pushed on through the night. The animals where tired, but they didn't dare to stop.

In the dark Captain Taylor was attempting to pick the smoothest route he could. He had the wagons stay in single file. He hoped to keep from hurting any of the animals or breaking any of the wagon wheels. They made camp around the little lake that had been formed from a spring and put the wagons end to end to make a half circle back to the bluff that overlooked the spring. It was about two hundred feet to the top of it. It was the darkest it had been all night. They knew the sun would be up soon.

Captain Taylor spotted a weakness with the defenses of the bluff. He then had ten men put on top of it to make sure they couldn't be attacked from there. As it turned out, there was only one route to get up there and only wide enough for single file. It would be almost impossible for anyone to rush them. The only problem was it was a long trip around. Once there they had tied some ropes together so they could pull their food and water up. Their horses had been brought back and put within the circled wagons to graze. The grass was plentiful and in good condition. They had been able to leave a few acres of grass for all the livestock to graze. The Indians hit them at noon and seemed like they were pretty upset. They did calm down however when all the best shooters brought there guns to fire on the largest group of Indians. It had been hard to estimate how many there were. But when the Indians retreated most of the people thought there had been around two hundred mixed Indians. They appeared to be Paiute, Pawnee, with a few Cheyenne. A couple of hours later the Indians found the back trail. They found out quickly though that it wouldn't work either. It looked like a stand off for now.

Captain Taylor called a meeting. He had explained that they needed to find the Indian camp and attack it if they could. There had been some opposition against that plan. He then explained even though they were pretty safe here they would be in a lot of trouble once they were back out in the open. Then there was the danger of trying to go through the pass before they made sure that it was clear. After the meeting he told Matt and Hawkeye to get some rest. He wanted to send them out to Scout around some as soon as it got dark.

After dark Matt and Hawkeye slipped out of camp they went by foot in different directions. They had made sure not to be detected. They returned just before the sun started its climb in the eastern sky.

They reported that the wagons were being watched and they still hadn't found the main Indian camp. Captain Taylor told them to get some rest.

Captain Taylor sat around by himself sipping coffee. In deep thought he ran one plan after another through his mind. He'd discarded most of them. Then he finely had settled on a couple them. Everyone except for the guards had started to relax. They kept their weapons close by as they made what repairs on the wagons and harness that needed to be done. Some of the women had decided to use up some of the supplies that were in danger of spoiling. It looked like they would have the extra time. Some blackberries had been discovered. Connie and Helen had decided to pick some. The Maxton's and the Gates had let them go only after it was decided that Billy Gates would go along. He was to watch for snakes while they picked the berries. The women had decided to use up what flour they had left to make some pies.

Captain Taylor had finally made up his mind. Seeing Tex close by he sent him after a few of the men. When they had showed up he said, "I think what we need to do unless someone has thought of something better. Is for a few of us to ride out like we are going to make a break for it. Hopefully the Indians will engage us. We need to keep them real busy. Just long enough for Matt and Flame to have a good chance to get through. With some luck maybe he can find their camp. If he can then we'll try to make a surprise attack on it. That's the best I've come up with."

Tex said, "Flame is well rested. But Matt's got to be tired."

Captain Taylor said, "Yes; I agree. It's the best plan I've come up with though."

Chris Maxton asked, "When do you want to do it?"

The Captain answered, "I think for Matt and Flame to see better. It would be best to give them as much daylight as we can. When they leave here they need to be able to pick the best ground so Flame can be at his top speed. At least until they can get by the Indians. Once they're in the open, I don't think there's anything on the prairie that can keep up with them."

Chris said, "Okay; I'll wake Matt up so he can get ready. Then I'll ride out with you."

Captain Taylor asked, "Are you sure? It's a lot harder to shoot off the back of a horse. All the shooting you have done so far has been from the ground."

"You want to show a good force out there to pull as many out from cover as you can,"

Mr. Gates said, "That being the case I'll ride along too. I guess the more we have after us, the better it will be for Matt."

Dan said, "Their right Captain. We should get as many to go along as we can."

"Okay, I guess your right. We don't need to do a lot of fighting. I just want to get the Indians to chase after us. The more we can get to come after us. The better it will be for Matt."

Chris eased away from the meeting to work his way to the quiet secluded place Matt had laid his bedroll out. When he got to Matt's shade tree in a quiet calm voice Chris uttered, "Matt."

Matt woke up instantly, "Yes."

Chris said, "Captain Taylor wants to talk to you."

"Okay thanks."

Chris went on to saddle his horse as Matt rose to find Captain Taylor. When Matt spotted Captain Taylor, he eased up next to him as he saw some of the men approaching with their saddled horses and weapons. Captain Taylor noticed Matt's approach. He met Matt on his way to get his horse. He said, "Matt, I want to try a little trick on the Indians. I'm going to ride out with some men to draw their attention. Hopefully the Indians will chase us. Then I want you to ride out like the devil was after you. Make it look like your riding for help. Then maybe you can Scout around and find the Indian camp. If you do, try to get back here without being spotted and then with some luck maybe we can put together a raid on the Indian camp. We may then be able to get through the pass before the Indians can get reorganized."

Matt said, "Okay, I'll get Flame saddled and be ready shortly."

As Matt went by Tex said, "Ride careful and good luck!"

Dan said, "You take care of yourself!"

Slade said, "Just shoot straight."

Bones kicked in, "If we do our job you shouldn't have to shoot."

Slim just said, "Ride cowboy ride."

Ben supplied a enthusiastic, "Watch your back."

Matt had a hard time controlling his emotions. He had seen how serious they had been. Matt suddenly realized that he had been accepted by them. He nodded to each one of them. When Matt got up to Flame he saw that Hawkeye had his horse about ready. Matt quickly saddled Flame and made sure his rifle, pistols and everything else was secure. After the raid on the last Indian camp he had added two holsters to his saddle. With the extra pistols he now had a dozen more rounds to fire before he had to reload. He double checked to make sure they were all fully loaded; even the chambers that were under the hammers. When he was done he looked up at Hawkeye. Hawkeye had watched him intensely. With a glint in his eyes Hawkeye said, "We get to have some fun now."

Matt said, "You take care. You have to big of a hunger for battle."

"Ho! You're one to talk. I know you. You have the hunger for battle also."

"See you in a day or two. Wish me success."

As Matt and Hawkeye came up with the rest of the riders they heard Captain Taylor explain, "I don't want to exchange the Indians fully. I just want to distract them. We'll make it look like were trying to get through to the east. With some luck we'll be able to draw some from the west. Even if it is just one it ought to help Matt to slip through. Then make sure the Indians don't get in behind us to cut us off. Everyone understand?"

They nodded. Captain Taylor then eyed each one individually and said, "Alright then. Let's get mounted. Matt! May God be with you and ride careful."

Chris leading his horse came up to Matt. Then gave him a big hug as he said, "Do be careful; there's a lot of us depending on you."

Matt nodded, "Yes sir! I'll be careful and do my best."

Matt took a good look around. But for once he didn't spot the girls. Chris had noticed Matt's searching look. "They're picking berries. The women wanted to do some baking. I'll try to save you some."

Matt then mounted Flame. He tied the reins to the saddle horn. Matt would guide Flame with his knees. He wanted both hands free. Matt watched Captain Taylor lead the men out. They scattered a little so as not to make one big target. Captain Taylor swung them to the East. Matt saw some Indians move out into the open. Captain Taylor must have seen them also. He had put his horse into a charge. The rest of the men followed. Some Indians rode to block them as they started to shoot. Matt noticed that most where a foot. However, a few had made it to their horses. A lot of dust had gotten stirred up. Matt thought that most of the Indians shots were short. Matt then noticed a good sized bunch of Indians approaching from the west. That was what Captain Taylor had hoped for. Matt still waited a little longer. He hoped that Captain Taylor along with the other riders spotted the Indians before they got cut off.

Matt checked the terrain to pick out the smoothest ground. With a quick glance back at the Indians Matt decided it was time. He felt sure that Flame could carry him past the Indians on their horses. He spoke a command to Flame. With a lunge Flame was off. Flame had sensed Matt's tenseness as he guided Flame with his knees. He urged Flame to his full speed. Flame's hoofs beat the ground like claps of thunder. Some of the Indians spotting him spun their mounts around to chase him. But Flame had put his whole heart into his run. Flame seamed to be reaching out as if he could pull the ground to him. With his belly close to the ground Flame was stretched out to his full speed. Matt's eyes watered from the wind hitting them. He squinted to help keep the wind out of them. As they started to clear up Matt then noticed how fast the ground was moving under them. He hadn't thought it possible any horse could go so fast. Not even Flame.

Captain Taylor had watched for Matt to make his break. At first, he thought Matt had broken too early. But when he saw Flame stretch out to his full speed he could hardly believe his eyes. There was shooting all around them now. Everyone returned fire at the Indians. Captain Taylor yelled as loud as he could. Then he made circling motions with his arm. He was able to get everyone turned back toward the wagons. That put them into a charge at the Indians that hadn't gone after Matt. Captain Taylor had everyone at a full gallop. They got closer than they wanted to before they got past the Indians. But they all made it back to the wagons. Captain Taylor double checked to make sure everyone had made it back then he looked west. Matt and Flame were out of sight all ready. It looked like some of the Indians had all ready given up the chase.

Captain Taylor then looked to the riders that had gone with him. A couple of horses staggered, then went down as their riders left their saddles. He could see a few men that were bloody. Captain Taylor looked back where they had been. A few Indians still lay on the ground where they had fallen. Six or seven Indian ponies were down also.

Captain Taylor said, "Make sure our wounded and horses are taken care of. Let me know if anybody is seriously hurt."

They helped the wounded under some shade trees where they would be more comfortable. It would make it nicer for the ones that took care of them also. At least for now they had lucked out. They had all made it back with just a few injuries.

Hawkeye rushed up, "Captain, I think I heard gun fire off in the direction Matt headed."

"How much could you tell?"

Coming up then Dan said, "I heard the gun fire too Captain. It didn't last long. There were quite a few shots and then it was over as quick as it started."

The Captain said, "Damn! Well, we'll just have to wait. Maybe after dark Hawkeye can sneak out to see if Matt made it alright."

Mrs. Maxton had finally found Chris. It had taken her awhile with everyone being so busy taking care of the wounded and making sure enough men were in place so they still had a good defensive position. She said, "Connie, Helen, and Billy haven't come back. I thought when they heard the shooting they'd be back to see what was going on."

Tex as he'd been going by heard her. He said, "Ma-am, I'll get a couple of men and go look for them."

Matt and Flame made it clear of the Indians in the immediate area. Matt then slowed Flame down to a lope. Matt looked for a place to hide out to let things settle down some. They rounded a little knoll right into a good-sized group of Indians. The Indians spotted them and kicked their ponies hard, heading right at them. Matt drew both pistols to let their lethal fire spit out a message of death. He'd done it so fast that he had dropped six braves off their ponies before the Indians had a chance to get their weapons into action. Matt knocked a couple more off their horses before the last three could get their weapons leveled at him. He shot one left then one right. An arrow grazed his left arm as he shot the last one. Matt then heard hoof beats off to his left. He kneed Flame back into an easy run. They worked their way through some brush to a little opening. They quickly crossed it into some more brush. He had been forced back the way he'd come from. Matt slowed Flame to a walk as he looked for a path they could use. The last bunch of Indians had stopped back where he'd dropped the first group of Indians. He had already sent a good number of them on the way to their happy hunting ground. Matt then spotted a little gully. He kneed Flame into it as he quickly reloaded his pistols. The gully turned slowly to the east then suddenly straight back to the south. Matt then spotted a draw running to the north. Even though it would skyline him for awhile he quickly guided Flame into it.

Just before they broke over the knoll going out of sight. Matt took a quick glance back. Some Indians just passed the gully they had just come out of. If he had stayed in the gully he would have run right into the Indians. Matt didn't relax much; he was sure some of the Indians would start to track them.

Flame had worked up a pretty good sweat. Matt had worked him hard the first couple of miles. But Flame wasn't breathing hard and still had a light step.

The draw soon dropped them into the side of a wide open valley. Matt sure they would be followed decided he had no other choice. He guided Flame out into it. The valley looked to be three miles across. Matt couldn't see either end of it. For it was shaped like a half-moon with both ends ending up to the south where most of the Indians seemed to be coming from.

Matt sure they would be tracked thought they couldn't be far behind. He then put Flame into an easy lope. They'd made it only a third of the way across when he heard a shot from behind them. Matt looked back and he saw about ten Indians on his trail. Then there was another shot. He glanced to his right and saw a bunch of Indians as they appeared around the bend. It looked like twenty from that direction. Matt took a hard look straight across to the other side of the Valley. He decided it would be too rough to take a horse out that way. With his knees he guided Flame left urging him into a slow gallop. Even at that pace Matt didn't think the Indians closed on them. The Indians were trying to work up more speed out of their ponies.

Matt was letting Flame choose the ground he wanted to run on. They followed the valley west. After a couple of miles when Matt checked on the Indians again, he could tell that Flame had pulled away some. Matt almost forgot what was happening when he noticed how fast the ground was going by. Matt listened closely to Flame's breathing for a few seconds and with a lot of heart felt relief Matt could tell that Flame wasn't laboring very hard at all. Even though Flame glistened with sweat he wasn't straining much at all. Matt was amazed with Flame once more. Matt then noticed that Flame seemed to be picking out the ground he was running on, that used the least amount of effort. As if he was attempting to conserve all the energy he could. Flame seemed to make use of every move he made.

Flame had eaten up another mile when Matt spotted another group of Indians appear in front of them. The Valley had turned more to the South. Matt guessed there were about thirty of them. Matt slowed Flame to a stop with his knees. He looked at the Indians behind them. The Indians had been joined by the ones that had been on his trail. It looked like some others from somewhere had gotten into the chase too. That then made the group ahead of them the smallest. The Indians had started to spread out to make sure he couldn't get past. As Matt checked back he saw that the group from behind was fanning out also. With his mind made up Matt leaned forward and then gave Flame a verbal command. Flame lunged into a burst of speed. Matt guided him straight down the middle of the valley. However, Matt did let Flame pick the smoothest ground to run on.

When Matt got into good shooting range he slowed Flame a little so he could settle into a smoother stride. The Indians with rifles had already started to shoot. Matt pulled his pistols then he started to shoot in slow evenly spaced shots at the top of Flame's stride. Even though still fifty yards away. Matt had already knocked a couple of Indians off the backs of their ponies. When Matt had emptied both guns he was already in among the Indians. None of the Indians directly in front of Matt had survived the lethal lead he had sent at them. Flame hadn't swerved left or right. The Indians ponies had to open up a path for Flame or be run over.

Matt quickly holstered his empty pistols. Then drew the other two pistols he had fastened to his saddle. He quickly thumbed them empty as they broke through the Indians line. Matt had caught some stragglers along with the ones that had lost control of their ponies. He shouted another command to Flame. In about four strides Flame had sprung nearly to his top speed.

Matt returned his empty pistols to their holsters. When they had covered about five hundred yards he slowed Flame to a stop with his knees. He turned Flame around to face the Indians. He'd been able to make most every shot count. There were Indians laid out all over the ground with the rider-less ponies scattering among them. It had confused the ones that survived long enough to slow the second group up. Matt pulled the seventeen-shot Henry rifle from it's boot. It was forty-four-caliber like his pistols.

Just when the rest of the Indians started around the confused chaos Matt had caused he started shooting again. With the distance a little over five hundred yards he took his time. After a few more ponies lost their riders under the deadly fire the rest of the Indians decided they'd had enough. The Indians stopped to circle back out of his range. When they had stopped Matt held his fire. The Indians started to pick up their dead and tend to their wounded. Matt quickly replaced the ten rounds he had fired from the rifle. Then he reloaded all of the pistols.

Matt checked the Indians one more time. It looked like they had lost interest in him. Matt kneed Flame into a lope on through the valley. They'd traveled another five or six miles when the valley opened up to a big wide open plane in front of them. From their vantage point it sloped down slightly. Matt eased Flame to a stop then with a careful look in all directions he surveyed all the land he could. With a closer look he could tell there where some rolling hills with little lazy gullies.

He kept checking his back trail. It still looked like none of the Indians had decided to take up the chase. Matt then caught some movement far away to the southeast. With a focused look he made out three spots. He quickly checked the surrounding area again. Matt then put his focus back on the three spots. With a nagging feeling that he was missing something Matt put his full attention on the spots. Just as the spots dropped out of sight it hit him that something hadn't looked natural.

Matt urged Flame into motion toward some lower ground. After a couple of miles a little peak appeared. He thought it would give him a good view. He hoped that they had continued in the same direction they had been headed. With some luck maybe they would lead him to the Indians camp ground. After another three miles he brought Flame to a stop and then dismounted. After a ten minute climb he dropped down and crawled the rest of way. As he eased up to the top he removed his hat. Then he gently parted the grass to peek over the top. As he spotted them Matt tensed when he saw that there were three Indians on horseback. Still a good way off Matt could see that each one of the Indians had someone held belly down in front of them across the front shoulders of their ponies.

Matt then got a sick feeling in the pit of his stomach for he was sure he had recognized two of them. Then he was sure he knew who the third one was. Not taking any chances Matt carefully back-crawled off the peak to return to Flame. As he climbed aboard Matt took a quick look at the sun. There was only about four hours of daylight left. He urged Flame to a slow trot as they kept to low ground. It had taken about five miles before he came across their tracks. He followed them for a couple of hours at a brisk pace. Matt did try to stay away from big rocks of thick brush as much as possible. He noticed that some mountains were starting to close in on them from both sides. He had gotten very cautious for he felt sure he was getting close to their main camp. He reined off to the side quickly when he spotted a lot of unshod pony tracks. They went in both directions making a new trail. He eased Flame into cover and then dismounted. He checked the wind; his luck was still running good. It was blowing into his face. There were strong gusts of wind every once in a while. Nice cool gusts that felt good.

Matt still had Flame's reins tied loosely to the saddle horn. He started slipping silently through the brush off to the side of the trail a little. Flame nearly as quiet, followed along. The valley had narrowed a lot. Not much over a mile the trail he'd been able to keep on his right turned into a narrow pass. He then hid Flame in some bushes. With one word Matt had backed Flame into them and was certain that he'd stay until given another command. The sun for the most part had left the sky. It was already letting the darkness settle into the pass. Using a lot of patience Matt worked his way along, until he spotted a couple of scouts. Then he stayed motionless until he had made sure there weren't any others. He was certain he could slip by them without being detected. But if he was to rescue the girls and Billy he needed to take care of them now. He made quick work of them much like he'd done a couple of nights past.

Then he gave a very soft whistle and Flame came up quietly. After a mile he spotted the cook fires of a big camp in another Valley that turned out to be fairly wide. Darkness had pretty much taken over the land leaving just streaks of light peaking over the mountain tops high in the sky. Staying to cover Matt was on the prowl. Soon he spotted what he was sure was the main part of the camp. Matt could see teepees along with the cook fires. He then spotted the horse herd, and decided he had to have three horses. He backed Flame into some brush again. Then Matt slide through the brush and grass in search of some more guards. He had come across one shortly. Matt had almost stumbled onto him before he saw him. Matt then was able to sneak up behind him. Grabbed his head hard with both hands and gave it a quick twist. Matt heard his neck snap then quietly laid him down. Taken more time than Matt wanted he came across three more. The best one had sensed or heard him. When he had turned Matt had taken him out with a blow to his heart. It had been hard enough to make it stop beating. Lee Chan had taught him well.

Silently Matt gathered three of the Indian ponies together. He led them back close to Flame tying them up with a slip knot. He'd had a couple of good looks into the camp. Matt didn't care at all for what he'd seen. He spotted Helen as some Indians had rudely tied her down to some stakes. They'd driven them into the ground to hold her spread eagle. Then they'd torn all of her clothes off and threw them into one of the fires close by.

Matt had used all of his will power to keep from rushing on in. He was afraid they'd kill them with the first hint that anyone was around to rescue them. Even though it was completely dark now with all the fires there was a lot of light. Matt could tell it was a new camp. There were still a lot places with some tall grass. That's when Matt made up his mind on what to do. He quickly took his gun rig off and then hung it around Flame's saddle horn. Then he took all of his buckskins off. He left his hat also. However, Matt did put his moccasins back on. Then he went to the closest Indian he had put on the trail to his happy hunting ground. Quickly Matt removed his loin cloth.

Matt tied the loin cloth around his hips with his knife still between his teeth. Then he reclaimed the pistols for each hand. Silently going to a little stream that ran through the area he found a place that had a lot of clay. He carefully laid his guns down, as he rubbed it all over his body. Matt had to put up with some pain from the wounds he'd already gotten from the battles he'd been in with the Indians. He didn't think anywhere serious but he had lost some blood and wasn't in his best shape. Most were just nicks, but he did have one through the fleshly part of his left shoulder. After he had a good layer of clay over his body Matt then pulled some grass and worked it into the clay. With some luck he hoped to blend in with the grass that was around. Matt made sure the knife was firm between his teeth. Taken up his pistols again he then set out with his rescue attempt. Quickly, but silently he worked his way up close. Then he got down to crawl. He crept up around some brush, then a couple of trees. Matt used the tallest grass he could find for cover. At last he had been able to work his way up to a position behind Billy. At least he hadn't had to go through the whole camp. Matt had been able to worm his way in from the East side of the camp.

He got another surprise for now he could see that Billy was tied to the tree. It was only about four inches through. Billy's arms were pulled behind him held there by a strip of rawhide around the tree. Billy's feet were pulled out in front of him tied to a stake. It made it so he had to turn his head or close his eyes to keep from looking at the girls. The big surprise was that there was another girl with Connie and Helen. It appeared that she was an Indian. Matt saw that there was a pretty good goose egg on the side of Connie's head. Helen had a pretty good bump on hers also. There was a handful of Indians with sharp sticks taking turns poking the girls. They'd been doing it hard enough to draw blood. It appeared that their breasts had gotten most of the attention from the Indians.

Mad clear through Matt had all he could do to control himself. He crawled up the last three feet right behind Billy. He was grateful he hadn't been spotted yet. While he kept close to the ground he whispered just load enough for Billy to hear, "Billy, don't let on that I'm here. It's

Matt. I'm going to cut your hands loose, then put my knife in one of your hands. You understand?"

Billy nodded just enough that Matt could see his head move.

Matt then said, "You'll have to cut your own feet loose then cut the girls loose, all of them! Then get out of camp straight behind your back. Circle around to your right just outside of camp. Got that?"

Again Billy nodded just enough for Matt to see.

Matt then told Billy where the horses were. Also, that they weren't to wait for him. Lastly, he said, "Billy, get ready. I'm going to distract them."

Matt had already cut Billy's hands loose while he was instructing him. He then made sure Billy had a good grip on the knife.

Matt then said, "Billy, give me a couple of minutes to get where I want to be."

He had to grit his teeth when the Indians started to poke the girls again. After five minutes Matt was where he wanted to be. He hoped to draw all the Indians attention onto him. With some luck he might distract them long enough for Billy and the girls to get clear. He took a deep breath. Then he lunged to his feet with as loud of a roar as he could make. He'd been able to startle them for they had looks of pure shock much like he was an apparition coming up out of the earth. They had been caught flat-footed and Matt didn't give them a chance to recover. He just started to work the pistols as fast as he could until they run empty. Then he moved in among them using his feet to kick. Matt let his momentum follow each kick. He was spinning so he could get all of his force behind each kick. He used the pistols as clubs and the satisfying cracks of skulls. A few had tried to get some lead or an arrow into him. Shortly the Indians realized as they missed. They were hitting there own people. Most then just took out their knives. A few had spears or tomahawks.

Matt didn't stay in one place long. He just let his body flow with his momentum. It helped him to get more force behind his kicks and punches. Also, it kept him moving, so he was never a still target. It also helped to keep him from being predictable. He used the pistols in place of his hands. He was determined not to lose them. Besides he noticed that they were doing a lot of damage. He tried to make sure each blow either crippled or killed. He had seen that Billy had finely gotten all of the girls loose and on their feet. Just in the nick of time for some of the Indians noticed that they had gotten loose. Matt then felt a sharp pain go across the back of his right shoulder. He then started to fight his way out of the mass of Indians in the direction Billy and the girls had gone. He had worked his way out from the main mass of Indians. When he was delivering a kick to an Indians throat that collapsed his windpipe, Matt felt a spear as it pierced his right thigh. Matt cracked another skull with a pistol barrel. Just then some shots made a loud roar above the noise of all the battle cries of the Indians. With a quick glance Matt saw that Billy and the girls had gathered up some rifles. They had thinned out the Indians from around him. He yelled, "GO!"

Then Matt dropped his pistols as he quickly took hold of the spear with his left hand. Then with the edge of his right hand he made a hard karate chop. It snapped the spear shaft. He felt the pain as it shot through him like a fierce bolt of lighting. He then quickly reached behind his leg. Then as he gritted his teeth he yanked the rest of the shaft with the spear head on it out. Just short of passing out he quickly bent over and retrieved the pistols. He spun as he rose back feeling the feathers of an arrow as it just brushed his head. A split second slower he'd have been a goner for sure. He then took out on a dead run after Billy and the girls. Matt almost made it out of the light from the camp fires when the Indians started shooting. Bullets crashed through the brush all around him. He caught up with Billy and the girl's real quick. Way too quick. Billy's expression showed the shock of observing the torturing of the girls and the violence he had just witnessed. Connie and Helen's facial expressions showed shock from their state of dress as much, as from their physical pain. They were having a real hard time of it from the sharp rocks and stones under foot. Their bare feet were already cut up something terrible.

Matt sure it was taking too much time whistled loudly. It wasn't long before Flame had thundered up. Flame had kicked up some stones and a lot of dirt as he slid to a stop beside Matt. Matt then quickly reloaded his empty pistols with bullets from his gun belt on Flames saddle. To Billy and the girls he said, "I know its rough, but hurry along the best you can. Billy, get them on the horses and be ready to ride. Connie Flames is used to you the most. I didn't know there would be four of you. So I got only three horses. I'll pick you up to ride along with me. I've got to slow them down some."

Matt then climbed aboard Flame. With a spoken command Flame lunged forward in the direction Matt was sure the Indians would be coming. Just as they hit the first opening Matt saw them rushing from the other side of it. So far it looked like none of the Indians had been able to catch up any of their ponies. They had spotted Matt also and made a running charge at him. With another command Flame again slid to a stop and lowering his head. Matt opened up on them. He fired as fast as he could. They had started to shoot also. He heard bullets whistle by his head along with the swish of some arrows. He felt a blow on his right side as he swapped pistols. The Indians had stopped their charge as they sought some cover. They tried to get away from the lethal wall of lead. As his pistols emptied Matt spun Flame around again. Matt guided Flame with his knees as the reins were still tied around the saddle horn. Headed back to where he'd left the horses. He hoped Billy and the girls had already made it. Just as Flame bounded out of the clearing Matt felt a blow just above his left hip. It didn't take more than five minutes before Matt and Flame caught up with them. Matt let out a sigh of relief as he saw that Billy had gotten the girls up on the ponies and ready to go. Matt guided Flame to a stop beside Connie then pulled his left foot out of the stirrup. Reached down for Connie's hand and helped her up behind him as Connie settled in behind to get a good hold on his shoulders. Matt said, "Billy! You need to be alert for any Indians that could have been drawn in by the gunfire. Go! We've got to hurry."

They had cleared the pass and made it a couple miles out in the open. Then pretty much in the clear Matt guided them to the northeast back towards where the wagons should be. Connie had a firm grip around Matt's waist now so as to keep her balance and to keep from being bounced off Flame's rear. She had given up some of her modesty. But with all the mud and grass that covered Matt's body. Connie tried to keep a little gap between them. The grass had already started to make her itch. She then thought she felt Matt weaken. She knew he had to be tired. Connie then tried to lean out and forward to look at Matt's face then she felt Matt start to sway. Connie then spoke to Matt in the hope of perking him up. It was then she realized what she had thought was sweat; was blood. Connie then realized Matt was out of it and riding by pure instinct. Then speaking softly she urged Flame to a stop. The others noticed and came to a stop also.

When Flame came to a complete stop it was enough to wake Matt up out of his daze. He asked, "What? Why have we stopped? We need to be going."

Connie answered, "Matt, you're hurt and bleeding badly."

Matt then responded, "We can't stop. They'll be getting horses, and be after us."

Connie said, "Matt, you're about ready to fall out of the saddle."

Matt said, "Okay tie me to the saddle horn. Use one of the ties from a holster. We have to go."

Connie hated it. But she knew Matt was right. Still she was sure Matt was in worse shape than he was letting on. With Billy's help Connie loosed Flames reins. Then took off one of the holster ties and tied Matt's hands to the saddle horn. Matt had already drifted of to sleep again.

After Billy climbed back on the Indian pony Connie yelled, "Billy! Do you have any idea on how we need to go to find our way back to the Wagons?"

Billy said, "Just to keep going as straight as we can the way Matt had us headed."

Helen with a concerned look at Matt just nodded in agreement. Just as they'd started to put the horses in motion they heard, "S-h."

They looked at the Indian girl to see that she held a finger to her lips.

They all became silent and completely still. Connie not hearing anything started using the sign language that Mr. Socket had thought her. She hoped that the Indian girl could see well enough in the dark. Also, Connie hoped she got her sign language right. She asked, "Why?"

The Indian girl smiled then signed back, "Riders coming. We go." Then pointed and led them off in the direction she had pointed. Connie just barely able to see in the dark nodded. She told the others what had been said.

If it was possible, it seemed like it had just gotten darker. Connie glanced skyward. She couldn't see a single Star or the Moon. She realized then that the sky had filled up with clouds. Not only had it gotten darker. The gusting wind had an awful cold bite to it. She knew that Matt's body was helping to keep her warm. She knew the others had to be cold.

153

CHAPTER TEN

WOUNDED

Connie was worried to death about Matt. She had never seen him when he wasn't just full of energy. He was still bleeding and she could feel the stickiness of the blood as it leaked out of him. Connie for the first time in her life felt completely helpless. Even when she had been staked out she hadn't given up. She still had hope. She hadn't figured out why, but something in her wouldn't let her give up. But if Matt died it would be a big blow. She'd rather be back yonder dead if it would make Matt all right. Now she didn't even know where they were headed or what they would do. It was a good thing Matt had been tied to the saddle horn. It took all she could do to keep him from falling left or right. Then when going up a slope or hill she had a hard time keeping herself from sliding off Flame's rump. She was very uncomfortable with all the sweat, blood, grass, and from Flame's hair. For it was irritating her bare bottom and the insides of her thighs.

They had dropped into a gully. The Indian girl pulled her horse to a stop and then slid off its back. Billy started to get off his horse. But the Indian girl motioned for him to stay on his horse. Helen had been able to see her motions did likewise. The Indian girl then motioned for Connie to ease Flame up to her. Connie not really comprehending reined Flame up next to her. Connie watched her bend over. Almost immediately she stood back up with her hands full of something. She rubbed it into the wound on Matt's right leg. Upon realizing the Indian girl was packing the wound with mud she got upset, and tried to get her to stop. The Indian girl gave her a fierce determined look. Then said something Connie didn't understand at all. She'd been able to see pretty clear. For the moon had showed through the clouds for a couple of seconds.

The Indian girl just bent over again to fill her hands with more mud. Taking the mud as the Indian girl handed it to her but with a lot of apprehension Connie did as the Indian girl directed her. Connie packed it in the wound on Matt's right side. Connie still not comprehending did as she was directed. With the Moon peaking through a couple of times Connie had been able to see pretty good in just three or four minutes his wounds that had been packed. Connie now understood for as the moon peeped through the clouds again she saw that Matt had stopped bleeding. Connie then realized why it was so dark, and cool. With the cloud cover it looked like they were in for a bad storm. With all that had happened, a storm was the last thing on her mind. But as that ran across her mind Connie felt her heart swell most to bursting as she realized Matt was in no condition to be out in a bad storm. It was then she admitted to herself how scared she was for Matt's life and that she was totally in love with him.

Matt had stirred a little and moaned when they'd packed the mud in place. Finished the Indian girl had gone back to the pony she'd been riding and grabbing the horse's main swung up on it's back. Taking the lead she motioned for them to follow. The moon stayed hidden to let the darkness envelope them fully. Staying close, afraid they'd get lost; they each in turn made sure they stayed on the heels of the horse in front of them. The Indian girl kept up a steady pace. Connie along with the others had gotten completely disorientated. To them though it appeared that the Indian girl did have a destination in mind. She led them in a straight line as much as possible as they traveled through the night. They did have to work their way through gullies and valleys. But as soon as she could the Indian girl made an adjustment in the direction she seemed to have a beeline on. After what seemed like a week Connie noticed that things had started to become visible. A few minutes later she could see that the sky was dark with clouds.

None of them had said anything all night. At first it was mostly because even with the relief of being rescued, they had become concerned for Matt's welfare. Now it was taking all of their concentration just to stay on the backs of their horses. Connie's head pounded so bad it felt like her eyes would pop out of her head. The goose egg on the side of her head throbbed with her heartbeat. Her arms and shoulders hurt from the strain of keeping Matt in the saddle. It felt like her bones were about to pop out of there joints. Also, it felt like her bare bottom had been rubbed raw.

Connie could see mountains all around them now with gullies and pass's going in a lot of different directions. As it started to rain she glanced skyward again and saw that the clouds looked like they where full of water. It was a cold rain that had put a chill in all of them already. She could feel Matt start to shiver as the rain fell harder by the minute. Matt was like lead in her arms. Connie had never been in so much pain, in so many places at one time. Where a muscle didn't ache she was either rubbed raw or badly bruised. Her breasts felt like the bare nerve of a tooth ache from all the puncture wounds she had received from the Indians. As she held Matt in place in front of her it had added to her discomfort.

Connie was sure the others had to be hurting as bad as she was. They had to keep on the backs of Indian ponies while holding the rifles they had taken from the Indians. They had been in a shallow valley for half a dozen miles when the Indian girl motioned for them to stop. She then guided her horse up a small ravine and disappeared. In a few minutes she returned and motioned them to follow her.

She led up the ravine for several yards before it gradually dropped into a deep ravine. Just a few yards after they had reached the crown Connie saw the tracks where the Indian girl had went up the steep bank and then returned. She motioned for them to follow then immediately put her horse at the bank again. The horses had a hard time pawing their way up as the rain had softened the bank into mud. Connie knew if Matt's hands hadn't been tied to the saddle horn, they would have fell off of Flame's back. She had tried to lean forward with Matt's body as she squeezed her legs tight to hold her fanny in place. Matt's weight had been too much and she had ended up holding on to Matt to keep from slipping off Flames back. Even though Flame was the last one up with the mud all churned up he made it easier than the other horses had. Then they dropped down into a little valley. They had ridden on a good mile when the Indian girl slowed their pace. She acted like she was looking for something that she had lost. Then with an immense look of gratitude she gave them a forced smile. As if to say she had found exactly what she had been looking for. She also spoke several words that none of them understood. She led them up a slight ravine to the right and then just as it started to make another right turn a half mile from the entrance. The Indian girl made a sharp turn left up a steep knoll. Not as bad as the previous bank though. When they cleared the top Connie saw a basin that was about the size of a thirty acre park. They went through what looked like the only way in and out; at least on horseback. It appeared that there was a lot of good graze for the horses.

They had just gotten down into the gradual sloped entrance when Indian girl spotted a ledge and stopped. She pointed at Billy and then the ledge. Then she pointed back to the way they had just come from. Connie started to explain to Billy what she thought she wanted Billy to do.

Billy tired, worn out, and cold said, "I know. I'll watch. Is Matt alive? He doesn't look good."

Connie answered, "He's still breathing."

Billy slid off his horse. The Indian girl reached for the horse's reins and Billy handed them to her. Then the Indian girl led the rest of them on down into the basin. When they had gone around an outcropping of rocks, to Connie's surprise she spotted a spring that ran into a nice clean clear pool.

The Indian girl slid off her horse then quickly disappeared into the rock formation. She returned shortly to motion Helen down. Helen comprehending fell off of her horse as much as anything then stood on shaking knees. Leaving the other horses the Indian girl motioned for Connie to guide Flame along with his precious load. The Indian girl helped balance Helen as she led them up through the rocks. The last few feet they had to go single file. With her circulation returning Helen had gotten her legs under her by then. Even though the passage was quite winding Connie was sure it wasn't more than forty yards from where they had left the other horses. Flame had just been able to work his way through in a couple of places. Connie had all she could do to contain her surprise when she saw an open space right in front of a cave. It was big enough for all of them too dwell in. It even had a ceiling tall enough for them to stand up in.

Connie comprehending then reined Flame up as close as she could. It took a little while to undo the leather ties as they were soaked and had been drawn tight with the strain of keeping Matt in the saddle. With Matt's hands untied the Indian girl and Helen stood on Flame's left side. Connie leaned Matt toward them. Matt's dead weight almost put all them on the ground. Connie had tried to slow Matt's decent but had to let go or she would have tumbled on top of them. She quickly slid off Flames rear to help drag; more than carry Matt into the cave. Leaning him against one of the cave walls they moved some rocks and cleared some other debris out of the way. To give them a good place to lay Matt out. When they had finished and had him lain out. Helen got her first good look at Matt. She then realized how badly Matt had been hurt and exclaimed, "Oh, my! He's all shot up."

With all the movement Matt had started to leak blood again. Connie said, "Oh, I know! And we don't have any medicine or a thing to doctor him with. It looks like we'll be here a while. Guess I better unsaddle Flame and take care of him."

Almost in a panic Helen said, "We need to do something. Matt will die if we don't."

Almost groaning out loud Connie said, "I know; but there's nothing we can do. Just watch, hope, pray, and comfort him as much as possible."

The Indian girl had watched them intently as they spoke so as to gather their thoughts. She then followed Connie and Flame back out into the basin leaving Helen to watch over Matt. Back out in the basin the Indian girl quickly walked off to where Billy was on guard watching their back trail. Connie with a glance at her unsaddled Flame, then picketed him out on some plush grass. Connie then picketed the Indian ponies out.

Connie hadn't thought she had taken so much time, but was surprised when she returned back to the cave. The Indian girl had already returned with what looked like sleeves from Billy's shirt. Helen was already at work cleaning Matt up. The Indian girl motioned to Connie then handed the sleeve she'd been using to Connie. Connie went to work helping Helen clean Matt up. Then Connie noticed the Indian girl as she picked up Matt's knife and stood. She had gotten

Matt's knife from Billy also. She quickly walked off taking the knife with her.

They gently cleaned Matt up as much as possible. It had been a hard job getting all the clay and grass off. They had been real careful so as not to start him bleeding anymore than he was. They had not much more than finished, when the Indian girl returned with her arms full. She had some kindling along with a bunch of other things. She laid all of it down and quickly went out again. When she returned she had a large stone. When she set it down they saw that the top of it was concaved enough to form a small bowl. She then squatted down and separated everything out. Finished with her sorting she took Matt's knife to cut his borrowed loin cloth off.

Connie and Helen had both gasped in surprise. She'd done it quickly before they realized what she was doing. Then realizing he was completely exposed they'd stared for a minute then looking at each other. They had gotten more embarrassed than they'd ever been in their lives. Seeing a man naked was not something that was proper unless he was your husband.

The Indian girl quickly cut the leather into strips. After that she tied one strip to a stick which made a little bow. Then she put another stick through a loop in the leather strip. Taking Matt's knife she made a hole in another piece of wood, then in the second one. Using the knife she sliced off some shavings onto one of the pieces of wood. Then she placed the bow with the stick in between the two pieces of wood holding them in place firmly. She drew the bow back and forth. The stick through the leather strip started spinning.

The Indian girl worked at it steadily for a few minutes till a tiny flame appeared. Then she added some twigs to it. As the fire grew she put some small limbs on it. After that it wasn't long before she had a good fire going. She laid stones around it to make sure it was well banked to get all the heat she could to flow straight up. Then she placed three good sized stones in place and made sure they wouldn't roll. She than carefully laid the large stone on top with the bowl facing up. She then stood and went out into the rain. When she returned she had piece of tree bark full of water. She did it by tipping it slightly and holding her hand over the low end. She poured the water into her makeshift bowl. She then started mashing some of the other things she'd gathered and added them in with the water. She then went out and returned shortly with some dry wood. She then stoked the fire up some more. She'd been able to get a pretty hot fire going already.

When the Indian girl stood to go out again Connie and Helen got up to follow her out. With the Indian girls direction they returned shortly with a lot of dry wood. It had been pulled out from under the rocks and from under the cliff. Even with the down pour the rain still hadn't gotten to it yet. The three girls then worked together to build another fire pit. By using a burning stick from the first fire it didn't take long at all to get the new one burning. They made the second fire pretty big to use for heat. They all needed it. For all of them had gotten chilled. Besides, Matt would need all his energy to fight his wounds. He didn't need to use any of his energy to fight off the chilly air.

The Indian girl had squatted down to check the water with her ground up ingredients in it. She had made a satisfying noise as she stirred it a little. The water had started to steam. She then made some motions to Connie and Helen. Not understanding Connie used sign language. With comprehension Connie looked at Helen and said, "She thinks it's okay for Billy to come in out of the rain."

Helen had been so concerned about Matt she'd forgotten all about her brother. He had to be cold. Helen just nodded as she stood to walk down through the rocks out into the rain. About to chew herself out for her lack of concern for her brother it suddenly hit her how much she loved Matt. She couldn't deny it to herself anymore. She felt a sickness hit the pit of her stomach as her heart skipped a couple of beats as full understanding hit her. The hard cold rain helped to revive her as she stepped out into the open. Even though with it being full day it was still quite dark. It was raining hard enough to make it difficult to see through.

The Indian girl's mixture had started steaming. She took Billy's sleeves out to the spring and cleaned them up good. Upon returning she dipped one of them in the stone bowl then started bathing Matt's wounds with her potion. After using the potion all up she started mashing up another mixture to be heated up. When the new potion had gotten pretty warm using the other sleeve and with Connie's help they dripped some into Matt's mouth. The Indian girl held it open while Connie wrung the liquid out of it. They repeated till it was all gone.

They had just finished when Helen and Billy returned. Billy spotted the dry wood and added some to the fire. With Helen he sat next to it to dry out and get warmed up. They were quite chilly. After a little as their bodies warmed up some they sat back to relax. With real concern Billy looked at Matt, and then asked, "How's he doing." Connie and Helen both looked at Matt with their love showing all over their faces for the entire world to see. The Indian girl had observed and felt something prick her heart. Then she had a fleeting thought as to why. She was sure that under the circumstances she had done all that she could. She prayed to the Great Spirit that it was enough, as she had never seen such a warrior. Nor had she even heard of one so great. She felt pride about to burst through her heart and was exceedingly happy to have been rescued by him. She hoped he lived. She would use all of her skills that her uncle had taught her. He was a Great Medicine Man among her people. He even had the power of being able to see into The Spirit World the same as she did.

That was how she had known how to find the place. She hadn't ever told her uncle or anyone. She had been uncertain how great her powers were or how to know for sure whether they were real visions or just something from the dream world. But as soon as she had seen the warrior, (Matt was the name they called him and she liked the sound of it. She had formed his name on her lips a couple of times and thought it even felt good as it rolled off her lips) leap up back at the Indian camp with a loud roar. Then she had seen how easy he had destroyed his enemies. She knew he had great power. Then she had seen some go down that didn't show any visible marks. The way their bodies had fallen she knew they were dead. So now she thought that the warrior had magical powers also. Her other companion's were decent for white eyes, but she didn't think of the warrior as a white eye. She didn't understand that thought, so she just shrugged it off. She was very proud of her companions, for not once had she heard any of them cry out like most white eyes did. Not understanding the white eyes talk she let her own thoughts run through her mind.

Connie had finely smoothed out a place to sit and relax. Maybe even a little dazed after spending the last few hours; with all her thoughts and energy on the care and concern for Matt. It had taken awhile for Billy's words to register on her mind. Matt labored hard as he breathed. He was hurt bad and had lost a lot of blood. With a glance at Matt as if to make sure he still breathed, even though they all could hear him. It was hard to believe he was still alive with as bad as some of the wounds were. Connie took a deep breath, then said, "I think the Indian girl has done all she can. It looked like she used some herbs and roots that have medical value to them."

Helen said, "I think you're right. It looks like we'll have to depend on her. I don't have any idea where we are or what to do."

Billy said, "I don't either. I do think the Indian girl does have our welfare and Matt's on her shoulders; at least it appears that way."

Connie tiredly responded, "Yes I think you're right, before this when things had gotten out of hand. I just followed Matt and everything worked out."

Helen said, "I think she knows what she's doing. She has already kept us from being recaptured or worse. Besides it was like she knew right where this place was."

Billy with a thoughtful look said, "To me it seemed more like she was following a map.

Both girls with some thought finely nodded. The fire had it's affect on them. They looked at the Indian girl as if to make sure she was still there. Connie and Helen seemed of one mind as they looked for a good place to lie down. Connie said, "Billy I'm all done in. Can you watch over Matt for a little?"

Billy said, "Sure I know you got to be tired. It feels like a year since any of us have been able to get any sleep. Even as tired as I am it still is going to be hard for me to go to sleep. I'm not used to being around anyone that is completely naked. I know it's not your fault and nothing anybody can do about it. I just got to work things out in my mind, that's all."

As Billy had spoken it had made all of them blush a little. The Indian girl had sat next to the fire as they spoke. As she listened to the tone of their voices she watched there facial expressions and felt better about her companions. She hadn't understood a word, but was able to recognize how concerned they were. It didn't appear to her like it was for them. But mostly for the one that was fighting to hang on to his life. He had gotten chilled from the cold rain and the cold floor of the cave hadn't done a lot to warm him up. But she thought that unless he caught the breathing sickness with him being cool, it would help him to fight the fever when it came. Also, it would slow down the flow of his blood. More determined than ever she would make sure to do every thing within her power to get everyone through their ordeal. After the other two girls had lain down and she saw that the boy was going to watch. She stretched out to get some rest also.

CHAPTER ELEVEN

HARDEST JOB

Tex, Bones and Slade had made their search. It hadn't taken them long to find out what had happened. They found the baskets with the berries scattered all over the ground. When they followed the trail they had a hard time believing their eyes. A narrow cut was found going into the cliff. It wound its way up and down as it worked its way through the little mountain range they were using to defend themselves. It opened out on the plains a couple of miles to the East of where they had made camp. As Tex led them back he knew he had the hardest job ahead of him; that he'd ever had to do. He hoped he never had another one even remotely as close. He heard some others coming and to make sure they weren't fired upon by mistake said, "It's Tex! Bones and Slade are with me." When they met Tex confirmed their worse fears and nodded as he said, "Yes they're gone."

Dan with the new group said, "Damn!"

Everyone just starred at each other, then at the ground as if to shield their own thoughts from each other. Tex took the lead as they continued back. When they returned to the location of the baskets, Tex paused.

Bones said, "I'll get them."

Dan said, "Tex, I'll tell them."

Tex responded, "No! It's my people; it's my job."

With heavy feet they walked back to the cook fires. Mrs. Gates and Mrs. Maxton saw them as they came up. When they spotted Bones with the empty baskets, they both exclaimed, "Oh, no! No!"

Tex with his back ramrod straight walked up to them. He stopped just a few steps away. Then took his hat off and held it in both hands as he said, "Sorry ma-am, but they're gone. Some Indians got them."

Mrs. Gates about to cry said, "They're alive then. They got to be."

Tex shuffled his feet as he said, "Well ma-am. They were when they left here." His thoughts were that they'd be better off if they were dead.

Captain Taylor, Chris Maxton, and Mr. Gates walked up then with a good sized bunch of people following them. Seeing how stressed their wives were, they went straight to them and took them in their arms to console them. Their wives put their heads against their husband's chest as their bodies started to tremble; they stood on weak knees.

Dan said, "Captain, the youngsters were captured. There's a gash that goes all the way through the bluff. You'd never guess it was there until you are actually in it."

Captain Taylor nodded then called out a couple of names and said, "Would you see that it's guarded please?"

The two men nodded as they rushed of to get their weapons, canteens and a little food. Captain Taylor looked at the two women with their husbands and then said, "Sorry, it's my fault. I didn't have the area scouted good enough."

Hawkeye said, "Captain I've been here before. I didn't know the gap was there. I don't know of anyone that did before today."

Chris said, "No Captain. We can't blame you. Things just happen sometimes no matter how careful we are."

Mrs. Maxton then put to words what was on everyone's thoughts. She asked, "Captain, what will they do to them?"

Captain Taylor had to clear the lump out of his throat before he could talk. He had really taken a liking to the youngsters. He said, "I don't know. Maybe they won't be treated to bad or the Indians might just kill them. The last thing I don't want to even think about."

With his words Mrs. Gates and Mrs. Maxton had turned as white as ghosts. Mrs. Maxton lips trembling said, "Thank you for being straight with me."

The men took their wives off to comfort them.

Then Captain Taylor said, "Hawkeye get some rest if you can. I want you to leave out as soon as it's safe."

Hawkeye replied, "Okay Captain."

The whole camp had gotten real quiet. The next morning they were all getting real anxious as Hawkeye hadn't made it back yet. He was to have returned before daylight. Captain Taylor had started pacing. Bones suddenly came rushing in from his guard post trotted up to Captain Taylor saying, "Captain, I think Hawkeye is coming in."

The Captain gave Dan a look as he walked up. Dan nodded, then turned to look in Hawkeye's direction stating, "I'll take his horse out and pick him up."

In a few minutes Dan had returned with Hawkeye. As they dismounted Hawkeye said, "They're all gone! That's why I'm late? I wanted to make sure they were gone. Their tracks go southwest."

Captain Taylor said, "Dan, that doesn't make sense. I think it's a trick."

Dan said, "I don't know. I could take some men out and get a good look around to see what we're up against."

Captain Taylor answered, "Yep, I guess that's the best thing to do. Get some men together, just a few. Hawkeye, did you see any sign of Matt?"

Hawkeye just shook his head in response. With a grim look on his face the Captain said, "All right! Sorry, but I need for you to go back out with them."

Hawkeye said, "I was going anyway."

Dan with Hawkeye and ten men rode out toward the rapidly darkening Sky. They returned in a couple of hours. The clouds had let go with a vengeance. It was a drenching windy storm they road in out off. The word was quickly passed to Captain Taylor. With his slicker on he stepped through the line of wagons to meet them. When he had cleared the wagons by a few paces the Captain stood waiting for them to ride up. They looked like drowned rats. Dan as he wiped some water off his face spotted Captain Taylor. Making a slight adjustment he guided his horse up to The Captain. After he had leaned forward on the saddle horn he said, "The rain has washed out all sign."

As Captain Taylor nodded he said, "I was afraid of that. Go get dry and warmed up if you can."

The next day the Sun had come out bright and warm. Dan led out in search of some sign from Matt or the Indians. He had Hawkeye along with the ten men he'd ridden out with before. They rode out at first light. Mostly they rode together until they came to a draw or gully. Then a couple of men would check for any sign that someone was in the area. The rain had wiped out all the old sign. So, anything they found would have to be fresh. It was hard to believe that the Indians had left. Dan had made up his mind it was about time to head back. It was a little pass noon when Hawkeye returned from a high peek he had been on to get a good look around to see if he could spot anything that moved. When he rode up next to Dan he said, "There's riders far out. I think there Blackhawk's. There not the ones we've been fighting. They act like their looking for someone also."

Dan asked, "How many?"

"About twenty."

Dan and Hawkeye had worked together for a long time. Dan gave Hawkeye a hard look then said, "You act like you want to meet them."

Hawkeye nodded as he said, "I think maybe it would be a good idea."

Dan just held tight rein for a little while. Then with his mind made up he just nodded in agreement. Hawkeye's judgment was usually good. Dan turned his horse to face the rest of the men, then said, "We are going to meet some Indians. They seem to be friendly. But make sure you have your guns handy; but keep them holstered and be alert."

Dan then nodded to Hawkeye. Hawkeye turned his horse and led them off in the direction the Indians should be. They rode for a couple of good miles when as they cleared a slight rise they spotted the Indians. Dan had everybody stop. Then he had them spread out a little. When he was satisfied he gave Hawkeye a slight node. They rode out in front a couple of hundred yards and stopped. They waited and watched as the Indians did the same. Two Indians rode up to stop within ten yards. Dan relaxed a little as they didn't appear to be looking for trouble. Hawkeye had grunted with satisfaction since he had recognized Runs Far. The son of Chief Strong Arm.

Runs Far held his hand out giving the sign of peace.

Dan responded in like manner.

Runs Far surprised them as he spoke good English saying, "You've been looking very hard. We have also."

Dan was able to hide his surprise except for the light that had appeared in his eyes. He answered, "Yes! We have some people that were taken from our wagon train, two girls and a boy."

Runs Far nodded as he replied, "We have been looking for some sign of a maiden. The Pawnee's took her when they stole some horses from our Village."

Dan said, "We don't know for sure, but we think maybe the same one's attacked us. They were Pawnee's and Paiutes." With a look at Hawkeye Dan continued, "Hawkeye thinks they where some Cheyenne with them."

Runs Far's eyes darkened as he said, "Maybe so; heard some bad ones had gotten kicked out of their tribe. Maybe they joined up with the others."

Dan said, "Well! You're the only thing we have seen today."

Runs Far said, "It's the same for us. We had been able to follow the ones that had taken the girl. We had gained on them. We were only a half day behind them, when the rain washed out all sign."

Dan said, "I hate it. But I guess there is nothing more we can do. We need to get back to the wagons. I'm sure the Captain will want to get them moving. He has a lot of other people he is responsible for."

Runs Far said, "Yes, life is hard. We do have to decide life and death sometimes. It's not easy. We will stay and look for the girl at least a week, maybe a little more. If we come across any of your people, we will care for them and make sure they are returned to you safely."

Dan said, "Thanks! We are headed for the Oregon territory."

Runs Far said "We'll take them to are lodges and keep them safe. Then we will get word to you or Hawkeye."

Dan replied, "Thank you very much. I'd like that. How do we find your camp?"

Runs Far said, "Hawkeye will be able to find us.

Dan nodded. After a little pause he said, "Guess that is the best we can do. We need to get along now. Thank you."

Runs Far said, "We go south in the direction the tracks were headed."

Dan and Runs Far held up their hands to show respect for each other as they made their final good-byes. It was an hour after dark before they made it back to the wagons. Dan then brought the Captain up to date. They were still apprehensive. They couldn't figure out why so many Indians had just ridden off. They'd been greatly out numbered. But it was like the earth had swallowed them up. The worst part was that the youngsters had vanished just like the Indians. They still new nothing about Matt. They hadn't worried about him a lot. Even the ones that didn't know him well had heard how good he was. For the most part they were just sure he was out doing his job. They finished some needed repairs and filled up all the water barrels. The wounded were on the mend. They had been lucky for nobody had been badly hurt.

The Gates family along with the Maxton's where still in somewhat of a daze. But they still insisted on doing their chores. They needed to do something to help them make it through the days and nights. Tex, along with the rest of the cowboys had taken the loss of Connie, Helen, and Billy real hard also. They had all become like a large family. They each felt the same about the Gates family too.

As the repairs and other chores were being done Captain Taylor had sent Hawkeye out to scout the pass. If it was clear he intended to have the Wagons moving at first light in the morning. Everything had gone smoothly for the day. The Maxton's, the Gates family, and the McBain's along with Bruce Hart had gotten together for the evening meal. They had solemn looks on their faces as they sat sipping coffee. None of them had felt like eating much.

Chris had requested for all the cowboys to stay after the meal was finished. After getting his thoughts together Chris said, "We need to talk a little. I know it would make me feel better."

They all became real attentive as Chris said, "The Gates have decided for me to speak for them also. We've had a hard blow to our hearts. I know we all have been blaming ourselves and feel like there was something we could have done to prevent what happened. Valerie and I have been back and forth over everything. We tried to get our thoughts together to get a little peace of mind as the Gates have also. For a while we even blamed ourselves for even deciding to come on this trip. Then as we looked at what we had planned for the future we knew that's what we really wanted to do. When you balance everything out we feel in our hearts that we have done the right thing. The Gates along with us have finally gotten everything worked out. No mistake we know there's always going to be a void in our hearts whenever we think of our children now. The reason we wanted to discuss this with all of you is we knew that in your own way that all of you have taken to the youngsters also. I know that each and everyone of you wish you could take their place and would have gladly given your life in place of theirs. That's what we all feel. None of us know the future. Some things happen we just can't prevent. Later we kick ourselves and think that we should have known what was going to happen. There's not anyone that I know of that can do that though. I know your hurting like we are and we all really appreciate that. But now we got to go on and just live day to day and do the best we can. Besides I believe that's what the youngsters would want for us to do if somehow, they could talk to us. I guess that's all. I'm just glad to have gotten the chance to meet all of you."

Captain Taylor along with Dan approached the fire. They had stopped to stand just within hearing distance. The cowboys stood with hats held in their hands. There was not a dry eye among them or any of them that didn't have a lump in their throat. Captain Taylor saw the emotions run through the cowboys. With a glance at Dan he could see he felt the same way. Captain Taylor felt the emotions run through his body. The Maxton's had been pure green horns when he first met them. They were pure westerners now. He was as proud of them as anybody he'd ever met. To himself he made a vow to get the youngsters back. Even if he heard just a hint that they may still be alive; even if it took the rest of his life. Captain Taylor with Dan, turned and slipped away from the fire. When he glance at Dan, Captain Taylor saw that his face was full of resolve also. He was sure that Dan had come to the same decision. Tex was the first one to get his emotions under control enough to speak. He said, "Thank you sir." With a nod at the ladies, Tex continued. "Don't give up hope completely; all the youngsters have a lot of spunk. Some way, some how; they may be able to pull through."

The other cowboys mostly of the same mind gave their encouragement also. The Gates and the Maxton's thanked them. Then they returned to the seclusion of their wagons.

As they left Tex said, "I don't know how you boys feel, but if they never paid me another dime I will work for them as long as they'll have me. Looks like I might never make it back to Texas. Not the way I feel right now anyway."

Hawkeye when he returned from his scouting trip had given a good report. He hadn't found a one sign of any Indians. The bad part was that he hadn't seen any sign of the three youngsters either. Matt still hadn't made an appearance. They made it to the mouth of the pass the next day. Things had gone smoothly, and there wasn't any sign of any Indians. Then just a little before dark a single Indian approached. He stopped just out of rifle range. Then in a loud voice in English spoke Hawkeye's name twice. He then dismounted his pony to wait patiently in plain sight of the camp. It was a couple of hours after dark before Hawkeye returned to report to Captain Taylor. After he slowly dismounted from a very tired horse he said, "They are all gone. It's clear all the way through the pass. I am certain they didn't go through the pass."

As Mrs. Maxton handed a cup of coffee to Hawkeye. Captain Taylor told him about the visitor they had. Hawkeye took a couple of swallows then went off in the direction of the Indian. It took some persuading before he was able to convince the Blackhawk brave that he would be safe. Carefully clearing the guards Hawkeye led him up to the Maxton's cook fire. That was where Captain Taylor and Dan were along with the Gates and of course the Maxton's. The cowboys had come to stand just within hearing. It had made the brave nervous, but Hawkeye assured him he was safe. Then to Captain Taylor, Hawkeye said, "He's brought word from Runs Far."

Captain Taylor asked, "Do you know what it's all about yet?"

Hawkeye said, "No." Then in a language none understood except Hawkeye and the brave they conversed for a couple of minutes. Then he turned back to Captain Taylor and the others and said, "Runs Far and his braves found the main camp where all the youngsters had been taken. All the Indians left except for one. Somehow, he had been left behind. He was dying, but had talked before he died."

Hawkeye paused to converse with the brave again. With the new information Hawkeye said, "As he was dying he was scared. He told them he'd seen a bad spirit. He had talked freely and explained everything to them. He wanted to be in good standing when he made it to the happy hunting grounds."

Hawkeye kept translating what the brave told him to the others. Hawkeye said, "They had three women captives and the boy. Then the bad Spirit came into the camp. He took the women and the boy away. Then left on a horse that was like a Flaming Spirit. They had all vanished. The Bad Spirit had called on the rain to wash away their tracks. He told them that many braves died that day. They had not known that the man and horse were spirits. Many of the braves felt that their medicine had gone bad. Many wanted to leave camp and hide. Many of them had been scared enough that they didn't want to fight him. They had no power to fight the bad spirit. Then he had died in peace. It was thought by many that he did make it to the happy hunting grounds."

Hawkeye translated as Captain Taylor, Dan, and others asked questions. It had taken quite a few minutes. They hadn't been able to come up with any other information, other than what they'd already been told.

After a short conversation between the Blackhawk brave and Hawkeye. Hawkeye then said, "The brave says that Runs Far and his braves will keep looking. Now that they know they are alive."

After another short conversation with Hawkeye the brave was ready to leave. Captain Taylor with the others had been trying to put all the pieces together while Hawkeye guided the brave past the guards. When Hawkeye returned he was just in time to hear Mr. Maxton.

Chris said, "Then they're alive. But where could they be?"

With disbelief in his voice Dan said, "Somehow Matt found them."

Slim said, "Not only that! I don't understand how one man could've put the fear of God in them. What's all this business about Spirits anyway?"

Hawkeye said, "If you had seen Matt in action like I have you would understand. Indians are superstitious and when they see something they don't understand they think it's from the Spirit World."

Slade asked, "What is it that they don't understand?"

Hawkeye answered, "It's his close in fighting with his hands and feet that's got them mystified."

Dan replied, "Yeah! He is really something to watch when he does that. I've never seen anybody move like that and man is he fast."

Tex said, "That being said. I'll bet he's just as fast with his shooting irons."

Mrs. Maxton brought them all back to earth when she asked, "Why hasn't Matt brought them back then. I can't believe he is lost."

With a pensive expression Hawkeye said, "I've been giving that a lot of thought. I've rode with him enough to know he's not lost."

Captain Taylor looked hard at Hawkeye as he asked, "What are your thoughts then?"

Hawkeye took time to look at everyone as he made sure of his thoughts. He took a couple more glances at the women. Mrs. Maxton and Mrs. Gates were listening intensively waiting for Hawkeye to reply. He was slow to say anything and acted like he wished he didn't have an answer. Finely, with dread in his voice Hawkeye said, "The only thing that would keep Matt from returning with Billy and the girls is that he's hurt bad enough so he's not able to ride."

Hawkeye's statement had brought them all back to earth. When they had heard that Matt must have found Billy and the girls and somehow had rescued them. They had some thoughts that everything was going to be fine.

Mrs. Maxton said, "Oh the poor dears. That's got to be it. Oh my! We don't know where to find them. There's not a thing we can do to help him."

Mrs. Gates said, "He always looked and acted so invincible. So full of life, it's hard to picture him not being able to take care of himself."

Ben said, "Arrows and bullets will slow anybody down."

Mrs. McBain said, "Oh damn!"

Startled; they all stared at her. For no one had ever heard her say a cuss word. Undisturbed she just looked back as she said, "Well! If he's hurt that bad the girls have to be just about out of there minds. You know that they both are completely in love with him."

That made them all feel melancholy. They just milled around without a word spoken, of their deep concern. Mostly they just kept to their own thoughts. Then Captain Taylor said, "If it was just them. I'd wait long enough to send out search parties. But I can't. We don't have the time. I've got to consider the whole wagon train and do what's best for it."

Chris said, "This really makes things hard. I know as long as Matt's alive that Connie won't leave him. Helen wouldn't either. Billy will watch over them. I'm sure, they will do the best they can for Matt. I hate the thought of it, but I agree we can't hold up the train. If he's alive and hurt real bad it could be a month before they are able to move him."

Captain Taylor said, "I hate the idea of leaving them, but we could spend a year looking for them and still not find them. I hate it, but I believe Hawkeye's probably right. They must be holed up someplace or I think Runs Far and his people would have found them by now."

Mr. Gates said, "Well! We need to pray and hope for the best. At least we know they where all alive when they left that Indian camp. And if Matt's hurt bad like you figure and he pulls through. He will start out after us as soon as he is able."

Silently they stood mostly in place, while they considered all the facts as they knew them. They felt helpless as no one could think of anything that would help the youngsters. After a little Hawkeye said, "Maybe their better off than we know. Runs far told us they were looking for a girl themselves. Maybe Matt was able to rescue her also."

Dan said, "If that's so, Matt should have a better chance to pull through. She would likely know how to find Herbs and to make some medicine."

Mrs. Maxton said, "Oh I hope so."

Mr. Maxton said, "Well I hope so too. As bad as my heart hurts I'm just dreading the idea of having to tell Mr. Saxton that his son is missing or dead. Right now it sounds like Matt is the one that really needs our prayers. "

Tex said, "Well like Mr. Gates said. We just need to pray and hope for the best. Mr. Maxton, if nothing changes by the time we get you where you're going. The boys and me will come back and try to find them."

Captain Taylor said, "You can include me in on that trip also."

Dan nodding said, "That goes for me to."

Hawkeye said, "You're not going without me. Count me in too."

Chris, Mrs. Maxton, the Gates, and the McBains all thanked them.

Chris said, "I'll just keep you on the payroll."

They all tried to refuse him. But he'd put his foot down and said that was the only way. He refused to let them change his mind. After things had been discussed and sorted out they started one by one to seek out their bedrolls. The others retired to their wagons. They all had a cautious hope that things would work out and everybody would live. They still had fear in their hearts, that they tried to push aside.

It had been two weeks since Billy and the girls had gotten Matt to the cave. Billy was on his ledge on guard duty. He'd taken over that responsibility. One of the girls would relive him for a few hours at midday. Billy knew he couldn't stay awake day and night. He wanted to make sure he didn't fall asleep during the night.

The hand they had been dealt was hard on each of them. When Matt had rescued them there hadn't been any time to do anything, except get away with their lives. They'd not had time to get any clothes for the girls. The time it had taken almost took Matt's life. Billy had worked some things out in his mind to some of the events. He had considered that it was probably his fault they had been taken. He had been sent to protect the girls. He had offered his shirt which they had decided he should keep as at least he was dressed. They had sort of gotten used to it except when he was near they felt a little uncomfortable. Billy was still uncomfortable when he was close to them. The Indian girl did not seem to be awfully distressed and even acted like they would end up being alright. Billy, Connie, and Helen were very uncertain of their future.

The days were still pretty warm. But the nights had started to cool off quite a bit. Billy had found a good spot just a little distance away from the cave. It was well-shaded, and stayed cool even on the hottest days. So, he had been able to sleep pretty well.

The first day the girls had attended to Matt mostly. Then they had helped each other take care of their own wounds. There hadn't been any that were serious. But they'd had a few puncture wounds that were pretty deep.

The next day Connie and Helen had started to clean all of the weapons. Billy had lost his shirt tail that day. Billy helped, but they wouldn't let him clean Matt's guns. So, he had gotten to clean the four riffles that they'd been able to get away with. Some luck had been with them. The four rifles were forty-four-caliber. The only problem was that they only had twenty three rounds of ammo left. Connie had stated, "Matt always made sure he had a hundred and fifty extra rounds in his saddle bags."

Billy had said, "He most of done a lot of fighting before he got to us."

"That's one thing about Matt from the time we were kids. I've never seen him, run from a fight."Billy watched out over the land all around as he recalled their conversation. He had decided to believe what Connie had told him. He still hadn't gotten over how Matt had attacked the Indian camp. Billy shook his head. He'd seen it and still had a hard time believing it. Of course, with cutting himself loose and then the girls he'd not seen everything that had happened. But what he had seen was Indians falling every which way. Some by gun some by hand and some by Matt's feet. Billy thought he'd like to have gotten a body count. But he knew no one would believe him.

They had been able to communicate with Bright Star fairly good the last couple of days. That was what the Indian girl had told them her name meant in English. Connie and Helen had been teaching her English. She was learning fast. Billy liked her accent when she spoke. Helen and Connie had learned some of her language also. The problem was they were making him learn it too. Well at least try. He had picked up on some of it though.

Star was something Billy thought. She made sure they had something to eat. He had been sure he would never ate a rattlesnake. But he had now and it hadn't been bad. Star had set snares and caught rabbits. She was working on making a bow and some arrows. They had seen some deer and antelope. She told them she wanted the hide as much as they needed the meat.

She found some clay and made a pot to cook in. Star had gathered some dark stones and built a makeshift oven of sorts and put the pot in it to bake for a couple of days. The pot was strong enough if they handled it real careful. She found some wild onions along with some other plant roots that were pretty good. The pot was used mostly for Matt. The girls had been mashing his food and force feeding him. Yesterday had been the first time he'd opened his eyes. It had been just for a few minutes. His eyes had been unable to focus. The first couple days had been touch and go. Matt had run a high fever and Star had worked day and night to get it down. Then they had to open the wound in Matt's thigh. It had gotten infected. A piece of metal had been found. It had taken all of them to hold Matt down. Even near death Matt was still a handful.

Billy was proud of all the girls. He still didn't know how they'd been able to cope with all they were going through. Billy was sure at first what had kept them going was their concern for Matt. Then he had seen a change in them. Connie and Helen had always been determined, but he saw a little bit of a steely glint in their eyes. Anybody would have there hands full if they messed with them now.

Billy had made up his mind to protect them as best he could. Star had already taught them so much. Connie and Helen did most of the camp duties now. They were taking care of Matt for the most part now. Billy had a lot of time to think while he was out on watch over the last couple of weeks. Star had picked out a good spot. Nobody had been seen and just to make sure, every two or three days Star would go out scouting around.

The biggest thing he had to adjust to was that nobody had any clothes except for him. He knew his face had to have been red for most of the first week. He thought all of them were the most beautiful creatures he had ever seen. Even with one of them being his sister. He knew it wasn't right seeing them all naked. But, also under the circumstances there was nothing any of them could do, but to survive. They had become determined to do that. Things had started to look up now. When he saw Matt last he had starting to get some of his color back. He'd been as pale as death for a long time.

Billy being out in the country away from the wagons had become acclimated to his surroundings. His hearing had improved and was still getting better all the time. He was getting so his eyes missed nothing. He took his job serious. His thoughts were interrupted as he heard bare feet coming up. He glanced to see that it was Star. She said, "You go eat and sleep. I watch."

He nodded his thanks as he climbed down and handed her the riffle. He then headed for the cave. When he got there Helen cut off a leg from a rabbit they had cooked and handed it to him. He ate then went out to get a drink of water from the spring. The water was cool and tasted good.

Billy returned to look down at Matt. Then he asked, "Did Flame come up to the cave today."

Connie answered, "No, I think he knows Matt is getting better. Billy, I think Matt's going to make it."

Helen said, "Yes Billy, his breathing is easier and his color is getting better all the time."

Billy, not sure he wasn't getting himself in trouble, but thought it needed to be said. "You know that Star looks at Matt and thinks of him; as some kind of God or something."

Connie said, "We know Billy. We've talked and her English is getting pretty good and we're picking up on her language pretty good. She says he's a Spirit and rides a Spirit horse."

Billy nodded, "Well, I guess I better go get my nap so I'll be ready for tonight's watch."

Helen said, "Billy, one of us can stay up and watch for you. You spend all your time on guard duty or sleeping."

"With you girls doing everything around camp, setting snares and cooking. It is about the only thing left for me to do. Besides, it's bad enough to sit out yonder knowing how you are. Let alone being with you and seeing you all with no clothes on."

Both girls blushed.

Then Helen said, "Well! There's nothing we can do about it unless we take your clothes. Then what would you wear?"

"We all know that. I just wonder if we'll ever get pa to understand. I did offer to give them to you."

Helen asked, "What do you think they are doing?"

Connie said, "If they are alright and the Indian trouble is over. I think they've gone on."

"I think she's right sis. Even if they knew for sure we're alive they still couldn't wait. They have to get through the mountains before the winter storms."

Helen said, "They must be worrying their heads off about us."Billy said, "Well, I just hope they are doing ok. I'm going to get some sleep.

CHAPTER TWELVE

ON THE MEND

The next morning a little before it was time for Helen to go relieve Billy of his guard duty. Connie along with Helen bathed and cleaned Matt up after they had fed him. He'd open his eyes a few times and had even started swallowing. Even better he acted like he wanted something to chew. They'd been half choking him to force feed him. So, mostly broth and water was all they'd been able to get down him.

Helen at the spring getting some fresh water heard Connie. It wasn't a scream really. It was more like she'd just gotten a big surprise. Then she heard Connie exclaim, "Ok, Ok, Oh My."

Helen hurried back to the cave. Star out checking on her snares heard also and rushed up to follow in closely behind Helen. When they got there, they stopped suddenly to stare. Just then Connie exclaimed once again, "Oh my!" Connie acted like she had a big problem and didn't know what to do about it.

Star said, "You scared me something bad. I was afraid something had happened to Matt."

Connie jerked around; she hadn't heard them come up. Then she said, "Ok, ok, Oh my." Connie making a great effort to soothe Matt as her words finely registered on her mind continued, "Something's wrong."

Helen asked, "What do you mean? With Matt?" Connie said, "Yes! I know you can see. It's growing and throbbing. He must be hurting awfully bad."

Connie continued to make a great effort to rub Matt's pain away. Helen as she fully understood fell to her knees and laughed like she would never stop. Tears had already come to her eyes. Star had started to giggle also.

Connie confused, was unable to get her thoughts around to what in the world Helen could see that was so funny. Connie was sure Matt had to be hurting. She thought maybe Helen had finely lost it. But Star was almost just as bad.

Helen, finely between gasp of air said. "He'll relax a lot quicker if you stop rubbing it. He may be hurting and throbbing. But it's not from pain."

Connie still confused, did stop messaging Matt's penis. It still stood up straight for a second then started to deflate. Slowly it lay down and then went limp.

Star still giggled as she said, "Good, Matt is restoring some of his blood. That's very good."

As Connie stood up she blushed. Connie still had failed to understand. She put her hands on her hips and stared at them as they tried to compose themselves. Then Connie said, "I don't see what's so funny. I was just trying to help him."

Connie's statement got both of them started all over again. Her innocence rendered her incapable of understanding. Helen had made an attempt to get up off her knees, but she couldn't make it. Star had dropped to her knee's holding her stomach.

Connie taken all she could take, turned and stomped out on her bare feet. Angrily over her shoulder she said, "You both have gone loony. I'll go relieve Billy."

With eyes already full of tears Connie's response made them laugh harder if it was possible. Connie heard them and stomped harder. She barely noticed the pain it caused her bare feet as she went on out.

Connie was still mad when she got to Billy's ledge. The mile walk had done little to ease her anger. However, she did find Billy perched on his ledge.

Billy took another good look around before he made a move to climb down. Down at ground level he cheerfully said, "Hi. I was expecting sis though."

"She's cracked." Then seeing that Billy didn't believe her as she knew Billy didn't have a clue on what had happened. So, she set out to explain what had happened without causing herself anymore embarrassment. Billy listened and as he comprehended what had happened. He tried to pay extra attention to the surrounding area. Anything so he didn't have to give Connie a direct look. He hoped he was succeeding at keeping a grin from appearing on his face. When she finished Billy asked, "You haven't been around boys much then?"

"Yes! I have. Matt and I have been friends for a long time."

"No, I mean like taking care of babies."

"Well no."

"If you had you'd have seen it happen before; then you'd have thought nothing of it."

"Matt hasn't done that before."

"Not that you've seen. It's a good sign that he is getting better. Even though he wasn't fully conscious, he was well enough to respond with you being there. He'll be waking up soon, I would say."

"Then he wasn't hurting?"

Billy almost groaned out loud. He took a minute as he thought on the most proper way to explain. He took a deep breath. He decided to take the bull by the horns and just say it, "Connie, you saw what happens when a man is aroused from seeing or being touched by a woman's body."

Connie's face instantly turned a scarlet red. Then she stammered, "Oh, my! I didn't mean, oh. I'm…I'm sorry Billy. Thanks. But it got so big. The way it throbbed I thought he was hurting."

Billy thought to himself, if Matt had been awake he would have been hurting for certain, "No he was just responding."

"Thank you Billy. I'll stay and watch. I need to be alone."

Billy nodded handed her the riffle. He could tell she was completely embarrassed. A proper lady did not talk so commonly about such things and she was certainly a proper lady. She was red all over. So red he would have bet his finger would have been burnt if he had touched her. But man; she was gorgeous. It was time to leave before he embarrassed himself. Well at least she knew now. She was beautiful with her nice long legs and a terrific shape. Then with her skin being exposed to the sun she was getting a perfect tan. He left her with her thoughts and quickly walked away.

When Billy got to the spring he dropped down to his knees to get a drink of water. Then went on into the cave. Helen was the only one in it with Matt. Billy asked, "Where's Star." "She went out to scout around some."

Billy just nodded, as he thought to himself he should be the one out scouting around. But, he did admit that Star could do better than he could. In the short time they'd been together he knew she was the only one he had seen that could move as quietly as Matt. She was able to blend in with the background like Matt could. Helen cut off half of a rabbit and handed it to Billy as he sat down. After taking a bite Billy said, "It's done just right. Stars snares must have done real good last night."

Helen proudly said, "One was mine."

"I thought you were going to relieve me."

"I was, but Connie got upset and needed some air. She decided to take the watch."

"I know she told me."

"Oh! What did she tell you?" Helen didn't feel at ease with where the conversation was going. Helen couldn't believe that Connie would have talked to Billy about such things.

With his face a little red Billy turned his head, so he wasn't looking right at her. His sister had become a well-shaped woman. Maybe with the skimpy meals they'd lost the excess fat any of them had. Not one of them had complained, however. All the girls were really well developed, he thought.

"I explained to Connie what happened to Matt and why." He paused a little then said, "You should have explained it to her."

"I was caught by surprise and I couldn't. I mean…I couldn't talk." She laughed just a little. Then she continued, "Billy, you should have seen it. She was really concerned and was going to rub Matt's throbbing pain away."

Helen burst out into another fit of laughter. Billy shook his head. But he did have a slight grin. As he got up with his meat he grabbed a couple of onions and roots they had cooked. As he left back over his shoulder he said, "Connie was right, you have gone loony." He just heard her laugh louder.

After Billy left she had been able to calm down. Then she felt the pull of eyes on her. She turned to look into Matt's stare. For his eyes were focused. When Matt saw Helen turn her head he tried to look away. He was able to a little bit, but his eyes hadn't followed his head. It had taken a lot of effort just to move it what little he had. He was still awfully weak. His lips had moved and Helen was sure he was asked for some water. His voice had just barely been audible.

Helen quickly got Matt's canteen which was kept fresh for him. She leaned over and put it to his lips. Matt swallowed three or four times real good. While doing so Helen saw that his eyes had been glued to her breast. She felt her body heat up with a blush. Matt must have seen her response. His face started to redden also. Helen then saw the light fade from Matt's eyes as they closed. With heart felt relief Helen sighed out loud. Matt's face had relaxed into a restful sleep. The tense fighting look was gone.

She settled back on her heels and took a deep breath. She could hardly breathe for her chest had tightened from the intense look Matt had given her. In those few seconds his eyes had flashed at her with the force of a lightning bolt. It felt as if it had gone right through her.

She looked around as if to see if they were alone. Then with some effort Helen stood on shaky knees. She felt weak trembling all over she kind of stumbled out of the cave. She had to get away even if it was just for a few minutes. Outside she sat on a rock in the shade of the cliff. A nice cool breeze helped relax her a little. Her heart still raced a mile a minute and it felt like her veins were about to burst. Unconsciously she touched herself to rub some of the soreness away. She was startled as she felt how hard nipples gotten. Much like little marbles.

She wasn't laughing now. This was the first time that she'd ever had any emotions affect her like this. She didn't know how she would survive such emotions if it happened to her very many times. But also, if it never happened again she thought she'd dry up emotionally and die someday. Helen felt like she needed some relief of some kind and along with that thought she felt some heat with a tingling down between her legs. Just barely able to control herself, she tried to think of something far away.

Star always did her scouting afoot. After making sure the horses were alright and everything around their camp was the same. She would wait awhile to watch the birds. To be sure nothing disturbed them. She even watched the bees for a few minutes to make sure they were in their normal routine. Afoot she'd found many ways out of the basin. A couple of them she had to scale a rock wall for a few yards. She made sure she never went the same way twice. It was harder not to leave footprints than it would have been if she still had her moccasins. Matt's were too big, so they had been cut into strips to make snares.

Today she planned on searching further out. She wanted to get a good idea of the terrain. They were running out of game and would have to move soon. Something had changed the pattern of the deer and antelope. It had been three or four days since any of them had returned to the basin for water. She was sure it wasn't her companions or her that had driven them away. She was being extra careful so as not to leave even one toe print if possible. She knew she had a miserable night coming for her. The days had gotten shorter and the nights cooler. She had told her companions that she wouldn't make it back to camp tonight. She wanted to check there surroundings farther out. Mostly she wanted to make sure she had a good route to travel, so they would not leave any tracks as well as being able to stay out of sight.

When they left, at least for a short distance she was going to do all she could, not to leave any sign at all. They wouldn't be able to travel fast or stand and fight. Matt wasn't strong enough to help himself yet. It took two or three of them to move him. She shook her head. Matt was a big man--big of shoulder, but slim of hip. He was very nice to look at even with the weakened condition he was in. But she thought he weighed heavier then he looked. It was like he was made of iron.

Sure, everything was as it should be, she stopped her day dreaming and set out on her scouting trip. She dreaded the cold night to come and was already missing the closeness of her new friends along with Matt, of course. She was more determined than ever to make sure they'd be safe. Carrying the riffle in her hand she was careful not to skyline herself as she moved into the landscape. She had eight hours of good sunlight and needed to use all of it.

The next morning Connie and Helen got up and went about doing their daily chores. Helen to check the snares. She was nearly as good as Star at setting them and was getting quite successful. Connie broke some big limbs for the fire. She used a big rock as an axe. By raising it high then letting it fall on the middle of the limb that had been placed on top of two flat rocks. They had been placed so when the limb broke it would be two or three feet long. The wood being real dry did make a loud snap when it broke. Star had insisted on real dry wood so there wouldn't be any smoke drifting into the sky. They had used quite a bit of wood during the night. It had gotten quite cool. Connie and Helen had taken turns putting wood on the fire to keep Matt warm.

Connie was concerned about Billy and Star. They both had to have gotten awfully cold. She was especially worried about Star. It was the first time she'd been away all night. Connie was concerned because Star had been hit on the head awfully hard. Connie noticed sometimes that Star would go into a spell or something like she was trying to see something that wasn't there. She would concentrate awfully hard for a few minutes. Then she would give up with a sigh as if she had failed at something.

Helen returned then Connie looked up at the sun and saw she'd been thinking too much. She hadn't gotten as much wood broken up as she should have. Helen went to prepare the rabbit. With Star's instructions there was very little of it that was thrown away. It was either eaten or used as a tool. They pieced together the fur to make a blanket of sorts to cover Matt up with on cold nights.

Working steadily for a half hour Connie thought she had broken up enough wood. Then she proceeded to carry it into the cave. When she laid her bundle of wood down she heard a raspy voice say water. She turned to see that Matt was watching her. Going to him Connie stooped and got the canteen. Then she leaned over putting it to his lips. Matt drank thirstily and after eight swallows he moved his head up. Connie drew the canteen away. Matt thanked her. His voice had almost been clear with hardly any rasp to it at all.

Connie was barely able to stand, yet she was able to kind of stumble out of the cave. She'd seen the way Matt had looked at her breasts; the intensity that had been in his eyes. She'd seen him blush, which had made her blush in return. But what had really gotten to her was the sparkle in his eyes that had shot right to the soul of her being. Back at the wood she'd broken up she was surprised as by reflex she touched her nipples. They felt nearly as solid as lead. She rubbed them to soften them, even if it hurt just a little bit.

Matt had affecting her a lot in the last couple of years, but never to this extent. She had been shaken to her core. She wanted something real bad not quite knowing what it was. She just stood by the stack of wood to catch her breath. She almost put her hand between her legs to rub the spot that seemed to throb with the pulse of her heart. She drew her hand back then turned her head to make sure she hadn't been seen. She didn't know what had made her want to do such a thing, but after yesterday she would really have been embarrassed if she had been seen. Helen probably would have had another good laugh at her.

Connie had known the difference between a man and woman, but admitted she knew next to nothing about cause and effect. Neither had she actually thought about how the parts of a man worked. Between schooling and what sewing her mother had insisted on she had spent the rest of her time with Matt. They'd been involved in one activity after another. There had been an attraction Connie admitted that to herself, but they'd never gotten around to acting on their feelings. Even out here on the trail they'd been to busy on the wagon train. Now all their effort was being put into getting Matt healthy again.

With what happened today and thinking about what she had been doing to Matt yesterday. With that thought she pinched her left nipple so hard it brought her back to reality. Perspiration beaded her forehead and circled her lips as she took quick breaths. Her thoughts tumbled through her head like a whirlwind. She'd almost moaned out loud as she took a deep breath and tried to get herself under control. She had no doubts now that she was in love with Matt. It brought her back to reality. She just didn't know how to deal with the intense emotions.

Helen had noticed what had happened to Connie when she had given Matt the water. She couldn't help but see how flushed Connie's skin had gotten. She'd seen how hard Connie's nipples were as she rushed out of the cave. Helen was sure that Matt had the same effect on Connie as he had on her. It was getting harder all the time to keep there pact to be friends and let Matt decide which one he wanted. They hadn't ever considered it wouldn't be one of them. Now that Star had come into the picture it started to look like things could really get complicated. Star thought enough of Matt to act like he was some kind of Great Spirit or something of like manner.

Helen was sure if it hadn't been for Star, Matt probably would have died. That made things more difficult. She liked Star. She was so capable and knew so much. They'd have been lost without her. Helen had noticed that Star did go off in her mind somewhere sometimes. As if she was some place else. Connie finally controlling her thoughts went back in with some wood. Helen saw she had gotten herself composed. A little blush was all that Helen could see that Connie had left over from her previous state.

Matt had drifted back to sleep after Connie had rushed out. But hearing the wood being dropped he opened his eyes and told them he would like something to eat. They both looked at each other uncomfortably. Helen rose, got the knife; then cut off some meat. She sat next to him to cut the meat into small pieces, then put each small peace into his mouth. As Matt chewed his meat he looked from one than to the other. Helen feed him half a rabbit before he had enough. Helen had gone out and refilled the canteen when Connie had left in such a hurry. Neither of them made a move for the canteen even though sure he would probably want some water. It was like they both hoped they wouldn't be able to hear what he would say next. But they did.

Matt said, "I would like some water."

They looked at each other. Both of them had a slight blush. Connie was sure the same thing must have happened to Helen. Connie said, "I'll do it next time." Helen got up and retrieved the canteen from the coolest spot they'd found inside the cave. She then squatted next to him leaned over and held it to his lips. As she held it she turned her head slightly so not to look directly into his eyes. He'd been able to raise his hands and help. She felt a slight tug, she lowered it and recapped it. Matt said, "Thank you."

Helen's heart beat hard within her chest, for just a split second; she'd seen his eyes. She stood up then went to a little ledge in the cave and sat down.

Matt asked, "Where are we?"

Connie said, "We don't know. Star dosen't know for sure either. She led us here in the dark. Well, it was dark most of the way."

"Star, who's she?"

Helen said, "She's the other girl that was with us."

"Billy."

Helen said, "He's fine; he's out on guard duty. It's getting about time for me to relieve him, I'd better go."

Helen didn't run, but as she stood to leave she was relieved that she had an excuse to leave. Matt had tried to divert his eyes, but she had seen how they had followed her. She hopped it was still a little cool outside.

"The one you call Star. Where is she?"

Connie said, "She's gone out to scout around. To make sure we are still safe."

"Guess you didn't have time to get any clothes."

Connie had been able to control herself for the most part. She'd seen his eyes as they had traveled her body. His words however, had given her a full blush as she calmly and resolutely said, "No. We just had time to get away."

"Sorry, I'm sleepy."

Matt had been asleep for a few minutes when Billy came in. Connie rose and retrieved the rest of the rabbit, then handed it to Billy. It was a little before noon. Billy said, "Sis was a little early."

Connie didn't want to explain. She had just gotten cooled off good. Like she hadn't heard Billy, she said, "Matt's much better. He even ate some and drank a lot of water. He talked a little bit too."

Billy shrugged just a little. He gave Connie a good look. Like his sister he felt she had held something back. "Yeah, Sis told me most of that. Boy it's good news. It looks like Matt is going to pull through."

"Oh! Yes, I have been so worried."Billy turned his head a little. Not from Connie's nakedness this time, but from the love that had appeared in Connie's eyes; for Matt. He had seen the same look in his sister's eyes. Star came into the cave and carefully laid her rifle down. Star had stopped several times to check her back trail and then took a complete sweep to study the surrounding area before she moved on. She had cooled off some, but she still glistened with sweat. Billy had started to get accustomed to the girl's nakedness. But with the shine of Star's beautiful body, he couldn't help but stare. As Billy tried to recover, Connie brought Star up to date on how good Matt had been doing.

Star said, "That's good. In two days, we need to move."

"But Matt's not ready yet."

"It's not safe here anymore."

The sun hadn't made an appearance yet as the girls went about breaking up camp and getting things ready to leave. Helen had gone to check her snares and bring them in. One rabbit only was in her snares. Star and Connie had used up the last of Matt's moccasins to put over the iron shoes on Flame's hoofs. With the Indian ponies not being shoed they'd leave little sign when they crossed hard ground. Star wanted to leave no sign at all if she could. She told everyone they had to be very careful. They were deep in the enemy territory, that her people were at war with.

Star had not told them that some of the enemy, had already started to search for them. She was sure that after they had calmed down, they had gone to their lodges to seek stronger medicine. Then they would be after Matt with a determined effort. If they could kill him, they thought it would give them unbelievable power; his power.

Spending the night away from her new friends, Star had been able to see into the Spirit World. Trusting in what she had seen, still she was very apprehensive. Her vision had showed her a place to look for, but it was to the south, then west of their present location. Farther away from where her people would be. She had scouted south then and planed her route. The way they would be going she hoped they might come across some of her people. She was sure that they would be out searching for her. They were in no shape to fight any enemies.

Matt had been awake six to eight hours the last day. Not all at once, but from time to time. He had ate most of their food, which he needed. But it had made it, so the rest had to go without. Star was proud of her friends. None of them had complained or even showed a bad face. Because Matt had gotten healthier she made a loincloth of sorts, out of the rabbit pelts. Matt had started to show them, that he was all male. When one of the girls took care of him or in doing their work had made a certain pose, the result was plain to see. He'd tried to control himself, but the natural beauty of nature had it's way with him.

They needed him to save all his energy to get his strength back. With himself covered he might be able to relax some.

Getting things ready they spent just enough time in the cave to take care of his needs. Matt was still weak, but insisted on going outside to relieve himself. It had gone fine until he actually had to go. With Connie holding one arm and Helen the other so as to study him he had been able to go. They all had gotten a little embarrassed. By the time they got Matt back to the cave he slowly collapsed into a nice deep sleep.

Helen had the rabbit cooked and ready to eat as the sun started to push the darkness away. Star and Connie had the horse's ready. Helen woke Matt up. Matt was able to feed himself now. Connie gave him the canteen telling him to drink as much as he could. Then the three of them studied Matt as he walked out. After he'd relieved himself again they helped him up on Flames saddle. They all drank as much as they could from the spring. Billy came up and drank from the spring. They had decided after he made sure it was clear to come in to camp at first light. The one canteen was all the water they'd be able to carry.

Star had gone over the route with Billy in detail. She had cut a good limb with a lot of branches on it. She was going to wipe out and cover up their trail as much, as possible. Billy would lead, then Connie and Matt on Flame. Helen was to follow them leading Star's horse. Billy and Helen carried the extra rifles. Matt's weapons were on Flame's saddle.

Matt had been in and out of sleep. The first couple of times he had opened his eyes, was the only time he had been confused. He had been surprised when the first thing his eyes saw was Helen's two lovely breasts. They had been the first for him. The next time he was just as happy to see Connie's breasts right in front of his eyes. He had taken them in completely. He knew it had embarrassed both of them. But he couldn't help it. They were so beautiful. He hadn't missed the flash of light that appeared in her eyes; that struck him like a bolt of lightning.

Then the last couple of days he'd seen Star. Star had beautiful long black hair that reached all the way down to hang just under her bottom when she was standing. Her hair had a beautiful shine to it. She had long glorious legs even though she was an inch or two shorter than Connie. He thought Connie had grown about four inches since they had left New York City. Connie had to be five-foot-nine now, he thought. He had always thought, but hadn't been sure that Connie's breasts were a little small. But not anymore! Helen was the shortest at five-foot-six. She didn't lack anything though. Helen with a shorter body made up for it, with her gorgeous legs. That would drive any man mad. Each of them had stirred up emotions in him that he had no business having. As his health improved the harder it got. He didn't know how much more he could take.

It had taken a lot of effort from everyone to get Matt up on Flame. At the time no one had worried about being modest. The effort had made all of them break out into a sweat. Connie with Helen's help had climbed on behind. Matt had thought to sit behind. But the girls told him that he didn't have his strength back yet. Connie was there to keep him in the saddle. They wouldn't stop unless there was trouble.

Matt had given in. But he wasn't ready for the sensation that had gone through him when Connie's nipples touched his back as she got on. He leaned forward a little as Connie settled in place behind him. Star handed Flame's reins to Connie. Flame had been a perfect gentleman with all that had gone on. Matt hoped he could be one; but thought it was going to be the longest and hardest ride he would ever have to do. He could feel the naked flesh of Connie's thighs against his bottom. He was glad when Billy showed up. He wanted to get the trip over with.

Helen gave Billy what meat Matt hadn't eaten. Billy nodded and then drank all he could from the spring. Billy then mounted the Indian pony and took the lead. It was then that Matt realized he was the only one that had eaten. As Connie put Flame into motion her breast touched Matt's back again. He decided the ride was going to be pure torment. Helen and Star mounted their ponies and followed. Star wouldn't start worrying about the trail till they got to the valley that lead into the basin.

Runs Far and his braves had searched everyplace they thought would conceal someone. They were careful to conceal any sign they'd been there. They were deep in enemy territory. Runs Far could have had more braves, but he had decided against a big group. It was hard enough to stay hidden with the few he had. He had picked the best trackers and fiercest fighters from among his people.

He was proud of his sister. He always had been. Father had named her right. Even as a baby she had out shined all the others. Even among his own tribe. They all knew and admitted that she was different from the others. When she had become a maiden she still out shined all the other maidens. As far as that she could hold her own with most of the braves. Unlike the other maidens she had learned the ways of the braves. She always did her duties around camp. But went into the woods every chance she got. His father had whacked her many times with a stick for not staying in camp. But after his arm had gotten sore and he had broken many sticks. His father told them that the woods were running out of sticks to use on her. He decided to give in and had his best braves teach her.

Star learnt to track and hide sign better than all of the braves except for one or two. She could hit the mark better than most with bow or riffle. There was only a handful of braves that could stay with her in a days run or a swift sprint.

All the braves would have come along if it had been possible. Many braves had come to her lodge baring gifts, but she had refused all of them. Father had started to make a fuss, but Star still refused. She then told of her ability to see into the Spirit World. That's when Sees Far had been summoned to put Star through some test to see if she really did have the gift. After some time he told them that he was sure that Star did. Then it had been decided that Star was to be taught in the ways of healing, also. She had learned quickly and had even amazed her uncle how quickly she could learn. It appeared she had the power of healing also. Star was a favorite among the people.

Many of them had wanted to come along to rescue her.

Most of the men had been off hunting that day. Star with some other maidens had been out gathering wood and berries. The enemy had been out raiding for horses and food. After the raid they had escaped with their catch when they came across the maidens. Star had seen that they were all about to be taken. Commanded the other maidens to drop everything and run. Instead of following; Star grabbing a good sized limb she attacked the raiding party by swinging it at the horses. The raiders had been surprised. They had thought too capture the defenseless maidens with ease.

It had caused so much confusion, that Star had almost gotten away also when one of the enemy braves, had hit her on the side of her head with the flat part of his tomahawk. One of the maidens had glanced back just in time to see what had happened. Then she saw the enemy carry Star off along with the ponies they had been able to catch.

Some of his people had been hurt in the raid. But none of them had died. Runs Far and his hunters had returned two days after the raid. His father had sent some scouts out to find him. As soon as he could get his things together and prepare his war horse he had gone out in search of his sister. There had been no pursuit before his return, because it would have left the village with hardly anybody to defend it.

Runs Far bringing his thoughts back to the present was relieved. They had found the enemy's war camp. It wasn't the main village though. But now he knew Star and the others were still alive. At least that was what the enemy brave had told them. Runs Far had been sure enough to send one of his braves to let Hawkeye know.

Again, they searched blindly. The hard rain had wiped out all sign. They were left to try trailing her in their minds. What they thought Star would do and better, try to think where she would be. It had gotten more difficult as several of their enemy was out scouting around searching for the escapees also. That gave him hope. If they were still searching. Star and the others with the flaming horse were still free. Runs Far wished that his uncle Sees Far had come with them. Maybe with his power he could lead them to her.

Capt. Taylor had circled the wagons. There had been a couple hours of daylight left. But he decided to stop early to give the livestock a chance to get revived some. They were near Bear Lake in Utah Territory. There was a lot of good graze in the area and they had fresh meat. A good supply of good tasting fresh water also.

They had made it through the passes and crossed the rivers pretty well trouble-free. The mountain trails and passes had been a lot of hard work. They had to camp on a couple passes over night. The people needed a rest as well. They had made good time sense their big scrape with the Indians. Another month or two would get them to their destination. The days had gotten shorter and the nights were cool enough that the fire had started to feel good. From the word, they had received from some trappers headed to there winter camps, the passes were still clear.

It was still quiet and sullen around the Gates' and the Maxton's camp. They tried to put on a good face, especially the cowboys. The cowboys went out of their way to do everything they could for the Gates and the Maxton's. Chris had asked Captain Taylor what he could do. They hardly let him do a thing. He'd told Chris that was their way of grieving and probably didn't really realize they were doing so much. Capt. Taylor knew Chris had written a long letter to Mr. Saxton and put it in the mail. Chris had told him that was the hardest thing he had ever done.

Capt. Taylor hadn't given Matt up for dead yet. He thought a lot of the people had though. No one talked about the youngsters and that saddened him. He knew Hawkeye felt the same. They both would have to see the body or bodies to believe; that they had perished. Or at least someone else that could make that claim. No! He would wait till he had proof. He had heard about to many stories of survival; at great odds.

Matt had tried to stay awake and sit up. Flame made it as easy for Connie as he possibly could, it seemed like. Connie hadn't ever rode a horse that had such a smooth stride. She was real thankful for that. It had helped her a lot. The only thing was when Matt had at last given in, he had fallen back against her chest. With it hot and sunny she was afraid he would get sun burnt. His back and her breasts were covered in sweat which made her uncomfortable. Flame's hair was giving her thighs and fanny a real workout. The sweat made it worse than before. It had to be bothering Flame also, but he hadn't showed any sign of it.

Billy spotted a little spring brought his pony to a stop. He slide off and drank. Connie got Matt's canteen and drank. She felt him stir a little. She put the canteen to his lips. Weakly Matt did drink, quite a lot. When Matt finished she handed it to Billy and he refilled it. Billy then looked back the way they had come from. Shortly Helen came up leading Star's horse. She got off and took a good drink also. When Helen had finished then one at a time Billy let the horses drink. Then with Helen holding the horses Billy sought some higher ground to see if anything stirred besides them. They had to wait a half hour before Star caught up with them. She was sweaty and covered with dust. They could tell she had worked hard to cover their trail. The horses had stirred up the water pretty good, but she went to where the spring was running into the pool and drank as much as she could.

Connie said, "I'm worried about Matt getting sun burnt." Helen and Star looked up; they nodded. They quickly mixed up some mud. Star handed Connie some; she rubbed it all over his back and arms. Star handed her some more which she rubbed on his chest and face. Matt hadn't liked it much; he had stirred a little. But he didn't wake up. He'd gone back to sleep right after drinking the water. Star finished by rubbing some on Matt's legs.

Star motioned to Billy that she would take the lead. Also, she wanted him to watch for marks left by Flames iron shoes. Billy nodded as Star lead out across solid rock for the most part. Billy thought Star had done a lot of scouting. The pieces of leather were still doing the job. As Billy dropped in behind he couldn't see any tracks. All they needed was for a good breeze to come up for a couple of hours. As light as the dust was a good breeze would wipe out any sign they left behind them to completely hide their tracks. Besides a good breeze would feel good.

Late in the afternoon the shadows had claimed most of the land as Star lead them up through a stream. They had been in and out of it for the last four or five miles. The banks were narrow which put them in the water at times. Especially when they came to a rapid. It twisted back and fourth up over some small rapids. One rapid had been a little steep. Star had waited on her pony until Flame came up close. By riding close together Star and Connie had been able to keep Matt in the saddle. Connie knew she wouldn't have been able to have done it by herself. The water hadn't been over three or four feet deep; most of the time just a foot or so. It was swift moving and very cold. It would wash away any sign they had been through in a short time.

Star back in front was taking her time. She was looking for a certain spot in the rock formations. She would know it when she saw it and didn't want to miss it. She was very apprehensive and was getting worried that she may have missed it. The ravine they were in had turned pretty dark. If she didn't spot it soon it would be to dark. It had been through her vision that she knew how to find the stream. The spot she looked for had come from her vision also. It was rough going and the horses were left to pick their own way. They didn't want any of them to come up lame.

The ravine made a turn to the west. Then in a short distance it turned back east. Within just a few more yards it made a sharp turn to the south again. The stream had gotten narrower and shallower. Star suddenly pulled rein and as she sat on her pony studying the east wall. She decided the spot on the wall was nearly a perfect V made by the sunlight. On the smooth face of the wall above them as Star watched the V disappeared as the sun traveled on to the west. The timing had been magical. If they'd been a minute later she would have missed it. Five minutes earlier she wouldn't have seen it either. As the others caught up she slid off her pony, then after a couple of steps to the steep west bank worked her way up into the chasm.

Helen and Billy had come up as Connie watched Star disappear. Helen asked, "What happened?"

Connie said, "I don't know. I got here just in time to see Star disappear." Star returned twenty minutes later sure she'd found a way to get the horses up. But it would be next to impossible to get Matt up in the condition he was in. When Star got back down to them, she said, "We'll have to lead the horses up and let them pick their way, but keep them at it. Don't give them too much time to think."

Billy slid off his horse as Helen asked, "Are you sure Star? It looks awfully bad."

"Yes, the Spirit World showed it to me."

Billy said, "It's just a little climb sis. Matt's going to be the problem."

Helen responded, "Oh yes, you're right."

Connie had just sat and watched. She was completely worn out. Star, Helen, and Billy were able to urge the ponies up without a lot trouble. By the time they made it back though, it was near dark. Billy turned his back then Connie eased Matt down with the help of Star and Helen lowered him onto Billy's back. Getting Matt's leg over the saddle horn hadn't been easy. Billy staggered under Matt's weight. He turned and started up. Star and Helen each took a leg lifting as much weight as they could off of Billy as he struggled along. He picked his way carefully, trying to make sure not to fall.

They banged their arms, shins and skinned their knees under Matt's weight. They had just been able to make it up where it leveled off. They were out of breath and covered with sweat. They eased Matt down and leaned him against the side of the chasm. They then dropped where they were to rest. Connie had taken awhile to make the climb after holding Matt all day. She'd had all she wanted. She saw Matt and stepped past him. Flame then scrambled up past them careful not to step on any of them especially Matt.

All exhausted it took a few minutes for them to recover. Connie got up and went to Flame and started to take his saddle off. Star got up and told them she would search for some food. Billy staggered to his feet and went to Matt's saddle bags as Connie laid them down. With Matt's knife and Star's little bow to start a fire, Billy searched for some wood. As much by feel as actually being able to see anything. Helen got up and went to Flame's saddle and got the rabbit fur quilt to cover Matt with. It had already cooled off quite a bit. There was a steady breeze coming through the chasm, that had a chilly bite to it.

The chasm they were in wasn't real level but it had widened out some. Billy, found some wood that lay around. He didn't see any trees. What wood there was must have been washed into the chasm. He found a short piece a foot thick and about six feet long. He could feel that it was dry under foot. He found out that the log was dry and after moving some larger rocks smoothed out a place for them. He then moved the log where he wanted it. Shaving off some pieces with Matt's knife and doing like Star had done built a fire.

After a few minutes having some light from the fire Billy helped Connie and Helen move Matt to the fire. It had been tough on Matt, who had lost most of the color he had when they'd started out in the morning. Star was gone for over an hour before they heard her signal. They signaled back like she'd taught them. Shortly Star came in with a rattlesnake, rabbit, and a good-sized lizard of some kind. She used Matt's knife to clean them, then hung the meat on sticks over the fire to cook. Billy sure Star would find something had ready prepared the sticks.

Connie with concern in her voice said, "Matt's wore out. His leg wound opened up and bled a little too."

They still took their time when they spoke. They still had some trouble understanding Star, like she did with them. So with a mixture of her own language, English, and some sign language they were able to conversed. Star said, "We'll get up early. There's a good place with food and water not very far from here. It will be a good place to stay also."

Helen said, "We should have stayed where we were."

Star then stated, "No. Our enemy was close by. It wasn't safe anymore."

Billy asked, "Where are we?"

Star said, "I don't know. We'll be safe now."

They took turns on guard duty, during the night. In the morning they woke up with the sun seeking what warmth it would give them. They had decided to let Matt sleep, but had saved him some meat to start out the day with. Connie woke Matt up to give him enough time to eat and drink. He tiredly chewed his meat, and drank some water. Not with the eagerness that he'd had before.

As the girls moved around camp Billy noticed that they limped or winced as they did their chores. Then he noticed spots of blood smeared around from their cut feet. The rocks of the bank had cut up their feet pretty good. With Billy making several trips to the stream to fill the canteen for them, they filled their bellies with water.

Star had Billy help her hide the trail. She told Connie and Helen to break up camp and to get the horses ready. Billy figured it took them over three hours. Star had insisted on putting some of rocks they could move into the creek. Because Flame's shoes had left scratch marks on them. Then, they carefully moved some other rocks around to replace them. With a lot of work they covered every sign they made when they left the stream to enter the chasm.

Star even dusted everything down as they made their way back up the bank the last time. If they had left any sign Billy hadn't been able to spot it. When Star and Billy returned back to join the others the camp had been wiped clean, like nobody had ever been there. Connie and Helen had taken advantage of the time.

Star looked around and seemed very happy. Then she looked at Billy intently she asked Connie for the knife. Connie got it out of saddle bag and handed it to Star. Star with knife in hand squatted in front of Billy. She quickly cut his pant legs off up to his knees. Billy's face had gotten beet red since he hadn't known what she had intended to do with the knife. So he had watched her closely and his eyes had a direct view right between her legs that left nothing to his imagination.

Billy looked up quickly saying, "Damn! You shouldn't have done that." Star quickly cut his pant legs up into four pieces. Going up to Flame she said, "We need to cover up his shoes again." Connie and Helen knew what had upset Billy so bad, but didn't say a thing. Connie still remembered how embarrassed she'd been over her ordeal. They woke Matt up and even though he was weaker than the day before he was able to help them some as he mounted Flame. With all of them mounted Star led off. They rode on solid rock with a few hard packed dry dirt spots once in awhile. With Flame's shoes covered they left hardly a trace of passing through the area. The chasm then started to widen out. Not steep, but a nice steady climb.

Shortly after noon still mostly on solid rock they toped out of the chasm. They saw a good sized lake in front of them. Star led them down a gentle slope. Then over onto some grass to their left, up and away from the lake. It looked like the gorge or chasm they'd come through was an overflow for the lake sometimes. They rode into a high valley with rolling hills. The grass looked like it had deep rich roots even though it had started to dry up some. All around them, the foliage was changing the fall colors. A sign that winter wasn't far off.

They rode along getting more cheerful all the time. Along with the good graze there were tree's scattered around. It didn't appear that many had visited the place. They had already spotted some deer as they eased into some slight cover. There was sign that there was a plentiful supply of other game around also.

They crossed what looked like a river that was a couple of feet deep. An easy crossing of eighty feet, the water didn't appear to be flowing in either direction though. They were still a couple of miles away from the lake. Star then continued to lead them along next to the river.

When they had ridden a couple more miles they could hear a roar that kept getting louder. It sounded like it was coming from within the ground. A good mile farther on a branch of the river ran to the west a short distance where it disappeared under a mountain. The water flowed toward the mountain, as if to point that was where the loud roar was coming from. They figured there had to be a pretty good-sized water fall within the mountain or on the other side of it.

CHAPTER THIRTEEN

A NEW PLACE

Ten miles past the branch of the river Star reined her pony to a stop. To the west across from them, the river made a loop in under the mountain. The river was divided by a twelve-acre island. The side next to them was only fifteen feet wide and a foot deep. The other side looked like it would be deep. It was a hundred feet across from the island to the mountain cliff.

Star motioned for them to stay, then guided her pony ahead for a quarter of a mile as she watched across the river on the far bank. Making a decision she guided her pony into the water and crossed over. The pony made it without losing it's footing, just barely. Headed back the way she'd come from, Star rode as close to the cliff as she could. The tree's and brush kept her away from it in a few places.

She was nearly back to where her friends where across the river, when she grunted and slid off her horse. As she walked to the cliff she spotted the cave she had seen when she had her vision into the Spirit World. She had trusted her vision to find each one of the landmarks. But she had followed her instinct a lot of the time also.

There was a six feet by six feet entrance. Then it opened into a circular chamber of about forty feet. There was a couple of other openings, how far they went she didn't know. They were just very dark holes was all she could tell at the moment. With what light she had she checked to make sure there wasn't a nest of snakes, cougars, or bears already inhabiting the cave.

Satisfied she had the place to herself, she returned to her pony, jumped on it and rode up the river. She'd ridden about a mile when she found a better place to cross. The river was almost two hundred feet wide but only a couple of feet deep.

Later that night, after they had settled in and had a good fire going they started to make themselves at home. They made some mats out of pine straw. They had some good grass close by to put their horses on. The smoke from the fire drifted up through a hole in the top of the cave somewhere. It drafted so good the only smoke in the cave came directly from the fire.

Star had been able to kill a deer with Matt's knife. She'd hung on a tree limb till she was able to drop on a small doe that wandered underneath her. Helen and Connie had found some onions and roots to eat. Billy had set up some stones to make a fire pit and carried quite a bit of dry wood in for the fire. They'd all gotten their bellies full for the first time in a long time. They woke Matt up to eat. He hadn't eaten much, after a drink he'd drifted right back to sleep. In Matt's weakened condition the last two days had completely wore him out.

Over the next few days Matt's color returned. He was awake for the better part of the day now. He was able to stand and walk out to relieve himself on his own. The trip left him completely exhausted though. He just fell on his mat when he made it back. Connie and Helen fussed at first, but Star told them he would get his strength back quicker. Matt had his full appetite back now. He liked the taste of the venison along with the wild onions and other roots, that Star had showed them they could eat.

They had made quite a few improvements in their new home. They moved some good sized rocks into the cave for seats and back rest at the end of their mats. There was a plentiful supply of wood for the fire, but they all wished for an axe. Star already had a couple of hides drying that she planned to tan the best she could, with what she had. With their meal done Matt had drifted off into a nice, strength building sleep. With their bellies full leaning on their back rest they relaxed as full darkness settled over the land. The fire felt good as the nights kept getting cooler. It had been the best day they'd had since they'd been kidnapped. With the light from the fire Connie gave Star a direct look as she asked, "Star, how in the world did you know this place was here?" Star, pretty certain they wouldn't believe her, paused a good minute or more as the others looked at her waiting for her answer. With her thoughts composed she said, "I'm able to see into the Spirit World sometimes. It's like I'm there, floating in the air. Maybe I'm there with my eyes only.

Helen said, "Well, it appeared like you had been here before. Star; are we lost then?"

"No. I have never been here before. But I know how to get back to my people"

Billy thoughtfully said, "Star, your saying when you guided us in here it was by your visions."

"Yes. Do you believe me?"

Thinking before he spoke Billy suddenly made up his mind that Star wouldn't lie. He replied, "Yes, I do. I do remember that a few times it looked like you where looking for something."

Star relaxed, she even smiled a little, then said, "Thank you." Billy got up, retrieved his rifle and as he left the cave he said, "I Better go check on the horses and then I'll be at the place I've been watching from."

They nodded to Billy as he left. They talked a little more before they stretched out on their pine straw mats. It was uncomfortable on their bare bodies, but it was better than lying on the hard rock floor of the cave.

Runs Far and his braves never camped in the same place twice. They had searched every place they thought someone might hide four or five people and their horses. They'd not left one stone unturned. To make it harder they had to be extra careful as the enemy was all around them. The last day they'd had to drift further to the south to keep from being detected. They were getting farther away from their own village. They had to return to their people soon. They had to hunt and gather enough food for the winter to take to their winter camp before winter claimed the land.

The next morning as they broke up camp to head out in different directions, Runs Far made sure everyone knew where they were to meet. The last brave to return last night told them he'd found some sign just before dark. Runs Far didn't have much hope that it was from his sister. Even if she had circled to get around the enemy it was way south of where he thought she should be. But with the white eyes being along with her they didn't want to leave one stone unturned.

The sun was midway across the sky when he found what the brave had described to him. He checked around to make sure he was safe. Then Runs Far followed the tracks the brave had left last night. After a fifteen minute ride he eased into the basin. When he spotted the spring he slid off his horse. He had a good drink. Then just stood and looked around.

Within a half hour a couple of his braves approached. One rode on in to report that a couple of braves had stayed back to watch at the entrance, so they didn't get trapped in the basin. Runs Far told the brave to find Bears Claw and have him come on in. Runs Far then just waited patiently for Bears Claw to get there. He was there best tracker and Runs Far didn't want to disturb a thing. He held the other braves back as they started to drift in. Word had already been passed that some sign, from Star might have been found. Something had to be up for Bears Claw to have been sent for.

Bears Claw had his pony at a trot when he rode in. He slid off his pony then had a good drink. As he stood he gave Runs Far a respectful look. Runs Far had showed him a lot of respect. Bears Claw slowly made a study of everything. Careful where he stepped he worked his way up into the cave. He was already sure that Star had been there and he was determined not to miss a thing. After nearly an hour of a detailed search he waved for Runs Far to come up.

He talked and pointed to different signs in the cave. Of all of the tracks on the trail going into the cave, then of the other things scattered all around inside. He then told Runs Far he was sure that it was Star along with four others. One wore boots, one was hurt, and the others had bare feet. The ones with the bare feet had left most of the footprints. They went through the cave again to make sure they hadn't missed anything that might identify for sure who had been staying in the cave. They had four horses and he assured Runs Far that he could recognize their tracks now, even though the sign was four or five days old.

But, as he started out on their trail he got a surprise when he saw that the tracks from the iron shoes had disappeared. He saw that Star had brushed away their tracks and even had dusted their trail some.

He'd expected that, but it did take him awhile before he figured out how she had made all sign of the iron shoes disappear. After that he was able to work out her trail a lot easier, once he knew what he was looking for. When Bears Claw started out on the trail Runs Far had his braves wipe out any sign that had left.

It was the third day after they'd found the trail from Star and her companions. They'd lost the trail and then found it a couple of more times. Bears Claw had worked the trail with as much care and determination as any he'd ever been on. But Star had been brilliant. They'd lost it completely now. He knew Runs Far was disappointed and so was he. He'd gotten up at daylight and worked diligently until dark. He'd found their back trail twice, but had been completely stumped when it had run out the next time. Runs Far then put everyone out to search in all directions again. After they decided where they should try to camp for the night. Runs Far then told them, they would have to give up the search after another seven days.

At the new place the hunting was good and with the fresh meat, berries and vegetable like plants Star showed them to look for. She told them the plants would be good for them. With full meals now everyone was getting healthier. Matt was up and taking care of himself now. He had started taking walks and was rapidly getting his strength back. They'd been at their new place for two weeks. Everyone had cheered up as Matt improved. Bringing him up to date they told him, if it hadn't been for Star he probably would have died.

Flame seemed to be happy that Matt was up on his feet. Flame always watched for Matt to come out of the cave. Then he followed Matt around much like a dog would have. Flame seemed to know that Matt wasn't back to full strength yet. When they had started to play around again Flame hadn't challenged Matt to be fast or strong. Flame was being extra careful.

With his strength and endurance improving Matt spent less and less time around the girls. No one had said anything, but they could see the effect the girls had on him. Star and the girls had tanned buckskin and made a loincloth for him. They were in the process of making him a pair of moccasins. Star had killed a doe to make loincloths for each of them.

Matt went out longer each time. He'd been doing a lot of exploring. Then he'd go swimming two or three times a day. The water was cold but the exercise helped him get his strength back. He felt refreshed as he let the sun dry him off. The others enjoyed the stream also. It was a big improvement over the sponge baths they'd had to take.

Star had found a limb and made a bow, then some small straight ones to make some arrows with. She had to hunt awhile before she found some pieces of flint to make the arrow heads with. But with the snares and Star's skill at hunting they had a good supply of food now.

Matt's thoughts drifted from one girl too the other, several times a day. He had to admit that he liked each and every one of them; what was not to like he thought. Due to the circumstances which he didn't hold against anyone, there'd been nothing hidden from his eyes. Connie was smart, daring, and really outgoing. She could do most anything a man could do. Helen was a little on the quiet side. But he could tell she missed nothing. Helen had the ability to do things right without a wasted move. He was sure Helen had a quick mind. But she did like to have all the facts before she spoke. Star, he had observed, was smart as well as quick of mind and body. She was very graceful and nearly had the strength of some men. But she didn't have the big bulky muscles to show it. She had a gorgeous sleek body in every way, as far as he was concerned.

Forcing his thoughts away from the girls and on to more important things, he knew that their families had to be worried about them. Especially if they thought the girls, Billy, and he were still alive. He got better each day now, a lot of the soreness had been worked out of his body. His leg and shoulder were still tender and hurt with any movement. He was in good enough shape to ride, but knew he was in no shape for a fight. They would have to make a move pretty soon. It had been cold the last couple of nights. With them not having an axe or at least a tomahawk made it awfully hard to keep a good supply of wood. They had used a lot the last two nights. Billy helped with the wood, as everyone took turns on guard duty now.

Matt was proud of Billy. A lot of men would have gone berserk to have seen and gone through what he had. The circumstances had made Billy a man overnight. You could see it in his eyes. Matt had the feeling that Billy thought he should have done more. Matt hoped he would be able to recognize that at the time everything had happened, he didn't have the knowledge or ability to have done different.

Matt made up his mind that they needed to move. He was sure by the time they got to the big Mountains, the passes would be snowed in. They would have to spend the winter at one of the forts, or someplace else. That wouldn't be so easy either. They'd have to find someone to take them in. They didn't have a dime between them. With his mind made up he would discuss it with them.

Star and Connie were working on a deer hide they were trying to get tanned, the best they could. Star wished for a buffalo to kill so they could do a better job. She wished she was back with her people. It was close to the time her people would go on the fall hunt, to supply their winter camp with meat. Even now they could be moving further away from them. As they worked Star glanced at Connie. She scrubbed some of the deer brain with a few other things into the hide to help tan it. She noticed how Connie's breasts had gotten firmer and a little bigger. All of Connie's muscles had firmed up as far as that went. Connie was so beautiful she could see why Matt would be attracted to her.

Star did feel Matt's eyes on her from time to time. Each time she felt her heart beat faster. No man had done that to her before, she wondered about it. He was white skinned which amazed her. She was sure Matt was the great warrior she had seen in her vision. The one she never told anyone about. The one that the Spirit World had shown her that was to be the father of her children. Since being rescued she had tried to recognize the person in her vision. But that detail of her vision had never been clear. Everything else had happened much like she had seen in her vision.

When Matt had sprung into action everything had fallen into place just like she'd seen in her vision. She had put her trust in the vision and followed it pretty much just the way it had come to her. Before the rescue she'd been sure it wouldn't be a white person. Now she had her doubts; she admitted to herself that she was confused.

After their meal as the sun disappeared, Matt said, "We need to talk." They looked up and gave Matt their full attention. Matt said, "I Think we need to get ready to move."

When he looked at Star he tried to concentrate on her face and not her breasts. He looked into her eyes. That was a mistake. They sparked and flashed like lightning which shot through his body to ignite his nerves. He tried to lay his arm in front of him, sort of as if by accident to cover his rising emotions. Putting his attention on the fire he tried to gather up his thoughts again. In the process he noticed that Star's nipples had grown and hardened like little acorns. Matt reddened a little, as he thought how difficult it was being around these girls. No, women! The others had been quiet as they had noticed what had happened. Each of them became uncomfortable. Helen and Connie had glanced at each other knowingly, but kept quiet. Matt finely got his thoughts back together, then said, "We need to move soon. To get Star back to her people and then the rest of us will need to find a place to spend the winter."

Billy, like Matt, had thought he had become a man, in just a few weeks. He had been able to stay outside the circle of the other four for the most part. However, he hadn't missed many of the emotions and looks that passed between them. It was like he was in tune with their thoughts. Not so much Matt, but the girls. When Matt had been critical, they had let their emotions show on their faces, for the entire world to see.

He liked all of them. But he was afraid there would be a big explosion someday. He didn't think there was a thing he could do about it. Billy watched the fire and made sure not to look at any of them. He did think, that maybe Matt had just lit the fuse to the powder keg.

Matt had expected a response, but when nobody said anything. He got a little tense as he concentrated on the fire. He missed the girls; as they gave each other a good look. Each of them had gotten tense and had clamped their jaws tight. Not noticing the girls' actions Matt said, "With nothing to cut wood with and as high up as we are we'll freeze. The game will soon be headed to better places for the winter also."

Everybody had still kept quiet. With a quick glance at the girls he saw how tense they were. He had no idea what had caused it. He thought they were being kind of rude not to respond at all. With an effort Matt kept his temper under control, because for some reason, they were making him mad. It was like they had just decided to ignore him for some reason. Then Matt thought maybe they just wanted him to take control; glad they wouldn't have to make the decisions anymore. Deciding that had to be it he said, "I better go out and scout around tomorrow to see if I can find a safe way out of here."

Before Matt could say anything more all three of the girls loudly said, "No!" Star stood up quickly, then said, "I'll scout." Connie and Helen got up to stand on either side of Star. Together they both said, "Yes."

Connie then said, "Star will do any scouting that needs to be done."

Matt confused and somewhat displeased said, "No, it's time I got back to doing something."

Star said, "You do need to do something. You need to eat and get strong. You're still weak. I've watched; I know." Matt knew he was weak. But he thought he had been able to hide just how weak he really was. But with the way Star looked at him he knew he hadn't fooled her.

Matt said, "It's not right. I should be the one or at least maybe Billy. It's a man's job." Helen surprised herself as well as the others when she said, "Star's as good as any man and just as skilled. If not for her, all of us would probably be dead. She has done just fine. I trust her completely."

Matt felt his words had been turned around and wasn't being understood. So, he said, "I didn't mean that Star wasn't good. I just think it's a man's job. And even if I am weak I'd be able to do a better job than Billy. Besides, you girls need to gather up enough stuff for us to eat on the trail so we can travel faster."

Billy had stood and just listened. He did step off a little, but he wasn't going to leave. He had a slight thought that it would be the proper thing to do. But he wanted to see how Matt got out of the hornets nest. Matt had really gotten them stirred up.

Connie said, "Matt, you are not strong enough yet. I know how stubborn you are and how much pride you have."

Star said, "If we have to we'll tie you up. You're not going. I will go."

Helen said, "Now you're talking. That's what we better do. He's stubborn enough to slip off when we're sleeping."

Nodding Connie added "Yes. He'll do something like that."

Matt stood up saying, "Now, everybody calm down." He could see in their eyes, they ment what they said. He said, "I was just. Well. It's not right for Star to be taking all the risks."

Connie said, "Like it or not; Star is the best to do what has to be done right now."

Matt said, "Well fine! but I don't like it. I guess you are right."

Helen said, "Matt, another thing. Until we see spring, if we are able to get Star back to her people, we'll stay the winter with her people."

"Well, I just thought we should get back to our families as soon as possible."

Connie said, "Matt we don't have any money or supplies. Star's people are probably the only ones that wouldn't mind taking us in. We would be safe there."

"I guess your right."

Matt then turned, and went out into the cool night. He needed some time to himself. They were right of course. That made him upset with himself. He didn't like being weak. He still thought he could've made it. He did admit that he probably would've been completely worn out when he got back.

After a couple of minutes Billy went out to check on the horses then on to take the first watch for the night. He wore a slight grin. Matt had backed down easier than he had thought he would.

After Billy left Star asked, "Are you two mad at me? Connie said, "No. Of course not. We just need to be real stern with Matt to protect him from himself."

Star said, "That's not what I mean. I know you saw when we looked at each other."

Helen said, "Oh yes, Star! We couldn't help it. Connie and I love Matt so very much, also." "Oh no, it can't be anything like that. It's just that he excites me."

Helen and Connie nodded with understanding. Then Helen said, "You'll see." Drawn together by a neutral force they embraced then hugged Star. At that time they made a lifetime friendship. (They didn't know it, at that time though.)

The next morning Matt was restless. Star had gotten up at first light and gone out on a scouting trip. After a time or two around the camp he told them he was going to explore around some. Connie and

Helen nodded. Then Connie said, "Just not too far. And remember, the more energy you save, the quicker you'll get stronger."

Matt nodded slightly as he kept to his own thoughts. He didn't want them to see it, but he was concerned for Star. She had decided to go on foot. She told them it would likely take her two days. He thought he shouldn't worry. She was just an Indian anyway. Then he was upset with himself for that thought. Not knowing why he knew right then and there that he'd kill anybody that insulted her. With his thoughts going to Connie and Helen, suddenly he knew he felt the same way about them. That upset him even more which left him in a very foul mood. Mostly because he didn't understand his emotions. Yes, he liked them. But why should he want be so protective of them?

Matt went on to check the horses. He spent some time with Flame. They played around a little in a game of tag. They had fun with each other, but did try to do it when they thought nobody else was around. It hadn't lasted long; he had tired out quickly. But it felt good and he could feel his strength returning.

He decided to go for a swim. He decided to go below the cave where a sandbar had been left because of a sharp turn in the river as it headed west into the mountain cliff. There he could just lie, soak in the water, or relax in the sun. Usually, Matt didn't do that sort of thing, but thought it would be very pleasant.

A good hour had gone by as Matt lay on the sandbar in the sun. With a quick dip in the clod water he cleaned up and was refreshed. As he stood up and was ready to go back to the cave he saw a twig float past him then disappear under the cliff. He watched for it to return. When it didn't; after he was sure it should have. He waded into the cold water. It came up his chest before he got to where he saw the twig last. He stood in amazement. There was a gap in the cliff wall four foot wide. The top of it was like an A-frame twenty feet high. The way it blended into the cliff the only place it could be seen was exactly right where he stood.

Some of the water flowed gently into the gap. Curious, Matt waded into the gap. He almost lost his footing just before his feet touched solid rock. Then it rose at a slight incline. The water was only half way up to his knees when he had gone on into the cliff forty feet. He reached up and touched the jagged top. It felt solid he didn't want anything loose to fall on him. The tunnel made a sharp right. It was just a real dark black hole from what he could see. But some water still flowed on into the tunnel. He returned back to the cave. He stood next to the fire to get warmed up some; he'd gotten colder than he'd realized. After he got the chill off he went in search of a pine limb with a big knot. It took Matt the better part of an hour before he found what he wanted. Then he had to work a little harder than he wanted, to break it in the right place. He did it between two big rocks.

Matt hadn't seen Connie or Helen. He was glad of that; he didn't want to be quizzed by them. They probably had gone to gather roots, berries, or wild onions to have with their meal. That was so they would have a healthier diet. Billy stayed on guard duty through most of the late night till the sun came up. The others took turns during the early night. That way they got a full nights sleep three out of four nights. With Star gone that would change a little. When Matt went into the cave to light his torch. Billy taking a little break stepped in to get a bite asked, "What's up."

With Matt's explanation Billy was curious. He got up and followed Matt. With Billy close behind Matt returned back to the entrance of the water tunnel. After an hour of twisting and turning up and down they were about ready to turn back. Then they saw daylight ahead of them. With the pine knot about consumed the pine wood would burn up fast. The tunnel quickly widened out to about forty feet and was twenty feet high. The water was only four inches deep. They carefully walked to the opening to stand on a ledge that overlooked a big open canyon in front of them. With a look at the sun they knew that they were looking west. They were sure it was quite a lot lower at the west end of the tunnel than it was at the east end.

The canyon floor was several thousand feet lower than where they stood. They saw four big rivers with a large lake. They could see some large animals. From there view point they saw a couple of good-sized forest. The canyon floor looked like it was pretty much level with some rolling knolls. The grassy plains still had a rich green color to them. Matt and Billy just stood and stared for a long time. They agreed that it was the most beautiful sight they had ever seen.

Matt still held the torch. Most of the pine pitch had been burnt up. He'd have to be careful to keep a gust of wind from blowing it out. To the south side of the ledge there was a thirty acre meadow with some grass and a few pine trees. The only break they saw down the mountain was the stream that flowed down a large twisting draw. Other than that the mountain was a mass of high cliffs stacked on top of one another. There was a good sized pool twenty feet below the ledge they stood on. Matt and Billy close to the edge of the tunnel with a couple of well placed steps made it to the meadow. They found a couple pine limbs with knots to use as torches.

When they got back to the cave Connie and Helen had the meal about ready. Matt and Billy had gotten a couple of looks; like where have you been. But nothing had been said and Matt was tired when they had returned. But he felt good as his body was getting stronger. He had worked up a real good appetite and ate the biggest meal he had since he'd been wounded. Billy had eaten well, also. After the meal they told Connie and Helen about what they had discovered.

Star had made good time because she didn't have to worry about covering up any horse tracks. It had been a chore traveling down the stream. She had tried to stay on the bank, but had given that up as it kept pushing her back in the water anyway. Once she got out on the open terrain she made a wide circle. It didn't look like anyone had discovered their trail yet. She'd been able to move along without leaving any sign of her passing. The moccasins she'd been able to put together had really helped. But being green because the doe skin hadn't had enough time to cure and be tanned properly they were about worn out already.

She had covered a lot of ground and was glad she had decided to come by foot. It made it a lot easier to find cover as she moved about. The enemies of her people were all around. She had to stay alert and move with a lot of stealth. She'd hoped she might come across some sign of her people. She was sure she would've recognized some of their pony tracks. But with so many out searching for her companions and her, her people would have to be hiding their trail.

With the time they'd had and probably some ceremonies, the enemy braves had gotten their courage up again. It would be big medicine to them, if they could capture or kill Matt. Then it had to be a thorn in there sides that they had been cheated out of the fun they'd had in store for their prisoners. Star had known that they were to have been killed. None of them had claimed a one of them. Star knew that they had been close to being violated. They had been working up to it. If Matt hadn't showed up when he had she would have welcomed death.

It had been cold last night. She had missed the warmth of her new friends as much as she did the fire. She tried to deny them, but her thoughts kept dwelling on Matt. She kept remembering what Helen had said. She admitted that Matt stirred her emotions. But she refused to believe it could be love. She was still troubled and confused about her visions. Some of them had been so clear that she knew without a doubt that she had the gift. Still there was some that hadn't been clear and they troubled her.

At great risk and taking a lot of time she had been able to steal an axe. She was able to make it appear like one of the braves had been careless, which he had. They hadn't searched long. She stayed till they broke camp and then went in the opposite direction to circle back around to the stream that led to the gorge. It was a lot harder going back in than it had been on the way out. The water flowed against her and her moccasins were in tatters. She could already feel a couple of cuts on her feet. The chill of the water wasn't as bad. She was close to breaking out into a sweat from her efforts.

As she made her way back to the cave she located it from the cliff above. She'd made sure on her way out that she would recognize it. She had five miles to go and made a beeline for it. She was tired and hungry enough to eat a bear. It was already pretty dark; it would be dark by the time she got to the cave. Holding the rifle and the axe above the water wasn't that easy, especially when she had to swim.

Billy took the midnight to daylight shift every night. Matt was taking his turn on guard duty and was sure he had spotted Star just as it was getting dark. He did know it was somebody on foot and headed straight for them. Matt passed the word. Connie, and Helen eased some meat closer to the fire to reheat it some. Matt watched Star as she made her final swim. He took the rifle and axe from her as she stood. Then they both waded on up the bank and walked on into the cave. Matt had watched Star real close, he checked to make sure she wasn't hurt. He saw that she sort of limped a little when she made it into the cave, he saw some spots of blood. Still wet her hair clung to her back. Star sat and removed her tattered moccasins. She left her loincloth in place. Matt, as he carefully laid the rifle and axe down continued to watch Star real close. He assured himself again that he just checked to make sure she wasn't hurt in any way. Star had noticed and her nipples had hardened as she felt her whole body warm up. She had a thought, that maybe she should return to the cold water.

They were all happy to have Star back with them. They waited for her to eat. When she was done they discussed the latest events. Star had learned to put sentences together in English now. A few words still gave her trouble, but not many. After Star reported about everything she'd seen on her scouting trip Matt said, "We should try to slip out and get Star back to her people."

Star said, "No. That's not a good idea. The enemy is all around. With all of us out in the open, we wouldn't be able to get through without a fight."

Helen said, "Matt, you're not strong enough to get into a fight. I think that's what you intend. We only have about thirty rounds of ammo left." With a little more insight into what Matt was thinking Billy said, "Matt, if we did try to sneak through and got into a fight one of the girls could get hurt, if not killed."

Matt started to say something then paused. Then, shortly he said, "Well! We could end up in a fight with them if we stay here. They could stumble onto this place." Connie then asked, "Do you think we could get the horses through the tunnel into your canyon." Matt and Billy then told Star all about what they had discovered. When finished, Matt gave Billy a look then said, "I'm sure I can get Flame to go through. Then maybe the other horses would follow him. But if we do go through it would probably be best to spend the winter in there."

A little bit smug Connie said, "We know that Matt." Matt then said, "I do think it would be hard for anyone to find the cave. Unless you stand in the water right where I was you would never see it. If we did leave there would be no smoke to lead them in here."

Star said, "Then we should wipe away any sign of our being here that we can and go into your valley."

Matt nodding, "With all things considered, I guess we don't have any other choice."

With a quick response which was out of character for her and maybe to taunt him a little going into a sensual pose Helen said, "You act as if your getting tired of us."

Matt had looked toward Helen as she spoke, getting ready to respond to her. Suddenly he couldn't speak. He'd been crossed up. With her sudden pose her breasts still jiggled. Also, as if doing a little curtsey, she bowed, which slightly raised her loincloth. Matt did have a quick response. His face got red as his loincloth was pushed up in front of him. It wasn't hiding much. Matt stood, turned, and quickly went outside. Billy was just a few steps behind him.

Helen blushed as she said, "Oh my! I don't know why I did that." Star asked, "Did you see?"

It was all she could get out as Connie started giggling. Soon all three of them were in deep laughter. After a couple of minutes they had cleaned up the scraps from their meal. Then they went to work on their individual projects. Clothing of some kind or making a tool that would help make their work easier around camp.

Matt and Billy heard the laughter from outside. Billy then heard Matt mumble something like the foolish girls had gone crazy. At least that was what he thought he'd heard. Billy decided to let Matt have some peace. So, he didn't ask him what he'd said. Besides, as he remembered the look on Matt's face he had all he could do to keep from laughing out loud.

CHAPTER FOURTEEN

GOING THROUGH

They all worked at removing all the sign they could from their stay at the cave. Then they went outside to do the same with the rest of the camp site. There wasn't much they could do about where the horses had grazed. They still didn't have a lot to take along. What they did have they tied to Flames saddle. This part of the trip everyone was going to be walking anyway. Star had replaced her moccasins with a couple pieces of leather and then used some strips of leather to tie them on her feet. They had quite a chore getting the horses through. They had taken a couple of extra torches along with them. It had been a good thing. It took nearly twice as long as it had before. Gently they'd had to persuade the horses along. They had talked to them and patted them to keep them calm. Flame hadn't been a problem. Most of the way the other horses had followed along pretty well. They had three problem places where they had to work with them awhile before they were able to persuade them on. Two of the places had a sudden drop of four feet. The third one was like a chute. It dropped at a thirty degree angle for three hundred feet. What made it bad was the loose shale under foot. It had even made Flame a little nervous. But with a little persuasion Matt was able to get Flame through it.

When Matt saw the daylight shining at the end of the tunnel he held back to let the girls go on. Seeing the light Star lead her pony on followed closely by Connie. Then Helen passed him as she led her pony by to catch up with Star and Connie. When Billy stepped up leading his pony Matt walked beside him with Flame close behind. Matt and Billy were close enough to hear the girls as they stopped on the ledge to get their first view into the canyon. They could hear the girls as they oh-ed and ah-ed. The first to speak after absorbing the enchantment of the canyon Star said, "It's pretty and big." Excitedly Helen said, "It's beautiful. Oh! I've never seen anything so wonderful." Connie said, "It's so big. Look at all the colors. Oh! It's so gorgeous."

Letting the girls take in the scenery Matt and Billy led Flame and the other horses to the ledge. The ledge was only two foot wide right next to the meadow. The horses had to jump a gap of six feet to land on solid rock three foot lower, that slopped slightly down. The shoes on Flame's hoofs wouldn't be any help to him. Matt tied Flame's reins to the saddle horn. Then went out into the meadow and called softly. Flame sniffed around a little then with a lunge he jumped. Flame landed softly and ran on a few steps until he was on dirt where he came to a stop. Matt couldn't keep the surprise off his face as he saw how slick and easily Flame had made it. It wasn't quite as easy to get the Indian ponies across. One had almost fallen down completely, but did manage to stay on its feet. Another one had slipped a little the last one made it fine.

The girls gathered some wood together while Matt and Billy rolled some rocks around to make a fire pit. Then used the last embers of the pine torch to start the fire. It was already late. It had taken the better part of the day to wipe away all traces of their presence back at the cave. Then it had taken awhile to bring the horses through. With the urging and tugging the horses they were tired anyway. They decided to spend the night in the meadow. They all sat looking at the western sky from their lofty meadow to watch the shadows claim the canyon floor far below. Everyone was completely relaxed. They'd had a nice meal and felt safe. They were sure it would be next to impossible for any one to find them. The sky was already pretty, but by the time the sun had finely disappeared they all agreed it was the most beautiful sunset they'd ever seen.

The next morning after their meal they started down the draw. There was no trail and they decided to lead the horses. It was steep in a lot of places with big rocks all around. It looked like at one time there had been a lot of water rushing down the draw. Most places they were able to get up on the side of one bank or the other. The ground was very rough with a lot of sage brush and a few scrub pines. They had to ease into the wash from time to time. There wasn't much water flowing down the draw now. But there were pools of water in places.

They'd been at it for an hour. They'd only made three or four miles when they came to a place where the water had cut a path through some softer ground. It left hard rock walls a hundred feet high on each side. Then they came to a ledge that had a drop of fifty feet. They had to backtrack far enough to find another way around. They finely found a way that was up close to the top of the south wall. They took it slowly because of a lot of jagged rocks. They ended up having to backtrack a quarter of a mile to find it. Two hours later they found themselves below the ledge. They were all wet with sweat and there wasn't much left of the moccasins the girls had made. The leather Star had tied to her feet was almost worn through. Billy was the only one that still had something halfway decent. Back in the washout they continued to work their way down the draw.

It took a day and a half to get out of the draw and onto the canyon floor. The grass was almost up to the Indian ponies bellies. Even as late in the year as it was, it was just starting to turn brown. It was a deep healthy green. The horses really enjoyed it. They deserved it. It had been a rough trip on the horses and everyone. They'd been able to ride the last two miles of the fourteen mile trip down the draw. The next trip wouldn't take so long. They knew how to go now and on the next trip they wouldn't have to do any backtracking.

Star walked all the way so no one had to ride double. She didn't stop to think why, but was happy to do it. Neither Connie or Helen had to ride behind Matt and be so close. They were all in wonder as they kept looking the canyon over. It was real lush and quite a bit warmer then it had been up on the mountain. They figured they were at least four thousand feet below their last dwelling.

They decided to spend the night at the bottom of the draw as they were all tired. Even though Matt tried to hide it he had about reached the end of his endurance. He was gaining strength and getting healthier each day. But he used up a lot of energy the last two days. They hadn't worried about covering their trail. Even if they'd wanted to hide their trail, as bad as it was they could have spent a month and still would not have been able to cover their trail. A good rain would do more than they could. They built a fire and cooked their meal. Finished with their meal as they rested Star said, "We need to hunt. We are running short of food."

Matt said, "I'm sure no one is using the draw. I've seen some deer tracks. Bigger than any I've seen before."

Connie responded, "Yep, I noticed them also."

"One or two looked real fresh." Billy replied. Helen said, "I think we got enough food for another day. I would like to go on." With a look at Star as Connie saw her nod she said, "We should be good for another day. Let's go on."

About noon the next day they reached a river that came in from the west then ran south to circle back west. Star was delighted. They'd seen some buffalo which hadn't run off, but just eased away like they didn't know what to think about the intruders. Star told them that with the buffalo she would be able to tan the hides properly. Then Connie, Helen and her could make some good clothing. They had seen some elk that hadn't run off very far. Flame had gotten excited and Matt had a couple of rough moments controlling him as they saw a herd of horses. They too just drifted away in the distance over a small knoll.

They rode on taking the northern part of the river as it headed west. Riding along on the north side keeping close to it. They rode on for twelve miles then crossed over the river as it headed north again. The water was only up to their horses knees. It was fifty yards wide with slow moving water. They were drawn to a mountain point that stuck out into the valley. There was a big cliff that rose up several hundred feet above the canyon floor. It had light greens, reds and brownish colors all mixed in layers along with the grayish background of the rock face. They could see a pretty good-sized forest with mixed trees. Though twenty miles away it was a beautiful sight to them.

There was close to three hours of daylight left when they got close to the cliff. They hoped to find another cave or something for shelter to spend the winter in. Star rode her pony which put Connie back behind Matt on Flame. Both Helen and Star had seen how flushed her face was. Neither of them had any doubts as to what caused it. They both envied her. For they thought each of them would have liked being up behind Matt. Billy had seen their looks. He saw that Connie had noticed, but tried not to show it which made things worse. Billy had smiled to himself a couple of times. Then he thought that it was going to be a real interesting winter.

Star with a sudden shout of glee slid off her pony then ran a short distance and jumped a little brook. Matt along with the others dismounted to follow along after her. They had been taking in the grandeur of the mountain and had been caught off guard. When they looked toward the cliff Star had disappeared. With the horses left behind they walked toward the cliff and then jumped the brook. It was then that they noticed the steam as it gently rose above the water. When they looked to find Star they saw the cave, then Star reappeared from the caves entrance. The sun was already far to the west. They were in the deep shadows as Star showed them the happiest face they had ever seen her have since they had been together. When they were up close to her she said, "We wouldn't be able to find anyplace better than this one."

With disbelief as Matt looked around he said, "The water in that stream is hot." Star said, "Of course. There's a hot spring in the cave with a nice pool. It will be good for baths. This is a very good place." They followed Star into the cave. The main chamber was fifty feet in a circular shape with a twenty feet ceiling. The big pool was off to the right of the entrance. It was six feet deep. There were other openings that lead into some other chambers with some more springs. They were hotter than the one in the main chamber. Helen exclaimed, "Look."

Kneeling down she put her hand into the water then said, "It is real cold; too." After taking a drink she exclaimed, "Oh! It tastes real good too."

With a close look they saw that the water seeped in from the face of the rock wall. The water then ran into a natural trough a foot deep and two feet wide. The trough was three feet long as it narrowed toward the cave entrance. The overflow then ran out at a trickle on the south side of the entrance to join the little brook. When they'd looked everything over good they were pleased with their new cave and their immediate surroundings. With the daylight fading fast they went to work setting up camp.Runs Far and his braves lost Star's trail. After an intensive search without finding a single sign he called it quits. When they returned to the camp of his people he handed the reins of his pony to Has Bear Claw. He then held his head high as he walked up to his father the Chief of the Black Hawks; Strong Arm. Runs Far told him all he knew, that he was sure that Bright Star was alive and well. Then he told him of the white eyes that were probably with her. Last of all, of the man on the flaming horse that had rescued her and the other captives.

Strong Arm nodding told him of the messenger. (A story teller going from village to village unharmed and what some called the Indian telegraph.) The messenger had spoken of the White Spirit on the flaming horse. How he could kill with a look. How he had shot and not missed. Strong Arm told Runs Far the messenger said that many braves fell in battle. It was already a great honor to have fallen in battle to the White Spirit. Their medicine had gone bad. They returned to their lodges to pray and work up some big medicine to fight the White Spirit. They would be big and powerful if they were the one that was able to kill such a powerful legend.

Runs Far continued, "He will have many braves of all tribes after him now." Strong Arm replied, "Yes; as his legend travels many more will be out after the White Spirit to capture his power." Runs Far said, "May the God of his and of our people be with him then." "Yes. Sees Far has already gone off to give offerings and many prayers to the Great Spirit for his protection. Sees Far told us he's had a vision. Not very clear, but that they are well."

Runs Far asked, "He don't know where they are, then?" Strong Arm said, "No the Spirit World hasn't given him much insight right now. "We need to hunt then go to our winter camp?" Runs Far asked. Strong Arm said, "Yes. I was just waiting for your return. Sees Far told me to tell you that you didn't fail. He's sure that the Spirit World helped your sister get away from our enemies."Captain Taylor brought the wagon train to a stop at the final destination for many of them near Portland Oregon. Overall it had been a good trip he thought. They had lost a couple of wagons over a cliff on one of the mountain passes. They'd lost another at a river crossing. He wasn't happy to lose any, but knew realistically all things considered, it had been a good trip.

Dan and Tex had both showed their courage and skill. When one of the wagons had gone over Tex had just been able to catch the driver before he went over. Then Dan had to grab Tex by the legs to keep him from going over. Tex wasn't going to let go. With the help of some others they were able to pull everyone back.

Everybody was tired and wore out, but overjoyed to reach their destination. Most were busy staking out plots on a section of land using squatters' rights. Some had money to purchase land that had been improved by some investors. It was already deeded and for sale. The Gates was one family that had been able to purchase a very nice plot. It had a stream running through it with a good stand of trees. The best part was the flat land with dark rich soil. It even had a twenty acre orchid of young fruit trees. They had to construct some buildings though. They still lived out of their wagon.

The Maxton's with his people were busy building a warehouse and their own house. Chris had been able to purchase a good piece of land. It was a good place for the ships he was expecting to arrive in the spring. There was deep water right up to the bank. Then it had a slight raise of twenty feet and then leveled off. Chris bought more than he had intended. Seeing a flat place on top of the bluff that overlooked the sixty acres he was building the warehouse on. He bought another forty acres to build their house on. He intended to build a good-sized house to have room for his partners when and if they came to visit. He found out there already was a sawmill in operation and had ordered his lumber.

Mr. Saxton had made sure he would have enough money with him. That had been why they'd had the sixth wagon that Bruce Hart had driven out. It had all their guns and ammo with the most important tools and supplies along with a chest of money that had been hidden in it. The rest of the wagons had been full of hardware and windows that they were sure wouldn't be in supply yet. The ships were to have more; at least that's what they hoped. That they would be the first, to be able to supply such things. They would be able to do it cheaper than bringing everything over land.

Capt. Taylor his scouts and the cowboys had been just relaxing since they'd arrived. They helped when someone needed an extra hand, as long as they didn't have to use a hammer or axe. They refused to use anything that had a handle. None of them would ride on a wagon seat again for all the money in the world. That had been repeated by each of them since they had arrived.

There'd been a little squabble over the cowboys pay. Chris had insisted on giving them some extra over the amount they'd agreed on. The cowboys told Chris they had already been paid more than they were used to. They soon learned that Chris could be real stubborn. After a heated discussion they gave in. Right then and there if not before, they made up their minds. That if the Maxton's ever started a ranch or anything close to it they would ride clean across the country to work for them. They still planed on heading out in the spring as soon as the mountains passes cleared; to find Matt, Billy, and the girls. Just before they arrived at Portland some riders told them that they had just made it through the mountains behind them. An early storm had already filled the mountain passes. With the news they knew that going back east was out of the question for now.

At times they all had talked about the youngsters. They kept telling each other that they would be alright. More like they were trying to convince themselves than anything. The youngsters did have three who insisted that they were fine. Capt Taylor, Tex and Hawkeye stubbornly said they would be fine.

Chris Maxton sent a report back east to his partners the Saxton's. On the success of the land purchase and all of the building that was underway. He assured them that they would be ready for the ships by spring. He had mentioned there was no new news about the youngsters. But did have high hopes that they were well. That's what he wrote even though he was not so sure of it himself. His wife was still pretty sure, but he had noticed that nobody mentioned their names anymore.

Coming over the trail had been rougher then he had thought it would be. Chris realized they had been real lucky not to have lost more than they had. For all of that when the Indians had them surrounded, they all had been sure that they would be lucky if anyone survived. Capt Taylor and Hawkeye couldn't explain why the next day after Matt had ridden out the Indians had disappeared. Valerie and Mrs. Grace Mc bane had been sure Matt would take care of the others then catch up with them. When that hadn't happened they were sure the only thing that delayed them was that Matt was badly hurt. That being the case they were all in jeopardy. They tried to stay hopeful, but it didn't look good.

Chris had seen that Matt was not just tough. He was more capable than anybody he had seen. Even compared to the men he'd met along the way. He'd had some on his crew. Tex was nobody to mess with and the rest of the cowboys could hold their own. Chris thought Capt Taylor for as calm as he was, would be like running into a tornado once you got him stirred up.

In the short time they'd been out west. Chris, Valerie, and the rest of his group that had come from New York City had won the respect of the others. But Matt had stood out above everybody on the whole wagon train. Matt in the time he had been on the wagon train was all ready being compared to some of the most dangerous people that were already legendary. Some had already died and a few still lived.

Hawkeye had finely told them what Matt had done in the fights with the Indians. Most anyone that had been close enough to see stated that they'd never seen anybody shoot as accurately as Matt did. Dan had been heard to say once; he doubted there was anybody faster than Matt. He had received some confused looks, but didn't expand any. So as Chris balanced everything out he was very happy with their progress. But he did have a deep sadness in his heart.

Randolph Saxton had had a real good day. He'd had a good meeting with some of the contractors he supplied. He was able to confirm that his suppliers had the products made and had been shipped to arrive on time. It looked like things were going as good if not better than ever. It was going to be a real profitable year. Even with the expense of the enterprise they had invested in out west. With it being Friday, he was looking forward to a pleasant weekend. He was glad he hadn't checked his mail till after the meeting. His sons had gotten the rest of the mail pertaining to their business. Randolph could tell that the writing on the envelope was Chris Maxton's and addressed to him personally. Upon spotting it he had a bad feeling and made sure it was the last one he opened. He was sure it had something to do with Matt.

So, as he opened it he wondered what kind of trouble Matt had gotten into now. As he read it his heart went up into his throat. With a lump in his throat so bad he could hardly speak, he told his secretary to cancel any appointments he had. That he didn't want to be disturbed. Not even by his sons. He reread the letter several times to make sure he had a clear understanding of everything. Matt had always gotten the best of him. Matt was always able to get under his skin. Matt was as intelligent as anybody he knew. Hs just couldn't get Matt interested in the business. Not only that, he knew Matt could have gone to any of the best colleges to be a doctor, lawyer or anything. But it had seemed like all Matt wanted to do was run around. He didn't seem to have a care in the world for anything.

It had been right after Matt had gone west that he'd found out Matt hadn't been where he was suppose to have been. Matter of fact it was learned that Connie Maxton had been his study companion. They had skipped classes and weren't at their friends' houses studying like they had been told. Come to find out the servants had been covering up for them for a long time between the two households. There excuse was that they hadn't gotten into a lot of trouble. So they hadn't seen a lot of harm in it. Somehow they'd both been able to keep their marks up it seemed. Both his wife and Connie's mother had never told him or Chris Maxton about the tardiness of either Connie or Matt.

Yes, he had to admit that Matt had a wild streak in him. That Mark and Michael had gotten so they didn't mess with Matt. He knew until they got to a certain age that they had for one reason or another ganged up on Matt and there had been several fights. To Matt's credit he had never told or cried. But Matt never ran from them either. Thinking back he thought maybe that was why the servants had let Matt get away with so much. He did admit he was proud of Matt. He just wanted Matt to be much more than what he was. Now, with another glance at the letter, he was afraid that would never happen. Not only that, he thought he hadn't let Matt know that he really did love him.

He dreaded going home. It wasn't going to be the weekend he had looked forward to just a short hour ago. He knew it was going to be the hardest thing he'd ever had to do in his life. He knew he had to let Ann read the letter. He was sure Ann would take it hard and probably Meaghan the worst of all of them. Meaghan thought the sun rose and fell with Matt. As far as that went his wife Ann had always held Matt as her favorite. Oh, she made sure to show no favors. But, everyone in the household had known. Randolph then thought to Matt's credit he didn't take advantage of it. Maybe Randolph thought that was why Mark and Michael had been so rough on Matt. He looked at his watch and saw the time. Deep in his thoughts he'd let the afternoon slip by and it was time to go home. It was a few minutes early and as he walked out he told the secretary to have one of the administrators lock up. He stopped just long enough at each of his sons office to tell them it was time to go home, that he'd hail a carriage for their ride home. They had given him strange looks, but he had gone on before they had a chance to question him.

They quickly stopped their work, and then went after their father. When they got to the street their father had a carriage waiting for them. Mark asked, "What has happened? You closed your office and cancelled all your appointments. You didn't even want to see us."

Randolph answered, "It will have to wait till we get home. I'm only going to go through it once. Sorry, but that's how it's going to be."

Both of the brothers saw their father's stern look, along with something else. So they kept quiet; they knew something serious had happened. When they got to their home and walked up the steps to their place Jim Fallon the head butler welcomed them and took their hats and coats. Mark and Michael said hello. They got a strange look from Jim. They just shrugged their shoulders. Their father hadn't said a thing to Jim which had never happened before.

Randolph on his way to the study spotted Jessie Fallon, the head mistress in charge of the house. He told her to get all the family together in the dining room. Then he went on to the study and poured himself a full glass of whiskey. He didn't drink much and had it for his guests more than anything. He was glad to have it tonight though and took a couple of good swallows then went on to the dining room.

Mark and Michael had gone on ahead to the dining room and sat down. Randolph glanced at them as he went to the head of the table and sat down. In a little bit the rest of the family started coming in one at a time. Seeing the mood they sat down without saying a word. Margaret came in and as she sat down next to Mark, her husband. She asked, "What is going on?"

"I don't know yet. Just be patient."

Margaret said, "Well, I don't know what could be so urgent. Mrs. Fallon told us that she thought it was urgent."

Mark poked her a little with his elbow, into her ribs as he said, "S-h...." Margaret's temper rose, but she did stay quiet. Coming from another part of the house Meaghan Saxton, Randolph's daughter, then

Ann arrived and sat down. Betty Green one of the servants came in and put each one's favorite drink in front of them. Then seeing that Randolph already had one she returned to the kitchen with his. Most of them liked lemonade. Ann liked hot tea and a couple of them liked water.

Randolph looked quickly around and noticed that the help had come and was standing in the doorway. Randolph said, "You may as well come in and listen also." He motioned for the servants to come on in. Soon all of them were in the room. It was very quiet and for once Margaret didn't say anything. This was the first time anything like this had happened. After Randolph saw that everyone was attentive he took another swallow of his drink then reached into his pocket and removed the letter. He paused and then read it to them. If possible, it got quieter. When he finished he was sweating. He wiped his brow with his handkerchief and took another swallow of his drink a big one.

Meaghan with her voice trembling said, "He's alright. He's got to be! Maybe he just got lost and didn't make it back to them. He's probably at some fort or town." Ann had taken the letter and read through it quickly. Then with her voice calm but strained said, "I'm sure Matt's alive. I think I'd feel a hole in my heart if Matt was dead. I don't. Somehow he's still alive. Meaghan the letter states that Matt must have gotten hurt not lost. That's why he didn't catch up with the wagon train."

Mark said, "Well it sounds like their depending a lot on an Indian to tell the truth." Randolph cut in, "Chris would have made sure of any information he sent, so as not to mislead us."

Jessie Fallon said, "Oh the poor dears. They got to be terrified. It must be rough on them. Oh, I do hope they are well."

Margaret frustrated, said, "All this fuss and everyone upset. And no one even knows if he is hurt or anything. Maybe he just wanted to have some company." Sue Saxton Michael's wife, with a wonder in her voice said, "Margaret, you should be ashamed of yourself. If you had listened, you'd know that Matt was somehow able to rescue the girls and the boy away from the Indians."

Margaret seeing the stern looks from Ann and Meaghan kept quiet. She hadn't seen the look her father-in-law had given her though. For Mark had elbowed her again; afraid she'd say something else. Michael thinking out loud with concern in his voice said, "Well I'm not giving up. I will believe he's alive until somebody with some facts tells me different. Besides if I know Matt he'd be awfully hard to kill."

Ann, Meaghan and Mrs. Fallon all nodded at Michael as they wiped tears off of their cheeks. Most of them tried to hide the tears that had appeared in their eyes.

Mark asked, "What I wonder, is what he was doing out riding as a scout anyway? Randolph said, "I'm sure he was doing a good job or the wagon master wouldn't have had him doing so. Remember, from his business report Chris told us the fellow was real good."

Ann said, "We should tell the Socket's and Chan's. You know that they think a lot of Connie and Matt too." Randolph exclaimed, "Damn! I forgot. Yes, I'll have to tell them. I had hoped I wouldn't have to repeat it again." Michael said, "Sir I'll do that for you." Randolph asked, "Are you sure? I should. But, I would sure appreciate it." Michael said, "Yes. It'll be alright. Somehow I think it will help me to get closer to Matt."

Meaghan her voice a little stronger said, "Michael I'll go with you. I think it'll help me too."

They solemnly broke off into small groups. The servants mixed in with them, as they tried to console one another. For the most part they spoke in hushed tones. Quite informally they settled down to pick at the food that had already been prepared. Only Margaret ate as much as she usually did.

The next day as Meaghan and Michael Saxton rode the train out to the Socket's, both were quiet with their own thoughts. None of the household had eaten much the last two meals except for Margaret, Mark's wife. Meaghan knew that Margaret had never liked Matt. But she hadn't thought that Margaret would be so cold-hearted. Meaghan had seen that her father had noticed Margaret's attitude. She was glad he'd never given her any of the looks that he had giving Margaret. Michael carried the letter. They thought it would be easier than trying to remember all the details. Randolph had told them that Mr. Socket would probably want all the details.

Upon reaching the station Michael waved for a carriage; the driver knew of the Socket place. After they had climbed in and sat down he guided his horse out of town. When they arrived at the Socket's, Vern and his son James were working with a young horse in a small corral. Vern had spotted them and as the carriage came to a stop he spoke to James. James released the horse, which gave a little snort as it went to stand off in the far corner.

As Michael helped Meaghan down from the carriage Vern and James had slipped through the railings. As they came up they tipped their hats to Meaghan as they cheerfully welcomed them. Vern said, "It's nice to see you. James and I needed a break anyway. Let's go in and get some coffee. By the look of your faces I think I'll add something to it."

Vern had noticed the grief on their faces. But it was what he had seen in their eyes, that had turned his stomach. As they stepped on the porch to enter into the house Mrs. Socket with Diane by her side opened the door. They both welcomed their surprise visitors.

Betsy saw her husband's eyes. She turned to Diane and told her to set out some cups and plates and some of the cookies they had just pulled out of the oven. Betsy escorted Meaghan and Michael to the table. She told them to sit as she went to help Diane saying, "Coffee will be right up, unless you want something else?"   Meaghan and Michael told her that coffee would be just fine. Neither of them were coffee drinkers, but thought it might be good today. They didn't want to put Mrs. Socket to work just to fix something different for them either. Meaghan thought as she sat down. That this household had responded much like theirs had. Neither Michael nor she had told them anything yet. But they knew something serious was up. It was quiet as if they were waited for a bombshell to drop.

Diane had put out cups and plates then a large plate of cookies. Mrs. Socket poured the coffee. When she had filled all the cups she put the pot back on the stove. Then with Vern's cup she took it to him where he stood against the doorway to the kitchen. Vern sipped his coffee a couple of times. He looked at it, then as he held it out he said, "Betsy I'm sorry. Just whiskey if you would please."

She returned to the cupboard got a small glass and filled it. She took it to him, than sat down as Vern took a good sip. Then in a drawl that Meaghan and Michael almost didn't understand Vern said, "I'm ready to ride your bronco."

Michael not comprehending just looked. Then Meaghan just as Mrs. Socket started to explain said, "Oh! Michael gives Mr. Socket the letter." Michael as he understood, took the letter from his inside coat pocket. He stood, went to Vern and handed it to him. Then said, "I'm Sorry sir." Vern took it looked at it hard for a couple of seconds. He walked to Betsy then handed it to her as he said, "Betsy you can read better. If you would, please read it to us."

Betsy was in tears by the time she had finished reading the letter. Meaghan after hearing it read the second time, finely broke down into tears and cried. Diane tears in her eyes got up and hugged Meaghan around the neck. Then she said, "They're alright. They got to be. They are like family. I love them both. Oh, I know they are okay."

Mrs. Socket, seeing their distress got up and held her arms out. Meaghan unashamed with Diane stood and went into her arms. Michael with his heart in his throat, was like Meaghan. After hearing the letter being read for the second time, he had less hope then he originally had had. As he looked at James he was sure that James's eyes were misty. He glanced at Mr. Socket and quickly looked away. He'd never seen so much fire in anyone's eyes. It looked like Mr. Socket was ready to spring off in any direction. His father had picked up on how much the Sockets thought of Connie and Matt. He now realized how well they were loved by all of the Sockets. Michael heard Vern clear his throat. Then he chanced a look at him. He saw a controlled stern look on Vern's face. Vern said, "I'm not much to talk. But let me tell you how I see it. I do think Matt probably got hurt. James can testify how instinctive Matt is with directions and distance. Second if Strong Arm sent some of his people out to look for someone it had to be a special person. If I remember right Runs Far is his son. It probably was a woman. If so and she was being held captive. Matt would have rescued her also."

After a short pause Vern continued, "The Reason I'm telling you all of this is that she would know how to take care of them and hide them. Also she should be able to get Matt back on his feet and healthy. Capt Taylor and the others are honest. I'm sure they wouldn't pass on any information that wasn't true or let false statements be passed on."

They all looked at Mr. Socket with fresh hope in their eyes. Diane wiped some tears from her eyes, then said, "Oh father. Do you really think so?" Betsy used her handkerchief to wipe some tears off her face then choked out, "I think maybe your dad is right. Vern you could always think things out better then anyone I know. After hearing you, it does make sense. Meaghan looked into Mr. Socket's eyes and asked, "Do you really believe it?"

Vern nodding his head answered, "Yes. Not saying Matt didn't get hurt. I think that's the only reason they would be late. I'm sure if anything else happened Matt would have gotten them back."

James a little cautious, but with some cheerfulness in his voice said, "I think my father has figured it out about right. I can see how he's thinking." With more assurance in his voice Vern said, "I'm sure I'm right. If Matt was dead the Indian maiden would have found her people. So, I really do think they had to find a place to hole up in, to give Matt a chance to mend."Betsy added, "Oh! That does make sense."

Then Vern with a hard look at Meaghan and Michael to be sure he had their full attention said, "I don't know how well you really know your brother. But I can tell you that Matt is the most dangerous person I know. He is peerless as far as speed and accuracy with his guns. I've seen him and Connie practice what he calls Ninja moves. I just can't see him going under very easy. So if he was hurt bad. I can tell you there had to be a lot of them. He would be awful hard to kill."

James excitedly said, "Yeah that's for sure. I've seen him up close. Father told me he felt like Matt held back some so as not to show off. Vern laughed as he said, "Yep I think so." Then getting serious he said, "It won't hurt to keep them in our prayers though. They still may not be out of the woods yet." They talked awhile then the Saxton's went out to their waiting carriage. Meaghan and Michael both felt a lot better than they had when they had arrived at the Sockets. They had a fresh new hope building in their chest thanks to the Sockets.

Their visit with the Chan's went much like their visit with the Socket's had. Su Chan had read the letter. She had spoke in Chinese to translate it for her family. After she finished Meaghan and Michael explained what Mr. Socket had told them. After a few minutes as each of them discussed the letter Lee Chan told them that he was in agreement with Mr. Socket. When they returned home they told their family about what they had learned. There was a cautious hope through the whole household now.

It was now the middle of October. They all had been busy in the large valley. They had walled up the entrance to the cave with flat stones and mudded the joints. They'd found some stone they'd been able to make into useful tools. They'd even scrapped out a couple of wood bowls sort of. The tools helped with digging the roots and wild onions.

Matt copied Star's handy work to make his own bow along with some arrows. He was out a lot now and doing most of the hunting. Matt had a good part of his strength back now. He was sure he was in good enough shape that they could leave now. Star had pointed out to him that snow probably had the high passes full. That they were low enough so that winter would come later to the hidden valley. Matt was getting well enough that he was quite restless.

He only killed enough to keep a fresh supply of meat on hand. It was getting cold enough that the meat would stay cool enough not to spoil. The next day or two they planned to kill enough game to get them through the winter. Not that game was scarce. But so they wouldn't have to be out in the winter chill that would come later. The girls had been able to tan only enough doeskins to make some leather skirts. Matt did have a pair of buckskin pants now. Well sort of; the pants only came down to his knees. The girls worked on a pair for Billy now. For what was left of his dungarees after many washings in the river along with the normal wear enabled one, to nearly be able to see through them. The girls promised the next thing they would make would be some blouses.

Their skirts helped a bit. But the girls weren't real careful when they were busy. Matt noticed many times when their skirts had ridden up their legs especially when they bent over to retrieve something. They unconsciously would completely expose themselves at times. He thought he'd get use to it after awhile. But it got worse if anything. He noticed that Billy spent a lot of time doing something away from the girls as they worked.

To make things even worse if it could be, all the girls had been given him knowing looks. Like he was welcome to whatever he wanted. Then when he made the mistake of looking directly into their eyes he'd get a flash of lightning that jolted his entire body. Then he had to walk away quickly to keep from embarrassing himself. For at those times he didn't feel like a gentleman at all.

Matt had spent a lot of time around the wild horse herd. They'd become used to him. He was sure in the next few days he would be able to start single ling out one or two to make friends with. Once they became friends he was confident it would be easy to train them. He'd kept a sharp eye on Flame. To make sure he didn't run off. Matt thought he could get Flame to come to him if he needed to, but was afraid Flame might get hurt or killed if he got into a fight with one of the other stallions.

They had used one bullet to kill a buffalo. Star told them that the buffalo would give her a lot of things she could use. She wanted the hide as well as the meat. That was what was keeping them busy the last couple of days. The weather had stayed cool and if it stayed as it was. The meat wouldn't spoil. Billy with the axe Star had stolen had been cutting wood for their fire. That's all Star and the girls let Matt and Billy do around camp. Star had convinced the girls that taking care of the camp was women's work; not for the men to do unless they were slaves. They decided to kill only enough to get them through the winter. They needed the hides more than the meat, so they could make some more clothing.

Matt had found a good sized flat piece of slate that he carried back to the cave. When they had questioned him what it was for, he told them after the snow came they would practice their reading and writing. Star doubtful had shook her head and told them it would be too hard. Matt told her she could learn. That she already spoke good English. She could learn the other things too. Connie had thought it a good idea. Matt had at least one on his side. Matt had pretty much caught up with the others as far as speaking in the Black Hawk language.

They had relaxed the last couple of days. After what few chores that had to be done each of them had gone off on their own. To do whatever they wanted or just to have time for their own private thoughts. Each of them found their own little place to spend the time alone. Mostly in the sun while it was still warm knowing there wouldn't be many more days that they'd be able to. The little separation had been good for all of them. To get a handle on their own thoughts and get some things squared away in there own minds.

That night there was a cool crisp bite to the air. Star assured them it was time to kill what game they'd need. With the return of Matt's strength his appetite had grown to. Billy had gone into a growing spurt also. They decided that even with the buffalo they had killed they could also use another four or five deer. They went to bed a little early as the next day would keep all of them busy.

The next day Matt was able to stalk three deer. He brought them back on one of the Indian ponies. It was all most not fair. The deer were pretty tame and didn't run off far. It did help that he used a bow and arrow instead of a gun. He'd ridden out on Flame away from the cave. He was doing so to keep from driving the game away that was close by, so if needed they'd have some game close to home. It hadn't taken him long before he had gotten to know the valley in the area real good. He'd been going out farther and farther too different places whenever the time permitted him each day. Billy had done the same the last few days. Matt had convinced him that he had enough firewood. So, Billy had been going out to see the sights. The girls had stated as soon as they got their work caught up they wanted to look things over also.

Matt's luck was still with him the next day. He'd gotten two more deer before noon. He had cleaned them out and taken them back to camp. They still had just the one knife. Matt ate while the girls worked at skinning them. They hadn't finished yet when Matt took his last bit. After a good drink Matt said, "Billy I'm going to the north for six or seven miles. I am sure that I saw some deer up that way. When they get done you can ride up that way with the knife. I think the girls could use another doeskin."

Helen decided to tease Matt, she got up from helping the others. On her way to the cave she walked a little closer to Matt then she had to. She paused long enough to lean toward Matt a little as she said, "It sounds like the great white hunter is getting awful sure of himself."

With a will of their own Matt's eyes became glued on her beautiful firm breasts. It took a little time before he realized what she had said. Matt then glanced at the others and saw that they'd been watching. His face turned a bright red. His loincloth was high in the air. He got up turned in the direction Flame was and followed it to Flame and climbed aboard. He grabbed the reins of the Indian pony that had been ground-tied. He had been using the pony for a pack animal. His voice was thick with emotion as he said over his shoulder riding off, "Just luck as much as anything."

He heard their giggles behind him, just as he was about out of hearing. Matt was uneasy with the praise. Was really uneasy with Helen's little display and especially the way it had affected him.

CHAPTER FIFTEEN

THE GRIZZLY

A couple of hours later Matt had made a clean kill on a big bull elk. It had taken the best part of an hour to sneak up on him. To make sure of a good shot with the bow and arrow. The deer had moved on somewhere. When he had spotted the elk he'd been determined to get him. After making sure of his kill he returned to Flame and got the Indian pony. He led them back to within sight of the elk. He left Flame there as Flame didn't like the smell of the blood. As he led the pony up to the elk. He heard the trotting hoofs of Billy's pony. He gave a loud whistle. Not the one he reserved just for Flame. He wanted to make sure that he never confused him. Matt dropped the reins of the mare thirty yards from the fresh kill. The mare had gotten pretty well accustomed to the smell.

As Billy rode in closer Matt looked back through the woods of poplar and oak, they were in. It was then that he saw it was Star and not Billy who rode up. He stood and watched as she rode up. He couldn't get his eyes off her. She was as graceful as anyone he'd ever seen. She was beautifully trim and muscular without being bulky. Her black hair offset her reddish tan body to perfection.

As the pony trotted up it made her breasts bounce. It was driving him nuts. He felt his makeshift breech cloth start to rise. He forced his eyes away. He got the reins of the mare to take her closer to the elk. Star slide of her pony than fell in step with Matt as she lead her pony. They tied their ponies to a tree just a few feet from the elk. Star with the knife still cut the elk's juggler vein so it could bleed out good. When it had, Star preceded to clean the elk out. Matt helped by rolling him whichever way Star needed. Star as she worked told him that it was a very good kill. That they'd have a lot of good hides they could use to make some more clothing.

Shameful of what he was doing while he held or moved the elk to make her work easier. He couldn't stop his eyes from watching every move she made. She didn't waste a one. But as she worked her makeshift skirt climbed up her legs. He didn't miss a thing as she squatted to cut push or pull the elk's innards out. Matt sure he saw some moisture, drop off of Star's lips. The lips between her legs, he felt himself go hard. Somehow with a great effort Matt had a thought about the elk. It would be very difficult for them to get the elk up onto the pony. His voice thick with emotion Matt asked, "Do you think it would be a good idea to quarter the elk and take half of it back to the camp at a time." Matt spoke in her language. She paused from her work. With a smile already starting on her face as she looked up. From where she squatted she had no problem seeing Matt's aroused condition. As she looked into Matt's eyes in her language with her voice thick with desire Star said, "Yes I think that's a good idea."

With her eyes directed straight up at him they had flashed with brilliant sparks that shot right through him. A hellish roar right behind him put Matt into instant action. Star's eyes drawn to the roar screamed like no Indian was supposed to. In a flash Matt grabbed the knife from Star. He spun took a step forward and leaped high into the air. Matt had moved so quickly that Star fell back on her bare bottom as all thought of her skirt was gone. She'd been startled by Matt's whirlwind movement as much as she had been by the biggest grizzly bear she'd ever heard of let alone seen.

The grizzly now stood on his hind feet. Star saw Matt crash into the grizzly's chest. He'd been just quick enough to get inside the grizzly's sweeping paw. Matt plunged the knife in as his left hand grabbed a handful of fur to hold himself tight against the grizzly's chest. The grizzly roared louder than ever. While Matt repeatedly stabbed the grizzly. Star couldn't see his hand. Because of the blood and fur that was flying off the grizzly's chest as well as from the speed of Matt's hand. As Matt kept up his attack, the grizzly finally realized that Matt was clinging to him like a tick. The grizzly with one front leg held Matt pined against his chest. With his jaws he reached down to clamp onto Matt's left shoulder. Meanwhile with his other front paw the grizzly had already taken three swipes at Matt. One across his shoulders one across the back of his legs with the third one across Matt's fanny. The grizzly's claws had made deep gashes but hadn't torn off any big chunks of muscle because Matt had stayed tight against the grizzly's chest. The grizzly staggered as his jaws started to clamp onto Matt's shoulder. Blood covered Matt now and was all over the front of the grizzly. The blood poured out of a huge hole in the grizzly's chest. With a better look Star was sure Matt had just about cut the grizzly's heart out. Suddenly the grizzly fell forward on top of Matt.

Transfixed by the fierceness of the scene Star watched the grizzly closely as she got up off the ground. She didn't see any movement from the grizzly or Matt. She'd never seen such a fierce battle or anybody with as much determination and courage as Matt. On her feet Star's mind quickly cleared from the trance like state she'd been in. Cautiously she rushed up to the grizzly to help Matt. He was pinned underneath the grizzly. The top part of Matt's head was all she could see. She paused a second as the grizzly let out a big gasp of air then she saw tremors run through its body. Then in earnest she went on toward the grizzly. The grizzly was huge and she knew Matt had to be in danger of being crushed. Star took the final step then pushed on the grizzly's shoulder tentatively. Star then lowered her shoulder against the grizzly and pushed with all of her strength. The grizzly hardly moved.

It had been about thirty seconds since Matt and the grizzly had crashed to the ground. Star took a deep breath and started to push again. Then she heard thundering hooves rush up. She looked up as Flame flew straight at them to kicking up dirt and stone as he slid to a stop three or four feet away. Flame snorted and stomped his feet. Then sniffed Matt's head. Nervously Flame took the last step to brush Star aside a little. Flame put his head against the grizzly's shoulder and pushed. Amazed Star put all her strength into a big shove along with Flame. To her relief the grizzly started to roll.

When the largest part of the grizzlies body rolled past its left leg and shoulder. The grizzlies own weight rolled him on over. The weight of the grizzly's right leg had held Matt tight against his chest. The grizzly's leg even started to lift Matt up off the ground. Matt's weight was enough though and Matt dropped to the ground. Star's heart went up into her throat. Matt hadn't moved. Then she heard a rush of air as it escaped from the grizzly. Just a couple seconds later she heard a gasp as air filled Matt's lungs. Matt was already pale, but his chest moved with his breathing now.

Matt was unconscious and it didn't look like he would be coming to any time soon. Star dragged him a body length away from the grizzly. Then rolling him over she gasped as she saw the damage the grizzly had done. Flame still nervous of the grizzly, stayed close by. Star went to him and got the canteen. She made a mud pack and rubbed it into Matt's wounds to stop the blood from leaking out of him. After she had slowed the flow of blood from most of Matt's wounds she took her makeshift skirt off. Getting the knife that had fell from Matt's hand. She made some holes in the skirt then cut four strips off of it. Using the stripes of leather she tied the skirt as tight as she could to cover Matt's lower back and fanny to compress the torn flesh tight to stop the flow of blood. She'd done as much as she could with what she had. The grizzly had bitten deep into Matt's shoulder though. It looked like the grizzly had bitten him nearly to the bone. Matt's arm was still intact though. The grizzly hadn't had time to tear it off.

Star looked around as Flame stepped up. He nickered softly as he sniffed Matt. Star rubbed Flame's gallant nose realizing he was worried about Matt. It appeared that he loved Matt as much as any human would. Star got up with the canteen and left Flame with Matt as she went in search of water. After a few minutes she found a little stream running through the area. She filled the canteen and returned to Matt. She made sure he was breathing alright and that he hadn't turned his face into the dirt. Star couldn't move Matt by herself. She hoped the Indian ponies had returned to camp when they'd broken free at the sound of the grizzly's roar. She hadn't turned to look, but she'd heard them leave. Star checked Matt wounds again. She found one that bled too much. She made, some more mud with some of the water from the canteen then patched it up better. When she heard a whistle she replied with her own. Directed by Star's whistle she soon spotted Billy, Helen and Connie as they rode up. Billy spotted Flame first then the grizzly. He realized then what had caused the ponies to break their reins and return to camp. With the ponies held to a walk the last few feet. Billy was finely able to pull his eyes off of the mountain of fur. Staring at the blood that covered Star's body. Billy instantly blushed as he realized his eyes had taken in the forbidden fruit of her nakedness. Billy jerked his eyes away. He started to ask where Matt was. As he spotting Matt he exclaimed, "Damn! How bad is he?" Star answered, "Very bad. We need to get him back to camp so I can make up some medicine to care for him."

Connie finally able to get her eyes off the grizzly as she looked at Matt said, "Oh my. Not again I cannot take much more." Her expression was full of stress. Helen with her voice full of wonder said, "Oh why? I don't think I can go, through all of the worrying again." Her expression was nearly a match with Connie's Star said, "Billy we need the axe so we can cut poles to make a traverse."

Billy spun his pony around and rode off. Connie and Helen slid off the other pony. Then with Star's instructions they took the knife and cut their skirts into strips to tie the poles together to make a traverse for Matt to lie on. They would need a long one to go over one of the pony's back. When done while they waited for Billy to return they went to work to finish dressing out the elk. As they started on the grizzly Star said, "Good. Now we have enough meat and a good hide for a warm blanket." Her face was with an expression of stern determination like she had some blame of the situation.

Neither Connie nor Helen replied. Sick with anguish for Matt they just did as Star directed them to do. When Billy returned with a quick glance at the girls he slid off his pony to cut a couple of long poles then a couple of short ones. They tied them together then rigged the traverse to the pony that Matt had used to carry the meat on. After laying Matt on the traverse, they decided Star and Helen would take Matt back. Billy and Connie would finish cleaning out the grizzly then skin the elk and quarter it. Then do the same with the grizzly.

Flame followed along behind Matt as Helen led the pony while Star walked along beside Matt; on the traverse. With concern all over their faces Connie and Billy watched till they were out of sight. In an hour with the help of the axe they had the elk quartered. Billy then told Connie to go retrieve the pony with the traverse. They would put the meat on it. He would work on the grizzly while she was gone. When Connie returned, Billy asked, "How is Matt doing?"

"I don't know. I didn't go inside."

Billy made no comment. He'd heard the stress in Connie's voice. They loaded half of the elk on the traverse. Then Billy led the pony with the traverse as Connie followed along behind. With the use of the three Indian ponies they made three trips. The last trip they'd been able to get only a quarter of the grizzly on the traverse. It was enough to put a real strain on it. Billy and Connie had all they could do to hang the grizzly quarter up in what they now called the cool cave. The cool cave was close to twenty degrees cooler than any of the others. They didn't know why. But it was excellent for storing the meat.

While Billy took care of the Indian ponies Connie unsaddled Flame. It was close to dark. They'd have to get the rest of the grizzly tomorrow. Billy and Connie went to the river to wash most of the blood off them. Helen had heard them and came out with her eyes full of tears saying, "I have never seen anyone tore up so bad."

Connie took a deep breath then went into the cave. Star had been busy. From time to time when ever she had spotted them Star had gathered her medical herbs. So all she had to do was crush and mix them. Star and Helen had carefully cleaned Matt up. Then Star had rubbed her medicine into his wounds. Star looking up to see Connie then she said, "I need the knife to cut some loose skin off. Matt has some places that will never draw back together. They will heal better if I cut the shredded pieces off." Connie asked, "Will it make him bleed more?" "Yes, he's lost a lot of blood again. But as long as it's not too much it will be good for Matt to bleed. The bear's claws probably had rotten meat along with some other things that could cause a lot of infection."

Star worked for an hour. She had cut then sewed. She used the bone needle she had gotten from the buffalo they had butchered. Matt's shoulder was the worse. His lower back and fanny had been clawed up pretty good. The back of his thighs had been clawed only an inch deep. Matt had been awful lucky with the bite wound. Even though it was deep the grizzly with a couple of more seconds would probably have torn Matt's shoulder off.

The others had done as Star directed as they watched her handy work. They kept busy to cover up their concern as much as they could. Luckily Matt hadn't regained consciousness while Star had doctored him. He had moaned and groaned a few times. Even stirred a little bit, but hadn't woken up. The others had gotten cleaned up. Star done with her doctoring went to the hot pool, and bathed. It had gotten dark out by then. Helen and Connie had started preparing their meal. Billy made a trip outside to get some firewood reported that it had gotten pretty cool.

Matt started to stir. Then let out a groan he turned his head far enough to see Connie. He asked, "Is Star alright." Connie said, "Yes Matt she didn't get a scratch. You need to be still so you don't open up your wounds." Matt said, "I'd like some water." Helen close by doing some cleaning went to the water trough then returned with a bowl of cool water and put it down under his chin. Laying on his stomach he sucked the water till he'd almost emptied the bowl, they'd hollowed out of a piece of wood. They could see that it hurt him terribly every time he moved. Even if it was just a little bit. Helen went to refill the bowl. Matt asked, "How bad is it?" then continued, "I feel like he tore all the hide off my back."

Close by Star said, "Some are real deep. The wounds aren't as bad as they could've been. Infection is what's going to be bad. It would have been better if you'd been shot.

Helen spoke before she thought. She said, "Why do you want him shot." Star said, 'I don't. Bullet wounds don't fester as bad as wounds from an animal." Helen said, "OH! I'm sorry. I just don't see why Matt has to keep getting hurt." Matt said, "I'm hungry I'd like something to eat."

Connie used the knife to cut up the meat for Matt. She placed each piece in his mouth when he was ready. He had eaten good which they were thankful for. Matt fell asleep shortly after he had another drink of water. All the water Star could persuade him too drink.

The next morning Billy and Connie went out to retrieve the rest of the grizzly. Star and Helen stretched the elk hide out along beside the deer hides to dry and cure. They kept checking on Matt. When he woke up with the help of Star and Helen he had been able to get up and make it outside to relieve himself. They'd gotten a little embarrassed. But with Matt being so sore and weak he needed their help. Back inside, he'd eaten well again. Star kept at him to drink as much water as he could.

With Helen's help Star got Matt into the pool of the hot spring. Star assured them that it would help Matt to heal. As they helped Matt they could see his face was flushed. Matt's skin had already started to warm up. Because of it Star didn't keep him in the pool very long. But she wanted to get the use of what minerals there was in the water. When they'd helped Matt back to his bed Star rubbed her mixture of medical herbs into his wounds as Matt moaned in torment.

That afternoon Matt had broken out into a sweat. Star used the knife as she checked each of his wounds. She used it to scrape away any puss she found. She opened up a couple of his wounds so they would bleed a little. They had been full of puss. For the most part most of the wounds had done pretty good. The bite wounds had become a problem though. Every two hours Star checked each and every wound. Cleaned and doctored them. Matt's fever finely broke on the third day. Star hoped she wouldn't have to heat the knife to a cherry red to cauterize the festered puncture wounds from the grizzly's teeth to get rid of the poisonous puss.

That evening pale and weak Matt had regained consciousness. He was real thirsty. He drank a lot then went back to sleep. That night as they quietly talked they felt some relief. It had been touch and go for Matt. Star told them she was sure that Matt would be alright now. Helen said, "Yeah until he gets hurt again."

Billy said, "Well! It's tuff to see him hurt. But we all know that we're proud of him and wouldn't want Matt to be any different." Connie said, "One thing I'm not going to do is to be without a gun from now on." Connie gave Star a look before she continued, "Don't take this the wrong way Star. But that's twice now that I haven't had a gun handy. And Matt's gotten hurt because of it."

Star asked, "Why would I take that the wrong way. But I do wonder how you could see and shoot from here to where the grizzly was when it attacked us."

Connie had spoken her thoughts out loud not realizing it. It took her a second to recall what had been said. As comprehension came to her she said, "Oh I'm sorry. I didn't realize that I'd spoke out loud. What I think is that all of us should carry a gun." Helen commented, "All the time." Connie said, "Yes! Or at least have one within reach."

Billy said, "Guess we did get awfully relaxed. It has been so peaceful here though."

Star said, "Yes. After all the danger we'd been in before we got here. It has been very pleasant not to have to be on watch all the time. Connie said, "Yes. But from now on I think we need to be armed. We've seen what happens when we're not. So far Matt has been the one who has suffered because we haven't."

Before anyone else spoke Connie continued, "Star you and the rest should know. I blame myself for Matt getting hurt. I could feel that we were being watched just before we were captured. But I just thought it was me, for we were sure that everything was secure."

Billy said, "No! If it was anybody's fault it was mine. I was sent to guard you and I messed up. I never knew they were there until it was to late. I should have. It was my job." Helen said, "Well that's behind us. Besides one good thing has come out of it. We've gotten to meet and know Star.

Billy said, "Yes that's what's kept me from being a real sour puss. Also Matt has never said or hinted that he blamed any of us." Connie said, "He never will either." Star said, "I'm glad also. I've gotten to like all of you too." Billy laughed and they all looked at him. When Billy hadn't said anything, all the girls together then asked, "What?" Billy decided to just say what he had thought. He said, "Seeing everybody is being so friendly. I was just wondered when Matt finely makes his choice. If you'll still be so friendly. I can see that you all love him." Each of them had started to speak. But then they stopped to look at each other. The girls had blushed a little and then smiled at each other. Star after she had heard it spoken out loud admitted to herself that Billy had spoken the truth. Star then said, "Maybe Matt won't have to choose."

Billy laughed again. With a look to make sure Matt hadn't been awakened he said, "Matt hasn't said anything, but I can see that he loves each one of you."

Even though it was cold outside the cave was kept warm from the heat of the hot spring. They didn't need a fire except to cook with. To change the subject Star said, "I'm good with a riffle. But I've never had anything to do with the pistols."

Connie said, "It's a good time to start then. In our extra time I'll teach you. Maybe I'll teach you how to fight with your hands and feet also." Each of them looked at her as Billy asked, "You know some of the things Matt can do?" Connie nodded, "Yes. We have trained with each other and had the same teachers."

A week had gone by. Connie had gotten her way. She had gotten them to take up their weapons. They made sure they had one within reach at all times. Connie had started to train them. With Star's help she had fixed Matt's gun holsters to a leather belt they had made out of some of the hide they'd tanned to make clothing out of. Then Connie made sure the pistol they used to practice with was empty. She had them draw and point like they were actually firing it. She watched real close to make sure they did it with a smooth motion. She had them keep at it until they got used to the weight of the heavy pistol.

Connie kept them at it to make it repetitious enough so that they got to doing it, by instinct. Connie had them pull the hammer back as they pulled the pistol out of the holster. Then squeeze the trigger as they brought the pistol forward hip high while they held it level, aimed at the target. Connie even though they just dry fired stressed accuracy over speed. Whenever Connie demonstrated for them they were amazed at her smoothness and speed. She told them after they got so they could do it by instinct without really thinking about what they were doing. That their speed would come along fast. To work at it till their hands could do it as if they had a mind of there own. The last thing was coordinating the pointed pistol at the exact place they were targeting with their eyes. It had been rough on them until their hands had gotten toughened up. Connie kept them at it until they had gotten calluses on their thumbs, palms and fingers. Connie was happy with their progress. She saw that they were getting faster all the time. She was sure that they didn't know it either. She had started to teach them the moves and balance that was required to fight with their hands and feet. Most of the days had been pretty cool. But it had been sunny. So they'd done most of their training out in the sun.

Mostly so as not to disturb Matt, as he rested and regained his strength. Matt with his fever gone had recovered quicker then Star had thought he would. He had to be careful not to move to fast or stretch to far to keep from opening the wounds up. Once a day Star helped Matt stretch a little farther each day. Just short of opening up his wounds. They could tell that it hurt Matt terribly. He'd be covered in sweat by the time he got done. Star explained that he needed to do it so his skin and muscles didn't heal up so tight it would restrict his movement. Star has also made sure Matt got into the pool from the hot spring at least twice a day. Then Matt rested or slept most of the day.

They were all amazed whenever they looked Matt over good. With all the scars that he had it was hard to believe he could actually be alive. From the bullets, knifes and the spear. The grizzly's teeth and claws had really done a lot of damage. Even with the trimming and all of the sewing Star had done. Rough ridges and grooves over his shoulders back and fanny left little doubt of the pain he must have suffered and the will to live. The girls thought he was still the most handsome man on earth. They were just happy that he was alive. They hadn't said anything, but Billy could see it in their eyes. Billy was sure Matt noticed. For as Matt healed and got better Billy saw Matt redden a little whenever he caught one of them look at him with admiration. Billy still couldn't believe that anybody could take so much punishment and still live.

Billy looked around at the rest and saw they were all asleep or close to it. He sat on a stone by the entrance where he could see outside and watch the stars. It was cold tonight. He noticed that the girls had covered themselves with deer hides. Billy was glad of that. Using the freshly tanned hides the girls had made some more clothing. They had made loin cloths for everyone except him. He had talked them into making a pair of buckskin pants. Sort of the pants only came down to his knee's. He just couldn't quite, get used to a loin cloth. At least not around the girls. He was determined not to let the girls see his flag raised. They couldn't help, but see Matt's flag when he responded to their beauty or some other emotion. Billy could tell that Matt was getting better. The last couple of days he had seen Matt raise his flag often.

The girls because of the limited amount of hide. Were in the process of making vest or something more like a capes for themselves. They'd made a shirt for Matt and him. The rest they decided to save for blankets until the elk and the grizzly hides cured. They had decided to keep the grizzly hide and the buffalo hide in one piece. The buffalo hide was almost cured. If it turned real cold they might need them to stay warm. The hot spring provided most of the heat.

Billy thought of the progress he'd made. With Connie's instructions. He was somewhat confident with the pistol. With the Martial Arts he'd started to get used to the control and balance along with the discipline that Connie required with each move. Not only was it new, it was strange. But with what he already had learned he started to understand how Matt had done so much damage, when Matt had rescued them. Even with that Billy had never seen anybody move so fast. He could still see the events of that night just as if it had happened a few seconds ago. For the most part he'd just seen the Indians fall to lie still. Billy had heard bones snap or a loud thump as Matt had delivered his blows. Recalling that night Billy had thought he was out of his mind when he'd heard Matt's whispered voice. With the Indian's all around that night. He'd been sure it was impossible for anyone to sneak up on them.

Billy was now sure that Matt could do anything. After all he thought how many could take a knife and kill a huge grizzly. Billy as he felt his eyes start to get heavy he stood then went on into his bedding. He glanced at the others in the flickering light, then felt his face redden. He couldn't help it and was glad they slept. For his mind had brought up the vision of the girls as they had trained. Billy had had a hard time concentrating. For he couldn't seem to take his eyes off the feminine beauty of the girls as he had faced them. They had realized what Billy's problem was and made some loin cloths which did help. However, when one of the girls made a quick turn or gave a kick his eyes drifted down. To solve the problem Connie took it upon herself to educate him. Instead of holding back she had delivered her blows. He still had the bruises to show for it. After a good beating from a few of her blows that he'd had no idea where they had come from. He had no problem with his eyes now. At least when it came to facing one of them for a fight routine. Until then he'd thought no girl could really hurt him. Connie had taken care of that though. He'd rather be kicked by a mule. At least he could get away from a mule. So he had learned to keep his eyes on the opponents moves, he had to. Connie had told him, if he didn't she'd give him another lesson.

With the passing of a couple of weeks. Matt was up and moving around gaining strength each day now. It had been murder on him to stretch his muscles. So that he had the same amount of movement that he'd had before.

During one stretch they'd had three to four days of real cold rain. Then a foot of snow had covered the ground before the storm blew on over the mountain. Since then it had been warmer. The snow had melted from the warmth of a southern wind the last couple of days. Matt had walked a lot the last two days. Then he'd been doing the exercise routine that Lee Chan had Connie and him do when they'd been back East.

That was the major reason that he'd been in such good shape. His speed and coordination had been vastly improved also. It felt good to workout again. He tired easily, but was determined to get in as good of shape as he had been; if not better. He was sluggishly slow he thought, but he was determined to get better each day. He made that promise to himself.

When he'd found out about all the training Connie had made them do, Matt had been pleased. But then as some time had gone by, it upset him that Connie had everybody training and practicing. He was happy that Billy had learned so much and was doing so good. What bothered him was that he didn't want the girls to ever have to fight. He felt like it was up to him to protect them. That he would make sure that not even one hair on their body would ever come to any harm. Not if he had anything to do about it.

It had taken a couple of days before he realized what had been bothering him. Then he had tried to figure out why he thought that way. He'd hardly spoken a word to anyone. They had thought that he had taken a turn for the worse. He assured them that he was fine. So he had spent a lot of time off alone. He'd spent time with Flame and thanked him for helping Star move the grizzly off him. He felt that Flame had understood him. They had gotten so it was as if they could read each other's minds anyway. Flame was a lot easier to understand than it was to know what was on the girls minds or his for that matter. It seemed like every time he decided he knew what the girls were up to. That they decided to change things. Like when they had waited on him and hadn't let him do anything for himself. Now they still waited on him sort of. But then, they took off as soon as they could. All they really wanted to do was train and practice. That's all they did with the daylight they had.

He had to admit Connie had done a fantastic job. She was demanding and gave clear instructions. They had little trouble understanding what she taught. She already had them so they could actually go through a fifteen to twenty minute fight routine. Connie worked with a different one each day. So she could tell how good each one of them were progressing. Matt thought in another week or two that he'd be back in shape good enough to go through one of his own fight routines.

Matt left them to train while he walked a good five miles before he found a place to set down and rest a bit before he started back. He was getting to know the immediate area pretty well. He really liked the valley. He'd take Flame out tomorrow to give him a good workout. Besides he wanted to explore and look around farther out. He hoped maybe he could run across the horse herd he'd been making an acquaintance with before he'd been hurt by the grizzly. He wanted too tame a few of them. There were some really good horses in the herd. The others had mentioned that they wanted to explore some also. But they were going to perfect their training first.

Matt rested up good now stood then started back. He even trotted a short distance, just enough to give his lungs a good workout. His legs weren't real solid underneath him yet. He slowed to a walk, but didn't stop. It was a little easier than it had been the day before. When he returned back close enough to see the area in front of the cave. Matt stopped to watch and rest again. It was Billy's turn to be in a fight routine with Connie. She really pressed him to his limit. Matt's heart filled with pride as he watched. He'd, almost forgotten how good Connie was. He was sure that for her to have been taken back at the wagons. That whatever had happened had to have been a complete surprise.

Billy was learning real good. He was just a little behind the pace and slightly off balance. As Matt watched, he realized Billy still had to think about his moves. That was the biggest reason he was a little late to block or to make a counter move. Matt thought they all were doing excellent. Especially for no longer than they had trained.

Matt didn't watch long. The girls naked except for their loin clothes. Made Matt harden. To relax he headed on toward the cave. By the time he reached the cave he was pretty much back to normal. Taken his vest and loin clothes off he eased into the pool that was below the hot spring. Matt realized it was getting harder all the time for him to be around the girls. He felt a huge attraction for each one of them. It had gotten so it took all he could do to keep them from seeing how he felt. He told himself that it was just because they were so beautiful. Then with them being naked or close to it most of the time. Showed him how close to perfection they were. At least as far as he was concerned.

With the hot water taking the soreness out of his body. Matt relaxed by the edge of the pool wondering if there was any meaning to the dreams he'd had. They were really strange. Some of it he'd recognized. For it had been some of the scenery not to far from the cave and a little beyond. What really confused him was at times it was as if he was seeing through someone else's eyes. He was sure it was a part of the valley he hadn't visited yet.

Matt eased out of the pool to be next to the fire to dry off. He put his loin cloth on then his vest. Then he sat down and rested. He'd walked pretty far today and had even run a little. He was tired and a little worn out, but it felt good. He could tell that his strength was coming back. He heard some steps and looked up to see Billy come in. Then go to the hot pool to bathe with his clothes on. Matt had tried to get him to take them off. But Billy told them it was bad enough that he had seen all them naked. At least they weren't going to see him naked.

Matt asked, "You OK Billy? It looked like Connie worked you pretty hard." Billy said, "Yeah, she works me to the best of my ability. I think I'm making it harder for her though." Billy paused then asked, "Matt how good is she? I know she's still holding back for me. I just wondered how much." Matt replied, "Well I think your about halfway there. You should be proud of yourself though. You've accomplished a lot in a short time." Billy said, "Well I'm sore, but I think I'm getting tougher." Matt said, "Your sister and Star are doing exceptional also." Billy responded, "Connie is just as rough on them when it's their turn. Connie's been awfully demanding. But she encourages us and gets the most out of us." Matt answered, "Yes, I've watched. There's only a couple of people that I know of that could teach you any better."

When they heard the girls, Billy eased out of the pool. He got the knife on his way out to the meat cave to cut up some meat for their meal. Even though it was cool the girls had gotten so they liked to clean off their sweaty bodies. With a quick swim in the cold river before they came in to relax in the hot pool. They told Matt and Billy that the cold water really revived them. They had relented to let Billy go back out in the cold to get the meat however. Matt had watched the girls as they went by. The water still dripped from their naked bodies. With a will of their own Matt's eyes saw that their nipples were as hard as little pebbles when they'd walked by. Matt thought they had to know how they affected him. What made it worse was like they were proud to have him look at them. When they'd gotten in the hot pool with his voice thick of emotion Matt said, "You girls are doing real good. You all have done a lot in a short time." Star said, "Connie told us that we've done good. And if we continue to do good she'll let us have a week off to relax." Matt said, "I don't see why she's put you through all the training though."

The girls looked at each other then Helen said, "We just decided it would keep us healthy and that it would be good to stay in shape while we spent the winter here." Star said, "Yes we need to have something to do to keep us active." Matt thought they sure were doing that. Their bodies were in perfect shape. Connie, Helen and Star had gotten so it irritated them every time Matt called them girls. They still always smiled nice at him and tried not to let him see their feelings.

CHAPTER SIXTEEN

THE GRIZZLYSPIRIT

A couple of days later it had warmed up during the night. They decided to take the day off from their training. They'd each gone off on their own to explore the valley.   It was a good break from their training. The horses needed some good exercise anyway. With Connie's insistence they all carried guns just in case. Most of the snow had melted. It had left everything with a real nice fresh smell in the air. It had gotten on toward nightfall when Billy rode over a little rise to see Star's horse. He soon spotted Star where she sat on a knoll a little higher up. She was looking off to the West at the sunset. It had to be one of the prettiest he'd ever seen. Then as he rode on up he noticed that Star didn't react until he got right next to her. She stood and turned to him with surprise still on her face. She said, "I was deep in thought. I didn't hear you until the last moment."

Billy said, "I can't blame you. I think it's one of the most beautiful sunsets, I've ever seen." Star turned back to watch the sunset. Then looked back at Billy after a pause. She said, "Billy! Well never mind. Well, I'd like to talk. Well maybe not that so much. I'd like to ask you something."

Billy slid off the Indian pony then sat down next to Star, as she sat back down. Billy said, "Sure, I don't know, if I can help you much. I've noticed that you've been a little quieter then usual." Star didn't say anything for a couple of minutes. Just sat in deep thought. Billy just sat patiently waiting to see what was up. He knew then that something really troubled her. Star finely took a deep breath then said, "Billy. I don't want you to tell the others. I'd like to keep it to ourselves."

Billy nodded then said, "I think you already knew that or you wouldn't have said anything." Star nodded then after another minute said, "OK. What I'm going to say I've kept to myself. Probably you won't believe what I tell you." Pensive Billy nodded then said, "I'm a good listener." Star then continued, "Well! whether you believe or not here it goes. I started to have visions of my future when I was only in my twelfth summer. Just bits and pieces though. It has always confused me."

Deep in thought Star didn't say anything. Given her a lot of time Billy finely asked, "Does it have anything to do with us?" "Oh! Yes. Well some of it. Well maybe quite a bit of it does. You see in my vision. Well one of them I was showed who my mate would be. Well that's not really accurate either. I didn't actually get a clear picture of what he'd look like." Billy started to catch on, "You think it's Matt." "Well in my vision he was able to kill a big Spirit bear." Billy asked, "Spirit bear? You mean the huge grizzly Matt killed."

"I know what you must think. But I was there. I know what I saw. It matched my vision. Well except I thought he would be of my own people."

Billy asked, "You really believe in your visions then?" "Oh yes; that was how I was able to get us away from our enemy. I didn't know that I'd be captured, but my vision showed me our escape route. It was just me that I'd seen in my vision. Now I've seen some things that I don't dare to relate to you. I've seen all of you in the future."

Billy attentive with his mind racing with his own thoughts over what he had just heard. His mind full of wonder as he tried to sort out the truth of her beliefs. With a doubtful look he asked, "What's the difference between a regular grizzly and a Spirit Bear?" "Oh that's easy. After Flame and I rolled the Spirit Bear off of Matt. I saw the bears Spirit leave him as he breathed out the last time. Then the Spirit entered into Matt, and brought him back to life. The Spirit had to go somewhere or be lost forever. So, it entered Matt's body.

Billy's mouth had dropped. He just starred at Star for a long moment. Then he said, "You really do believe what you just told me." "Oh yes. I've no doubt about it. The doubt I have is Matt. You see if he doesn't ask me to be his mate. I still owe him my life. With my people

I'm honor bound to serve him, the rest of my life. In anyway, he wants to use me."

Billy really dumbfounded now just starred at her. After a couple of minutes he said, "Matt won't like that."

"It's not his choice." Billy realized that Star was dead serious. He said, "Damn. Now I see what your dilemma is."

Hearing a new word Star asked, "What does dilemma mean?" "Oh sorry it is like a problem with several different thoughts. And then make things worse. You know Connie and Helen are in love with Matt the same as you are." If possible, Star got redder as she said, "You've said that, before." "I was just teasing all of you then. This puts a whole different picture on things. I've no idea how to help you or what to say." Star said, "I guess I didn't really expect that you would have an answer. But it helped me some to talk to you." Billy then said, "I'm serious, I don't think Matt knows it himself yet. But I think, he's in love with each one of you. If that's the case he may never choose any of you. Because he would not want to hurt any of you. I guess if I know him any at all, when it finely hits him, he'll never choose anyone."

Star quiet for awhile, then said, "Yes he has much honor. I think the last is what he would do. Oh! That's not good." Billy said, "Sorry. I shouldn't have said anything." "No Billy. Don't be sorry. That's what I needed, to help my thoughts. Is for you to be honest with me. Even if you don't believe me." "Wish I knew more." Star then stood up, when Billy got up to stand next to her he was surprised when she hugged and kissed him on the cheek. Then she said, "Thank you. You've helped me a lot. If nothing else just to talk my problem out with someone. You really did help.

Billy uncomfortable from their brief contact. Said, "Oh that's OK. I just wish I could've helped you more." Star nodded saying, "It's time to go I'm hungry."

They swung up on their ponies then headed on home. They hadn't gone far when they saw Connie walking home. Helen and Connie had took turns going out. They still had only the four horses. After returning from her ride Connie had decided to walk around some. It looked like darkness would settle over the valley about the time they got home.

Chris and Valerie Maxton had already moved into their new house. The contractor they'd hired had been able to hire some extra men. They had built it in record time. The Maxton's were pleased with the workmanship. The house was bigger than they needed. But they thought probably they'd have visitors from the East. It had two floors with a full basement. It had a kitchen dining room and parlor on the first floor. There was five bedrooms on the second floor.

They really missed their daughter and the Saxton's son. They talked about them very little. When they did their personal names were never used. Just the youngsters was all they'd say out loud.

The Mc Bain's had bought a little cottage. Brad helped with the warehouse and other construction. He made sure that the work was done correctly. He coordinated the supplies to match the work that was actually being done. He'd proved to Chris that he was very efficient. Better then Chris had realized. Bruce had been a good addition to the workforce also. He'd decided to stay at a hotel.

Grace Mc Bain at least twice a week went to the Maxton's. To help Valerie with the house work along with some other things. They had started to make a quilt some curtains and other things to add to the decor of the house. They planned on planting a garden in the spring. They talked often with some of their neighbors. To find out how to prepare the soil and what things grew the best. They tried to keep busy so they didn't have a lot of time to think.

They were pleasantly surprised by the weather. It had rained often. But it had snowed only once. They would've enjoyed it if the sun had shown through the clouds a little more often. But it wasn't anywhere near as cold as they had expected.

The Maxton's, Mc Bain's, Bruce Hart and the Gate's had started a routine of having dinner at the Maxton's after church. Sometimes one of the cowboy's would drop in. Capt. Taylor had been going to church with them almost every Sunday. Tex went along sometimes. For the most part none of the other cowboys went to church. But they did at one time or another end up at the Maxton's for dinner. Tex and the other cowboys had found some work. They helped out doing some odd jobs for some of the people. Like breaking horses or moving some cattle. But nothing that required riding on a bench of any kind.

The Gate's had been busy. They worked from sunrise to sunset to prepare the fields for the spring planting. With the fields done they'd started to build a house and barn. They'd done most of the work themselves. They 'd told the Maxton's that they were doing fine. They wanted to save their money. So, they would have enough to get them through until their crops came in next fall. Chris had offered to help.

Chris had spent most of the day in his office at the warehouse. Writing out a report to send to his partners back East. The work crews had shut down for the day. But, he wasn't in a hurry to go home. His wife and some other women were together to place what foods each of them were going to cook. They'd been planning a Christmas and New Year's Party for the next weekend. They'd made sure that all the cowboys had been invited. Everyone was looking forward to having a grand old time. Everyone had been putting a cheerful expression on their faces. He noticed that the cheer never quite reached their eyes though. He thought it was getting a little better on everyone. He was sure that they all missed and wondered about the youngsters like he did. He thought it was strange. That Capt. Taylor, the scouts and the cowboys were still determined to go back and look for the youngsters.

Chris felt that they thought of the youngsters like they were their own kids. Many of folk from the wagon train made it a point to ask if they had heard anything from the youngsters whenever they happened to meet. They had been well liked by a lot of the people. Chris had been proud of each one of them. That they had made such a good impression. They'd looked good without drawing attention to themselves. Each of them had done more than their share without a single complaint. Chris finished his report and sealed the envelope. He hadn't mentioned anything about the youngsters. He decided that if he had nothing new to report. It would be best not to remind them.

At the Black Hawk's winter camp. They were having a mild winter. It was because for many years they'd made their winter camp on the mountain range called the Yellowstone's. Because of the hot springs all around. It was warmer than a lot of other places. Better than the bitter winds out on the open prairie. The winter camp was a time that they all enjoyed. The families were together at this time. It was at this time that most of the teaching was done. The tribes heritage along with their customs. The braves took turns guarding the camp. Which was the only time they weren't able to be in their warm teepees.

Strong Arm always made sure that someone was on guard. He was determined not to have a surprise attack on them. Strong Arm enjoyed sitting by the fire with his wife Late Bloom. Frequently their thoughts had been of Bright Star. Sees Far told them that Bright Star and the others were alright. The White Spirit Warrior had been badly hurt again, but was well on his way to a full recovery. That was all he knew. He would seek a clearer vision. Sees Far's words had comforted them. They had learned to trust in Sees Far and his visions. But they did miss their daughter. Their grandchildren usually visited them at least once a day. They helped carry wood or went after some fresh water.

Runs Far had been able to spend a lot of time with his family. His duties at the winter camp didn't require much of him. They didn't have any raids to plan or have to do any hunting. Unless someone wanted to go out in search for some fresh meat. This was the time he spent training his children. They played games with them and some of the other families. Runs Far and his children missed Bright Star as many of the other people did. She was one of the better players. Sees Far had been away for a week on a vision quest. He wanted to get away so he would have nothing to distract him. Then maybe The Spirit World would appear to him with some clearer information. Strong Arm warm in his teepee heard a little commotion outside. Getting up with a buffalo robe, to wrap around him he stepped outside. He liked to watch the children at play. It was Sees Far's return that had stirred up the children. They loved to hear his stories. Strong Arm had just been thinking about Sees Far. It was as if his thoughts had made him appear. Sees Far saw Strong Arm. As he acknowledged the children he worked his way up to Strong Arm. Then he said, "We need to talk."

Strong Arm just nodded as he motioned for Sees Far to go ahead of him into his teepee. Sees Far said, "I would like Runs Far to hear also." Strong Arm nodded again. He spotted one of his grandchildren. Getting his attention, he sent him after his father. Then Strong Arm entered his teepee. He saw that Late Bloom had already given Sees Far a drink. She was already busy preparing something for him to eat. Runs Far came in shortly. He sat down at his appropriate place. They waited patiently as Sees Far ate. He had been fasting like he usually did whenever he sought information from the Spirit World. After he drank again, he thanked Late Bloom. She gathered up her utensils and set them aside. She then took her appropriate spot by the fire. She saw Strong Arm look at her. But unless she was commanded to she had made up her mind to stay.

Sees Far after everyone had settled into their places paused a moment to choose his words carefully. He said, "The Spirits have been good. Bright Star is very good. The others with her also." Then he paused again to make sure he spoke the right words.   Sees Far then continued, "The White Spirit Warrior has taken on the Spirit of a Grizzly. He is now more powerful than ever. It is for our people to honor him. We need to gather together the best leather from among our people. Then the best cutters and sewers. Three of the costumes must be made from doeskins. The other one from buckskin. By the time you get the leather together I'll have the measurements and designs that are to go on them. Very special designs. Now! I'm very tired."

Sees Far then stood and left for his teepee to get some much needed rest. After he'd gone Runs Far asked, " Did you understand everything he told us?" Strong Arm answered, "Yes. But he left out a lot he could have told us. Get the word out among our people just like Sees Far told us. Remember to let them know of the honor we're to show. Also that it's with my blessing."

Runs Far nodded then got up to do as he'd been directed. He nodded at his mother as he left. He saw the dumbfounded look on her face as he left. She wasn't the only one. Sees Far had lifted their spirits with his news. But he had also raised many questions that had went unanswered. They knew that he would let them know when it was time. Sees Far had learned that sometimes when the Spirit World enlightened him that it was better that he didn't tell all he knew until it was the right time to do so. Runs Far couldn't help but wonder how the White Spirit Warrior had captured the spirit of a grizzly or for that matter what it really meant.

The Saxton's had planned a big New Year's party. A lot of the most prominent citizens had been invited. With Mrs. Saxton's and Meaghan's insistence the Socket's and the Chan's had also been invited. Mrs. Saxton had made sure that a good band had been hired to play at the party. The house had been rearranged so there would be lots of room to dance. Everyone had been enthusiastic as they'd put up the decorations. Margaret Saxton Mark's wife mostly just gave orders to the servants. Then acted like she was the one that did all the work. Everyone had decided they'd have a good fun time. So they just kind of let her have her way. But in the end Mrs. Saxton's wishes had been carried out. Everyone had been happy with the results.

Jim Fallon had been busy welcoming all the guest for the last hour. Everybody dressed up in their best. When they got inside one of the hosts would take their coats and hats to be hung up till they left. Mrs. Saxton had all the servants dressed in the colors of the season in uniform dress's and suits. So no one had any problem knowing who the hosts were. Jim Fallon had a good heavy overcoat on. It had been a cold day and was even getting colder. He thought nearly everyone had made it. He'd decided to wait outside for a few more minutes. Then he would go inside were it was warm to wait for the late arrivals. The Saxton's had told him to stay inside as much as possible. But he'd made up his mind that it was only right to assist the women and young children out of their carriages. Nobody had to leave any of their children home. The Saxton's had hired extra help to keep a nursery and fixed up another room for the toddlers.

The Saxton's had always had big celebrations. But they'd decided to really go all out this time. The business had done so well that Randolph thought it only proper to share. So a lot of people he and his sons had done business with had been invited. Jim thought that some of it was in the hope of having such a good time. That not knowing the fate of Matt and Connie they all were putting on an extra effort to celebrate so the youngsters would be lost from their minds for a short time. That seemed to be what was driving everyone in the household. At least to make a huge effort like they were all having a good time.

Jim saw another carriage enter the driveway. As the carriage came up he recognized Vern Sockett and his family. Even though they'd meant only once Jim knew he'd never seen anyone else like him. Jim had taken an instant liking to him. Vern he thought could crush a man's hand if he wanted to. Vern didn't show it though. But Jim had felt the hardness. The way Vern walked and sat, set him apart from any others he'd ever seen. Jim had noticed that his eyes always moved. If he ever missed anything Jim would have been surprised. He thought Vern's eyes were the most direct and honest he'd ever seen.

When the carriage came to a stop. Vern got down then shook Jim's hand. Then they helped Mrs. Sockett and their daughter Diane out of the carriage. James their son climbed out last. Jim said, "Careful ladies, it's a little slippery." Vern said, "Hope we're not to late. The train was running a little behind." Jim said, "Everything's fine. The festivity's haven't started yet." Vern said, "Well! I'm not much for parties. But the rest of the family wanted to come." James said, "Don't let him fool you. If ma hadn't have threatened him he wouldn't have come. He doesn't like to be around so many people." Vern quickly cuffed James. Jim had just barely seen the movement. James laughed as he staggered back a step. Then said, "See what I mean." Mrs. Sockett said, "You two behave. Diane and I have been looking forward to this."

When they entered the house their coats were taken and hung up. Then another host lead them on to the large room. Meaghan Saxton had been keeping an eye out for the Sockett's and the Chan's. For she was sure they'd be out of their usual environment. She was determined to make them as comfortable as she could. As she spotted them she excused herself from the people she'd been talking to. As she hurried up to them she said, "Oh, I'm so happy you made it."

Mrs. Sockett said, "We're so happy to have been invited. You have decorated everything up nice. I just love the bunting of red, blue and yellow. The green ribbons mixed in have really highlighted everything."

Meaghan saw that they were a little underdressed in some nice attractive gowns. Vern and James had nice clean inexpensive suits. She said, "Each of you look very lovely tonight. Make yourselves at home. If you need anything at all just ask one of the hosts." The Sockett's were a little uncomfortable as they saw all the beautiful gowns and suits the others wore. They were determined not to show it. They thanked Meaghan. Then as she pointed, she said, "There's drinks over there. We'll be eating pretty soon. I've arranged for you and the Chan's to sit close to me." Meaghan talked with Mr. and Mrs. Sockett while James and Diane went to get some drinks. As they talked Mrs. Saxton came up. It was then that the Chan's came in. Their dress was different. But very nice and expensive. Mrs. Saxton welcomed them, it took a couple of minutes as they all shook hands with the Sockets also. Mrs. Jessie

Fallon spotted Mrs. Saxton. After filtering her way through some people she told her the meal was ready. Mrs. Saxton then told the Sockett's and Chan's, "Meaghan and I insisted that you would be seated next to us as our special guest." Not given them a chance to respond she lead them to some tables that had been put end to end to make one big table.

Within a few minutes everyone was seated. Randolph Saxton at the head of the table with his family seated on his right. Except for Ann who was on his left. Then the Chan's and the Sockett's with Meaghan being the last before the other guest. With the food of salted ham, beef, an assortment of vegetables, bread, pies and cakes being brought out to be served, it had quieted down quite a bit. They had nearly any type of drink that any of the men, women and even the children would like, that had made it to the party. It took several trips for the five servants to bring out the food and drinks. Then they stayed in attendance to wait on anyone's needs.

They all ate heartily. As the food was very good. Many commented on how good it was. The Chan's and the Sockett's had noticed that they'd gotten several glances at them during the meal. After making sure everyone had fresh drinks to make a toast with. Randolph Saxton stood up then everyone quieted down.

Making sure he had everyone's attention Randolph said, "On behalf of my wife and family. I would like to welcome each of you. I just want everyone to have a grand time. Our family has invited some very special guests here tonight. Not to embarrass anyone. But if you haven't heard a very close friend of the family and my son are missing from the wagon train that took them West in a move to expand our business. Our family just wanted to show our gratitude to our special guests. For I think that without their help we wouldn't have much hope of seeing either of them again. But with their expert instruction in training Connie Maxton and my son Matt in how to take care of themselves and what they would have to do to survive in their new environment out West. We have high hopes of them returning to us. After I make the introductions I'd like for all of you to join me in a toast to them."

Randolph then introduced the Chan's and the Socket's. After that and the toast he had the band start. The party really got going then. Some started to dance. Most realized that something out of the ordinary had taken place. They tried to gather around the two families to hear what was said. They all wanting to learn more about them. Vern was upset at first. He didn't like being in the spot light. He was calmed down however by Betsy patting him on the shoulder. Vern hesitantly answered their questions. Within a few minutes a interested crowd had gathered around as he explained what he had taught Connie and Matt. Mostly men, but some of the women listened intently also. After a little they had Vern telling them about the West. Lee Chan with the help of his oldest son had gotten a good gathering around them also. They described the way that someone could fight with a lot of practice.

Mrs. Saxton watched to be sure everything went well. Seeing that the men were occupied. She captured Mrs. Sockett and Mrs. Chan. She took them off to one side so they could get better acquainted. When they'd gotten a little separation from the other people Mrs. Saxton said, "Betsey! I thought maybe Randolph had made a mistake. By drawing so much attention to Vern. He looked like he was about to really explode for a moment there."

Mrs. Sockett smiled as she kind of sighed with a little nervous laugh. Then she said, "He does get tense sometimes. But now that they got him going. He'll talk all night. I had hoped I'd get at least one dance with him." Mrs. Saxton laughed then said, "I'm sorry. But I think it would be easier for us, to use our first names. I hope you don't think I'm being rude."

Mrs. Sockett answered, "No, not at all. It's fine with me. I'm glad. It's such a nice party. You've done everything up so nice. That there's only one thing that I can think of that would make it better."

Mia in broken English said, "Yes, First name is good with me. Like Betsey I can think of only one thing that would make the party better." Ann saw the wistful looks on their faces as they had spoken. Busy as she was, she tried to be a good host, it took a couple of seconds for Ann to get their meaning. When it hit her, with a sigh she said, "Yes! That would make it the best ever." With their own thoughts for a moment. Mrs. Saxton then asked Mrs. Chan if she had enjoyed the food. Mrs. Chan nodded then told her yes it had been very good. Sue Chan had come over to help when they had a little problem understanding each other. Their guests had started to break off into little groups. As the band played some had started to dance. James and Diane Socket had joined the dancers as had Lee and Sawn Chan.

Randolph as he oversaw things, was relived that everyone seemed to be having a good time. He had felt a little bad about putting so much attention on the Socket's and the Chan's. But after a few anxious moments he was glad he had. Not only that if Connie and Matt somehow survived because of the training the two men had given them. It gave him some space to just relax and enjoy the party. He was kind of able to be on his own.

It was a good band that Ann had been able to acquire. The band had a fiddler, piano bangle player and drums. They took a few minutes to set up and finish tuning their instruments. Most of the young people had paired up too dance already. Randolph walked around to check on the punch bowls and snacks that had been put out just in case anyone did get hungry. Happy with the status of the food and drink. Randolph decided to mingle in with his guests. With a glance all around to make sure nothing was amiss he spotted Margaret. She'd just removed her stare from the group of people that surrounded Vern Socket and Lee Chan. With a turned up nose she spoke to one of her friends. Randolph had never really taken to her. But he had been able to be sociable with her. But after her comment about Matt he had done his best to avoid her. He could tell she was displeased. She had gone out of her way to out dress everyone, in an attempt to get all of the attention. Randolph smiled to himself. It hadn't been his thought to do so, but with the introduction of the special guests. She hadn't been able to get the attention she looked for. Some of the wind had been taken out of her sails.

The party went on well past midnight. Most everyone had proclaimed that it was one of the best they'd ever been too. Randolph and Ann had made it a point to thank their guests for their kindness and support as they departed. Many of them had left their best wishes behind for Connie and Matt. Randolph and Ann had been able to persuade the Socket's and the Chan's to stay over for the rest of the night. The Sockett's would have had to go to a hotel or wait at the train station. The Chan's had quite a ways to go to get to there home. Besides Randolph wanted to talk with them.

The next morning Vern found his way to the kitchen. In search of some coffee. His nose had lead him to the kitchen. He was surprised however to see that Bob and Betty Green were already up. Vern hadn't been able to break his habit of being up with the Sun. He was just in the hope of finding some leftover coffee. He sure hadn't expected to find freshly made coffee. The Green's looked up as he quietly came in. Bob said, "Good morning Mr. Sockett. Your almost as quiet as Matt. Betty will have some strong coffee ready soon. My name is Bob."

Vern said, "Thanks Bob. Just call me Vern. As far as Matt. I've never seen anyone that could come close to moving as quiet as him." Betty with deep emotion in her voice asked, "Do you really think that Matt and Connie are alright?" Vern said, "Yes, I don't expect you to understand. But I just don't feel like I think I would if, Matt had already gone under." Bob said, "Well, we've been hopeful." Betty with the coffee ready poured some into a couple of cups. She handed a steaming cup to Vern. Then said, "I hope it's how you like it. That's the way Matt liked it." Vern took a sip then said, "It's just right." Betty asked, "Want some cookies." Vern answered, "No just coffee will be fine."

The rest of the Sockett's and the Chan family along with the Saxton household had eaten a late breakfast in the dining room. Several of the extra servants had stayed over. They had eaten in the big parlor so as not to bother the main household and their guests. Then they would help put the home back in order before they left. Margaret and Mark were the last to arrive. The meal was a simple one. Some even ate some of the leftovers from the party. When everyone had gotten filled up they had pretty much stayed at the dining room table. For the most part the children sat in their own group.

The grown ups had then just sat around close so they could talk better. They'd discussed Matt and Connie in great detail. Vern had been asked a lot of questions. Betsey had been a big help in explaining some of the details so the Saxton's understood better. To close with Mr. Chan and Vern both stated that Matt had a strong will. Enough to survive where others would've given up. Randolph had then nodded as he agreed along with Ann. They both acknowledged how strong minded Matt was. The Saxton household felt much better after the discussion. Margaret had put on a expression of boredom. She had listened intently however and somehow had kept quiet. Maybe it was because of the frown that she saw on Randolph's forehead every time she glanced his way.

Before they'd departed for their homes. The Chan's and Socket's talked awhile. They struck up a quick friendship and decided they'd try to spend more time together. They shook hands all around before they climbed into their waiting carriages. Betsey and Mia even hugged each other. They all waved at the Saxton's who'd come out to make sure they'd gotten off alright.

Helen and Connie had worked together with Star to plan a special celebration for them. They had explained to Star what Christmas meant. That it had to be close to that time of the year when it was appropriate to celebrate it. Matt and Billy had spent a lot of their time out in the valley when the weather was nice. So the girls were able to get things ready without Matt and Billy knowing, so it would be a big surprise to them. After Star had understood she had come up with some excellent ideas. Connie was sure that Christmas had already come and gone. Helen had stated that it didn't really matter. That it would just be nice to celebrate. They had gotten all the things together that they could come find. They decided that they could have everything ready for tomorrow. There had been a couple of cold spells, another snowstorm. But for the most part their valley hadn't been cold. They didn't know it, but it was into the end of January.

They had kept up with their training. With Matt's help Connie was pleased with everyone. She thought they'd become nearly as good as the Chan children. That was a real accomplishment with no more time than they'd had. Connie thought she had seen a vast improvement in Matt once he had gotten back to full strength. She'd thought that he couldn't ever be any better than he had been. But she was sure that he was. He was even more alert than she had ever seen before. Sometimes it was like he saw something far away. When that happened, he looked dead at you. But his eyes seemed to be focused on something else. The others had noticed also. Then a couple times Connie had been thirsty. When she'd gotten up to get something to drink. She saw that Matt wasn't in his bed. She hadn't heard a sound or felt him leave like she used to.

They'd been busy. Matt true to his word with Connie's help. Had made sure that everyone could read and write. He had them work on math also. Star had some problems at first. But once she grasped something she didn't forget. With the daylight hours Matt and Billy had spent a lot of their time out in the valley away from home. Connie with that thought was full of wonder as she realized they had been referring to the cave as home. She even stopped doing what she was working on. Helen and Star when they noticed, looked at her as they paused with their work. Then Helen asked, "What?" Connie caught by surprise said, "Do you realize that all of us have been calling this place home." Helen said, "Yes. It's better than saying the cave. Or what ever else you can think of." Star completely stopped doing her work then. With a direct look at Connie she said, "I feel like you do. It is like I'm home."

Helen looked at one then the other. She then realized what they meant. She said, "You mean like home. Well! That doesn't make sense. Like this is where we belong." After Helen had put it to words, they both nodded at her. With understanding coming Helen paused a little. Then in deep thought she said, "It does doesn't it? I do feel like I belong here."

Connie said, "I never was going to stay with my mother and father forever. So I think I would really like to settle in this valley." With enthusiasm Helen said, "I feel the same. Of course I will miss my family. But this is such a beautiful place. I would like it fine."

Star burst their bubble as she said, "It wouldn't be home without Matt." It was real quiet then as they looked at each other. Each of them realized the truth of her words. Everything had just been brought out in the open between them. Each of them now knew that they had the same feelings and desires. Not just for Matt. But that each of them had fallen in love with the valley also. They just sat as they looked at each other with love, hurt, passion, desire and respect for each other; and the one they loved. Each of them left their emotions unguarded as they sought for some kind of comfort in each others grief. It was several minutes before anyone spoke. Then Helen asked, "What are we going to do? I love both of you better than sisters. It's like you two are part of me now."

Sadly, Connie said, "I feel the same. And I've grown so fond of Billy. He's just like the brother I've always wanted. It would be nice if there was some way that each one of us could all have Matt. That would solve all our problems."

Star gave Connie a hard look then said, "Maybe that's possible. Not many times has it happened. But among our people. It is not prohibited, no, what do you say, oh-h not forbidden."

Connie responded to help Star. She said, "Prohibited or forbidden." Helen's mouth dropped as she said, "You mean like each one of us could be Matt's wife." Star smiled as she nodded "Yes! we could be Matt's mate."

Helen said, "Oh yes, we could do that." Then as she realized what they were discussing with a frown she said. "Yeah, I think we'd be fine with it. But I don't think Matt would ever go along with such an arrangement." Then Helen looked at Connie as she asked, "What would God say? Even if Matt did agree." Connie answered, "I know what you mean about Matt. He could be a problem. But I remember reading in the Bible that Moses had two wives. King Solomon was suppose to have had over a hundred wives."

Star asked, "Who are they?" Connie answered, "People of our God. That lived a long time ago." Star said, "Our God is the Great Spirit." Connie said, "We worship our God in the Spirit also." Star said, "Maybe they are the same."

They had talked about many things. But this was the first time they had shared their souls with each other. They discussed each other's God and customs. Helen said, "I think maybe Star is right. It feels like to me we just got a lot closer in our feelings for each other. Well, at least I feel closer to you two. Then somehow, I feel closer to God. Maybe it's just because we have been discussing him." They both nodded. Then Star said, "It hasn't been clear. But I believe in one of my visions that I have had that we were all one family."

Star told them of her visions. How they had been true to her. But they were still mystified. She hadn't told them of their doubts though. Star had kept many of them to herself. The ones that didn't make any sense to her. Back to work fixing up the things they wanted ready for the next day they had settled down to their own thoughts again. Then Helen asked, "Connie what about our families? Oh! I know we could work things out between us. But even if Matt did go along with it. What would they think."

Connie answered, "Since we've gotten everything out in the open. Remember before we met Star that our agreement was to let him choose. But as you now know that each of us here would just rather be dead if we knew we could never have Matt." After the other two nodded their agreement. Connie continued, "Guess they'll just have to except it or disown us."

Helen thought about it for a while. Then said, "Yes! Your right. I feel that way too."

Then for some reason as if they had been prompted; they stood as of one mind. And hugged each other. After that Star said, "We need to finish they will be back soon." As they got busy Helen asked, "How are we going to let Matt know?" Connie said, "I'll talk to him. I'll try to time it right. Poor Billy. We'll probably be a disgrace to him. But we need to flirt with Matt as much as possible to soften him up."

Star asked, "What does flirt mean."

Helen said, "To move so that Matt notices us. To let him see everything and excite him."

Star said, "Oh! Yes that should be fun."

CHAPTER SEVENTEEN

THE COMMITMENT

Matt, and Billy had worked a lot harder than the girls knew. After Matt had completely healed. It felt like his strength had just poured into his body. Billy and Matt, had worked at taming some of the wild horses they'd found. It seemed to Matt that not only had his strength returned to normal. But beyond what it had been before. His ability to work with animals had even increased. They didn't need the meat. But just to try out his new power. He had approached a couple of deer. He'd been able to walk right up to them. Almost like he'd been able to put a spell on them. He hadn't told anyone. But Billy had been impressed by the ease they had with the horses.

Billy had heard about how Matt and Flame had meet. So he hadn't asked a lot of questions. He had watched very close so he could gain some of the ability that Matt had. Matt's ability with the horses was something to watch. But Billy saw what really set Matt apart from most of the others was his patience and that Matt let them know he wanted to be friends with them. But Matt hadn't had it as easy with Flame, as it had been with the horses here. Matt thought that none of the horses in the valley had ever seen a man. Matt, and Billy had used all their private time to work on their big surprise for the girls.

They knew nothing of the plans that the girls had come up with. They had decided that it would be nice if they could just give the girls something nice. To make up for some of the hardship they'd been put through.

They had picked out four of the best mares they could find. One of them Matt had reserved for himself. She was a roam. Nearly the same color as Flame. With a big deep chest and long legs to match. Not slim but well built. She had a long body. She was tall for a mare. She stood a good fifteen hands. What Matt liked the most was how intelligent she looked. He hadn't been wrong and Flame had taken to her right off. Matt was sure that she was already bred. They had picked along the same lines for the others. One was a bay. With a white blotch on her forehead. That looked almost like a star. Another one was a light tan. But she did have white from her hooves up to her knee joints on all four legs. The last mare was white. With a black mane and tail.

The first few days they just made friends. After that Billy was really impressed on how quickly the horses learned. Matt had him to pay attention to them, to learn what each one liked and then what they didn't like. That way they learned to make a trade off to work out an understanding with each of them.

Billy had spotted a stallion he liked. He was a solid bay color. Except for three white socks that ran up to his knee joints. His left front leg was of the bay color. He had long solid legs. With a deep chest and long body. Fifteen hands tall. It had taken a little longer. But Matt had been able to persuade him to accept their attentions. It had really helped that the mares had already been pretty much broken, to ride by then.

They all were fleet of foot and fast. They were sure they would have a lot of endurance also. Matt still didn't think there was any that he'd ever trade Flame for. They had been training them be ground tie. Matt and Billy had trained them to neck rein and knee reign. Matt and Billy had just had a real good day with them. They had rode each one of them. They had nice long smooth strides. They were quick to respond to any guidance given to them as Matt and Billy put them through some routines. The horses were real pleasant to work with. They each had developed their own personality's already.

Billy and Matt had found a little cove to train them in. It had good grass and water so they had tried for the most part to keep them in the cove. The first few times when Matt and Billy returned. They had to go out and round up one or more of them, especially the stallion. They'd been pretty content the last few days though. The cove had been used to keep the horses out of sight from the girls more than anything. Just in case one of them had been out riding around. It did have some nice soft ground. The grass was a dark rich green. The horses had really taken to it now. It helped them as they trained to separate them from the rest of the wild horse herd. To do away with any distractions. Like the stallion that watched over the horse herd the mares had come from. They were real happy with finding the little cove, for it had been very beneficial. Matt and Billy were very happy. Each of the mares had done exceptional. They even felt that the mares had gotten so it was a fun game to be put through their paces to change directions by neck or knee reining. Then a command to speed up or slow down by either method. It was close to dark as they rode back to the cave. Matt wore his pistols and Billy carried one of the riffles. Bringing them out of their own pleasant thoughts Billy said, "Boy! It has been hard not to say anything to the girls about the horses." With a pleased smile as much for Billy as anything else. Matt had become very fond of Billy and couldn't be happier. Billy never complained and did everything Matt suggested without a single back word. Billy was eager to learn also. Matt smiled again as he said, "Yeah we'll give them their gifts soon." Billy said, "I still can't get over how quick we've been able to train them." Matt said, "They seem to be smarter than most. I don't think they've had any people around to mistreat or scare them either." "Matt, do you miss our people?"

Matt took his time to make sure of his words. He was sure everyone probably had the same thoughts. He said, "Yes. I guess the biggest thing is that I keep thinking about how worried or sad they are because they probably figured we were dead or worse." Billy's mouth dropped a little. He'd been thinking of his own feelings. Not how their people would be worried or hurting.

The girls had adapted to all the different things that had been thrown their way. Matt's statement after Billy had contemplated it, had made Billy feel better and more determined than ever to get out. To let their family's know that they were alright, Billy said, "It'll sure be nice to see them again."

"Yeah! It sure will be nice to see them. I'll bet the girls will be glad to be able to just sit back and relax. With everything that has happened to them it must have been awfully rough on them, even for Star. Billy couldn't help it as he gave Matt a long look. He made no comment though. They were close to the cave. It was almost dark now. They dismounted and took care of their horses. Then turned them out to be with the other two Indian Ponies. As they took care of the horses Billy thought yes, it had to be really tough on the girls. But not the way Matt had it figured.

Then do away with all pretences of modesty. Billy had a hard time believing that Matt still didn't realize the girls wouldn't want to be any other place than by his side. Billy was still worried about which one Matt would choose. Also, how bad it would hurt the ones he didn't choose. For Billy was sure that they were all crazily in love with Matt. He couldn't help but see it. It had amused him most of the time. It had helped get his mind off their troubles, several times.

When they had taken care of the horses and entered the cave. They felt like something was up. But they didn't let on. They'd felt it for about a week now. They'd talked about it. But hadn't let the girls know that they suspected anything. Tonight, they'd felt it more then usual. They went to the freshwater basin and drank. Then after they sat down the girls served up the food.

There was some small chatter from the girls as they ate. When they'd finished the girls asked how their day had been. They told them about their day leaving out the details about the special horses they picked out for the girls. The girls then asked a lot of questions. Most of them directed at Matt. Then in a pleasant manner they kept him in conversation about the valley. How wonderful it was, the hot springs and the fresh water. The beautiful tree's and how good the grass was. Matt looked a little puzzled. But kept up with them. He didn't want to do anything to upset their surprise, that they had for the girls. Billy amused just sat and listened. Matt didn't seem to realize that a trap had been set and that he had just stepped into it with both feet.

That night Matt's heart was full as he laid down. He liked the valley. He'd thought about making a home out of it if he could; somehow. It would take a lot of work and money. It pleased him that the girls seemed to think of it as he did. He knew he had to get the girls back to their families. As the thought ran through his mind he felt a sharp prick in his heart. It kept him awake as he wondered about it for quite a while. In an attempt to put an end to those thoughts he wondered about his new strange ability to see things far away. He couldn't explain it. It was like he was using someone else's eyes. Sometimes it was from high in the air. Other times it was like he was on a cliff. Like a Mountain Lion waiting on some prey. He thought he'd seen places in the valley, then later in his travels he'd come across the area he had seen. But he knew that he'd never been there before. It was weird; he hadn't told anyone. Because he thought the others would think he was crazy. Well except maybe for Star, she wouldn't.

The next morning as Matt and Billy were about to go out, the girls told them to be back at noon. The girls then told them they were going to prepare a special meal to celebrate. That's why they hadn't fixed much for breakfast. They just nodded in agreement as they went on out.

When Matt and Billy arrived at the horses they'd picked out for the girls they went right to work. Using some hay they had bound together to use as a curry comb they brushed them till their hides glistened in the sun. It was a nice warm day and they were really cheerful. For they'd decided it was a perfect day to take the horses back to the girls. As they approached their home cave they did so cautiously in hope of catching the girls inside. They'd been able to. Jubilant they ground tied the horses just outside the entrance to the cave. They looked at each other with big satisfied smiles on their faces as they entered the cave. They smelled the pleasant aroma of the food that had been cooked. They licked their lips unknowingly as they noticed that the girls had made the fire a little bigger than usual. They had made candles out of something. The girls had made the cave as bright and clean as a cave could be. They'd both looked all around. Then just as they got into the main part. Billy ran right into Matt's back with his nose. Matt's back was like solid rock. Matt still hadn't moved. Billy grunted as he rubbed his nose and wiped the tears out of his eyes. He stepped around Matt to see what had froze him in place. Billy as he got a full view of the girls almost spoke out. He had all he could do to keep quiet. Billy didn't know how they had done it. But the girls had fixed their hair so it shined and somehow it was like their bodies glowed. They didn't have a thing on. As they stood they looked proudly right at Matt. Like they waited for him to say something. Billy then looked at Matt to see his lips move, but not a sound was heard. Billy a little flushed himself started for his seat. But before he got there. Helen said, "Billy get all cleaned up. Everything will be ready in a half an hour or so."

 Billy just nodded as he decided the hot pool would feel real good. As he walked off he glanced at Matt. He couldn't help but notice the big bulge between Matt's legs. It was Helen's voice or Billy's movement that finely snapped Matt out of his astonished state. He finely said, "Boy you girls are really beautiful. I can't think of anything that would even compare. I do appreciate it. But I think it would be proper for you to put something on."

That's what had gotten him so tongue tied. He wanted to praise and flatter them. But still in some way he wanted to warn them, that after all he was a healthy man with desires. At least that's what he tried to tell himself. For once he didn't try to hide how he felt. They would have to be blind not to see how he had responded. He was completely surprised. When Connie stomped her bare foot on the cave floor as she put her hands on her bare hips. Which resulted in making her breasts bounce. From her emotions her nipples had hardened completely. As she showed her feelings with a little disgust and anger in her voice she said, "Matt if you haven't noticed. Not a one of us is a girl. We're women and we're tired of you calling us girls."

Matt eyes were glued on her as he followed every move. This time he couldn't regain his control no matter how hard he tried. Hard he thought. It was so hard it hurt. The only thing he could think of was somehow he had to try to be a gentleman. Also, he didn't want to make any of them any madder. For he had seen that somehow, he had hurt their feelings. He said, "OK! I'm sorry. You are very beautiful women."

Then he made up his mind not to say anything else unless he was asked something. That way he hoped he wouldn't say anything wrong. He thought his comment had smoothed things over. But in just a second he found out he was in more trouble. For Star came up to him then with a thick voice full of emotion she said, "We clean." Matt saw that her breast had swelled. And her nipples were rock hard also. Matt could hardly talk but asked, "What?" Helen now in the same state as her skin took on a reddish glow the same as Connie's and if possible Star's skin was a deeper color also. They all were aglow with the blood that rushed through their veins. Helen said, "Star's got some final preparations to do before the meal is done. Connie and I will bath you." As she spoke her voice thickened with emotion. Matt beside himself almost spoke. But just before he did he saw something in their eyes. Especially Connie's and Helen's. He'd almost groaned out loud. He just nodded as they walked up then Connie took one arm as Helen took the other. They lead him toward the hot pool. Star turned back to finish her meal preparations. Billy saw them as they headed his way. He got out of the pool with his buckskin pants still on. He had washed his shirt also. Taking it he went and hung it on the clothes rack they had made not far from the fire.

Matt was so stressed that his muscles had become stiff. Which made it difficult for him to move. He was determined to be decent. It took all the power of his mind to do so. When Connie and Helen got him to the hot pool they started to remove his clothes. He almost jumped out of his skin. As Connie stooped to remove Matt's moccasins while Helen took off his shirt. Matt from all the emotions that went through his body. Had all he could do to keep his knees from giving out on him. Connie and Helen both had hesitated. Then to Matt's surprise Connie unfastened his buckskin pants. And slid them down. Till then he'd thought they were bluffing.

Both women blushed a little more as they formed a big O, with their mouths. Not a sound was heard though. Matt felt a little satisfaction as he saw their response. For his manhood was standing up and out. He didn't have to look to know that it was bigger than it had ever been. The women recovered. Then lead him to the pool then together they eased on into it. Then immediately they went to work scrubbing him down with something like soap. From somewhere and somehow, they had made some soap. It had a wild berry fragrance to it. Matt then realized that was one of the new smells he'd noticed when they entered the cave.

They scrubbed every inch of his body. Their touch was driving him out of his mind. Finely he thought they were done when they paused. Then he looked at both sets of breasts that floated so nice right in front of him. He then felt Helen. He knew it was Helen for Connie hadn't moved. And Helen's face had filled with excitement. Beyond his belief she was actually scrubbing and cleaning his throbbing manhood. To his surprise and as hard as he tried not to he finely lost. He saw

Helen's face really redden as she licked her lips. Matt was able to relax a little as the throbbing stopped as he got a little smaller.

No one spoke as they got out of the pool. As they went to their usual places to eat his body dried fast. The water had been hot. But nothing like his body felt. Matt then noticed that Star had replaced the rock he usually sat on with a wood seat that had been padded then covered with some leather. As he sat on it he was pleased with how comfortable it was. He had looked for his loin cloth that he usually wore after he'd cleaned up. It wasn't anywhere to be found though. He still kept his silence he didn't want to make any of them angry. The women started serving Billy then him. Matt noticed that they kept their distance from Billy. But when they served him and it didn't matter which one it was. They put their breasts right in front of his eyes, or what was even worse. They would stand straight up and hold what ever it was they served him, just below their private area. It was really working havoc on his manhood.

He was sure that Billy couldn't help but notice. But Matt embarrassed had glanced in his direction to plead for some help from him. Instead he could have sworn that Billy had just hid his face with a smirk all over it.

Matt ate like he had never eaten before. They had turkey, venison, wild onions with some other roots that was very good . They had made some kind of pudding with berries. It all tasted good. Very good. He was amazed. With what they had it was almost as good as any meal he had ever eaten before.

Billy finished patting his belly, as he stood up. He said, "Thank you. That was a very good meal. I'm stuffed, I guess I need to stretch some and get some fresh air." Helen then stood up as she said, "Just a minute Billy."

She went to her things then picked up something and brought it back. She handed him a new leather shirt with some design work on it as she said, "Merry Christmas."

Billy felt it between his fingers as he held it out to look it all over, then said, "Thanks, it is beautiful and soft."

Then he put it on and walked out. On his way out he glanced at Matt. Billy then thought if anyone ever had the expression on their face, like someone holding a tiger by the tail; holding on for dear life and not having any idea of what to do next. Matt's face was the perfect picture. He couldn't keep from laughing as he rushed outside.

Star then got up and returned with one for Matt. As Matt felt it he could tell it was much better then his others. And was made to fit him. It had some designs on it also.

Matt had almost choked on a lot of the meal. Because he had eaten out of reflex trying to get his mind off the women. Matt got up then started to put the shirt on. He glanced around to find something else to wear. Then he cleared his throat and with a real husky voice he said, "Thank you. This is sure a big surprise. It was a very good meal also. You've all outdone yourselves."

All the women got up. Connie took Matt's new shirt before he could put it on. She smoothing it out then put it on the pile of stone that served as a clothes rack as she said, "It's warm enough you don't need it now. It's heavier then the ones we made before." Then as if on signal they all walked right up to him and hugged him. While giving him a kiss. One on each cheek as Connie kissed him right on the lips. Matt was afraid he was going to loose control all over Connie's belly. For she had put it right up against him as his emotions were growing again. All of them with a lot of emotion told him Merry Christmas.

Matt stuttered a Merry Christmas. Then after a second said, "Billy and I have something for you girl's; f-for you women. It's outside." They had started to tense up. He'd caught himself just in time. They recovered before he did. Together they asked, "OH. What is it." Matt thought that they did act like girls now. They all acted like they'd never received a gift of any kind before. They started for the entrance. Then Matt said, "Ladies, wait just a little please. Let Billy and me get things ready for you." They did wait as Matt went on out. He found Billy just outside of the cave a little. He told him the girls were ready for their gifts. He caught Billy's glance. Matt's condition was apparent. He felt his body heat up with embarrassment as they lead the horses up closer to the cave entrance. Then ground tied them there. Matt went back in as Billy stepped back off to the side. But made sure he would be able to see their faces when they came out. Matt still had a personal problem and it didn't seem like it was ever going to go back to normal. When he was back inside he said, "OK ladies! We're ready. Billy and I wish you a Merry Christmas."

Then he waved them on ahead of him. As they got outside with him close behind, he heard them quietly exclaim. For they'd had sense enough not to scare the horses. They said, "OH my. There beautiful. Oh Matt, Billy; this is the best ever."

Matt was pleased. And he saw by the look on Billy's face. That he was very pleased, also. The women then asked. Star first then Helen and Connie. Which one is for which? Matt waited as Billy told them, "Matt and I decided to let you make your own picks."

The women looked at each other. Then Connie said, "OH. Matt Billy this is the best gift ever. Helen I think it's easy for Star. The bay with the star on her forehead should be Star's."

Helen nodded then said, "I agree."

Star replied, "Thank you. She is the one I had picked."

Star then looked at Connie and Helen and waited for them to make their choices. Connie then said, "Helen I kind of like the white mare with the black mane and tail." Helen responded, "Oh good! I do like the tan with the white socks." In unison they said, "They look like their already trained."

Matt nodded. "Yes. Billy and I have been working our butts off. They neck rein and knee rein."

Star took up the reins to her horse. Matt and Billy had made simple halters. Matt had seen Star leap up on a horse. She had also taught Helen and Connie how to do it. Matt was surprised when she said, "Matt. Help me up please."

Matt started to say something then not wanting to spoil their mood just nodded. He walking up knelt down and made a step with his hands. Star smiled her thanks as she put her left foot in his hand. With her hands she grabbed the mares mane. Matt tried but without success. His eyes went right between her legs. When she raised her right leg up over the mares back he saw her lips part. It made him swell so bad he thought it was about to split. Mounted and full of glee she rode off. Seeing the performance Star had put on. Connie and Helen had Matt do the same for them. By that time he was at his limit. He didn't even look at Billy. As they rode off he just went the shortest route possible to the cold water of the river and stood in it. He stayed in it for about fifteen minutes. He was about frozen when he got out. But at least it wasn't standing straight up and throbbing now.

Billy saw the goose bumps on Matt as he said, "I think we did good. They really liked the horses."

Matt was relieved that Billy didn't say anything about the events of the day. Matt said, "Yeah. They really seemed to be overjoyed today."

They had been gone for quite awhile. Matt had started to get concerned. He said, "They don't have any weapons. Do you think one of us should get armed and go make sure their OK."

Billy nodded, "Yeah probably should."

He started to go inside. Then Matt said, "Never mind I hear them." Billy stopped and listened. It was another five minutes before he heard them. They spotted them as they rode over a rise. Then down into another low spot. As they rode up Matt and Billy could see that all three of them had big pleased smiles on their faces. Matt and Billy started forward as they headed toward the cove they had boxed in to keep their horses. The women waved them back as Helen said, "We'll take care of them now that we know we have them." So Matt and Billy just stayed and watched. Matt knew he was getting himself in a fix again. But he just couldn't take his eyes off them. Their breasts were bouncing. It started to get him all worked up again. After a few minutes the women came up. They each gave Billy a kiss on his cheek and thanked him. Billy flushed and a little red from the nearness of them said, "Your welcome." Then each in turn hugged Matt real close. They'd put their bodies tight against him and kissing him full on the lips. Connie was the last one. After her assault she turned to Billy then said, "I'd like to talk to Matt please."

Billy nodded, then with Star and Helen went inside. Matt after the assault on him was so filled with emotion and passion that he was dizzy. He was afraid if he moved he would fall down. He was trying to control his desires and hadn't heard what Connie said. He was just barely aware of being left with just Connie. Connie was completely aroused from her contact with Matt. So it took her a little while to get her thoughts back. When she had them in place again she said, "Matt. We have another gift to give you today."

Matt after his contact with all the women. Was in a worst state than he had been in all day. He was sure that even a gust of wind would finish him.

Matt in pure torment with a strained voice just above a whisper asked, "Did they go in to fix it?"

"No. They wanted me to explain."

Matt didn't understand, he tried to think. He got some of his awareness back as he asked, "Explain what?"

Connie knowing Matt since they were young. Knew it was best not to make a long story out of it. So she just said, "Our next gift to you is us."

Matt's mouth formed a great big OH.

Connie continued, "I know your beliefs. Star told us it's not usual for a man to have more than one wife. You know from the Bible, that it is not completely out of the question."

Matt with everything that had happened today. Now realized they had been setting him up on purpose. He tried to get mad at them. But couldn't do it. All he could think of was the hardening going on between his legs. His voice was real husky as he said, "It's not right. There's nobody here to marry us. We shouldn't even be talking about such things before there is.

Connie asked, "What do you mean by we?"

Matt usually clear minded. Was really having trouble with his thoughts. Connie, was unnerving him. She was proudly standing right in front of him. She had even spread her feet slightly apart and his eyes seemed to have a will of their own. They traveled from her breast nipples, then to the patch of hair between her legs. He stuttered as he said, "Us. I guess well all of us."

With a great effort Connie kept her joy and amusement to herself. She knew what they had done. They had really worked Matt over. Matt usually had complete control of himself in any situation. Right now his control was at it's breaking point if not already gone. Her control was on the verge of being completely gone also. She felt feverish. Choosing her words carefully she asked, "Is it a preacher that would make us married, or the commitment that we would make to each other."

Matt's face showed his confusion as he said, "Well that's simple. It is the commitment that is the most important."

To keep her advantage Connie said, "That's the way we feel. I'm glad we're all in agreement. After Billy comes out. You come in and one of us will be ready." She walked off before he could say anything.

Being left alone gave him some time to think. What had he agreed to? He thought things through again. Then knew he had to talk them out of it. It did seem like they had everything worked out. But it wasn't right now that he'd had time to get his thoughts straightened out. He'd made up his mind that he would never ask or marry anyone unless he was really deeply in love with them. When the word love registered on his brain it shocked him. He then realized he was in love with each one of them. Connie and he had been together ever since they could walk. But they had never mentioned the word love. He loved Helen and Star also he just realized. He supposed he had fell for them at first sight. He couldn't think or see how it was right to love all three. But there it was. He really did.

Inside the cave Connie went to Star and Helen. They had a quiet conversation. Billy knew something big was up. He didn't say anything just observed. In a short time the women had gone to their bed. They'd fluffed it all up then covered it with the buffalo hide that had been completely cured with the hair left on. Then out of the corner of his eye he saw them rub something on Connie that made her skin glow. Billy could smell the pleasant fragrance also. Then Connie and Star did the same with Helen. Star was touched up also. They all smelled real sweet. They had the same glow they'd had when Matt and him had returned earlier that day. Then as Star and Helen started to walk toward the entrance Star said, "Billy would you walk with us."

Billy just nodded. Stooped grabbed his rifle then followed along behind them. When they got outside. Helen said, "Matt Connie is ready."

Matt had made up his mind to talk them out of a hasty reaction. He had hoped he would have to do it only once. But it looked like he would have to explain it to them one at a time. He went into the cave and was lost. For Connie laid on the bed her skin with a fresh glow and her legs slightly apart. Matt felt himself get harder if that was possible. He stopped then as he started to say what he'd been thinking. Connie said, "I'm ready for you." she had then hesitated a bit, "I think."

Then she licked her lips as Matt's eyes devoured her. She moved slightly opening her fruited passion a little bit. He saw that it was glistening, invitingly. He looked into Connie's eyes then. They were full of passion. They flashed lightning bolts that went straight through him. Matt hurried to her. They both greedily reached for each other. Not gentle at all he was on top of her. They were both beyond foreplay. Both of them long past any embarrassment now. By instinct Connie reached down grabbed Matt's hardness and guided it into her own hot volcano. She'd felt the hard throb of it in her hand. It had excited her beyond belief. Nature now had control of both of them.

Matt wanted to plunge all the way in. With the last thread of control he held rein on his desire as he eased into her. He was so excited that he was afraid that he'd lose control before he even got in. As he started to enter her she removed her hand. Then she put both of them on his backside as she pulled him into her. He didn't know why. But he decided to let her guide him in. In a second he was glad he'd done so. For he felt her tense up. He'd stopped and started to pull out. Connie with her voice thick with passion, said, "It's OK. Just a second. I've got to have you in me."

She had her hands firmly on his backside slowly urging him all the way in. Matt felt Connie tense a time or two more. But finely he was all the way in. He'd felt Connie spread and raise her knee's up beside his hips.

Connie had felt some pain. And was glad that Matt had been so gentle. But she had felt a spark of something as it shot through her body. It hinted at something yet to come. Something intense and so good.

Matt then moved in and out. He tried to be gentle. But after three or four strokes. He was in full rhythm. His strokes had gotten harder and harder.

Connie had felt some more pain the first few strokes. But as it eased some she relaxed. Then it really started to feel good. She felt Matt tense then thrust real hard a couple of times. Then she felt him as he started to spurt into her. As she felt Matt soften a little she was disappointed. Matt moved into her again, as she felt him stiffen she urged him on. After a minute it had completed it's enlargement. Connie started to feel something like electrical sparks all through her body. Her body took over to raise her hips up to meet his thrust. Connie worked as hard as Matt now. With each shock wave that shot through her body she demanded more. She felt Matt as he intensified his efforts. As Matt thrust into her really hard a couple of times. With Matt releasing his passion into her, she felt wave after wave of an electrified sensation as it shot up through her body. It started between her legs, up her belly, then through her chest.

As Matt finished, he groaned with the effort of his passion. Connie had moaned and gasped for the last few minutes. He was afraid he'd hurt her some. But his body had been beyond his control. When he'd caught a flash of the desire and passion from her eyes that matched his. He'd thrust into her vigorously. They were both out of breath. Matt's member softened then deflated. He'd slowly eased off of Connie to lay on his back beside her. Matt had nothing he could compare with the love making Connie and he had just done. But it was by far the best feeling he'd ever had.

After Matt withdrew from Connie she felt as if a part of her had been taken from within her. But she was aglow with the warmth of her passion. She'd never felt so good. Connie snuggled up to Matt on his left side. He wrapped his arm around her. Then pulled her tight to his chest. Her breasts against him. Connie kissed Matt on the lips. Then laid her head on his shoulder. They rested their pleasure filled bodies as their breath, returned back to normal.

After a short rest when they sat up. Connie saw a worried look on Matt's face. Connie asked, "What's wrong?"

"I've hurt you."

"At first a little. Nothing to be upset about though." "Your bleeding a little."

"Oh! I'm sorry I forgot. It felt so good. Star told me to expect it. Her people, discuss sex openly. Come lets get cleaned up."

Taking hands like the lovers they'd been. They went to the hot pool. They playfully cleaned each other. After all they had just shared they had become so much more then just friends. It was a relief of sorts. That they didn't have to worry about the guilt of their thoughts anymore. They had done it. Right or wrong.

Connie after their bath. Was still a little rubber legged from their love making. She got a little bit to eat. She was hungry. She gave some to Matt. He thanked her as she headed toward the entrance. Back over her shoulder she said, "Set, and rest. Helen will be right in."

When Connie looked back she saw that her comment had the affect she'd wanted. For Matt's manhood had started to grow. Matt decided he had less control over the events and his body then he ever wanted to admit. He hadn't realized he'd get aroused so easily. Just at the mention of one of their names. He couldn't help himself. For as good as it had been with Connie. He already looked forward to making love with Helen. He'd gotten pretty well aroused by the time Helen came in. She was all aglow and smelled good. Matt saw she was excited. She was a little flushed. Which he thought made her even more beautiful. As they embraced Matt felt her rock hard nipples against his chest. He was pleased to see a startled expression of anticipation as his manhood let her know how she had affected him. They laid down as they kissed and soothed each other with their hands. Matt knew what to expect now and he was ready.

Helen's excitement had grown. She was still a little apprehensive. Being around women a lot more then Connie had. She'd remembered some of the gossip she'd heard from the women folk. How they had complained and talked about how bad sex was. So when Matt started to mount her she reached for Matt's manhood. More out of defense than anything else. A thrilling shiver ran up her spine as she felt the throbbing pulse and the firmness of it between her fingers. She guided him to the spot of her budding desire. Matt felt her tenseness. He had also noticed she wasn't as wet as Connie had been. He'd eased up and started kissing her breasts. He teased her nipples with his lips. Helen responded and started to moan. As her passion grew Matt eased into her moistening desire. Helen as her excitement grew relaxed and opened her legs wider. Then she let go of his manhood letting it into her. She felt the pressure as she was opened wider and wider. Matt felt the restriction as he had with Connie. He gave a slight thrust and felt a pop. He had stopped then. He'd felt Helen tense she'd started to clamp her legs together. He kissed her breasts as he waited for her relax. As the excitement built up between them he was able to enter her all the way. Helen felt as if she was completely stuffed. Matt then started to move inside her. Slow as he watched her eyes. When he saw them take on the same expression as Connie's had. Filled with passion. He realized that their eyes looked exactly the same. Not in color. But the same intense sparks of passion. It made his passion grow to the fullest. When Helen started to moan. Matt increased his thrust. Helen as if she had caught fire started to gasp, "Go, go harder, go, yes, yes." Matt built up to his peak. Helen had now lost all hesitancy. She was thrusting up to meet him. Matt had all he could do to stay on as he rode her hard now. She moaned uncontrollably as her head rolled from side to side. Then she erupted with uncontrolled spasms as Matt spurted into her. She kept repeating, "Oh! So good."

Matt started to ease out as he felt his member start to deflate. Helen reached up and pulled him all the way down on top of her. She kissed him several times. Then said, "Oh Matt that was so good. I wanted you so bad. But I let the wives tales that I had heard frighten me." Matt knew he had to be heavy. He rolled them over and was able to succeed in keeping Helen tight to him. She smiled as she looked into Matt's eyes saying, "Oh Matt I'm so happy."

Matt relaxed his hold on her as he said, "You've made me happy also."

Matt felt Helen try to raise up so he took his arms from around her. She then carefully brought her legs up on each side of him. Too his surprise Matt saw that Helen sat on him with his softened manhood still inside her. She then started to move back and forth just a little bit as he started to grow again. It didn't take long before it was hard again. She then started to move faster and faster. When Matt got close to shooting his load up into her. She must have felt it. For she'd slowed down almost to a stop. He'd been about ready to go nuts. He'd been close to going over the top. She then went into motion faster again. Then slowed down again. She repeated it a couple of more times. Finely she didn't play anymore. Which Matt was glad of he felt like his emotions where about frazzled. Then she started to ride him harder and harder. Matt thrust up into her, hard. She moaned as she rode him like some wild thing. He noticed as her eyes went wide open then glazed over. As his load shot up inside her she said, "OH YES."

Her eyes closed then she fell forward on his chest. Matt could feel her as she was spastic around his manhood. He felt spasms from her belly also. She breathed hard but steady. Matt breathed hard, also. They both glistened with sweat. Matt said, "Oh baby, that was so good."

He hadn't gotten no response. Matt said, "Helen."

Still with no response Matt gently rolled her over and looked at her worriedly. She was breathing so he knew she was alive. He was about to go out to get some help when her eyes fluttered open. She smiled at him and said, "Oh Matt. Thanks! That was so good. I love you."

Matt said, "I love you. You sure your OK. You scared me."

"Oh Matt I feel great. I'm just tired."

"Good." He stood on shaky legs. For he had used a lot of energy. And had climaxed real hard also. He then said, "Guess we should get cleaned up." Helen smiled and nodded. He reached down and helped her up. Holding each other they went to the hot pool. After they got clean and revived a little. They got out and stood by the fire as they dried. Mostly dry after a few minutes Helen said, "I'm going to get a bite to eat. Then take some out to Billy. You want something?" "No I'm fine thanks."

Helen said, "Thank you! thanks."

Then walked on out putting a extra sway to her hips. She peeked back to see that she'd gotten the desired results she'd wanted.

It wasn't long before Star came in. Matt upon seeing her was amazed at himself. He was getting aroused again. He smiled and spoke in her language as he said, "You're beautiful."

As he gazed upon her and all of her beauty her eyes flashed with bolts of lightning that shot right into his soul. She answered in her language very pleased at the respect that Matt had just given her. She said, "Thank you, you are very handsome."

She was not as shy. She'd waited to meet her mate and actually mate. She was ready and full of desire. To stretch out his muscles as well as giving himself time to get some more of his energy back. Matt said, "I'm thirsty I'll be there shortly."

As he returned he noticed that Star's gaze was right between his legs as he strode to the pallet the women had made. For some reason it gratified him as Star had looked a little apprehensively. He'd never compared, but he'd always thought he'd been blessed. He stretched out beside Star. They playfully teased each other. Matt was hard. Star was aroused. More than ready. He'd sensed that Star was already well stimulated. He wanted it to be real good for her. So he took his time stoking up the fire before he rose above her to enter her. As he did so she reached down instinctively guide him into her.

She opened her legs wide for him. Her people had been plain in telling her about sex. With her fingers she held him in position till he started to ease into her. Star then reached up to grab his backside. With her legs spread as wide as she could get them. She pulled hard with all her strength. Matt at her urging plunged all the way into her. She had expected the pain and wanted to get it over with.

Matt all the way in was throbbing as he looked into Star's eyes. He'd seen the touch of pain in them. He waited for the pain to subside. When he saw pure passion light her eyes up. He was astonished as he noticed, that her eyes had done as Connie's and Helen's had. The same lighting storm that flashed from them right into him. He started to move inside her and heard her gasp. Then felt her hands urging him on. As their passion grew they adapted to each others movements. Star was insistent and they reached their peak quicker than Matt intended.

They rested a little then Star reached for Matt and played with him. It didn't take long before she had it growing again. She was then eager for Matt to mount her again. As he positioned himself over her she raised her legs up to put her ankles on his shoulders. He hesitated then she nodded and urged him on in. As he did so he really got turned on by how wide she had opened up for him as he watched until he was all the way in. He then moved in and out of her. He was turned on by the action as he became more intense with each move. Star with the intense angle and the deepness of Matt's thrust was getting real hot with passion also. Matt had learned a lot already. He brought them both to the brink of their passion three times and them slowed down. Star rocked her head back and forth and wasn't saying anything except a babbling that she repeated. At last he reached his limit and started thrusting hard and deep into her. Then he felt her finger nails dig into his back. He was thankful that she didn't run them up and down. She just pulled at him as if she could force all of him into her. Matt felt her muscles start to spasm. That's all it took for him to release his passion deep into her. He relaxed some as he had shrunk, then he slowly drew out of her. To his surprise Star had passed out with her passion. He eased her ankles from his shoulders to stretch out beside him. Matt knew he was spent now and laid on his back. He drew Star close and put her head on his chest. After a couple of minutes he saw her eyes open. She smiled and snuggled closer to him if possible. They were both sweaty. That's one thing Matt didn't like about himself. He sweated enough for two people.

After a little while they got up and went to the hot pool. They cleaned each other completely. Then went and dried by the fire. With the passion still showing in her eyes Star said, "I love you."

They spoke her language Matt said, "I love you."

He saw her eyes sparkle with warmth. He thought she hadn't expected him to say so. She turned to the padding they used as a bed and started to remove the buffalo hide to clean it. She said, "Maybe the others are getting cold."

Matt nodded then said, "I'll go get them."

It was good that he had. It had gotten dark out and had cooled off a lot. Connie and Helen were both cold and went to stand by the fire.

Billy not being dumb knew what had happened. He hadn't made up his mind on the right or wrong of it. But one thing for sure he'd never seen such a happy look on their faces that just glowed from their love making. Matt even had the most relaxed and satisfied look Billy had ever seen him have. Billy got a drink and went to his bed. As he laid down he noticed that Matt was completely relaxed. Billy thought it had been a long time since that was the case.

Helen and Connie warmed up some helped Star. Shortly their bed was remade. Matt started to head to his when he heard a noise and looked back. The women shook their heads and motioned for him to come to their bed. He looked at Billy's place and then back. They motioned again and then he went to join them. They had him lay in the middle one on one side. The other two on the other. Matt had been sure he'd be asleep in five minutes. He wasn't so sure of that now.

Captain Taylor, Hawkeye, Tex and the rest of the cowboys had gotten restless and were ready to go. It was the end of March. They all had, had enough of the settlers lives. They still had money. For not like most they didn't spend all their money on women and booze. They had spent some, but had managed to save most of it. They had set up a camp a little ways out from the main settlement.

They still had done things to help when they could do it from the back of their horses. They were now ready to go look for the youngsters. Chris Maxton still wanted to pay them but they still refused. He had however finely gotten them to except his offer to supply them. He had insisted that they take most of the rifles, pistols and the ammo for each gun they had with them. He was sure that if Matt had to have holed up someplace or any other problems Matt and his party may of had. That they probably would need the weapons and the ammo. Captain Taylor agreed. They had gotten everything packed and were ready to go. They wanted to get through the passes and over the mountains as soon as possible.

The Maxton's and the Gates' had come up to see them off. Chris was still hopeful, but just couldn't help having some doubts. He asked Captain Taylor, "You really think there's hope and you are not going on a long trip for nothing."

Captain Taylor in a firm voice said, "We'll find them you'll see."

The women became worried when they heard Mr. Maxton put their fears to words. A hopeful spark came to their eyes however with Captain Taylor's response.

Tex, Hawkeye, Slim, Bones, Slade, and Dan Wade in like words had told them that they were sure that Matt and the others would have made it through the winter.

When they got through the mountains they hoped to join up with the Black Hawks. Hawkeye was sure he could find Strong Arm's winter camp in the Yellow Stones. They said their good-byes and mounted their horses.

The Maxton's and the Gate's watched until the cowboys rode out of sight. The Gate's then headed home. They had their house and barn built now. They just waited on the weather now to do their spring planting.

Chris was just waiting for the first ship to come in and open up for business. The warehouse was finished. Chris already had people waiting on some of the trade goods. The local people were pleased with the prices he had quoted. They were as anxious as he was to get opened up for business. Not all were happy. There was a couple of mercantile businesses that were having trouble already, because of their higher prices. People just bought enough of the necessary things to get by on, until the warehouse and store opened up.

CHAPTER EIGHTEEN

GOLD APRIL 1879

Matt was cutting fire wood. He had already rolled some stones into place. He had built a melting pot of sorts. He had found a large stone that had a trough shape on top. He had braced it up by putting two other stones underneath it. He had to let the fire burn a long time to get enough heat from under the stone trough to melt the gold. Then it would run off into the molds he had made. He was able to break the soft quartz rock loose with a pointed piece of stone that was a lot harder. It weighed a hundred pounds however. So that was why he made sure when he dropped it on the quartz he was well out of the way. Matt had set everything up on the clay bank next to the river. Then he was able to form some molds out of the clay. He already had five bars. He guessed they weighed about forty pounds each.

Matt had made his discovery by accident. On nice days they all had started to ride out away from the cave. He had been out for a long ride, just to see a new part of the valley that ran northwest from the cave they lived in. He'd covered quiet a lot of ground that day. But when he'd been about ready to turn around and go back he'd spotted a bright reflection. He could see he was in a box canyon with a water fall coming off the top of a mountain ledge at the far end of it. Then he decided to see what the sun was reflecting off of. So far he was sure that he was the only one that knew about it. On some of the warmer nights he had even stayed at the river bank next to the fire. He did have a cover of sorts that the women had tanned from one of the deer hides.

Matt had been on cloud nine for the first couple of weeks after their little party and making love to the women for the first time. They had repeated their union many times. It seemed like they just couldn't get enough of each other. The women couldn't get enough of Matt. They had let their sexual desires run wild. With no one to say what was right or wrong. They had just done what they felt. Even if it was a little wild.

When he'd been on his first ride away from them to get some fresh air and explore the valley. That was when it really hit him; on what they had done. At first Matt was real mad at himself, for letting things get out of control. He had a hard time then to understand how he had in one night, become the husband of three beautiful women. Now that it was done. As far as he was concerned there was no other way to look at it. He'd then determined that it was up to him to care and take care of all their needs. How he had no idea, because he wanted each one of them to be treated like a Queen. If it was at all possible for him to do so. He'd made up his mind that he would never let anyone slander or insult a one of them. That he would take the blame for letting things get out of control.

Billy had found and made a place for himself, at another little cave not far from the main one. It was big enough to sleep in with enough extra space to have a fire. He needed the fire as some of the nights were still pretty cool and none of them had any extra clothing to keep warm. Billy still had his meals with them. They had agreed with his decision. They had apologized to him to be the cause of him moving out. He had told them that it was alright. That he'd get more sleep anyway. His comment had made each of them blush even Matt. Matt could tell that Billy had become a man already as far as he was concerned. Mostly because he'd had to or go crazy from all that he'd had to witness.

As he worked Matt reflected back. It had taken him a few days before he finally got his thoughts together. He'd felt bad about what had happened between the women and him. But not so much from their love making, because that was fantastic.

He was concerned what people would think about the women. Then the big problem of how he was to support them in the manner he thought they should have. Matt wanted them to have the best of everything and to make their lives the easiest, he could for them. He knew his family was wealthy. But he was determined not to use a dime of their money.

So when he'd found the ledge of gold he hoped it was the answer to his problem. It had raised his spirits a lot. Maybe it would be enough at the least, to give them the money for a good start. With the discovery of the gold Matt had a much better attitude. He'd been quite solemn back at the cave. The others had picked up on it and asked him if anything was wrong. Billy had even been concerned. Matt had told them he was fine. Things had gotten strained from time to time though.

Through all that had happened Matt couldn't understand how the women got along so good. He'd never seen them fuss. He knew it had to be rough on them. Away from their families then just living in a hole in the ground. Nothing that amounted to anything good to wear. But, they seemed cheerful most of the time. It amazed him that they were able to keep their hair so shiny and clean along with the rest of their bodies. As he thought of each of them and their bodies it started a reaction in his loins. Concentrating back on his work again. He thought that it seemed like the women had become so much a part of him that he couldn't exist without them. Matt didn't know the exact time or when. But now he knew that he loved each one of them very deeply.

With his fire built up from the coals left over from last nights fire he added some more wood. In a few minutes the stone with the trough in it had heated up enough for the gold to melt and start to run. As the gold dripped down on it's way to the molds he had made. He took his rock hammer to the ledge and broke off some more chunks of the quartz. With a dull thud his rock had gotten caught. He had to wiggle it around to loosen it up. When he was finally able to pull it out the point and the next ten inches had a golden shine to it.

Excited Matt pulled the loosened quartz out of the way and in a short time he uncovered a vain of gold with some traces of something else going through it. The ore then came up in bigger chunks. They were quite a bit heavier and melted down faster.

When he saw how quick it melted he used a stick to form another mold on each side of the others. Cutting a little ditch to each of then he soon had them ready. When one of them filled up Matt put a stone in the ditch to the mold so the melted gold ore then had to run to another mold. When it cooled off enough he took the gold bar out then removed the stone to let his mold fill up again. Matt worked steady for the next three hours. He ended up making four more molds which were full. As the fire had cooled down he cleaned the scrap rock out of his trough with a stick. Before the gold cooled off enough to stick to it. Matt was the happiest he had ever been in his life.

He then let the wildest dreams imaginable run through his mind. He pictured building up the valley into something real special. He let his mind run wild with his thoughts. Oh he just hoped the women would like what his racing mind had already thought of. As he thought of them he was nervous. For he thought that they would probably want to be around their families which he could understand.

Matt's circumstances were different though. This was just the chance he had been waiting for. To make a break from the rest of the family. He guessed that was why he fought with his father so much. He had been determined to make his own way. To make is own mistakes, right or wrong.

When he finished cleaning up his camp. He double checked to make sure there wasn't any hot spots from his fire. He didn't want to start a wildfire. He mounted Flame and headed for the cave and the others. He let Flame set his own pace and just sat back in the saddle relaxed. It was around seventy miles back to the cave. At Flames easy pace which would've worn out most horses. They'd be there in seven or eight hours. That would make it around midnight when they got there. He couldn't wait.

He let his mind drift back to his previous thoughts. He was worried what people would think of Connie, Helen, and Star. For himself he wasn't that concerned. He'd kind of gotten used to people not expecting much of him. Matt knew one thing though. If someone didn't like the arrangement they had made they'd better keep it to themselves. For he wasn't about to let the women be insulted or even as much as an unkind word spoken against them if he could help it.

Billy after Matt and the women had made their union together. Knew that things had changed. Matt and him had become closer than brothers. He had learned more than he ever thought possible, since he met Matt. When Billy had first seen Matt he knew that Matt was different. How much, he had no idea. For he was not sure anyone could do some of the things he had seen Matt do. So at the time he just knew, that he wanted to be around to see what would happen next, whenever he could. He had no idea he would be right in the middle of the action though. With Matt it wasn't just his physique and demeanor. Matt was highly intelligent. They all had found that out. Because when they'd settled down for the night. Matt would make sure they learned something. Math, English, History, or something. He had insisted on it.

Not only were the studies bothersome. As far as he was concerned the training of using the guns and caring for them was just plain work. They never got to shoot them. What he did like was what Matt called Martial Arts. After the moves had become natural to him, he was pretty quick. Billy thought yes he was fast, but compared to Matt he was slow. Connie made him feel a little better when she had told them Matt was much faster than he had ever been. The statement had embarrassed Matt. Billy had then wondered about Matt's childhood. It seemed like Matt got completely flustered with any compliments. Matt acted like he'd never gotten much praise at all.

Billy like the others when the weather had been nice went out to explore the valley. He'd spent a night or two away from the cave on a couple of the warmer nights. It looked like the big valley was void of anything with two legs except for the five of them. They all felt safe, but Connie still with an iron will made sure they were always armed with their guns. After Matt's fight with the bear he made sure he was within reach of one at all times. The rest had followed suit, with Connie's insistence.

Billy was in love with the valley. It was so big it would take three or four weeks to ride around the outside perimeter. There was all kinds of game. Each of them had spotted mountain lions, wild horses, buffalo, deer, antelope, wolves, coyotes, plus all sorts of small game. Billy had gotten so he hated the idea of having to leave and go back to farm work. After being taught how to handle himself and the guns. It would be awfully hard for him to settle down to farm life again. He missed the rest of his family. But the thing now was that it would be awful hard when it got to be time to part ways with the women and Matt. They were such a big part of his life now. As his thoughts went to them.

Maybe it was all the danger and trouble that they'd been through in the short time they had been together, that made them feel so close.

The courage that every single one of the women had, was apparent when they were being tortured. He still hadn't gotten over that. He was so proud of them. Billy had a real problem, for he couldn't see how his heart would take it, when it would be time to separate from them. He was afraid he would be in their way or unwanted. That was one of the reasons he had found his own place to sleep in. Each one of the women had all there concerns for Matt only. He had never seen them so happy. He would never let anybody harm or say anything bad about any of the women if he could help it. But he just had to be there when they told his parents about their arrangement with Matt. That promised to be a real good show. Billy had finely decided that under the circumstances that they all had been through. That he didn't have a problem with it.

Billy then thought about Matt. There just wasn't enough adjectives to explain about him and his abilities. Billy felt like Matt was almost a God. Matt had been friendly with him and taught him how to track along with the other things that it would take to survive out here. Billy was proud of the fact that he was able to track better than the rest. Well except for Star and Matt of course.

Billy let his thoughts drift as he rode back to the cave and home. Well he met the women as he rethought. But it would be nice if it was home. He couldn't think of a place he would rather be. Billy had been out to explore the valley often. He had almost finished training the young stallion Matt and he had captured. He'd been away six days this trip and would make it back just before dark. He had been a hundred-fifty miles from the cave. Billy had found, what looked like to have been at one time a trail that ran up the face of a big cliff. It had at one time gone all the way to the top. But a giant rock slid or earthquake had wiped it out. He was sure then that was how most of the animals had gotten into the valley. He really looked forward to getting back and telling everyone about his knew discovery.

Billy let his thoughts drift to Matt as he guided his stallion with his knees. He was used to riding bare back and comfortable with the stallions stride. He wondered what Matt was up to. Matt had been in a better frame of mind when he had returned to the cave the last couple of times. Before that Matt had been tense with a gloomy frown, like the war of the worlds was going on in his mind. Then things had suddenly changed. Matt had returned more like the active person they were used to. Billy knew that Matt was up to something mysterious. It was a dead giveaway when he had taken the axe with him. Matt's lame excuse hadn't fooled any of them. At least that was what he thought.

Connie, Helen, and Star, had spent a lot of time working with their horses. Matt, and Billy had done a real good job of training them. They'd really fell in love with them. The women got to the point of really babying them. The mares had gotten so they watched for anyone of the women to come out of the cave. When they spotted one of the women they ran up, like big house dogs would've.

The meat was about gone. Some of it had spoiled. They had agreed not to kill anything else until they needed it. The next day or so they would need some fresh meat. It would taste real good. Matt and Billy surely, had to have been eating fresh meat, Connie thought. The stinkers.

They had decided for her to tell Matt of their new surprise. They were not to surprised on their part. It fell into place that with each of them being healthy and with Star's knowledge of the roots, herbs and berries they had been able to store. They had something to supplement their meat diet with, so they could eat good and stay healthy.

Connie tried to decide if it would please Matt or if he would be upset. She was worried about that. She knew how much Matt valued his freedom.

None of them had been regular since they'd been taken captive. Star had told Helen and her that her life's flow hadn't been regular either. They'd been sure that with the stress of caring for Matt and the worry that each of them had for him. Had probably, caused them to miss. They knew now that wasn't why they had missed the last couple of months. Besides they could already tell that there belly's had started to swell.

Connie was a little surprised that Matt, nor Billy had noticed already. Well with whatever it was that had troubled Matt. Maybe that's why he hadn't noticed. It had been tense for all of them, as they'd tried to comfort Matt. Which just seemed to trouble him more. So they all had been quiet, deep with their own thoughts. Oh, their love making had still been good. Maybe Matt had been a little ruff. But that had pleased them in another way, deep within them.

Connie, Helen and Star had talked openly and freely whenever Matt and Billy had gone out on there trips. They had worked out a lot of things. As good as things had become between them. They had to rationalize things out with each other, to have a good understanding with each other. There had been a danger of them being jealous of each other. The thing that had helped them the most was that they noticed Matt made no preference to a single one of them. So after a lot of talk, they'd worked most everything out in there minds. They'd become closer to each other than they would ever have dreamed possible. They liked to kid each other and just spoke of whatever came to their minds. There wasn't anything they hadn't talked about or hid from each other. Star had even opened up about her ability to see into the spirit world.

Connie and Helen believed her. Star made sure that they understood that she had no control over her powers. That sometimes she could see things real clear and then sometimes it was like things were hidden in a thick fog. But, her visions did help from time to time. They were convinced that they'd already been helped by her visions. Within all their conversations they'd come to the conclusion. That they loved each other nearly as much as they each loved Matt. Connie with a thought of Matt had decided she would just come right out and tell him.

Helen deep in her thoughts was a little apprehensive, but she was excited also. They'd all worked on preparing a real good meal for the night. Star had assured them that Matt and Billy would be back tonight. Helen had never been as happy as she had been the last two or three months. The other two agreed also. They each loved their horses and worked with them until they had become, like big over grown dogs. They had made pets of them. But, they had agreed that it was what Matt had done to them each time he'd been with them. He really made them glow with the warmth of their feelings that was apparent on their satisfied faces.

They'd been busy through the winter months as they had made some more clothing for each of them out of the hides. Matt and Billy first, they had enough buckskin, to make each of them a jacket and some leggings. The leggings weren't long and the jackets didn't have sleeves. But, they did provide some warmth. Then with the doeskins they'd made a couple of loin cloths for each of them and then a long leather wrap that was like a skirt and shirt combined. At least they had their breasts and private area, covered most of the time out of respect, for Billy. Of course they where glad of the warmth the skins gave them as they worked outside or went for a ride out into the valley.

Helen like the others had thought about her family often. Now however it was more to let them know that she was fine and they didn't need to worry about her. Oh; she missed them, but she had what see wanted and was where she wanted to be. She thought maybe that Billy was the one that was out of place. He hadn't said a thing though and seemed to be enjoying himself now. Especially since Matt and he had caught the young stallion. Billy had done a real good job of training him. He'd told her it was pretty easy if you did as Matt taught you.

Billy had then told her how much he thought of Matt. Billy had told her that he didn't think there was anything that Matt could not do. Especially when it came to fighting. She'd cautioned him as she told him that Matt had almost died twice because of his fights. Helen would never forget Billy's response. Billy had paused a minute then told her, I think he just needed to rest up some. I don't know of anything that could kill him. Helen pretty much knew then that Billy thought of Matt, nearly as much as he would a God. Then she also thought as bad as it would effect Connie, Star, and her. If something was to happen and they lost Matt. Billy might be the one that would have the hardest time recovering if they did lose Matt.

Helen purposely changed her thoughts to more pleasant things. She thought of her unrestrained love for Matt and the others. Connie, Star and her were closer than she'd ever been with her family. And she thought that her family had been closer than most.

Bright Star was exceedingly happy. She couldn't think of a thing that would improve her state of mind. She had ended up with a warrior beyond compare. Her people, after hearing of the feats he had already done, would be very proud. He would bring much honor to her and her people. She knew that if Matt chose to do so. That he could have all the braves he wanted from among her people. If he needed them to go into some battle or most any other quest.

She wasn't worried about whether they'd believe her or not. For he wore the scars of his exploits on his body. At the thought of his body, her body instantly warmed up. Star thought he had a magnificent body. Then to make things even better his male member was magnificent. She felt like it reached deep inside to stir up one emotion after another, so intense that it felt like it was about to destroy her. Then when about to pass out from the intensity of it something changed. Then it was as if the life was being pumped back into her to explode with a big eruption. Connie and Helen had told her that making love with Matt had effected them nearly the same way. It was like the three of them were of one body and mind as far as Matt was concerned.

With a big effort Star concentrated back on her work. Her thoughts of Matt had made her wet between her legs. Her thoughts then went to her new sisters. That's how she'd come to think of Connie and Helen. She loved them as much as she did Matt. She also realized that she had a lot of love for Billy. She was real proud of him. In the few short months she had known him, he had become a man. She knew he was still growing, but Billy was already a man that would standout in any crowd. Star thought if it came to action, a lot men would be hurting. As far as that went, Matt had seen to it that they all could take care of themselves. Bare hands, against knives or any other weapons.

The thing that Star still didn't understand was why Matt had insisted on teaching them all to read, write and do arithmetic. Star hadn't liked it much and didn't see any need for it. But with Connie and Helen's help she did very good. That's what they told her. Billy hadn't cared for it much either. But he did good also. She did get her reward though. They had learned her language and all of them spoke it without to much trouble now.

Star knew that her people would be proud of her for saving many of the girls when her camp had been attacked. Now though with what Matt had taught her she knew that it would be very hard for anybody to get the upper hand. Even against many she thought she could hold her own.

With her mind back on her work. Star like Connie and Helen was excited, even a little uncertain at how Matt would take the news when he returned. She was sure that it would be tonight.

Captain Taylor with Dan, Hawkeye and the cowboys had made it through a high pass during one of the winter thaws. It was a pass not often used even in good weather. It wasn't much more than a game trail as it wound its way through the mountain. With a cliff on one side, then down a little to raise up again with a cliff on the other side. They'd worked up a good sweat by the time they'd pulled, pushed and fought with the horses to get them on through. From nervousness as much as the physical strain. Everyone had gotten impatient when they thought they would have to turn back. Hawkeye had told them about it and how dangerous it was. He hadn't exaggerated any. Some of them told him he could have told them a little more. But they'd made it through the pass without any misfortune.

It was on the trip from Portland Oregon to the pass that they'd had their problems. They'd been set upon twice by some bandits. Because of the extra pack horses full of supplies they had attracted a lot of attention. The first fight had been fierce and deadly.

When it was over they'd left eight body's with a couple more that might not live and three others slightly wounded, to care for them.

Captain Taylor had gotten a bullet through his left shoulder and Hawkeye had received a burn on the right side of his neck from a passing bullet. Bones had taken a bullet in his right thigh that had stopped against the bone. Hawkeye the handiest with a knife dug it out, while Dan, Tex, Slim and Ben held him still.

Dan figured he was pretty handy with his six-shooter. But he saw that Tex, Slade and Ben were not to be trifled with. For when the bandits had rode into camp all sure of themselves because of their greater number they acted like they were pretty tough. They found out in a hurry how wrong they'd been. When the first one made a move for his pistol. Tex, Slade and Ben had cleared leather first and started to empty saddles. Dan didn't know which one of the three was the fastest. Only that he was behind them and he was sure the Captain, Slim and Bones been the last to get into action. Hawkeye had a rifle on them from some brush he had been hidden in. Hawkeye hadn't been in the line of fire. Slim had told him that the burn on his neck might have come from a ricochet or maybe, even one of them. Hawkeye had just grunted then commented that with all the lead that had been flying around it wouldn't surprise him.

Seeing that there was no real hurry and having a good camp they'd spent a few days there until they were sure their wounds were healed enough so they wouldn't open up and become infected when they started to travel. Hawkeye had followed the bandits for a day to make sure they would not cause anymore trouble.

The second time they had been confronted by another band of bandits that were passing through the area. Ben spotted one of the bandits as he tried to sneak a gun out on them. Ben blew him out of his saddle before anyone else hardly knew what was up. The rest of the bandits had been taken by surprise as much as anyone. When they had looked back up from where their friend had fell, they were looking into the gun barrels of Tex, Slade and Ben. There'd still been a few tense seconds, then they'd just turned their horses to leave. Captain Taylor stopped them, then told them to take the dead man with them. They'd looked at the guns being held on them , then had done as they were told.

The biggest reason they had decided to push on through the dangerous pass that they didn't want to wait for the snow to thaw enough to use a safer pass, that was at a higher elevation. They had made a little mistake. They had gone too far into the mountains and couldn't find any graze for the horses. They had almost used up all the grain. They decided to go on, instead of going back down the mountain to start over again.

When they cleared the pass Hawkeye found a meadow with a lot of tall grass showing through the snow that was only about a foot deep. There was a stream going through it. They'd cut a hole in the ice to get some water. Then they'd cut another one so the horses could drink. From a stand of pine and cotton wood near-by. They'd cut some poles and made a lean-to. They draped a canvas over it to make a temporary camp. Hawkeye had gone in search of Strong Arms and his people. He had been gone a week, Captain Taylor and Dan thought it to be the middle of March. They were very pleased. It had been brutal on both man and beast. But they had made it a month, if not two ahead of the spring thaw.

Close to the blazing fire they all rested on their blankets and saddles. Except for Slim and Ben who were out on guard. Tex said, "I'm sure glad that we let Mr. Maxton, talk us into bringing all the extra supplies."

Dan answered, "Seemed like, I heard you complain about packing and unpacking, all the supplies the whole trip,"

Captain Taylor, said, "There was a time or two, that I wished we hadn't brought so much. But I think we'll be lucky if we have anything left over. You cowboys eat a lot."

Bones said, "It's getting warmer. We should be able to start hunting as some of the game should start to move around again."

Tex said, "Captain, I haven't seen you miss any meals."

Dan said, "The way the food has been cooked, I would almost rather have missed a couple of meals."

Bones answered, "Oh, I'm sorry. I didn't think I had done that bad."

Dan said, "A...h, your cooking has been fine Bones."

Tex looked at Dan, then asked, "You mean my cooking."

Dan saw that he had got to Tex a little, as he carefully said, "Well, I'll say this. You can handle your shooting iron a lot better than you can cook."

Tex a little perplexed tried to decide whether he had been given a compliment or an insult. Finally smiling a little he said, "Yeah, I guess boiling coffee is about the best, thing I do around the cook fire."

Slade asked, "When was your coffee the best?"

Tex scooped up some snow and threw it at Slade saying, "Well, you fix it then!"

Slade ducked, then responded, "No, I pass, I know my limitations. I burn just plain water."

Everyone then just chuckled.

Slim came in from his guard position to stand next to the fire, then in a low voice said, "There's some riders coming in."

They all made sure of their weapons and spread out, away from the fire. They looked to the south end of the meadow. In a couple of minutes they saw about a half-dozen riders came into view as they cleared some brush. They appeared to be Indians. But, they weren't riding in at them in a threatening manner.

Captain Taylor said, "Don't loose your caution, but you can relax some. Hawkeye is with them."

Dan answered, "You're right, Captain. It sure looks like him. He's on a different horse though."

Tex said, "Yeah, that's what threw me."

They waited as Hawkeye and the Indians rode up. When they'd gotten up pretty close in a low voice Dan said, "I think it is Runs Far and a few of his braves Captain."

Captain Taylor, answered, "I thought so. I couldn't think of anyone else that Hawkeye would bring back with him."

Hawkeye led them into camp. After they jumped off their horses he introduced everyone. Hawkeye interpreted and after a short conversation it was decided that they would stay the night at the cowboys camp. Then leave for Strong Arms' village in the morning. The Indians made quick work of setting up camp. A couple of them took care of the horses as the others built up a fire and laid out their blankets. Then two of them, skinned out a deer they'd jumped up out of a thicket that day. In a short time they had it over the fire. Runs Far told them they would share. When Hawkeye had explained what Runs Far had told him it pleased the cowboys. For there wasn't a good cook among them.

Captain Taylor said, " That's a relief. I don't think my teeth could take much more of that hard tack."

The Captain didn't get a response. The cowboys acted like they wanted to make sure they didn't do anything wrong. It had been quite awhile since they'd had any fresh meat. The cowboys shared some coffee with the Indians. Most of them liked it real sweet though and used up most of the sugar they had. After their meal as they sat around the fire sipping coffee. Hawkeye said, "Runs Far and his people were looking for us. Sees Far told them we had made it through the mountains and were in the area."

Tex with awe showing all over his face asked, "How is that possible?"

Runs Far had joined them. He could speak broken English and understand most of it. He answered Tex, "Sees Far has the gift of being able to see into the Spirit World."

Captain Taylor asked, "Has he seen the youngsters and know if they are okay?"

Runs Far said, "Yes, Sees Far told us that they are well. He did say that the Spirit Warrior had been sick again, but had recovered."

Captain Taylor, Dan Wade and Hawkeye nodded. The cowboys looked at Runs Far, then Captain Taylor and his scouts. They had doubtful looks all over their faces.

Tex looked at his partners seeing the doubt on their faces. Then as he gave a hard look at Captain Taylor he asked, "Do you believe him? Are you taking him serious?"

Hawkeye cut in saying, "Yes, they found me before I made it to their camp. I've heard of the power that Sees Far has."

Tex was still doubtful as he asked, "You, didn't put Runs Far up to pulling a joke, on us; did you?"

Runs Far seeing their doubt just said, "In time you'll see the power of Sees Far. Then you will believe. He doesn't see everything. But what he does see and tells you about, will come true."

Tex and his partners looked everyone over good. They hadn't seen a smile. So they decided to be contented. But they were still along way from being convinced.

Slade asked, "Who or what is the Spirit Warrior?"

Now it was Runs Far's turn. He gave them a cautious puzzled look. Then he said, "He is one of the people that you are looking for. He has much power he is already become a, what's the word you people use? Oh, yes. A Legend! He is already a legend among our people. He is already being talked about at many camp fires throughout the Indian nations."

Runs Far had everyone's interest now. Tex asked, "Then you know where the youngsters are?"

Runs Far answered, "Oh, no. We still need to search. But Sees Far will go with us this time. He will be a big help. But we will need to be real careful. We won't be the only ones looking for them. The Spirit Warrior will be hunted by many braves from different nations. They believe that if their the one that is able to kill the Spirit Warrior they will have great power. If he is killed by the Spirit Warrior. Then it will be a great honor to have been killed by such a great warrior."

Dan asked, "Are you talking about Matt?"

Runs Far was unsure. For it was the first time he had heard of a name other than the Spirit Warrior. He said, "He is a big man. Very fast. He rides a Flaming horse. If that describes your Matt. Then it is the same person."

Captain Taylor said, "Yes, that's him. Matt is the name he goes by."

Runs Far said, "The Spirit Warrior is what the people of the Indian nations are calling him."

Runs Far then told them of all that was being told about Matt and his exploits. About his fighting ability. It seemed that the Indians that had attacked the wagon train and were killed by Matt. That they had been laid to rest, with great honor. Seeing that he had such great power they had died with honor.

After they spent the night it took them three days to reach Strong Arms village. It wasn't real big. They had around filthy teepees. Strong Arms had some of his people, move in with there families so Captain Taylor and his men could have the use of a couple of teepees. The Indians treated all of them with a lot of respect and honor. The whole village already knew that they were friends of the Spirit Warrior. Bones attracted a crowd of children as they hadn't seen anyone with his skin color before. Some Indian maidens, had been appointed to make sure they had all they wanted to eat. They had the free run of the village and attracted a lot of attention wherever they went.

Captain Taylor was told by Hawkeye. That by Sees Far's recommendation that the whole village would move out in search of Matt and the rest of the youngsters. He'd, told his people that he'd seen into the spirit world. That he'd had a vision of how they would be rewarded for doing so. They had spent many nights in discussion before most of the people of the Black Hawks had reached an agreement. There still was a couple of families that had decided they would go their own way when the village departed.

Depending on the weather a little. They had decided, they would leave in a couple of weeks. They would head south out of the Yellowstone Region. They needed some fresh meat. Some scouts would be sent out in the morning in search of a small herd of buffalo that hadn't migrated to the southern plains.

Billy got home just before dark. As he took care of his stallion and rubbed the sweat off with some wads of dry grass he suddenly stopped. It was then that he realized what his thought had been, he wished it really was home. He'd never seen any place like it. For that matter he'd never heard of any place like it. The valley was huge. The main part had a big open area with gentle rolling slopes with some of the best grass he'd ever seen. A big lake to the southwest of their home. There were four streams that flowed into the lake with one main stream that flowed out, to run mostly west then circle south and back to the east. It made it along ways back toward the lake before it went south. There were six smaller valleys that ran out from the main valley. Two went off toward the west, two toward the south and two toward the north.

Besides the buffalo and horse herds there were all kinds of game around. From bears and mountain lions, to rabbits and squirrels. Billy thought he had traveled around the valley more than any of them. He just couldn't get enough of the beauty of it and wanted to see something new each time he went out. It seemed like the valley was protected from most of the bad weather. For it hadn't been awfully cold, nor had they much more than a foot of snow. It had mostly melted in between storms.

Billy had already seen some good stands of trees at the foot of some cliffs that looked like they would be good sized forests. One, that he had seen was mostly of evergreens. Most were mixed with willows, birch, oak and some cottonwoods. With spring coming on he thought it was really going to be colorful with the blossoms of the wild flowers and buds from the trees.

His thoughts were interrupted by his sister as she came up greeting him with a little hug and a little peck on his cheek. He brushed his young stallion that he'd named Three Socks a few more times. Then he took the halter off and turned Three Socks loose. All the women did it now every time he returned after being gone a few days. He'd gotten used to it, but it had embarrassed him at first.

Done he looked at his sister. He thought she looked real pretty and had spiffed herself up more than usual. So Billy asked, "What's up?"

Helen replied, "Why nothing. Just happy to see you back again."

Billy had watched Matt and the women when they'd had a little spat. He had learned it was just a waste of time to ask again when he knew almost for certain that she had understood him completely. Matt still hadn't figured that out yet or was being stubborn. So Billy just said, "Oh, thanks. That's nice I didn't know you really missed me that much."

Helen's eyes brightened some, nearly sparkling. She smiled, but didn't say anything. She did think Billy was getting too smart for his own good. For he had just turned things around on her. She decided she would have to really concentrate and catch him on something to put him back in his place.

Neither of them said anything more as Billy shoo-d Three Socks and the mares away as they had all come up to Helen. Billy then closed the make shift gate to the barricade of vines and brush they had looped together to close off the grassy little hollow they kept the horses in. If the horses really wanted to they could get out through the thick woods that covered the east side of the hollow. But they seemed to be content with the rich grass in their meadow.

As they walked to the cave. Helen put her arm on top of Billy's and let him guide her to the main cave. That's another thing they'd started. Before that the only place he had seen it done was at dances. He was used to it now and had to admit, he did kind of like it. He never knew which one would come out to greet him first. He thought it had become like a game for them. Inside the cave he knew for certain that something was up. He could smell the aroma of something special being cooked. He kept his thoughts to himself though.

Connie and Star stopped what they were doing and repeating Helen's welcome Connie said, "Your clean buckskins are laid out by the hot pool for you."

Billy did bath in the nude now. The women made sure that they kept their backs to him. He had watched them like a hawk the first couple of times. He trusted them now. As he turned toward the pool He said, "Thanks."

Star said, "We cooked a rabbit to snack on until Matt gets here later tonight. We'll have it ready by the time your are done bathing."

CHAPTER NINETEEN

DADDY

They could hear Flame as he brought Matt up the valley. Flame usually light on his feet, did like to show off sometimes. It seemed like after they'd been gone for a few days. That Flame would stomp the ground hard with his hoofs to announce their return. Matt agreed, for he told them that it made a rough ride. He told them he let Flame keep it up because Flame seemed to enjoy it so much.

After a few minutes Matt finished rubbing Flame down. Then he turned Flame in with the other horses. Billy knew it when Matt approached the cave. All Billy had to do, especially after Matt had been away for a few days, was to watch the women. He'd noticed that they would get tense or even get excited enough that their skin reddened a little, just before he came into sight.

When they turned as one Billy let his eyes follow them to the entrance. Matt, stood with a surprised look on his face. Just then Billy realized that with all the time he had spent with Matt, the only time he ever saw any thoughts on Matt's face, was when Matt was around one or all of the women. Any other time he never had a clue.

Billy noticed that Matt was excited about something and was the happiest he had ever seen him. The women had picked up on it too, for when they'd reached Matt they started their chatter as they gave him hugs and kisses. Billy couldn't help but see a little foreplay, as they reacquainted themselves with his body. One of them must have remembered that Billy was still there waiting for the special meal they'd prepared. The chatter had stopped as they grudgingly broke up their cozy huddle. Star then told Matt "Get your bath. The food is ready and we're all starving. We waited for you so all of us could eat together."

After the meal, which had amazed him again. With no more than they had on hand. Billy wondered how Star and he was sure Connie and Helen had helped also. But with the different herbs and roots from the plants that were in abundance all around. They seasoned the food a little different, so it didn't have the same taste. They'd made a cake of some sort with a lot of nuts they had gathered and mixed everything together. He decided it was more like a bread. But it was good. Even if you did have to be careful when you chewed. To keep from chipping a tooth on a stone chip. It couldn't be helped, the heat as it cooked probably broke them off as much as the grinding did.

They were all in a festive mood and Billy couldn't remember how long it had been since he'd had such a good time. He had picked up their mood and everyone was jubilant. After the meal the four of them had gathered close together. Billy listened to them as they conversed. Then like something had finely reached it's limit. Connie cut in on their conversation. Billy heard the excitement and joy in her voice as she said, "Matt, we're going, to have a baby. All of us are. Star, Helen and me. We're all going to have a baby."

Billy saw that Matt had been completely caught off guard. When he responded, after it got through to him he was as excited as they were. Then there was another round of hugging and kissing as they rejoiced together. When their exuberance had dwindled some Matt said, "All of you! Okay. I'm going to be a father. Wow, I should have known. I can see it now, its very apparent. I've got some news too."

Helen asked, "You're not upset, your happy to be a father?"

Matt answered, "No, I'm not upset. I just hadn't thought about it. But don't worry, I can take care of you now."

Star said, "We know that, we'll just have to make sure you don't have to fight very often. Making love is better than fighting."

Connie said, "Billy."

Star's lips formed a big O as she looked at Billy and got darker than her normal color. Connie and Helen mostly because of what they hadn't had to wear most of the time were almost as dark, as Star was now. Matt been pulled off track when Star had mentioned making love. He tried to gather his thoughts together as he said, "No, no. I've, well I hope, if you. Well darn. I had my thoughts together, but your announcement has messed me up."

Billy still hadn't interrupted, he just sat and watched the show. They'd quieted down some then Connie said, "Okay, we're listening."

Billy saw that Matt looked like he had regathered his thoughts. Billy could tell that Matt chose his words carefully as he said, "Star, I hope it doesn't upset you, but I've found gold. Lots of it."

Billy in spite of himself along with Connie and Helen were excited. Before they could respond Matt motioned with his hand for them to keep quiet. Then Matt continued, "Star, with your permission I'd like to use it to make a home here for all of us and build the valley up into something real special."

Star asked, "Why do you ask me and not others?"

Matt answered, "It's your land. I mean well; It belongs to the Indians."

Star smiled at Matt's thoughtfulness. The others even had more respect for Matt. Star was thoughtful, as she said, "No, that's not so. I don't think any Indians have been here. If they have it was a long time ago. You found it; its your land."

Matt with caution in his voice as he said, "Are you sure? Do you think that is how your people would look at it?"

Star nodded, "Yes. You found it, its yours. No one knew about it before."

Matt then thought back over his words as he said, "Well, what I'd like to clarify is that I want to make this our home. All of you, Billy you too. We'll all be partners and make this into the grandest place possible. Finding the gold makes it possible."

Billy suddenly burst out with, "That will make me an uncle."

They all looked at Billy with puzzled looks. They'd been talking about the gold and the valley. The first to catch up with Billy's thoughts Star said, "You're as a brother to me. You'll be my babies uncle too."

Connie said, "Oh yes Billy. I'd like it to be the same with my baby and me." Billy was drawn into the circle of hugs and rejoicing. They all confessed to each other how much they cared for each other and looked forward to the birth of the babies. Then how much they'd come to love the valley and that they already thought of it as home. Matt had asked, "What about your families?"

Matt was quickly put to ease about that. They all wanted to let everyone know that they were okay and to see them for a short time. Then they wanted to be back here at home. They all told him, Billy included that they already felt like they belonged here.

The next couple of weeks they'd all gone to the gold mine. They'd took the Indian ponies along to use as pack animals. After a couple of trips they had twelve bars at home. No one referred to it as the cave anymore.

The next week they explored the valley. They all traveled together now. It had warmed up and was quite pleasant now, even at night. They noticed that there was less snow on the mountain peaks. So far the only entrance to and from the valley, that they had found was the one that they had used. As they returned home they made the trip to the east to check the dry wash. It was still pretty full of rapid running water. They knew it would have to be almost dry again for them to be able to get through the tunnel. It did look like the water level had gotten a little lower. They thought it would be another week or more before they could leave. None of them liked the idea of leaving now. The more they saw of the valley, the harder it was going to be to leave it. But they knew it was only right to visit and let there families know, that they where alright.

It had been real warm the last couple of day's and with the warmth their leather outfit's they'd been wearing started to smell. They'd not been able to tan the leather completely with what they'd had and the hides had been a little green. Star had insisted that if nothing else, the bear hide and the buffalo hide had been done proper. They had made sure of the two hides. They had to go back to just loin cloths again. Even Billy had taken to wearing a loin cloth. Star had found just enough good leather to make one for each of them. Except for Star they had to be careful of the sun till they got their tans.

Matt as the women's bellies started to swell. Had tried to get them to do less and not ride as much. But he'd been told in no uncertain terms that they would do what they had been doing. Star the most insistent had told him it was better for them to stay active. That It was better for the health of the babies also. Billy had watched another good show. Matt had tried hard to hold his ground. But Billy mused that Matt was out matched or at least out numbered.

Strong Arms with his village and Captain Taylor along with his men had been on the move for a week. The villages medicine had been good. They had found a small heard of buffalo and made a few kills. Just enough to feed them.

For the cowboy's it was the first buffalo hunt they'd been on. It was one of the best time's they'd had. Captain Taylor told them he had enjoyed it, also. They had run them instead of making a stand and shooting them from a knoll like most of the white people usually did. Only a couple of horses had gotten injured. They'd only run them a mile or just over. Then let the rest run on out of sight. They'd be moving on and the meat would've spoiled if they'd killed anymore. The cowboys were amazed at how efficient, the women had been in butchering the huge animals. They spent a couple of days processing the meat. A big portion of it had been put on the fire and eaten as they didn't have to ration any of it anymore. The fresh meat tasted good to everyone and they'd, gorged themselves. When they moved out again, just about the whole animal had been used in one way or another.

In another week it was thought that they would be where Runs Far and his braves. Had lost what little sign they'd been able to find that was left behind by the youngsters. Then it would be left up to Sees Far to find their trail. The Indians had no doubts about Sees Far being able to lead them to the youngsters. Tex and his partners were still skeptical. They admitted that the Indian scouts had found the buffalo where he'd told them to look. They were sure he'd just made a good guess.

Near the end of the next week they'd made it to where Runs Far and his braves had last seen the trail of the youngsters. They'd been held up some because some other Indians were active in the area. They appeared to be searching for something. Strong Arms made sure he always had enough braves stay to protect the main party and that the scouting party was big enough to discourage any attacks. They had to many people to just sneak through. Tex along with the other cowboys knew that they where well south of the trail they had used when they'd gone west with the wagons. The direction that they were headed in made no sense to them at all. If Captain Taylor hadn't been with them they would have already gone off on their own. Captain Taylor told them to be patient. They tried to, but they were sure that they were on a wild goose chase.

Runs Far had just told Sees Far were he had found the enemies camp and where Star and her friends had temporarily stayed. Runs Far pointed as he described all that he could to Sees Far. Hawkeye told Captain Taylor and the cowboys what was being discussed. When all of the talk had stopped. Sees Far after a good minute just grunted. Then he concentrated for a few minutes. He even closed his eyes and turned his head. Then he opened his eyes and kneed his horse off to the south.

They where in the southwest part of Wyoming getting close to Utah. Toward the end of the day. Strong Arms had the main part of the village stay. Then with a few braves, Runs Far and Captain Taylor with his men followed on after Sees Far. Who acted like he was on a trail he'd used all his life. They where in a valley with a river along the west side, of it. It had narrowed quickly with rock cliffs on both sides. They followed the river as the shadows deepened. One of the cowboys had made a statement that he hadn't seen any sign at all. Runs Far told him that Sees Far wasn't following a trail that was on the ground. They made camp next to the river just before dark.

The next morning Strong Arms sent word for the rest of the village to come on. Near the end of the day they were in a small stream that had branched off from the river. The water was ice cold. The water was up to the horses bellies with the spring run off from the snow capped mountains. It was ruff going and took a lot of time. The current, was swift and strong, in many places. The cowboys had cursed as their boots had been splashed full of water. When Sees Far spotted a gorge that had six inches of water rushing into the stream they were in. He dismounted and started to lead his pony up into it. His pony didn't like it, but he patiently urged him on up. The rest of them followed. The cowboys cussed some more; it hadn't taken long for their boots to become, completely full of water. They also found out that their boots slipped on the rocks a lot more than the Indians moccasins did. After slipping and sliding they made it up. Many had sore shins. The horses hadn't done much better. A couple of them had come up real lame. When they'd cleared the steep part the floor of the gorge was pretty smooth. It was still slippery, but not bad. When the gorge opened up they went to high ground on the south side. The gorge led them into another valley with a small lake. It was decided that they'd spend the night there. A couple of braves were sent out to hunt for some meat and the rest went about setting up camp. A brave was sent back to the main village with instructions for them to follow the next day.

During the evening after their meal Tex asked, "Runs Far. How are you going to get all of your people up that gorge? Especially the young and old people."

Runs Far hadn't showed it, but he was surprised with the concern he'd heard in Tex's voice as he replied, "They will help each other. They'll be here tomorrow you'll see."

They rode out in the morning with everyone except the ones that had the lame ponies. They followed Sees Far till midday when he stopped and looked west to where the stream they'd rode next to had split around an island. The part to the west ran right up to a big cliff. It was the second time the river had run right up to a cliff. But this time they didn't hear a big roar coming out of the ground. Sees Far spoke to Runs Far who in turn sent Has Bear's Claws with a couple of braves out ahead of them.

Captain Taylor asked, "Runs Far; what's up?"

Runs Far said, "They've gone out to look for a good place to cross the river."

Close to two hours later Has Bear's Claws returned with the two braves. The cowboys retightened their cinches as the rest of the Indians climbed back on their ponies. Then they were guided to a good crossing. As soon as they crossed over Sees Far headed south. Back in the direction they had just come from. Only on the other side of the river. Captain Taylor even looked surprised. For they'd been able to see the cliff on their trip north to the crossing and hadn't seen a living soul except for some wild game. The cowboys were perplexed nearly to the point of protesting. They had even started to lag behind when one of the braves raced ahead a little then jumping off his horse and gave a happy yelp.

When they rode up many of the braves talked excitedly with each other. When they'd pulled reign and dismounted Runs Far walked up to them. With excitement all over his face which he didn't even try to hide he pointed as he said, "They were here. There's a cave. Then they kept their horses over there,"

The cowboys looked around and sure enough somebody had camped here. They could see many places were someone had used an axe. Then they went in and checked the cave. It looked like in deed, that five places had been made up to sleep on. The numbers added up. But there was not a sign left behind of who it had been, that the cowboys could see.

Tex asked, "Do you think, it was the youngsters?"

Runs Far answered, "Yes, there's sign of my sister all around."

Bones asked, "Where are they then?"

Runs Far lost some of the light from his eyes as he said, "We don't know, they've moved again. Maybe the game got to scarce for them. Also we are up very high. There's still a lot of snow in the wooded areas. It wouldn't have been a good place to spend the winter."

Sees Far told them he was going to camp at this place. Runs Far then sent out three scouts to look for some more sign of the youngsters and to see if there was another way out. Sure enough the rest of the village showed up the next day. Many of them looked beat. But they had satisfied looks of accomplishment on their faces. The scouts had returned also. They hadn't found any other sign of the youngsters or another passage.

Runs Far told Captain Taylor that some of the people had gotten upset. They had decided to stay on the other side of the river. Sees Far with many of the advance party would stay in camp here. The Indians had split up into several groups. With emotions high among the Indians. Captain Taylor and his men decided that it would be better to have their own camp fire. More out of the language barrier than anything else. The Indians had quite a few heated discussions going on.

That evening after the sky had turned dark. The Captain with his men huddled around their fire as they sipped on their after meal coffee. Bones said, "It's a sorry thing when your own people loose faith in you."

Tex said, "I thought it was too good to be true. I didn't expect to ride right up on them anyway. Did you? With all the mountains and everything we'll be lucky to find them in ten years."

Hawkeye said, "Matt will find us before then."

Dan said, "Yeah, I'll bet Hawkeye's right. Matt will probably find us before we find him. I think maybe we jumped the gun. Its just that their parents are so decent and have kept up such a good front I thought searching for them was the right thing to do."

Slade said, "I'm kind of thinking along with Bones. Everyone was so happy yesterday."

Slim said, "Well, nothings lasts forever. One thing is for sure though. If it was them they aren't here now."

Ben replied, "Well, that's for certain. Maybe Matt is a spirit and made all of them vanish."

That quieted them down with their own thoughts for a little bit. For about half of them took him a little serious. Matt had always been a little spooky to them around camp.

Captain Taylor had gave a lot of thought to their circumstances as he said, "I Think Sees Far has brought us to the right place. I don't think the youngsters are far from here."

They all gave him a hard look to determine if he had spoken with hope. But they could tell he'd been serious.

Hawkeye said, "I also feel like we are on the right trail. I think we're close to them."

Both Hawkeye and Captain Taylor received stern looks from them, but no one spoke. They didn't believe in magical powers. They just decided that it was hope that had made them speak up that way.

CHAPTER TWENTY

PEACEFUL VALLEY

In Peaceful Valley. That's what they'd started to call their valley. Matt and Billy had returned from their trip to check on the wash out from the tunnel. They'd told the women that they should be able to get through after a couple more days. They all had mixed feelings. They wanted to see and let their families know that they were fine. But they had fallen in love with the valley so much that it would be hard for them to leave their home. On the trip Matt had taken a bow and some arrows along with one of the Indian ponies. They had run out of meat. Some had spoiled and been thrown away. On the way back they had spotted a small herd of deer. While Billy stayed with the horses Matt stalked them. After an hour he'd made a nice clean kill. He was getting the hang of using the bow and arrows.

When they got home the women made quick work of skinning and cutting the deer up into strips to hang and dry. They intended to use the meat on the trail so they wouldn't have to hunt along the way. Also Matt had told them he couldn't see killing something. Then use just a portion of it, then leave the rest to spoil.

Billy had a good tan along with the rest. He still wasn't used to being naked except for his loin cloth. He kept his distance from the women when he could. After Matt and Billy had taken care of the horses. The women told them to get cleaned up. When they got the hide stretched and the meat on the rack they'd made. That they would get cleaned up while the meat cooked.

Star said, "It would be nice if you put some wood on the fire. Then the fire should be ready to cook with when we come in."

They had a quiet meal. It had been a busy day. They each had their own thoughts to keep them busy. There seemed to be as much dread as there was excitement. Shortly after he was done eating Billy went to his bed in his private cave. He was used to the women being mostly naked now. But he left to give Matt and the women their privacy. Also whenever he entered the main cave he made sure he'd been heard as he went in. He didn't want to embarrass them or himself. Billy thought that their love making had picked up the last few days. Like they hoped to store it up so it would last them on the trail. Billy then drifted off to sleep.

The next morning Billy made sure he'd been heard. He found Matt and the women nearly finished with their meal. He quickly gathered up some food and joined them. When they'd finished eating as Billy still chewed on his food. He heard Matt ask, "Star, do you feel alright? You seemed awful restless last night."

Star took some time before she said, "I feel fine. I just kept waking up. It was like something or someone tried to take the thoughts out of my mind."

Connie said, "Maybe you just had a bad dream."

"No! When I was awake, it still felt like someone tried to gather my thoughts."

They talked some more as they went over everything they needed to do to get ready for their trip out. Matt and Billy left the cave to do their part. They went to check the horses over good. They made sure all their hoofs and legs were intact. They scraped the hoofs clean to check for pebbles or bruises. Then they sharpened the axe and knife, with a piece of sandstone. Matt looked at the knife and decided he would replace it as soon as he could. It had gotten awful thin from all the use and sharpening it had been through the last few months. Finished with their jobs Matt asked, "Billy if you could find some piece of any your clothing. I'd like to use it to clean the guns to make sure they are in the best shape we can get them."

Billy thought a little then said, "Star wouldn't let me burn them when I'd started too. I'll ask her. I'm sure she kept what was left. She dosen't let anything get wasted."

Matt nodded as Billy walked off. Then he thought about Star's restless night. Just then his thoughts were interrupted by a screech over head. He looked up to see an eagle as it drifted on an updraft above the mountain cliff. Matt thought to himself and wished he could see through the eagles eyes. Startled Matt caught his breath as he unconsciously moved his feet to feel the ground. Reassured he closed his eyes. Suddenly he was high above the mountain. Then he concentrated all of his thoughts on the outer entrance to the tunnel that came into the valley. Then the ground started to move swiftly under him as he traveled east. A few minutes had gone by and the washout to the tunnel had started to become visible.

It was then that Billy returned with some rags and a couple of the weapons that had been inside with the women. Surprised that Matt hadn't acknowledged him Billy stepped past Matt so he could look at Matt's face. Matt stood with his eyes closed. When Matt still didn't acknowledge he was there, he said, "Matt, I got the things to clean the weapons with."

Matt hadn't responded. Billy looked closer and saw that Matt really concentrated on something like he was, in a trance. After a few minutes Billy started to get scared. Billy had already laid everything down he quickly returned back inside then he went up to Star saying, "Star; I need your help for a minute."

Connie and Helen looked at him as he turned and went outside. Star shrugged her shoulders to them as she followed Billy out.

When they where up close to Matt Billy said, "See he's been like that for twenty minutes, I'd guess."

Star answered, "Matt's alright I think. I've seen my uncle concentrate like that. Sometimes for a long time. The only thing is my uncle usually sits down when he does it."

Billy said, "Oh, I was worried that he had suddenly gotten sick in his mind or something."

Matt while he concentrated on what he was doing. For once never heard or realized that Billy and Star where right next to him. It was about forty minutes before he was able to see the outside entrance to the tunnel. When he saw all the Indians that were there Matt had seen enough and opened his eyes. He received another shock when he realized that he still stood where he had been, before he took off up into the sky. He looked up above and the eagle was no where to be seen. He looked toward the washout and the tunnel. He still didn't see the eagle and decided that somehow it was the eagle's eyes that he had looked through. It was then that he noticed, that Billy and Star watched him. Matt, had no idea, what had happened. No way that he could see to explain it to them, that would make any sense to them. He was sure of that. Matt looked at the weapons and rags, then in a gruff voice said, "I'd like to clean them over there sitting on that rock."

Billy and Star both curious, could tell that whatever had happened to Matt. That he didn't want to discuss it. They took everything to where Matt desired. Then Star returned to the cave. Matt went to work cleaning all of the weapons. He checked them over real good as he made sure they worked smoothly. He wished he had some oil. But after awhile he was finally happy with them.

Then he made a check of how many rounds there were after all the guns had been loaded. Billy and the women watched Matt as they worked on getting everything ready. They could tell that Matt had suddenly made a drastic change. He was all business now. After he arranged everything he pointed and said, "Whenever any of you go out make sure you have your weapon with you and take the extra rounds that I've divided up with you also."

Star asked, "Why?"

Matt said, "There's a big group of Indians at the outer entrance of the tunnel."

Connie puzzled asked, "How do you know that?"

Matt said, "I don't know. I can't explain it. I just know."

Helen looked from one then to another, then asked, "Do we still prepare to leave or what?"

Matt thought for a minute, then said, "Yes, we may have to move out of here anyway. Billy, I guess until we know one way or the other, we need to hide the gold."

Star said, "Put it in the bottom of the hot pool and put some rocks on top of it."

Matt and Billy both looked at her, then Matt said, "That's a good idea."

After thirty minutes they had the gold moved. They decided that they would have someone on guard duty. There was a ledge that was a hundred feet up a little to the south of their home. It wasn't a bad climb. But you had to be careful. Billy told them he would take the first night watch and went to his bedroom to take a nap. Minding what Matt had told them he took his rifle and the extra rounds. When the evening meal was ready Helen went and woke her brother up. It was another quiet meal as their peacefulness had been disturbed. Matt's demeanor hadn't helped any either. After their meal that night as they settled down to rest with Billy on guard duty. It was the same night that Captain Taylor and his men had their conversation about Sees Far and the youngsters.

The next morning when he'd finished his meal. The sun had just started up when Captain Taylor with a steaming cup of coffee left camp and walked along the river to the south of the little cave they had found. Nobody had stayed in it. Either out of respect or because they might have become spooked by it. Captain Taylor followed the river around the bend that carried it underneath the mountain, before it turned back out headed toward the little lake by the gorge. He stopped often to sip his coffee. When he had gone about as far as he could without getting his feet wet and about to turn back. Captain Taylor spotted Sees Far in the receding shadows. Sees Far stood and looked at the side of the mountain with it's giant cliff.

He turned and acknowledged Captain Taylor then went back to studying the cliff. Captain Taylor still hadn't picked up on their language. So he ended up just doing the same. He thought they had stood there for nearly an hour when Sees Far gave a sigh and started to turn back up river. For some reason Captain Taylor was drawn to the spot also. When Sees Far turned to leave Captain Taylor touched his arm to hold him there.

They stood for another ten minutes and then Captain Taylor, more by instinct than actually knowing anything stepped into the water close to the side of the cliff. He'd expected the water to be deeper. But to his surprise it only came to the top of his boot. He brought his other foot down and after taking another step found it wasn't any deeper. Man the water was cold though. Captain Taylor worked his way around close to the cliff. After he'd gone thirty feet he couldn't hold his surprise as he exclaimed, "Well, I'll be damned."

Sees Far hadn't understood. Sees Far just watched as Captain Taylor sure of himself now. Because the water depth stayed about the same. But he still couldn't believe what he saw. When he seemed to walk into the cliff and disappear. Sees Far exclaimed something that Captain Taylor didn't understand. Sees Far hurried after him and when Sees Far caught up with Captain Taylor and saw the entrance to the tunnel. Sees Far couldn't hide his amazement, either. They returned back to the bank and stepped out of the water. They smiled at each other as Captain Taylor took his boots off and dumped, the water out of them. Then he put them back on. Sees Far had waited and they walked back to camp together. Back at the camp they separated. Sees Far went to his fire and Captain Taylor to his. Captain Taylor poured himself, another cup of coffee as Dan asked, "What happened to you, did you fall into the river?"

Captain Taylor said, "No, we just found the entrance to a tunnel."

Dan asked, "Where?"

Captain Taylor replied, "Just down the river a bit. Where the water goes in under the cliff."

Hawkeye quickly stood and walked off. The others more doubtful followed along. Captain Taylor sat down on a rock and relaxed as he sipped his coffee. He looked down river and saw some of the braves headed toward the entrance. After a little his men returned and told him that some of the braves went to find some pine knots to use as torches. That Hawkeye and Dan had decided to go with them.

Tex said, "I'll be surprised if it leads to anywhere."

Captain Taylor said, "Oh it goes through. That's where we're going to find the youngsters."

Bones said, "I think the Captain's right. It's the only place they could be."

Slade asked, "How do you figure that?"

Bones answered, "Runs Far had tracked them to the little stream before he lost all sign of them."

Slim said, "Yeah, he's right. I think I heard someone say that."

Ben said, "Well, if they went through I wonder how they ever found it."

Slim said, "Maybe Matt is a Spirit."

Bones tried to chuckle along with the rest as he said, "That's beginning, not to be so funny."

They talked of pleasant things while they waited for the explorers to return. Tex along with his fellow Texans were still doubtful. They hadn't spoken out though. Because it was easy to see that Captain Taylor expected the youngsters to be on the other end of the tunnel. It was close to four hours before any of the braves returned. It was a few minutes later when Dan and Hawkeye reappeared. Wet up over their knees they got their cups and filled them. Then they stood close to the fire as Dan said, "Wow that water is cold. I can't feel my feet. I'm sure glad you saved us some coffee."

Before, anyone else spoke Hawkeye confirmed, "The water sure is cold. The youngsters made it through though. We saw where they'd cut a couple of pine knots. We also found an old campfire pit."

Tex said, "You're kidding! You can get a horse through there, then?

Dan nodding, "Yeah, it's going to be tough. But they did it."

Captain Taylor said, "Well, I guess we're going through, then."

Dan nodded again, as he said, "Yeah; In about an hour. Their feet got cold too and they wanted to grab a bite to eat. I guess everyone on this side of the river is going. That is if you fellows are going."

Captain Taylor said, "Good! It's a wonder we found them so quick."

Ben said, "We haven't found them yet."

Slim said, "I didn't come all the way here to turn back now."

Dan said, "Oh I think we've found them. For the first time in a long time I feel real good about it."

Tex asked, "You mean you had your doubts and still came all the way back here?"

Dan said, "Oh! And I suppose you never had a doubt."

Tex finally called to task, said, "Yeah, I guess I did. I just hated to call it quits. I didn't want to admit it. Besides I thought maybe it was my fault."

Bones said, "It's been a long trail. I just hope their alright."

Slade said, "I hadn't thought they had a chance to survive. With all the other Indians after them."

Captain Taylor said, "I'm sure we all had our doubts from time to time. But now I'm sure we'll be seeing them soon. It's time we got saddled up and ready. A couple of you see if you can find some pine knots. We may need them if we have to wrestle with the horses. It my take awhile to get through."

Word had reached the main village and everyone rejoiced. They had decided that they would stay until someone returned to tell them to stay or to go on through. A lot of the Indians didn't like the idea of going into a cave, let alone through a long tunnel. It took them three hours to get through the tunnel with the horses. By that time the sky had already started to darken. They decided to camp in the meadow.

It took them a couple of days to work their way down the washout. They had to back track and tried to be real careful so none of the horses came up lame. The rapid water, though not deep hadn't helped them any either. They were astonished as they took in the valley. They were impressed at the beauty and the size of it. Tired they made camp, on some plush green grass that was a couple of inches high. The camp sight was on the valley floor just a little ways from the washout. The water had flowed less each day. In another day or two it would be down to a trickle.

It had been three days since Matt had seen the outer entrance to the tunnel. He knew how hard it would be to find the entrance. But he was worried that with as many Indians as he had seen that they wouldn't move soon. They'd been taking turns on guard duty. It was Matt's turn on the ledge. After he checked to make sure nothing moved. He let his thoughts go to the washout. He wondered how much water was coming down it now. If it was nearly dry yet. As he thought about it he saw a vague image, as if he looked through a heavy fog. He was startled. He looked way out and saw that everything, was still clear. He was confused then he decided to close his eyes and concentrate on the wash again. To his amazement he could see it. He almost fell off the ledge. For as he watched it was like he had just jumped from a ledge to the top of a big rock. Then it was like his eyes raised just above the level of the rock to look down the washout. Amazed he saw a good sized band of Indians. Matt opened his eyes and found himself back on the ledge.

He looked out across the valley. But he couldn't see any movement or anything that was out of place. From the way things had seemed when he had been able to view the washout. He thought it had to have been through the eyes of a mountain lion. He was bewildered at what was going on with him. Matt didn't understand his new ability. But he was sure, what he'd seen was true. When he had seen the Indians they were already on the move. Headed straight toward the cave.

Around mid day Connie climbed up the little trail to the ledge. After carefully swapping places Matt said, "Keep a sharp eye out. Some of them have made it through the tunnel and are on the valley floor already."

Connie looked out across the valley. She hadn't seen anything that looked out of place. She said, "Okay, I'll keep my eyes peeled."

When Matt made it down he walked around the whole area. He spent a good hour as he checked every rock and ditch. He also checked every bush that was in the area.   Lastly he went and checked on the horses in their little basin. Then he walked through the stand of thick trees that was on the east side of the basin. Done with that he went in and told the others that they were not alone in the valley anymore.

Helen asked, "Do you think they'll find us?"

Matt said, "Ask Star, she should know. She can see into the Spirit World."

Star said, "I told you. I only see from time to time. When I do it just happens. I can't control it."

Things had been so pleasant. But with the threat of danger they'd all gotten tense.

Matt snapped back, "That's great! That does us a lot of good; dosen't it?"

With hurt feelings, Star said, "Well! like you can do better."

Matt spat out, "I can! Billy there's some things. I want to do outside."

Matt spun around and left. Billy somewhat set back just followed Matt out.

Helen seeing that Star was upset said, "Star, he don't mean it. We all know if it hadn't been for your gift, we could have all perished. He's just worried about us."

Star nodded, "Yes, I know. He's not worried for himself. But he dosen't know that if something happened to him I'd rather be dead."

Helen listened to Star in her language. When Star got excited or upset, which wasn't often. She spoke in her native tongue. Helen spoke Stars language as she said, "We all know that. Connie and I feel the same. Matt isn't moody often. What has him upset more than usual is that he's probably extra worried about us, because of us being with child."

Star nodded, "Yes, that's probably what's gotten me upset, also."

"Yes, you're probably right. I have been having trouble with my temper also."

Matt and Billy worked hard when they got outside. Billy had picked up on Matt's sense of urgency. They moved some rocks and dug a few holes. They wanted to make it awful rough for someone to rush them on horseback. By the time the sun had set. Matt told Billy they had done as much as they could. When they went inside they were surprised to see that it was Connie and Helen who worked on their evening meal. Still with a heavy tone to his voice Matt said, "Connie, I thought you would still be on guard duty."

"Star told me that she would watch. So I let her; alright?"

Matt just nodded, then went with Billy to the pool for their baths. When Matt was done he stood and went outside. Then climbed the trail to the ledge; as he sat next to Star he saw her tense up. He said, "Please forgive me, I've no excuse. It's just I don't want any trouble now. Things were so nice and all of you are with a child. I just don't want anything to happen to any of you. I also know if there's any trouble. I probably wouldn't be able to keep you ladies out of it."

Star sighed then put her head on his right shoulder as she said, "That's the way we all feel. None of us want anyone to get hurt. We love you just as much as you do us. That's why we will all fight if we have to. Don't forget Billy either. He would die for you."

Matt sighed, "I just didn't think anybody would find the entrance. I know it has to be rough on you ladies. I mean there's not a single comfort here for any of you. But because of the gold, that's all about to change for you."

"Matt, all we need is you. Don't you know that?"

"Yes, I know. Well, I hoped that, but I want the best for all of you. Well and the unborn babies too."

Star kissed him, then said. "Go and let me watch now, go get your rest."

Matt returned to the cave and to their amazement he apologized to them for his actions that day. Billy went out to his bed as the others settled in for the night. At midnight Matt took Stars place.

The next morning after Helen had relieved him and he'd had a short nap. Matt and Billy improved their defenses a little more. They cut some poles six feet long and left them pointed on one end. They buried the other end at a forty-five degree angle with the ground. They put them where the ground was the smoothest so anyone that rushed them would be directed into holes and onto the rocks they had moved. They left a path that made three turns. No one could make a straight run at them now and they had a good field of fire.

The sun had just started on it's trip west, about midday. When Helen came down from the ledge and told them she had spotted some riders headed straight toward them. Matt then told each of them where he wanted them. He made sure they knew where each other would be. Then he made sure they knew where they could shoot so as not to hit each other. He stressed to them to stay in place and to keep their heads down. That he'd be where he'd told them so they wouldn't have to worry about hitting him. Everyone except for Connie had been amazed at how cool and calm Matt had suddenly gotten.

CHAPTER TWENTY ONE

ONE FOUND

From the camp at the bottom of the washout, Sees Far led them to the northwest. Captain Taylor and his men just settled down to a pleasant ride along with the Indians. They all were taken in by the enormous size and beauty of the valley. The grass was already green and plush. The cowboy's were so taken in that they had to remind themselves why they were here. To a man they all commented that it would be the best cattle ranch ever if someone wanted to develop it, into one.

When they came to a river they stayed close along the south bank as they followed it northwest. After an easy twenty-five miles they decided to camp. The Indian's ponies and even the cowboys horses from the long trip and the long winter were not in the best shape.

When they started out the next morning they rode for a mile or two to where they crossed over the river to head a little more to the north. They were close enough now that they could see the mountain. They noticed that it came a point in the direction they where headed. The mountain looked like it was straight up and down.

Besides the wild life, they hadn't seen any sign of another human being anywhere. There'd been a little excitement when a single horse track with a shoe on its hoof had been spotted. Strong Arms braves were sure it was from the Spirit Horse. Hawkeye was sure it was Flame's too. A little after midday Sees Far pulled his pony to a stop. When Strong Arms and Runs Far came up beside him they conversed for a few minutes. They'd been riding in one group. They had not worried about any enemies being in the valley with them. When Sees Far had stopped speaking. Run's Far reined his pony around up next to Captain Taylor. Then he said, "Sees Far thinks it would be better if you go first. Your people may not take us as friends."

Captain Taylor nodded, "Yeah I think maybe you're right. The only thing is I haven't seen anyone."

Run's Far smiled then pointed, "Just keep headed in the same direction. Sees Far told us he had recognized it. He is sure they're there. He's also sure that they know we are here."

Captain Taylor said, "Okay, We'll go check it out. Dan get our men together and lets ride on in."

Dan responded, "Okay Captain."

Dan made a couple motions with his hands. Then eased his horse out from the main body of riders joined by the cowboys. When they all gathered around he explained to them what was up. While Dan explained Captain Taylor conversed some more with Runs Far.

Captain Taylor saw that Dan and the others were ready. He told Runs Far that he'd see him in a little while. The Captain then joined Dan and the rest of his people. Then took the lead as the rest fell in behind him. The Indians waited till they had a mile head start. Then they slowly followed them.

Within an hour Captain Taylor reigned his horse to a stop. He had spotted the stakes stuck in the ground. He looked all around and hadn't spotted a soul. The things that had been done were real fresh. The Captain felt sure they were being watched. He quietly asked, "Hawkeye, have you spotted anyone?"

"No, I'm not real surprised about it either.

Captain Taylor didn't yell. But in a clear loud voice he said, "Matt, its Captain Taylor with the cowboys. The Indians out yonder are the people of the Indian girl you rescued."

Matt said, "Hello, I recognized you right off. I wondered when you were going to announce yourselves."

To a man they all spun their horses around. For Matt had spoken from behind them. No one spoke as they looked at Matt for the first time since he'd rode off. Then they had never seen him with nothing on except his lion cloth and double pistol rig. He held a rifle loosely in his left hand. But what they saw for the first time was Matt's physique. Matt's muscles rippled with the tiniest movement. Not big bulky muscles. But with hard powerful muscles that didn't show any fat anywhere. They all had been caught off guard and were unnerved. Matt's appearance had as much to do with it, as surprising them from behind like he had. Matt saw a slight smile start on Hawkeye's face as a glint appeared in his eyes. He started to turn his gaze back toward the area around the high cliff.

Captain Taylor finally getting some of his wits back asked, "Where's the others?"

Billy said, "I'm right here Captain Taylor."

Hawkeye relaxed now to watch the show. He'd caught onto Matt's scheme. He watched as the rest spun their horses around again. They started to have a hard time controlling their mounts. Not only because of the treatment they were getting. But the horses had picked up on the tenseness of their riders.

Matt said, "You ought to go ahead and step down. The horses are getting nervous from your treatment and will be unseating you anyway before long."

No one spoke as they dismounted. Billy didn't have on anymore than Matt. He had grown from the last time they'd seen him. He had to be five-six now. The biggest growth they saw was that he was now a man, no matter what his age was. That he'd been tempered by the fire and found to be made out of good stock. They could see it in his eyes as Billy walked up to them. With a little smile on his face Billy said, "It was Matt's idea. Once we knew who it was, he thought it would be nice to give you a welcome you would remember for a long time."

They looked from Billy to Matt. Then as Matt walked up to them Tex said, "Well, damn! You two surprising us like that are lucky you're not dead. We could have just started shooting."

Hawkeye enjoying himself still watched the area around them. With Tex's brash statement he couldn't hold back anymore and started to laugh.

Tex asked, "Now what do you see that is so funny?"

Captain Taylor and Dan hadn't quite caught on yet. Boones had a thoughtful look on his face.

Hawkeye looking right at Tex's glare took a deep breath of air, then said, "If they had wanted to we'd be the dead ones."

Tex's face got red with embarrassment as he realized the truth of Hawkeye's words. Then he remembered the stories the Indians had already told about Matt's ability with guns. Even if a fellow believed only half of it. That person would be nobody to mess with and there Matt stood, alive and well. As Tex tried to get a handle on his emotions Dan asked, "Where's the girls?"

Connie, Helen and Star with all the attention drawn on Billy and Matt. From the stand of trees that made a half circle to their little horse basin. They stood just out from them in plain sight. Together they said, "We're right here."

All the men turned as one. They couldn't help it. Their eyes had bugged out and their mouths had dropped wide open. They had never seen such a beautiful sight. Then, as they realized that the girls were nearly naked, they'd reddened a little. But they still hadn't been able to get their eyes off the girls. No one had spoken they couldn't. Matt Billy and the women had held their positions. But Billy was still close enough that he could see every ones actions and expressions. Billy had watched everyone closely to practice what Matt had taught him. He was sure Matt would question him later to find out if he had paid attention to all of the details. It was good that he had. He saw that Matt had gotten real tense. With a guess as to why he put his thought quickly into action, with a slight movement of his hand Billy motioned the women toward the cave as he said, "Gentlemen, why don't you let me show you around?"

Hawkeye quick of mind saw where Billy had looked. Something in Billy's voice had alerted him. Then he saw Matt's eyes. Hawkeye looked at Billy as he said, "Yes, I'd really like that. Wouldn't you fellows like to see how they made it through the winter?"

Hawkeye saw the trail Matt and Billy had left and led his horse on through. The women had moved from view a little as they headed for the cave. The men with their thoughts scrambled form the events of the last few moments unable to say anything just followed Hawkeye.

As they moved off Matt watched them for just a few seconds. Because he'd sensed as much as anything that some of the Indians had started in again when they'd seen the cowboys get off their horses in peace.

When they'd gotten through the fortifications. Billy had made it there to meet them. Billy as many thoughts rushed through his mind made a quick decision. He stepped up close to meet Hawkeye. With a quick handshake he said, "Take your horses and put them in the basin over to your right. You'll see the gate. Keep everyone there, I'll be right back. But make sure you do keep everyone there!"

Billy quickly walked off not giving Hawkeye a chance to respond. He caught up with the women close to the cave entrance. They had puzzled looks on their faces. With a stern voice he said, "I don't have time to explain. Star go out with Matt. Connie, Helen go inside the cave. Give me a few minutes then I'll come get you."

Again Billy walked off without waiting for an answer. Billy hurried to the basin. When he arrived the cowboys had already spotted some of the best horses they had ever seen, next to Flame. They had finished unsaddling and a couple had just asked Hawkeye why they had to stay there. Billy had been just close enough to hear said, "I told him to. I need to explain something to you and you better listen good."

Billy covered the last few feet as he spoke. When he stopped Billy stood with his feet slightly apart, his weight balanced equally on both feet. He held his rifle pointed to the ground in a non threatening manner. They all looked at him and could tell that he was real serious. They were a little put out and a couple really resented being talked to that way from a kid. Hawkeye however stayed cautiously calm, he was sure he knew what was up. He had seen Matt's eyes.

Billy reading their thoughts said, "I'm sorry, I don't have time to be polite. I wanted to make sure everyone understands though. None of us have anything to wear, but what we have on. But the important thing you need to know is that Matt will not let anyone slander or do any offensive action associated with the women. So! If there are any of you that have a problem with that I'm suggesting that you saddle back up and leave. Oh! Just to let you know I'll be standing with Matt."

Billy hadn't stopped to keep anyone from interrupting him. They all stood quiet for a minute. Then Captain Taylor said, "I understand; you did a good job of explaining things to us and I agree. Now that I've had time to think on it a little."

Ben said, "Well, I don't. What right does he have to tell us how to act?"

Slim said, "Ben, partner. I can't say that things are right. I can't even say they're fair. But we can't change them once they happen."

"What are you saying?"

"Ben, Helen made up her mind a long time ago. Let it be."

"I never told anyone," Ben said as his face reddened.

"Didn't have to. We've been partners long enough. I saw how you acted whenever she came around and how you watched her."

Ben didn't say anymore. he just looked off.

Tex said, "I'm sorry Ben. I never knew. I'm just happy that they're all alive and I admit that I had my doubts that all of them would make it."

Captain Taylor said, "Well, I agree with everything Billy said and I'll stand by him."

Hawkeye said, "Me too."

They all agreed. Even Ben after his partners counseled him some. He told them he agreed. With that settled Captain Taylor said, "Good! Billy. Let me shake your hand. I'm proud of you."

They all shook hands then while they told each other how good it was to see each other again.

Star had made it to stand proudly behind Matt as her people approached. Matt turned and gently moved her up by his left side as he said, "I don't care if it does offend your people, you never have to stand behind me. Never!"

Strong Arms, Sees Far and Runs Far stopped their horses a few paces from them.

Matt spoke in their language as he said, "Welcome, step down and rest from your long journey. You didn't have to search for us. I was going to bring Bright Star back for a visit with you."

While they slid off their ponies Runs Far had looked at his sister and saw the slight swelling of her belly. He understood why Matt had spoken like Star wouldn't be staying with them.

Sees Far said, "Yes, I see. But I see others also. It would be best to start the new family right. Even if it is a little late. We should have a big ceremony to make things right with the Great Spirit."

Matt asked, "What things need to be made right? We have already reached an agreement and are happy."

Sees Far asked, "Bright Star. You haven't told him of the wedding ceremony?"

"No! No one was here to have a ceremony for us. Besides we have done nothing wrong. Many of our people never have a ceremony."

"Yes! You are right. But they are not the chiefs daughter!"

Matt exclaimed, "What?!"

Strong Arms stepped past his brother and took his daughter into his arms in a big hug. Star then introduced him to Matt. He gave Matt a big hug also. Matt had been uncomfortable with the affection. Some of the other Indians had slid off their horses while they had talked.

Then to Matt Strong Arms said, "This is Sees Far. He is our Medicine Man. He does take his responsibilities serious." Runs Far had watched Matt and Star closely. Bright Star just glowed while she stood next to him. He decided he liked his new brother-in-law.

With a passing look at his nephew Sees Far said, "Yes! And our people couldn't be more proud of her choice. You are already spoken of over many camp fires. You have very strong medicine."

Star knew that Matt had become uncomfortable with praise while her uncle hugged her she said, "Come let us show you around."

To Matt's surprise her uncle hugged him as she hugged her brother. Then Star introduced Matt to Runs Far. Runs Far had seen that Matt had been uncomfortable with the hugs. So he just shook Matt's hand.

Matt and Star turned to lead the way on the path that Billy and Matt had left. Strong Arms, Sees Far and Runs Far left their ponies with some of the braves. Then followed Matt and Star on the path. Then as they walked on just loud enough for Star to hear Matt said, "You never told us about being a Chief's daughter."

"It was never important to me."

All the Indians that had been close enough had checked Matt out pretty good. They had noticed the fresh scars from the battles he had been in. But they hadn't been prepared for all the scars they saw on his body from his shoulders and down his legs. Many of them really did believe that he was a Spirit. They thought no man could have lived through all the punishment, that they had seen represented by all the scares that covered his body.

When they reached the end of the path through the fortifications. They met Captain Taylor with his men as they returned from the basin. Being up close Matt shook hands and introduced them to Bright Star. They all were pleasant and except for saying hello they had held their tongues in check. For indeed they all had seen something in Matt's eyes that would put caution to any person that had any sense.

Hawkeye smiled at Bright Star and shook her hand as he spoke in her language giving her praise. Captain Taylor and Dan shook hands as they gave their acknowledgements in English. They had no idea if she understood.

When she responded in better English than they spoke they were pleasantly surprised. The rest all shook hands with her while saying their "Hello's." They all tried to divert their eyes from her mostly naked body. They all realized then how beautiful she really was.

Matt had not realized how highly keyed up and on edge he was. He didn't know it. But he just waited for someone to scorn anyone of the women.

Strong Arms had Sees Far, Runs Far and the rest of the braves bring their ponies in and take them to the basin while Matt got reacquainted and introduced Strong Arms' daughter to the cowboys. They had finished and just returned. When Matt in a voice loud enough for everyone to hear said, "Everyone, make yourselves at home. We have fresh meat, there should be enough for everyone to have a good meal tonight."

Then Runs Far turned and explained what Matt had said. Matt turned with Star and led off toward the entrance to their home, which was four hundred yards to the south of the basin. For the first time Captain Taylor and his men saw all the fresh scars that covered Matt's back side. To a man they almost lost step as they thought it was a miracle that he was alive. Billy watching Matt closely said, "I think It's nice enough to cook outside. I'll start making a fire pit to cook by."

He gave a significant nod to Hawkeye as he quickly walked off. He was rewarded as he saw Hawkeye ease up close to Matt. Hawkeye then got him into a conversation. Billy picked out a spot that already had a slight hollow with a lot of good sized rocks around to sit on. He started to lay out some smaller rocks around the hollow as he made a rock wall for the fire. It was to be a good sized fire. A couple of the braves started to help along with Slim and Bones. Tex spotted the stack of wood and got some to build the fire with.

When Billy saw that things were well under way he went up to Star and told her they may as well get some meat ready to cook. Star nodded and with Billy they went toward their cave. Billy glanced back to see that Matt and Hawkeye still talked. He saw Matt give him a glance as he and Star reached the entrance.

Star still hadn't figured out why Billy had sent Helen and Connie inside the cave. She wanted to introduce them to her people. Connie and Helen had waited. With Star beside him Billy walked up to Helen and Connie then said, "I rushed you off to make sure there wouldn't be any trouble."

Helen and Connie along with Star gave him puzzled looks. Billy finally used to how the women dressed. In turn they'd gotten used to their state of being undressed and didn't realize what he was talking about. Billy said, "I just wanted some time to make sure all the men understood that not even by accident that none of them say anything that would be taken as slander or an insult."

Connie said, "Oh I'm sure none of them would do that. They have always been perfect gentlemen."

Billy knew they hadn't gotten his meaning yet said, "That was before they saw you naked. Well pretty much so. Also I wanted to let them know how protective Matt was of you."

Connie and Helen turned a little red as full understanding came over them. They all formed a big "O" with their mouths. Then Helen asked, "You told them?"

Billy answered, "Yes, That I wouldn't put up with any slander about any of you either."

Connie said, "We don't deserve such good men as you and Matt. We decided together a long time ago we would accept what anybody said about us, as long as Matt was happy with us."

Billy blushed a little with the praise as he said, "Thank you! But do be careful. After all the cowboys aren't used to seeing so much bare skin. Star's people didn't act like anything was out of place.

Star said, "They wouldn't they already think we belong to Matt. There won't be any trouble from them. I did notice that your people watched me a lot with their eyes."

Connie said, "Okay, we'll just have to be as careful as we can and keep our distance as much as possible. But I'm not going to stay in here hiding."

Helen said, "Me neither."

Billy said, "I didn't mean for you to. I just wanted to give the men and you some time to reflect on things to make sure no trouble got started."

They all thanked him again with a big hug and kiss on his cheek. He was still uncomfortable when they did that. Sometimes he was sure that was why they did it. But he did like the warm feeling it gave him. Star had gotten the knife then said, "We'll get the meat ready."

Star with Connie and Helen went to cut up some of the fresh meat they hadn't stripped yet. It looked like most of it would be used. Billy followed them out and when they turned toward their meat cave. Billy saw that most of Captain Taylor's men had spotted the women and watched. Billy took a deep breath and walked on as he made sure that both pistols were loose in their holsters. Matt had his own gun rig on. Billy wore the one that had been on Flame's saddle.

When they left the cave the girls and Billy had left their rifles. Matt still held his rifle in his left hand. Billy glanced at Matt as he walked back to the growing fire and the cowboys. Matt talked with Strong Arms, Runs Far and Sees Far. A hand full of the braves stood close by. As the cowboy's glanced at the women, Matt's eyes had turned to them. Billy saw that Matt watched them intently. Billy walked up to Captain Taylor who like the rest looked at the women. But he had taken his eyes off as soon as he realized what he'd done it. Billy asked, "The last time you saw my folks were they doing okay and well?"

Captain Taylor caught up in his own thoughts was a little surprised to see Billy standing in front of him. He'd been trying to understand what Matt and the Indians were talking about. He'd been able to pick up a word here and there. But for the most part he'd been lost. Like the others his eyes had been drawn to the women as they came out. As he looked back to answer Billy he glanced at Matt and saw something in Matt's stance and look. Captain Taylor had picked up on the danger signals. So a little louder than necessary he said, "They were all in good health and have built a real nice place. They have worked hard and have a real good start on really making it into something grand."

Drawn by Captain Taylor's voice most of the cowboy's looked at Billy. They studied him some. It was then that they realized he was not the youngster that he had been when they last saw him. He stood straight and he had grown. Of course they hadn't seen him nearly naked. His shoulders weren't really broad, they had a nice build to them however. Slim of waist with no fat.

Now that they had taken an interest, the biggest difference they noticed was his eyes. They had the look of someone that had seen a lifetime of violence and survived. Of someone that had been tempered by the fire and come out stronger for it. Also, even with the lack of proper clothes the pistols didn't look like they were out of place. They had been adjusted to hang much like Matt's with the pistol butts even with his hands so it wouldn't take much of a movement to clear their holsters.

As Captain Taylor and Billy conversed with a few of the cowboys were drawn into their conversation. Soon most of them took turns exchanging information with Billy.

By the time Connie, Star and Helen had returned with some meat. With the help of a couple of braves Bones had gotten some limbs together to hang the meat on over the fire. Bones then put some coffee beans in their coffee pot and set it on fire. That broke up the groups some as they went to retrieve their cups. Even some of the Indian braves that had them went to get their cups. They'd gotten so they liked the coffee.

The cowboys glanced at the women without being seen if they could. After a couple of times when the women caught them. The women just looked back at them and smiled. Whichever one it was would get red-faced and tried to make sure not to get caught again. They tried to find something to do or made sure of where they looked. With time things got more relaxed. The women could talk with everyone and had really started to enjoy themselves. When the meat was done the women passed it out. As Helen and Star sat down with their food. Connie took the second pot full of boiling coffee around to refill their cups. The women had been able to serve everyone without showing any sign of embarrassment. Some of the cowboys had red faces when the exposed breasts were only two or three foot in front of their eyes. Connie then got her food and sat down next to Star and

Helen. All three of the women must have been more tense than they'd realized. Because as soon as Connie Sat down with surprise all over her face she asked, "Where's Matt?"

They all looked at one another. When the question had been repeated to the Indians they looked around in astonishment. Not a one of them had seen Matt leave. Of course it could be blamed that everyone had their attention on the women. But with Matt just vanishing as if into thin air like that, made a lot of the Indians uncomfortable.

Matt had to do some soul searching. He'd thought that he was ready to handle things. With the Indians everything had been fine. He liked Strong Arms, Sees Far and Runs Far already. Most of the braves had been pleasant. He was uncomfortable with the honor and respect along with the pride that they'd had in their eyes. As far as he was concerned he had just done what any man would've done to protect his people. He admitted that he'd been awful lucky to survive.

However it had taken all the control he'd had to abstain from the violence he'd wanted to distribute out. He couldn't help but see how the cowboys had looked at the women. He'd about lost the battle with himself when he had eased away from the fire.

He'd been able to slip out easily on his bare feet. He hadn't used a halter or saddle on Flame. He'd just leaped on Flames back and rode of. He guided Flame with his knees. They'd gone out through the thick stand of trees to the East. It was still a little cool at night, but if felt good to him. He needed to cool off some anyway. He was able to relax more as Flame carried him away. Matt let Flame pick the course he wanted and the pace he wanted. It would be dark in another hour. It had been warmer that day. But it already felt like it would be cooler tonight.

He put his thoughts back to the reason he had rode out of camp. He couldn't blame the cowboys for looking. In their place he probably would have also. He knew he loved the women. He just hadn't been prepared for how jealous he had gotten. It had been a feeling he'd never felt before. Not like when one of his brothers had gotten something he would have liked. It was a much deeper emotion when it came to the women. Nobody had done anything out of place. Which he was glad of.

He considered Captain Taylor along with all his men to be his friends. But he'd been so keyed up that it would have taken very little for him to have lost control. So he'd rode off to keep from making a fool of himself. He wouldn't go back till he was, completely calmed down. He let Flame continue to pick their course and speed. Flame moved at an easy gallop that covered a lot of ground. The wind in his face was pleasant as he took in the fresh air. Matt than dwelled on his ability to see things from someone else's eyes or something other than his own. It was easier for him each time. Matt's new line of thought kept him busy as Flame moved across the valley.

Connie had gone to the cave to let Matt know that the food was ready. When she didn't find him in the cave she then went and checked the basin. When she got there she saw that Flame was gone also. She went back to the fire and told the others. With Star and Helen they decided not to worry. They had already learned that he liked to be by himself, from time to time. Especially if something was on his mind.

When they had finished eating the women borrowed some cups and sipped some coffee. Star found out that she liked it. They told her that it was better with sugar.

Connie and Helen were brought up to date about their families. The Captain had done most of the taking then. The talk finely got around to how and what happened to Billy and the women. They all had been curious. It was Tex who had finally asked.

Billy and the women had gotten awful quiet. The cowboys waited patiently for a couple of minutes as Billy and the women gathered their thoughts. After they'd gotten their composer Billy started the conversation. Then Star, Connie and Helen joined him. They left nothing out as they covered everything from their capture to the present. Well! Nearly. Their love making they'd left out, of course.

As one of them spoke their words were translated to the Indians that didn't know English. By Hawkeye or Runs Far. Most of them except for a hand full didn't understand English. Once they had started Billy and the women hadn't been interrupted. Then they had warmed up and had even gotten a little excited. They were proud of Matt and each other. They wanted their guest to know how much Matt had done for them. Billy and the women told them the truth about all of the events that had happened. They hadn't exaggerated any. If anything they had down played some of the events. With some questions that had been asked they'd talked late into the night. Wood had been added to the fire a few times. The coffee pot had been well used also. When they finished it had gotten awful quiet as they tried to absorb all they'd been told.

Even the Indians seamed reluctant to break the silence. They didn't want to miss a word either. After a while the silence was broken as Captain Taylor said, "I don't know what it was. But the first time I saw Matt, I thought he was something special. Um! You ladies are something special also."

He'd turned a little red-faced as he'd spoken. He'd looked straight at them to let them know that he really ment it. Connie cut the Captain a little slack as she nodded her thanks saying, "I grew up with Matt. For as long as I can remember I've heard talk of how different he was by our families and some other people."

Some of the Indians started to talk excitedly among themselves.

Tex asked, "What's gotten into them?"

Helen listened a little before she answered, "They think that Matt has powers. That with the things he's already done that he is more of a spirit than a man."

A little reddish of face Dan looked at Star as he asked, "Bright Star, right?", she nodded. "I've never heard of anything called a Spirit Bear. But you really do believe that Matt ended up with his Spirit."

Star nodding, "Yes, I saw it when it happened."

Some of the braves asked what they'd said. When it was repeated to them. They'd nodded among themselves with a respectful reverence expressed on their faces.

Captain Taylor and his men just kept quiet. It had been a pleasant evening and they didn't want a dispute with Bright Star. Some did have doubtful looks on their faces though. With the pause in the conversation the women stood and excused themselves. They told everyone that they were tried and needed to get some rest.

The first to respond. Maybe a little quick Captain Taylor said, "Oh! Yes ladies. I'm sorry we shouldn't have kept you up so late. In your condition you need all the rest, you can get."

That was what finally embarrassed the women a little. Even Star had been a little self-conscious. She didn't know why, but she wanted them to think well of her. Especially Captain Taylor. They said their goodnights and went to their bed in the cave. After a little while Billy told them goodnight then he retired to his cave. The rest found places to unroll their bedrolls and retired for the night. Some close to the fire. The rest just snuggled deep in their blankets.

The next morning Runs Far sent a brave out with a message for the rest of the people to join them. He also sent out some braves out to hunt for some fresh meat. The morning meal had been a little skimpy. Hawkeye and Bones had gone along with the hunting party.

The women had gotten their horses and proudly showed them to everyone. They showed them how well they'd been trained. Then they'd gone out for a little ride. When they returned Captain Taylor had already had his men move the supplies to the entrance of the main cave. After the women had rubbed their horses down and turned them loose. They were surprised when they approached the cave and saw all of the things stacked in front of it. Helen turned and retraced her steps back to the fire where Captain Taylor and his men sat sipping coffee, then asked, "What's all the stuff that's in front of our cave?"

Captain Taylor said, "I forget to tell you last night. Mr. Maxton sent all that stuff along. He told us if we found you that you would probably need some things."

Helen asked, "Oh what all did you bring?"

Captain Taylor looked at his men and saw blank looks on their faces. Then he said, "We know what some of the stuff is. But not most of it. We just packed it and brought it along."

"Well, thank you. I guess we might as well find out what Mr. Maxton sent us."

As she turned to go back to Connie and Star. Who looked like they had already started to paw through some of the things. Ben asked, "Would you like some help carrying the stuff on in?"

"Oh, that would be nice."

Slim said, "I may as well help also."

Dan and Tex decided they would help.

Captain Taylor was concerned, but he didn't show it. As if reading his mind after they had gone Slade said, "I think they'll be alright Captain. But I'm glad Ben didn't go by himself on that errand."

Captain Taylor said, "Yeah! Me too."

Slade then voiced his thoughts a little as he said, "I was caught off guard last night. But I have had time to think things over. After what the youngsters told us and of what all they've been through. Well! Probably some preacher might say their not decent. But he better not say it within my hearing."

Captain Taylor gave him a good look, then said, "I agree. I don't know how. But it seems like they've got things all worked out. I was worried about Ben though."

"Yeah, that was a surprise. I never knew a thing though. He's old enough to be her father. I think he has things worked out though. He was better this morning."

"I thought so. But I was concerned when he asked to help. Usually he don't say much."

Slade said, "I just think he wanted to make sure she's happy."

"Well, that's easy. Every one of those ladies act like their the richest people in the world."

Slade said, "Yeah; But it's harder for some people to see, than it is for some others though."

They had watched as everything had been carried in. When Dan and the other men started to return. Captain Taylor and Slade were silent as they waited for them to walk up. When they arrived Dan said, "If, you get an invite you ought to go in and see that cave. It's the neatest thing I have ever seen. It's got a hot spring that runs into a pool and cold fresh water from another spring. Nice and roomy. Never saw or even heard of such a thing."

Captain Taylor said, "I'd like that. I'm beginning to think that there's nothing that would surprise me about those youngsters."

Billy returned then rubbed down Tree Socks after his ride. He wasn't worried about Matt. But he thought if Matt wanted to talk he would let him. Billy had rode out with the hunting party then split off to see if he could spot Matt and Flame. He was sure that They 'd spot him first which was what he'd hoped for. Billy knew that Matt had been tense. But hadn't realized how much. Billy knew that with everyone around Matt had to have a good reason to take off. Shoot he hadn't even stopped to put Flames bridle or saddle on. Billy had just gotten close enough to the fire and the men to hear Captain Taylor's last statement. Billy decided to test the waters a little and said, "I guess I ought to give you a little advice. I wouldn't be calling the women girls or youngsters where they can hear you. Matt just about got run out of the country the last time he mentioned the word girls."

It got the results he'd hoped for. They chuckled a little. After a little bit Ben even had. Captain Taylor glanced at Ben and relaxed as he chuckled. Billy much like Matt had thought him, hadn't miss the little glance Captain Taylor had given Ben and wondered.

Captain Taylor with a little grin said, "Yes, Matt is going to have to really be on his toes now. I wonder if he still thinks he's the boss."

They all laughed at that. Billy glanced all around as he made sure Matt wasn't there. Then with a smile on his face he said, "Oh, Matt's tried. He hasn't given up yet."

They really laughed then and some of the Indians that had stayed around with Strong Arms, Sees Far and Runs Far looked at them as they wondered what was up.

Runs Far had been close enough to hear and repeated it to them. They had erupted into laughter also. The laughter had just died down some as the women came out of the cave carrying some cooking utensils. Connie asked, "What's funny?"

They all had been caught with the amusement still on their faces. They stopped suddenly and acted like they hadn't a clue to what she wanted to know. They all tried to look around innocently like they didn't even know where they were. Even the Indians. Thoughtfully Captain Taylor said, "Sorry! But I don't think it would be decent for your ears."

The women were suspicious that a joke had been played on them. Connie said, "Well we've unpacked all the stuff my dad sent to us. He even sent a Dutch oven. Some flour and spices. So if you was to behave we were going to make some biscuits and some other things."

After hearing her statement they got serious looks on their faces and a few of them said, "Yes, Ma'am."

Quick to pick up Connie's mood the women just looked at each other. The Indians had sobered up also. Dan stood then took one of the large pots the women had brought out. Dan went to the little stream to scrub it out with some sand. Then Slim, decided to help. Soon even a few of the Indians went in search of wood for the cook fire. The women returned to their cave to prepare some other things to cook. As the camp filled up with activity. In English Runs Far proudly told Captain Taylor, "Maybe it's not a good idea to make them mad. Even my braves are busy doing what many think is women's work."

Captain Taylor thoughtfully said, "Yeah, I can see that. I think maybe we better heed to Billy's warning."

The hunting party returned with fresh meat. They had quartered it then wrapped the quarters in the hide. The women worked steady to prepare the other things to go with their meal. Most everyone was busy doing something. The men cooked the meat. The biscuits would be a treat they didn't get very often.

Matt was hungry. He hadn't eaten since the morning before. He could've hunted for something. He'd chosen not to though. He had drank a lot of water to pacify him. He had finely gotten things worked out in his mind and was in a good mood. It was late afternoon and the shadows already ran far out into the valley. Flame and Matt had explored some more of the valley and really had a good time. They'd taken time out to play some. So as they approached home. Matt was completely relaxed and cheerful. He guided Flame back much the same way they'd left. As he let Flame pick his way through the dense stand of trees. He noticed that Flame was being careful and quiet. It helped that there was a lot of pine needles under foot.

When they reached the clearing in the basin Matt kneed Flame to a stop. Then he pulled some tall hay left over from last fall and rubbed Flame down good. Finished Matt eased along on his bare feet. Like Billy and the women his moccasins had worn-out. As he approached the camp of his guests he got a whiff of the food that was being cooked. It made him hungrier. It smelled like a real good meal was being prepared. The cowboys must have brought some flour and spices. Then he was sure he could smell coffee. Then it hit him that made sense. He knew if nothing else, the cowboys would make sure they had coffee.

It had been a good day at the camp. Everyone had gotten reacquainted with each other again. They had made new friends. The Indians had even mingled in with them. Once in awhile someone that understood both languages had to interpret a little. Everyone was cheerful as they finished preparing the meal. The men had cooked the meat again.

The women had finished sorting out the supplies Mr. Maxton had sent. He had sent guns and ammunition holsters and oil. They found candles, canteens, bowie knives, dried fruit, blankets and a couple of axes. He had sent almost anything that they might need. He had even sent some clothes which they had tried on. However they found out that they didn't quiet fit. Especially around the waist. They were too tight. As they sorted through the things Connie thought. That her father must have picked out most of the stuff. He hadn't sent any under things at all. They probably wouldn't have fit anyway she decided as she looked at her belly which had started to swell slightly. Her father had sent some hair brushes. They had been busy as they watched over the food and brushed each others hair out real good. Connie and Helen were in control mostly as they taught Star how to use the flour and the dried fruit. Along with the Dutch oven and the other stuff. They'd cooked inside as everything had already been taken in anyway.

The women had brushed their hair out real good. Then they had cleaned up the guns and adjusted, the gun belts to fit them. They had tried on some wool shirts. But they itched so bad they'd taken them, off. Their skin had gotten used to being uncovered. Besides they had already exposed most everything to everyone anyhow.

When the last batch of biscuits had cooked. They started taking them out along with a couple of pots of beans and stew. They'd made quite a few batches so everyone could have a taste. So as they carried out the last of the finished meal the women wondered if Matt would show up. With everyone around they didn't see a need to wear their new gun rigs with their new guns. They had fastened the bowie knifes with their sheaths on their hips. Held there by their loin cloths.

Billy had enjoyed the day. His thoughts had gone to Matt often as he wondered what he was up to. With the new friends and the old friends they had talked about many things. He had answered a lot of questions about all that had happened after being captured. The

Indians after they knew he spoke their language had been as inquisitive as any of them. He had spoken honestly and factually. They'd been impressed by his detailed explanations. Also, even though he was young the Indians and the cowboys a like. Were impressed by the man he had become. A few of them sipped their coffee as the women brought the last of the biscuits up to their cook fire. When nearly there Helen asked, "Is the meat about done?"

Bone's with the help of a couple of braves he'd gotten chummy with. Had thrown on a couple quarters of venison then turned them every half hour or so. Bone's nodded as he said, "Yes Ma'am! We all thank you. They smell real good."

Connie cheerfully said, "Good this is the last of the biscuits. Besides I'm starved."

"Me too."

They heard as several jumped. Indians and white men both. Some had spilt some of their coffee. For once the women hadn't even sensed him. In all fairness several of them had been listening to Billy explain some more details, as the women came up. When they'd quickly turned their heads, they saw Matt in the flesh as he took the last few steps to join them. By the look on some of the Indians faces they weren't so sure that it was flesh they looked at. Matt looked completely relaxed and even showed them a slight grin. All three of the women's countenance had taken on a sudden glow. Their eyes especially brightened. Matt's appearance brought a hush over all of them. Then Matt said, "I can smell some things I haven't smelled in a coon's age. The coffee is a real treat. I hope you've got a lot of it."

Most everyone except for Billy and the women still hadn't recovered from Matt's sudden appearance. Most everyone knew how quiet he could move. But they thought that they should've seen him come up. They where in the shadows, but it hadn't been that close to dark, yet. Hawkeye said, "We've got lot's of coffee and the women have fixed a feast for us."

The women had set the food stuff down for everyone to help themselves. Then Helen got a new cup and filled it with coffee. When she handed it to Matt she glowed with pride. Connie fixed him a plate of food while Star ladled some stew onto another plate for him. Then they fixed their own plates and sat next to Matt. Everyone else had been left to help themselves to the food and coffee. After the meal they sipped coffee and talked till the sun set. Then the women and Matt went into their home.

Within four days the rest of the Black Hawk Tribe with Star's mother arrived. They set up camp as the sun started to go down. The camp was a mile below the cave beside the river that came out from a smaller valley. The river flowed south from a gap between two mountains. From the gap the smaller valley went northwest for a hundred and fifty miles to it farthest point. Star and her mother Late bloom rejoiced when they got together. She introduced Matt, Billy, Connie and Helen to her. Matt and Billy had left after a little while to let the women get acquainted. They weren't much on women's talk anyway. Which is the direction the conversation had gone in as the girls had mentioned how they were looking forward to having their babies.

CHAPTER TWENTY TWO

THE GRIZZLY SPIRITS WEDDING

The next morning Runs Far announced his arrival at the entrance of their cave. They'd cooked just for themselves as everyone had made their own camps. With all the new utensils that Mr. Maxton had sent the cooking was a lot easier for them. With all the people there they had stayed close to home. They'd talked late into the night, then slept late. Star grabbed her lion cloth and tied it on as she went to welcome her brother. Matt, Connie and Helen got up and put there's on. Matt put some wood on the fire while Connie put a fresh pot of coffee on the fire. Helen got some biscuits that had been left over from the night before. Which had used up the last of the flour.

When Star returned with Runs Far he declined the offer of a biscuit. He told them he'd eaten. They spoke in his native language. They talked a little and when the coffee was ready. Runs Far did except a cup of coffee. When they'd finished their coffee Runs Far said, "Strong Arms and Sees Far would like too talk to all of you."

With questioning looks they nodded, then Matt asked, "When?"

"When the sun reaches midday."

They had agreed. Then after Star followed her brother out, she returned to get in the hot pool with the others. They decided to walk to Strong Arms village. The Indians had set up their tepees already. When they arrived Runs Far met them, then led them to a large tepee. They saw Strong Arms and Sees Far along with a couple more elders and five other respected braves. They sat patently as Runs Far brought their guest in. Matt spoke their language as he said, "I'm sorry we are late."

Strong Arms answered, "Your not late. You were seen. We just got everyone together."

Then they sat down as Star and Runs Far directed to the appropriate places. Women usually didn't set in on the meetings. When everyone had sat down according to their status within the tribe with their special guests and the women. Sees Far lit a pipe and started the ceremony. After the pipe was passed around and everyone had done the same. Matt and the three women were told too do the same. Then they were served a meal of buffalo stew that was excellent. When they'd concluded Sees Far said, "We have talked much and agreed that it would be proper to have a special wedding ceremony to honor the Great Spirit. Then also to give honor to the Great Grizzly Spirit and his women."

Star so as not to embarrass her people had all she could do to control herself. She knew now not only had her people excepted Matt and the two other women. But they were to be honored beyond anything she had ever heard of. Matt, Connie and Helen kept their emotions contained. They showed little sign of what they'd heard. They didn't fully comprehend what was to take place anyway. Matt just wasn't crazy about all of the attention. When about to protest he saw the stern looks then changed his mind and just nodded. Sees Far then went ahead and outlined what was to take place for the ceremony. It was decided that the purifications would start the next day.

The next few days the Indian village was full of activity as everyone got ready for the big event. Captain Taylor and his men. When they found out what was to take place helped out doing what they could. Runs Far had joined Matt in the new constructed sweat hut to go through the purification with him. Matt told him he didn't have to. But Runs Far told him he didn't mind. That it was good for him anyway. Besides it would give him a chance to learn more about his brother-in-law. Matt was kept away from the women as they went through their own rituals.

Finally the big day had arrived. Captain Taylor and his men had even gotten cleaned up the best they could, under the circumstances. They had even bathed. From Hawkeye and a few of the other braves. They learned how important of a ceremony it was. That it was in honor of The Great Spirit as well as Matt and his women. They had prepared a lot of food and there was to be a big feast.

Captain Taylor and his men picked out a good place to observe the ceremony. They'd not been any to early. As the sun was nearly overhead, the little knoll had started to fill up. The children and all that could were encouraged to witness the special event. Their excitement showed in their eyes. But were respectfully quiet. Their was a little movement as some strived to find a better spot. When the sun was overhead. Chief Strong Arms and Sees Far walked up the lane that had been left for them to the top of the little knoll.

They were brilliantly dressed in buckskins with the bright symbols and the beads of their tribe. Chief Strong Arms wore his headdress full of eagle feathers. When they got to their places. Runs Far in a brilliant buckskin outfit with Matt beside him started up the lane. Matt was dressed in buckskins that had the same beadwork and symbols of the Black Hawk tribe. But some other symbols had been added. Then from each shoulder in brilliant colors was the scratch marks of a bears paw. The art work made the claw marks look fresh. Bright yellow like freshly parted skin. Then bright red as if blood flowed out of the wounds. Some spots were all the way down Matt's buckskins. Like they had dripped down from the wounds. Even onto his new moccasins.

Runs Far walked with a purposeful step. He showed a lot of pride and walked as tall as he could. It was a big honor for him to be next to someone that was so great. Matt was impressed with the buckskins and with all the respect he was getting. He noticed that a lot of Chief Strong Arms' people were in awe of him as he saw the looks from their eyes. Being with and after a lot of pleasant conversation with his knew brother-in-law. Matt had made his mind up to go along with everything, even though he thought. They made to much out of him and the things he had done. Everyone had been so nice he didn't what to make a fuss. The only thing he'd done was what any man would have done in his place, he thought. When they arrived up in front of Sees Far. Runs Far stepped next to his father. Matt was left to face Sees Far.

Within five minutes though no one heard a sound it was as if a quiet moan had passed through all of the people. Matt turned just his head as he looked down the lane. He almost let things get the best of him. They were beautiful. Strong Arms' wife in her ceremonial costume led Star, Connie and Helen with three maidens beside them. All of them in ceremonial costumes. The maidens had been chosen to get the honored women ready. Their hair had been brushed till it glistened in the bright sun and was loose down their backs. As they got closer Matt could see that their doeskins had the same pattern of beads and symbols just like his. Their leather dress's had been cut with a deep V in front to show most of their breasts. He was sure they had a purpose for doing so. But he didn't figure out why until they were a lot closer. Then he saw the polished white bear's claws that were attached to the inside of their breasts. Two on the their left breast and one on the right. They pointed down to curve under each breast. Taking his eyes from their breasts he noticed the design on their shoulders. Up from the top of their breasts over to their backs like scratch marks from a bears claw. The colors matched his buckskins. He knew theirs had been imbedded into their skin though.

Matt looked into their eyes as they got close. His heart skipped a beat. For their eyes flashed with brilliant lighting bolts that shot right through him. He felt the sensation down to his toes. He had seen the pride and excitement that they were expressing to him. Matt was glad his buckskins were a tight fit. Oh, it hurt. But he was pretty sure he didn't stick out much, at least he hoped not. He'd never been so hard. With the tight leather it felt like it bulged all the way down to his right knee. It felt like if he took a quick step it would break. Late Bloom led them up to Matt then put them in line in the order they had mated on Matt's left side. Matt then noticed that the backs of their gowns had a deep square cut. The gowns were held up by the tightness of the sleeves. The claw marks ran down their backs. Nearly to their fanny's.

Sees Far then started the ceremony. Hawkeye and a couple other braves translated for Captain Taylor and his men. Billy could have. But he decided that he wasn't going too miss a word. He stood just off a little from Strong Arms and Runs Far. He was a guest of honor and had a buckskin costume with the design of the Black Hawks. They had lent it to him for the ceremony. Sees Far honored The Great Spirit. Then highlighted the great deeds of The Grizzly Spirit. Billy noticed that Matt stood tall even though he seamed to be embarrassed by the story and the praise.

The Indians when out of Matt's and the women's hearing. Had passed the story around the camp until all of them knew it. Almost as good as Sees Far did. However they learned that Sees Far must have had some insight from some of his visions. He told them of some new things that Billy hadn't even known. He watched closely and from Matt's expression was sure they were true. Matt normally wouldn't show any sign. But Matt was swept up by the beauty of the women and their emotions along with the ceremony.

Then Sees Far explained that each one of the women had excepted and would join together with The Grizzly Spirit. Then the women of The Grizzly Spirit had humbled themselves with respect. That they have honored him by accepting the claws and would wear them forever. Therefore not only have they been joined as man and women. But they also have been joined by the claws of the Spirit Bear. Therefore from this day forward let there be a curse on anyone. That brings any harm to any one of The Grizzly Spirits women or offspring. Sees Far then honored The Great Spirit again. When he finished the drums started and everyone started to shout and rejoice.

Some of the braves danced in honor of the newlyweds. The celebration went on late into the night. Everyone had a good time. They had received some personal gifts given to honor them. Captain Taylor and his men promised to get them some gifts as soon as they got some place to get something. Matt and his ladies told them that being there was enough. They still insisted on getting them something. Strong Arms had a tepee set up. It was specially done for Matt and his wives. When the celebrations had died down some. Matt was finally able to get rejoined with his ladies.

As the week transpired Matt had done a lot of thinking. With several discussions with Billy and the women. He finally had a format worked out in his mind. Together they'd rode and planned as they tried to project in their minds what they wanted to build in Peaceful Valley. Matt had tried to persuade Billy to be an equal partner. Billy had told him as long as they would put up with him, he would just work for them in whatever status they saw fit for him. Matt thought that Billy was being about the most stubborn person he knew besides his wives. They'd gone back to wearing just their loin cloths. They weren't going to ruin their ceremonial costumes. The clothes that Mr. Maxton had sent was to tight for their bellies.

The Indians had explored and rode a lot to look the valley over. They were amazed at the size and beauty of the valley. Also with all the deferent varieties of wild game that they'd seen.

Matt, Billy and his wives had set up a meeting. With Strong Arms and some of the elders. They hurried back so as not to be late. It was close to dark and they'd arranged to meet them at sunset. They were just a few minutes early as they approached. They could see a large group had already gathered. Most of them were the elders. But quite a few men with a few women curiously stood around.

After they'd been invited to dismount. Matt then explained what they'd decided and hoped would be acceptable to them. Then he told them of a good sized valley to the south that ran south from the main valley. That it had a high plateau with a big lake. He told them about the river that ran through most of the valley. Then of the forest in some places throughout the valley. That there was a lot of good grass. Especially on the lower section. That the main water supply came from a tall waterfall that came from the mountain up high near the top.

Matt explained that if they would he'd like for them to slowly move all of the buffalo and most of the wild horses into the valley. That he hoped the Black Hawk Nation would make it their home. Matt promised them that he would make sure that nothing ever happened to Ceremonial Knoll. That he would be proud to see them keep to their old ways and customs.

Matt told them he intended to develop the main valley into four good sized ranches. With some farm land scattered throughout the valley. That a lot of people would be brought in to help build and develop the land. He then stressed that the Black Hawk Nation would have no trouble. That the people brought in to do the work would be told that their valley was off limits. Matt told them any of the brave or woman that wanted to help with the ranch or any of the other jobs that came along. That they'd be welcomed to try out for any of them they wanted. They would be paid. He expressed the need for some scouts that he could use on the cattle drives and trips to town for supplies. He explained that there was no hurry. That it would be months before other people would be in the valley.

Matt then told them of his big request. That none of the people who decided to stay in the valley. Would go to war against the white man or any of the other tribes. That he knew of the honor that braves received from going into battle. But he hoped that they would be able to receive enough honor and respect from their people by scouting for him.   Matt told them that he and his wives wanted to leave in five days. That they wanted to let their families know that they were alive. Then Matt paused. Not knowing how they would receive the next bit of information. He told them of the gold he'd found. Then explained that he wanted to use it on the valley and to take care of his wives. That the gold would be returned to the valley in the shape of goods, and materials to build up his ranches. Then Matt told them he was finished.

The Indians had listened passively. They'd not shown their emotions on their faces. There was a good five minute silence before Strong Arms still in deep thought said, "Some of the braves and I will look over the valley you've told us about. Then we'll see how the people decide."

Matt said, "That will be good. If you decide to stay I would like to have the entrance guarded to keep anyone else form getting in. White eyes or Indians.

Matt's words had put a sparkle to his father in-laws eyes as he said,, "Unless they are friends or work for you."

Matt nodding, "I still think it will be many months before that happens. Unless I can hire Captain Taylor and his men to stay around and help me. I don't know anything about ranching. So I could use their help."

Strong Arms nodded as he said, "Okay, maybe it'll be good. We'll look then see how the people decide. Then I'll let you know."

Matt said, "That'll be good. If some braves would like to, I would like to have them ride scout when we leave."

Runs Far said, "I will help. I'm sure there will be plenty of others to help also."

Matt with his wives and Billy thanked them for listening. Then took their leave as the Indians broke up into small groups to discuss what they'd heard. Matt, Billy and the ladies. Reclaimed their horses and rode quietly to their home. Each of them rode with their own thoughts. When they'd taken care of their horses and as they walked toward the cave Star said, "I think my people might accept there's not many that want to go to war. My people have tried to be peaceful with the white eyes "

Connie said, "Oh, I hope your right. I like your people and would feel bad to see a lot of them die. Even though I know it is a custom for them to receive honor that way."

Billy said, "Well if that's the case, from what I've heard from the cowboys and after getting to know Matt. All they have to do is stay close to Matt and they'll have their hands full."

They all stopped with Matt. As he gave Billy a hard look Matt asked, "What do you mean by that?"

Billy smiled a little, then said, "Why Matt we know how much trouble there is when other people try to take what they can from you or mess with one of the girls. I just know you'll never back down from anything."

Helen and Connie almost together exclaimed, "Oh, my! Yes, Billy is right. Matt we'll have to make sure that one of us is around to make sure you don't get into trouble."

Matt said, "No! You don't have to worry about me. You just take care of yourselves and our babies. I'll be careful."

Star just grunted in disgust. Matt glanced at Billy as he eased on toward the cave, with a slight smile on his face. Matt said, "Really, I'll be careful. I'll probably have lots of help anyway."

Connie said, "I've heard that before and what matters to us is that your our husband. We need you just as much as anything else. So we'll just have to make sure that one of us is close by to try, too keep you calm."

Matt said, "Okay, that's enough. I love all of you very much. But I'm not going to have you around me like a bunch of nurse-maids babysitting me."

Matt got a big surprise when they all talked loudly at him at the same time. He only picked up a word here and there. He couldn't make sense of any of it as they vented their opinions. He'd picked out something about love then food. Which reminded him that he was hungry. After their onslaught on him they all turned and stomped into the cave. He hadn't been able to get a word in. With some satisfaction their stomps weren't that impressive. Maybe it even hurt their feet a little. Matt with his ears still tingling tried to recall what he'd said to upset them so bad. He decided it would be best to stay outside and let them cool off.

Billy heard the new pots and pans being banged around as he finished bathing. He decided as he put his loin cloth on that he'd be better off to keep quiet. Forty minutes later Helen walked up to him and gave him a plate of food. Then took his cup and refilled it. After that she got her food and sat down next to Connie and Star. Five minutes later Matt came in and was surprised when none of the ladies got up to get his cup to fill it with coffee. He gave them a look, but he didn't get one back. He got his cup and filled it. After a couple of sips he put it down. Then he got a plate for his food. When he got to the pots and pans by the fire he saw that they were empty. He looked around to see if he'd missed one. Then he asked, "Where's the food?"

Connie said, "Oh! If there isn't any left in the pot or pan then it must be all gone."

Helen said, "I think there's some meat left. You just need a knife to cut off a piece."

Matt's temper rose as he put the plate down. He reclaimed his cup off coffee and walked out. Did they think he was blind he wondered. He'd seen the meat and knew that you used a knife to cut it. Matt had felt like stomping his feet. But he knew that it would have just hurt his feet if he had. With a touch of satisfaction. He thought I can control myself better than they can.

Billy had felt a little bad about what he'd said as Matt left. He'd met for the statement to be a joke more than anything else. But he knew that he hadn't been far from the truth either. He just ate his food and tried to relax. The women were pretty tense. Billy decided that they'd have to work things out on there own. He knew Matt would do anything for anyone of the women. Even gladly onto death if it was called for. The problem was that the women felt the same way about him. They probably felt like it was their fault that he'd been hurt.

Billy felt like he was partly to blame for some of it. Then he realized at the time they'd been captured he hadn't known how to defend himself like he did now. Trained as he was now Billy knew that they wouldn't have captured him. At least not alive. Bill had realized over time that it was nobodies fault. That things just happened even if you were sure of everything. The best laid plans didn't work out sometimes. Especially out here in the wild west. Billy knew the women would have their hands full if they thought they could protect Matt from all the harm that would be directed at him.

Billy glanced at them and saw that they were mad clean through. Matt really had them stirred up. Billy smiled to himself as he thought. Yep it sure won't be boring now that things were about to be put into motion. He was ready. It had been a long winter. Even as beautiful and new as the valley was. He was ready for some excitement. Finished with his meal Billy cleaned his plate off then refilled his cup. He thanked the women as he left.

They'd nodded then after Billy had been gone a minute Connie said, "Oh! Matt makes me so mad. I've never seen him scared of anything. He just thinks there is nothing he can't survive. Even after almost dying twice."

Star nodded as she said, "With him taken on the Spirit Bear's Spirit he probably feels more powerful than ever."

Helen said, "I just wish he would understand that the babies deserve to know their father and that he'd be extra careful."

Star said, "I know he dosen't want any of us to be harmed in any way."

Connie said, "Yes! But dosen't he know that he hurts us when he says things like he just did. That it just scares us to death."

Helen said, "He just dosen't think we need to watch his every move. But I still can picture how fearless he was at the Indian camp and how he attacked right into the thickest bunch of them. I still don't know how he was able to get away from them."

Star nodded, then said, "Yes! That was the most amazing thing I have seen until the grizzly attacked us. Matt wasn't even scared then. He just grabbed the knife and attacked him. Yes! We do need to watch over him, somehow."

Connie said, "Well, I've cooled off some now. We wouldn't be able to stay mad at him. But lets just kind of make sure at least one of us is close by. Especially once we're on the trail."

Helen said, "Yes, lets. We don't have much here yet. But I already dread leaving. This is home for me." They then stood and hugged each other in agreement.

CHAPTER TWENTY THREE

HIRED

Matt got some funny looks as he approached Captain Taylor, Tex and the rest of the men as they laid around their camp fire sipping coffee. Matt just ignored them as he refilled his cup. He'd spotted what was left of a hind quarter of elk above the fire, just close enough to stay warm. Matt asked, "Is it alright if I cut off a piece."

They looked at him wonderingly then nodded. Matt pulled his new bowie knife from its sheath he had attached to his gun belt. Matt had touched up the edge so it went through the meat like it was butter. Matt when he'd finished the first peace cut off another and ate it. Then he refilled his cup again and sat down to sip his coffee. He had just got his mind back on the scene in front of the cave as he tried to figure out what the devil had happened. Then Hawkeye asked, "You don't have any food in your lodge?"

Matt gave him a hard look, then said, "It's not that. I just wanted some Elk meat."

He wasn't about to let them know that the women hadn't fixed him anything. Hawkeye had picked up on the tenseness of Matt's voice however. He couldn't help, but dig the spur in a little deeper. He said, "Maybe you should have done like Dan told you to. You should have rode Flame to the ocean and caught a boat. It's too late now."

Dan as he listened sipping his coffee suddenly choked and coughed. He'd just caught Hawkeye's drift. Then he burst out laughing. When he saw Matt's face redden and his jaw tighten. Dan quickly held up his left hand as he said, "I'm sorry Matt. Hawkeye caught me off guard."

Matt was flustered; for once he didn't know what to say or do. He realized that Hawkeye had figured out that he'd had a fight with the women. Before he really got his thoughts together Matt said, "It's just that they want to be so protective they hardly let a man breathe."

Hawkeye after seeing Matt in action and hearing the story. That Billy and the women had told them, could almost figure out what had gotten them all upset. He said, "Well, if that's what there're worried about. I'll just have to tell them, that there's not enough people here to keep you out of trouble. Not that you look for it. But it always finds you and I can't see that you'd ever run from it. It would be a full-time job to watch over you."

Matt was glad that the Ladies hadn't heard Hawkeye. He was still perturbed as he tried to ignore most of what Hawkeye had just said. But quick to grab a opportunity Matt asked, "Would you like a job?"

Hawkeye looked at Matt. Then saw that Matt had really meant it. He asked, "What! What kind of job do you have?"

Everyone of them perked up as Matt explained what he had in mind. When he'd finished they stared at him amazed at what he wanted to do.

Captain Taylor after a short pause said, "If someone did have the money they could really make something special out of this valley. Say, your family is wealthy right. Do you think they would lend you the money?"

Matt said, "I don't intend on asking them. I need a lot of help to get everything done. But money will be no problem."

Captain Taylor heard the seriousness in Matt's voice. He asked, "Then how do you plan on doing it. All of the things you want to do will take a lot of money."

Matt said, "Well! I've found some gold and will use it here in the valley to make it into something real special."

They looked at him to see how serious he was. They saw that he ment what he'd said. They were sure he wasn't playing a joke on them.

Matt said, "I could use all of you to help plan and build this place up. There'll be jobs for you as long as you like."

Tex said, "I work cows, I'm not doing anything that I can't do from the back of a horse no more."

Matt asked, "Where would you get the cows from if you had the money?"

Tex said, "Deep in Texas. They're cheap and there's still a lot of them running loose that no one's rounded up after the war."

Matt asked, "If you had the money and men could you start gathering them up so we could move them up in a couple of years?"

Tex said, "Yeah! But if we were able to get them up this far. You'll play hell trying to get the cattle through that hole in the mountain we came through."

Matt said, "Yeah I was afraid of that. Maybe we can find another way in by then."

Tex asked, "You're serious aren't you?"

Matt said, "Yes, we decided this is where we wanted to make our home. Then when the gold was found we started making plans. With all of you here it makes it a lot easier if you want jobs."

Captain Taylor said, "I don't think I'm much for pushing cows anymore."

Matt said, "Captain that would be fine. If you would I'd like for you to hire some men and make the trail good enough to get a wagon through. I know it will be a lot of hard work. If Star's people agree to it, they will watch the entrance to let in only the people that belong in here."

Captain Taylor asked, "Have you told them about the gold?"

Matt nodded, "Yes, I knew I wouldn't be able to keep it from them. I have asked them to stay and inhabit a valley that's south of here for themselves. I want them to drive the buffalo and most of the wild horses into it also. I want them to watch and be careful so there'd always be a herd of buffalo. I Told them not to kill to many. That if they needed meat I'd give them all the beef they needed."

Captain Taylor nodded, then said, "Sounds like you've made a lot of plans. Guess you've hired yourself a man."

Billy back from his walk to the basin, to check on Three Socks and the other horses. Had come up just close enough to hear the last part of the conversation. It looked like things were being put into motion now. Dan, Hawkeye, Tex and the rest of the cowboys decided to join up. There decision as much as anything was that they wanted to be around when the fireworks went off the next time. They were sure that Matt would keep them entertained.

Everyone was busy for the next few days. Connie and Helen had stripped some more meat form an Elk that Hawkeye had killed. Then they'd hung it up to dry. With all the extra mouths too feed they would need it. Tex and his cowboys had checked harness's shoes and hooves of the ponies that didn't have shoes. If at all possible they didn't want a single horse to come up lame. Especially out of neglect. The horses would be heavily laden and it was an extremely ruff trail in places. They had constructed some crude racks to strap on the ponies to hold the gold in place.

Matt had decided that with the extra help. He wanted to take out some more of the gold. With Captain Taylor, Dan and Billy they'd left the next morning after the night everyone had decided to work for him. Star insisted on going. Things had calmed down between the women and Matt. Matt didn't want to stir things up again, so he'd relented with out much of a fuss. But it seemed that Star was just along for the ride. He still had to wait on himself. Matt now knew how much he'd gotten used to all of the catering the women had done for him. He decided that somehow he had to get back into their good graces, as soon as possible.

They covered the seventy miles to the ledge in a day and a half. With the pack horses and everyone else it was still a quick trip. Everyone helped and even with the crud set up Matt had made they had enough gold bars to load on the pack horses in another day and a half. With the gold it would take them two long days on their return trip.

Tex and his men had most everything ready that they could. They had finally understood that they would have a fortune in gold with them on the trip out. They had cleaned all their pistols and rifles. They oiled them real good, then wiped off the excess oil to keep them from gumming up when fired. They worked on them till they worked smooth and easy. Ben and Slade had even worked the insides of their holsters to make sure their pistols slid out smoothly without any drag at all. It was still a wild land and many outlaws waited a lifetime, just for an opportunity to get their hands on such a large amount of gold .

The last couple of days. Connie and Helen had made some new moccasins for them all. Matt, Billy, Star, Helen and Connie. They had used up the last of the tanned hide. They carefully rolled up and packed all their ceremonial costumes. They weren't about to leave something so nice and valued by each of them, behind. Helen and Connie had used the same cook fire as the cowboys and ate their meals with them. As the evening of the fifth day approached they watched for Matt and his party to return. The shadows had run far out into the Valley and were just about ready to be taken over by the approaching darkness when they were spotted. Connie and Helen put the meat and some other things on the fire to cook. Everyone at the fire had already eaten not knowing when Matt and the others would return. Tex and the rest of the men went to help take off the heavy laden packs. After Matt and Billy had eaten they got the gold bars out of the pool and put them with the rest. They'd just sat down with a cup of coffee when Strong Arms, Runs Far and Sees Far came up to the cook fire.

Strong Arms said, "We like the valley you have given us. You have given us much honor. Yet already you honor us. We have given you many gifts. But the gift that you've given us we'll never be able to return."

Matt said, "You are family my people. I would just like for you to enjoy and live a long life. Also, we'll have someone to watch over things when we are gone."

Strong Arms said, "You honor us very much. It will be as you say. Also many braves will ride beside you when you go."

When Strong Arms had spoken, they all turned and left before anyone could respond.

Hawkeye said, "They must have fallen in love with the valley you've given them."

Star said, "Wait till you get a chance to see it. I fell in love with Matt all over again when he suggested it for my people. It was made for them and will be a good place to preserve."

Matt turned reddish and got uncomfortable when she'd declared her love and praise openly.

Captain Taylor said, "Guess, I'll have to wait till the next time. But it does sound like a place I'd like to see. They were impressed and that's not easily done."

Matt with Connie, Helen and Star left for their home when the conversation dwindled. Shortly after Billy gave them his goodnight as he retired for his last night in his room for awhile. He'd made the little cave into a nice comfortable and homely little room. Even though somewhat crude, he really liked it and would miss his little cave he now called home. They had a long trip ahead and he was excited about seeing his parents and the rest of his family. How his brother and sister had grown and what kind of place they had settled in. He missed his mother and father very much.

When Matt and the women had made it inside, Matt said, "I can't remember exactly what set all of you off. But I can't stand the tenseness that is between us.

Unlike her Helen quickly responded, "You said you didn't want us to watch over you like a bunch of nurse maids."

Matt thought he understood as he said, "Oh, I'm sorry. I admit it. I got so I loved the way you took care of me. That's not what I meant. I just don't want any of you to get in the way if there is any trouble. If a fight develops let me handle it. That's all I meant, besides with you all being with child. There is even more of a reason for you to stay out of harms way."

Connie was exasperated; then too the other two she said, "See! Just as we thought." Connie turned back to Matt with a stern look as she continued, "Matt, you get it through your thick head. If there's a fight we will be in it. We have almost lost you twice. We don't want nothing to happen to our children or any of us. But we would rather be dead than to be alive without you. We love you that much."

Matt taken back by her statement, understood now what they really meant. They had touched on it once before. But he hadn't realized the full impact of what they'd told him. As full comprehension settled in, before he could respond Helen said, "Matt, that's the only way we could decide for the three of us to share you. None of us could picture our lives without you. When we realized how each of us felt and tried to figure a way out of the circumstances we were in. Then when Star mentioned that even though it was rare. That it was permitted among her people. For a man to take more than one women. That was how we decided to try and make it work between us. You see we each fell in love with each other as well as you. We just don't what to see any of us getting hurt."

Matt had let his emotions show in his eyes. Then with a moan he said, "I don't understand how. But I'm so lucky. I don't deserve to be loved so much by all three of you. I can hardly believe it. But it just scares me to death with the idea of any one of you, getting hurt."

All three of them softened their expressions and relaxed. Matt was finally about to fully understand. They snuggled up to him. Then in English Star said, "That's how we feel. We're all scared to death that we'll lose you. Even with your new power from The Spirit Bear. We still fear for your life and even though the honor of you being killed in battle would be great. Our lives would end."

The emotions Matt read in their eyes and heard in their voices was almost over-whelming. It was hard for him to speak. But he did manage to say, "Ok, I well. I see, I'm sorry. We'll just have to watch out for each other. It just scares me so."

With the heat of their closeness and with the emotions from their discussion. Matt's response was felt. Matt's lion cloth wasn't doing much good. Star felt his man hood as it throbbed against her swollen belly moaned as she quickly removed his lion cloth. Then said. "Oh, good. I've missed you between my legs so much."

Early the next morning as Matt and the women finished their meal. They cleaned up their home putting everything in place. They'd gotten very little sleep. But they were happier then ever. Their strange union was fully understood by all of them now. The deep commitment the four of them had made was a joining of souls, as well as a union of bodies.

When they stepped outside everyone was ready and waiting. Billy had gotten up early and put his things together. Then he had breakfast with Captain Taylor and the others. Billy was the first, to spot them. He noticed that they looked like they hadn't slept much. But he'd never seen them happier. The women made quite a picture as they approached with everyone looked at them. With the supplies that Mr. Maxton had sent they'd reworked their gun belts so they had a holster on each hip. Then their bowie knife in it's sheath was fastened a little behind their right hand gun. The gun belt hung on their hips over their loin cloths. While their bellies hung slightly over their gun belts. The holsters were tied down and adjusted so they were even with their hands. They carried their rifles in their left hands. When a grin started to appear on a couple of faces. The women responded with stern looks back at them. The men then tried to keep out of each others way as they looked, for something to do. The women all looked like they meant business. Matt did grin a little as he noticed the glances between the cowboys and his wives. He was glad he wasn't involved.

Billy was armed like the women. They had tied a strip of leather to their rifles so they could sling them across their backs. They would keep their weapons within reach. All five of them had on the new moccasins that Connie and Helen had made. Of the five horses Flame was the only one that had a saddle. The three women and Billy would have to ride bareback. Matt had offered to trade off on the use of the saddle. But the others had refused and he decided that he sure wasn't going to stir things up again

The gold and all of the trail supplies had already been packed on the pack horses. Matt helped the ladies mount up as the others respectfully turned their heads. They'd gotten somewhat used to the women's attire. The sun had just cleared the horizon as they put their horses in motion. Later Tex had told some of the men it had been unnerving when he first saw the women. Then in a stern voice he'd told them that he felt like they were the most dangerous bunch he'd ever seen. Those that heard him just nodded in agreement.

With the heavy laden animals it took them two days to reach the washout. It wasn't dry yet. But there wasn't any rushing water either. There were some pools as the water trickled down from the tunnel high up on the side of the mountain. The weather had been pleasant. Matt, Connie, Helen and Star snuggled together away from the cook fire a little in a couple of blankets to keep warm at night. The nights were still a little cool.

The next morning. When they'd gotten the packs on and about ready to ride they heard the sound of hoofs south of them. Matt helped his women aboard then climbed aboard Flame. Then they saw Runs Far and thirty of his people appear out of the dark shadows as sun light started to drift into Peaceful Valley. They led three horses that pulled some poles with their teepees on them. Captain Taylor moved the pack train out in single file as Runs Far rode ahead of his people to converse with Matt. Runs Far told Matt that some of the people would guard the outside entrance. Then that Runs Far with the other sixteen would be his scouts. In a couple of days a few more would be along to guard the inside entrance at the meadow. He explained that his braves wanted to see their new home first.

Matt nodded, then explained to Runs Far that he wanted an advance group out around them ten to fifteen miles. Two to angle out in front, then two angled out behind. Then one on each flank. That he wanted them afoot to keep from leaving any sign for anyone to find if it was possible. Matt told Runs Far to use another six on reserve to swap out every third day. The last four he wanted half way between the scouts and the pack train. Matt told Runs Far to workout with his people how they would signal each other. Matt expressed to Runs Far that the scouts were not to engage anyone unless it was a matter of life or death. That he needed them out there to be his eyes. If there was any trouble the out riders and the main body would handle it.

Matt knew as heavy as the pack animals were loaded once out in the open they would be easy pickings if they didn't have advance warning. It was still dangerous territory and he was going to do all he could to protect the women. Especially now that he knew for certain. That any danger that came along; that they would be sharing it with him. It took them eight days to get out of the mountains, to some open land. They had a terribly rough time getting the heavy laden pack animals, through the tunnel. Most of the trail was easy, compared to the tunnel.

The advance scouts had already signaled back that some enemy tribes were out in small bands, searching the whole area. One of the guards from the outside entrance had gone along with them. He had been sent back with a message to be sent to Strong Arms for him to increase the number of people to guard the outer entrance. Around their camp fire with four men from the pack train on guard. The six outer scouts slipped out in the darkness to relieve the other six scouts. Matt and the rest had a quick meal, then four of them went out to swap with the ones on guard duty, so they could eat. The women took turns on guard duty too. Tex and a couple of the cowboys had grumbled some. But the women had gotten there way. Seeing that trouble was about they all made double sure, that their weapons were in working order.

As they settled in around the fire with a cup of coffee before seeking their blankets. Captain Taylor walked into camp after being relieved from his guard duty was just in time to hear Matt as he asked, "From what the scouts have reported, its like they're out there searching for something. Do any of you have any idea of what it could be?"

Run's Far looked at Matt. For most of his adult life he had been able to keep his emotion's from showing on his face. This time however, with amazement showed allover his face he said, "Yes! You and your Spirit Horse."

Now it was Matt's turn. He said, "That's hard to believe. Why would they be looking for me?"

Captain Taylor had filled his plate and cup. Then sat with the rest of the men. He glanced at Matt's face and was sure, that Matt hadn't realized yet how famous he was among the Indians.

Hawkeye as if he'd waited just for such an opportunity said, "The Spirit Warrior and his Flaming Spirit horse have much power. Many have died in battle against them. He is a Legend now and would bring much power to the lodge of the one that was able to find and defeat him in battle. It would be a great honor to die by the hand of The Spirit Warrior."

When he was done Hawkeye gave Matt a big smile. As if to say doubt my word's. Matt looked around and from a couple of Runs Far's Braves that had understood Hawkeye he saw the respect and awe on their faces. As far as that went none of his men acted like they had any doubts.

The women hadn't been very modest at all since they had made their peace settlement. When ever close and when they felt like it they just kind of gave him a quick kiss or hugged him whenever they took a notion. It made him red faced. But he loved it. Even when they did it out in the open. Star close by leaned into Matt pushed her left breast hard against his back as she whispered in his ear, "See love. That's why we are so worried about you. You have many enemies."

With Star's touch Matt was more worried, about exposing his hardening condition than any enemies. He then said, "Well! I guess we should be getting our rest."

Matt got up and with the women beside him headed for their bedrolls. As they watched them leave even though somewhat used to it by now they were still amazed that Matt and his women could come and go so quietly. If you didn't watch them carefully, they did seem to just appear or disappear on you. Billy was getting to be nearly as bad. To some, especially a few of the braves it was unnerving and had been said that the Spirit Warrior was turning his women into Spirit's.

Matt with just a little sleep had been in deep thought most of the night. He'd decided he was responsible for the safety of all that rode with him. Not just the women.   He decided that he would do all he could to keep any of them from coming into any harm. The next morning as they finished their morning meal. He explained to Runs Far that he wanted the scouts to keep track of all the people inside the circle. If they started to group up he wanted to know where they were. They wanted enough time to send out the other six scouts to get behind the group. Then knowing where they were. Except for a hand full to stay with the pack train. Matt and the rest of his men would attack them. Hopefully they would catch them in between and wipe them out. Then Matt had exclaimed, "If they can't see fit to leave me alone, I'll make them pay for it."   Matt had spoken in English so his men would understand. Runs Far translated for his braves so they would understand. Hawkeye just in after being replaced on guard duty grabbed a quick bite and gulping a cup of coffee, then said, "Good, all this quiet was making me bored."

Captain Taylor said, "You blood thieving hellion. We haven't really gotten started yet. I don't much cotton to the idea of fighting every mile along the way."

Dan said, "If the scouts are right. It does sound like most of the Indians in the territory are out after Matt."

Slim said, "Well, I guess we're as ready as we can be and that's half of the battle."

Tex said, "Well, I don't see anyway to avoid a fight. It's always best to hit them head on if we can. Matt is right about one thing. After today we'll be leaving a trail a blind man could follow."

Matt stood and with the rest started putting their packs on the pack horses and saddled the rest of the horses. The women made quick work of cleaning up the camp. They had taken over the camp chores over the protest of the men. The men had gathered the fire wood and made the fire pit for them. Then carried what water they'd needed. As Matt helped the women up on their mounts. Tex and Slim packed the utensils on the horse they used to carry them on. The horse had gotten used to al the clatter they made.

From information gathered from Captain Taylor, Dan and Hawkeye they were headed for Rawlings Wyoming. It was the closest place they knew of that smelted gold and would be able to handle such a large quantity. The next two days went by without any problems. But word had come in from the scouts that they'd been spotted and that three bands of Indians had joined together to total about fifty. One of the scouts had gotten close enough to hear The Spirit Warrior and his Spirit Horse mentioned. That was all he'd needed to know. He'd quickly left and gotten word, back to The Spirit Warrior.

CHAPTER TWENTY FOUR

AMBUSH

That night as the scouts came into the camp fire. Matt questioned them thoroughly in their language. He wanted to know all he could about the trail they'd be taking. Then how close the Indians watched them and where the Indians had camped. How the Indians would have to travel to get ahead of them to set up an ambush. When he was sure he had all the details. Matt told them to get a bite. The last scout that would be coming into their camp arrived as Matt finished his plate of food. As he sipped a fresh cup of coffee that Star had just refilled, Matt made some plans.

With Runs Far, Tex, Captain Taylor, Billy and the women, except for Connie. As she was on guard duty. Matt laid out his plans to the protests of the women and Tex. But he finally persuaded everyone to agree. He and Hawkeye would ride out in the morning in advance of the pack train. Seeing them do so, Matt told them he was sure they would be seen. Then he and Hawkeye should be able to draw them out. If it was him they were really after. It would be to good of an opportunity for the Indians to pass up. The women still upset with the plan settled down. When Matt guaranteed them he wouldn't attack until he had their support. Matt stressed to Runs Far. That Runs Far and his scouts had to be sure the Indians didn't spot Tex, along with most of the men as they slipped into place. If all went as planned. He and Hawkeye would be able to lead them to Tex and the men. The women were still upset that Matt would put himself out as bait. After Matt had assured them patiently for the sixth time. That he wouldn't attack on his own. They unhappily at last relented.

The next day three hours out from camp Matt had gotten Hawkeye's attention, then motioned him to close in. They worked their way towards each other then. Hawkeye had been a couple of miles away and they'd acted like they were looking for the easiest route to bring the pack animals through. They'd even made some markers, which in reality ended up helping them. They'd made sure not to ride close to anything that would hide a man or animal. When they'd rode up close to each other Matt looked at the terrain all around them, then said, "Hawkeye, keep an eye out. I want to concentrate on things for a couple of minutes."

Hawkeye nodded as he checked the landscape. Matt closed his eyes and concentrated on the area northwest of them. Matt had thought he'd detected some movement from that direction thirty minutes earlier. Sure enough from some small creature in what must have been a small scrub oak tree. Which he'd determined by its leaves he saw a bunch of Indians go by. By the shadows they'd cast he could tell they were headed toward Hawkeye and him. Matt then concentrated on where Tex and the ambush party should be. He almost lost his concentration as he realized. Instead of an animal he'd seen through the eyes of a human. He didn't know who and the picture had blurred a little then cleared up. He saw Runs Far and his women. Each of the women had as fierce of a war look on their faces, as anyone he had ever seen. He'd laughed out loud as he opened his eyes and saw Hawkeye with complete astonishment all over his face as he stared at him. Matt explained, "The women have the most determined war face on of anyone I've ever seen. Hawkeye! If something did happen to me, I think they'd wipe out all the bad Indians in the territory. The way they looked, I'm a baby compared to them."

Matt spoke so serious and with such conviction. Hawkeye spun his head around and looked for them as if they were there. But he just couldn't see them. He looked back at Matt and saw the same expression Matt had when he'd spoken. The expression of seeing someone you loved. Not in thought. But by sight, like actually being able to touch them. In spite of himself Hawkeye asked, "Where?"

Back to his actual surrounding Matt said, "Ok, lets ease back toward the pack train. Everything's going like planned. Don't act concerned. But it shouldn't be long now."

A few minutes later Matt spotted a horse and rider as they broke cover a couple of miles off to their right. Hawkeye and Matt were headed back southwest. It had to be one of the enemy. Matt said, "Get ready, they're about ready to attack. See that knoll ahead slightly to the right? Our people are there. When I say head straight for it. When about there break off to the left of it. When our people start shooting you're on your own."

Hawkeye looked then nodded. With a look to the northwest they saw the big band of Indians as they broke cover to catch them. Matt eased Flame into a lope with Hawkeye and his horse beside them. Judging the distance Matt said, "Now."

Hawkeye urged his horse to the best speed he could over the broken terrain. Matt held Flame a little behind them. After a five minute run as it looked like they would be able to reach the cover of the knoll the Indian's had started firing. Matt had timed it almost perfect. The Indians were still a good three hundred yards away. On the backs of their Indian ponies. Nothing, but a pure luck shot would hit them. Matt yelled to Hawkeye and they broke left.

That gave encouragement to their pursuer's and they'd started working their ponies harder. In less than a minute the knoll erupted with gunfire. That was the cue that Matt had waited for. He kneed Flame to a stop as he dropped his reins. He kneed Flame around as he drew his rifle from its boot. As Flame completed his turn Matt spoke and Flame lowered his head as he stood still.

Matt shouldered his rifle drew a bead and squeezed off a round at the nearest Indian farthest from the knoll. The Indian grabbed his chest and fell. Matt grunted his satisfaction for a good many of them were already down. The rifle fire from the knoll had completely blind-sided them. The trap had worked. It was over in ten minutes. Hawkeye had gotten off eight shots in the battle and Matt had fired a dozen times. Most of the damage had come from the knoll.

None of Matt's people received a scratch. There was a little grumbling as Matt passed the word for no one to take any scalps. He was able to carry it off by a sudden inspiration when he told them that The Spirit Warrior had no use for them. But Matt did instruct them to make sure the dead were dead. He wasn't going to give no quarter to anyone that attacked him or his. His eyes had flashed brilliantly as he spoke. No one had responded as they immediately carried out his wishes. Matt then instructed them as a few shots went off to keep the good weapons and what ammunition they could use. Many of the Indian ponies had run off. The ones that did stay, if they were better Runs Far's braves swapped. The ones they caught they removed their halters and turned them lose. It took slightly less than an hour for them to pick out the best rifles as they made sure of the dead. The scouts of the inner circle had been sent back out.

With Connie's guidance after the battle. She was able to persuade Helen and Star not to rush up to Matt to see if he was okay. She explained that after a fight it took a little while for him to relax and shake off all the tension . That once he got into action it was like he wanted to destroy anything that moved. Besides, from their advantage point as the gun smoke drifted away they could see that he looked fine. Real fine as far as they were concerned. So when the rest went to get their horses the women did likewise. But, they drifted along behind the others a little. They heard Matt as he gave the order to make sure the dead were dead and what to do with the weapons. They noticed that no one hesitated. For everyone knew he'd meant what he said and by the tone of his voice. That he expected to be obeyed.

The women hung back on the fringe of the carnage they had helped create. They were all a little pale, even Star acted a little apprehensive. As a few shots rang out they rode around toward Matt. They noticed the flashed look Matt gave them as they approached. Helen and Star saw what Connie had told them. They'd never seen eyes that held as much intensity and rage as his did. When he'd spotted them some of the fire had left. But as he'd glanced back toward the carnage his eyes had started to flare up again.

The women held back a little as they just stayed close by. Even when Matt headed them out back toward the pack train, they stayed a little behind Matt. It had been a quiet ride back. Except for the horses and the gear that squeaked. Mostly from the saddles and the leather harnesses of the cowboys.

Matt's intense demeanor had dissipated by the time they'd gotten back to Captain Taylor and the rest. Captain Taylor's face had lit up when he saw them approach. Matt let the men go by and watched as they took the ropes of the pack animals they'd been leading before they'd gone out on the ambush. Dan rode up beside Captain Taylor then leaned forward to rest his arms on his saddle horn, then he said, "It went like clockwork. They never knew what hit them. Man if those ladies can use a short gun as well as they can a rifle they are the rip snort-ness gun hands I've ever seen. Smooth and calculating to boot as far as I can tell."

Dan talked in a low voice as he knew Matt didn't care about discussing or rehashing his exploits. As Runs Far rode up Dan asked, "Runs Far. Did you see Matt's face and eyes right after the battle?"

Runs Far answered, "Yes, even without any war paint. It was the fiercest I have ever seen. His eyes flashed like intense bolts of lighting set on total destruction."

Dan looked at Runs Far with a confused look, then asked, "Where were you educated? I never heard an Indian talk like that, not even Hawkeye."

Captain Taylor interrupted them as he said, "I guess we better get these animals back in motion. Matt just gave us a look like he's ready to go."

By the time they had reclaimed the leads of the pack animals and were ready to start out again. The women had settled down and their color had returned. They'd gotten a lot of looks and nods. All of the looks had been of respect. They tried to figure out what it was about. For they hadn't done anything different from the others. If anything they hadn't done as much. As the pack animals were put into motion. Billy rode in among them and in a low voice he said, "Each of you did real good. They're already saying that your the best shots around."

Billy reined Three Socks off before they could respond. They sat on their horses with their mouths open. Billy's eyes had been full of excitement. They didn't know whether from surprising them or left over from the battle. Maybe both. There'd been pride in his eyes, also.

After they'd made camp and eaten their meal. They sat around the cook fire with coffee cups in hand. Then not able to contain her thoughts any longer. Helen said, "Matt, I was scared to death that you would turn and attack the Indians before they rode into the ambush. I thought maybe you'd try to wipe them out, all by yourself."

Matt, a little embarrassed teasingly responded, "When I saw the look on your faces. There was no way I was going to get anywhere close to being in front of your rifles."

Hawkeye flashed him a look of weird bewilderment. It was like he'd tried to put something together. But had lost the handle. The women had a look of complete bafflement. Star's eyes showed a spark of perception. But it hadn't registered on her mind. The rest around the fire had been completely confused. They knew that there was no way that Matt could have seen any of the women. But they themselves, had noticed the looks of the pure concentrated determination that had been on the women's faces.

The next couple of days had gone along pretty well. They hadn't pushed the animals hard, because of the heavy weight they carried. When they had easy going they made about twenty-two miles. When they ran into some gullies and passes. That they had to work their way through. They only made fifteen to seventeen miles. On the third night one of the scouts reported. That a couple of white eyes had come across their trail and had followed it for a couple of miles. Then they had left toward the northeast. Dan and Hawkeye agreed that the direction they had taken. Would take them to the Green River settlement.

The next day turned out to be real unpleasant. The temperature had dropped during the night and with the daylight there was a mixture of rain, snow and sleet. The wind had picked up and really made it miserable for them.

Billy, Matt and the women had wrapped themselves up in blankets the best they could. Their teeth had chattered most of the day and when they'd made about twelve miles. They came upon a ravine with a stand of cottonwood and some scrub oak around. They drug the pack animals off the muddy terrain and made camp.

They found a place a good ways up from the bottom of the ravine. That wasn't covered with mud. They all went to work setting up camp. Some helped put up a piece of canvas for a wind break. Some others made a fire pit while the last of them found some wood. They'd built a big fire. It had been done to get the women warm more than anything. But everyone had crowded in to get warm from time, to time. They built a couple of other fires up close to the west bank. Where it was down out of the wind. With the fires going they took care of the animals and put some coffee on to boil. The women went to work preparing their meal. As the evening cooled off it had turned to a wet snow. It wasn't long before it cooled off enough to change to a fine powder that started to pile up into drifts. As the wind increased the horses even started to crowd the fire. After their meal a lot of hot coffee was drank. Even Runs Far's braves had drank more than a cup of it. The only thing was, that they liked a lot of sugar in theirs. The sugar was long gone though, none of them complained.

Billy, Matt and the women still didn't have much in way of clothing. Billy and the women had been able to put some jeans on. The women had been able to cover their legs. But, because of their swelled bellies they had to leave them, unfastened. Matt, because of his leg size hadn't been able to get into any. He'd gotten awfully cold and was really glad for the fire. But, as he warmed up his thoughts turned to the outer scouts and knew that they had to be real miserable. They wouldn't have the heat of a fire tonight and nothing but a cold meal. Also, he was sure they wouldn't ever complain about it either.

He still didn't quite understand how Star's people had taken to him. They acted like all he had to do was ask and it seemed like they would gladly do anything he asked of them. It was like they would even be proud to die for him. Oh he admitted he had been lucky in his fights. Especially with the huge grizzly. But he didn't think he'd done anything that someone else wouldn't have done, being in the same position.

Besides with the training he had received from Vern Socket and Lee Chan. He felt like it was them as much as anything that should be praised. Once they'd started to train him, they'd been hard task masters. He was glad of that, once he had gotten his strength back. He had worked extra hard to get his body back into condition. He felt like he owed it to them.

It had been a cold night and everyone had covered up with their blankets as snugly as they could. They swapped guards every two hours so they could get warmed up again. Late in the morning the wind changed to come from the south. It warmed up quickly and the snow had started to melt before the sun came up. The temperature climbed up to about sixty degrees and gave them a bright sunny day. It had been hard on the animals that day. They'd sunk into the mud nearly eight inch's most of the day.   They'd just eased along so they wouldn't have any mishaps from a broken leg or some other incident. The pack animals slipped and slid along leaving a trail, that left little doubt of what was on the pack animals.   They'd been a little blind the last twenty-four hours, because of the weather. Matt was real glad he had the outer scouts out on foot. They still shouldn't be leaving any sign that they were around. If anybody took an interest in the pack train. Matt and his people would be alerted long before anyone could cause them any trouble. Runs Far and his braves had worked out some signals they could use with a mirror, or a covered directional fire at night. When they made camp Runs Far sent some braves out to replace the outer scouts. It was a day early. But he wanted a full report before they moved out in the morning. When the replaced outer scouts came in they told Runs Far there was nothing to cause them any trouble.

It had been pleasant weather the last two days. As they set up camp for the night. Runs Far received word from one of the scouts that rode the inner loop. He'd been northeast of the advancing pack train. He reported that the two riders that had come across their trail four days ago had showed up again. They had twenty-seven other men with them. Then he told Runs Far that two riders were out ahead of them like they were looking for something. He reported that they all pushed their mounts hard. Runs Far had told Matt as they'd about finished eating and sipped some coffee, which they were getting short of. Matt asked, "Do you think they are looking for us?"

Captain Taylor said, "That's what I would figure. They are probably bandits and figure you have a fortune. They think we'll be easy pickings."

Runs Far said, "Yes, that's what I think. They'll probably cut our trail tomorrow. Then they'll know where we are."

Dan said, "They'll probably try to get in front of us to set up an ambush."

Tex said, "Yeah, I hate outlaws. They never fight you head on, unless they absolutely have to."

Matt as they talked ran his own thoughts through his mind, mostly just listening.

Ben, the quietest of the cowboys said, "We'll just have to make sure the women are protected."

Star said, "No! We'll fight also.'"

Connie said, "Yes, we don't carry our weapons just for looks."

Helen said, "Yes, I agree."

That hadn't been what Ben had expected to hear. He looked around with enquiring eyes as he tried to get some support from the others. He didn't see any though, they looked like they didn't dare to say anything. By the tone of their voices, the women sounded dead serious.

After he'd eyed his partners, Ben said, "Well, I just wouldn't like to see any of you ladies get hurt."

Connie said, "We don't want to see anyone get hurt. But we're part of the outfit and will do what we have to."

The others had decided to keep their own thoughts. Ben was a little uncomfortable with a reddish face. Not one to say much. But set in his ways he said, "Well, I just don't think that it's proper for women to be in a gunfight."

Helen spoke spontaneous as she said, "Well! Under the circumstances I can't say that we have been very proper."

Her statement made all of the men reddish in the face. Captain Taylor, Dan and all the cowboys as well as Ben. No one was about to say anything more then. They had agreed to work for Matt and his women. They rode for the brand. They'd talked about the way things were. They'd decided that as strange as things were. That it was a miracle that they were alive. That everything was alright as far as they were concerned. They thought the world of the young women and none of them had nothing but respect for them. After they had seen how Matt and the women interacted with each other they decided that they did seem to fit together somehow. Even Ben had seen that and had gotten things settled in his mind. He was still protective over Helen, Connie and Star. As far as that, the rest of them thought that all of the young women; were something special. No matter how they were attired. It had taken some time to get used to it. But they hardly thought anything of it anymore.

The Indians had taken to them right off and seemed to think of the women much like they did Matt. There wasn't a one of the Indians that treated the young ladies, like they did the women of their own tribe. They'd helped around camp as much as the other men had. Usually the camp chores would be left to the women. But, it hadn't been that way at all.

After a couple of uncomfortable minutes Captain Taylor said, "Well, with the scouts out watching them they won't be able to surprise us."

Billy just sat and listened. He'd been slightly amused and was real contented. It looked like the men had come to an understanding about Matt and his women. At the least it looked like anyone that tried to take on the outfit, had just dug their own graves.

Matt with his own thoughts listened to the others as they hashed things over. Then it came to him again that he was responsible for the lives of all that rode and worked for him as well as the women. He completely understood then why Captain Taylor had chewed him out. He thought Captain Taylor should have scolded him a lot more than he had. When he'd sorted out the things on his mind Matt said, "We'll be careful and not look for any trouble. But we won't run from it. If someone comes looking for us then we'll take care of them, if we can't persuade them to leave us alone. If it comes to that we shoot to kill and take no prisoners. I don't want anyone to get hurt needlessly waiting to see if anyone wanted to quit or give up. Once it starts we finish it."

They'd looked at him to see that his face had been just as hard as his voice had been. His eyes had shined black with the intense heat that they could almost feel. Matt's statement brought an end to their conversation. Some of the braves hadn't understood. They were told what Matt had said and just nodded as they quietly left for their bedrolls or to relieve the guards around their camp. The rest of the men drifted off to their blankets after they finished their coffee. Soon Billy, Matt and the women were the only ones left by the fire. Connie said, "Matt if you could you should try to tone yourself down a little and not be so harsh."

Matt said, "I meant what I said, I won't harm a soul if they leave us alone. But dammed if I'm going to let anyone take anything away from me. Anything!"

Billy looked at his moccasins. Usually he didn't mind stirring the pot a little. He knew it wasn't a good time start something. In a quiet calm voice he said, "Matt we feel the same. After all the time we've been together the last few months, we all have the same thoughts."

With his words Matt relaxed a little. He hadn't realized how tense he'd gotten.

Helen saw the affect Billy's words had on Matt. She said, "Oh, yes, Matt. We've all had a real hard time. But now it looks like we've all been blessed and have had a lot just handed to us. But it doesn't mean we have to let someone help themselves to it."

Star said, "It's not right for someone to try too take it away."

Matt said, "It has always upset me to see someone steal from someone or bully someone."

Connie nodded as she said, "Yes, Matt. That's one of the things that I've always loved about you."

Matt's stature softened a lot more after her statement. They conversed until it was good and dark. After Runs Far told Matt that the guards were set for the night, they headed for their blankets.

The next night it was confirmed that the two outlaws had cut their trail and followed it for a while. Then they had rushed off to join the main gang. When they'd gotten together they rode off to the northeast at a rapid pace. When he'd received the information. Runs Far sent two of his relief guards out on foot to find and keep track of them. Matt enquired what the terrain would be like the next couple of days. If there was a good place the outlaws could use to ambush them. Runs Far said, "I'll signal the scouts. To make sure they check the area real good and to watch for such a place."

Matt replied, "Good, if so. Maybe we can turn the tables and have something ready for them. We can plan more tomorrow night. Just make sure we know where the outlaws are."

In the morning they'd woke up to a spring drizzle. It lasted for most of the day. That evening the ones that didn't have any duties as they sat around the fire. Cleaned their weapons and made sure they were dry. The warmth helped dry them up too. When the weather was overcast and the sun wasn't shinning. Runs Far and his scouts had to wait for darkness to pass there signals. The inner scouts usually didn't get in to give a report till an hour after dark or more. Runs Far came in with his report that had been passed in from the outer scouts. He sat next to Matt, then said, "Unless we change the direction we're headed in. We'll be funneled into a draw that'll take us into another valley that opens up wide."

Matt asked, "How far are we from it."

Runs Far said, "Ten, twelve miles. Be about midday or shortly after when we get there."

Matt asked, "What are the outlaws doing?"

Runs Far replied, "They have circled to the north riding hard."

Matt said, "You do think they intend to ambush us then?"

Runs Far answered, "Yes."

Matt asked, "Do they still have someone watching us?"

Runs Far said, "Yes, he hasn't signaled to the others yet."

Hawkeye said, "I guess it wouldn't do any good to go another way. It would just be delaying the inevitable."

Matt had his thinking cap on while they'd talked. Then when Captain Taylor said, "It looks like there's no other way. But to take them on and get it over with."

Matt said, "Yes! We'll start out in the morning just like we've been doing. Runs Far if they have planed on ambushing us at the draw. I'm sure they'll have someone there on watch to alert the others."

Runs Far had admiration in his eyes as he nodded. Matt then continued, "After we've been on the move for an hour. I'll take a few of you and see if we can't get into the draw before the outlaws do."

Dan said, "Then we can set up an ambush for them."

Matt gave Captain Taylor a hard look, before he said, "I've tried to decide what's the right thing for us to do."

Then Matt glanced at Runs Far, Hawkeye and some of the other braves. He just hoped they would understand as he continued, "It's not fair or right. But I don't think we can just ambush them?"

After his statement he'd gotten a lot of puzzled looks. They tried to put a loop on Matt's thoughts. Captain Taylor just asked, "Matt. What are you thinking?"

Matt said, "I remember what Mr. Socket told me. First, not to ever back down. But he also told me to make sure, that I was in the right."

Tex said, "We'll be in the right when we wipe them out. That's what they plan on doing to us."

Matt said, "Even though we're sure there nothing but outlaws and are sure they plan on robbing us, they are white. We'll have to let them make the first move"

Dan asked, "What do you plan on doing then?"'

Matt answered, "We'll have to confront them and ask them what their intensions are."

Slade asked, "You just plan on giving all of our advantages away then."

Matt just nodded.

Tex said, "I don't believe it. That's crazy. It will increase the chances of one of us getting hurt."

In deep thought as he listened cutting in on the conversation Captain Taylor said, "Oh! I do see where Matt is coming from. Right now there's not much law out here. But Matt's right, as much as I hate to say it."

Dan asked, "How many do you plan on taking with you when you go up to confront them?"

Matt looked at Run's Far as he said, "It can't be helped. But a hand full of the scouts need to find anyone that'll be in the draw and take care of them before we get there."

Runs Far nodded. Then Matt said, "I guess we can get by with eight or ten."

Tex with astonishment all over his face said, "They'll have us outnumbered more than two to one."

Ben said, "The women can stay with the pack horses then."

Matt just smiled a little as he heard the expected outburst from the Ladies. For in unison they said, "Oh No! We ride with Matt."

Slade said, "No ma-am! It's not right for women to be in a gunfight. For that is exactly what it's going to be. Everyone will be face to face. It's no place for a women."

Star just stated, "We'll Go! We're not going to stay behind."

Runs Far even groaned. As he had a mixture of pride and concern on his face.

Tex said, "No ma-am, I agree. You ladies need to stay behind."

Connie stated, "Maybe! But we're going. We're as much of a part of the group as the rest of you. We'll not ask everyone to take on all the risk for us."

Slim protested. "I don't want to disagree with you ladies. But I agree with the others."

Helen said, "There's nothing to decide. We already made our minds up before we left home."

Her statement put confused looks on many of their faces. Until they realized that she meant that her home was in the valley where they'd spent the winter. In a firm voice Matt said, "They'll ride with us. I know you don't like it. But I have come to an understanding with them. And I'm not going to get involved in another argument with them, over it." Matt had gotten a little embarrassed as he admitted, he had giving into his women's wishes. But he was rewarded by the loving grateful looks he got from them.

Captain Taylor had a look of admiration mixed with deep concern. The rest of the men gave Matt the expected looks of disapproval. That was short lived though as they got into a heated discussion on who was going to stay with the pack animals. Or who was going to ride forward to confront the outlaws. After he'd listened a few minutes to the friendly bickering among his men. Matt had mixed emotions. He was proud of them. For to a man they were all willing to put their lives on the line. He knew it was his job to decide which ones would go. And which ones would stay. When it started to get real heated, Matt said, "Tex, Slade, Dan and Ben will go with me. Captain Taylor will be in charge with Hawkeye out in front to make sure everything is clear."

Matt saw some of the light leave Hawkeye's eyes. So he said, "I'm sorry Hawkeye. I just want the best gun handlers with me. Hopefully to avoid, anyone getting hurt. If it comes to gunfire I hope to get as many as we can before they fire a shot."

Hawkeye grudgingly nodded. Then Matt said, "Runs Far, you can sneak out and help make sure we don't have any surprises in the draw. It's getting late. Time we got some rest."

There was a couple of men that acted like they had something more to say. But slowly, one by one they went to their bedrolls. Matt and his women as they went toward their bedrolls. Carried on a little in a loving conversation. When they reached there bedrolls they cuddled together in their blankets for the warmth.

389

CHAPTER TWENTY FIVE

GUNFIGHT

It was warmer the next morning. They broke camp the same way they had been doing. With everything ready as they mounted up. Runs Far told Matt that the scouts had reported that the outlaws had set up camp three miles from the other end of the draw. Runs Far then slipped away to join his scouts. An hour after they'd left their camp. Matt motioned to the ones that were to ride with him. They handed the lead ropes of the pack horses to another rider, then galloped off with Matt. Because of the rain they'd gotten the day before. They didn't stir up a dust trail.

They came within sight of the draw in a couple of hours. Runs Far came out of a thick grove of cottonwoods to meet them. When he'd reined his pony in next to Flame. He told Matt that the outlaws had two men watching the draw. They were being watched and when it was time they would be taken care of.

Matt decided that Runs Far should ride along with them. They made sure all of their pistols had their hammer loops off and were loose in their holsters. Matt then eased them along through the draw. It was covered with sage brush on both sides. The sides higher up were pretty steep with a rock face exposed on top. They climbed a gentle slope most of the way. The draws floor had been a couple hundred yards wide most of the way. Some places it had narrowed to fifty yards. They rode light in their saddles, ready for anything. They all watched for anything that was out of place. As they went around a slight bend Matt thought he had glimpsed a rider going out of sight riding hard. He quietly warned them and led them at a slower pace. In a low voice just loud enough for Matt to hear Runs Far said, "We've got to be getting close to the other end."

Matt nodded. Then motioned for them to walk their horses. Then he made sure everyone was spread out across the draw. In five minutes the draw started to open up some as it sloped down from them into a higher valley. The gang of riders appeared riding hard. One of the outlaws spotted them. He yelled as he motioned for them to stop. The outlaws fought their mounts as they jerked them to a stop. Then Matt spoke just loud enough to be heard by his people. He Said, "Keep you horses at a walk. Don't stop until I do. If anyone makes a move for a gun. Blow them out of the saddle."

As they approached they saw the surprised looks on the outlaws faces. They'd started to spread out. Matt said, "If they go for their guns get the ones straight in front of you."

Billy and Star where on Matt's left. Helen and Connie were on his right. Tex and Slade were to the right of Connie. Dan, Ben and Runs Far were to the left of Billy. As Matt and his people slowly approached they had their eyes glued on the outlaws. Most of the outlaws had astonished looks on their faces. They heard some of the comments the outlaws made as they got closer. As they'd realized there were women that rode at them. With not much more on than gun belts and a pistol on each hip. Most of the outlaws had trouble getting their eyes off the women.

At fifty yards everyone felt the tension that flowed between the two parties. The outlaws had finished spreading out and pulled their horses to a stop. They watched as Matt and his riders approached. With the tip of his right toe Matt nudged Flame behind his leg. Flame lowered his head nearly to the ground. Billy and the women did the same with their horses. Matt dropped the reins on Flames neck and forced himself to relax. Matt concentrated on using his peripheral vision as much as he could. He wanted to catch the slightest movement if he could. When were within twenty-five yards Matt used his knee's to bring Flame to a stop. Everyone along the line stopped also. As the tension mounted Matt wanted to keep them off balance if he could, before the outlaws got set. He got right to the point as he asked, "What are your intensions?"

An outlaw slightly to Matt's right looked at Matt, as if he was surprised that Matt seemed to be the one that was in charge. He said, "We're just riding through. What's the meaning of you stopping us?"

Bluntly Matt asked, "Why have you trailed us? Then how come you rode so hard to get in front off us?"

There was some mumbling among the outlaws. The outlaw that had spoken tried to hide the surprised look that appeared on his face. He said, "I don't know what you are talking about."

Matt said, "Your lying, I know you are after the gold."

Because of Matt's bluntness the outlaws had been surprised. Not many people just came out and told, someone they lied. Some of the outlaws still had a hard time keeping up as they were still distracted by the women. As their looks intensified Matt spotted one of the outlaws to his left that had his right side turned away from them. Matt saw his elbow jerk back.

Matt knew the verbal conversation was over as he drew his pistols a split second later to break the silence with there loud report. The outlaw never cleared leather. The one next to him was hit with a slug from Matt's right hand gun. As they started to fall out of their saddles. Matt switched to the next two to the right of them. Billy and the women had gotten into action as Matt blew the next two riders out of their saddles. Matt put his sights on the outlaws in front of him as he worked his way to the right. Slade and Ben were next to get into action. Tex and Dan right behind them as some of the outlaws got their guns out of their holsters. Runs Far had gotten his rifle lined up as the outlaws started getting off some shots. The noise was deafening as Matt knocked two more out of their saddles before any of the outlaws got their guns leveled at any of his riders. Matt swapped guns as the last of the outlaws got off a few shots before they were blown out of their saddles by the devastating gun fire from Matt and his riders.

From the time Matt had started the fracas. The gunfight was over in less then a minute. Four horses were down with the twenty-seven outlaws. As the echo's died off. Matt checked to see if any of his riders had gotten hit. The other's also checked the ones closest to them. As they started to move around, Matt commanded, "Check and make sure they are dead. Be careful."

Most of the frightened horses had run off a short distance. Some were wounded from bullets. A couple had broken legs as they'd gotten tangled up when they'd tried to get away from the commotion that had went on. There were a few more shots as they completed the gruesome task of putting the hurt animals out of their pain and suffering. They found two outlaws barely alive. They had died within five minutes. By that time two of Runs Far scouts trotted up with satisfied looks on their faces. One from each side of the draw. They reported that none of the outlaws had gotten away. Satisfied that everything had been done to make them safe. Matt replaced an empty cartridge with a loaded one in each pistol and returned them to Flames saddle. Then he reloaded his other two pistols as he commanded, "Get the good weapons and horses that you'd like to have. With the others just take the bridles and saddles off them. Then let them go."

No one spoke a word. At least not to Matt. He had his grim war face on again. His eyes were a reddish on black color. They just did as he commanded. Most of them dismounted as they carried out their task. Then there was the sound of some gagging. When Matt looked over his shoulder he saw Helen as she bent over and vomited. Matt dismounted leaving Flame's reins draped over his neck. As Matt walked up to Helen to comfort her Connie started to vomit. Star was pal, compared to her usual complexion. Matt put his arms around them and drew them close as they wiped their lips with the back of their hands.

Matt said, "I'm sorry. It's a lot different when your close enough to see everything. The first time is the hardest. Just remember, it was them or us."

With her voice still strained Connie said, "Yeah, I remember; Mr. Socket told us something like that. I thought I was ready. But it's still pretty sickening."

Matt nodded as he said, "Yes. Each of you did very good. I'm proud of you and I'm glad you were along to help.'"

Helen as some of her color returned, with a great effort to control her voice said, "Thanks! I needed to hear those words."

Tex had seen a little of what had happened. He'd quickly retrieved a canteen from the nearest horse he came to. Slowly and apprehensively he approached as he said, "Here's some water. If nothing else it'll help get the taste out of your mouth."

The women's color returned rapidly as they were embarrassed that they hadn't held up. They sheepishly took the canteen an rinsed there mouths out with a swallow of water then spat it on the ground. Tex handed them his handkerchief. He'd noticed their embarrassment and told them that they'd done real good. He'd gotten grateful looks, from all three women as Connie said, "Thank you."

Helen and Star nodded their thanks also. Then Star handed the handkerchief back to him. Tex had gotten a little embarrassed from their grateful looks as well as being so close to them. For loin clothes were still all they wore except for their moccasins and guns. He said, "You're welcome."

Tex turned and went back to help the others. Busy with his concern and comforting the ladies. Matt's demeanor softened. He pulled Star in close with Helen and Connie. He hugged and comforted all of them. Twenty minutes had passed when Billy came up to them, then said, "Matt we're done. Unless you want us to bury them."

With some of the hardness still in his voice, Matt said, "No leave them where they lie."

Billy nodded then turned and walked back to the rest of the men. When he'd returned he told them they were done. They'd used some of the horses as pack animals. They had all the weapons and extra saddles tied on top of them. They gathered up the reins to the extra horses then mounted their own. Matt escorted the women to their horses and helped them up. Matt and the women followed along behind his men as they rode slowly back toward Captain Taylor and the gold. The scouts had slipped away, back toward their positions. Matt's Ladies stayed next to him as they rode back. Billy and Tex led them back toward the pack train.

Billy and Tex met Hawkeye a couple of miles ahead of the pack train a little past noon. Matt and the women stayed with Hawkeye as the rest went on to help with the pack animals. Captain Taylor, Slim and Bones had their hands full with all the pack animals. Just as soon as they rode up with a smile of deep concern Captain Taylor asked, "Is everything OK?"

Tex said, "Yes. I don't think a one of us got a scratch."

Captain Taylor said, "We heard all of the gunfire. Sounded like it was pretty hot and heavy for awhile."

Not one that spoke out often Slade said, "Man! I've seen a lot in my time. But nothing like today."

After he'd made his statement. Slade just rode on to help with the pack animals. As the rest rode by to reclaim their pack horses. Tex said, "I'm sorry. I know how curious you are. But after being in battle you know how Matt is. It takes awhile for him to get all the way back down to earth."

Tex kicked his horse into motion as Captain Taylor nodded. He was full of questions. He'd seen the grim looks on their faces. Maybe a little astonishment had been on their faces, also. Captain Taylor knew that the cowboys were hardened riders. It was strange. But Billy seemed like he was almost contented. Much like he'd just been out for a Sunday stroll. They made it only fifteen miles from their last campsite when they found a good place to camp. It was just short of the draw. Matt stayed close to the women as he'd turned control of the pack train over to Captain Taylor.

On the sixteenth day from the outside entrance of Peaceful Valley. They were in camp a little early as the sun had just started to set. They were within eighteen miles of Rawlins. The last few days Matt had tried to work out a problem he'd had on his mind. He hadn't been able to come up with an answer yet. As they sat around and sipped the last of the coffee that Mr. Maxton had sent. Matt finally just asked, "Do any of you know of a good place we could camp for a few days. I need to go in and get something for us to wear. Also I'd like for Runs Far and his braves to camp with us. Until you are ready to go back to Peaceful Valley, Captain Taylor."

Hawkeye said, "Five miles a little south of here is an old abandoned army fort. The pony express used it for a little while then left it. An old couple that lost their children and place to a Indian raid took it over. I think they are still there. They don't get many customers. Most people go on into Rawlins. So they barely scratch out a living."

Dan said, "Yeah, that would be a good place. It's not real big. But it might be just what you're looking for Matt. We'll still be sixteen miles out of Rawlins."

Matt said, "Good. Do you think it'll be okay for Runs Far and his braves to be around?"

Dan said, "Oh I know the Young's. They trade with drifters and Indians. I don't think it'll be a problem at all."

Helen asked, "After they got wiped out by Indians. They still welcome them?"

Captain Taylor said, "As you've found out. Life is ruff out here. Even with what you've been through. Some of your best friends and mine are Indians."

Helen a little stunned, nodded as she said, "Oh! Yes, your right. I wasn't thinking."

Matt said, "Runs Far, we will still need to have the scouts out around us. At least until we get the gold sold."

They hadn't started early the next morning. But they still made it to the Young's, by ten in the morning. After a short visit by Dan after he'd explained the circumstances of his arrival. He was told to bring everyone in. As Dan led them in they'd seen the holes in the walls where some upright timbers had fallen down. The gates were in need of repair. The stables roof had holes in it. Other than the building they used as a store the officer's quarters building was in the best shape. It looked like the Young's used it for their living quarters.

Dan guided them through the gate then led them forward to meet the Young's. They were in their late fifty's. They were white haired. Mrs. Dawn Young was five foot four with a thin build. She had brown eyes with a wrinkled face. Mr. Fred Young was five foot six. Thinly built with broad shoulders that looked like they'd once had a lot of strength in them. Dan introduced Matt, Billy, Connie, Helen, Star and Captain Taylor as they rode up. They all nodded to each other saying their hello's. Mrs. Young as her mothering instinct took over said, "Oh my. You girls get right down here. Lets get you a nice hot bath and see if we can find something for you to put on."

Connie said, "Yes ma-am. We need to take care of our horses first though."

Mrs. Young said, "Fiddle sticks. That's nonsense. The men can take care of the horses."

Matt said, "Yes ma-am. We'll be glad to."

Matt put action to his words quickly dismounted Flame. Then helped his women down. They followed Mrs. Young as she lead them into her living quarters. They heard her chattering to the girls as they went out of sight.

Mr. Young said, "Wonder's will never cease. I haven't seen her take to anyone like that sense we lost our youngsters. She's taking an instant liking to them. Come on, I'll show you where to put your horses and give them a bite of grain."

Matt saw Mr. Young glance at the scars on his chest and back a couple of times. He got a little uncomfortable. But he tried to ignore the feeling. After a few minutes they'd took all the packs off and unsaddled all the horses. Mr. Young explained that they didn't have any extra beds, just enough for the women. He invited them to lay their bedrolls out wherever they liked.

An hour after Mrs. Young had taken the girls in they reappeared as Matt, Billy, Dan and Captain Taylor left the stable and corral. Mrs. Young had a approving smile on her face. The women looked uncomfortable with the sheets that Mrs. Young had pinned on them. She looked at Matt and Billy as she said, "We need to get you two cleaned up and see if we can't find something fitting for you two to wear."

Matt said, "Yes ma-am. I was going to make out a list of things and send Captain Taylor with Dan into Rawlins if you don't have what we need."

Mrs. Young not to be deterred said, "That's good. I'm sorry most of the things you youngsters need we don't have. If you don't mind I'd like to make out a list of things to send along?"

Matt answered, "That'll be fine. I'll pay for everything. You just figure out what your charges will be."

Mr. Young said, "We don't have much. But whatever you need just help your self to it. We can tally things up as we go along. We'll treat you real fair."

Matt said, "I'm not worried about that. You've already been real good to us."

After a late noon meal. Captain Taylor and Dan put the saddles back on their horses. Tex and Bones got a couple of pack horses ready for them. Matt had given Captain Taylor some gold nuggets he'd carried in Flames saddle bags. With the list of thing's from Matt and Mrs. Young they rode out toward Rawlins.

Matt and Billy after their baths had been talked into having sheets pinned on them. Matt even though the cloth made him itch was glad to have something on that covered him. The Young's hadn't mentioned a thing. But he'd noticed the looks and with each one he saw the amazement grow in their eyes.

Runs Far had gone out and killed a deer. The men built a fire pit and with some irons that Mr. Young provided they had the venison over the fire roasting. Mrs. Young and the women had fixed a big pot of beans to go along with it. The night had closed in on them as they enjoyed a pleasant evening of food and some small talk. The Young's filled them in on what had happened with the rest of the country. After the meal Mrs. Young rushed the girls off to bed as she said, "You girls need to be getting your rest now. Seeing that we roasted outside tonight it won't take me long to clean up."

They'd protested, but she'd ended up persuading them to do as she whished. It had been awhile since Matt hadn't spent the night with his women. The Young's had been so nice and ment well. So Matt decided not to make a fuss and just stayed with his men. They conversed in some light conversation. After a few minutes Matt decided to go on to his bedroll. Some of the others soon left to go to their bedrolls.

The next day Captain Taylor and Dan returned around noon time. Upon their return they unpacked the pack horses at the Young's living quarters. Mrs. Young had insisted and when she had the packages she wanted. She had the women help her take them inside. Matt and Billy sorted through the rest to pick out their clothes that had been purchased for them. Matt's clothes were tight on him, especially the pants around his thighs. He'd been able to get them on though. But after wearing his boots for an hour he'd decided to put his moccasins back on.

That evening they had some warm bread with their meal, along with a couple of fresh apple pies. The women had on plain cotton dress's that where a little over sized. But they did fit over their bellies.

They had brushed each other's hair out until their hair shined. It had been forever since Matt had seen them all dressed up. They looked beautiful to him. Star had quite a time getting adjusted to some of the new things. She'd never worn anything like the new shoes. What she thought was even worse, was something she'd been told were stockings. Then the under things weren't comfortable at all. Billy's cloths were a little large. The women, Matt and Billy scratched a lot as they tried to get used to wearing clothes again.

CHAPTER TWENTY SIX

NO INSULTS

Matt told everyone he wanted to move the gold on into the smelter the next day. That he wanted to get an early start. Then he inquired of Mr. Young if there was an honest banker in town. Mr. Young had advised him to see a Mr. Cliff Benson. Then Mr. Young told Matt where he was located. Not to cause a fuss Matt still hadn't the heart to tell them how thing's really were, between him and his women.

The next morning as they worked on getting the pack train ready. Matt along with most of the others were surprised when they heard the clatter of a carriage as Slim drove it up to them. Matt looked at Captain Taylor as he said, "I didn't know about this."

Captain Taylor said, "I just thought. That the ladies ought to go to town in style."

Matt nodded, then said, "It's a good idea."

Captain Taylor said, "We would've brought it back with us yesterday. But it was the only carriage we could come up with. It had, already been rented out. So I had Slim slip in last night so as to have it here this morning."

Matt turned to Slim as he said, "Thank-you Slim. You can take some time off and get a nap."

Slim said, "No, I'm fine boss, no problem. I'll get my horse and be right along."

Matt said, "If you feel that way. How would you feel about driving the Carriage in then?"

Without a thought he said, "It would be my honor, boss."

Matt didn't say anything. But he was real uncomfortable with being called boss.

Matt just said, "Good, you got it."

Slim just nodded as he reined the horses into motion then stopped the carriage up close to the Young's living quarters. The Ladies had surprised looks on their faces as they came out noticing the carriage. They still had their holsters and guns on over their dresses. The only thing they hadn't done was tie them down to their legs. Mrs. Young had complained. But they as politely as they could told her, that they needed their guns. Matt walked across the compound. Then he helped them into the carriage. Matt whistled softly and Flame ran up. As Matt mounted Flame Captain Taylor motioned for everyone to start. Slim sat proud as if he had the most valuable thing in the world in the carriage. In reality that's the way he felt. Matt thought so too. When everyone was in motion toward the gate Matt said, "Slim! You and the ladies go ahead of us."

Slim nodded as he maneuvered the carriage in front. They got to Rawlins around two in the afternoon. Captain Taylor guided them to the smelter. When the owner came out inquiring what he wanted Matt explained about the gold they had. Then Matt told Captain Taylor to make sure it got unloaded. But don't let them take any inside till he got back with Mr. Benson.

It had taken Matt forty minutes to find the bank then wait while Mr. Benson finished with another customer. When Matt explained the need for his services Mr. Benson told his clerk he'd be back shortly. Outside at the tie rail he tightened the cinch of his saddle then mounted and rode along with Matt back to smelter. Mr. Benson was around forty with a slight pouch belly. Five foot five with black hair, a long nose with large ears, small hands with a short body for his long legs. Matt liked him instantly. He'd watched his eyes and face closely. Matt was sure of his honesty. Mr. Young told him that he was as honest of a banker as he knew. Matt had seen a couple of other banks that looked like they were doing a better business in there bright new buildings.

Mr. Benson was all business when he saw all the gold bars laid out. Twenty four of them. Mr. Benson and the owner checked the scale together before they started weighing them. They found out that they averaged ninety pounds. Mr. Benson haggled with the owner for a few minutes before they agreed on a price of five hundred fifty four thousand dollars. Mr. Benson double checked the receipt for the gold. Then he said, "Matt you'll be down to the bank shortly so we can get things squared away."

Matt nodded, "Yes, I won't be long."

Mr. Benson hurried off back to his bank.

Matt said, "Billy, I think if Slim let's the Ladies off in front of the bank. That you'll be able to take Flame to the stable and see that he's taken care of."

Billy said, "I think Flame will let me. Sure."

When they arrived at the bank Matt opened the door and escorted the ladies through. As they stepped on in Matt started to guide his women toward Mr. Benson's office when the teller at the counter asked, "Can I help you?"

Matt said, "Yes, we're here to see Mr. Benson."

Mr. Benson hearing the voices opened his door. When he saw Matt and the Ladies he said, "Oh, Matt come on in. I didn't expect so many. Excuse me."

He had a short conversation with the teller. Then he said, "Please come into my office."

No sooner than they'd gotten into the office the teller came in with two chairs. When the Ladies were seated the teller left the office and closed the door.

Matt sat down then said, "I know I didn't introduce anyone at the smelter. I want you to meet Bright Star Saxton, Connie Saxton and Helen Saxton."

He had introduced them in the order they sat from him on his right.

Mr. Benson had a confused look on his face as he asked, "Are they your sisters? Oh sorry, Well Hello"

Matt said, "No, their my wives."

Mr. Benson unable to hide the surprise on his face said, "Oh."

As if reading his thoughts Matt said, "No, none of us are Mormon. It is just the way things have worked out."

Mr. Benson said, "Oh-h, sure no problem. You-u just completely surprised me. That's all. Do you want joint or separate accounts."

Matt said, "A joint account please."

Mr. Benson said, "Excuse me. I need to get a different form. I'll be right back." When he returned Mr. Benson handed Matt a paper as he said, "I need all of you to sign this form or put your mark on it."

Matt leaned forward and signed the paper, then passed it to Star. When they'd all signed it Helen handed it to Mr. Benson.

Mr. Benson took the form and looked it over. Then as he looked at the Ladies he said, "Very good. Each one of you, have good pens men ship."

The Ladies said, "Thank you."

Then Mr. Benson asked, "Would you like some spending money?"

The Ladies had nodded, as Matt said, "Yes, I would like four thousand. I got some riders that could use some money. Then we could use some money to purchase some more things that the Ladies would like to have."

Mr. Benson stood as he said, "No problem. Excuse me Ladies I'll be right back."

In a few minutes he returned. Then he counted out the money for Matt. When he'd finished he said, "It don't matter which one. But I need one of you to sign the receipt and balance sheet."

Matt signed them then stood up. He helped the ladies up then said, "Thank you Mr. Benson. You've been very helpful. I believe you've already saved me a lot of money."

Mr. Benson said, "I thank you for your business. It's been a pleasure on my part. It's not often that I get to see such beautiful Ladies. I hope you don't mind me saying so."

Matt assured him that it was alright. That was the way he felt. The Ladies had acknowledged them with a slight bow as they blushed a little. They'd talked a little while, then said there good bye's. Matt, escorted the women out of the bank. On the boardwalk they waited for their eyes to adjust to the sunlight.

Matt brushed the hammers of his pistols with his thumbs to make sure the hammer loops where off. When he wasn't in the saddle he made sure they weren't. He'd instructed Billy and the ladies to do the same. Matt then escorted the ladies along the street toward a General store. That Mr. Benson had advised them to use. In some places they had to step down as the wood boardwalk ended. Then a couple of buildings later the boardwalk continued on.

They weren't in a hurry as they still hadn't gotten used to their foot wear yet. It gave them time to look the city over as they strolled along. Star had all she could do to contain herself as everything was new to her. All the Ladies were excited as Connie and Helen took turns explaining the different things to her. Mr. Benson had told them of a decent hotel a block further up the street from the general store.

They'd nodded at some of the people that seemed friendly, for the most part. They'd attracted a lot of attention as they traveled up the street. Even with the plain clothes they wore they still looked attractive. Also, because of the guns strapped on each hip over their dress's. They had attracted a lot of attention. Matt spotted the General Store and said, "Ladies, we need to cross the street."

As he'd spoken, he pointed. They'd nodded, then after a couple of riders and a buggy had gone by they crossed over. On the boardwalk they continued on up the street. As they approached a saloon Matt saw Billy and Tex as they came down the street. Suddenly two cowboys bust through the swinging door's just a few paces in front of them. One of them yelled some obscenities back into the saloon. It was obvious they were drunk. The one that had yelled nearly fell as he turned back to join his partner. His partner loudly said, "Yippee! Look what we have here. Three young fillies, ripe and ready to ride. Just the way I like them."

When he had focused his eyes and gotten his look. He started to say something,   when he was cut off by Matt. With an intense voice Matt said, "Mister you got one choice. That's to apologize to each one of them. Right now!"

The puncher laughed as he focused on Matt then asked, "Well, just who do you think you are?"

Two shots almost as one rang out. Two holes appeared dead center on the unlucky punchers chest within the space of a dine. The bullets had cut his spinal cord and he dropped like a sack of potatoes. When his partner heard the shots and saw his friend fall he went for his gun. The twin pistols spoke again with the same results. The gun play had taken just a couple of seconds.

Tex rushed up as Billy cautiously followed along behind. A small crowd had started to gather as Matt returned his guns to their holsters. Then as he escorted the ladies around the bodies he said, "Excuse us.

Someone get the sheriff or Marshal. I will be at the General Store." He pointed as Tex helped clear a path for them to walk through. Billy stayed just outside the gathering crowd as he watched everyone intently. Someone in the crowd asked. "What happened."

Another said, "They insulted the women."

Another person said, "I never saw him draw. His gun's just appeared in his hands."

There was more talk as they left the scene. Tex as he dropped in behind Matt and the ladies heard some of the talk. Billy had joined him by the time Matt and his women had gone inside the General Store. Tex looked at Billy then said, "Back at the draw I didn't see that much. I just know everything happened real fast. But today I saw Matt in action. I'm considered pretty fast and have been able to hold my own. But Matt is faster than I ever thought anyone could possibly be, let alone seen."

Billy grinned slightly. He had seen Matt when he'd practiced. Billy knew that the way Matt had taught him, he was quick. But nothing like Matt.

Billy said, "Yeah. He is sudden. Isn't he?"

Tex stated, "Sudden. He's like a flash of lighting."

Captain Taylor, Dan, Slim, Hawkeye, Slade, Bones and Ben rushed down the street. When they spotted Tex and Billy in front of the General store they slowed down to a walk. Slightly out of breath as they joined them Captain Taylor asked, "What's going on? Somebody told us there was a shooting over three women. We were afraid that it was Star, Connie and Helen."

Tex said, "Oh! You don't need to be afraid for them."

Billy as he quickly caught onto Tex's drift just kept a sober face. If they'd noticed his eyes were twinkled though. Captain Taylor said, "Oh! Good. I was afraid they were involved."

Tex answered, "Oh. They were."

All the men had listened to every word. They had dumb founded looks on their faces as Dan said, "You just told us they weren't."

Tex said, "I just told you that you don't have to worry."

Slim as he scratched his head under his hat asked, "How's that? Anytime there's gunplay. Is a time you need to be concerned."

Tex put some more bait out as he said, "There was only two of them."

Captain Taylor and Hawkeye had caught on to Tex's play then. They waited patently for the punch line. Bones said, "I still don't see why you're not concerned."

Tex stated, "I finally got to see with my own eyes how quick and easy Matt can get into action. Boy's, I still can't get over how fast he is. Like some of the other people. I saw him with his guns in there holsters. Then the next thing they were already in his hands smoking."

Captain Taylor asked, "What started it? Matt wouldn't just shoot someone for no reason."

Tex answered, "I Don't know. I Wasn't close enough to hear. I did hear someone say he heard them insult the ladies.

Billy said, "That would do it.!"

Right after Billy had spoken a slow moving man with a sheriff's star pinned on his vest approached. He asked. "Did any of you do the shooting."

Tex answered, "No. Our boss is inside with the ladies sheriff."

The sheriff nodded, then got under motion again as he said, "Thank you."

When they'd made it inside where they had a little privacy all the women confronted Matt as Connie asked, "Matt, why did you do that?"

With a surprised look he answered, "They insulted you."

Connie said, "Matt, we expected that."

Matt asked, "Why."

Star said, "We were sure that people wouldn't understand our relationship."

Matt said, "They didn't know. Besides that make's no difference."

Connie said, "Matt you just can't shoot everybody in the whole country."

Matt answered, "I'm not going to. But I won't stand by and have any of you insulted. In any way!"

The way Matt had stated his last words the ladies knew they wouldn't change his mind. They were proud of him. But worried about the trouble it would cause. The proprietor slowly approached. He had seen them when they came in. But he noticed that they'd gotten into an intense discussion. He asked, "Is there anything I can help you with?"

Matt glad for the interruption explained what they needed. The owner nodded, then informed them that he did have a dressing room and was sure with his wife's help, the Ladies could find what they desired. They wouldn't be able to tailor them though.

As the owner took the ladies off to introduce them to his wife. Matt started to look for some more things for himself. He noticed the sheriff when he came through the door.

Matt caught the surprised look on his face, when he spotted Matt and slowly walked forward. When he'd made it up close he held his hand out and said, "Hi, I'm Ed Blane. The local Sheriff."

Ed was five foot four, a little heavy built as he'd started to put on some pounds the last few year's. He was forty Five with a pleasant face. He had black hair with brown eyes that missed nothing. He had a short thick neck. Ed Blane had a reputation for being fair. Very tough and determined though. Despite his slow pace it was known that he never backed down from anyone. He still was considered to be very fast and accurate with his pistol. He was excellent with his rifle.

Matt nodding said, "I guess you're looking for me. I'm Matt Saxton."

The Sheriff said, "I am if your the one that did the shooting."

"Yeah, I'm the one!"

"Well, I'd like to hear your side of it."

Matt gave him a detailed explanation. After he was done the Sheriff said, "Ok. That's pretty much what I was able to put together. They've always been a little ruff. Never anything serious. But they have always picked fights. They'd just had a big argument with the bar tender. They'd had to much to drink. Still there was no excuse for them to do what they did."

As they'd talked the sheriff looked Matt over good. Even though it was just a couple of glances. Most of the time they looked each other in the eyes. Matt thought that the Sheriff would be about the hardest person to lie to, that he'd ever met. Ed Blane usually didn't make snap judgments. But he had to admit that he already liked, the young man, that stood in front, of him. Matt had spoken plain. He hadn't added anything or left anything out either. Most would have tried to brag or left something out so they wouldn't be at fault. Matt had instantly liked the sheriff, he said, "Sheriff, I don't want to cause you any trouble. But I won't let the ladies be insulted."

The Sheriff nodded as he said, "I'm glad you gave them a chance to apologize. If not I'd have to take you in."

Matt answered. "I understand. I'll be careful."

The Sheriff laughed, "I've looked you over pretty good and that's one thing I haven't spotted."

Sheepishly Matt said, "I do try."

The Sheriff said, "I guess that concludes my business with you. I hope our people are more hospitable to you. Be careful, the two punchers had some friends. I don't think they'll bother you though. Not if they listen to the talk, they won't."

They said their good-bye's. When the ladies finally finished their shopping. Matt and the men carried their purchases as they escorted them to the hotel. Then Matt paid them back to when they'd left Portland Oregon. They'd told him that Mr. Maxton would pay them. Matt told them he'd take care of that problem. Matt then started Billy's time back to when he'd been captured by the Indians. Billy told Matt he wasn't working for him then. Matt told him sense he didn't want into the partnership he wouldn't hear any more arguments about it.

Billy, Captain Taylor, Dan and Hawkeye got a room in the same hotel. Tex wanted to also. But had ended up going with the others to a different one because they had run out of rooms. Matt and the women received some strange look's when he asked for their largest room and bed.

They'd agreed to meet Captain Taylor, Dan and Hawkeye for supper. That evening after their little shopping spree to get a few things they wanted. Billy and Captain Taylor waited for the others. They'd gotten a place in the back of the restaurant with a big table. Billy and Captain Taylor had stayed together most of the day and shared a room. It wasn't long before Dan and Hawkeye made an appearance to join them. As they sat down Dan said, "The word has spread all over town how fast Matt is with his guns."

With concern Captain Taylor said, "You haven't added anything to it, I hope."

Understanding the Captains concern Dan said, "No. You don't need to worry about any of us either. Tex; well all of us know that Matt doesn't like to hear any talk about him. We're smart enough not to spread any stories. Well unless maybe it's a good friend."

Captain Taylor said, "Good. Oh may!"

The others had followed his eyes and were astonished as the women being escorted by Matt approached the table.

The Ladies wore evening dress's. Star's was a light blue, Connie's was a light red and Helen's was a light green. Their hair had been brushed till it shone. The dress's had the same six inch square cut down the front. Not being tailored they had a loose fit. The dress's flowed down to the floor. The Ladies got a few intense looks as some people noticed the design each of them had on the front of their shoulders. Billy and Captain Taylor helped Matt get them seated as Dan and Hawkeye stood while they took their seats. Then Matt sat down with his back to the wall.

They ordered and had a pleasant meal. From time to time there'd been a lot of look's directed at their table. Captain Taylor and Dan had decided to have a glass of whiskey to finish their meal off with. The rest sipped coffee. They were having a pleasant chat as they sat back in their chairs and relaxed. It had been along time since they'd not had any chores to do. Their conversation was interrupted by a burst of gunfire off in the distance. They were quiet with their own thoughts for a minute. They had picked up their discussion when five minutes later Matt spotted Slim as he looked around the restaurant. Matt motioned and Slim rushed up. Before he'd stopped he said, "Ben's been shot."

As he quickly got up Matt said, "Captain Taylor, Dan, Billy, you stay with the women. Hawkeye you come with me. Slim let's go."

Slim led off at a trot. They rushed further into the city. Past the center of town then into the ruff part of town. It took them a little over five minutes of trotting and sometimes they slowed to a fast walk as they waited for a horse and rider to go by.

There was a crowd gathering in front of a big saloon. Matt passed Slim and pushed his way through. Slim close behind Matt saw him use his hands as he gave short jabs to open up a path for them. There was a lot of grunts and some cussing. But with Slim staying right on Matt's heels they didn't have much of a problem getting through.

When Matt got inside a big circle of people he spotted Ben. A saloon girl had his head in her lap as she sat wiping blood from Ben's lips. Taking a quick glance around Matt knelt down next to Ben. Matt saw that he'd been shot several times and was bleeding bad. Matt said, "Hang on Ben. We'll get you to a doctor."

Ben's breathing had a bad rasp to it and he coughed as the blood came from his lips. Between gasp's Ben said, "Matt, I needed to talk. I was jealous of you. I'm in love with Helen. Glad she choose you. Take care of her."

Matt tried to keep Ben quiet and told him to save his strength. Matt had Slim find some bar cloths. Then he tore them up and plugged the bullet holes with them.

There was another stirring in the crowd as another person yelled and pushed his way through. He could be heard saying, "Let me through, I'm the doctor.

When he got through Matt said, "Doctor over hear, quick. Do all you can for him."

Matt eased out of the way as the doctor knelt down and opened his bag. Then he said, "I can't believe this man is still alive."

The doctor worked feverishly. A couple of minutes later an authoritative voice made it through the crowd. He told them to clear out and go home. As he'd thought Matt saw that it was the sheriff. The sheriff looked around then started to send everyone out that hadn't witnessed the shooting. The crowd had thinned out quite a bit, then it was stirred up again by a group pushing it's way through the crowd.

Then Matt saw that it was Captain Taylor, Billy, Dan and Hawkeye with the ladies and the rest of Matt's cowboy's. The women had their guns strapped on over their gowns. Matt had mixed emotions. He was proud, angry and filled with sorrow. The sheriff saw them also. Right off he knew the women weren't from the saloon and shouldn't be there. He recognized two of the cowboy's that was with them and was sure they were the one's that the trouble had been over earlier. Matt moved to block the women from getting any closer. At the same time he noticed that Billy and Tex made sure the cowboy's had spread out. They watched the dispersing crowd closely. They had their hands close to their pistol butts.

The sheriff about to step forward to keep things from getting any more tense. Saw that suddenly a lot of the people acted like they needed to do something and had just remembered what it was. When they started to rush off. The sheriff took another look at Matt's crew. After a closer look at their faces he could see why. They all were deathly intense.

Connie knew what Matt's intensions were and just stepped around him as she asked, "Is there anything we can do to help doctor?"

Matt said, "The doctor is doing all he can."

Then they heard Ben as he grasped, "Helen!"

Helen heard and rushed to him then knelt down beside him as she said, "Yes Ben. Is their something I can do for you?"

Ben gasped, "One last look."

Ben coughed and spit up a lot of blood. His eyes started to glaze over as he said, "Thanks."

Ben went still then and the doctor said, "I'm sorry folks. He's gone. I don't see how he lasted as long as he did."

The doctor then reached up and closed Ben's eyelids. Then he checked the others. There was seven of them. Five of them didn't move. Two were hit hard and still breathed. The doctor worked on them and did what he could. The sheriff questioned the witness's to find out what had happened.

Matt then turned to face Captain Taylor. He said, "I thought I told you to stay with the women."

Before the Captain could respond. Star said, "Like you could've kept us from coming here."

Matt just clamped his mouth shut and grimaced. Then he concentrated on listening to the sheriff as he questioned the witness's. As they pieced everything together they learned that Ben heard the men as they talked about the women. He'd gone to the bar to get another bottle of whiskey. The one's that had been shot had declared that the women were the cause of their friends being shot. That they were probably nothing more than high class whores. In short order Ben had informed them that he rode for them and when he took a job he rode for the band. After a few more words the gunplay had started. As they'd gone for their guns Ben had been quick enough to get two of them before any of their guns cleared leather. After that they were told even though Ben was taken lead. He had just kept firing his pistols until they were empty.

Slim pointed as he guiltily said, "I was over there at the corner table. I didn't get here till the shooting was over. Ben just told me to get you Matt. That he needed to talk to you. I didn't think we'd make it back in time though. He was tougher than I thought."

Connie asked, "What did he say Matt?"

Matt said, "We'll talk later. I do have to tell you though."

Matt then turned to the sheriff asking, "Is it okay if we take my man and see to it that he is taken care of properly?"

The sheriff said, "Yes. I think I got most of the story now. Go ahead, I would like to talk to you in the morning though."

The doctor to anyone and everyone said, "This one is done for. I don't think the other one is going to make it either."

Tex and three of the cowboy's gently picked Ben up and carried him off.

The sheriff called a name and said, "Be good enough to show them where the undertaker is."

He nodded as he stepped in front to guide them.

Matt asked, "Sheriff, is there anything we can help you with?"

The sheriff looked around and saw that the saloon was nearly empty, then he said, "No. Take your people and put them up for the night."

Helen had gathered up Bens pistols before they left. Matt with his women and the rest of his crew quietly left with a few looks from the few people that were still there. As they walked down the street it looked like most of the people had gone home. The street was mostly dark except for a few stores and saloon's that still had some lamp's lit.

Back at the hotel Matt said, "See you in the morning."

Captain Taylor, Dan, Billy and Hawkeye nodded as they headed for their rooms.

When Matt got the ladies up to the room he told them what Ben had told him. All the women were teary eyed when Matt had finished. Helen first, then Connie and Star even seemed a little misty eyed. Then Helen said, "I didn't know. He never said a thing. I did notice that he had looked at me a few times. But I never paid it much attention. I'm so sorry."

Matt said, "Brace up. I'm sure Ben didn't want that from you. He just wanted to square things with me. It proves to me that he was one honest cowboy."

Matt wisely didn't say anything about them showing up at the saloon. Restless with their thoughts they didn't sleep well. Matt had even slipped out to find that the night clerk did have access to a pot of coffee, that the cook left on for him. One by one the Ladies had joined him.

The next morning up with the sun as they'd gotten accustomed to it. Captain Taylor and Billy found Matt and the women already at the big table. The restaurant had been open for a half hour. They'd waited for a fresh pot of coffee to boil and had just gotten their coffee when Captain Taylor and Billy showed up. Captain Taylor and Billy hadn't much more than gotten their coffee when Dan and Hawkeye came up to the table. They ordered breakfast and for the most part ate their meal in silence. They had finished when Tex and the rest of the crew showed up. Tex told them they had eaten. But they wouldn't mind having some more coffee. There was only a handful of other people up. They pretty much had the place to themselves. When everyone had coffee Matt said." Captain, I'd like for you to take Ben back and bury him on ceremonial Hill. I think it will be alright with the Indians. Tell them he died with a lot of honor."

Hawkeye nodded as Helen said, "Oh yes. I think that's the only place. It's better than some boot hill."

Tex said, "I do think Ben would have liked that."

Slim said, "Yes. He was my saddle partner. I am sure he would."

Matt said, "Slim, order a headstone. You knew Ben the best, so you have them put on it what you think Ben would like.

Slim, a little chocked up as he answered, "Yes Sir."

Then Matt went on to other business. "Captain, I'll get you squared away with Mr. Benson at the bank. So you can draw on the account and hire some people to build the trail. You'll need to purchase some wagons and some animals to pull them with also."

"Tex, I know you and your men want to be driving cow's. But, that's a little way's off yet. I need to build a ranch house and stable before we get a herd in. It'll probably be eighteen to twenty month's."

"Captain Taylor can concentrate on the construction part. Dan, between you, Tex and the rest of the crew bring the gold into the smelter."

"Billy will be going with us to see his folks. We're sending telegrams out to our families today. Just make sure you have Run's Far and his scouts out when your traveling. Remember, this outfit don't back down from anyone. Keep it that way. Just be sure that you are in the right. I'll see if there's a Marshal or someone that should know about our fight with the outlaws."

Matt saw the sheriff as he slowly came into the restaurant. Matt finished as he said, "That's all, unless there's some questions or something I need to know."

They finished their coffee as they absorbed everything he'd been told. They tipped their hats to the Ladies as they left. Matt had been all business and in a way, it had made them feel better. They were saddened by Ben's death. But Matt had reestablished a plan of action for them.

The sheriff ordered some coffee as he nodded to Matt's crew as they left. Then he tipped his hat to the Ladies and nodded to Matt.

 Matt introduced him to the ladies, "Sheriff I'd like you to meet Connie Saxton that's on my right. Helen Saxton on my immediate left then Bright Star Saxton. I should've done it yesterday. But with them shopping and then at the saloon last night. I didn't feel like either time was appropriate."

The sheriff had shook hands with the Ladies as he'd been introduced. He nodded to Matt as he sat down. Then he said, "I agree. It was a busy day yesterday. I just wanted to know how long your going to be in town?"

Matt had gotten a steely look in his eyes as Connie put a hand on his arm. With a crisp voice Matt said, "The Ladies, Billy and I will probably catch the train tomorrow."

The sheriff had seen Matt's eyes. He already knew, that he never wanted to be the one that would have to confront him. He'd just found out, how fast Matt's dander could be raised. With a quick thought he decided that the punchers never had a chance. He chose his words very carefully as he said, "You and your people have done nothing I wouldn't have done in your place. After meeting these Ladies I can see what the stir was all about. I think the people have wised up now. At least I hope so."

Matt's demeanor calmed nearly as quick as it had risen. He said, "I don't look for trouble. But I won't stand for the Ladies to be slandered or let anyone cheat me. Nor will I let anyone take something that belongs to me."

The sheriff nodded as he said, "That's kind of what I expected. Well I guess I ought to make my morning rounds." As he stood he tipped his hat to the ladies then said, " I hope the rest of your stay is a lot more pleasant."

With an after thought Matt said, "We had a run in with some outlaws southwest of here."

The sheriff said, "I'll let the Marshal know. He should be back in town sometime today."

Matt thanked him, then they said their good byes. Matt paid for their meals and all the coffee. When they left the restaurant they went to the telegraph office as it was just opening. After they'd sent a telegram to their families to let them know they were fine. They'd gone to the undertaker's to make sure, that Ben was being taken care of properly. Matt made arrangements for a preacher, to say some words over Ben before he was taken to the valley. Early the next morning.

Matt with his Ladies searched for Billy as they looked the city over some. Star was still excited with all the new things she saw. When they'd found Billy they went to a saddle shop where they picked out some saddles. They still got a lot of looks directed their way. But the people were pleasant or kept their distance. They decided to take their horses with them on the train. To ride them on the trip through northern California to Portland Oregon. After they made their purchases at the saddle shop. Billy went in search of a couple of men to move the saddles and tack to the stable. Billy came across Bones and Slim. They decided they'd like to go along with him to the Young's, to bring in the Ladies horses for the train ride west. With some persuasion Matt finally convinced the ladies to let Tex go along and escort them. While they bought some more things they decided they needed from the General Store. Matt assured them that with Captain Taylor along, he wouldn't get into any trouble. With Captain Taylor Matt had visited the bank to see Mr. Benson and made the necessary arrangements. So

Captain Taylor could draw money from the account. Captain Taylor then went to get a hair cut.

Matt spent an hour writing a detailed letter to his mother. Matt had gotten a few looks from the bank clerk as he wrote the letter. When he was done he got with Mr. Benson again. Then Matt went to the telegraph office. They handled the mail service too. Matt got an envelope then put the letter with the large draft for his mother in it. The letter directed her to purchase the Bingham Mansion in New York City if it was still available and make the necessary repairs, so he would have a place for his Ladies to stay while the building was being done at Peaceful Valley. Also, to keep it a secret between them. Matt then went back to the saddlery. It took him and the proprietor over forty minutes before they'd made a deal. After Matt explained what he wanted they'd spent most of the time fitting as they tried different things, till Matt was happy with the design and fit of the special harness. It would hold his forty fours snug, under his arm pits. He knew that back east with the guns on his hips. Would make a lot of people nervous, as well as the police. He was going to have his guns with him though. When he was about to leave he changed his mind and ordered four more. For Billy and the ladies. They'd pick them up on their return trip.

Star had gotten somewhat accustomed to all of the people. Also, she had put up with the friendly teasing, from Helen and Connie. As they had taught her about women's clothing she had never seen, let alone put on. Using a knife and fork had been a real experience also. She'd stated that she didn't like it. Connie and Helen agreed with her. They were having a hard time getting used to wearing all the cloth's again.

They had agreed to meet back at the hotel at noon. Matt had arrived a few minutes before the ladies had. When they arrived he helped carry their purchases up to their room. He'd seen the rest of his crew as they approached. Matt told Tex to find a place for them, in the restaurant. Matt and the Ladies joined them shortly, then they had a pleasant meal. Matt informed them about the service for Ben that was to be held in the morning. Also, that the train was due to leave at ten in the morning. That they would probably need help getting the horses into the box car, with it being the first time any of them have being in one. Tex then asked, "Who is going to take care of them?"

Matt answered, "Billy has volunteered too."

Tex said, "You ought to take Slim. He's gotten to know the horses pretty good. Flame is even used to him. Billy could use the rest."

Matt thought a little, before he said, "Alright, I think that's a good idea. I did purchase a boxcar just for us. One more horse will be no problem. If it's okay with Slim."

Tex said, "When he gets back I'll check it out with him. I'm sure he won't mind though."

They talked for another few minutes as they completed their plans. With the talk about the things that needed to be done their spirits grew. They all missed Ben.

The sheriff had been catching up on his reports and filing away some papers when he heard foot steps in the hall. He looked up and saw Ralph Crampton on his way to his office. Ed said, "Ralph, I would like a word with you."

The Marshal turned and stepped into Ed's office. Ralph Crampton was a U.S. Marshall. He was six foot one, thirty years old. He had broad shoulders, long legs and arms. A slight limp from previous injury to his left leg . Reddish sandy hair and brown eyes. He had a scar from a knife cut on his right check from his chin, almost up to his ear lobe. He had a long nose that was bent to the left, after it had been broken. He was noted for his fairness as well, as his honesty. It was said once he went after somebody he was able to track them down and bring them back, dead or alive. Ralph backed against the door jamb as he asked, "What's up? I was hoping to sleep the clock around."

Ed said, "You need to talk to a Matt Saxton."

"Do you know what it's about."

"Yeah. Something about a shoot out with some outlaws."

The Marshal asked, "Why would outlaws bother them?"

"I heard they brought in a fortune; in gold."

"Oh. Yeah that would do it. Where will I find him."

"Over at the Grand Hotel. Maybe you'll be lucky and catch them eating supper. Oh Ralph. Use caution."

The Marshal had started out. He stopped and turned back, then asked, "Why's that."

The sheriff took his time as he carefully choose his words saying, "I really like the youngsters. But there has been two gun fights since Matt and his crew have come to town. I don't think there is anyone in the crew that will back down, from anything. Don't let their age fool you. I saw something in the youngsters eyes that told me they'd seen and lived through something that most wouldn't have."

"Their not on the prod then."

"No. There nice people, really. Oh! Don't say anything that's even close to an insult to the ladies."

"Ladies."

"Yeah. There is three of them and I think they can handle their shooting irons as good as anyone in the outfit. Well except for one, maybe."

The Marshal said, "Well thanks. I guess I'll go see if I can find them, then get some sleep. I'll see you."

"See you."

The Marshal as he headed toward the hotel was in deep thought as he walked along. He was very tried. But he'd become excited. The sheriffs judgment of people was as good as anyone he knew. When he arrived at the hotel he was informed by the clerk that Matt Saxton was in the restaurant. When he stepped through the doorway, his eyes where drawn to a set of eyes looking directly at him. He knew instantly without a doubt, that the young man behind them was Matt Saxton. He hadn't expected him to be so young. As he slowly approached their table he looked the rest of the crew over. He thought he recognized a couple of them. If so it should be a good outfit if he remembered right. He saw they all wore guns. Even the women had one on each hip. Because of their dresses they weren't tied down. But they did look like they belonged there. When he realized they were just young girls. He remembered what the sheriff had told him and was glad the sheriff had prepared him.

The Marshal walked up then stood by their table as he said, "I'm looking for Matt Saxton."

Matt said, "I'm Matt. Pull up a chair and set."

"No, That's alright. I might not get up. I was headed for my bed when the sheriff told me you wanted to talk with me."

Matt introduced everyone, then explained about the gun battle they'd had with the outlaws.

The Marshal said, "Captain Taylor, I thought I recognized you. I just couldn't place you. Do you agree with the details as Matt told them."

The Captain said, "Up to the battle it self. I was with the pack animals. Dan was up there though."

As the Marshal looked at Dan he nodded as he said, "Matt got it right as far as I can tell."

The Marshal said, "I guess that's all I need. I'll go check them out."

Matt said, "Marshal we took their weapons. Most of them were real good. We kept the best horses. Then turned the rest loose. Other than that we left them were they fell."

The Marshal said, "Thanks. I guess you've brought me up to date. I'll go see what the critters have left for me."

Matt said, "Captain Taylor will be headed back out tomorrow afternoon with the rest of the crew. If you don't mind riding with Indians they can take you right to the spot."

The Marshal said, "Thanks again. I'll catch up with them. See you."

The next morning they ment at the undertakers and said their goodbyes to Ben. After the little service they put his box with him in it on a wagon they would use for most of the trip back home. Runs Far and his scouts were to meet them south west of town. They did have a few problems getting the horses into the boxcar though. They had thought to put Flame in last as they figured he would be the hardest. After a couple of attempts with the horses. Matt just talked and comforted Flame as he led him up the ramp. The other horses followed with out much trouble then.

They rented a buggy to transport all the ladies things to the train. When they'd gotten everything aboard, it was just a few minutes before the train was to leave. Billy had decided he would stay with Slim and the horses, till the first stop anyway.

They all said their goodbyes. The whole crew got a surprise as each of the ladies gave them a hug and a peck on their checks. The Ladies where helped aboard the train. In a couple of minutes they waved to their crew as they departed from the train station.

After his long sleep Marshal Crampton caught up with Captain Taylor and the rest of the crew. He'd looked around some with surprise on his face as he saw Runs Far and his braves riding along with the cowboys. The pack horses had empty packs except for a few that were loaded with the new supplies. The wagon had just the box with Ben in it. Captain Taylor had already hired some men to work on building the trail good enough to get some wagons over it. He'd decided to concentrate on the tunnel first. Then the washout down into Peaceful Valley. There was a couple other places that would need a lot of work, also.

The Marshal carefully approached, then said, "Matt told me something about the Indians. I Didn't know he met they were part of the outfit."

Captain Taylor said, "Yeah. Matt made an agreement with them to ride scout for us. We know about anyone that could cause us any trouble long before they can get set up to attack us."

The Marshal asked, "How in the world did he ever talk them into doing that?"

Hesitating a few seconds, then choosing his words carefully he said, "He gave them a great gift. He's highly honored and respected buy them. Lastly some of them are family."

The Marshal took his time as he sorted everything out in his mind. As he remembered some of the events that had happened in town he said, "I see. Who do the other two young ladies belong too then?"

Captain Taylor had known that question would come sooner or later. But he still hadn't figured out a good way to explain. As he tried to form something up in his mind. Runs Far had rode in close and listened. He proudly said, "They are his women. He is very powerful. He is The Great Grizzly Spirit."

The Marshal couldn't hide the bewilderment that showed on his face. At first he thought a joke was being played on him. However he recognized the serious prideful tone to Runs Far's voice. When he'd glanced at him the Marshal saw he was dead serious. He'd decided it was better to talk about something else.

Early on the third day out the Marshal got his look at the carnage that had been left. The buzzards and other critters hadn't improved things either. It had been pleasant ride with Captain Taylor and the rest. The evenings had been real nice with the talk around the camp fire. Most of the talk was about The Great Grizzly Spirit and his women. The Indians liked to talk about them and the Marshal had gotten most of the details about the shootout before he had arrived at the sight. He just couldn't picture the girls in a shootout. Yes he admitted to himself that he had seen the guns on their hips. He still had a hard time putting them in the middle of what he looked at.

Knowing there was no rush Captain Taylor and his crew stood off to the side away from the stench of rotted flesh. The men that had been hired to work on the trail stood off by themselves. They saw the facts of the outlandish story they'd been listening to the last couple of days. Tex with the others that had actually been involved, were off in there little group as they went over the battle, in there minds. They left the Marshall to himself as he pawed through the bodies. He had, a handkerchief tied over his nose. The Marshal, had stuffed his saddle bags full with the most recent wanted posters he'd received. He'd spent a good hour going over the bodies. He'd checked there pockets and had found a large sum of money. Both paper and coins. He had a hard time comprehending that no one had taken the money. It was just the way Matt had told him. They'd taken the weapons and some horses nothing else. From what was left over of the bodies he was sure he had identified fourteen of them. A couple had big rewards. The other's ranged from a couple hundred, to five hundred dollars. The Marshal was quite pale when he finished and walked up to Captain Taylor and some of the others. Captain Taylor came up with a little bottle of whiskey. He handed it to the Marshal as he said, "Here Maybe this will help."

The Marshal took a big swallow, then said, "Thanks. I needed that."

The Captain, said, "We couldn't help but notice. I don't see how you stayed out there so long."

I was afraid if I didn't. I wouldn't be able to go back out there."

Captain Taylor asked, "Did you recognize anyone?"

"I'm confident I matched up fourteen of them with their posters. What should I do with the money I found and the reward money from the posters?"

Captain Taylor said, "I guess just have Mr. Benson deposit it in Matt's account."

The Marshal said, "Alright. It's hard to believe that none of you got hurt. It looked like the lead had to be as thick as a swarm of bees out there."

Tex said, "Like we told you. The hail of lead was going at them. Matt, Billy, and the ladies had them so full of lead. Before they'd gotten their gun's into action, there was noting for them to do. But to fall off their horses."

The Marshal finally excepted the story at face value. He, said, "I had determined that Matt would be a dangerous person to mess with. But I still have a hard time with the idea that the women are that good also."

Slade stated, "Well Marshal. Seeing is believing."

Before the Marshal had a chance to respond Dan said, "We have learned when it comes to the youngsters and trouble, there's nobody better to be riding with. You just have to be awful sudden or you miss it."

The Marshal nodded as he said, "Okay; I'm getting used to it. Well I guess I need to get back and fill out my report, to send it in. It should make a lot of law agencies happy."

After another fifteen minutes of conversation the Marshal departed and headed back to town. Captain Taylor and the rest of the crew headed on toward Peaceful Valley.

CHAPTER TWENTY SEVEN

ALIVE

It was the middle of the day when Mr. Maxton rushed into the house then yelled, "Valerie, Valerie, their alive! Their Okay!"

Mrs. Maxton rushed out of the kitchen as she wiped her hands on her apron. She asked, "What are you talking about. Was there an accident at the warehouse?"

"No, no, Connie, Helen, Billy and Matt. They are okay and coming home."

Valerie stopped in her tracks, as she held her right hand over her heart. With her face already pale she said, "Okay. Chris are you sure? I couldn't stand it if it's not so."

Chris rushed up to her then handed her the telegram as he said, "Here read it."

Valerie became teary as she read through it. She held the telegram in her left hand as she embraced her husband, then they gleefully did a little dance.

Then they heard footsteps as they rushed up the steps of their front porch. As he came through the door Mr. Mc Bain asked, "Chris! Is everything alright. I saw you run by the office like something was on fire."

The Maxton's rushed up to him and grabbed him as they turned him to join them with their little dance. Then Chris said, "Brad their all okay. Connie, Helen, Billy and Matt are coming home."

Brad said, "Glory be, Oh my. Good, good. When should they be here?"

Chris stopped, then said, "Oh, I don't know. Connie just said they were all fine and would be here as soon as possible."

Brad said, "Man that's so good to hear. It's going to be hard waiting for them to get here. But it is the best news I think, I've ever heard."

Valerie said, "Oh yes. The best ever. I guess I'm glad it will take them a little while. It will give me time to fix her room up. Oh I got so much to do."

Chris said, "Brad, I'm going to saddle my horse and take the Gates's their telegram. You should be alright at the office till I get back.

Brad said, "Yeah I'm be fine take your time. I'll let Bruce know."

As Chris rode up to the Gates house he was impressed of how good their crop's looked. They were doing a fine job. The whole place was neat and well taken care of. They had been real busy. Judy Gates saw him and paused to see who it was. Then continued on to the house with the basket of eggs she'd gotten from the chicken house. She yelled into the house and as Chris reined his horse to a stop Mrs. Gates came out onto the porch.

Always happy to see one of the Maxton's she worried, about what would bring him out in the middle of the week. She wiped her hands on her apron as she cheerfully said, "Won't you get down and have something to drink."

Chris dismounted then tied his horse to the hitching post. He said, "Thank you, some water would be nice."

Violet said, "Judy, Mr. Maxton would like some water."

Judy had just gotten to the doorway. She nodded then went back inside.   Chris asked, "Is Robert around?"

Violet said, "Yes. Joe and him are down behind the barn building a dam to catch some rain water. Just in case it gets a little dry later on."

Judy came out, then handed Chris a glass of water. Mrs. Gates then told her to go tell her father we have company.

Violet with a reserved cheerfulness said, "We may as well have a seat while we wait for them."

Chris knew his visit was a bit of a surprise. He concentrated hard to keep from grinning; from ear to ear. He said, "Yes, thank you. I can see you have really done wonder's with your place."

Violet with her eyes full of pride said. "Thank you. Robert and Joe have really been busy."

Chris said, "It show's."

After a few minutes Judy returned with Robert and Joe. Chris and Mrs. Gates had discussed some of the local events. Mr. Gates walked up and as Chris started to get up Robert said, "Stay relaxed." Then he smiled as he shook Chris's hand, then sat in a rocking chair while Joe sat down on the top step. Judy had gone into the house and returned shortly with glass's of water for Robert and Joe. They thanked her.

Robert said, "It's nice to see you. But I know you didn't come all the way out here just for a pleasure ride."

Not trusting himself to speak as the suspense was about to get him; also. Chris stood reached in his shirt pocket as he took a couple of steps, then handed the telegram to Robert.

Robert looked Chris in the eye, he hadn't been able to read anything from them. Then he unfolded the telegram as Mrs. Gates and the rest of the family had drawn look's, on their faces. Robert with pressed lips started to read. Then with disbelief on his face first to be replaced with a smile. Chris saw him as he reread it.

Robert jumped out of his rocker then rushed to his wife and pulled her up from her chair as he said, "Their alive; their fine. Their coming home."

Violet sighed as she held her husband then said, "Oh may; all this time and not a word . Are you sure?"

Robert, "Yes; it's right here."

Chris just stood back as Judy and Joe joined their parents as they celebrated the good news. When they had calmed down some, Robert turned toward Chris then said, "You rascal if there weren't any women present I'd give you a good piece of my mind. I thought for sure you had brought bad news. You knew what was in that telegram."

Chris smiled then said, "Not for sure. But I did suspect that it was the same as Connie's.

Violet said, "Oh! I had expected the worse. But this is such good news."

Chris said, "I think we all had. I know their are not here. But, I think we should have a little get together, to sort of rejoice some."

Violet said, "Yes. Oh, that would be so good.

Chris smiled and said, "Yes, this is such good news, we should celebrate some. We can have a big home coming when they get here."

Robert said, "Yes, I agree. I noticed she didn't say when or how they were coming.'"

Chris agreed, "No, Darn; Connie didn't give any details either."

Robert said, "Well, I'm just glad their alright."

Everyone agreed to that and after a little Chris departed. They'd made plans for a little get together after church Sunday. As he headed for home. He was happier than he'd been in a long time.

Mrs. Saxton had taken to visiting a lot and when at home did help around the house. She did anything she could to help get her mind off Matt. She still felt in her heart that he had to be alive. Just had to be. The threat of his loss had awakened her heart to how much she loved him. She just hoped for the chance to let him know. She was surprised as the carriage she'd rented brought her home to see their family carriage at the front steps of her home. She quickly paid, then rushed up the steps as she wondered what could have gone wrong now. James Fallon the head butler opened the door and welcomed her home. He took her light coat from her. It had been a cool windy day the third week of March. She thought it had been a warmer welcome than usual. She also thought he tried to keep something from showing on his face.

James said, "Your just in time Ma-am. The men are in the den."

She said, "Thank you."

Her heart skipped a beat as she hurried on. As she entered the den she smelled cigar smoke. Then heard glass click as Randolph poured some more whisky into his glass, as well as his son's.

When he heard her steps he turned with his drink and a giant smile appeared on his face as he gleefully said, "Ann! Oh good." He started to rush to her, then stopped and said, "Oh! Let me fix you a drink. Then we can really celebrate."

Ann looked at her son's who smiled from ear to ear. Well at least the thought of doom had been lifted from her heart. She smiled a little for she couldn't remember ever seeing Randolph as excited and confused before. She asked, "What are we celebrating?"

Randolph as he was in the process of pouring her some sherry stopped. Then as he gave her a dumbfounded look, his face illuminated again. He handed her the drink as he said, "I'm Sorry, I got ahead of you. Matt's okay. Connie and the others are fine. He's alive!"

Ann saw her sons nod, as tears filled her eyes. Randolph hugged her tight against his chest. As the emotions ran through her she was glad he held her so tight. Her knees had gotten weak. When Randolph felt her unsteadiness he eased her into a chair.

Michael said, "We couldn't stay at work, once we got the telegram."

Mark said, "Yeah! it's a glorious day."

Ann had taken a big swallow and as some color returned to her she said, "My prayer's have been answered. I never gave up on them. I just couldn't let go. Just give me a minute. I'm just so relieved right now. I don't have any strength and my thoughts are all mixed up."

Michael leaned down and kissed her on the cheek. Then said, "Yes, it's such a relief. Take your time. We kind of went through the same thing."

Just then, Margaret and Sue Saxton came in along with the rest of the house hold servants. They saw the jubilation and the drinks. Randolph saw James as he came up and shook his head. Randolph understood, he gave James a slight nod as he said, "Everybody, you can take the rest of the day off to celebrate or whatever you want to do. Matt, Connie and their friends are fine."

They gave a small cheer as relief crossed most of their faces. They took turns as they congratulated the Saxton's. Margaret a little put out whispered in Sue's ear as she said, "All this excitement is just for Matt?"

Sue looked around to see if anyone else had heard. With disbelief she said, "I'm so happy. We were all worried for him. You've got to be glad."

Margaret just said, "Humph."

Sue then went and gave Michael a big hug as she said, "Oh! I'm so glad."

Michael answered, "Yes, I think we all have come to realize how much we love Matt."

Ann with some of the women servants wept tears of relief and joy. Most of the women had acquired some glasses poured some sherry to sip while the men sipped whisky. As the celebration calmed down some. Ann more like herself stood and leaned against Randolph as she'd put her head on his shoulder asked, "Has anyone gotten word to the Sockett's or the Chan's?"

"No! But, your right. I can't remember ever being so relieved about anything before."

Ann looked at his face, then saw the intensity in his eyes. She gave him a big hug and kissed him full on the lips. Then said, "I love you."

Randolph a little uncomfortable, returned her hug and quietly said, "I love you to."

Ann asked, "You gave everyone the day off. What are we going to do for supper?"

Randolph said, "I guess we'll rent a carriage and eat out."

"Yes, that does sound good. I do feel like going out."

"Well I guess we ought to get ready. The others can fend for themselves. I'd like to be alone with you tonight. Let me have a word with Michael. Then I'll be right along."

She nodded and went to get ready. It had been along time since Randolph and her had gone out by themselves. First knowing that Matt was okay and now a chance to be alone with her husband. She couldn't be happier. As she got to the stairs for the second floor. James their head butler caught up with her. He reached up on a shelf as he said, "Ma-am, this came for you while you where out."

Ann took the telegram. As she thanked him. She saw that it was addressed to her. Wonderingly she went up to her room. When she'd read it, she was in complete amazement. She was to expect a large daft with all the details of what she was to do with it. She wondered how Matt could have so much money. It made her heart glow, that Matt put so much faith in her.

Randolph asked Michael if he would make sure, that the Sockett's and the Chan's were told of the good news. Then as he reached the top of the stairs he heard Meaghan as she was welcomed home by James. Randolph turned and went back down the stairs. Then embracing her with a big hug as he asked, "Did James give you the good news?"

"No, But I noticed he was awful cheerful."

"We got a telegram from Matt. He, Connie and their friends are okay."

"Oh dad! That's the best news ever. It's well. I'm just so happy."

With her eyes teary, she laid her head against his chest as he handed her his handkerchief. She sobbed quietly for a couple of minutes. When she calmed down and relaxed some. Randolph said, "We all feel the same way. I'd have sent for you. But no one knew where you were. I'm taking your mother out to celebrate. Michael is going out to let the Sockett's and the Chan's know."

Meaghan said, "Good; they should know. Do you think he would mind if I went along with him?"

"I think he would like it. I think he plans on leaving soon."

Meaghan kissed her father on the cheek saying, "Oh, thank you. I want to see if I can catch up with Michael."

"Yeah, run along."

Meaghan went in search of Michael as Randolph went upstairs. When he got to their bedroom Ann had changed into a pretty bright red gown and was busy brushing her hair. He walked up behind her saying, "Let me brush your hair. Meaghan's home. I told her the news. She's probably going to go with Michael to the Sockett's and the Chan's."

She answered, "Good I'm glad. What are the rest doing?"

"I don't know. I haven't heard a thing. I think they can take care of themselves though."

"Oh yes, I just wondered. Where are we going?"

Randolph asked, "How about the Diplomat steakhouse and pub."

"That'll be great. Thank you."

Sue decided to go along with Michael and Meaghan. They'd already left by the time Randolph and Ann had changed and spruced up. They were still an attractive couple. Randolph flagged down a carriage then helped Ann in. He told the driver where they wanted to go.

Michael had their driver take them to the Chan's. He told the driver to wait for them as he helped Sue and Meaghan down. After being welcomed into their home Michael told the Chan's the reason for their visit. Mrs. Chan and Sue Saxton hugged each other as Sue Chan and Meaghan did a little dance along with their gleeful hug. Lee Chan Jr. and Sawn Chan smiled as they congratulated them.

Lee Chan had just let a big knowing smile appear on his face as he said, "I didn't really expect anything different."

Meaghan asked, "You were really that confident?"

"Yes, I've seen the intensity and determination in his eyes."

Michael said, "I wish we could have had that much confidence. We've been worried a long time."

Sue Chan said, "We were worried too. But, dad told us he was confident they would be alright."

Sue Saxton said, "I'm just stunned, that you had so much confidence in Matt. Mr. Chan."

In his broken English Lee Chan said, "I trained him to fight in a special way. He ended up being the best I've ever seen. He would be able to take on a large number of people and defeat him."

Michael knew first hand, his brother was a fighter and never liked to give in. He was sure if Matt had really learned some special way to fight, he would be awful dangerous. He said, "Yes, if Matt has been highly trained in a special way, he would be a hand full."

Lee Chan smiled as he said, "Yes, he is very good and very fast."

The Saxton's after a few minutes departed with warm goodbyes. They returned to the waiting carriage. When Michael gave the driver their next destination he put the horses into a trot. They still had to make a run for the train. They'd just made it. It was the last one going out toward the Sockett's place.

When they arrived at the train station it was already late. They decided to visit the Sockett's before they looked for a room. With each of them carrying their own overnight bags Michael was able to flag down a carriage, to take them out to the Socketts. It took them thirty minutes to get there and were relieved to see their place lit up.

When he heard the horse and carriage. Vern had gotten up and stepped outside. He stood in the shadows as he waited to see who his guests were. Old habits where hard to break. As the driver brought the carriage to a stop in the light. Vern recognized the Saxton's. He asked, "What's got you folks out here this time of night?"

It had startled them when they'd heard his voice, coming in out of the dark. Until he had spoke, they hadn't realized that somebody was outside.

Michael said, "I'm sorry we're visiting so late. But we've got some news you should hear."

Vern stepped into the light with a guarded smile as he said, "Welcome. Come on in and make yourselves at home. You'll stay the night of course."

Michael said, "Oh no sir. We'll get a room in town after our visit."

Vern said, "Nonsense grab your bags. You'll spend the night here."

After they'd gotten out of the carriage Michael paid the driver. Vern took Meaghan's bag over her protest. Michael got his and Sue's bags, then followed Vern inside. When they were inside Vern said, "Jimmy, Diane take their bag's up to the guest rooms. Then hurry back. They've got news."

Mrs. Sockett heard them and had composed her expression. Vern's face was unreadable. They quickly carried out their assignments as Betsy welcomed them and gotten them seated. As Jimmy and Diane returned Mrs. Sockett set a tray of drinks and cookies on a small coffee table in front of the Saxton's. As all of the Sockett's sat down except for Vern, who stood patiently on balanced feet as he waited.

Michael said, "We received a telegram today. Matt, Connie and their friends are fine."

The Saxton's were startled as Mrs. Sockett, Jimmy and Diane jumped up, hugged, jumped and danced around gleefully. After a minute Betsy hugged her husband as she said, "Vern, you can show some emotion. I know your just as relieved as we are."

He smiled and hugged her back as he said, "I guess your right. Damned if I don't feel like doing a little jig."

The Sockett's joined hands and danced around in a little circle. After a couple of turns, Vern motioned for the Saxton's to join in. After a few minutes mostly out of breath they all sat down. Then Mrs. Sockett said, "That was the best news we've had in a long time. We have just about worried ourselves to death, over them."

Sue said, "Mrs. Saxton was so relieved, they thought she would have a heart attack. Well at least that's what Michael told me. She was still pale when I first saw her."

Betsy said, "I can understand. We sort of adopted Connie and Matt into our family a long time ago. We think as much of them as any other member of our family."

Diane said, "Yes. I have missed them terribly. I can hardly wait to see them again."

Meaghan said, "Oh me to. Now at least my mother can relax and rest. She's tried to stay busy and I know it was just an attempt to get her mind off Matt."

Betsy said, "I can just imagine. I've gone through a spell like that before. This was almost as bad."

The Saxton's had noticed the meaningful look she'd given Vern. They'd ended up talking for over an hour before they went to bed.

The next morning by the time the Saxton's were up, Vern had already gone to work. Jimmy worked with his father now and was gone also. Mrs. Sockett wouldn't let them leave until she'd fed them. Then she had Diane take the Saxton's to the train station. When Diane returned, she unhooked the horse from their buggy. After putting him in the corral she found her mother in the kitchen. She said, "I like the Saxton's that where here last night. Especially Meaghan."

Betsy said, "Give them time. Maybe you'll end up liking all of them."

Diane said, "They seemed more like real people, last night."

"I think their concern over Matt and Connie may have made all of them think more about their love, for each other. Sometimes it takes a disaster for some people to realize how much, someone mean's to them."

Mother and daughter had a pleasant day as they worked around the house. They discussed many things as the day had gone along. It was a better day than they'd had in along time.

Billy stayed with Slim for a little over twenty four hours. To make sure the horses had settled down. With the sway of the boxcar and the clatter of the tracks they had been nervous for quite awhile. They had gotten used to Slim being around them by then. Billy was sure Slim would be able to handle the horses. When the train stopped to take on water and coal, Matt and Billy made sure Slim had food and water as well as the horses.

On the third day they reached Sacramento California. They had no problem getting the horses out of the boxcar. They were more than ready to get their feet on solid ground. They found a hotel not far from the train station. When the three men had carried everything from the station up to the rooms they realized how much the women had brought with them. They got directions to a stable, then took the horses and put them up.

As Matt, Slim and Billy walked back to the hotel they spotted a general store were they could purchase their trail supplies. There were a lot of Spanish people around that looked them over good. Much of it was because of all the hardware, they wore. Slim was the only one that had a single pistol. Matt then made arrangements to store most of the things the women had brought. They were to take only what they needed for the trail. They would pick them up on the way back.

Rising early the next morning. After breakfast they packed their things on their horses. Matt, Billy and Slim had gotten them ready before they ate. The women had packed away all their clothes, except their trail clothes. They wore pants with flannel shirts. They all wore their moccasins except for Slim. So they wouldn't have to pack any more than they had to. They had decided to hunt for most of their food. When they got to the general store they purchased some spices, coffee and a few things to cook with. They wanted to travel light and planned on moving along at a fast pace.

After they'd visited the general store they made it twenty five miles out that day before they made camp. After caring for the horses they made a quick meal. Matt had gotten a couple of rabbits as it started to get dark. He'd been leading at the time and Slim never saw him draw. It was like the rabbits had fallen over from the noise. They did have bullets in them, however.

The next morning they were some what surprised by the women when they rolled up their bedrolls. They had decided to wear only their Moccasins and loin cloths they had brought along. Matt was learning and didn't say a thing. But as they observed the women Connie said, "The pants were to tight and it's warm enough for us."

Neither Matt or Billy said a thing as the coffee started to boil. They went to saddle the horses and pack everything up they didn't need to use for breakfast.

Slim said, "You can't go into a town or meet your folks like that."

Helen said, "We know that." She bent over and stirred the pot some, then said, "The foods about ready."

Two weeks out as they made camp that night they where a little over half way to Portland Oregon. They'd made good time. The horses had been on good grass most of the time. It had rained a couple times. All the women had done was put a slicker on over their shoulders. Matt, Slim or Billy would go into town for supplies whenever they got close to a town. Billy had scouted out ahead of them and had gotten a nice deer. They'd have something besides rabbit the next few days. They skirted around anyone they'd seen as they had decided they didn't need to advertise there presence. They had quickly set up camp. Then skinned the deer enough to cut off what meat they wanted for the next couple of days. They cooked up quite a lot and ate till they were stuffed.

Slim had been trail partners with quite a few riders. But the youngsters he rode with, were as good as any he'd ever rode with. They were very efficient at camp and on the trail. Slim had shook his head several times. They were like ghosts most of the time. He discovered, that if he wasn't careful, it seemed like they could be out of camp without him actually seeing them do it. A couple of times he would have sworn he had been looked right at them, when one of them appeared or disappeared.

Toward the end of April four days out from Portland, as they worked their way through a low mountain pass, they ran into seven wild looking riders headed south. The direction they had just come from. Slim had been out front scouting and returned back to let them know. After he'd questioned Slim. Matt decided to confront them a quarter of a mile further up the pass, where it widened out some. So they could spread out and not be bunched together.

When they got to the place Slim had described they spread out and waited. Matt was in the middle with Connie, Helen and Slim on his right. Star and Billy were on his left. They had to wait forty minutes before they heard the hoof beats. When they'd cleared a little rise and came into sight, they drew rein when they saw Matt and the others scattered out in front of them. With a command all the horses except for Slims had dropped their heads.

The riders as they approached spread out as much as they could. But the pass was narrow where they had stopped. It kept them pretty close together. They eased their horses ahead till they were within forty yards. A man with a big barrel like chest, that had been in the lead.

Looked at Slim as he asked, "What's the meaning of you confronting us like this."

With all of his riders highly alert, Matt said, "I'm sorry; I don't mean to alarm you. I just wanted to make sure we could pass each other safely."

The seven men looked Matt and his riders over good. Some showed amazement. While the others had lustful greedy looks, on their faces.

The one that had spoken before said, "At first glance I didn't see anything we could use. But now that I've had a chance to see better. You have some fine looking mounts and maybe something else that would give us a real good time.

Matt in a stern voice filled with malice said, "Be careful of what you say or do. If it comes to gun smoke we'll just leave you laid out on the ground where you fall."

Matt's statement had frozen them for a minute. A couple of them looked around nervously. One of the riders next to the big man said, "That's big talk for someone that has only one man among you, a child and three girls. Your almost a man. To bad you won't live to be one."

Matt said, "You've declared your intentions. You have got to count of five to change your minds and ride on through. That's it."

Some of them saw some humor in Matt's statement and chuckled a little. The big man chuckled a little saying, "You do have nerve. I'll."

That's all he got out. Matt had counted to five. He had his pistols out and fired each of them twice as the women and Billy drew their pistols. Some of the strangers had tried hard. But none of them had cleared leather before they were blown out of their saddles.

Slim had gotten his pistol out. But he never fired a shot. He just sat on his horse as he gaped at them. Then at the riders laid out on the ground. He didn't know who had shot who. But all of them had been shot at least four times. From what he could tell all of them had been hit dead center, in the chest.

Matt said, "Lets gather up their horses. I see a couple that look real good. Check out the weapons, there's probably some good ones."

Billy reined Three Socks after the other horses. Slim dismounted and started to check the bodies. Not a one had moved, since they had hit the ground. Slim found some good weapon's. Slim found a lot of money also. Fresh paper money and some gold coins. The women a little pale just stayed mounted then rode on a head to help Billy round up the loose horses. After Slim finished throwing everything of value into a pile he asked, "What, are we going to do with all of it."

Matt said, "We'll pack everything along and turn it over to the law."

Slim asked. "What do you figure? Bank money?"

Matt said, "Yeah, that's what I think."

Billy returned with a couple of horses. They packed all the valuables on them. Star, Connie and Helen with the reins of the other horses waited for them. Matt then rode up and led them on through the pass. Early in the afternoon they found a good place to make camp. It was early. But they'd decided it was to nice to pass. They all thought they could use a good break.

It was a quiet camp for the most part. They just sat around and sipped coffee while the food cooked. After he'd eaten Matt took his cup of coffee and relieved Slim who'd been on guard duty. Helen, Billy and Connie had to be in anticipation of meeting their parents. Matt was sure the days events were on their minds, also. As he'd thought about it. He knew that in reality, he hadn't given them a chance. He wasn't going to either. Not when any of the women were involved.

CHAPTER TWENTY EIGHT   HOMECOMING PORTLAND

On the third day after the shootout. They had about a two hour ride to Portland when they'd made camp. It was still a couple of hours before dark. But they'd found a good place to bathe and get cleaned up. They brushed out the cloths they planned on wearing in the morning.

The next morning after their meal. Billy, Matt and Slim saddled the horses and packed everything up while the women got ready. When they had finished and made an appearance. They'd brushed their hair and their ceremonial dresses on. Matt, Billy and Slim couldn't help, but smile. Connie asked, "What are you grinning at."

They hadn't realized they were. As they looked at each other, Billy said, "I guess, that it's. Well, you look real uncomfortable.

Star said, "We are."

Matt said, "Well I guess the sooner we leave the better then."

When they arrived at Portland, Slim guided them along. As they rode through the city they received a lot of looks. Especially, with the women being straddle, they showed some leg. They still insisted on wearing their holster belt and guns. Slim pointed out the warehouse. When Matt spotted the house. He was sure it was the Maxton place. Matt could see Chris's touch, illustrated by the way it had been built. Slim verified it for him as he pointed it out. Matt led them up to the tie rail in front of the house. Then he helped the women dismount. While Billy and Slim tied up the horses they had accumulated from the shootout. Slim then tied his horse up. Flame and the other horses that belonged to Billy and the women would stay ground tied.

Connie said, "Oh; I'm so nervous and excited too."

Helen said, "Me to! But, let's see if anyone's home."

Star hadn't said anything. But they all had seen how tense she was. The noise of their horses as they settled down around the tie rail announced them as they climbed the steps up to the porch. Connie with the rest of the women approached the front door with Matt, Billy and Slim behind them. Connie raised her hand to knock when she heard footsteps as they crossed the floor inside. Mrs. Maxton opened the door and saw Connie. She exclaimed, "My Lord, when! Oh! It's so good to see you. You look good. Are you alright?" She'd spoken as she hugged Connie like she'd never let her go. She started sobbing as she wiped tears from her eyes. Then she spotted Helen and said, "Oh my dear, give me a big hug. We've been so worried about all of you."

When she'd finished hugging Helen she turned to Billy and gave him a giant hug as she kissed him on the cheek. She said, "Oh you've grown. My your solid too."

Billy was a little embarrassed. Mrs. Maxton then put her full attention on Matt. She looked up at him with admiration in her eyes. She made Matt bend down so she could hug and kiss him. Then she said, "My, Oh, My! I didn't think it was possible. But you've spurted up. You must be six four now if not more. Oh! Thank you so much. I know if it hadn't been for you we'd have lost them."

She had embarrassed Matt with the compliment as much as anything. When Mrs. Maxton looked at Star Connie said, "Mother, I'd like you to meet Bright Star. She was a captive with us, also. We have been calling her Star."

Valerie embraced her saying, "Oh! You poor dears. It must have been real hard on all of you."

She stepped back and gave them all a good look as if to verify that they were really there. Slim stood back on the edge of the porch as he had kept away from the on slot of affection he was witnessing. He looked like he'd tried to hide a tear or two. Mrs. Maxton then said, "My, my. You all look like a bunch of desperados. Oh; come on in, all of you. If your dad comes home for lunch, he'll be here soon. Sometimes he gets a little something at a place next to the office."

She led them into the living room and as they sat down, she said, "You'd probably like something to drink. Oh! You've got to be hungry also."

She hadn't waited for an answer. She spun around and headed for, what they figured was the kitchen. Connie, then Helen with Star followed after her. Matt, Billy and Slim heard her tell them she could get everything. That they should relax. Then they heard a lot of chatter as they got reacquainted and made new acquaintances. Within a few minutes they returned with a tray of drinks and another tray of some home made cookies and donuts. Valerie said, "It's not much. It should be enough to get you through till supper."

After she paused a little she said, "Helen, Billy; if you want to you can spend the night here. We would be glad to have you."

Helen said, "I think I'd like to. I don't know what Billy wants to do?"

Billy said, "Ma-am, not to just rush off. But after I get some more of those fantastic cookies. I'd like to ride on out to see my folks, if you'll give me some directions.

Valerie said, "Oh I forgot. Yes, I can give you directions. I'm sorry, I'm so excited about seeing all of you again. I'm not thinking straight. Oh! Slim can tell you how to get there better than I can."

Slim caught with his mouth full, nodded then swallowed. He then said, "Yes Ma-am. I'll be glad to Billy."

Billy nodded as he helped himself to another cookie. Connie, Helen and Star felt Mrs. Maxton's eyes on their bellies with a wondering question in her eyes. She hadn't asked anything yet. Mrs. Maxton told them how good things had come together for them. As she'd talked Matt noticed that Star relaxed more and more. Mrs. Maxton had always been friendly and understanding. Matt started to feel the walls closing in around him and realized how much of an adjustment. Star had to be going through, being around the towns and all the people. When Billy finished and excused himself. Matt got up and went out with him. Slim not to be left alone with the women grabbed a cookie as he followed them out.

When they were outside, Billy asked, "What are we going to do with all of the horses?"

Matt said, "I've been giving that some thought. You go on a head, Slim and I will unpack them and picket them out. Tomorrow I'll see if I can't find the sheriff and let him decide what's to be done. Flame and the others won't be a problem.

Billy said, "I can help you."

Matt said, "No, go on. It'll give us something to do. There's no rush."

Slim told Billy how to get to his folks place. As Billy mounted and rode off. Matt and Slim led the horses to the Maxton's barn. Removing the saddles and harness they stored them away, then picketed the horses out to graze. They took their time and had just finished when they saw Mr. Maxton riding up. Slim had made up his mind to find a hotel room. Matt made sure Slim had money and for Slim to let him know where he was, in case something came up. Slim mounted and rode off. He paused a minute to talk with Mr. Maxton, then rode on. Matt stood by the tie rail waiting. Mr. Maxton rode up with a grin from ear, to ear. After dismounting and tying his horse up. Chris gave Matt a huge hug and patted in on the back. He said, "I can't believe I'm looking at you. I guess as hard as we tried I didn't think we would see any of you again. Lord it's good to see you."

Chris then stepped back and looked Matt over from head to toe. Then he said, "Well, you don't look any worse, from all the wear and tear."

Matt said, "No, I feel fine."

"Good. Good. Man it was a big relief, when I got that telegram. It is great to see you again."

"It's great to be here to. You've got a nice place. You've been busy."

Chris said, "Well, I guess we've done pretty good. Now, that Connie and you are here, it's the best thing we could have done."

Matt saw the questioning look in his eyes. He said, "Their inside. Don't worry about me, go on in. I would like to just sit in one of your chairs and look things over."

Chris nodding said, "Yeah okay. Just make your self at home."

Chris climbed the steps, crossed the porch, opened the door and went inside. When Connie heard his steps with her mothers nodded assurance, that it was her father she got up and rushed to embrace him. They'd met at the threshold of the living room were they hugged and kissed each other. Chris said, "Lord, it's so good to hold and feel you in my arms."

Connie said, "I've missed you so much."

Holding her out he said, "Let me look you over. It's still hard to believe your okay."

Connie turned as she said, "Father you remember Helen and I want you to meet Bright Star, who was a captive with us."

Chris looked at Helen as he smiled. Then he stepped up to her and they hugged. Helen then said, "Star is a very good friend of ours now."

Chris glanced at Helen as Star timidly approached. Chris hugging her said, "It's good to meet you. I can't imagine what all of you have been through."

Connie got a little nervous as her father kept glancing at her belly, as well as Helen and Stars. Connie got the tray of cookies as she said, "Dad, you must be hungry. We found out already, that mothers cooking is better than ever."

Chris said, "I'm so glad to see all of you. Thanks, I am hungry."

Mrs. Maxton said, "Well, everyone sit and relax. Chris, I've been catching them up on what we've been doing."

Chris answered, "I was a little late today. I had an invoice I wanted to finish. I'm glad I did. Brad can take care of things the rest of the day."

Valerie said, "Oh good, I'm glad. We need to make up some beds and get their rooms ready."

As the women looked from one to another. Chris said, "Oh sure. I saw the things packed on the horses. I'll get Matt to help carry them up to the guest rooms."

Valerie said, "Yes, that will be good. Us gals can fix up something real special for supper tonight. Connie I've been fixing up your room, ever since we got your telegram. I hope you like it."

Connie wished Matt was present. Just having him near always made her more confident. She'd decided to go ahead and get everything out in the open. As she composed herself, she gave Helen and Star a meaningful look.

Connie said, "Matt and you can take everything up and put it in my room. We should have time to fix everything up before it's bedtime."

Thinking he knew what she met, Chris said, "Oh, you girls want to be together."

Connie smiled nervously as she said, "Yes, with Matt; also."

Chris still not quite comprehending said, "I know you all have probably gone through a lot and are used to being close to each other. But Connie you know that wouldn't be proper."

Valerie looked from one to the other with some relief, as understanding started to appear on her face. Connie wanting to make sure there wasn't any misunderstanding said, "Father, Matt is the father of our children. Also, in a certain sense he's our husband."

Valerie understood. She tried to put things together in her mind. She was relieved though. It seemed at least, that her worse fear hadn't happened. Realizing her thoughts she glanced at Star, then felt a little guilty for the thoughts she'd had. She liked Star already and decided she had to think things through, a little more. Chris was going through a lot of different emotions. As he tried to keep under control. Finally with his face red, he said, "Well! I will. I like Matt. I know I probably owe Matt for your life. But, It's not right."

Connie had been impressed by her fathers control. She had excepted a lot worse. Encouraged by his control she stepped up to him and gave him another hug as she said, "I didn't say it was right. But thank you for understanding."

Connie then turned and said, "Mother, lets start fixing something real special for tonight."

As the women left him headed for the kitchen he had trouble finding the words he wanted to say. He finally got out. "I didn't say that I understood."

They kept going as Mrs. Maxton motioned them on. When they were in the kitchen she said, "I think you did just fine, Connie. He'll be alright once he's over the shock of it. Once we hear the whole story we'll probably understand a lot better."

Helen said, "That's a comfort Ma-am. I guess in a way that's why I was glad to stay here. Well also, I figured Matt would stay here."

Valerie said, "That's fine. I'm happy to have you. Bright Star, I'm happy your here also. Something's are not as strange, as they were to me when you first got here."

The women did take off their gun belts to hang them up on some peg's. They chatted women's talk as they worked.

Chris stared at the entrance of the kitchen for a couple of minutes. Then he took a couple of deep breathes of fresh air and composed himself. Then he walked out on the porch. He looked at Matt where he sat in a chair, out of the sun. He said, "We may as well carry your things in and get you settled."

Matt stood, then said, "Yes sir, that sounds good."

After they'd carried everything in and took them up to Connie's room. Mr. Maxton said, "I guess while we're up here, we may as well move a bed in from one of the other rooms."

Matt surprised at his composer wisely didn't say a thing. In a few minutes they had moved another bed in and put it beside the other one. Finished they went down stairs. Chris persuaded Matt to join him in the living room. They randomly discussed some the things that were going on around Portland. The women came into the living room and they all chatted pleasantly for a while. They told the men they would be having chicken, potatoes and green beans. They decided to bake an apple pie, for desert.

Billy followed the directions that Slim had given him. He made good time as Three Socks moved along rapidly on his own. He had picked up on Billy's excitement. With his farmers eye, he could see that his family had a real nice place and had all ready done an enormous amount of work. Billy kneed his horse up the lane leading to the house and barn. He could hear some noise coming from behind the barn. He saw some movement in the house. When Three Socks eased up to the tie rail, Billy just stayed in the saddle as he looked the place over. He heard some movement in the house as someone was busy fixing the evening meal; it sounded like. He had caught a couple of whiffs of something, that smelled real good.

He crossed his arms and leaned on the saddle horn as he just took in the sights and sounds of the place. As he looked toward the barn he caught the movement and sound of the front door being opened. He looked back to see his sister caring a bucket of water. Upon seeing him she stopped and asked, "Can I help you mister."

Billy smiled as he said, "Hello sis. How are you doing? Let me carry that water for you."

Judy froze in her tracks. As Billy quickly dismounted; she finally said, "Billy; It's really you."

As she started to yell inside. Billy said, "S--h, Walk with me and show me where you want the water."

Having all she could do to control herself she asked, "Billy, are you sure? I know what you plan. Mom will be awfully startled if you sneak up on her."

Billy said, "I'm not going to sneak up on her."

Judy handed him the bucket and as Billy carried it. She grabbed his other hand and led him to some rose bushes she'd been watering. She asked him a bunch of questions that he never got a chance to answer before she'd asked him another. When they'd returned and gone into the house. Judy led him into the kitchen and motioned for him to put the bucket on the floor at the end of the counter. Judy had stopped at the door way. His mother was busy with something on the counter. She said, "Thank you dear. I need you to start fixing the potatoes now."

Billy said, "I don't mind carrying water. But messing with potatoes isn't for me."

Mrs. Gates gasped, dropped what she was working on, onto the counter. She quickly turned, rushed to him, then hugged and kissed him. She held him for about two minutes as she wept all over Billy's chest. Then she stepped back as she wiped the tears from her eyes, she mixed flour into them. Getting a towel Judy helped clean her eyes. Mr. Gates gained control of her voice saying, "We have been expecting you. But you completely startled me."

Judy said, "I told him ma. But he wouldn't listen."

Mrs. Gates said, "You've grown. I think your shoulders are broader also. Billy, you sure look good."

Judy said, "Ma, you should see his horse. He's beautiful. He is your horse; right?"

Billy nodded, "Yes. I trained him my self. I'll tell you, all about it. But it is a long story."

Violet said, "Judy, go get your father and brother."

Billy said, "I'll get them mother. It'll give me a chance to look things over some more. You've done good."

Violet suddenly asked, "Billy, where's Helen? You shook me up so bad, I forgot all about her."

Billy turned back and looking at her, then said, "I was wondering when you'd get around to her. She's fine. She decided to stay at the Maxton's. I'm going to let her know, that you had all, but forgotten her."

Violet said, "Billy, you better not. It's your fault anyway."

Billy laughed, "Yeah maybe. But it'll be fun watching you try to explain it to her." then relenting some Billy continued, "Helen wanted to stay with Matt and you'll get to see her soon."

Before she could say anything else he'd turned, and left. She frowned as she thought. It didn't sound like Billy had laughed much, at all.

Out side Billy led Three Socks to the barn and unsaddled him. Billy spent a good fifteen minutes rubbing him down with a curry comb and brushing him off good. Billy then led him to the corral and turned him loose. Billy still looked the place over and admired it. He went the long way around the barn, to where all the noise was coming from. As it turned out it took him right up to the back corner of the barn. The corral ran a little past the barn, then made a right angle down to a little stream. His brother and father had their backs turned as they were busy building, what Billy was sure would be a hay rack when it was finished. When he stopped Billy said, "By the time you get your tools put away and washed up, mother should have supper ready."

They'd turned as one to look at him. Joe said, "Billy!"

Joe ran up to his brother and gave him a big hug. Robert looked his son over good then walked up as he wiped his hands on his pants. They shook right hands, then Robert gave Billy a big hug with his left arm. Then Robert took a step back as he released Billy's hand. He smiled as he said, "You've grown and by what I see in your eyes. You have grown into a man. I take it. You have been through a lot and seen even more."

Billy said, "Yes sir."

Robert said, "Well! We'll gather up our tools and be right along."

Billy helped them gather up their tools. After he'd cleaned up he waited in the dinning room part of the big front room, they used for there living and dinning. Robert had observed his eldest son. He'd watched the way he moved. Billy noticed everything he thought. Billy's whole posture had changed. The biggest thing though was his eyes. Robert could see, that they were eyes, that had seen a lot of pain, violence and only the Lord knew what else. Robert thought Billy was already all the man he would ever be. Billy still had a lot things to learn. But Billy's nature had already been developed to make him the man he was at fifteen. It was past Billy's birthday by a couple of months. Robert was sure the way the guns were hung on Billy (Much like Matt) that he was real efficient with them. Evidently he had learned how to use them in a short time. Robert was not enthused about that. But Billy was alive, that was the important thing. They'd had a good meal, and talked late into the night. The only thing that had put a damper on the fire. Was that the Gates wondered why Helen had stayed at the Maxton's, instead of coming on home with Billy. Billy was sure he knew the reason why. But he decided, that it was up to Helen to deal with it. The Gates had kept up with the crops and took a few days off. There wasn't much to do, except for someone having to milk the two cows and gather up some eggs.

At The Maxton's they'd enjoyed their meal and after they'd had a little conversation. Mrs. Maxton got some towels and night gowns for the girls. With the girls help she heated some water for the bath house. They'd built it behind the kitchen. The girls cleaned up in warm water for the first time in about forty days. It had been so pleasant and had relaxed them so much. They were sleepy and ready for bed. When they had given their goodnights and headed up stairs. Matt took a quick bath in the lukewarm water, then joined them.

They'd slept late the next morning. Well except for Matt. He'd woke up with the sun. Then he had just laid still, watching them sleep. Their blankets and sheets had crept down around their hips during the night. It had been a nice comfortable night. He'd watched as their breasts rose and fell with their breathing. Knowing what caused it he even liked the swelling of their bellies. He still had not sorted things out in his mind. He couldn't see how he could be in love, with all three of them. He just knew that he was. They were so brave. They were as determined to protect him, as he was to protect them. He was so proud of them. Then they were just gorgeous also. One by one they'd started to stir and wake up. Connie murmured, "I slept so good. I'd forgotten how good a nice soft bed was."

Helen yawned, "Yes, it's so nice. I've never slept on one this soft.

Star awakening said, "Maybe it's not so good. The sun is high in the sky."

Connie laughed, then teasingly said, "Listen to you. I don't think your happy, unless you got some work to do."

Star spoke her language as she said, "That's not true. I know something that makes me very happy."

She looked directly at Matt. He'd gotten her meaning right off and before he knew it, their covers were thrown aside. It was a couple hours later, before Matt made it down stairs. He started to heat up some water. Mrs. Maxton came into the kitchen then said, "I'll fix some breakfast for all of you. I know you've got to be starved. I think you need to keep your strength up."

Matt glanced at her. But hadn't caught her expression as she had already turned away from him. He was glad because his face felt like it was red hot. He'd just, gotten the water warm when the women came down stairs. Mrs. Maxton asked, "Did you sleep good?"

All three of them simultaneously said, "Oh yes it was beautiful."

Mrs. Maxton looked them over good and decided she'd never seen anybody, any happier. They seemed to glow. She thought she'd better make sure to give Matt an extra portion. Valerie said, "I'll have breakfast ready by the time you finish your baths."

They nodded as they cheerfully went on to the bath house. Valerie then decided right or wrong she was all for the relationship the girls and Matt had. She was convinced it was right for them. They took their time with breakfast. Matt told them he was going to find the sheriff to take care of the horses and the other things they saved for him.

Matt got the horses and all of the other things. It took him awhile to saddle and pack everything on them, then string them together. When he arrived at the sheriffs office. He tied the lead horse to the tie rail. The sheriff was in and he explained what had happened. Matt told the sheriff that they hadn't messed with the saddle bags other than filling up a couple of them with the stuff they'd taken off, the dead men. The sheriff explained if the horses were stolen, that he might not be able to find the owners. That he couldn't take care of them. Matt told him to sell them and give the money to an orphanage or some other good cause.

When Matt returned back at the Maxton's. He unsaddled Flame and turned him loose in the small corral. There was still some fresh grass in it. Mr. Maxton had returned as he was walked to the house. He tied his horse to the tie rail, then said, "It's a nice day. Isn't it?"

Matt nodded. It was sunny with a nice cool breeze coming in from the ocean. He said, "Yes. How often is it like this."

"Oh, it's usually quite pleasant here. Sometimes it's a little rainy. But the temperature is usually mild, it doen't get very hot and it's rare that it gets down to freezing."

They'd gone into the house as Mr. Maxton talked. He got a quick bite to eat and something to drink. Then he told them he had some things that had to be done at the office. After he'd gone Mrs. Maxton asked Matt to hook up their carriage. He didn't have long to wonder why. She asked him to drive her and the girls into the city. She directed him to a women's shop. Then she told him she wanted to buy something for her daughters.

Matt had been surprised by her comment. But decided not to say a thing. After a couple hours they came out carrying their purchases. Matt got out and helped them aboard. When they returned home the women went in to fix supper. Mr. Maxton returned shortly and helped Matt take the things upstairs. Matt then put the carriage and horse up. During supper Mr. Maxton told them he had a surprise for them in the morning and that he would like to get an early start.

Early the next morning Billy showed up. Right after Matt and Mr. Maxton had hooked up the carriage. Matt had already saddled Flame. The ladies had on new dresses. They had fixed up their hair and looked very pretty. Matt had noticed what they'd decided to put on. He had gotten out his black jeans and black shirt with a string tie. Mr. Maxton had a few things he kept at the house and Matt had been able to find a black Stetson to go with his outfit. The women thought he looked very handsome.

Billy had dressed up in black dungarees and a burgundy double breasted shirt with a string tie. Mr. Maxton drove the carriage. He took the lead as Matt and Billy followed. In a hour after a good climb, he stopped at a lake that was beautiful. There was some snow capped mountains off in the distance. Then he took them to one view point after another. The scenery had been beautiful. Mr. Maxton looked at his watch then said, "I hope you have enjoyed the sights. I'm getting hungry. We can see more some other day."

They all agreed and turned to head back. It was three o'clock when they returned to the Maxton's place. Mr. Maxton with Matt helped the ladies out of the carriage. Then he said, "Matt, Billy, lets get something to drink, then we can take care of the horses and the carriage."

They agreed and stepped up on the porch. Mr. Maxton opened the door then stepped back as he motioned the women on in. He still held the door as he motioned for Matt and Billy to go on a head of him. Suddenly the room came alive with a loud. "Surprise!"

The living room was full of people. It had been decorated. They'd hung up a big sign that said welcome home. The Gates's rushed to Helen. They hugged and kissed her. The Mc Bain's, then Bruce Hart had hugged and kissed Connie. They'd swapped from one girl to the other. Some people they didn't know welcomed Bright Star. They were friends of the Maxton's and the Gates's. That they'd made after they'd arrived at Portland. Some of the people were friends they'd made on the move west. Mr. Maxton, made introductions as things quieted down some. They shook Matt's and Billy's hands. They had lots of food and drinks. Slim had made it to. They had been asked quite a few questions about their ordeal. Everyone had been respectable though and it had turned out to be a grand party.

Mr. Gates had noticed Helen's condition. When a few minutes had gone by he'd motioned for her to go outside. Mrs. Maxton had noticed and as Helen headed out after her parents she hurried and was only a few steps behind Helen as they went out. Chris noticed that something was going on and drifted out behind them.

Robert had gone out and stopped under a big Douglas Fir tree. When he'd turned back and saw the Maxton's. He acted like he was a little displeased, that they had joined them. Valerie usually not one to meddle into other families business. Had decided she didn't want to see the party get ruined. So she decided she would let them know where she stood. When Robert acted like he was about to say something. Valerie surprised them when she cut him off, as she said, "Matt is the father of her baby, as well as Connie's, and Star's. They are all one family and after you see how they interact with each other like I have. I'm sure you'll agree with me."

Valerie had stunned them. Helen was the first one to get her senses. She hugged Valerie as she said, "Thank you ma."

It was more than Valerie had hoped. She hugged and kissed her check.

Robert's face had gone through a bunch of different expressions. With his lips like a fish out of water, he finally formed some words. He asked, "You really, don't have a problem with it?"

Valerie answered, "Not in the least."

Violet said, "Well, it's all ready done; Robert."

Robert took a deep breath, as the truth of his wife's statement had gone through him. He looked at Chris, then asked, "You don't have a problem with it?"

No-o. I've been around them, more than you have. I've come to think, that somehow they do belong together. Don't get me wrong. I had to sort things out in my mind too."

Robert paced a little then said, "I don't think it's right. But it is done. It is not a good thing to my way of thinking. It was not the way you were brought up and you knew better."

Helen said, "None of us have said it was right. But it has happened and there's no way to hide it."

Robert relented then, "Alright. But it's going to take some getting used to. I will not admit that is alright with me. But like Chris said, it is already done."

Helen hugged him as she said, "Thank you father, I love you."

Valerie said, "Let's get back to the party."

Robert hugged Helen again, then said, "I love you too. It's just that, I'm not used to you being all grown up. Let's go."

They'd eaten and drank. Then sat around and talked. They'd been asked a lot of questions. Finally after Connie had confided with Billy, Star and Helen. Connie raised her voice loud enough for everyone to hear said, "We'll tell you everything that happened. It will take awhile and some may not like what you hear. So, we'll give you a little time to get some drinks or whatever. Then after you get settled we will tell you our story."

After a few minutes after they had started to tell them their story. Connie saw Matt as he slipped outside. Billy had started the narration. Slim stayed, he hadn't gotten tired of the story yet. No one had left. There had been a few oh-s and ah-s as everyone listened, intently. Darkness had claimed the land by the time Billy and the women had finished their story. At times there had hardly been a dry eye, as they'd heard some of the details. They were amazed at all Billy, Matt and the women had gone through. There was not one look of condemnation as they'd finished their story. Then they got another round of hugs and kisses from most of the people. It was then, that some wondered where Matt had gone. But they hadn't let it ruin the mood.

Matt had taken care of Flame, unhooked the carriage and put Mr. Maxton's horse up. After that Matt had gone for a walk and hadn't returned until all the quests had gone. The girls had already gone to bed.

Billy, Matt and the women spent two weeks in Portland. Then they decided that it was time to go. They had many things that needed to be done. They had already put some things in motion. It was time to get on with the rest of their future plans.

Billy had spent most his time at his parents place. Billy told his family that he would be leaving with the others. His father told him, he had realized that right off. Then he'd stated that Billy had been changed, by the events he'd gone through. His biggest concern was, that Billy would stay on the right side of the law. Billy assured him that he would. Matt and the women had visited the Gates's often.

The families were emotional with them leaving so soon. They were just getting used to having them around and had admitted their fear, for the youngsters safety. There was concern for the girls, because of the their condition also. The Maxton's and the Gates's had insisted on a big send off. So they had another party the last night they stayed. The

Maxton's had hired four musicians. They'd danced and enjoyed another big feast. Matt had even started to warm up to the parties some. He had kind of taken to the dancing part of it. It had been a grand time, that had gone on well after dark.

Billy and Slim had stayed over at the Maxton's. It had been a short night for them. Billy, Slim and Matt had everything tied and packed on by the time the women were ready to go. Matt had purchased a couple of pack animals to carry the things that had been given to them. They had gotten up early and had hit the trail at the crack of dawn.

Captain Taylor and the rest of Matt's riders. With Run's Far and his braves had made the trip to Peaceful Valley and back a couple of times. They had dug a grave and laid Ben in his final resting place. The head stone had been finished and they'd set it in place the last trip. Captain Taylor with Dan's help, had purchased a couple pieces of sheet metal and took them to the gold ledge. They then made a trough with holes in it to sort out some of the gravel from the gold. They had bought a larges cast iron pot to melt the gold in. Then poured the melted gold into the trench to the clay moulds.

There had been, a couple more attempts of robbing the gold. They had handled them much like Matt had done. Hawkeye had gotten a shoulder wound. Tex had been hit just over his right hip. Slade had gotten hit by a slug through his left thigh. Which had hit his horse that bucked him off and broke his left arm. He had yelled and cussed some as they set it. They tied a couple of short branches to his arm to hold it in place. Three horses had be put out of their suffering after they'd been hit. They had been replaced, with the outlaws mounts. Marshal Crampton had ridden out to check the bodies. Then make out his reports to send to his headquarters. He told them they were making a fortune in reward money.

The work on the tunnel was coming along good. Captain Taylor had forty people at work on the tunnel and the washout going down into Peaceful Valley. It looked like the next time they came out, a wagon would be able to make it through. Then he would have them start on the draw, where it dropped into the creek. The trail along by the creek would take a lot of work also.

When they were in town the last time. Captain Taylor had given them a week off to unwind and get healed up some. Captain Taylor had stayed at the Young's. Quite a lot had happened at the Young's, also. They had complained some, that Captain Taylor had paid them to much. Captain Taylor explained to them he was just followed orders. Fred had hired a couple of farm boys, who's families had been having a hard time making ends meet. They were good workers and had already made a lot of repairs. The old forts walls had been repaired. They could close and open the gates. They had cut hay and put it in the stable.

There was an addition to the Young's family. It had been caused by a Comanche raid on his youngest brother's little ranch in Texas. Everyone had been killed except for his niece. She had survived because her father had seen them coming. She'd been at the well. He had thrown her in the well and instructed her not to come out until she knew for certain it was safe. The bucket had been left outside of the well. The water had been four feet deep. It had taken her over a day of making hand and foot holds to climb the sixteen feet to the top. The place had been burnt to the ground and the rest she hadn't talked about.

What family there was in Texas had sent her on to Wyoming. Thinking that a change of scenery would go along way in helping her to recover. They hadn't the means to take care of her, anyway. She was a good worker and obedient. She talked very little. But what everyone noticed was that her eyes were kind of dull. Her expression hadn't changed one time since she'd been there. Her name was Jenna Young. She was five foot one, a hundred thirty pounds. A little heavy boned. But with a very shapely body with arms a little longer than usual. A pretty pleasant face, that was a little pale. Blue eyes and long blond hair with a reddish tint. She was eighteen.

Captain Taylor, and Matt's riders where always a welcome sight at the Young's. Run's Far and his braves were no problem either. There had been some concern for Jenna, when she first arrived. The Young's had prepared her, not knowing how she would react with a lot of Indians around. She had just kept her distance. Sometimes she would go to her room to stay, until they left. It had surprised everyone when it was Run's Far, who in his calm voice seemed to have won her trust, as much as anyone. For they thought she would be afraid, because she was the only one that had survived an Indian raid. She liked horses and it was found out that she was real good with them. So when Mrs. Young didn't need her. She was assigned to help take care of the horses and the tack in the stables. She was a top hand, at repairing harness.

Mrs. Saxton had gotten Matt's draft, a couple of weeks after she had received the telegram. She was surprised at how much it was for. She opened an account in his name. But made sure she would be able to draw funds from it. She already had made some inquires about the Bingham Mansion. So it had taken her only a week to make the purchase. Matt hadn't given her a hint why he wanted it. The detailed letter he sent with the draft had given her a rough outline to follow. That was all; she hoped that she would have it done like he wanted. The property had a eight foot stone wall all the way around it. One gate with a driveway going up to the front of the Mansion. There it made a big circle in front of the wide steps that went up to the main entrance. The Mansion was made mostly out of stone. It had a huge basement for storage under most of it. It had four huge pillars that held up the balcony that came out from the third floor. The third floor had six large bed room's, of equal size. The second floor had a large room that could be used for a den or library. Then there was couple of rooms that could be used for den's sitting rooms or offices. The first floor at the top of the steps up from the driveway. Had a big patio across the front. Inside the main entrance of the big double door's. There was a big foyer with big walk in closets on each side. A grand hall went from the foyer all the way back to a big kitchen. Next to the kitchen there was a huge dinning room. From the dinning room there was a solid wall except for another set of double doors close to the foyer. The doors opened up into a huge banquet hall with a massive fire place at the far end. The fire place provided heat for the dinning room also. There was a cast iron baffle so it didn't demand a huge fire, for the dining room. The other side of the hall on the left in from the main entrance. There was a wide spiral staircase from the foyer up to the other floors. From the staircase back toward the kitchen there were eight small rooms. Lastly there were two large rooms next to the kitchen. All the rooms had been used for live in quarters, for the servants

She'd hired a contractor to fix the place up and to modernize it with all the latest conveniences that had come along the last few years. They were busy installing plumbing for hot water as well as cold. Then something called D. C. electric for the lights. They had made sure the chimneys were sound. A coal burning boiler to heat water, was to be installed in the basement. Next to the kitchen, a big cooler to keep ice and other perishables was being installed.

Matt had asked her to keep it a secret. She trusted Meaghan and she was doing well in college learning the ins and outs of engineering buildings. She'd decided to ask for her help. Meaghan had been able to get her professor to go out and look it over. He thought it was a good project for her and left it to her. She asked for his advice. He told her no. He then told her he would let her know if she started to do something wrong. If he was real happy about one of her decisions he'd let her know.

The builder had been a little unsure at first. Not with having a college student on the project. But, that it was a woman, which he didn't care for. But after a few day's he'd relaxed. After a few week's he even acted a little impressed. As part of her assignment Meaghan had to keep detailed reports and turn them into her professor. On a Saturday toward the end of the construction when the professor had some time he revisited the project. He'd wanted to have time, to go over it good. When he finished his inspection and Meaghan had answered many pointed questions. He'd told Meaghan that she'd quite well. He even left a note for the contractor, to congratulate him. That if he ever needed a reference, he would be happy to give him one. The professor then hailed two carriages. After they'd said there goodbyes and Meaghan was on her way home, she was elated. She didn't think the professor would give her false praise.

Mrs. Saxton and Meaghan had hired some caretakers to get the grounds back in shape, fixing some washed out areas and trimming and replacing shrubs, where it was needed. It was the middle of June with the hardest part yet to do. Ann had to find and hire some good servants. Matt had requested at least one cook, a butler, a head mistress, three personal maids and three or four others servants. To clean and run errands. Neither Meaghan or her, had figured out why Matt wanted the place. Especially why he wanted so much help.

Mrs. Saxton and Meaghan had put the word out that they would start interviewing the next Monday at the Bingham Mansion. They still kept it secret and as far as they knew. They hadn't spent much time at home, before they'd started on Matt's project and sure hadn't been home much after they started. They were sure no one had noticed anything different while they had been worked on Matt's project. The contractor was nearly done. All he had left was getting the finishing touches done. Cleanup mostly and some wax on the hardwood oak floors that had been sanded and freshly stained. He was going to scrub some of the stones, that had been stained by run off from the rain.

CHAPTER TWENTY NINE

ANOTHER COMMITMENT

Matt, Slim, Billy and the women had made it back to Sacramento without any incidents. Matt had purchased some tickets and made arrangements for a boxcar to load the horses in. They'd had a speedy pleasant trip, except for three or four day's of a hard rain and then some drizzle. The women had gone back to wearing just their loin cloths and moccasins. Even though it had gotten a little warm. Matt had worn his trail clothes and always made sure he took his baths away from everyone. He didn't mind if one of the women were around. He just liked to bathe with some privacy. He was still uncomfortable with people gazing at all of his scares. They had to spend two night's in Sacramento waiting for a boxcar to hook to a east bound train.

When they arrived in Rawlins it was the middle of June. They didn't have any problem unloading the horses. They were getting somewhat used to train travel. With everything they'd brought from Portland and picked up from a couple of shopping excursions in Sacramento. It had taken them awhile to pack everything on the horses. Then they'd headed out toward the Young's. Matt had made a quick stop at the saddlery shop. He told the other's to wait, that he would be just a minute. He returned shortly, carrying a balky package that didn't seem to weigh much. He had left room for it behind Flames saddle. As a crowd started to gather Matt led them out of town. They attracted a lot of attention as they had some of the best horses around. The Ladies bellies had started to protrude over their gun belts even though they'd let them out a couple of holes. Also being astraddle they showed a lot of well tanned legs. They'd looked a little uncomfortable. They never complained; but Matt figured they had to be a little stressed. For their sake he was glad it was a short trip out to the Young's.

When they arrived they were astonished at the change. They stopped their mounts and sat for a minute, as they looked over all the work that had been done. Then they'd eased their horses on into the complex. Matt led them up to the Young's living quarters. As they pulled up attracted by the noise of the approaching horses, Mrs. Young came out. Upon spotting them she'd immediately went into her mothering ways. She said, "You poor dear's. Let's get you inside and cleaned up. You need to get some rest."

After that she gave Matt a condemning look as she'd clicked her tongue. As they dismounted the women smiled at Matt; he wisely stayed silent.

Mr. Young had come up by then. He'd reached out and shook Matt's hand as he said, "I'm glad your back. Your paying us to much. I've held back the overage's to return them back to you."

Matt said, "No, It's fair. For I'm sure it makes some of your neighbors a little nervous with all the Indians being around. I just appreciate having a place big enough to have a little shelter and be able to get all of my people together."

Fred shuffled his feet a little, then said, "Well, seeing it in that light I can see a little of what your getting at. I still think it is too much."

Matt said, "No sir. I'm just glad for your hospitality."

Fred said, "Well okay, let's get your things unpacked and put your animals up. I'm glad to see you. She hasn't said anything. But I know ma has missed all of you. Don't let her fool you, young man. I've noticed she always gives you a hard time. She thinks the world of you; though.

Matt said, "I have been thinking, that she didn't care to much for me at all."

Fred as his eyes sparkled said, "That's what she wants you to think. You let her know I told you different, she'll have me sleeping out in the stable for week's."

Matt said, "I'll be careful."

Billy and Slim had most of the girls things unpacked and stacked on the little porch. Matt had kept the package he'd picked up at the saddlery. With Fred's help Matt Billy and Slim led the horses to the stable. As they unsaddled the horses they put the saddles up on the new saddle racks. Everything was neat and in order. It was as clean as a stable could be. Matt took Flames halter off and hung it up, as he knew Flame would go on to the corral with out it. As Flame went on toward the back of the stable toward the corral. Matt took off the pack rack, from one of the horses. Then he led the horse toward the corral. Flame had waited at the rear entrance. As Matt got to the rear entrance of the stable. He was leading the horse around to Flames left side. About to speak to Flame. Someone just outside the left of the entrance spun and stepped right into Matt.

He heard a grunt as the person hit him head first right in the chest. The person tumbled back as he tripped over his feet. By reflex Matt dropped the reins then quickly reached out and caught the person. As Matt gathered the person in his arms he stepped forward to keep his balance. Straightening up Matt lifted the person off the ground, tight against his chest as he gained his balance. There was a sudden flurry of movement as if a bunch of critters were trying to go in different directions; all at once.

Instantly he knew it was a woman. He felt her breasts against his lower chest. As a startled voice said, "Stop. Let go of me. What are you doing?"

He felt her fist as she beat against his chest. Then he lowered her down to her feet. Immediately; she stepped back, then with startled eyes she looked up to meet Matt's surprised eyes. With their gazes riveted on each other, her eyes sparkled to life. Matt's eyes immediately responded, to shoot brilliant hazel flashes of lightning at her. Her eyes widened as they shot back blue lightening flashes at him. Matt's body responded as his heart started to race. As he watched her face, flushed red with it's own heat. She gasped, "Oh, S-or-Sorry. I just. What, who are."

To Matt's amazement as her lips had formed a big Oh. She started to collapse. He quickly caught her again stooping down catching her in his arms. He had one arm under her back with the other under her leg's as he'd straightened up. He held her to his chest as he'd turned back inside the stable.

Billy heard the scuffle and saw the tail end of the action. With a word to Slim Billy tossed the rein's of the pack horse to him. Then he quickly went and gathered up the reins of the pack horse Matt had been leading. Which had begun to get nervous.

Then Billy asked, "What happened to her. Who is she?"

Matt responded, "Don't ask me. I don't know. She just passed out."

Fred as he'd led a horse up heard Matt's comment. He said, "She's my niece. I didn't know she was feeling bad. While we put these horses up you can carry her in and let Ma take care of her."

Fred caught up with Matt as he'd stepped up on the porch to the officers quarters building. Fred shouted, "Ma, Ma! This way Matt, her rooms farther on."

Fred walked on down the porch with Matt behind him. Mrs. Young's voice come from the room they used as a bath house. She said, "I hear you. You don't have to yell. What's the problem?"

Fred answered, "Jenna has passed out. I don't know why."

As Fred opened the door for Matt they heard footstep's behind them. Fred said, "Lay her on the bed. Ma will be right here."

When Matt gently laid her down she'd opened her eyes as he'd straightened up. They locked eyes again. They crossed sparked gazes again and with a gasped; Oh. She, had passed out again. Matt stood to his full height and looked away from the bed as Mrs. Young came in asking, "What happened?"

Fred said, "She passed out."

Dawn said, "I can see that. Why?"

Fred said, "Well, I don't know."

Dawn as she'd felt her forehead said, "She's hot. It look's like she has a rapid heart beat too. Get me a towel and some cool water."

Matt followed Fred out asking, "Is there anything I can do?"

"No, I'm sure Ma can take care of her."

"Well, let me know if you need anything."

Fred said, "I sure will."

When he was back at the stable Matt unsaddled Connie's horse. Billy and Slim had taken care of the others. They waited until he'd put the mare in the corral. When he returned Billy asked. "Is she alright?"

Matt said, "I don't know. She started to come too then passed out again."

Slim asked, "What happened?"

Matt said, "I don't know for sure. All I know is that she ran into me head first. I think I frightened her. After I caught her to keep her from hitting the ground. She fought to get away from me. Then she just passed out."

Slim said, "Well, maybe she just got to hot."

Mrs. Young loosed Jenna's clothing to give her some air. Then she sponged her forehead with some cool water. Jenna's eyes flickered then glanced around the room as if she was looking for something. Mrs. Young had seen the sparkle in them. There was a deep intensity in them. Dawn hadn't seen her eye's show anything, but a dull glaze ever since she had arrived till then. Jenna's normal color had started to return. She asked, "Where is? What's his name?"

Dawn thinking maybe she had been frightened said, "Who honey? There is no one here except us. Everything is alright."

Jenna said, "The stable. The big man. The flaming horse. Who carried me?"

"Oh Matt. What did he do?"

Jenna said, "He caught me. I was falling down."

"Oh. Did he hurt you?"

Jenna's thought's raced as she ran the events through her mind. She said, "No, not yet."

The girls had finished their baths. They heard some of what had gone on. They followed the noise till they found Mrs. Young in Jenna's room. The door had been left open. Star peeked in asking, "Is she alright?"

"Yes I think so. I think she was just a little flushed. Come in. All of you. Jenna I want you to meet some dear friends of ours. Connie, Helen and Star. This is my niece Jenna."

Then they began to get a little bit acquainted. The Saxton Ladies had put on house coats that Mrs. Young had gotten for them. Suddenly some of the brightness had left Jenna's eyes as she said, "Oh! The Spirit Warrior and his women."

Dawn surprised, asked, "You've heard some of the stories; then?"

Jenna's voice a little wistful as she said, "Yes. That's about all his men talk about when there's someone new around, to tell it to. Run's Far assured me, they were true."

Star nudged Connie, then Helen as she said, "We have got a few things to do to get settled in. It's nice to meet you."

Connie and Helen told Jenna the same then followed Star out. They'd heard Jenna tell her aunt she was alright. That she just wanted to rest. Star had detected a wistfulness to her voice. Star led Connie and Helen to the officer quarters for a married officer. That Mrs. Young had fixed up for them. With a little persuasion they had been able to talk Mrs. Young into letting Matt stay with them. She agreed with out much of a fuss at all. They thought that she would have been a little harder to convince. When they arrived Star explained what she thought had happened. Connie and Helen just looked at her in amazement. But they didn't say anything for a couple of minutes. They had thoughtful look's. Then Connie said, "Maybe, you are right."

Thoughtfully Helen said, "I think she is. We need to be careful."

They talked for a half hour until they came to an agreement and had put together a plan. Then they unpacked some of their most pliable cloths. They picked out the dress's that were big enough to have a loose fit over their bellies. Then Helen and Star went to help Dawn, who was busy in the kitchen. Dawn told Helen and Star they could set up the big table. Fred and his helpers had built a large table in the old mess hall. Dawn told them that Fred and her had planned on using it the next time Captain Taylor and all the men came in anyway.

Connie in search of Matt just strolled along. As she looked over all the improvements that had been made. Mr. Young's helpers had just come in with a load of hay and started to fork it into the loft over the stable. As they worked she noticed that they kept glancing at Flame in admiration. Billy and Slim were soaking up the last of the evening sun as they helped Fred a little as he was painting a carriage he had repaired.

When Connie was up close to them, she asked, "Where is Matt?"

Billy said, "He went for a walk outside. He told me he might work out some. That he was feeling a little stiff. He told me he'd clean up at the pool down in the creek."

Slim said, "Billy's been trying to explain to us. What it is that Matt does when he work's out. It doesn't make much sense to us. Then he told us, you Ladies work out also."

Connie said, "Yes. When I get my shape back, I'm going to get back into my routine again. Gun's aren't the only thing we're good at."

Fred looked at Slim as he said, " I think, I'll take her word for it."

Connie deciding it was best to leave Matt alone for now. She told the men bye, then went to help Mrs. Young.

Matt had found a secluded place, in a shady area. Then he stripped down, then put on his loin cloth he had tucked under his shirt. He worked out real hard for over an hour. His body was glistened in the sun as he made his way to the pool. He carried his weapons and a change of cloth's. There he laid down his things then eased into the water wading to the deepest part of the pool. He just soaked for along time as he let the cold water take the heat from his body. The problem was most of the heat hadn't been caused from his workout. He didn't know what had happened. Whatever it was he was sure that it wasn't right. As he thought of Connie, Helen and Star he felt cheap. That made his thoughts even more troubled. He had suddenly become confused all over again. What had he done? He had them all with child. It wasn't right. He thought to himself that he'd had his eyes open. Lord he thought. The Maxton's and the Gates had excepted the arrangement. How he had no idea. He felt right when he was with the women. It was only when he was alone with his own thought's, like now that he could see. He had thought everything was okay, until he had ran into Jenna. Lord, her eyes had just shot their sparks into the depths of his soul. That thought made his body hot all over again. Even in the cold water. He cussed in an under toned voice as he eased out of the pool. He used the edge of his hand to flick the water off his body. The workout had been some what of a waste. He felt just as tense as he had been before his workout.

When he entered the compound, he put up his dirty cloth's. Then he retrieved the package he had brought in from the saddlery. With the package Matt walked to the Young's household. He smelled the food long before he got there. As he entered Dawn said, "Oh! Your just in time. I was getting ready to send someone out to find you. Everything is ready. We've got it set up in the old mess hall."

Matt said, "Yes Ma-am, thank you."

Matt turned and crossed over to the mess hall. When he entered he saw that a place had been left for him at the far end. As he sat down with Connie on his left and Helen and Star on his right. He glanced at Jenna who had kept her head turned down toward her plate. He felt his body heat up. Then he noticed that everyone of the women was watching him intently. It had made him feel real uncomfortable. It was like they had read his mind.

Mrs. Young joined them shortly. Then Fred said grace. Matt just realized how hungry he was. But the food just seemed to make a big ball in his gut. He noticed that Jenna hardly ate anything. She just picked at her food, leaving most of it on her plate. She excused herself saying, that she didn't feel good. As the others finished eating they started to talk. Matt was inattentive as he was busy with his own thought's. Dawn tried to give Matt another serving. She'd told him there was plenty. He told her he had enough. Then he'd excused himself saying he wanted to stretch his legs. He gathered up his package and left.

After most everyone had headed for their beds, Connie had gone in search of Matt again. She found him at the corral. She explained that they had set things up so they could all be together. He hadn't responded. He just followed her through the compound then into the quiet building. Once inside he'd spotted Helen and Star completely naked in their low lit room. He was been lost then and had peeled off his cloth's as fast as he could.

The next morning Matt got up with the sun. He felt good and relaxed. He dressed, then went in search of some coffee. The Young's always made sure there was a pot on the stove. He had just filled a cup, when Fred came in giving him a hard look. Fred shook his head as he filled his cup, then sat at the little kitchen table. Matt as always, had his gun rig on decided to stand.

Fred finally asked, "Did you sleep good?"

"Yes."

Matt heard Fred mumble something that sounded like, "Um-ph."

Slim coming in said, "Coffee does have a way of starting the day out right."

Fred said, "That's for sure. I don't like to start without it."

Matt had eaten an enormous breakfast and never felt better. Jenna had not made an appearance. She told her Aunt she didn't feel good. The young women helped Mrs. Young clean up as the men went about their daily chores. Matt, Billy and Slim had gone out to the corral and were discussing their plan's. It was the first time they had nothing they needed to do. Matt was debated on going out to meet Captain Taylor or wait a couple day's to see if they showed up.

Even back in New York City. Connie and he always seemed to have something going on. The only thing that had kept him there, was that he was sure the women would persist on going along also. In their condition he didn't think they needed to be on the back of a horse. He'd decided he'd wait a couple of day's. Then if they still hadn't made it he would need to try to talk to them and hope they would let him Billy and Slim ride out. With his mind made up he'd told Billy to meet him in the mess hall. Then he gave Slim the day off. After that he'd gone to get the package he had taken back out to the stable.

When he arrived at the mess hall he saw, that the women were there too. Then he set the package down and opened it up. They looked on with wonder as they saw the leather straps with buckles and two holsters fastened to them. Using Billy he'd made adjustments until he had the holsters under each arm pit. Then he had Billy put his pistols in the holsters. He explained that with a jacket or coat on, the guns would be hidden. That way they could wear them, even in New York City.

Slim and Fred came in and watched in amazement as he did the same with the women. Then they went and got their pistols, putting them in their holsters. Matt after he got his new rig the way he wanted it, took them all out to a little cliff, around behind the old fort. They walked about a half mile from the main gate to get there.

With the gun's unloaded, Matt had all of them practice as if they were firing the guns. After a couple of hours he had them load the guns. Then he had them draw and shoot. After they had emptied both guns twice, he'd told them that it was enough. He didn't want the women to get to tried and he was happy. At least without a jacket on in the way, they had gotten accustomed to the new rigs. Good enough, that they weren't much slower than they were, with their normal gun belts. Tomorrow he decided to have them practice with jackets on.

After Matt had walked them back, he'd decided to work out again. Billy decided to join him. They practiced for three hour's with only one break midway through their routine. They each received a few bruises from the exchanges of light contact. Billy told Matt he felt good, though. That he'd needed it as he felt a lot looser. They then went to the pool to bath and cool off some. Billy noticed that Matt seemed uncomfortable about all his scares and tried not to notice. But he did glance at them a couple of times. Anybody seeing them would swear there was no way anybody could have lived through it. But there he was in the flesh to prove otherwise.

Jenna didn't put in an appearance at supper that night. After the meal as Fred, his helpers, Matt, Billy and Slim chatted. The young women helped Dawn clean up. They did saved a plate of food for Jenna. When they had everything dried and put away. The three women excused themselves as Dawn sat with the men to listen for a little. The three women went to Jenna's room. Star sat on her bed saying, "You need to eat."

With a voice that sounded like it was far away Jenna said, "I'm not hungry; really."

Helen said, "We think you should go for a walk. Maybe the exercise will do you some good."

Jenna said, "No; just leave me alone. There is nothing you can do."

Connie said, "We were going for a walk. If you go along we promise not to bother you anymore."

Jenna didn't respond for a couple of minutes. Then she said, "Okay Alright!"

They'd waited for her to put some shoes on then led her out. Connie a little behind grabbed the plate of food and a fork. They led her out the gate and down along the creek. There was a half moon to see by. They talked and pointing out things. Just hoping to find something that would interest her.

Star said, " I guess this is far enough. Connie brought a plate of food in case your did get hungry."

Jenna said, "No; I would like to go back now. I'm tired."

As they turned Star and Helen positioned themselves on Jenna's right. As they started back they'd both pushed Jenna hard, right into the pool. She'd went flying and only had time for a quick squeal just before she splashed head first into the cold water. With a whole lot of flailing arms and legs. When Jenna's feet touched the bottom of the creek she gave a hard thrust. She shot up out of the water in search of some air. As she got a mouthful of air she gone submerged again. Taking time to get her feet under her Jenna's head appeared and she was able to stand. With the water a little over her waist she wadded to the creek bank as she coughed and spat out some water. Star had gotten a glimpse of her eyes, which had been blazing with anger. When Jenna got control of her breath, in an angry voice she asked, "What's the idea; are you trying to drown me?"

Helen said, "We just thought you needed to clean up some."

Even more angry, Jenna said, "If I'd wanted to, I would have taken a warm bath. This is crazy."

Star said, "Well, we just thought you'd like to bathe in the same water Matt dose; completely naked."

There was just enough moon light, for them to observe her expression. As it changed from anger to passion. They even seen the flashes of light in her eyes. She stopped shivering also. With an excited voice she said, "What. He's. No. I saw-w; okay. You know. That is cruel."

When she finished the last part of her statement the light left her eyes and her voice turned wispy. They persuaded her to sit which hadn't been a problem. It seemed like all of her strength had left her anyway. Connie said, "We kind of have an idea of what happened. First thing, it didn't happen to just you."

Confused, but with a spark of interest Jenna asked. "How do you mean?"

Star said, "It happened to Matt also."

"Oh no, nothing happened."

Helen said, "Jenna, we don't mean that. We are sure you effected Matt the same way he did you and we know how you feel."

They had to watch close as a small cloud covered the moon some. They saw some interest return to her expression. Connie said, "Yes, when Matt was so close to death. We'd felt like if he'd died, we would have also."

Jenna had completely agreed with that. With her voice a little livelier she said, "Oh yes. That is exactly how I feel."

Helen said, "We were pretty sure of what happened. We have decided there is only one thing to do."

Apprehensive Jenna asked, "What is that."

Star said, "For you to join us. To be a wife to Matt, also."

The cloud moved on enough for them to see the complete amazement on her face. Her eyes brightened as she said, "Your not jealous. Okay! There is nothing I would like better. But my Aunt and Uncle would never let me."

Connie said, "As for the jealous part. Look at us. We have gotten along fine. It is strange, we know. But we haven't had a problem. As for the other, it's your life and there will be some talk probably. We decided we would rather live. How about you?"

"Oh yes. Ever since it happened, I have felt like I would rather be dead. But what will Matt say. He acts like he is happy with the way thing's are now.

Helen said, "Oh yes. After he kept us up all night. He has been fully aroused. Oh, it was wonderful. We are sure you were the reason for it."

Confused Jenna asked. "Caused what?"

Star chuckled lightly, then said, "Sex. He just couldn't get enough. I don't think we will have a huge problem, getting him to agree."

Embarrassed, with a passionate hopeful glow on her face, Jenna said, "You really think so? I wish I was as confident as you are."

With confidence Star said, "We'll make it happen. Connie give her the plate of food. I know you have to be hungry."

They'd talked some while she ate. Then they chatted some more on the walk back to her room. Connie stepped into the kitchen to get some more food. Dawn had been in the kitchen tidying up some. She had seen Jenna, Star and Helen go by. Dawn asked, "Is she okay. She looked like she was all wet."

`Connie answered. "Yes. I think she is going to be fine."

The next morning Jenna was up with the rest. Dawn was surprised with the brightness she saw in her eyes. They had not been like that, sense she had come to stay with Fred and her. Jenna's eyes had shined much like Matt's ladies did. Something nagged at her. But she'd shrugged it off as she returned with some fried bacon back too the mess hall.

Matt couldn't get over the change that had come over Jenna. She acted like she was full of life. He had been sure, that she was aware of him. He did catch a couple of glances from her. When he had, he noticed the sparkle in her eyes. Then he almost sworn out loud as it made his heart beat faster. Damn; he thought he had himself under control. He ate quickly and excused himself. He got a couple of strange look's as he left. He caught a smile from Jenna as she looked straight at him with eyes that sent sparkled lightning bolts right through him. He almost missed a step as he stepped out. He was glad his back was to them. For he had a big bulge between his leg's. He was sure the best thing to do was to saddle up Flame and ride out to meet Captain Taylor. After walking awhile he made up his mind to do exactly that and was headed toward the stable. Then Connie, Helen and Star appeared wearing their jackets and carrying his jacket. When they were up close Connie said, "We thought we may as well go ahead and get our practice done. Before it gets hot; since you wanted us to practice with our jackets on today."

A little grumpy Matt said, "Yeah, that is a good idea."

When they headed for the gate Billy joined them. Doing much the same as they did the day before. After a couple of hour's of practice they loaded their weapon's. Then they drew and fired up thirty rounds each. On the walk back Matt looked each of them over good. Unless you looked for them, you wouldn't notice that they had guns on them. His thoughts were interrupted when Connie asked, "Matt. Are you alright."

`"Yeah fine. Why?"

Connie said, "Well; you act like you are tense."

"I'm fine. I don't know what your talking about."

Not letting up any Helen said, "Well, you do sound kind of moody."

Billy gave each of them a good once over glance as they approached the main gate. Something was going on. He didn't know what it was. But Matt had acted different the last couple of day's. Also he realized that his sister and the other two were up to something. Connie took Matt's jacket as the women went on to their room to put them up. Matt decided to work with Flame some. Billy decided to work with Three Socks.

As they walked up Slim asked, "Is it working the way you wanted it too?"

Matt just grunted. Astounded Slim just glanced at Matt. As Billy said, "Yeah. We're nearly as good, as we are the other way. It did take some time to get used to the difference though."

Billy decided to stay and chat with Slim a little first. Matt kept going on and had been nearly through the stable. When Jenna came in leading a horse that had a slight limp with it's right front leg. Jenna stopped the horse, then smiled pleasantly as she said, "It sounded like you got some good practice in."

Surprised; Matt stopped and asked, "What are you doing."

Cheerfully she said, "I'm going to doctor his hoof. He'd stepped on a sharp stone which we had to dig out. I'm just making sure it hasn't gotten infected,"

"Need any help?"

"No. He dosen't give me any trouble."

Matt then had glanced into her eyes. They sparkled with blue flashes, that seemed to go to the depths of his soul. He her as she took a peek down between his legs. His response had been immediate and he was sure she had seen it. Matt knew he had to get out of there. He just spun around to go back out front. Over his shoulder he said, "Be careful."

As she'd watched Matt walk away, she took a deep breath. She was proud of herself. As the heat started to build in her body, she felt a strange reaction from her loins. She was sure Matt hadn't noticed. The timing had been just right. She was sure she wouldn't have held out another second.

As Matt passed Billy and Slim. Billy asked. "Is there something wrong?"

Without the slightest hesitation as he passed them. Matt said, "No. I just remembered something."

Billy and Slim looked at each other. Then Slim said, "He acts like his got a bunch of bees under his bonnet."

Billy nodded, then he glanced into the stable to see Jenna lead a horse into a stall. Billy said, "Maybe he does at that."

Slim asked, "Do you know what's up?"

Billy took some time before he answered, "I might have an idea. Not good enough to say anything though."

They looked in the direction Matt had gone. They watched him go out the main gate. Fred and his helper's on the way in with a load of hay waved. Then watched as Matt just strolled on off.

When Fred guided the horses up so the wagon was in front of the hay loft. He asked, "Is there something troubling Matt?"

Billy said, "I do think he's got something on his mind."

Matt practiced his routines for most of the afternoon. He finally rested and was drained as much, as he could ever remember doing so before. He glanced at the sun, then grabbing his gun belt he had taken off before he'd started his routine. Then he walked to the pool. When he got there he put his gun belt on the creek bank, then took his boots off. He had been wearing them to save his moccasins. He took his shirt with him into the pool. The cold water felt good to him. He took his pants off and had just finished, washing his clothes. When he knew someone was coming. He sensed it as much as actually hearing. Helen appeared shortly carrying some fresh clothes. She said, "I thought you might like these things."

Puzzled, Matt asked. "Now, how did you figure that."

Mischievously Helen said, "If someone takes the time to notice, it's as plain as the nose on your face."

"Okay, what is that?"

Helen answered, "That your in love."

"Of course. I've let you know that."

"With Jenna; also."

Surprise all over his face, he didn't try to hide Matt said, "Oh yes; damn it! Your right."

Matt with his wet clothes eased out of the water. Helen had read his eyes and knew what he wanted. When he was out of the water, there was no doubt. A little ruff he'd grabbed her arm as she dropped the clothes she had brought. He led her to a place that little more secluded. She helped him remove her clothes. His desire made her hot and with very little for play they cleared out a place and were ready. Matt plunged in just as she opened for him. It was more vigorous than any other time she could remember. She didn't know how long it had taken. But when they finally finished she felt fantastically fulfilled.

They had been a little ruff. As she cuddled up to him she said, "U-um. That was good."

Concerned; Matt asked. "Are you alright? I didn't hurt you?"

"No, I'm fine. I do think we know how things are."

As Matt held her in his arms, he asked, "Your not mad?"

"No. It is strange, though. Isn't it?"

Wonderingly, Matt said, "Yes, I don't know what happens. It is just, when I saw her eyes. Well, it was over. It happened in an instant."

Helen asked, "What do you think, happens to us?"

"Well before, it was just the three of you that affected me."

Helen looked to the west, then said, "I guess we should get dressed. Supper will be ready soon."

"What about Jenna. Dose she know what has happened."

Helen said, "Why do you think she was felling so bad."

"Oh. I guess I need to talk to her then. What should I tell her?"

"Just let her know it's alright."

Matt asked, "Alright. What do you mean?"

"That it's okay. That you want to take her to be your wife also."

"What! I thought you meant for us; to let her down easy."

Helen said, "The way you just made love to me. You can't tell me you don't want her."

"Lord it's not right."

Helen asked. "Is that the way you feel about us."

Quickly Matt said, "No. No. Your right. Well it's fine. Lord, we have made out okay. Gee. This is getting to be a mess."

Helen smiled, then said, "One more won't make it anymore right, or wrong."

"You really mean what your saying. Lord, people will never let us alone. What about Connie and Star?"

"We have already talked. Matter of fact we have already told Jenna it wouldn't be a problem."

Matt asked, "When? How did you know I' would go along with your plans?"

"The cat was out of the bag after you kept us up all night. When we put our heads together, we figured out what happened."

Matt said, "Oh! well I guess we ought to go."

She nodded and Matt helped her up. Gathering up all of their clothes they quickly dressed. Matt then gathered his wet clothes and they walked hand, in hand.

They made it just as Mrs. Young put the last of the food on the table and sat down.As Helen and Matt had gone to their end of the table, they got a few puzzled looks. Jenna was a little flushed. Star and Connie gave them knowing looks. The others tried to adjust to Matt's quick change, back to his pleasant cheerfulness. Helen just seemed to have an outer glow to her countenance.

Fred said grace and everyone dug in. Again after the meal, as the men started to talk the women started to clean up. After they had washed and put up all the eating utensils. With Helen's persuasion they had gone out to walk around some in the cooling air of the evening. When they got a little distance away from the Young's living quarters Helen said, "Jenna; it is all settled. Matt has agreed to let you join us."

Jenna had all she could do to control herself. She exclaimed a little loudly, "Oh I can't believe it. I didn't think he would. I hoped he would."

Star said, "Well I guess there's not much to do. But to get you two together."

"Oh; I've got to decide how to explain it to my aunt and uncle."

Connie said, "We can help you explain it to them, if it would help."

Jenna said, "No, they've been so nice to me since I've been here. It's up to me to let them know. I just hope they don't end up being disgusted with me."

Star said, "If they consider your happiness. They won't. They should be happy for you."

Jenna said, "I guess I should let them know, soon."

They all agreed and gabbed a little as they got to know their new sister in-law to be. When they were back inside. The men had started to break up and head for their beds and bedrolls. They couldn't help, but notice the light step to Jenna's walk. Also, her whole countenance seemed to glow.

Mrs. Young had a nagging thought. But, at the moment she'd never seen Jenna look so lovely. Jenna had the same cloth's on. But, a drastic change had come over her.

The others had noticed also and had given her admiring looks. What really sent her blood to rushing though, was the approving glance she had received from Matt's intense gaze. She was barley able to keep on walking. But she made it to her room.

Just before noon the next day. When Fred and his helpers came in with another load of hay. They were told that some riders were coming in; Indians. They didn't know which tribe though. At their pace it would be an hour before they arrived. Matt, Billy and the girls had gone to the main gate. They looked out toward the rolling valley that lead to the southwest. As they watched, way off in the distance a bunch of riders topped a rise to drop out of sight again. With a sure voice Matt said, "It looked like Hawkeye. I don't know the others."

Star said, "It looked like Sees Far and some more of my people."

They returned back inside and it was just over an hour later when the riders approached the fort. Sure enough Hawkeye, Sees Far and some of his people entered the fort. Fred welcomed them and Hawkeye explained that they would be staying a few day's. Fred told them to make themselves at home. Billy, Slim, Matt and his women all exchanged welcomes with the new arrivals. Matt was told by Hawkeye, that captain Taylor and the rest should be in before dark. They had decided to take the gold straight into Rawlins. As they started to separate, so the Indians could get settled Jenna made an appearance, as she was taken a break from her chores. Sees Far spotted her when she come into view. In his language he said, "Your new women is beautiful. We will set up the lodge and start her purification soon. The ceremony will be in five days. That will be good. Yes?"

Having his thought's confirmed, Billy patted Matt on his back saying, "Congratulations."

Fred and Slim had puzzled looks as they listened. Billy's word had been the only one they had been able to understand. Slim asked, "What did he say?"

In Sees Far's language Matt said, "Oh! But I don't know? Well okay. I completely believe in your power now."

Sees Far said, "The power is not mine. It Comes from The Spirit World like yours."

Matt had decided to answer in Sees Far's language. He asked. "Now I don't understand? What do you mean?"

Sees Far said, "I have seen you use the gift that you have received from The Spirit Bear."

Matt sure he knew what Sees Far meant said, "I just thought that it was something strange. I was not sure what it was."

Sees Far said, "You need to trust it. It is not bad. It is a good gift from The Spirit World."

Matt nodding said, "Yes. Thank you."

Sees Far nodded, then went off to make sure the preparations were being done right. Billy hardly heard Slim. He was listening intently as some understanding came to him. Billy realized he had just learned something. But, wasn't sure what it was.

Hawkeye kept his face expressionless as he let many of the same thoughts. Fred and Slim looked from Matt, to Sees Far with questioning looks on their faces. Billy had become slightly amused. Matt finely just told Fred and Slim that Sees Far wanted to make sure he wasn't going to be a problem. After Matt spoke, Hawkeye and Billy hadn't said anything. But, both of them had amused expressions. Matt then excused himself with the idea of taking Flame out for a good run. Billy liked the idea and decided to go along. Star, Helen and Connie decided they had better let Jenna know what was up and explain what the next few days would be like for her.

That evening as Runs Far scouts had started to come in from their scouting duties. They reported that the gold had been delivered and the others would be along soon. Runs Far and his scouts had waited just outside of Rawlins. They'd stayed out of sight. Then they'd joined Captain Taylor and the rest of the riders as they'd headed for the old fort. The sun had lacked only a couple of hours before reaching its azimuth when they'd entered the fort. Star and the rest were surprised. Sees Far hadn't told them anything about Strong Arms and Late Bloom being with them, along with a few prominent people of the tribe. They had decided to see some more of the country and had rode along with the scouts. Fred was amazed at all of the Indians that appeared. They were setting up camp near the creek outside of the old fort. After Matt, Billy and the women welcomed them warmly, Strong Arms and most of his immediate family, had gone out to join the others. Fred commented, "They all act like they are going to have a celebration."

Matt said, "Fred, I need to talk to you and Mrs. Young."

Fred recognized the seriousness of his voice nodded as he led them off in search of Mrs. Young. As Matt along with his women followed. After taking care of his horse Captain Taylor had been just close enough to hear Matt. To no one in particular he asked, "What's up."

Billy asked, "You don't know why Strong Arms and his people are here."

"They just told me something about wanting to go along and see how we did things. That it would be good to do some riding."

As some more of the crew came up, he hadn't elaborated. Billy just said, "Well, that is true and with all the family together there is going to be a celebration."

Captain Taylor said, "I hope it doesn't cause a problem with Fred's neighbors. It could make them a little nervous."

Billy responded, "Not if they know what's good for them. There is enough gun's here to put a stop to things, without getting any of the Indians involved."

Tex said, "A fellow could get used to this. We always eat good when they put on a celebration."

Bone's worriedly said, "Yeah. All the good food is going to make me fat."

For his reflective comment he had received some scoffed chuckles. They talked and joked as they led their horses into the stable. They continued gabbing as Slim and Billy helped take care of the pack horses and hung up the pack saddles.

With Matt and his ladies as they entered the Young's living quarters Fred said, "Dawn. I guess we need to talk."

They had then crossed on over to the mess hall. Dawn had entered followed by Jenna as Fred along with Matt and his women sat down around the big table.

When Fred had seen Jenna come in with Dawn. He had started to say something, when Matt cut him off. Matt said, "It's okay Fred. She's the reason we need to talk."

Matt had seen Jenna's eyes sparkle with relief and gave him a big smile of gratitude as she sat down. Dawn sat down next to Fred with a questioning expression on her face. Jenna had received encouraging looks from Connie, Helen and Star.

Matt remained standing. Then got right to the point. He said, "Jenna has agreed to be my wife."

Fred had been completely blind sided. He couldn't say a thing. Dawn with the hints that had nagged at her brain. Was hit with understanding. She said, "I saw it happen. I just didn't know what it was."

Grumpily Fred expelled, "Saw what happen?"

Dawn said, "Jenna falling in love. I know it now. I've never seen it hit someone so quick and hard before."

Fred asked, "Your not upset? Your not worried about what the others may say?"

Dawn answered, "No. When it gets right down to it. It should be Jenna's decision. I can see with my own eyes that she's all for it."

Jenna relaxed as she realized that everything was going unbelivingly better, than any of them had ever hoped. Fred said, "Well, I guess things are settled. I do whish the best for all you youngsters. I can't say that I understand. But, we won't give you any trouble." They all thanked the Young's. Then the women had gone to the kitchen to finish preparing the evening meal. With Captain Taylor and the rest in they'd fixed a lot. They were all busy.

During the meal Captain Taylor and the rest of the crew couldn't get over the change that had come over Jenna. Most had finished their meal when Runs Far and his mother had knocked then entered. Late Bloom had been uncomfortable with being inside with just white eyes, for the most part. She had kept a friendly expression though. In English Runs Far said, "Sees Far is ready for the young maiden to start her purification."

Star whispered in Jenna's ear, then they got up excusing themselves. They followed Runs Far and his mother on out to the Indians camp. They had received astonished looks from around the table. Matt had slipped outside while Connie and Helen had filled everyone in. They explained to the Young's what the wedding ceremony would be like.

The place had been busy the last few days with all of the activities. Some of the Indian scouts had been off on a hunting trip. They'd boasted about who would bring back the best kill to honor The Grizzly Spirit and his women.

Being close to town, Matt's riders not to be outdone had gone into Rawlins to get some gifts for them. They'd decided to get something for all of them, not just Jenna.

When the day of the wedding ceremony had arrived, all of the riders had gotten cleaned up and dressed in their best outfits. Runs Far had joined Matt in the men's purification hut again. Not only did he enjoy being with The Grizzly Spirit even though most of the time was in silence. It also gave him a break for his own thoughts. They were dressed in their ceremonial costumes. Star, Helen and Connie hadn't been able get into theirs. So they decided to wear the dresses that Mrs. Maxton had bought them.

When Jenna did appear in her new doeskin costume, which had been made just like the other three. She blushed noticeably as it revealed most of her breast to show the two bear claw's attached to her left breast then one to her right breast. Also her back was exposed to show the newly decorated claw marks. They went from just above her breast, over her shoulders and on down her back. She spotted Matt and was encouraged. She walked with a determined step toward them.

Runs Far and Billy beside Matt watched as Fred led Jenna up. Hawkeye had made sure to be next to the Young's so he could translate for them. Fred joined Dawn after he left Jenna with Matt,

After the ceremony the Young's thanked Hawkeye and told him to tell Sees Far that they'd enjoyed the ceremony. That in some way's they'd thought it had been better than a church wedding. They realized the word's Matt and Jenna had committed to each other. If anything was more bidding than most church weddings.

Hawkeye promised them he would tell Sees Far. The big feast started along with handing out gifts. Mrs. Young with all the things happening at once, finally got close to Jenna to say, "Honey; you look very pretty. I have never seen your hair shine like it is now. I have never seen you so happy. You're beautiful."

Excited Jenna said, "Oh! thank you, Aunt Dawn."

Mrs. Young looked at Matt as he put an arm gently over Jenna's shoulders saying, "Don't worry Ma-am. I'll take good care of her."

Mrs. Young said, "OH fool-e; I know that. I just wish all kinds of happiness for you."

The Indians would celebrate late into the night. From passing messengers from one tribe to another. The story tellers had told them. The Grizzly Spirit or The Spirit Warrior was already a legend throughout most all the tribes. Some still hunted for him. But, had found it hard to find him. The words that were being passed was that if you let it be known. That if you were hunting him, he would find you. Not many liked that idea.

As the shadows had grown. Matt eased Jenna away to the teepee that had been set up for the newly weds. Upon entering they'd both became timid. Jenna had never been with a man and even though. Star, Helen and Connie had explained and tried to comfort her, she was nervous. Matt had just realized that Jenna, had never seen his scares. As far as that went you didn't have to see them. A lot of them could be felt without any problem at all through his shirts if that was all he wore.

Matt's confusion hit him again as he'd turned to embrace her. For an instant, all his doubts hit him and he was sure it was all wrong. Then as he looked into her hungry timid eyes, his desire overrode his concerns. Matt leaned down to kiss her lips, timidly at first. But, it had turned into a deep passionate kiss in no time. Both of their hearts started to pound. As the blood rushed through their veins. Matt had felt his manhood throb to it's full growth.

Jenna felt his hardness against her belly and responded with her own desire. Even though she was still a little timid. Matt unfastened the tie that held her costume together at the shoulders behind her neck. He slipped the costume from her shoulders then down her arms. Revealing her body down to her hips where the costume just barely hung.

Jenna found it hard to breath as she'd looked into Matt's eyes and saw in the depth of them the intense hungry flashes of his passion. Then it was as if the flashes were going through her, connecting them. Matt started to feel her grapefruit sized breasts. Pure pleasure shot through her as he took one nipple, then the other in his mouth and ran his tongue all around them. As Matt felt her weaken from the intense emotions shooting through her body, he slid the costume off her hips, then eased her onto the soft pad of buffalo robes.

In the process he'd gazed into her eyes. As she had looked back she had seen him glance down between her legs. She had seen his passion grow in his eyes. Matt then quickly unlaced her beaded and decorated moccasins. Still kneeling Matt removed his, leather shirt. Even though there wasn't much light. He heard a gasp as Jenna saw some of his scars. Jenna sat up quickly then went to him. As she traced some of his scars she said, "Oh Matt. I have heard them tell how bad you had been hurt. I never dreamed that it was so bad."

Unconsciously Matt had started to pull back. She'd said, "Oh Matt. It's okay. I don't mind. In a way it's made you even more attractive to me."

Kneeling in front of him she'd hugged him to her. Then she started to kiss each scar as she'd traced them with her fingers. Her fingers had traced over his shoulders and down his back. Over the grooves and ridges of the scar tissue. She felt how hard Matt's muscles were, which probably made the scars more prevalent. They just rippled with any slight movement he made.

With her first reaction Matt felt dismay. She was about driving him out of his mind though as she seemed to cherish each and every scar. He had taken all he could. He stood and removed the rest of his costume. Jenna had been determined not to be startled by anything else, from Matt's body. However her control had been put to the limit as she saw his male organ. It had been much more than she'd expected. Completely naked they came together again and kissed. They felt and touched each other as their passions grew. With Jenna back down on her back. Matt raised over her into position. As she instinctively spread her legs and put her hands on his hips, she pulled him down to her. She sighed as he started to rub her entrance with the head of his organ. Her passions had climbed the scale as the organ worked it's way between her lips and started to stretch them. She tensed slightly as her lips parted. Then she had gone higher up the scale as she felt her lips encircle the knob of his organ.

Matt gently pushed knowing what was ahead for her. It had taken all of his control not to slam it into her. When he felt the expected resistance he pulled back a little as she had tensed up. With a quick thrust he entered. She gasped a little as he looked into her startled eyes without moving. He waited till he saw some desire appear back in her eyes. Then he started to move in and out slowly. She tensed a little. Then slowly she started to relax. After a little she started urging him on. Then he started to make deep thrust into her. She started to respond to every move. When their passions had climaxed Matt laid down beside her. As they caught their breaths and rested. Matt held her in his arms cuddling her.

After a little he'd started kissing her all over. The only place he didn't was between her legs. When a few minutes had gone by she was surprised when he put his lips right on her lips. Startled at first, then after a minute she put her hands on the back of his head as she urged him on. Not awfully long after that she begun to beg that was enough. She wanted him deep in her. When he gave into her desire, it was a race to see which one would make it first. He felt her start to tense with organisms as he exploded into her.

The next morning, late as they awakened together, they where still intertwined. Matt cuddled her as he said, "Jenna, I love you. Are you, all right? Maybe I got a little to ruff a couple of times."

With a soft dreamy voice she said, "I love you. But, no. Everything was just wonderful. I do have to admit. I'm a little sore though."

She turned in his arms and positioned her chest on top of his as she looked into his eyes. With her hips by his side she'd reached down between his legs with her left hand. She asked, "How about you. Are you alright."

"You do that much longer, you'll find out."

She had seen the passion start to grow in his eyes as his organ started to grow in her hand. She played with it until Matt was moaning. When he started to raise up she held him down. Then she raised up in position over his organ. Then slowly sat down on it until it was completely inserted.

She had caught on to how Matt had teased her. He had played her like a drum until she was about ready to explode, then slowed down while she begged him to finish. She decided it was her turn. Matt tried to urge her over the top. But, she worked him over real good. He almost made it several times. When the passion finely burst like star's flashing in their eyes together. She collapsed on top of him, not moving except for her breathing. He hadn't moved as it had felt good still being in her. When his organ had shrunk out. She raised her head up, eyes still filled with passion. She said, "Um-h. That was the best ever."

"You sure took your time."

She laughed, "Like you would never try to tease me."

"I guess we ought to make an appearance."

"Yeah! Besides I'm as hungry as I can ever remember being."

They got dressed. Then run into an onslaught of friendly teasing from Strong Arms and his people. Matt and Jenna were embarrassed when they'd been told how loud they'd been. Not many had gotten much sleep. Then Connie, Helen and Star had teased them. Making their way through all the well wishers they'd gotten something to eat. There was still a lot of food around. They still received quite a lot of teasing. After they had eaten, they bathed then dressed into their normal clothing. They parted then as Jenna had gone to help her aunt or do her chores. Matt had gone in search of Captain Taylor. When Matt found him they'd discussed how things were coming along at the tunnel. Then with the road work down into the wash. Last they discussed the draw on the outer trail going to the tunnel. Captain Taylor told Matt that the road should be in good enough shape to get wagon's in and out after the next trip. Captain Taylor kept a ledger of the expenses and had showed it to Matt. Then Captain Taylor brought Matt up to date with the attempted hold ups of the gold. It had taken them a couple of hour's to go over all of the details.

CHAPTER THIRTY

THE WARNING

When they'd concluded there talk Matt had decided it would be a good idea to register the gold mine. Also he had made it plain to the Indians that were on guard at the tunnel, not to let anyone in that didn't belong to the crew or were actually worked on the road making improvements. Runs Far and Captain Taylor both assured him that no outsiders would get in. With a look at the sun Matt had decided he had enough time to ride into Rawlins to register the claim and check on his growing bank account. He wanted to take another large draft east with them. He would then get the train tickets for the trip while he was in town.

The biggest thing he hadn't worked out yet was for someone to take care of Flame and the other special horses. It was going to be hard to find someone who would be able to exercise them. It was going to be hard to leave Flame behind. They had become real close. Billy decided to go along with him to Rawlins also. As they started to saddle up Tex told them he would go along and quickly left to get his horse.

When they left the stable Sees Far walked up to meet them. Matt quickly dismounted as Sees Far asked, "Are you going into the city."

He had spoken in his language. Matt answered in the same, "Yes, I have some business I would like to get done. I should be back before dark."

Sees Far said, "I have seen an evil Spirit that watches you. Be careful."

Matt asked, "Who."

"I do not know. When I have seen it. It is always in a deep shadow."

Matt was confident in Sees Far now as he replied, "Thank-you. I'll be extra careful." Sees Far thoughtfully nodded, then said, "I think he will never face you. He will hide and try a sneak attack."

Matt had nodded then again thanked him then they said their good byes. Matt mounted Flame and guided him out through the main gate. Once outside he slid the leather hammer loop's off of his pistols. Billy noticing did the same. Tex had picked up on there actions and followed suit as he asked, "What was that all about."

As they rode along Matt put all his senses on full alert. Billy responded in like manner as he told Tex most of what Sees Far had said.

Tex asked, "Do you think we should go back and get some more men."

Matt answered, "No!"

They had a uneventful ride into town. However no one had spoken another word. They all were highly alert however. When they made it to the edge of town Matt kneed, Flame to a stop. Then he said, "It always pays to listen to advice. You two stay back to watch and see if you can spot anyone that seems to be more interested in me, than they should be."

They nodded as he kneed Flame into motion. Matt or anyone of his riders always attracted attention. For they all looked like they would be trouble if anybody was to mess with them. Some of the local residents had already seen an example of what happened, when you tangled with them. There had been a lot of talk and people where curious. Matt went to the bank first to see Mr. Benson. After a good hour they had gone over the account. They also discussed a lot of some other details as Matt told Mr. Benson about some of his future plans. Then he got a bank draft and some cash for some spending money. His account had a lot more money in it than he had thought possible. Captain Taylor and his men had been busy. He told Mr. Benson goodbye then left his office.

As he stepped out on the boardwalk Matt spotted Billy across the street. Then he spotted Tex a hundred yards down on his left. Matt then mounted Flame and headed up the street toward the saddle shop. As he passed another bank that was new it looked like a lot of money had been spent on it. Out of the corner of his eye Matt had seen a man come out and stand. Matt felt the stare that was directed at him and glanced over quickly to catch a look of pure hate in the strangers eyes. It quickly changed to curiosity as Matt nodded, then received a node back. The man then quickly turned and walked off.

Matt rode on the few hundred yard's to the saddle shop. Then he dismounted and entered the shop. He returned shortly with a shoulder rig for Jenna. He'd had Captain Taylor order it when he had been in the purification hut. Mounting Flame again he rode on to the train station and purchased the tickets for the trip east. With his business done he headed back out to the old fort. With his highly state of alertness he spotted a ruckus at the far end of an alley he had just passed. He had observed as four older kid's had ganged up on a youngster that appeared to be about thirteen.

As Matt quickly dismounted he gave Billy and Tex a sign that he was alright. Then he rushed down the alley. The youngster had been putting up a good scrap. But he was down and taken a lot of punishment. Matt controlled his blow's as he quickly, disposed of them. He had hurt them good. But he had been careful not to break anything or do any permanent damage to any of them.

The youngster was bruised up real bad. But he didn't seem to have anything broken. His clothes were a mess. His shirt was just barely hanging on him. He had black hair and brown eyes with long pointed nose. He was slimly built with a stringy muscular body. He was four foot ten. One of his eyes was already swollen shut. He had a pretty good cut on his left cheek. His lip's had been split and his knuckle's were all skinned up. As Matt finished checking him out he groaned and his eye lid had flickered. With his one good eye he'd looked up at Matt and with a tired weak voice said, "Thanks!"

Matt asked, "What was that all about."

"They wanted the money I made from cleaning out the stable."

"You didn't let them get it then?"

"No sir."

"What's your name."

"Johnny Miller"

"Well let's get you home so you can get patched up."

With a shameful look he'd hesitated a little then he said, "I don't have one. No family either. I'm on my own."

Matt saw the pride in his eyes. He chose his words carefully as he said, "If it's alright with you. I would like you to come along with me. I can promise you a steady job."

Johnny's eye lit up as he said, "I'm a good worker. I'll earn it; you'll see. I don't care what I do."

Matt then helped Johnny up among some tight lipped groans. They walked back up the alley slowly as Johnny favored his left leg, like he had all he could do to put his weight on it. When they where up next to Flame Johnny held his hand out so Flame could smell it. Even though it was bloody Flame had stayed calm. Johnny said, "Man that is some horse you have. I don't think I have ever seen any better."

"Thanks, I named him Flame."

Nodding Johnny said, "That fit's him like a glove."

Matt mounted then he removed his left foot from the stirrup and helped Johnny, up behind him. There had been plenty of groans then. Matt guided Flame out of town. About a mile out of town Johnny said, "We're being followed."

"Yes, It's okay. They are my men."

When they made it to the old fort Matt had guided Flame right up to the Young's living quarters. Mrs. Young and all the ladies had heard them approach. Knowing it was unusual for someone to ride up so close, they'd come out to see what was up.

Seeing only Matt. Mrs. Young asked, "Something wrong?"

"Yeah I got an injured rider."

Mrs. Young stepping to the side a little. Then as she spotted Johnny she said, "Okay my. He's a mess."

Matt had helped Johnny off. Johnny had a hard time of it. He had stiffed up some on the ride out. He groaned bad when his left leg kind of collapsed and he fell off Flame more than anything. The women had started forward. Seeing the look's on the women's faces Johnny had started to protests. When he just slowly slumped to the ground. Flame just stood patiently as they helped Johnny. He had adapted to being around people he knew. Matt quickly dismounted and gathered Johnny up. Mrs. Young said, "Lets put him, in Jenna's bed."

Star said, "I'll get my medicines."

Connie asked, "What happened."

Matt said, "He was fighting to keep his money. His name is Johnny Miller. He is homeless and has no kin."

Mrs. Young said, "Not any more."

Matt then left the women to care for Johnny. He went out to take care of Flame give him a good rub down. After that he compared observations with Billy and Tex. They both had noticed the stranger also. Billy being on that side told Matt that the stranger had looked back at Matt several times. Then he had disappeared into a saloon. Billy had the advantage of observing him the most. He told Matt that the stranger had been unarmed unless he had a hidden gun. That he had been very well dressed with dark hair and dark complexion. About six foot, well built and well groomed. Also Billy thought he looked like he was used to giving orders.

They agreed that he was the only one that had stuck out from among all the other people. Matt decided that they would keep the information to themselves. What Sees Far had told them along with the stranger in town.

After a couple of day's Johnny was up and about. Fred had put him to work in the stable. It turned out that the animals seemed to take to him. Matt then made a decision and with Fred's permission he had Johnny work with Flame and Three Socks a little. Then Matt had him work with the ladies horses as well. When it was seen that he hadn't had a problem with any of them. Matt then made arrangements for Johnny to care for them and ride them from time, to time. To make sure they stayed in shape. Matt had agreed with Captain Taylor that they should keep a few of the scouts around to protect the horses. Anybody in the country would like to get there hands on them.

Johnny finally told them what had happened to his family. They had moved from the east after the war. His mother and father had been the only one's that had survived. Their parents had been the owner's of a couple of large plantations in South Carolina. They'd gotten together then moved west. Married then had started raising horses and had done pretty good. They had been raided by outlaws. Both of his parents had been killed in the raid and he had just barley gotten away without receiving any harm. He had buried his parents and made his way to Rawlins. He had been begging for food and sleeping in the stable and alleyways for over a year.

The third day after the latest wedding. Captain Taylor led Matt's riders out along with Strong Arms and most of his people. The family had spent several minutes getting there goodbyes done, before they'd actually left.

Fred had gotten the carriage all fixed up. Where it had come from, he had no idea. It had been there when he had taken over the fort. He never had a use for it, until Matt and his people showed up. It two seats facing each other with a drivers seat in front. It took two horses to pull it. With Johnny up beside him Fred had been ready for awhile. Fred had volunteered to drive Matt's ladies in to catch the train. When the ladies finished their tearful goodbyes with Mrs. Young. Matt helped them into the carriage. Then Matt and Billy mounted their horses. They were going to make a quick stop at the bank. Matt wanted to get Jenna's signature on record.

The Ladies had their weapons on. But they were hidden under their jackets. Even Jenna had done the same. Even though she was not gotten comfortable with the weapon's yet. She was safe with them. But, the only way she had ever fired one was by using both hands and using the sights. Then most of the time she could hit what she'd aimed at. If she took her time.

As they had done the last time in town. Matt and Billy watched extra careful like.

Fred waited while Matt and his ladies had gone into the bank. The carriage along with Ladies, Three Socks and Flame had attracted a large crowd. Matt escorted the women through them back to the Carriage. As Matt mounted Flame to head toward the train station he'd seen a face as it had looked out from the bank window across the street. He was sure it had been the same eye's that had stared at him before. Fred made sure everyone was seated before he put the carriage into motion. Billy rode up next to Matt saying, "He watched most of the time. He kept looking at the women. But, your the one that really draws his attention."

Matt nodded as Billy dropped back a little to give them some separation. When they arrived at the station with the help of a couple of porters they got all of their luggage aboard the train. Matt had made arrangements for a private sleeper car. Most of the luggage had been brought in the day before and put aboard the car. It had been guarded over night on a side track. It had then been added to the rest of the train. After getting everything aboard the car and everyone settled in, it was only fifteen minutes before it was hooked to the rest of the train and after the caboose was attached.

They all had said their goodbyes to Fred and Johnny. Matt then said his goodbye to Flame. Matt had patted him and told him what a good friend he was. Then Matt turned and helped his women aboard the car. Flame hadn't liked the idea of going off without Matt. Matt had to admit that his chest was tight also. After a couple of hundred yards it looked like Johnny was doing alright with Flame and Three Socks. After they disappeared Matt and Billy had gone in with the ladies to help them get settled in for the long ride to the east coast.

It was close to dark when the train made a stop at Cheyenne. Matt, Billy and the Ladies were enjoying a meal in the dining car. Most of the people had rushed off to get something from a store. Crackers and cheese if nothing else could be found. Then hurry back on. The dining car had been a recent addition and was a little expensive. The Ladies did attract a lot of attention. Matt and Billy hadn't helped any as they still wore their double gun rigs on their hips. Star, Connie and Billy sat on one side of the table while Helen, Jenna and Matt sat on the other side. Matt watched everyone he could as they had come and gone. Then Matt had spotted a couple of tough looking characters as they'd gone by on the depots platform. Especially the gun's that had been tied down low. They appeared to have been well used.

The dining car was brightly lite from the oil lamps and as they'd walked by they seemed to be making a great effort of not appearing to be looking into the dining car. Matt nudged Billy's knee with his. Billy looked up into Matt's eyes. Matt just flicked them at the window. Billy glanced, then made a slight node.

When they finished their meal the train had picked back up to it's full speed again. Billy led them back through the passenger cars toward their private car. Matt had followed close behind them. In the second passenger car, Matt had spotted the two men. They had picked seats apart from each other. Matt noticed as they had gone past they both made sure they were looked anywhere, but at them.

The next morning on their trip to the dinning car. Matt noticed that the two men acted like they were asleep. Matt was sure that they weren't. After they had eaten and just sat enjoying some coffee. Star said, "To keep from getting bored to death we thought we would start teaching Jenna, some of what you call instinctive shooting."

Matt said, "Okay, after we have finished our coffee we'll go on back."

Helen said, "We thought she'd like it better if we worked with her some first. Just take your time and enjoy your coffee."

Matt said, "Well at least take Billy along with you. Don't leave our car unless Billy or I am with you."

They gave him a wondering look. But they just nodded obediently as they got up. Billy said, "I'll be right back. If the waiter comes by I'd like another coffee."

Connie decided to stay with Matt. Matt watched closely as the others left. When they had made it to the next car Connie asked, "Okay, what's up."

"What do you, mean?"

"Oh Matt. Maybe the others don't quite see it, yet. But you are as tight as a well strung fiddle."

Matt forced a smile, then said, "I don't know what your talking about."

"You don't fool me."

Just then before she'd finished. They had their hands full to stay seated. They heard the screeching of steel on steel. As the train tried to come to a sudden stop.

Matt got to his feet, then fought to keep his balance. He said, "Stay here and I mean that."

Matt had just made it to the second passenger car when there was a another sudden jar as the train came to a complete stop. Matt grabbed the back of a seat to keep from getting thrown down. Just then a man burst in from outside with his gun already drawn. He shouted, "Nobody! make a move; this is a holdup."

Matt saw that another man had entered the third passenger car next to their private car. Billy had just gotten his feet under him also. The other two that had gotten on the night before had their guns out. They were the only one's of the bandits that hadn't worn a mask. The one closest to Matt held his gun steady on Matt's middle. He said, "Go ahead and be quick. I'll keep them covered."

Matt just stood still as he'd watched the bandits eyes. Matt wanted to be able to read the bandits intent, if he could. Matt was worried about Connie. He was sure he had heard someone enter at that end also. Suddenly there was a loud snap, then the sound of metal hitting the floor. Just then Matt saw the intent come to the eyes he watched so closely. That was the switch that had made Matt's right hand move. There was a loud roar then another a split second later as a bullet had gone through the wood floor between Matt's feet. Matt quickly triggered off another shot at the robber that had worked his way up the car. Matt got him in the head just before he was able to dive behind some seats. It had been over in a second.

There had been a couple more shots. Matt hurried up toward Billy who stood with a smoking gun. Star had a gun out and held it on a bandit that was holding his right arm that was bent off at a bad angle. He moaned loudly at any slight movement. Helen started to pack Billy's handkerchief in a hole on Billy's left shoulder. Billy had turned pale and was gritting his teeth. Steadying Billy some, Matt took him on to the sleeper car and sat him on one of the bunks. Then he looked each of them over again. Jenna was a little shaken. But seemed to be holding up pretty good. He said, "You stay here. Take care of Billy. I need to go check on Connie."

As he had gone out Star came in as some of the men took the bandit off. Matt saw that the aisle was full. He went out; then stepped down on the track bed and hurried toward the front of the train. When he was up next to the dinning car. In a loud clear voice he said, "I'm friendly. I'm coming in."

Connie answered, "It's clear Matt; come on in."

As Matt entered he saw her eyes go all over him. He had done the same thing with her. He asked, "You alright?"

Someone said, "Alright I'll say. She just broke the bandits arm and the next thing she had a gun out holding it on him. I have never seen anything like it."

As the talk burst out around them. Matt walked Connie into the dinning car. She asked, "How about the other's? Are they alright?"

"Billy got hit high up on his left shoulder. I'm sure he'll be okay. But the bullet will have to be dug out, unless it went all the way through."

The conductor came in then saying, "Man! I've never seen shooting like that. We have a doctor on board this trip. He told us you cut that fellows spinal cord right in too. The doctor told us that's why his shot missed you when he had you dead to rights. The doctor is working on your young man and said he was sure that he would be fine."

Matt said, "Thank-you!"

The conductor said, "Oh no I thank-you. Oh and you to Ma-am. Everyone is saying his gun appeared just like magic. I have never seen anyone so fast."

Matt said, "Well that's fine. Maybe you ought to check and make sure all the other people are alright."

The conductor upon looked at Matt decided that maybe he was needed somewhere else. He'd turned and left. Connie had gotten the waiters attention and ordered some more coffee for them. It had taken a few minutes for some men to un-stack some log's that had been placed across the track's. The bandit's horses had been found unsaddled and turned loose. Then the train had started heading east again.

After the doctor and Star had patched Billy up and laid him out on his bunk. They'd thanked the doctor and asked him how much they owed him. He said, "For what you people have already done you don't owe me a thing. They'd have gotten my money also."

Helen said, "Well thank-you, your very kind."

"Well just let me know if theirs any problems. With the laudanum he'll sleep awhile." Helen asked, "With the bullet hitting his shoulder bone, will he be alright?"

The doctor said, "Oh! The bone is probably bruised and will be sore longer than the rest of his wound. But in time I think he'll be fine."

Matt and Connie had finished their coffee and made it to their private car. They stood aside as the doctor left to be ambushed by the questioning people, as he'd tried to return to where the two injured bandit's were being held. If nothing else, he knew their arms needed to be set. After the doctor had gone and they sat down. Connie asked, "Okay. What's going on? You, and Billy, knew something was up."

Jenna, Star and Helen looked up with questioning eyes at Connie, then Matt.

Matt said, "Well, we saw the two that didn't have mask on get on the train last night and thought they were acting awfully suspicious."

Connie was listening intently and looking Matt in his eyes trying to read them. She took her time as she digested his words. Still not quite certain she said, "There's more to it than that."

Matt said, "I don't know what it could be."

Jenna said, "Just some bandits and their luck ran out.

Helen said, "Yeah. I'm just glad that Star was in position to take care of the one she close to her. Billy wouldn't have had a chance, if she hadn't."

Star hadn't made a comment. She just listened.

Connie however, more sure of herself said, "That's it. They had Billy and Matt dead to rights. It wasn't by accident."

Connie's temper had grown and looked right back at Matt, then continued. "Now, what's up?"

Matt said, "I don't know what you mean."

Star was on the same trail as Connie as she said, "I do remember. I saw the man's eyes. He had intended to kill Billy, no matter what happened."

Connie's voice rose with her anger as she said, "You can bet on that. Matt's man had the same intent. Matt you tell us the rest of it. Now!"

Seeing that all of them, except for Jenna had grown angry he persuaded them to set back down. Then he said, "Well it appears that it was a holdup attempt to cover up their true intent. From what everyone saw they think the bandits were out to kill Billy and I. You ladies should not have gotten involved. Billy and I could have taken care of it so as not to put any of you in harms way."

When he had finished Connie turned to Jenna as she exclaimed, "You see. He and Billy think that we should not do any fighting and always try to handle everything. Even if it puts them in more danger. We have to watch them like hawks."

Jenna, not quite sure asked, "You really think they were sent to kill Matt and Billy?"

Star answered, "Yes, I don't think it will be the last time, either."

Jenna asked, "What will we do?"

Connie still angry said, "We need to watch over them and try to keep them out of trouble."

Matt said, "Oh no! You ladies have all you can do, to take care of yourselves right now.'"

Matt was thinking of there condition as they were heavier with child. In just a second he found out he had said something wrong. After an hour with them, all mad at the same time. He decided that they weren't going to calm down, no matter what he said. He decided he needed some coffee. As he went gone out Connie instructed Jenna to go so she could watch Matt's back and if she had to shoot, to take her time and make it count.

As Matt escorted Jenna to the dinning car he thought for awhile. That he had jumped from the pan into the fire. For everyone wanted to congratulate him and asked how Billy was doing.

When they made it to the dinning car things had calmed down. But he found out that he couldn't pay for anything. He was told that for the rest of the trip, him or any of his Ladies would not be charged for anything. The conductor told them that the bandits been put off at the first town and handed over to the sheriff.

After a couple of days most of the people that had been on the train from Rawlins Wyoming had gotten off. The few that were left quickly passed the story around to the people that got aboard. The story kept circulating. There was a lot of disbelief. But everyone was being real respectful. Even to the women and Billy as he was on the mend and up on his feet.

It was now Ma-am, sir, or Mr. Saxton. It made Matt tense with all of the unwanted attention. To make things worse the women hadn't decided to forgive him yet and never let him go without a body guard. Even though they gave Billy the cold shoulder, he just seemed to be amused at Matt's discomfort. That hadn't helped him any either.

When they had crossed the Mississippi River Matt swapped his pistols to his shoulder harness rig. Jenna was working hard as she practiced handling the pistols. She was getting used to there weight and had improved a lot.

Mrs. Saxton and Meaghan had been interviewing people for a week. Then after comparing notes they finally made up their minds. For the most part they decided on married couples to fill the positions.

For Butler and Head Mistress they settled on Lee and Grace Knight. Lee was in his forties with black graying hair and brown eyes. Medium slim build of five feet four inches. Very well groomed with a plain face. But he always had, a pleasant smile. His wife Grace was in her early forties with blond hair that had a tint of white showing. Blue eyes behind a natural rosy complexion. Five feet six with a slim build. She still had a youthful appearance.

David and Mary Allen they had decided on for cooking, with his wife helping the other servants whenever she could. David was five feet two. A little heavy with black hair and gray eyes. He had a well trimmed mustache. He was forty and Mary was thirty eight with light reddish blond hair. She had green eyes with a cute petite build. She was five feet one.

For caretaker and gardener they decided on Clifton Jones along with his wife Linda for another servant. He was thirty on a well built frame with broad shoulders. He had a slim waist. His neck was little long. He had a dark outdoor complexion with brown hair. Also he had direct brown honest eyes. Linda was twenty six and five feet two inches with a slender build, brown hair and green eyes.

The last servant they decided on was Patty Hall. She was twenty with a medium built body. Five feet five with brown hair and brown eyes. Long nose on a cute face.

Once they made there decisions they mailed out notices to them. They had wrote that they could move into the servant quarters anytime after the next Monday. They would be paid from that time on. It would give them a chance to get used to the place before the owner arrived.

Mrs. Saxton and Meaghan had talked several times and still hadn't figured out, why Matt wanted the place and all the help. The refurbishing had been completed along with the cleanup. The mansions care takers would have the place all to themselves. Meaghan had received high marks from her professor after he had gone over the place with the contractor. Mrs. Saxton received another telegram from Matt. The message she received informed her that they would arrive sometime around the first week of July. It was good they hadn't been slack. The household servants would be in place just three or four day's before Matt arrived.

The Saxton household knew that Ann and Meaghan were spending a lot of time together. But nobody thought much about it. Mr. Saxton and his son's were busy at work as business was good. As far as her daughter in laws, they seemed to like ruling the house hold. Especially Margaret. Ann had noticed that the servants hadn't seemed very happy about it.

The Maxton's had been busy also. They'd done better than any expectations they'd hoped for. Connie had sent them a telegram from one of their stop's to let them know everything was fine and that they would be in New York City in a couple of day's.

They missed their, daughters. That's how they'd looked at it. Of course Matt had in many ways always been like a son to them. As worried as they'd been. They thought they had received extra blessings now. Mrs. Maxton had even started helping out at the office. Doing book work or whatever else that she was able to do.

The Gates's had rejoiced also when they received a telegram from Helen. They had already started putting up some of the early vegetables for the winter and some of the crops would be ready to be harvested soon. They were glad they had made the move. They did miss the youngsters and had finally, a little at a time excepted their arrangement. That they were adults. More so than a lot of people that were twice their age.

Mr. Saxton was puzzled as he read the telegram. He had gotten it over an hour ago. It was from Mr. Maxton. It was personal and he had just reread it for the tenth time, as he'd tried to comprehend its meaning. He could tell it was a warning. It told him in so many word's not to make a rash judgment and to control himself till he had heard the complete story. Also that his son was fully grown and wasn't one to trifle with.

If they hadn't been so busy he would have already gone home to see what Ann could make of it. He was sure she would be there, for all of a sudden the last couple of day's she had been staying home. He was glad of that, things were back to normal. Even to the point of Margaret's pouting. Because she wasn't in control any more. Everyone was happy except for her. Randolph pushed his personal thoughts to the back of his mind as he'd concentrated on his paper work.

CHAPTER THIRTY ONE

HOMECOMING NEW YORK

It had taken them six day's to make the trip to New York City. With the stop's to get coal and water along with the stops at each station it had taken more time than most would thing. They all decided that they would be real happy when they could get their feet on solid ground. Matt finally had been able to convince them that he wouldn't ever hold out on them again. A couple of nights before there arrival at New York City.

Matt could've let his family know what day they were supposed to arrive. But he decided that if there had been a problem along the tracks and there had been any delay's, he hadn't wanted them to worry. Besides, he was sure they would attract enough attention as it was. The last people that had gotten aboard had been told about Billy, Matt and his women soon after. That even though they looked and acted nice. They were not to be trifled with. It was Friday, the first week of July around noon when the train slowed down for their stop.

Billy was mending quite well. But he was still pretty sore. They decided to be highly alert though. Billy stayed with Helen and Jenna as they made sure they were safe. The porters were taken care of all the luggage. Star and Connie had stayed by Matt's side above his slight protest as he went to flag down three carriage's.

They had decided to use one carriage to carry all of their luggage and two to ride in. It took them forty minutes to flag down the three carriages they needed and to load everything aboard. Except for Connie and Matt as they got into the carriages the new visitors were amazed wit the large buildings and all the people. Matt helped Star and Connie aboard with Billy. Then he went to the other carriage with Helen and Jenna then helped them aboard.

It was hard for them to concentrate on watching the people. When they wanted to take in all the sights. It took them nearly an hour to reach Matt's parents home. As they had passed the Maxton's home place Connie pointed it out as she said, "It looks like someone has bought the place and already moved in."

Star said, "Oh that's to bad. I would have liked to have seen your place."

Connie sort of hugged herself as she said, "I would've liked for you to have seen it. It was nice."

Matt directed the carriages into his parents place. Then he had taken a good look all around them. James Fallon the Saxton's butler came down the steps to greet them.

When James made it to the bottom step. The carriage's had come to a stop. When James got a good look into the carriage's. He spotted Matt and then Connie. He had broke out with a great big smile all over his face and rushed to the carriages as he exclaimed, "Oh lord-y. You've made it at last. You don't know how good it is to see you."

Matt had stepped down and was met by James's hand as he grabbed Matt's hand and started shaking it. Then he'd pulled Matt to him giving Matt a big hug. With wonder showing all over his face James had stepped back and looked up into Matt's eyes. He said, "Wow! You've grown too."

Matt turned and walked back to the next carriage, then had helped Connie down where she was met immediately by James. He hugged her then kissed her on the cheek. He said, "My; my. You have grown some too."

Connie said, "Oh, it's so good to see you. I hadn't realized how much I have missed you."

Matt helped Star down. Then as Billy with his good arm climbed down Matt returned to the first carriage to help Helen and Jenna down.

Then to James Matt introduced everyone. James looked a little bewildered as Matt gave only first names, except for Billy. They shook hands all around. Then James said, "I'll get someone to help carry all your things in. Let's get you inside first though. It has been a little warm lately. It's nice and cool inside."

Matt said, "That is not necessary. We won't be spending the night here."

James had taken Connie's arm and had started leading her to the steps. He stopped with Connie. Along with the others they gave Matt a questioning look. They all had thought they would be staying at the Saxton's. Matt made sure not to show any expression at all as he said, "I'll explain a little later." Then he made sure all of the carriages wait and explained that he would pay them extra for waiting.

James then led them on up and into the house. When James closed the door behind them. He startled them a little when he shouted, "Hey everybody! We have company."

Sally Ballas a servant that had been dusting in the parlor stepped into the hall, then gave a squeal and had rushed to Matt hugged him, then Connie. Soon all of the servants showed up doing much the same. The head servant Gail Slade and another servant Dawn Oates, Jessie Fallon head mistress and James's wife. Billy Green, another servant and kitchen help soon surrounded them. They wiped tears as they broke out into a lot of joyful chatter.

Matt embarrassed from all the attention was brought back to reality as he heard a voice ask, "What's all the excitement about? Oh. Hi Connie." As Margaret Saxton following her voice into the hall then stopped.

Sue Saxton continued on to give Connie a hug and a kiss. She even surprised Matt when she hugged him. Then said, "It is so nice to see you. We have all been concerned and have missed you."

Margaret hadn't said another word. She shook Connie's hand then she stood back and looked at the other's like they were imposing. Mrs. Saxton and Meaghan along with Jeff Blane, their gardener, had come in from the garden to see what was up.

Mrs. Saxton had stopped and put her left hand to her mouth. Meaghan rushed into Matt with a big squeal and unashamed hugged him with all of her strength. After a minute she let go of Matt. Crying and with tears flooding her eyes Meaghan made it to Connie to hug her. Matt had gone to his mother then said, "Mother it's good to be home."

Upon taking her into his arms she put her head against his shoulder and sobbed. Her body shook as Matt held her. He felt her emotions as they flowed through her. He had a lump in his throat and become afraid that his eyes would start tearing. His mother raised her head and waved Connie to her. She put her left arm around her and kissed her. Finally able to speak she said, "I have prayed and prayed. God did answer my prayers. But you took so long to get here."

Matt as his mother got her emotions under control shook Jeff's hand to be welcomed home by him.

Mrs. Saxton said, "Oh! where's our manner's. Gail they've got to be tired, thirsty and hungry. Let's set them up in the dinning room. Then Matt can introduce us.

Jessie helped Gail organize the rest of the servants as they cheerfully went to get drinks and food. Mrs. Saxton, Meaghan, Sue and James led their guest to the dinning room and soon had everyone seated at the table. Matt really felt welcomed for once except for Margaret. She still was true to form. Probably the thing that hurt her the most was that she wasn't the center of attention. Matt remained standing. He excepted a drink as the table had been quickly filled with snack's and drink's.

They were about to settle down when the front door burst open and they heard "Where is everybody at. What the devil is going on. Why are all the carriages out front."

James rushed out into the hall toward the door as he said, "Their here. In the dinning room. Welcome home sir. Mark, Michael. They look good."

Randolph as comprehension showed on his face said, "Oh, It looks like there's quite a lot to carry in."

James just said, "Yes, sir."

Matt not sure of his response or how his father would react, wanting to get it over with. He went out and met him in the hall. He was surprised to see the joy in his father's eyes. He received a huge bear hug and then was welcomed by his brothers in like matter. Matt relaxed. So far things had gone along good.

Randolph explained that they had decided to skip lunch so they could finish up and get home early. He was glad he had now. As they entered the dinning room Connie got up and waited for them. She received a hardy welcome. Randolph looked over all of the people in the dinning room. Then he said, "You don't know how relieved all of us were when we received your telegram."

Randolph took it upon himself to set Connie back down. Then he took a seat next his wife while Mark and Michael sat down next to theirs. Matt glad that everyone was present so he would been able to introduce everybody at once. As he looked over his family and the household of servants. He saw a lot of wondering gazes. Just as he got ready to speak he thought, he noticed some comprehension appear on his mother's face. Meaghan's face lit up, as if she had just been told a big secret.

Matt then introduced everyone to each other. He omitted the last names for Connie, Helen, Star and Jenna. After everyone stood, shook hands and been welcomed. They'd all took their seats again. Matt noticed when Margaret told Sue something and they'd looked at his women's left hand. He was a little apprehensive as he sat down. When everyone had sat down again and it was quieter, Randolph said, "Matt, you neglected to give us the young ladies, last names."

Matt could have delayed the coming argument. He decided he would rather get it over with. He said, "Saxton."

Randolph with a pleased expression looked at Connie. Then he said, "Good! We've hoped it would happen for along time. Matt, you still haven't told us the last names of the other three ladies."

Matt said, "Theirs are Saxton also."

Apprehension was going around the table. Randolph's neck and face had reddened. Then angry he said, "What the hell are you talking about. Why! That just isn't decent."

Before anyone else spoke. With a clear steady voice that was been full of deathly promise. Matt said, "Before anyone say's anything to insult or slander anyone of the women. I won't stand for it."

Randolph had been fishing for some word's. He hadn't been able to put any together. He already said something about not being decent. He also heard Matt's tone of voice. Then he had to look away when he saw Matt's eyes. Matt's eyes looked like they held the promise of death it self. When they had been directed at him. The shock that he was suddenly afraid of his own son, kept him from speaking.

Matt heard Margaret snicker and when he gave her a look. She suddenly turned pale as she saw his eyes. She had grunted as her husband Mark kicked her hard. She sat stone still and didn't say a thing after that. Then Matt got to his feet and as he headed for his fathers study. He said, "Let's talk. But not here."

Randolph nodded. Not saying anything. He slowly got up and followed Matt. The pleasant mood had changed to a statically charged environment. Not only had everyone been quiet. Some held their breath.

When they were in the study Matt closed the door behind his father. Then Matt said, "I'm going to explain it to you just once. I'm not proud of what I've done. If there's any blame put it on me. It's done now and I admit. I don't have an answer. But I'm absolutely sure of my love and pride I have for each one of them."

Randolph then hit by the warning that Chris Maxton had sent in the telegram. He was suddenly surprised as he'd realized, that Matt wasn't mad. He was just being deathly stern. Matt's eyes still had showed some intense heat in them. But nothing like the fire they'd had at the table. Maybe he had gotten some wisdom from Chris's warning. He hadn't been able to think of anything else to say. He said, "Okay. I'll try to understand. Also I agree that there will be no insults coming from this household."

Randolph was surprised when Matt stepped forward. Then he held his hand out as he said, "That's all I ask. I don't expect understanding or agreement."

Shaking hands he'd answered. "I'll make sure of it. I guess we've kind of made an agreement."

Matt said, "Yes sir."

Randolph was surprised again as that was the first time Matt had addressed him that way. With a little laugh he said, "Let's go back and join the other's before they have a heart attack."

Matt smiled, then said, "Yes sir. That sounds good."

When they turned to go Randolph instinctively patted Matt's back. He was surprised again. He had never felt muscle so solid before. Matt opened the door for them. It still was quiet when they got back to the dinning room. When it was observed that they were calm. It seemed like almost everyone drew a breath of air at the same time.

Randolph said, "Jessie, Betty. It would be nice if you would fix up something good to celebrate Matt and his new family. If you wouldn't mind, I'd like a good stiff drink."

Matt said, "Sir. While their doing that. I would like to go out and send the carriage that has all of our things, on to our lodging for tonight."

Randolph asked, "Your not going to stay here?"

"No. We have the means of taking good care of ourselves. Don't you think it would be better not to mix two big families together."

Randolph answered, "Yes, you've got a point. Your welcome here anytime though."

"That's more than I ask, Thank you."

As Matt stepped out and went down the hall. Everyone was stunned at the turn of events. Randolph and Matt getting along so good was the last thing anyone could have thought possible. The servants finally broken out of their surprise and had quickly gone to prepare things. Jessie fixed a drink the way Mr. Saxton liked and handed it to him. Slowly conversation had broken out as some had started to ask Billy and the ladies some questions. Randolph spotted Margaret and Mark. He made a quick decision. He said, "Margaret. I'd like a word with you."

Margaret hadn't liked things at all. She couldn't believe the way they had turned out. She didn't want to follow. Mark not knowing what was up persuaded her to go and they followed his father to the study. When they were inside Randolph had closed the door. It surprised both of them. Then he looked hard at Margaret as he said, "Margaret, this is mostly for you. I think I know Mark well enough. There will be no second chance. As long as you stay under my roof you'll not disrespect or say one word of insult about anyone from Matt's new family."

When she started to respond Mark had put his hand over her mouth and said, "If I have to I'll slap you. I agree with father."

With total disbelief she kept quiet. Mad they knew she was. Randolph said, "I know it will be hard for you. If you can't be nice. It would be better if you went to your room."

She looked at her husband and saw him node in agreement with Randolph. He removed his hand and she had to grit her teeth to keep from giving them a peice of her mind. Then at the thought of her and

Mark having to find a place of their own. She knew they would never be able to have a place anywhere near as grand as this place. Also they wouldn't be able to have servants. So as furious as she was she just nodded.

Randolph said, "Good."

Then he opened the door and let them out. He had again been surprised. This time it was by Mark's sudden back bone. He suddenly become proud of all of his son's. He was surprised however with the new thought though as Matt had been foremost in his mind. Matt on his way back up the hall as Randolph had stepped out of the study. He waited then joined Matt to walk back to the dinning room. To Randolph's surprise, although solemn Margaret had appeared to be respectful. but her facial expression was one of restrained petulance. He caught a look from Ann as she'd flashed him a smile of amazed gratitude which caused him to square his shoulders a little more.

The new guests were being quizzed about all that had happened. They'd given them bit's and peaces with a promise. That they would tell them everything when they had more time. Meaghan was having the time of her life. She had already taken to her new sister in-laws. It was obvious that three of them were already heavy with child. When Helen asked where they needed to go to relieve themselves. She took and showed them the toilet.

Ann was relieved that Randolph and Matt had finally come to some kind of agreement at last. Also, she liked the three other women that Matt had brought back with Connie. As she listened and watched she noticed that each of them deep in the back of their eyes had knowledge of events and things that had been hard to go through. The young man Billy Gates had the same look, deep in his eyes also. Connie had changed so much. But it was her eyes, that had changed the most. Above it all they'd seemed to be happy though.

After an hour they'd been served a good meal. The guest had been told about some of the attractions they should see in the city. Connie had been enthused also. Matt, had finally gotten his mother alone for a little while. He asked, "Is the Bingham Mansion ready and staffed?"

She smiled, then said, "Yes. You haven't told the other's. Have you?"

Matt's eyes glowed with mischief as he answered, "No! I wanted to surprise them."

"I think they'll be pleased. Meaghan helped and did a fantastic job. I'm real proud of her."

Matt asked, "You didn't have any problem's then."

"No, not really. My biggest concern. Is that I hope you approve of the help we've chosen."

Matt said, "I'm sure they'll be fine."

They rejoined the rest. When another hour had gone by. Matt decided it was time to go if they were to get settled in before dark. As he announced it was time for them to go. Meaghan said, "I'd like to go if you don't mind. I would be glad to help you get moved in and unpacked."

They agreed when Randolph said, "The only thing that concerns me is for Meaghan being out so late."

Matt said, "If she would like to she can stay the night."

"Yes, I'll get an overnight bag. It'll take me just a minute."

Randolph nodded then, as she ran off to get some things. Randolph asked, "You sure you have enough room?"

Matt said, "We'll be fine."

They said their goodbyes, then gone out to the waiting carriages. Several followed them out. Michael and Mark had helped the Ladies aboard. Meaghan rushed out and got into the carriage with Billy, Helen and Jenna. Matt with Connie and Star had the driver head out. Matt had told the drivers where he wanted to go when he had come out and sent the other carriage along with their things. Again everyone was alert. Matt pointed out a few thing's as they traveled along. After a few minutes Connie asked, "Where are we going. I don't remember any hotels out this way?"

Matt just said, "I heard that a new one was built."

Connie gave Matt a funny look. As she tried to think when Matt could've heard about a new place. Maybe somebody on the train. She settled back and enjoyed seeing some of the old sights. As she alertly watched any people they went by for something out of place. Connie was about ready to say something. She was sure nobody would build a hotel out here. Then their driver turned into the Bingham Mansion. Her mouth clamped shut as she realized that somebody had done a lot of work. It looked like it had been completely refurbished. It had been run down real bad the last time she had seen it. Maybe somebody had made it into a hotel.

As they came to a stop in front of the step's. Connie saw a neatly dressed man come down them to wait on the bottom step. As he spotted Meaghan he said, "Hello miss. I take it these are the new residents."

Meaghan smiled as she said, "Yes, let's get them inside and I'll introduced you."

Lee Knight said, "Yes, Ma-am. That sounds good to me."

With Lee's help Matt helped the women out of the carriages as Billy with his one good arm had enough to do caring for himself. Taking a good look around after everyone had gotten out of the carriages. Matt paid the drivers and thanked them. They'd been overjoyed at what he'd paid them. They told him to let them know when he could use them again. When they were inside they were met by the rest of the staff. Lee had alerted them before he had gone out side. Meaghan introduced everyone. After they had all shook hands and a little bit acquainted. She said, "Welcome home."

Matt hadn't been able to keep from smiling at how elated Meaghan was. Billy and the women tried to understand. The servants realized that this was the first that the women knew about it.